PATH OF THE
STONEBREAKER

By R.D. Renworth

Published by
Ashen Gate Fantasy & Sci-Fi

Copyright © 2023 R.D. Renworth

All rights reserved

The characters and events portrayed in this book are fictitious. Any similarity to real persons, living or dead, is coincidental and not intended by the author.

No part of this book may be reproduced, or stored in a retrieval system, or transmitted in any form or by any means, electronic, mechanical, photocopying, recording, or otherwise, without express written permission of the publisher.

ISBN: 9798358094031

Cover artwork design by: Katerina Belikova (Ninja Jo Art)
Map artwork design by: R.D. Renworth

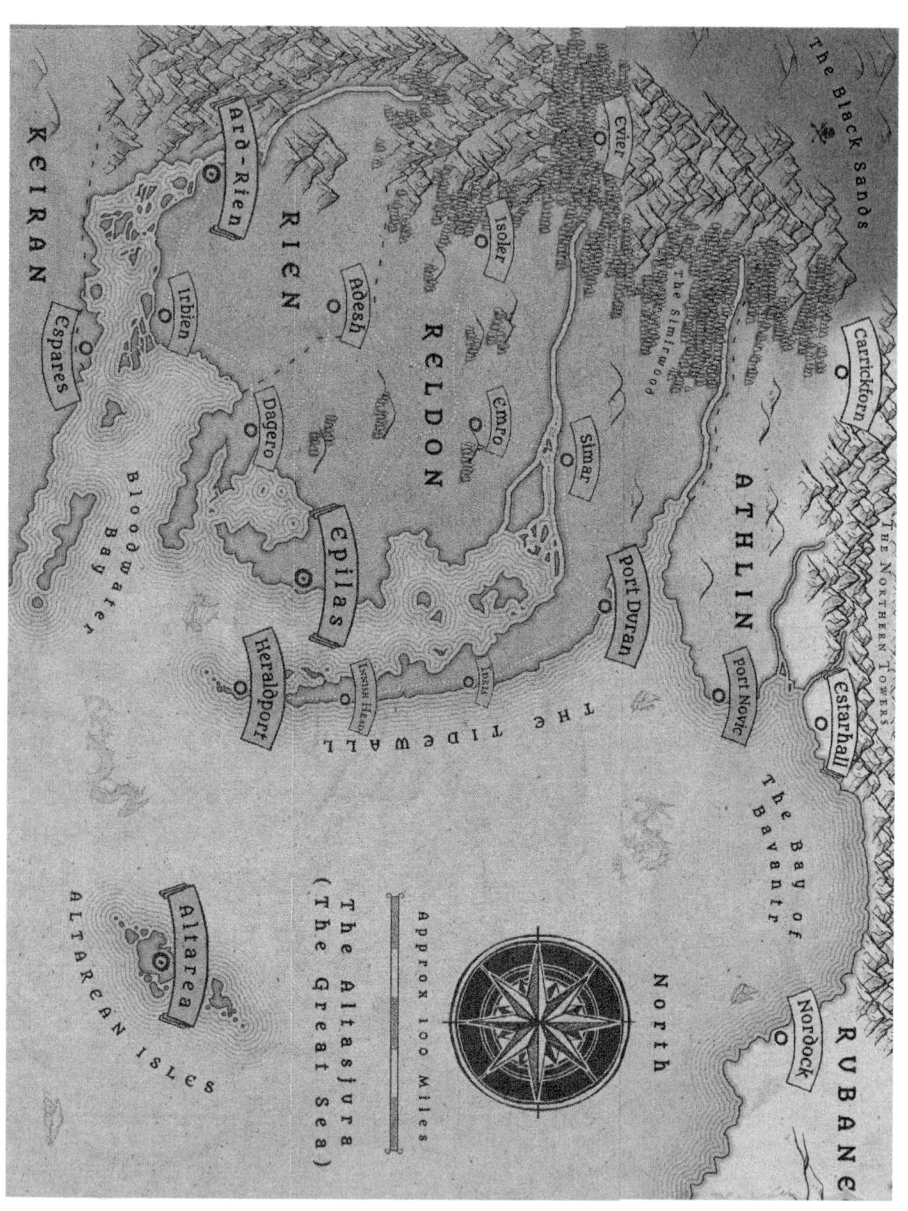

PART I

A TASTE OF POTENTIAL

CHAPTER 1

An Opportunity

A t the foot of the cliff wall, Femira stumbled to a stop before the corpse of a stormguard. In the glow of the burning palace above, she could see bones protruding from his gilded armour.

His face was slick with blood.

You've seen people dying before, she thought. She tried to look away and quell the lump in her stomach. He wore a blue cloak and from that, Femira knew he would have an amethyst on him. That alone was more than enough for a single night's work, but she was here for a bigger haul, not some chip of aeristone stolen from a corpse.

The wind raged and violently broke against the walls of the palace. It tore at the few remaining banners on the towers and threatened to shatter the stained glass windows. Above, more stormguards flew about with their wings of wood and sailcloth. They wouldn't be looking for a thief tonight—not with half the palace burning to the ground. *Opportunities like this don't come around every day,* she reminded herself.

Femira edged around the body and made her way through the jagged outcrops of rock to the base of the cliff wall. It was an imposing height, far taller than anything she'd climbed before. The palace was built right on top of the cliff. The palace walls were made of stone but beneath that would be wood, reinforced with steel. *Only the poor build with stone,* Lichtin had taught her. *Those with something valuable are smart enough to use wood and steel to protect it.*

Femira patted the pouch on her waist for reassurance that she had her climbing spikes. It had been a long time since she'd needed them but only a fool would come unprepared.

She took a deep, steadying breath and placed a hand against the stone. Femira forcefully pressed her palm against the black surface, her expression locked in concentration. Her hand began to vibrate, the familiar humming pulsation running up her arm. The earthstone hanging from a leather cord around her neck began to glow with a slight amber light.

She smirked as she felt the rock beneath her hand weaken and crumble. Her hand sunk inside the solid rock as if it were sand. She pulled it away, leaving a perfect handhold in the wall. There was no dust or flecks of stone the rock had simply vanished at her touch.

She stepped up, placing her foot in the hole she had created. Both her hands tingled with the earthstone's power as she reached up and carved out another set of handholds. She continued in this pattern, climbing higher and higher.

Femira could remember what it was like to climb before Lichtin had given her the earthstone, wedging the climbing spikes between bricks and hoisting herself higher, her feet always searching for holds and ridges in the stone. It had been easier to go barefoot back then and the soles of her feet and toes were still thick with calluses as a result.

Femira was halfway to the top when the crashing began. She twisted her neck to look across to the bridge that connected the island palace to the rest of the city.

Shit, they've reached the gate already. If the Reldoni invaders got there first then all the good stuff would be snatched up. Femira quickened her pace, leaving a trail of perfectly formed footholds in the wall. The flashes of lightning intensified and the winds picked up, pushing her against the wall. Her dark hair—tied back in a tight braid—slapped against her face. *Can't make mistakes now, keep going.*

Femira pressed herself out from the wall, pushing against the force of the wind. She reached up, climbing higher. She passed beyond the rough cliff wall and onto the brick stonework of the palace. She was sweating, her breaths short and ragged.

Heights had never scared Femira, but she'd now climbed two hundred feet with the full force of the Altasjura sea storms threatening to throw her off. She could hear the surf crashing against the rocks at the base of the palace, but looking below she could only see darkness. Neither Ecko nor Luna's moonlight could break through the storm clouds.

Almost there! Femira couldn't see the top but she knew it couldn't be much further. She climbed higher, her shoulders and arms straining. Her exposed hands were numb from the rain and wind, dulling the thrum of the earthstone's power in them. She could feel it stronger now in her chest, as if someone were playing brass instruments not too far away. The earthstone shone more brightly than it had when she started. On a normal night the stormguards would have long since spotted her.

Her brothers would have said it was too reckless, sneaking into the palace when it was under attack but Femira was desperate. She *needed* something valuable. Something that could pay her way out from under Lichtin's boot. Her debt to him was far too high for her to pay off by cutting purses. This was her best chance at finally being free of him.

Femira reached up, placing her hand against the wall, expecting it to disintegrate as she pressed against it. But it held firm. Confused with fatigue, she almost slipped. She looked up, there was no more rock and the wall rose only a few feet higher. The parapets at the top of the wall were steel. The earthstone could dissolve metal like it did rock but the process was much slower, it would take her hours to form a single handhold in the metal. *Too slow.*

Beneath her, she could see that the invaders had broken through the gate and were swarming inside. *Shit!* She could hear guards running across the top of the wall only a few feet above. *Time for a gamble.*

"Hey!" Femira's voice broke, it was weaker than she expected.

"Help!" she called louder. "Please someone help me!" There was no reply but she could hear the sound of men above.

"Someone please help me!" she shouted.

"What are you doing?" A reply! *You can do this Femira.*

"Help! The wind—it pushed me off the wall, please I don't want to die!"

"We're all going to die," another voice added.

"Leave her, we don't have time," a different voice. *How many of them are up there?*

"You go on ahead, inform the captain they've breached the inner gate, they're going straight for the mines," said the first voice, though it was hard to tell with the wind. "I'm going to pull you up, hang on." Femira waited, she could hear the clanking of the steel as the other guards continued on.

Within moments a rope dropped beside her.

"Thank you," Femira shouted, in a perfect imitation of a highborn Altarean accent. She gripped the rope with both hands. They were still numb and Femira didn't fully trust them with her weight but she'd committed to this. She pushed out from her footholds and let the stormguard pull her to the top of the parapet.

"What were you doing out here?" he asked, stepping back after pulling her over the lip of the parapet, "can't you see we're under attack? Get to the mines with all the other—" he cut off. With her dark skin she could never pass for an Altarean highborn and her black fitted climbing gear was clearly not the garb of a servant.

His curved sword was already out from its scabbard. She reached into her belt pouch.

"Sorry about this," she said and threw her climbing spikes at his face as she spun and ran. She didn't bother looking back to see if they landed.

Femira was no fighter, fleeing was her best option. She raced along the battlement, her legs were weak from the climb but adrenaline was kicking in. Femira felt a very sudden and strong wind smash against her face, slowing her pace. *Oh fuck, right. He's a stormguard.* She glanced over her shoulder, the stormguard was chasing her, his blade raised.

Time for something drastic.

Femira dropped to her knees, the parapets were steel but the walkway itself was stone paving. *Please let me be right about this.* Her hands vibrated as she pushed down against the floor, pulling as much power from the earthstone as she could. The stone beneath her began to crumble, the weaker stone between the tiles disintegrating faster. The floor shifted but didn't fall through.

Come on!

The stormguard leapt at her, his sword raised above him. She pushed down with all of her physical force and the power of the earthstone. She could hear the stormguard shouting over the howling wind. Her braid whipped about and then she was falling.

Femira's limbs flailed through the falling debris. Instinctively, her arms shot up to protect her face before she hit the ground with a thud. Pain flared in her hip as she landed.

Regaining her wits quickly, Femira rolled to the side, a cloud of dust surrounding her. *No time to wait.* She jumped to her feet, her injured hip protesting at the sudden movement.

The room was dark, but Femira had the faint light of the earthstone to guide her. She ran, glancing up to the ceiling where she fell through. As she did so, Femira tripped over something hard and stumbled back to the ground. Her hip screamed out in pain but she didn't waste any time, rolling and climbing back to her feet, she kept running.

Then she hit a wall. Her face squared against the flat stone. There was a sharp blinding pain in her nose and she fell back. Disoriented, she rolled to avoid any oncoming attack from the stormguard... nothing came.

She remained frozen on the ground for a brief second, but there were no immediate sounds. There was wind outside, the thrumming of battering rams against gates in the distance but there was no noise inside the room short of her own ragged breaths. She looked about, the dust was settling in the rays of moonlight beneath the hole she had created in the ceiling.

Where's the guard? Tentatively, Femira rose to her feet and limped slowly back to the hole, carefully staying in the shadows as she peeked up. There was nothing up there.

A crash sounded in the distance along with the faint cries of fighting men. She looked around again but the room was empty. *Handled that well.* She grinned smugly. *Best thief in all of Altarea.* She scanned the dark room looking for an exit. *Broke into the palace itself and didn't even get caught... well, barely caught.*

Using the amber light of the earthstone, Femira inspected the room. Furniture was piled about haphazardly and she couldn't tell what the room had ever been used for in the past. *Probably just a storeroom.* This wasn't where she was supposed to be. The stormguard that Lichtin had paid off said that they keep the best stuff stockpiled in the mine. That's where she needed to be.

***

The Altarean palace was built atop two enormous sea stacks. Captain Darza watched the swirling blue and black clouds of the storm from atop the arcing bridge that stretched out over the crevasse that connected the two stacks. Half the buildings were ablaze. Darza could see that the palace was lost.

Lightning flashed and thunder peeled.

The Reldoni had breached the gate and men were fighting atop the battlements. It would only be a matter of time before they reached the bridge.

For three decades, Darza and his division had guarded the bridge and never in those thirty years had a force breached the palace walls. In truth, his men were more of a ceremonial likeness than they were fighters. Their blue stormguard cloaks were clean and pressed, their gilded armour never suffered a scratch. Darza's spear had a silk cloth tied beneath the blade and had never shed blood. Darza himself hadn't even used the aeristone that hung from a silver chain about his neck since his promotion to captain.

From shattered doorways, the invaders flooded into the central courtyard at the base of the bridge. In the dim light, their armour seemed made of darkness. They were like an army of draega demons, swarming on the remaining defenders and swiftly overwhelming the stormguards. Some of Darza's people were beginning to flee, using their aeristones to lift themselves out of the courtyard and up to the castle walls, most fell to archers and the few gunmen. The rest died at the hands of the invaders already waiting on the battlements.

"What do we do, Captain?" Enoi aked, his voice strained, frightened.

"There's nothing we can do. The palace is lost... it's only a matter of time," he turned to face his companions, men he had known for most of his life. There were eight of them and normally they stood in pairs at the gaslamps spread across the expanse of the long bridge. Now they were clustered at the centre of the bridge, all wore worried faces.

"I won't ask any of you to stay," Darza began, "though I'm not sure where else you could go." They all wore glowing purple aeristones around their necks but none of them were particularly skilled flyers. "Those archers will get you if you go up, and down there," he indicated the mammoth stone doors on their side of the bridge, "there's nothing in there that can help us. But there are innocent people in there;

the children, the old, the weak. I don't know what it is these bastards want but I don't want them cutting down all those people to get to it." There were murmurs of agreement. They weren't heroes but they were good, honest men.

"Do you have a plan?" Enoi asked, like Darza, he was a greying man and far past his prime.

Darza kept his voice neutral, trying to sound calm, "at each of our stations there's enough dragon-oil to power these lamps for a year," he could see some of them nodding, understanding where he was going.

"If we gather all of it here—at the weakest point—we can blow this damn bridge up, and hopefully burn a few of those bastards while we're at it." They didn't need convincing, this was the only way they could defend the mines, and one of the few ways that didn't involve them actually having to fight.

"It won't hold them off!" Juren shouted from the back of the pack. "The palace is lost, we should run!"

"To where?!" Enoi shouted back. "You heard the captain, you've seen how those gunmen picked off the others. And besides, Juren, I've seen you fly and I doubt you'll even make it over the chasm. I'm with the captain!"

Enoi wasted no time and opened the base of the gaslamp, pulling out the casket of dragon-oil. With the only opposition stilled, the others swiftly returned to their posts to retrieve the caskets. Within minutes all were back, and the caskets piled together at the center of the bridge.

Darza and his men retreated back to the entrance of the mines. He held a bow with a notched arrow, the tip wrapped in cloth. He hovered it near the gaslamp, waiting. It didn't take long for the Reldoni to make their way through the courtyard, picking off the last of the stormguards. *Those brave souls,* Darza thought with a confusing blend of jealousy, pity and fear.

The first of the soldiers began to race across the bridge. The chasm was wide enough that their archers and gunmen wouldn't be able to hit Darza and his men, not with the storms still raging, blowing projectiles about every which way. He wasn't sure how well rifles aimed in the wind but from what he'd heard their precision was poor at the best of times.

They neared the center of the bridge, some of them slowing as they saw the pile of wooden crates. The zenith of the bridge was where it thinned, it was the best place to ensure there was a collapse.

Darza tentatively danced the arrow over the gaslamp, the rag caught alight quickly. He took a breath, trying to calm himself. He reached out with his aeristone and felt the rush of its power flood over him—the command of the winds. The winds picked up behind him and he let loose, the torrent carrying the flaming arrow onward, guiding it—protecting it.

***

The blast was deafening, Femira watched as the only bridge to the mines erupted in a blast of green and purple flame. Chunks of stone disappeared down into the dark chasm below, along with her plan to sneak into the mines by climbing along the edge. She had already made her way along the side of the inner wall, leaving behind a trail of earthstone-carved handholds.

Femira wasn't far from where the bridge connected to the palace wall. She couldn't see the invaders from where she clung, but she knew they would be planning to get across the crevasse so she would have to act quickly. She changed her course, now climbing up to the top of the wall.

She crested the top of the inner wall where the bodies of stormguards littered the walkway. Some of them looked like hedgehogs they had so many arrows protruding from them. She raced along the battlement at a crouch and reached where it joined with the main walls at the central courtyard. She could hear incoherent shouting and clanking of armour and swords.

Hesitantly, she peeked over the parapet. The courtyard was full to the brim with the invaders. She watched as more began to enter from the gates, carrying broken doors, furniture and other scrap, they were stockpiling it in the center of the courtyard. *They're building a bridge.* She realised. *Good, that gives me more time.* Femira looked over the horde, she would never be able to count how many there were but there was enough that they would have the bridge ready soon. *So maybe not that much time.*

She crept away from the edge and back along the walltop, giving herself a safe distance from the courtyard to think. *Is it really that far?* She looked out across the chasm to the mines. It looked to be about three hundred feet to the outcrop of the mine entrance, not really that far and it looked even closer further to the right. However the dark chasm below was a foreboding sight, there would be no coming back from a fall down there.

If she had a bow, Femira could shoot a rope over and slide across, but where would she find a bow? She would never have thought to bring one, or even buy one for that matter. Where do you even buy a bow? Or in her case steal one. *The barracks I guess, but that's in the palace.* She paused and looked around at the bodies, there were bows littered everywhere. She grinned and picked one up.

This would be easy, she'll do one test shot to see if it can reach the distance and then look around for some rope. She held the bow and tried to knock an arrow. *How is this thing supposed to work? There's not even a notch for the arrow to fit on the string. Am I supposed to hold it in place?* She fumbled for a few moments before managing to draw back the bowstring. She pulled the string back as far as she could and kept the arrow mostly straight with the same hand.

Ok, let's do this. She closed one eye and aimed toward the mines. *It's just like a slingshot.* She released the bowstring; it snapped back and whacked against the hand holding the bow.

"Shit, that hurts," she grumbled, dropping the bow and rubbing her hand. The arrow didn't even clear the parapet wall, it lay within arms reach in front of her. *Maybe archery's not my best skill.* Or it could have been a dud bow. *Maybe one of these other ones would be better.*

She picked through bodies, looking for a better bow. They were all the same. However, one body seemed a little different, his armour was made of lacquered wood and he wore strange goggles. There was also an arrow sticking out of his head, but that wasn't that unusual considering she was the only person on the wall without an arrow stuck in her somewhere. His body lay atop a large contraption of wood and thick cloth.

A stormsail! She realised with excitement and began unclipping the straps of the man's armour and poking around underneath. People liked to keep their runestones hidden, but nearly everyone always kept them in the same place, hung around the neck on a cord or in an inner pocket. *Best place to keep your stones is in your boot,* Lichtin always said.

That's why this one always smells like feet. She glanced down at the runestone around her neck.

Her hand clasped around a small lump in a secret pocket in the stormguard's shirt. She pulled out the chip of aeristone, it glowed with a faint purple light and was about the size of her fingernail. An aeristone this size was worth a fortune to a girl who lived in a cellar.

She jumped up with a grin and lifted out the stormsail from beneath the dead guard. Hefting it over her shoulder, she walked to the edge of the battlement.

The stormsail was a large wooden kite with a light sailcloth, the stormguards used them to ride the winds. Femira looked over the edge, down the chasm and felt her chest tighten. *You can do this.* She looked at the aeristone in her hand, she had never used one before. Maybe it wasn't much different to her earthstone? With her earthstone, she would feel a vibration in her hand when touched against rock. If she pressed against the rock it would dissolve away. Maybe with the aeristone it was the same?

Except instead of dissolving rock, it's making the wind lift her into the sky. *Simple!* Maybe she could dissolve the air above her, and that would cause wind to push her into the empty space where the air had been?

That makes sense, right?

She clasped the aeristone tight in her hand and reached her other hand out into the air. She waited… *Nothing.* No vibrations, no tingling, just the feeling of the wind blowing about as it had been.

"How do they do this?" Femira muttered to herself.

She closed her eyes and squeezed the stone tightly, its jagged edges biting into her palm. She waited for a few moments but she still felt nothing and then there was a crash.

Femira's eyes snapped open, the noise was to her left. *Oh no, they've finished the bridge.* It was the sound of the makeshift bridge dropping against the other side of the chasm. *Out of time.* She made a rash decision, she always worked best with quick decisions. She tucked the aeristone into her waist pouch, and climbed over the parapet wall, clutching the stormsail. The wind still raged; it was coming from behind her.

Now or never.

She might not even need the aeristone's power for this. She gripped the two handles of the storm-sail and lept out.

***

Darza sat in the antechamber of the main hall. The children and the elderly were inside, the safest place in the entire palace. Never before had this place been penetrated by an invading force. *Until now.* The room was large and like all the rooms in the Osiri Mines it had been carved directly out of the rock by stoneshapers.

At first the invaders had entered quietly, with rifles and crossbows raised but they did not shoot.

Before Darza, sat a tall man with dark hair and a kept beard. He was young, he couldn't be older than thirty and that was being generous but he had a dangerous gait. He was the kind of man that Darza had spent his career avoiding, the kind that would kill you before you even released that you were in a fight. He wore black armour with a hawk clutching a blade embellished on the breastplate.

Darza knew who this man was even before he was introduced. This was Prince Landryn Tredain, Lord Commander of the Reldoni army. Seated next to the prince was another man, older and larger with tight blond hair—he had been introduced as General Hannis Garld. Both had the tan skin and sharp features of Reldoni.

General Garld had a hand resting on the table they sat around. In it, was a wheel-lock pistol. The weapon was not pointed at Darza but the threat was indicated all the same.

"What kind of deal are you looking for?" Darza asked, trying not to let his voice betray his fear. He had nothing to bargain with, they were already in the mines, and the royal family were in their custody on the other side of the palace. *Surely they already have what they came for.*

"We have reason to believe there is a sizable cache of aeristone in the mine," Prince Landryn said, "I can imagine that a considerable amount of the stone has been well hidden. If you cooperate with my men in finding all of the caches, we will spare the people in the main hall."

"They cannot be trusted!" Enoi snapped from behind him. General Garld didn't hesitate, he raised his hand holding the revolver, and shot. The sound was as loud as a thunderclap and the bullet tore through Enoi's head, spraying blood against the wall behind him. The force propelled the man's lifeless body to the floor. The other men in the room gripped their spears tightly.

Revolvers were a new weapon and the people of Altarea had yet to understand how they were made. From reports, they could operate *without* the use of runestones.

"No... we cannot be trusted," Garld said evenly, "but you do not have much choice. We will overrun you and your men, and we will kill every soul in this mine. We can also easily tear this place apart ourselves in search of the caches." He said it all so calmly.

"But," the man added, "we are impatient men, Captain, and with your help, we can take a much swifter approach to our search. Cooperate with us and we will have what we need faster. And you, your men, and the people in this mine, will all be allowed to leave this place unharmed. The palace is now under Reldoni occupation, it would be far better for you to work with us than against us."

Darza thought for a moment. Enoi was right, of course, these monsters couldn't be trusted, but Enoi's brains were currently spilling out on the floor. Being right hadn't kept him alive. At least this way Darza might have a chance to survive this.

"Your King," Prince Landryn spoke again, "we offered him the same deal when we first arrived at the city. If he had agreed, much of this bloodshed could have been avoided."

Darza knew that King Amenia would never have surrendered the mines willingly. He was too proud... and too greedy. Also, who would have thought that these Reldoni scum could have so easily overrun the legendary stormguard.

Darza didn't take his eyes off the revolver, it was silver with a wooden handle. *Such a small thing that can cause so much destruction... much like an aeristone in the wrong hands.*

"What do you plan to do with the aeristone caches?" Darza asked, he didn't attempt to hide his loathing. The men remained silent, their bodyguards still had their rifles and crossbows pointed at him.

"You are not in a position to be asking questions, Captain," Garld replied, "You have two options; agree to help our men, or refuse and perish."

Could Darza really allow these men to claim such an amount of aeristone? The runestones were what made the Altarean army such an elite force. He had no doubts as to what use the Reldoni warmongers had in mind for the aeristone cache. They would use it to reap more death and destruction. But if he refused... Garld still had the revolver levelled at him. There were so many children inside—all of the Altarean highborn youth. Darza had no children of his own but he couldn't have all of those deaths on him, not when there was a sliver of a chance.

"We will do what we can, sir," Darza said eventually, "we will help you... if you spare us."

***

Femira crept through the dark corridors, Lichtin's informant said that she should make her way down to the lower levels of the mine, so she did, deeper and deeper. There had been some noise above as the first of the invaders had ransacked storage rooms. But it would take them a long time to make their way down this far. Still, Femira moved quietly, and used only the amber light of her earthstone to guide her.

Femira's knees burned where she'd scuffed them on the landing on the other side of the crevice. The feeling of soaring through the air on the stormsail had filled her with an exhilarating blend of terror and excitement. It was a reckless move, she knew, but then again, everything she'd done tonight had been reckless. *That was definitely top three at least.*

She came up to a large steel door with crossed spears emblazoned on it—the crest of the Altarean royal family. *This must be it.*

"They keep something good in there," the informant had said, "I'm not sure what it is but they don't let no one but the highest officials inside. Not even the stormguards are allowed in. The thing is completely sealed."

True to his word there was no keyhole to try to pick. Femira pushed against the door but it didn't budge. She pressed her hands against it and felt the thrum of the earthstone's power as it slowly began dissolving the metal. That would take hours... maybe even days to carve a hole big enough to crawl through.

Well I don't need to carve a hole through it.

She reached down and pressed her hands against the stone floor, she pushed down hard. Slowly, Femira began to form a tunnel beneath the door, dissolving the rock. It was a slow process but quicker than trying to pick a lock on a door with no keyhole. After a moment, she realised that the frame around the door was also steel and it expanded far below the floor. She tried dissolving the rock beside the door but it too had a layer of steel beneath. *They really don't want people to get in here.* The entire walls were likely steel, but maybe they weren't smart enough to line the ceiling.

Femira hurried back up the nearby stairs, counting her steps excitedly. *They can't keep me out, I'm the best burglar in all of Altarea—probably the best in the world.*

She hadn't heard any noise from the floors above so Femira was certain the invaders weren't even close yet. Once she was on the floor above the room, Femira traced her steps back along the corridor. There was nothing haphazard about these tunnels, they all followed a strict grid pattern. *Not really what I would expect of a mine.*

Femira reached a point where she was confident that the steel door was below her. There was a wall of rock in front of her. She confidently pressed her hands against the stone and began to dissolve it with large sweeping gestures, pushing out with the power of the earthstone as she had done before. It was a narrow tunnel but

Femira was quite small herself. She crawled inside and continued to push forward another few feet before angling downward.

The earthstone was slowly beginning to glow brighter and it was becoming significantly heavier. *I won't have much more power left.* Normally when it got like this Femira would have to return it to Lichtin; he did something with it that made the light fade and made the earthstone weightless again. Soon it would be too heavy to carry and would stop working.

"Runestones are like people," Lichtin had told her once, wearing his smug, knowing smile. "If you feed them too much they become fat and useless." *What is that even supposed to mean?* This is how Lichtin kept her coming back to him, the promise of so much more to learn.

Femira continued to tunnel down, sifting her hands through rock, it was like digging through dry sand. She dissolved more until her hands brushed against something solid. The thrum of the earthstone didn't stop and she scowled knowing it was now dissolving steel again. *They've even lined the ceiling with steel!*

Femira crawled out from her tunnel, and slumped back against the wall. She wasn't giving up—if anything the measures made to keep her out only fuelled her desire to break in. But her body was beginning to feel the exhaustion of climbing the wall, and the weight of the earthstone around her neck wasn't helping.

Her best option was the door. The informant said there was no keyhole but just because there wasn't a place for a key, didn't mean there was no bolt. Something had to be holding the door in place.

Femira made her way back down to the lower corridor. The door was completely smooth apart from the crossed spears engraving. There was obviously a way to open it so she began feeling around the etchings but she couldn't find any hidden cavity or anything that could be the unlocking mechanism.

Femira held out the earthstone using its light to peek through the seam of the door. The door was thick but there was an eerie light inside. *Perfect.* She followed the seam down the floor and then along the base. At the center, there was a break in the light, a thick black spot. Femira felt a grin pull at her mouth. *There's always a bolt.*

She pressed her fingers against the pinhole gap beneath the door. Dissolving metal was slow but not impossible. *I've got time.* She pushed her fingers hard against the gap and forced her way in with the power of the earthstone.

I climbed down at least two dozen sets of stairs to get to this floor. I have plenty of time before they get here. The thought didn't stop her glancing over her shoulder to the dark stairwell every few moments.

The vibrations of the earthstone helped dull the pain of the metal scratching against her fingers as Femira slowly pushed them further into the gap. The hole was tight and she didn't want to waste time making it more comfortable so she only dissolved enough to force her fingers in further. Femira wasn't sure how much time had passed when she managed to get her fingers about two inches deep. There was already blood running down her palm.

Femira pushed harder, gritting her teeth.

"Dissolving metal takes days, it's not worth your time," Lichtin always said but he was wrong, this wasn't taking *that* long. She couldn't have been at this for more than an hour now and her entire forearm was already underneath the door, her shoulder resting against the smooth steel. Her fingers had long since gone numb with the pain so Femira wasn't sure if she had even begun wearing down the bolt.

And then the door groaned. Slowly, the door shifted under the weight of her shoulder. Delicately, she pulled out her hand; there were shallow cuts leading from the tips of her fingers down to the wrist. She pulled out a bandage rag from her pouch and wrapped it around tightly to stop the bleeding.

Despite the pain, Femira could barely hold in her excitement. The hunger to know what was inside motivated her to ignore all the pain in her bruised, cut and fatigued body. Femira pushed against the door but it resisted. She let out a grunt, and pushed with more force until door groaned open.

Unlike the dark corridor outside, the brightness of the room forced Femira to squint as her eyes adjusted. Mounds of aeristone were piled everywhere, each stone giving off a deep violet hue. Collectively, they created a garishly bright purple light.

The room itself wasn't very big but there were columns leading to the end of the room where there was an altar. It almost looked like the inside of a very small temple. *Well this place is weird.*

She crept into the room, pushing the door closed behind her. *Why would they keep so much aeristone in one place? Surely it would be smarter to stash it in different locations... They're hiding something else.* She smirked with the realisation. *They know that if someone were to break in then they would carry as much aeristone as they could, and run for it before they got caught.* Rich people always thought they were so clever, but a good burglar is always a step ahead. "What are you hiding..." Femira whispered quietly to the room.

She walked up to the altar, instinctively crouching although there was nobody around. There was a book lying open on the altar but it was written in Common Tongue so it was useless to Femira as she only knew the letters of her homeland. She checked over the altar for any secret compartments but there was nothing.

Then she scanned through the room but couldn't find anywhere that something could be hidden.

"Maybe I'm wrong?" she muttered, her brow knotting in frustration. *No! I'm never wrong.* Femira did a second sweep, this time pushing over some of the mounds of aeristone, looking for hidden treasures.

Despite her annoyed expression, Femira loved this. She felt like Vagar the Bold, from the old stories, creeping through some Sorcerer King's tomb. Maybe there would be stories about her someday. *Femira the Vreth, she stole treasures from the heart of the Altarean palace without ever being detected.*

There was nothing beneath the mounds. *Maybe the columns?* She inspected each pillar, searching for signs of hidden compartments. She noticed that at the back of the room, one of the columns was a little unusual.

This section is darker, why is it darker?

Most people probably wouldn't have even noticed the slightly darker shade of stone. *It's a different type of rock to the rest... why are the columns rock to begin with? Why not use steel?*

She pressed her hand against it, and it immediately began to disintegrate. *It's weak rock too... really weak.* Femira grinned excitedly, heedlessly pushing her hands into the stone. It fell away so easily, as if she were simply swatting away dust, until her hands brushed against something solid.

It was a wooden box. Femira pulled it out, and stepped over to the altar, dropping it down carefully on top of the worthless book. It was seamless, she'd seen it's like before. *A pressure lock, probably.* Femira began pushing at various parts of the box in different patterns like she had learned to do years ago. She didn't want to risk smashing it against the wall—not without knowing what was inside.

Coming all this way and then breaking the treasure. Lichtin would be furious. *Well, it's not like I'd be coming home empty-handed,* she thought looking about at the trove of aeristone, there was enough here to buy the entire city. She considered leaving now and trying to open it when she got back to the crewhouse. She forcefully fit the box tightly in her pouch along with a handful of aeristones, and made for the exit.

The door swung open.

Instinctively, Femira dove to the side and scrambled behind one of the glowing mounds of aeristone.

"Well it seems that the rumours that Osiri is empty are unfounded."

Femira curled up behind the mound, trying to make herself as small as possible.

Shit, shit, shit, shit!

The voice was a man's and he had an accent that Femira didn't recognize. *Must be the invaders—the Reldoni. How did they get down here so fast?* She was holding her breath, and could feel panic rising. *Relax, panicking just gets you caught.* She steadily allowed herself to breathe quietly.

"I can assure you, sir, the mines are indeed spent. The King hordes the last of it because he knows there's no more left to be dug out." That accent was Altarean. Femira could hear footsteps moving about the room and armour clinking.

"I want this whole level guarded. We will begin moving the aeristone to the ships immediately." Against all her rationality, Femira peeked over the mound and caught sight of the speaker. The man was handsome, with black hair that caught the purple light of the aeristone in a strange way. There were a half dozen of them in the room. Five Reldoni all in dark red uniforms with black armour, and one unarmed Altarean stormguard.

"I will assess the quality of the stones," a large blond Reldoni said. They were all looking toward the back of the room, where the largest pile of aeristone was.

"Good, do that," the dark-haired man replied, "I'll post guards in the hallway and make preparations to move it all to the ships." He left with the other men, leaving only the blond man. Femira was unsure if his uniform was just so stained from blood that it was red or if it was always supposed to be that colour.

Femira assessed her options, they would be clearing out the stones soon so she couldn't stay hiding. She couldn't tunnel her way out, not quickly enough and certainly not through steel. She could wait for him to leave, and then sneak past the guards outside, it's darker out there so she could stay in the shadows.

Femira the Vreth could disappear into the shadows. That's what they'll say.

The blond man was showing no signs of leaving. She couldn't fight him, the guy was huge and she was exhausted. He also had a shortsword hilted at his waist and she didn't even have her climbing spikes to throw in his face.

The man was inspecting the column that she had taken the box from, she was aware of its weight in her pouch. It was clear that something had been hidden inside the column.

"You can come out now," the man said casually. Femira froze, her breath catching in her throat. *I can run for it,* she thought, glancing toward the doorway. Maybe the other man hadn't set the guards yet, maybe the hallway was still empty.

"Trust me, you won't get far... come out from behind that mound," he said as he made his way to the altar, not even looking in her direction. He knew where she was... if he knew where she was he could have killed her already.

Femira worked best with no plan. He didn't know what she had found, she had all the power. He's just a thief like her... *a thief that came too late. All he has is muscle... and a sword... and an army.* She took a breath, stood up and walked out into the center of the room.

The man was looking through the pages of the book and didn't look up. Femira felt awkward just standing there but she wouldn't be the one to break the silence.

"You have something I want," he said eventually, still not looking up.

"You'll have to be specific," she said, her heart pounding, all rationality screaming at her to run. He looked up at her and, to her surprise, he wore a friendly smile.

He was old, not *very* old, but still old enough that his face had creases at the eyes and the forehead. He had a tight blond beard and pale eyes that glowed purple in the light of the aeristone.

"You're a thief," he smirked. "Very bold of you to sneak into a palace that is under attack."

"I would say opportunistic." That's the word that Lichtin always used when dealing with buyers. *We're not thieves, we're opportunists.* He would say.

"Opportunistic indeed. I'm happy to have provided this *opportunity* for you." He walked around from behind the altar, carrying the book. "But Osiri—and everything in it—now belongs to the Kingdom of Reldon. Thieving from the crown is a tremendous crime."

"Well, we're not in Reldon, and I'm not Reldoni, so I think this is a bit of a grey area." The words just came out, Femira was starting to feel oddly relaxed, her panic easing.

"No... you're not Reldoni—or Altarean for that matter. You look like you might be Keiran."

"How much are you willing to pay?" she said sharply, they were wasting time. *What does it matter if I'm Keiran?*

"And what is it you're looking to sell?" The smile was gone, his purple-cast eyes watching her hungrily. Slowly, Femira pulled the box from her pouch, taking a step back. He was far from arm's reach but Femira wanted to be closer to the door in case she needed to bolt.

"A thousand gold marks," she said with confidence. It was an insanely high number, a single gold mark could buy her a permanent room in the city. "For the box..." she could tell by the look in his eyes that he would pay any price for the box. She then added with a raised finger, "and how to open it."

"You don't know how to open it," the man said.

"Yes, I do!" she retorted in offence.

"You're a good liar," he smiled, "tell me, are you working alone?"

What kind of question is that? Was he probing to see if she had backup? She didn't want to give any credit to Lichtin or the crew, all they did was pay off the informant that *she'd* sourced.

"If you kill me," she warned, "you'll never find out how to open it."

"I won't kill you," he replied and pulled out a small metal device from his sword belt, "if you answer me truthfully." He pointed the device at her, it was small and metal with a wooden handle. "Do you know what this is?"

"It's a pistol... I think," she had heard the crew talking about them. They were like the cannons on ships, only they could fit in your hand. Femira had seen—and heard—cannons firing against the palace walls in the early days of the invasion. She didn't particularly want one fired at her face.

"Who are you working with?" he asked again.

"Nobody," she replied.

"Who are you working *for*?"

"Nobody," she snapped. He clicked something on the pistol gently. Femira could feel herself starting to sweat. "Nobody! I swear. I sometimes work with a crew in the city, but not on this job."

"Do you know what's inside the box?"

Femira paused. She didn't want to give up her only bargaining chip. She had to make him believe that she could open it.

"No," she replied, "but I *can* open it."

He walked forward, still holding the pistol pointed at her. "I believe you," he said, and gently took the box from her. Fear began to rise in her. *He needs me to open that, he can't kill me.* She could run for it now, she *should* run. She still had a handful of aeristone, and with all the aeristone going back to Reldon, it would sell for a high price. Memories of the cannonballs exploding against the palace walls stopped her from running. *He needs me, he can't open it.* Neither could she yet but that didn't matter right now.

"I'm impressed that you made it here before me," the man mused, "what is your name?"

"Vreth," she replied. *If you get caught, never tell them your real name.* Lichtin always said. *Never tell them my name either! In fact, just say nothing and run.* She should be running, why wasn't she running?

"Vreth," he smirked, "clever… I like that. My name is Hannis Garld, Lord General of the Reldoni army," he clicked on a section of the box and it popped open.

Femira's chest tightened. *Run! Run now!* Femira dashed for the door, but it slammed shut. *How?* She turned to look at the man, panic rising in her. He was still smiling, the pistol was no longer pointing at her.

Garld reached into the box and pulled out the tiniest chip of a glowing runestone, smaller than a halfpenny. It was clear—like a diamond but at the same time *not* like a diamond. She didn't recognize it and she'd stolen her share of gemstones.

Garld had a terrifying smile. "You have no idea how long I have searched for this, Vreth," he didn't take his eyes off the fleck of stone.

"And yet… *you* got to it before me," he said. Femira got a sinking feeling in her chest.

"I want to offer you a job."

"What kind of job?" she asked carefully.

"I can see what you did to unlock the door… you're skilled with that—" Garld nodded to the glowing earthstone around her neck, "—despite being obviously untrained. Working for me, you can learn how to wield its power properly. You will be serving a *real* purpose. You will be respected… and feared." She couldn't deny that it was a tempting offer even if there wasn't the unspoken threat of being killed for refusing. Lichtin had lured her in with a similar promise, but he'd only taught her a little, and she was beginning to suspect he didn't know much more than that.

"And what do you need me to do?" She asked, uncertain. He smiled, the same knowing smile that Lichtin so regularly used.

"I want you to kill someone."

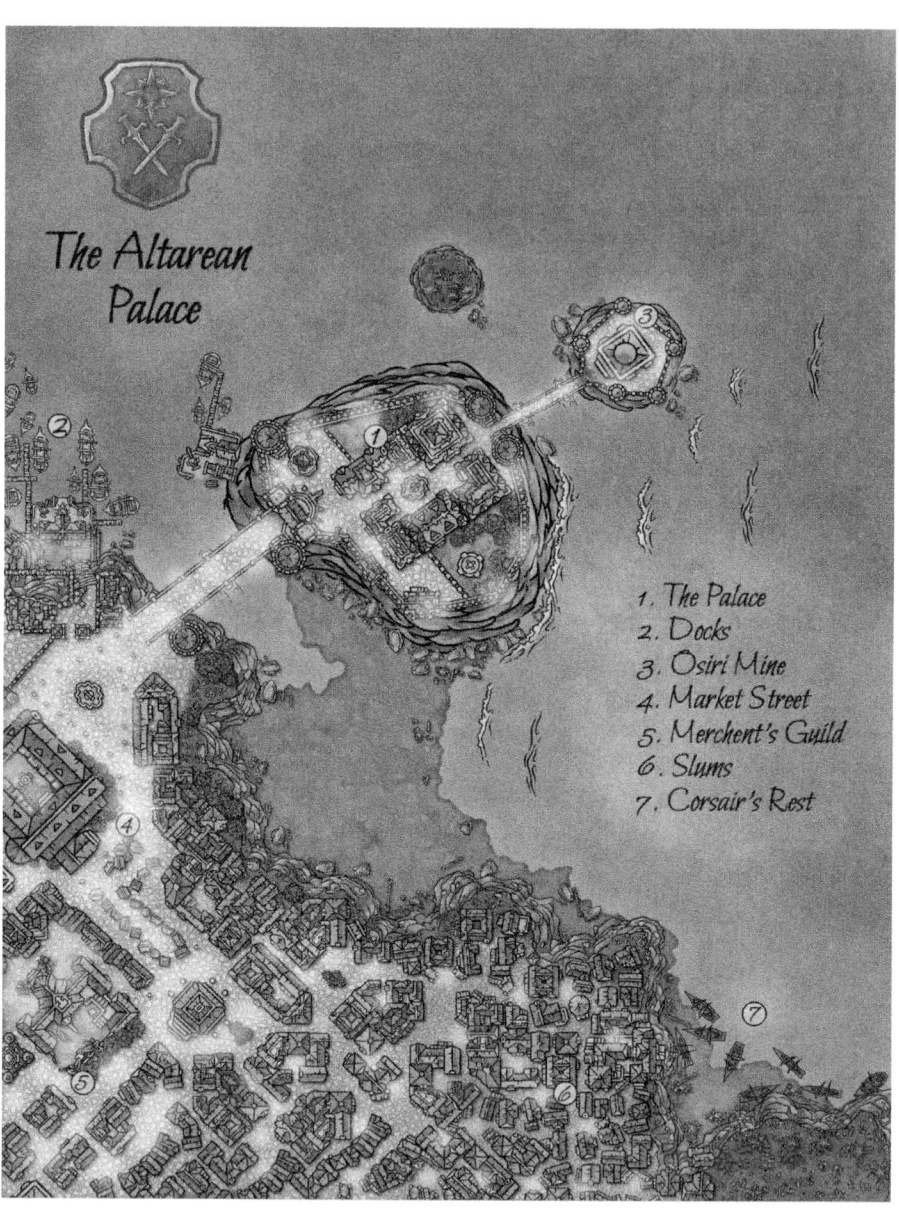

CHAPTER 2

An Efficient Sacking

Garld escorted 'Vreth' to the upper chambers of the Osiri mines. The chambers Femira had so carefully avoided when making her way to the sealed room. Femira was shocked by the number of soldiers running about. To her it seemed chaotic, but Garld calmly laid out orders as he passed soldiers, many of whom were to assist in moving the aeristone cache.

Femira could feel her pulse throbbing against the weight of the earthstone cord around her neck. She couldn't shake the thought of it being a noose. She'd never been caught thieving before—well, at least not in any situations that had actually mattered. She still wasn't certain whether this Lord-whatever Garld actually meant what he said or if he was just planning to lock her up. *But why lie in the first place? He would have no reason to, I'm already caught.*

"Stay quiet when I speak, and go along with whatever I say," Garld instructed. He had that kind of voice you just didn't disagree with, the kind that was well used to telling others what to do. Femira nodded and followed him into a small chamber. There was a corpse pushed against the wall and a horrific amount of blood and fleshy bits on the floor that Femira couldn't bring herself to look at. There was a mix of Reldoni and unarmed Altarean soldiers in the room.

"Darza, your men have assisted admirably." Garld said to a grey-haired stormguard. The stormguard's armour was so ostensibly ornate that even Femira could tell this man was not a real soldier, the breastplate was gilded with small decorative wings inlaid and he wore a fanciful blue cape. It was a stark contrast to the simple black and red uniforms of the Reldoni soldiers.

"Thank you General... and our agreement?"

"Your men will continue to assist until we are sure we have unearthed every cache," Garld replied.

"And the others?"

"They will be kept safe. You will find, Captain Darza, that the Reldoni are a merciful —"

"—*Merciful!*" Femira heard a woman shriek. She had not noticed the other woman in the corner of the room, she had the same dark Keiran complexion as Femira—and looked to be similar age, perhaps a bit older. The woman's face was contorted in a knot of revulsion, "you would call this invasion *merciful!* You murdered my husband, he would have surrendered if you allowed him, he—"

"—Lady Annali," Darza interjected, "please, if you would only—"

"—And you," the Keiran woman rounded on Darza, "you coward! You're a *disgrace* to the stormguards, you would stand here and treat with them. *They killed your King!*"

"And they will kill you as well if you resist, my Lady," Darza implored, "I beg you, please. The palace is lost and they are offering us our lives."

"If your men had been fighting with the rest of the stormguards—"

"—That is enough," Garld said, holding up his hand and gesturing to two of his own soldiers. "Put Lady Annali with the other *less co-operative* nobles. Perhaps a few days in a cell will help give her some perspective." Annali spewed more insults as two of the Reldoni soldiers not-very-gently escorted her from the chamber.

"Another we found in the lower levels," Garld said, nodding towards Femira, "she was hiding in one of the larger storerooms, see her put with the other highborn." Femira felt the weight of all the eyes in the room on her. If she hadn't felt so uncomfortable under all those eyes she would have laughed hysterically at the prospect that they would think her highborn. Captain Darza did not look pleased, his dark eyes the heaviest of all. "My lord, forgive me but this girl. She is no highborn. I think she may be—"

"—A relative of Lady Annali's, I'm sure," Garld cut him off sternly, "have her put with the group to be brought to the *Ambition*."

"Of course, my lord," Darza said, bowing his head. The grey-haired man beckoned Femira to follow him and together, with a Reldoni soldier escort, they moved into a far larger chamber.

Unlike the smaller rooms and hallways of Osiri, this room had lines of thin windows along one of the walls. At this hour there was no light from the outside and so the chamber was lit by long rows of braziers. The chamber was packed full with terrified, rich, little snot bags and their more rich and equally terrified parents.

"You were either incredibly stupid or incredibly desperate to have chosen tonight to sneak into the mine, thief." Darza said to Femira as he walked her down the lines of braziers.

"What makes you think this was the first time, old man?" Darza bristled visibly at the comment and Femira felt a smirk pull at her mouth. *Hit a nerve, did I?*

"Regardless," he continued, "you're likely in more danger being highborn tonight than a thief. Consider yourself very fortunate should you see the morning." He seemed satisfied when she didn't respond. They walked on, some of the highborn calling out to Darza as they passed, all of them distressed.

"Darza! What are they going to do with us?"

"Darza! have you seen the King?"—or lord whats-his-face, or lady whatever.

"Darza! Are they going to kill us?"

Whenever Darza did respond, it was with calming—and completely futile— words, for the people were not in anyway relieved after they passed. Occasionally, someone would accuse Darza of being a traitor or a coward for helping the invaders but the Reldoni soldiers were quick to take them away in the same manner as that highborn Keiran lady.

The commonfolk in the city knew who Lady Annali was; she had married the King's younger brother Lord Reselas the past unionsday. Femira herself had not joined the unionsday celebration on the sand, all those people heading out past the city tidewalls had meant that the city was ripe for thieving. Not that any commonfolk could have gotten anywhere near any of the highborn weddings, a kindly contingent of bluecloaks were tasked with making sure that the rabble from commoner weddings didn't flow over into their fancy celebrations. Even more of a reason for thieving.

It was well known that Annali and Reselas' marriage had been an arranged bond between Keiran and Altarea. *Little good it did them when the Reldoni warships appeared on the horizon.* The Keiran alliance it seems was as much security as a stone wall; when someone with a hammer or an earthstone came, it fell to dust.

Darza left Femira with a large group of very anxious highborn. All of them wore fine clothing of silk or linen. Femira stuck out like dog's balls in her black climbing gear. None of the others tried to make conversation with her, just the occasional suspicious glance. That suited her fine, *don't want to talk to any of you pompous shitbags either.*

When the nobles spoke to one another, they did so in hushed tones, "what do you think they'll do with us?" or "where are we going" were the general themes of their discussions. The conversations did little to ease Femira's own ever-growing concerns. *Why did I agree to this?* She began questioning herself after sitting on the tiles for a while. Perhaps, she should be finding a way to escape, to sneak away. The effort of the arduous climb earlier in the evening, in addition to her bruised hip, and the cuts on her hand, had left her exhausted.

After a few hours, a woman in palace servant livery passed by. She offered Femira fresh bandages for her hands. The woman didn't question how Femira had gotten the injuries, she simply washed, bandaged and moved on.

Femira fought against the urge to lie down on the tiles and sleep, fatigue threatening to overwhelm her. If she could make it back to the other side of the destroyed bridge, she could still climb back the way she had come. She could summon enough energy for that, couldn't she? Femira could just disappear into the night like a real vreth. She could just return back to Lichtin's crew with her tail between her legs, achieving nothing but a few scrapes on her hands for her bold burglary of Osiri itself. *Not entirely true,* she thought, patting the handful of aeristone she had pocketed.

Surely, the job Garld had offered her wasn't real, why would a General need someone like her to kill someone? Didn't he have an entire army to kill a whole bunch of people?

"*Are they taking you to their warship also?*" It took Femira a moment to realise that the speaker, a younger pretty highborn girl, had asked Femira the question in her own Keiran language. *Warship?*

"I'm not sure," Femira responded in Common Tongue.

The girl vanished among all the other highborn faces when Femira didn't offer anything else for conversation.

As the night pressed on, Femira moved to one of the walls and sat with her back against it.

The nobles were grumbling about not having comfortable seating, but Femira had spent more nights than she cared to remember sleeping on the street. She remembered the times where the rainwater from the makeshift shelters that her once bigger—now forever little—brothers had built in alleyways.

The sky outside started to lighten; light blue at first, and gradually growing into the stronger purple and pinks that often came with the morning after a storm.

Eventually, more Reldoni soldiers arrived and began taking groups of people out of the room. At first, there was some mild opposition from the highborn, scared people just looking for answers on what might happen to them. However nobody openly spoke out against the armed men.

Femira was huddled along with those around her. They were brought out of Osiri, and across the wooden reconstruction bridge that connected the stacks.

The Reldoni were already at work clearing away the bodies, piling the Altareans into huge pyres. The fallen Reldoni were carted off elsewhere for funeral rites. Femira wasn't sure if it was the light of the rising sun casting the courtyard in red, or if it was just the stains of blood.

The nobles wailed as they passed the pyres and although Femira had not known any of the fallen soldiers personally, she couldn't help but feel their loss. The sulfuric smell of the burning bodies made some of the highborn wretch as clouds of smoke drifted across the courtyard. Femira herself tried to stifle the stench with her hands but it did little good to mask it. In all the stories she heard of great battles and wars fought, she never considered what happened *after* the battle. Who cleaned up the mess left behind by the fallen?

The people cleaning up didn't look like soldiers as they weren't wearing armour or the black and red tabards the soldiers had. These were just regular men and women with blood stained tunics and masks getting on with their work. *Was this just an everyday job to them?* To just follow along and clean up the bodies of their enemies... and friends. They were grim thoughts that Femira couldn't shake as they passed by more bodies.

When they reached an open area of the courtyard, they were told to empty their pockets. Femira considered resisting when a soldier ordered her to hand over the handful of aeristone. Reluctantly, she made the wiser choice and handed them over. She still had the one she'd looted earlier from the corpse of that stormguard tucked into a secret pocket and—more importantly—the soldier hadn't spotted the glow of her earthstone tucked under her shirt.

The soldier's eyes widened at the handful of aeristone and he excitedly ran off. It reminded her of when the other thugs in the crewhouse would take a cut of the things that *she'd* stolen. The highborn around her looked relieved when the soldier had left, she could see some had pendants of aeristone—status symbols for them rather than any functional use. *Don't worry he'll be back for those too.*

Femira figured that now, while they were being moved, would be the best chance to slip away. She didn't know what Garld's plans were for her, and she didn't particularly feel like sticking around to find out. Despite the tempting offer to train her how to use her earthstone. *But then again, would Lichtin ever be able to live up to his promises?* Maybe she was better off taking the chance here.

As they passed through the courtyard and into the palace buildings, Femira tried to decide when her best opportunity would arise to sneak away. They passed dark hallways where she couldn't see any soldiers loitering but every time she thought to do it her legs wouldn't run, she just kept in line with the Altareans as they were marched to—what she guessed—were the lower levels of the palace.

Her exhaustion once again tried to crush her, but she lumbered on step after step. They were led down to the palace docks, on the northern side of the stack—the opposite side of where Femira had climbed earlier that night.

The enormous warship dwarfed the tiny palace dock. It was a great beast of a ship, constructed of wood and steel. There were four imposing masts for sails, and rows of cannons along both sides.

Those cannons had spewn fire and chaos on the walls in the days leading up to the capture of the palace. The city itself had been spared such treatment, having already been under Reldoni occupation for weeks. When the warships first arrived almost two months before, the King had refused to treat with the invaders and sealed himself—along with his most important highborn—in the palace to hold out for Keiran reinforcements that would never arrive. The city mayor surrendered when the first warships arrived and had been rewarded with minimal casualties in the city.

Through her haze of fatigue, Femira couldn't fully grasp the scale of the warship or the hundreds of soldiers and sailors moving about. She quietly followed along as her group was taken to one of the holds inside the bowels of the ship. She was shown to a sleeping roll, where she was finally able to collapse into sleep.

***

Any prospects of escaping became a distant thought.

Femira wasn't sure if she even wanted to escape. *What do I have to escape to? A bunk in Lichtin's safehouse?* Safe was not an apt description of the place either as most of his crew were thugs. Her brothers had protected her from some of the worst, but they were both gone now. They were in the ground, like everyone else who ever tried to care for her. Lichtin's protection wouldn't last long either. She'd found comfort in his company after her brothers died but the relationship had grown sour. She was heavily indebted to Lichtin for months of food, board and protection. Lichtin had made it very clear that he would make her suffer if she tried to flee the city without paying him his due. *Well, try and find me on this warship, you bastard.*

Femira wasn't sure how long she had slept, there weren't any windows in the hold so she couldn't even tell if it was still daylight or not. Soldiers came and left, dropping off crates of looted spoils from the palace.

She heard the soldiers argue over 'quarters'—sounded like the shit end of the stick to Femira. You risk your life in a battle and for everything you find, you only get a *quarter* of it, and the rest goes back to the army, or your boss or something like that. *I suppose it's not much different to me having to give half of what I steal to Lichtin.*

Femira toyed with the earthstone still around her neck.
"If you run off with that, trust me, girl I will find you. And you'll be fucking sorry you crossed me," Lichtin loved to remind her of all the things she'd be sorry for doing or not doing. *Well, you've been crossed Lichtin and I'm not sorry... yet.*

Soldiers would come, take some people from the group and leave. Sometimes they dropped new nobles off. All of them were confused and terrified, as if this was the worst place in the world to be. *A lot of worse places right here in your own disgusting city, trust me.*

Altareans in palace staff uniforms came with food every few hours. Being escorted by a Reldoni soldier, they often brought news for the group. From what Femira gathered; there were still remnants of stormguards holed up in different parts of the palace fighting. *Still!* The King was definitely dead as were most of the royal family. Most highborn had either surrendered or were captured. That Keiran highborn, Lady Annali, had finally stopped resisting and was apparently aboard one of the warships. King Amenia Solodan's infant son was now the only member of the Altarean royal family still alive.

An important looking soldier came after a while and announced he was looking for 'Vreth'. It had taken an embarrassingly long time for Femira to remember that *she* was Vreth.

The soldier took her to another similar hold in the ship but with nicer bedding. She was fed again, slept more and when she awoke, the ship was heaving in repetitive lurches.

She woke to General Garld entering the hold. He told the other Altareans and soldiers to leave and made his way to her sleeping cot, pulling a wooden chair from the single table in the room. He was still wearing the same stiff dark red uniform she had seen him in before.

"I had half expected you to slip past your guards and disappear, little Vreth," he said with a smirk.

"I considered it," she replied, sitting up on her sleeping mat. She felt unrested despite the amount of sleep she'd had. "But you've made a tempting offer. Besides, why would I give up *all* of this," she said, gesturing around the room; a dozen sleeping cots aligned in a tight row, each with its own grimy bucket for washing with, there was a shared table and a couple of chairs that they ate at. Adjoining the room was another privy where they could shit in a bucket and have one of the Reldoni soldiers empty it over the side of the ship. *If that isn't luxury, I don't know what is.*

"My apologies, I couldn't find you sooner. As you might guess, I was preoccupied with the take-over administration"

"Take-over administration," Femira mused, "is that fancy talk for ransacking and stealing—don't get me wrong, I'm all for it—Never liked the Altarean highborn much myself. And I can't exactly judge someone for stealing now can I?"

"Your work for me will be much the same as it was before," Garld said, "I was impressed by your skills in Osiri. To make it that far on your own, with such little resources... you're from Keiran, yes?" People loved to point that out all the time, her dark skin was like holding a big sign that said 'Hey! Just so you know, I'm Keiran!' So why did people always have to state the fact to her? She didn't respond and they spent a few uncomfortable moments just watching eachother.

"If we're to work together, we'll need to learn to trust one another," Garld said eventually.

"Why do you need *me*? Do you not have a thousand soldiers out there to kill for you?"

"On this ship, not so much as that," he replied with a smile, "but there are some tasks that require a more subtle approach than a team of soldiers swinging swords. I saw what you did in Osiri, how you opened that door. Pulling in that much metal so quickly, even for my most talented stonebreakers, it would have taken days, yet you managed it in—what?—a few hours, if even?"

She nodded, "maybe an hour," she replied.

"And I'm going to hazard a guess that you have yet to learn shaping," he said, looking pointedly at the still glowing earthstone around her neck.

Femira had thought once that maybe it just re-charged over time and so she had avoided giving the runestone back to Lichtin for a week. But the time hadn't dulled the light even slightly. *Don't run before you can walk,* he would chime at her whenever she asked him how to drain the light. And so, she was bound to always return to him.

"Of course I can," Femira lied. Garld narrowed his eyes at her. Then, he got up from his seat, "I will not work with you if you continue to lie to me," he said, and moved to leave.

"Fine," she said hurriedly, "I'm sorry! I don't know how to use it properly, not yet. Lichtin, my boss—former boss—wouldn't show me. I'd been trying to figure it out on my own but..."

Garld sat back down on his chair, and leaned close to her. "May I?" he asked, reaching for the earthstone around her neck. She nodded stiffly, uncomfortable with the idea of him taking her only valuable possession.

His hand clasped around the runestone but he didn't make any moves to yank it from its cord. Instead, he raised his other free hand in the air and in it, black sand gradually began to appear from nothing. More and more of the sand coalesced, floating and twirling above his open palm. The sand began to consolidate into a rough black rock—the same type of rock that the Altarean palace was built on, that Femira had climbed, sinking her hands into. Gears in Femira's mind were aligning for the first time as the runestone finally made sense to her. *It just moves the stone. It doesn't dissolve or destroy. It holds it!* She leaned back on her cot stunned, not in awe of what she had seen, but in shock over her own stupidity for not realising it sooner.

"You have never seen stoneshaping?" Garld asked, seeming genuinely surprised.

"He never showed me this,"

"I can teach you, nothing will be held back, I promise you. But you must learn to trust me"

"How?—Not the trust part—How do you do *that*?" Femira asked, eagerly pointing at the lump of black rock in his hand. Answers to the secrets she'd been craving ever since Lichtin had first loaned her the earthstone.

"It's a simple technique, once you know the basics. It will take time to learn and very few can master it... I, myself, would be considered an amateur. But I have stonebreakers in my ranks that will teach you." Garld said, and then abruptly changed the conversation, "*Can you speak Keiran?*"

She was so rapt by his promise of knowledge that she didn't even notice that he had switched to Keiran to ask the question.

"*Yes,*" she answered in the same language, "*I was born there.*"

"Good," he replied, switching back to Common, "how are your fighting skills? I'm guessing you haven't had much formal training, but have you ever fought armed before?"

"Fist fights, yes. A lot. With knives, not so much," she answered quickly and then continued before he had the chance to push her with further questions. "Does stoneshaping make the light fade from the stone? And when can your stonebreakers show me how to do it?"

"This is called the *transference*, when you draw in the mass of rock or metal it is converted to energy in the aradium gemstone—earthstone, as you call it. This energy is the light that you see. When you syphon the energy away, and back into physical form, the light fades. When we return to Epilas, your true training will begin. But first, my questions. How long have you lived in Altarea?"

"My mother took me and my brothers here when I was very little—younger than ten, maybe—I can't remember," she said and then salted with her customary lie, "she died soon after we arrived." She might as well have for all the woman had done for Femira.

"I see," Garld nodded, "I'm sorry to hear that... will any of the Altarean highborn recognise you?"

"If they did, I wouldn't be a very good burglar now, would I?"

"You've never worked for any of them before is what I mean."

"No, I only worked with Lichtin. He would get the jobs and assign them."

"You said you worked alone when you broke into Osiri, did you know what you were looking for?"

"I was working alone—I paid off a bluecloak for information on the layout of Osiri. He was the one who told me about the room with the metal door," Femira didn't want to tell him that it was Lichtin that had strong-armed the bluecloak with his skaga addiction to garner the information. A part of her loved that Garld thought she had done it all on her own. *And I pretty much did. I did the hard part of actually getting inside the palace.*

Femira continued, "I didn't know for sure what would be inside, but it's pretty clear if someone makes a big door out of metal, they've got something valuable to hide."

"How did you know where the soulstone was hidden?" This topic gave him an intensity that made Femira withdraw slightly.

"The diamond chip?" she asked.

"Yes."

"I knew they were hiding something," she responded truthfully, "it didn't make sense to store all that aeristone in one place. Even if you do have mounds of it, it's smarter to stash smaller caches. The whole place just seemed *off* and then I noticed that column just looked out of place, it was just a guess that it was hidden in there."

"You have good instincts," Garld remarked, "those columns didn't look stoneshaped, not many people would have guessed something was hidden inside. The jobs I have in mind for you will have need for this ingenuity."

Femira suspected in the back of her mind that Garld was similar to Lichtin, he would use her desire to learn more of stoneshaping to get her to keep coming back to him. Despite his promise that he was offering this knowledge up front.

"Are any of your stonebreakers on this ship?" she pressed, "can they show me now?" Garld leaned back on his chair, assessing her. He was silent a moment before calling out to the soldiers waiting outside.

"Misandrei," Garld introduced a tall Reldoni soldier who entered, "is one of my elites." The woman had short burnt-red hair, and striking blue eyes, one had a distinctive scar running above it. She had a strong build and Femira noticed that her uniform differed from the other Reldoni soldiers slightly. It was entirely black and was trimmed with silver. She had steel pauldrons emblazoned with a shield. It was not unlike Garld's own uniform but seemed more practical.

"Misandrei is one of the most skilled soldiers in our ranks," Garld continued, "adept in stonebreaking, and the other elemental runestones. In our ranks, she is what we call a bloodshedder." Femira couldn't help but feel intimidated by the imposing woman. Misandrei nodded to Femira in acknowledgement.

"Lady Annali will be training with you, Misandrei, for the duration of our return trip to Epilas, she is already quite an accomplished stonebreaker but she will require assistance in mastering stoneshaping, along with the other runestones. Her bloodshedder training will begin in earnest upon our return to Epilas," Garld said.

"It would be my pleasure to train you, Lady Annali. The other highborn are far more reluctant than yourself to learn our ways of runewielding."

Femira was dumbfounded. *Lady Annali?*

She recalled the other Keiran woman she had seen in the palace, the one who had argued with Darza and Garld. She remained slightly agape, looking between Garld and Misandrei. Garld nodded slightly and rose from his seat.

"I will check in on you again in a few days, Lady Annali. I hope you find the journey to Epilas to be… educational," Garld winked, and then left the room, leaving her alone with the bloodshedder.

This woman has answers.

"I want to learn how to stoneshape," Femira said, abruptly sweeping aside her concern over Garld calling her Annali. Femira held up her glowing earthstone, "how do I drain the light from this?"

"You can stonebreak already?" Misandrei asked, stepping closer to her. Femira was not tall to begin with, and sitting on her small sleeping cot, Misandrei towered over her. Femira nodded in response.

"The transference, the feeling you get when you draw rock into the stone," Misandrei said.

"The vibrations?" Femira asked.

"Yes, some describe it like that. Like a pulsing… you can feel it now?"

Femira closed her eyes, and tried to feel the vibrations. She gripped the earthstone in her non-bandaged hand, the familiar pulsations running up her arm as she did so. She nodded.

"Good," Misandrei nodded, "this is the transference. You already hold the energy in your body, now you need to make it take form in your mind. Hold out your other hand." Femira did as commanded, and held out the palm of her bandaged hand.

"Concentrate," Misandrei instructed, "*feel* the energy move through your body, and guide it into that hand." Femira kept her eyes closed and felt the pulsations moving up her arm. She brought her attention to other parts of her body and the pulsing seemed to *shift* through her. *Why had I never tried this before?* It seemed so obvious now. She focused on her chest and felt the vibrations thrum against her heart and breastbone. She shifted her focus to her open hand and felt the vibrations congregate there. Her hand shook with it.

"Good," she heard Misandrei's voice, "now *force* this energy from your body."

Femira wasn't exactly sure how but she focused on expelling the vibrations out. A cloud of dust and sand exploded from her hand. Femira let out a shameful yelp and jumped at the sudden burst, getting a mouthful of grit and dust. Misandrei, calmly brushed the dust from her uniform and bits of gravel from her hair.

"Interesting," she said, "you're not as practised as I thought."

"Well I have—"

"—Not a question," Misandrei interrupted, holding up her hand, "you are clumsy… but not without talent and—with practice—you might be useful."

Clumsy! Femira thought incredulously, she was Vreth! She climbed the Altarean palace wall undetected, she had stolen Lady Haresta's jewels when she was in the *same* room… albeit she was asleep—and Femira had in fact woken the woman when she had crept back out the window, but still!

"You will practise more, and I shall have you moved to a private cabin as befits your station." Misandrei spoke while looking around at the tightly packed sleeping cots, "this will also protect your Altarean friends from stray chunks of rock flying into their faces, I think."

CHAPTER 3

A Man's Hate or His Pity

Smoke rose from the ironworks of Rubastre.
No one throughout history could ever describe the city of Rubastre as beautiful. Even during the reign of the Sorcerer Kings this settlement's primary purpose had been the production of iron and steel. The hills to the north of the city were dense in iron and the Fahren river was wide enough for larger vessels to dock, and ferry it all away to the more important parts of the world.

Soot stained the buildings, the sky was a constant grey—and not to mention the ever present snowfalls—the entire place had a very depressing atmosphere. At least that was what Prince Daegan of Reldon thought as he stepped off his longship. He was eager to finally be off the vessel for the first time in weeks, but none-too-impressed that this was his destination.

Daegan had read descriptions of the city, looked at the maps and depictions but none could truly grasp the air of misery in the place. The settlement was organised in a circle like a giant carriage wheel left to freeze and rust in the snow. The Farhen river cut directly through the centre.

The inner sections of the city housed the ironworks where the powerhouse of Rubane produced most of the steel in the northern kingdoms. The outer rings were for the houses of all the soot-stained people that worked in the mills along with fishmongers, markets, brothels and everything else that makes a city like this limp on.

Why the Arch-duke of Rubane chose Rubastre as his capital city baffled Daegan. *Surely with all the steel this place exports, he could build himself a suitable palace someplace else. Any* place *else.*

"Well, we've arrived," Daegan announced to his companion, another Reldoni man. Like Daegan, he was tall with light tan skin and dark hair, "welcome to our new home, Captain Ferath."

"Maybe you, my lord. I'm only here until you get settled then I'm back to Epilas," the soldier replied, waving the escort of six more bodyguards into position around them as they made their way through the busy port.

"Nonsense," Daegan grinned, "what's for you in Epilas? Hours of training drills? My brother would put your talents to waste fighting Altareans or Reinish or whoever it is my father is most bothered with. You're much better off here with me," Daegan gave an extravagant wave to the city before them, "and this wondrous place. The jewel of Rubane they call it."

"Do they now? I wouldn't call it a jewel myself."

"No? Look how the fires in the ironworks light up the sky in pockets of that orangey-brown colour. You'd swear we were inside the heart of a topaz."

"What happened to Rubastre being the 'very pit of human civilization at the edge of the world' as you described it?"

"Don't know what you're talking about," Daegan replied as they passed a fishing vessel pouring the day's putrid catch right out onto the dock, "seems like a delightful place."

Waiting for them at the base of the pier was an escort of a dozen Rubanian guards wearing the grey livery of Arch-duke Edmund. *And why choose grey of all colours at your disposal! As if your city wasn't depressing enough.* They had the white bear of Dal'Regan House emblazoned on their tabards. *A hammer and anvil would be more suitable, considering that's all you do up here.* At their head waited a long haired man, his alabaster skin as light as his white hair.

"Honourable Prince," the man bowed, he was armed with a longsword strapped to his back. As were the rest of his soldiers. *All men... No surprises there.*

"I am Captain Keltin, Captain of the Dukesguard. The Arch-duke would have come himself but a matter with the Ironworker's Guild has delayed him." *Yes, yes I'm sure the Arch-duke personally comes down to this disgusting dock every chance he gets.*

"I hope you had a pleasant journey here, my lord," Keltin continued.

"Oh yes," Daegan replied with a smile, "I do love retching up my breakfast every morning. If only I were not bound to your lovely city I would have stayed out at sea forever."

"Um, indeed, my lord," Keltin replied. *That Rubanian wit living up to its reputation, this is going to be wonderful.*

Daegan declined the offer of a carriage. After six weeks at sea, he was restless and eager to finally be able to use his own feet again. It also gave him a chance to truly absorb all of the sights and smells of his new home. His servants were still unloading his luggage from the ship and would follow after him.

The Rubanian guards assured him that it would be an hour or so walk to the Arch-duke's Palace. Daegan had come to regret his decision not long into the walk. He wore his finest boots however the slushy grey-black snow quickly permeated through the velvet. His purple cloak did little to repel the cold so Daegan picked up his pace so as to try to get warmer from the movement.

Keltin and the other members of the Dukesguard seemed perfectly at ease in the chilly morning air. *Well they should be used to it, living here your whole life.* He glanced over at Ferath, the man showed no indication that the cold bothered him even though his black uniform was less protective than Daegan's own garb. *But then again he probably has a topaz tucked away somewhere he can pull heat from,* Daegan thought bitterly.

As they passed the main thoroughfare of the city leading up to the Arch-duke's palace, Daegan asked, "where might a man find the best wine in the city?"

"Grapes don't really grow this far north, m'lord," Keltin replied. "But you'll find plenty of reputable whitewhiskey houses this close to the palace. This part of the city's heavily patrolled, you won't get any of the roughs or ironworkers around here. Mostly all highborn in these parts, along with wealthy merchants and engineers. Some of them import fancy Reinish wines and the like, so you might find a bottle or two in some of these places."

The buildings closer to the palace certainly looked *less* soot-stained. Daegan noticed there were workmen cleaning away the grey slush from the streets and alleyways. The gaslamps were also lit even though it was only late morning.

"And if you were looking for something a little *less* reputable," Daegan probed.

"Um," Keltin seemed uncomfortable, "there are some taverns at the lower end of the street... poker games and the like."

"I don't suppose there are any vicedens?" Daegan asked bluntly.

"Er—Again, you will only find reputable establishments closer to the palace. But the bordellos would be closer to the lower end, the women in those places though, m'lord. Well, it's not the place for a gentleman such as yourself." *These Rubanians really are frigid aren't they.* Even the idea of only women in a viceden seemed strange to Daegan. *This is Rubane after all,* he reminded himself.

They passed through a large set of palisade gates and into the palace grounds. The Arch-duke had made a good attempt at replicating the grandeur of southern palaces; a large open courtyard and an impressive central building with sheltered bridges connecting to the outer buildings and towers. The spired towers and tiled roofs were tall, reaching up to points, likely so that the snow would slide off more easily. At the centre of the courtyard was a large bronze statue depicting a man wielding a giant hammer.

Daegan felt a wash of warmth as they finally entered the main building of the palace. He was already envisaging a hot bath to soothe warmth back into his toes. Inside the palace, to Daegan's surprise, he spotted no open braziers yet somehow the large courtroom was heated. The palace wasn't as opulent as Daegan's father's palace in Reldon, or even the mansions of the other Reldoni highborn, but there was subtle beauty to the place.

There was a gaudy network of brass pipes fed along the walls with brightly shining topazes inlaid into the pipes. The topazes themselves gave out amber light, but not nearly enough to fully illuminate the hallways alone. *A strange decoration.*

To his disappointment, Daegan was brought directly to the Arch-duke's offices rather than to his new apartments in the palace.

"Prince Daegan," the Arch-duke said as he entered the large office, "my apologies I could not greet you at the dock. My, you've grown so much since my last visit to Reldon." *You didn't see me when you visited.* As Daegan recalled, his father had him hidden away from the foreign dignitaries. The Arch-duke wore fine silver thread clothes and had a long stylised white moustache.

"Arch-duke Edmund, I'm honoured to be placed here," Daegan said, inclining his head, "my predecessor had nothing but the highest of praise for your city." *If you consider 'a cold frozen hell'—as Ormand described it—to be a compliment.*

"Ambassador Ormand was much loved here," the Arch-duke replied. "He had an unfathomable way with both the ironworkers and mercantile guilds." Bribes had been Ormand's only seed of advice to Daegan. *Bribes and a fur-lined cloak.*

"I assure you," Edmund continued, "the honour is entirely ours, a Prince of Reldon will always be welcome in my halls... although I see you have learned the first lesson of the north."

He nodded to Daegan's sodden boots, "the cold gets inside you quickly up here. My steward will escort you to your new apartments, you will find all the luxuries you would expect, I'm sure."

"You are too kind, Arch-duke," Daegan replied, eager at the prospect of having warm, dry feet again.

"There is a feast planned for this evening, a welcoming for our new Reldoni Ambassador. We will do great work together, Prince Daegan, I look forward to it." The Arch-duke smiled and was already on his way out of the office to his next appointment before Daegan could say anything more.

***

"These will do," Daegan said as he inspected his new quarters. He did have to admit, they were rather nice rooms. More than what he had expected. A large antechamber with space for both dining and lounging, a set of bedchambers and side rooms for his senior servants and guards—even a balcony in case he wanted to step outside for a taste of the cold biting air.

The master bedchamber also had a brass tub for bathing in. He fervently unlaced his boots and discarded them as the last of the servants unpacked his things. His own manservant—Thalan—was elsewhere being introduced to the other important palace attendants. The ageing man had been even more put out moving to a new palace than Daegan had been.

"Do you want to take the other guestroom, Ferath?"

"You honour me, my lord," Ferath replied, "but I think one of the side rooms would suit my station better."

"Nonsense, you're captain of my guard. It would do for you to be close."

"You're just trying to convince me to stay."

"Well of course that's what I'm doing. If you go, who will I beat at kalah?"

"Two months, my lord. That's all I'm here for then I'm headed back."

"How about I play you?" Daegan gestured to the kalah board on a table in the lounge, "If I win, you stay. If you win, I'll give you Thalan. That's a good deal, wouldn't you say Kerala?" Daegan asked the other soldier, standing guard at the door.

She wore a red uniform—unlike Ferath's black—with the Tredain House insignia, a design that looked like two curved Reldoni crossblades with a shining stone above them.

"I wouldn't really want Thalan following me around, my lord... but I suppose," she had a light voice, one that conflicted with her tall height and hard face.

"You see?" Daegan said, "even Kerala agrees."

"It would be easier to keep the Prince out of trouble if you stayed, sir," Kerala offered to Ferath.

"You see, Ferath! You have to stay. It's for my own safety."

It was well within Daegan's power to simply command Ferath to stay. He was reasonably certain that Landryn wouldn't be concerned with Daegan poaching away one of his lower ranked officers. *The almighty Lord-Commander Landryn has far more important things to worry about than his troublesome little brother.*

"I'll consider it," Ferath eventually conceded, "but there's no point playing you. We both know you'll win."

"Excellent—you'll love it here, I promise you. Well, with that all decided, think I'll have that bath, try to get some of this damn cold out of my bones."

He dismissed Ferath and Kerala—the latter of whom staunchly remained at her post by the apartment door—and made his way into the main bedchamber.

"You there," Daegan called to a servant who had been unpacking one of Daegan's trunks—a young blond man in the Arch-duke's grey livery—"fetch me some hot water for a bath."

"Oh," the boy said as if shocked that Daegan would address him directly, "m'lord, it's already, uhm, ready, sir." The boy waved a hand at the empty tub.

"I'm not sure how you Rubanians typically bathe, but in the south we tend to use water."

"Apologies, m'lord," the boy stumbled moving over to the tub and gesturing at the small shelf at the side. The shelf held two gemstones glowing with a faint light; one aquamarine, the other topaz.

"The water cools so quickly so we leave it stored in the runestones," the servant said. *Of course they would,* Daegan thought darkly. Unconsciously, Daegan felt a pressure against his throat as the boy looked at him expectantly.

"Well then," Daegan snapped, "fill it up."

The servant looked confused, even a little put out at being asked. He hesitated a moment before asking, "um, right now, m'lord? It cools quite quickly."

"Yes, now," Daegan said, sharply, "I'm intending to take it right now," he took off his tunic to demonstrate the fact. Thalan, of course, would never question the command nor would any servant in the Reldoni palace, but the Rubanians wouldn't know that about Daegan. *Not yet.* And he wasn't in any rush for that.

The boy jumped at Daegan's harsh tone and promptly took the aquamarine stone in his hand, "apologies, sir. I don't use waterstone much so this might take me some time." His face scrunched up in a frown as he held his other hand over the tub. A slow unsteady stream of water materialised, guided by the boy's hand, feeding into the tub. As the boy had warned, it took him some time, the stream fluttering occasionally, stopping and starting again. *Like pissing while someone's watching.*

Once the tub was filled, the boy picked up the topaz and had been about to proffer it to Daegan, but wisely thought better of it and again held his hand over the now filled tub. After a few moments, light steam began to rise from the water and the glow of the topaz diminished. The boy looked awkward as if Daegan had asked him to do something very improper. *It's just bathwater, get over it.*

"Off you go," Daegan said as he unbuckled his belt. The tightness in his throat had not dissipated even after the servant left and closed the door. Daegan undressed fully and slipped into the hot water. The sharp change in temperature burned at his feet and legs as he stepped in and lowered himself.

Finally warm again, Daegan let out a sigh of bliss. He was *almost* fully relaxed, if not for the knot in his throat. *Idiot boy... it's a simple task, what is wrong with you?* He felt tears welling up, so he dipped his head under, letting the hot water sting at his face.

***

The palace boasted a fine feasting hall. A grand staircase led down to the main hall where sets of circular tables were arrayed. The more important highborn nobles were seated at the front of the hall where the Arch-duke sat. Prince Daegan, being the guest of honour for the evening, also sat at his table.

Mixed among the tables were giant gilded fire pits that provided heat. While the walls were lined with fire sconces and the chandeliers above provided ample light, the firepits gave a satisfying crackle of the burning logs.

The feast itself was a disappointing affair. Daegan had heard stories of raucous Rubanian drinking halls, where Northmen clad in furs and steel would gregariously drink themselves into a stupor. However the guests at this feast were all unsatisfyingly proper. They were definitely drunks; throwing back the Rubanian whitewhiskeys as if it were water, but they were that genteel kind of drunks—the kind that threw about words instead of fists. *One of the few things I had been looking forward to.*

Daegan had to admit that the whitewhiskey was remarkable. It gave a satisfying burn at the back of his throat and lit a fire in his stomach so warm that it made his heart flutter. The courtesans in Reldon had teased that Daegan might find love up in the north and never wish to return. With how the whitewhiskey tasted on his tongue, they might not have been wrong.

"Most southerners can't stomach whitewhiskey, but be careful. You'll find this will go to your head a lot quicker than a Reinish wine," Arch-duke Edmund said with a smile as Daegan knocked back his third glass.

"We have an old proverb in Reldon," Daegan replied with a grin, "the remedy of fire is fire."

"I have heard this before, but I don't think the meaning relates to our whiskey," Edmund responded, offering his crystal glass to the waiting attendant to pour him another.

"No, but I think it's more fitting when discussing whiskey than when used in war, wouldn't you agree?"

"Indeed. Ask any man in this room, you will find the belief that there isn't is any ailment that cannot be cured with a glass of Rubanian whitewhiskey," the older man smiled admiring the clear liquid in his glass. The light passed through the crystal, causing it to shine and glitter.

Another of the Rubanian highborn at the table—Duke Jared Harfallow as he had been introduced—said, "An old friend of mine would say that whitewhiskey was much the same as a beautiful woman… it demands appreciation." Lord Harfallow was also an ageing man, his light brown hair and beard streaked with grey.

"Well that's a sentiment I can certainly agree with," Daegan replied.

"You are unmarried, I hear, Prince Daegan," Duke Harfallow continued. "Tell me, how you have managed to evade the clutches of a wife for so many years. Have you simply hidden under a rock every unionsday for the past decade? You are what? Thirty?"

"Twenty-six," Daegan corrected him, "it is not so unusual, in my country, for men and women to marry later in life." It was not the reason Daegan was unmarried but Daegan preferred to avoid that topic.

"A young Prince like yourself, I can imagine you will attract the attention of many of the ladies of court," Duke Harfallow said.

"And their fathers," Duke Edmund commented. "I must admit that another bond of marriage between Rubane and Reldon would be a welcome blessing."

"It's common here then," Daegan said, "for parents to arrange marriages."

"Probably more so than in your own country," Duke Edmund said, "quite traditional for us highborn here."

"I might be forced to do that soon for my eldest, Danielle," Duke Harfallow said, pointing a few tables down to a pretty blond woman, "she'll be twenty-one before the next unionsday."

"She has plenty of time I'm sure to find a husband," Daegan commented, not particularly enjoying the direction the conversation had taken. She was certainly attractive, but Daegan had no interest in the prospect of marrying some Rubanian girl—which was likely what Duke Harfallow's agenda was.

"In your country, maybe," Harfallow said wistfully, "perhaps I should arrange a meeting for you. She's strong-minded, that is trait you Reldoni find appealing in a woman, I hear."

"Perhaps, I—" Daegan had been about to start proffering excuses, but was happy when one of the Arch-duke's guards stepped into their conversation.

"—My lords, forgive my intrusion," the man said. He had a strong build, with long blond hair tied back in a knot, the sides shaved. He bore Edmund's grey tabard with the arctic bear emblazoned across the chest, a Rubanian greatsword strapped to his back. *Nothing like a big unwieldy sword to complete one's dinner attire.*

"Master Grimsworth had been hoping to join your table for the fourth course. Shall I bring him?" The guard asked. An odd thing to interrupt a conversation with, Daegan thought, but then again these Rubanians were a strange people.

"Ah yes, thank you for reminding me, Tanlor," Duke Edmund replied "please, do fetch him. Master Grimsworth is the head of the Ironworks Guild," Edmund added to Daegan. "He and Ambassador Ormand had a favourable relationship. I believe he wants to continue that accord with yourself, Prince Daegan." *Line the pockets of the Guild Masters,* Ormand had advised Daegan, *and Reldon will continue to see a steady supply of the finest Rubanian steel.*

"Was that Tanlor Shrydan?" Duke Harfallow asked in surprise, his face becoming flush with the whitewhiskey.

"Indeed," Edmund replied, "joined my guard three years ago. A fine young man and an excellent swordsman, Keltin tells me."

"I've not seen him since he was a wee greenhorn," Harfallow said, a wide grin splitting his face, "Aye, a good lad as I recall. Visited my castle in Hardhelm once—entertained my entire hall with the stories of his father; Taran the Hunter."

"Taran the Hunter?" Daegan asked, "I've not heard of him? Was he a knight?"

"Oh, it's a great story, Prince Daegan," Duke Harfallow began, beckoning the servant holding the bottle of whitewhiskey for another, "but Taran was no knight. Lived up in the far north—"

"—Master Grimsworth," Edmund cut across as Tanlor returned, escorting a short, balding man in fine linens. His appearance surprised Daegan, for some reason he had envisaged a large blacksmith of a man instead of this well-dressed man that looked more like a wealthy merchant.

"Arch-duke Edmund, Duke Harfallow," Grimsworth bowed respectfully. "And you must be our new Reldoni Ambassador. I am pleased to make your acquaintance, Prince Daegan. I am Harald Grimsworth, Head of the Ironworks Guild. Your predecessor and I had a very mutually beneficial relationship," he said with a shrewd smile. *He bribed you and you ensured that the Reldon military had exclusivity to most of the Rubanian steel exports.*

"You will find that Lord Ormand and myself are very similar in our dealings," Daegan replied.

"I should hope so," Grimsworth said, taking a vacant seat at the table, "an urgent matter I wish to discuss with you is the administration subsidy,"—*the bribe* —"Lord Ormand was unfortunately quite late in his last payment. Five hundred gold marks, to be exact."

Five hundred gold marks! That was ludicrous, even more surprising that he was openly discussing this in front of the Dukes. Ormand had told him that a hundred gold marks had been the agreed yearly price for the arrangement.

"He wasn't *five years* overdue," Daegan replied, not attempting to hide the displeasure in his tone. How dare this lowborn weasel of a man try to swindle an extra four hundred gold marks. *Even one hundred is a considerable amount.*

"In fact this subsidy was something I was hoping to discuss with you also," Daegan said, feeling irritation rising, "one hundred gold marks, I have decided, is too high for administration. We will reduce this to fifty."

"Let's not be unreasonable here, ambassador, the Ironworks of Rubastre have long held a good relationship with Reldon."

"As have the Ironworks of Garron. And Duke Harfallow's own city of Hardhelm," Daegan replied coolly, nodding toward Duke Harfallow. "The Ironworks of Rubastre have suited well for the past few years, but we have found your quality *slipping* of late."

"The river to Hardhelm freezes in winter, this halts the supply. And the Garron Ironworks is far too small an enterprise to cater the ever growing needs of the Reldoni army," Grimsworth was visibly irrate. *Good.*

"Let's not be hasty here, Prince Daegan," Grimsworth shook his head. "I believe we may have started on the wrong foot here. I have brought a welcoming gift for you." Grimsworth took a small ornate box from his coat, and offered it to Daegan.

"The latest innovation from our engineers," Grimsworth continued as Daegan opened the clasps on the box. Inside was a wheel-lock pistol similar to the ones that had started being produced in Reldon in recent years, although this was one considerably more decorative. The steel barrel had intricate patterns in the metal and a polished rosewood grip. Inlaid on the barrel were two gemstones; one was a topaz and the other had the appearance of tiger's eye. Aradium, Daegan recalled. *You don't often see earthstone as ornamentation.* Both gemstones were far more valuable in runewielding to be wasted as decoration.

It was a fanciful gift, to be sure. One to show wealth, and also trust. *But they know that we have already discovered the art of crafting these weapons.* If anything, it had likely been a Reldoni engineer that had leaked the schematics for the weapon design to the Rubanians in the first place.

"Thank you, Master Grimsworth. It is a fine pistol, similar design to my own country's handguns," Daegan said, lifting the weapon from the box and feeling the weight of it in his hand. He hadn't practised much with these new weapons, but from what he had heard they were far easier to kill a man with than a crossbow. "The topaz and aradium are a curious embellishment."

"That is the innovation, Prince Daegan," Grimsworth said with a sly smile. A knowing smile. It made Daegan feel nervous and gave him a slight tightening in his throat.

"Your Reldoni engineers may have broken new ground with this design, but it was *my* engineers and expert runewielders that have perfected it. Much like a crossbow, your Reldoni pistols require reloading. A dangerously time-consuming task when faced against an armed opponent. With one of these new designs, the need for reloading is a distant memory. Once you've fired your round, the aradium runestone is already forming your next bullet in the chamber. From our tests, the draw time has been reduced to mere *seconds...* And that's not even the best part, Prince Daegan." His eyes took on a wicked light, "one doesn't even need to be an accomplished runewielder to use it."

Daegan felt his legs begin to shake. *He knows.* His throat closed, making it difficult to breathe. *This fucker knows.*

"Why," Grimsworth continued, "it doesn't require any runewielding at all. Even a *cripple* can use it." Daegan's heart pounded in his chest. It throbbed against the pressure on his throat.

When Daegan didn't say anything, Grimsworth went on. "Now the matter of the subsidy, I think we could negotiate potentially raising it, wouldn't you agree?" *You slimy little man.* This man was sorely mistaken if he thought Daegan would simply back down and be blackmailed. His secret would eventually get out... it always did.

"Fifty gold marks," Daegan managed to croak out.

Grimsworth scowled. "Fine!" Then he flashed his malicious smile, "I felt it was a suitable gift for a cripple such as yourself."

"*Harald Grimsworth!*" Duke Harfallow boomed with outrage, "How *dare* you make such an insult to a Prince. You forget *your place*." The Duke's voice had such a deep and angry resonance that it pulled the attention of everyone in the hall.

"Oh, I meant no offence," Grimsworth said, his face a mask of mocking innocence, "perhaps I was mistaken, Prince Daegan?" he asked. *Don't you make me say it, you fucking swine.* Daegan's silence was evidence enough for all within earshot. Some whispered to each other, most had enough tact to avoid meeting his eye. Daegan wanted to use the pistol to blow a hole in the man's face. It was more the fear of it not working that held him back.

"My apologies, Duke Edmund. I find that I am weary from my travels... I think that I'll retire." Daegan said, and rose to leave. Edmund nodded graciously, saying nothing, he didn't give any emotion on his face. *He knew too.* The other highborn at the table all awkwardly bid him goodnight with Duke Harfallow very clumsily shaking his hand and apologising.

Daegan did not bid goodnight to Grimsworth but as he walked away from the table, the man called out, "I do hope you enjoy the gift, Prince Daegan. Better to be a cripple than always sitting down, eh?"

Daegan worried that his legs were shaking too much to carry him out of the feasting hall. As graciously as he could manage, he walked the length of the room, gripping the handle of the pistol with such intensity that his arm shook.

It's a simple task, Daegan's father's voice rang in his ears.
No son of mine is a cripple.
What is wrong with you?

***

"My lord, perhaps you should come inside?" Ferath asked, stepping out into the frigid night air. Ecko was a thin blue crescent but Luna was full, her reddish light working with the city's gaslamps to cast the city of Rubastre in a dim orange hue. Unlike at home, there was no warmth from Luna in this wretched place but Daegan was far past any measure of sobriety for the cold to affect him.

"The whitewhiskey does light a fire in you," Daegan said. He felt the slur in his own words but didn't care, "far more than a topaz, I'd wager."

"I haven't tried the stuff yet," Ferath said, purposefully not taking the vacant seat opposite Daegan.

"And I've no way to try the topaz, have I?" Daegan replied bitterly, "so you'll be the judge." Daegan had been swigging the clear liquid directly from the crystal decanter.

"Sit. Drink." Daegan said, pointing the decanter at Ferath, sloshing the drink.

"I'd rather not, sir."

"Kerala's on duty tonight, so you can have a drink with me, can you not?" Kerala stood guard by the balcony door like a cast bronze sentinel. *A topaz on her too.*

"Bet you've got a hidden topaz somewhere on you, as well, eh, Kerala?" Daegan said, and she nodded impassively. "I'd get more words out of a bronze statue," Daegan said, and was disappointed the others didn't seem to pick up on his joke.

"You look like the miserable fucked the hopeless," Ferath said, finally sitting down and taking the decanter.

"*There he is,*" Daegan smiled, "*I knew* you were still the same."

"You know, Daegan," Ferath said, all formality now thankfully shaken off, "of all your vices; I didn't think that self-pity would be the one that would control you. You didn't hate yourself this much when we were boys."

"Hate is not the same as pity," Daegen replied, "I'd much rather have a man's hate than his pity. *You* used to hate me... don't pretend you didn't. You hated Landryn and me. *You* were the better swordsman—and the better runewielder. Yet *we* got all the promotions, all the advantages. And they left you to rot as a low-ranking soldier... I preferred you back then, when you hated me."

"You're right," Ferath replied, "I did hate you." He didn't seem to have taken any offence to Daegan's rant, "and Landryn too. I beat him in *every* bout in the sparring yard. And yet when the time came, he became *my* Captain."

"—And now he's your Lord-Commander, and you've only just made it to the rank of Captain. Surely it must seethe in you each time he arrives home victorious from another battle." *As it does in me.*

"It did," he admitted, "... for a time."

Ferath's face took on a distant expression and he was quiet for a moment. Just before Daegan could press him further, he spoke, "He saved my life once, you know. It was a skirmish along the river Remen and I was leading a charge against a line of pikemen. This big ox of a foebreaker bursts from their line, swinging an axe in each hand."

Ferath spoke animatedly using his fists as if to somehow express the size of the man, "I'd never seen a charge break so quickly. Most of my men were barely more than boys—hells, I was barely more than a boy myself—and we hadn't expected a foebreaker to be hiding within such a small party of pikemen... He smashed their morale to dust. Even mine, with all my resilience training," Ferath said, still with that far off look on his face.

"I'd never felt such crippling fear," he continued. "Waves of unrelenting certainty that this man would kill me if I charged at him. They train you for it... to resist. But in training, the real fear isn't there. You have the safety of knowing you're not in any real danger..."

Daegan wasn't sure if he'd ever truly felt the effects of a foebreaker's control, his own training hadn't progressed that far. He had undoubtedly been manipulated by someone using a mindstone before but he'd never—and thankfully was unlikely to ever—experience what Ferath had.

"Then your brother," Ferath went on, "clad in his black armour appeared like some hero from the fucking stories. He fought like a draega demon... far more skill than he ever showed against me. The foebreaker must've been crushing Landryn with every ounce of fear he could muster but your brother fought through it. He never once faltered, not once! Landryn tore through the line, not a single swing of his sword was wasted, each one taking down another pikeman until he faced the foebreaker himself. I've watched runewielders fight my entire life and I can say this with absolute certainty that the two men I watched were the most skilled I will likely ever see."

"I had been wrong to resent your brother," Ferath admitted holding Daegan's gaze. "It may have been your father that got him those initial promotions, but any man who would throw himself between a powerful runewielder and group of novice boys, is someone I would gladly follow. It's not someone deserving of hatred."

Daegan—even if he were sober—couldn't truly grasp how Landryn's actions could have instilled in Ferath such fervent loyalty and admiration. An accomplished mindstone wielder pushing a terror into him so strong that he couldn't run —couldn't move—was something Daegan simply couldn't comprehend without having experienced it himself. His training had ended long before the boys were taught the techniques that could be used to defend against such attacks against one's psyche.

Daegan liked to believe he could tell when a secretive mindstone user was attempting to manipulate his emotions, that he would be able to recognize such an affrontive shift in his own emotions, an abrupt denial of what he truly felt... But the truth was; he had no idea. Daegan barely knew how a mindstone worked nor could he ever hope to learn.

"I didn't know that," was all Daegan could say. And it was true, Daegan had long stopped paying attention to the accomplishments of his brother. His victories in battle, his promotions and honours.

"I envied him for a long time," Daegan admitted, "I wished so hard that it had been him and not me that was cursed with this... *affliction*."

A deep part of him still did.

Ferath nodded in understanding, "If the secret sorrows of a man could be read on his forehead, how many who now cause envy would become the objects of pity?" he said.

"Such similar emotions; hatred, envy that becomes pity," Daegan said.

He eyed the wheel-lock pistol that Grimsworth had given him, discarded on the table next to the decanter. A soft glow emanated from the aradium and topaz gemstones. Daegan picked it up, and pointed it out toward the cold darkness beyond the balcony.

He pulled the trigger and there was a loud crack as the bullet was fired from the barrel. In quick succession, he fired all five rounds in the barrel until the trigger clinked uselessly. The light in the aradium stones had faded to nothing.

Five bullets is all I get before I have to go crawling to a stonebreaker so that they may grace me with their superior ability.

Ferath leaned forward, one hand resting on the chamber of the revolver, the other on the steel balcony palisade. Within seconds the light returned.

"I thought metal was slow to dissolve," Daegan said, looking at the crumbling patch on the balcony where Ferath's hand had been.

Ferath did not respond, instead he rose from his seat.

"It's a good weapon, my lord," Ferath observed and then made his way to the door, "don't let the prick that gave it to you be the reason not to use it. Don't give him that power over you."

Dark clouds dimmed the night further, blocking out the moonlight. Daegan remained in his seat and, after a while, the snow began to fall lightly on the city of Rubastre.

He kept the pistol gripped in his hand, staring into the swirling light of the aradium gemstone with a resentment that he wished he was strong enough to overcome. Indignantly, he tossed the handgun off the balcony—or rather, he *attempted* to. The weapon clattered against the palisade and bounced back, landing on the floor.

Not for the first time that day, Daegan felt the familiar tightening in his throat. *There is no ailment whitewhiskey won't cure*, or something along those lines Edmund had said. And so, Daegan reached for the crystal decanter and tried to burn away the pressure on his larynx.

CHAPTER 4
The Cripple Prince

"I'm tired," Daegan groaned.

"Tredains don't tire" Landryn replied, and shot forward. The first clash of steel on steel made Daegan's heart leap in a conflicting blend of excitement and worry.

Landryn knocked Daegan's sword aside, and then as quick as a snake, whipped back and whacked the flat of his blade against Daegan's shoulder.

"You're going to have to do better than that if you're going to challenge Ferath," Landryn said. Daegan jumped back, raising his blunted sword in his fighting stance. Landryn came at him again, each clash leaving Daegan with either rapped knuckles or a slap of Landryn's blade on his arm.

"Don't swing so hard," Landryn said as he easily evaded one of his younger brother's offensive moves.

"Swordsmaster Garld says you need to throw a lot of strength to cut through armour," Daegan retorted with a petulant frown on his boyish face.

"Yes—but I'm not wearing armour. A big strong swing is fine when your opponent is all clad in steel and moving slow," with a condescending flair, Landryn plucked at his cloth tabard to demonstrate the difference, "but you know I'm going to move quickly, so you've got to adapt and be quick too." Landryn leapt at him again, and Daegan clumsily parried the attack.

"Why would someone go into battle without armour?" Daegan asked, managing to back step out of his brother's range.

"Most of our soldiers don't have any," Landryn said.

"Do we not give them armour?"

"Steel is expensive," Landryn shrugged, then shifted into an offensive stance, preparing another attack. "So most of the lower classes wear dragonshide, it's cheaper."

Landryn jabbed and Daegan deflected but his older—and faster—brother allowed the movement to carry him into a spin and came around to whack against Daegan's shoulder with the flat of his blade. Pain flared and Daegan dropped his sword to rub at the shoulder.

"Ow!"

"*You* won't always be wearing armour either. If this was a proper fight, I'd have taken your arm off. Now pick that up," Landryn instructed, nodding to the fallen sword.

Reluctantly, Daegan picked up the sword and assumed an offensive stance of his own. Gritting his teeth, Daegan tried a similar jab and spin, but Landryn had been prepared for it, and easily knocked his little brother back. They carried on in a series of parries, most ended with Daegan stumbling after a shove or deflection from Landryn.

Daegan's shirt billowed, the tip of Landryn's sword just catching the material as Daegan jumped back to evade a side swing. Daegan's heart lurched with excitement at the near hit. Landryn reset again into his stance and drove in again for another jab. Daegan finally saw an opening, assuming that his brother was intending for another parry-and-spin attack. This would be Daegan's first chance to land a hit, he grinned as his brother put his weight into the jab. Daegan sidestepped and performed an efficient swing of his sword at Landryn's shoulder.

And then Daegan felt it; a rush of wind pushed him off balance, causing his sword to swish up, and miss its target. The manoeuvre made Daegan stumble and trip.

"Hey!" Daegan said accusingly, jumping back to his feet. "No runestones, that's cheating!"

"Sorry, I didn't mean to, it just happened."

"Don't apologise for simply using your talents," a voice called from the edge of the duelling ring.

"Father!" Both boys dropped their blunted swords and stood to attention. Their father stood at the entrance to the private duelling ring alongside Swordsmaster Garld.

Landryn spoke first, "I'm sorry, father, I know it's late. We just—"

"—thought you could ring *steel swords* against one another in the middle of the night and no one would notice."

"Daegan is facing Ferath tomorrow. Ferath's the best in our rank, he needed to practise," Landryn said.

"And so you thought you would draw steel in an unsupervised bout?" Garld admonished the boys, his disapproving gaze making Daegan squirm.

"Where is your aeristone, Daegan?" His father asked. Terror rose in his chest.

"Here, father," Daegan pulled out his runestones. Hanging from a silver chain around his neck were all four of the elemental gemstones; aradium, topaz, aquamarine and amethyst. Each of the runestones glowed with a faint light. Daegan had made a point to learn the proper names for the elemental gemstones. In truth, Daegan studied harder than all the others in his rank. He needed to.

"So why—when your brother windpushed your blade—did you not push against it with your own aeristone?" His father's grim expression and icy tone made Daegan want to shrink away.

"I-I didn't know he was using it," Daegan explained.

"Landryn's edir is wild and uncontrolled, a *toddler* could detect it," his Father scolded, Daegan noted that Landryn too was ashamedly looking at his feet. "You are telling me that you couldn't feel him drawing in the air, and then pushing it against you? Are you lacking in your senses as you are your wits?" he asked disdainfully.

Daegan trembled. *I'm trying. I'm trying as hard as I can.*

"Windweaving *is* the most difficult to grasp, your Highness," Garld offered.

"Don't make excuses for him, Garld," Daegan's father said. "He's a Tredain. Landryn was *half* his age when he started using runestones. So tell me, boy, *why* do you continue to fail?"

"I don't know, father," Daegan said, tears had begun welling up in his eyes.

"We have coddled you long enough," his father confessed, "give me your sword."

Daegan jumped to obey, offering the blade which the King snatched.

"Landryn, resume your attack," his father commanded.

Landryn hesitated, "but father, h-he's unarmed."

"No," their father said bluntly. "He isn't. Your brother is a Tredain, just like you and me, and all of our ancestors back to Queen Elyina herself. Our edir bends water to our will, rock forms at his command, the very air *itself* should rush to obey him. So.
 Resume. Your. Attack."

"Yes, father," Landryn said, wincing as their father spoke. Once again, Daegan's older brother assumed his fighting stance, he looked at Daegan with worry. "Please, Daegan, j-just defend yourself."

Daegan was too shocked to move, a boy not yet even twelve years old, facing his armed brother two years his senior. His only defence was four glowing stones.

In the same manoeuvre as before, Landryn shot forward. His attack had a fraction of his previous spirit but Daegan had no means to parry, and so he raised his arm in defence. The blunt steel bit into his arm, pain flaring as the sword broke his skin.

Daegan felt the impact rattle the bones in arms. Muscle and bone were not meant to take the full brunt of steel. Daegan cried out and staggered back clutching his arm.

"Again," the King commanded.

Landryn resisted, "Please, father—"

"—*again!*"

Before Daegan could grasp what was happening, Landryn struck him again. The same instinct took over and Daegan raised his bloodied arm to shield his face. This time the sword belted against Daegan's shoulder.

"Defend yourself!" Landryn shouted in frustration as he hit his brother again. All Daegan could do was weather the attack, pain blinding him as his brother repeatedly struck him again and again, until eventually Landryn lost patience and kicked the younger boy square in the stomach, knocking him to the ground.

The stone floor of the duelling ring felt cold against Daegan's face, nausea from the kick welled up inside him. The sharp cold of the tiles on his face helped distract him and avoid vomiting.

"Lan, sto—" Daegan started, only to have the breath knocked out of him as Landryn's foot slammed into his chest, pinning him to the floor. Daegan gasped, trying to suck in ragged breaths.

"Lan, please!" Daegan shouted at last. Landryn was panting heavily, his face flush with fury. Daegan looked up through watered eyes at the tip of the blunted blade hovering above his face. *Please Lan.*

Landryn stared at their father for a long moment before turning his gaze back to Daegan, flat on his back. Daegan could taste copper in his mouth, his blood ran hot from his nose and the gashes on his arms. Landryn held the blunted sword hovering above Daegan's face, and for a split second Daegan truly believed that his brother was going to slam the tip of the sword through his eye.

With pained effort, Daegan raised his bloodied arm and weakly tried to bat the sword away. Landryn gritted his teeth and threw the blade across the duelling ring. Father said nothing, he just stood watching with disapproval while Daegan groaned on the floor.

"Tredains do not yield," the King shouted at Landryn. "We do not bend nor cower. We cut down the enemies before us or we die in the effort." His father's fists clenched tightly around Daegan's sword. "We do not have *weakness* in our family," he growled "now get up, Daegan."

Daegan coughed, he could barely grasp his father's words through the confusing haze of pain. The ground felt sticky from his bloodied hands as he strained to push himself up off the ground. Daegan got as far as his knees before stopping to retch.

"You are dismissed, Landryn. Return to your room," their father said, not taking his gaze off Daegan's struggle to get up. *No, please, don't go, Lan.* Daegan looked pleadingly to his brother, 'please,' he mouthed looking at him.

Landryn held his gaze for a moment, his face scrunched in anger. He turned away from Daegan, and walked to the door. Daegan closed his eyes, could feel his entire body begin to tremble. He heard the door of the training room slam.

Landryn had abandoned him.

Daegan managed to stagger to his feet. His father was a mountain of a man when he stood directly over him. Garld next to him was equally domineering. Daegan's entire body shook from both fear and the beating he had gotten.

"Idiot boy," his father spat at him, "what is wrong with you?" Daegan didn't respond, his lip began quivering but managed to stem any tears from actually escaping. *I don't know, father, I don't know why it doesn't work for me.* Daegan wanted to scream it at him. Father held the sword so intently that Daegan feared any words he said would be seen as weakness, and his father would punish him for it.

"Are you now mute *and* dense?" Father asked.

"N-no, father," Daegan replied.

"So tell me, have you been slacking in your studies?"

"No father, I read the archives on runeweilding every night. I swear it," Daegan said quickly, and it was true, he had.

"So you are confident in how aradium can be used to stonebreak? To turn stone to dust and pull it into your edir?"

"Yes, father."

"We shall see," he said bitterly.

Daegan felt the tug on his neck roughly jerk him forward as his father grabbed at the runestones around his neck. Daegan's head snapped back and he kicked wildly as he was lifted by the chain. The silver links bore into his neck, not enough to choke him but enough so that his breaths wheezed as he laboriously tried to suck in air. His body flapped and thrashed ineffectively against his father's resolute strength.

Through bleary panicking eyes, Daegan watched as his father raised his free hand; summoning jagged pillars of rock that broke up through the tiled floor. Six stone spikes crept up from the ground around him. Daegan felt the jagged edges of the stone pillars slowly press into his shoulders, biting into his skin. Four of the pillars of rock pinned him in place, his feet dangling just a few inches off the ground, unable to find purchase. Two columns with sharpened points pressed unbearably against his throat.

More pillars began to rise, all of them working to pin Daegan in place, pinching and biting into his skin. Only when his father released his grip on the chain did Daegan feel his full weight push down against the pillars. He was left suspended in the air by the jagged pieces of rock all pointing inwards at him.

Instinctively Daegan tried to let out a cry of pain—but with the two pillars pressing against his throat, his airways were too tight and only a barely audible squeak escaped him. Daegan's lungs tried desperately to pull in more air but it came in thin rasps. He tried to beg his father—to plead for release from the prison of stone, but the words came out as an incomprehensible wheeze.

His father still gripped Daegen's aradium in his hand. Its amber light had completely faded. The runestone looked like just a regular piece of brownish jade. "Your aradium is now empty," his father said, if he showed any remorse for the pain he was inflicting on his son, his face and voice did not show it.

Please, father, please let me go. Daegan thought desperately. *Free me.* Daegan's eyes frantically searched his father for understanding, for some sliver of caring. But he knew he wouldn't find it. Tredains show only strength, never weakness. To show emotion was a weakness. So his father was—and always would be—cold and impenetrable.

"-leese-" Daegan managed to croak, "hree"

"There is only one way you're getting free, Daegan." He shook the aradium in front of him, "You *know* how to use this. You are a *Tredain*. You are not some s*kragling halfbreed*. The blood of Elyina flows in you."

Daegan looked desperately to Garld. The man had stood solemnly beside his King, wordlessly allowing the abuse.

"Harrd," Daegan wheezed, "ease" was all he could manage. Garld said nothing. And then his father—King Abhran Tredain of Reldon, Protector of all Reldoni People—turned his back on his suffocating son.

"No son of my mine is a cripple," he said, "you will get yourself out—or you will die here."

***

Daegan wasn't sure how much time had passed. The exertion of his beating from Landryn, in addition to the strain on his breathing was more than enough to push him into unconsciousness. These spells were brief however as he would find himself gasping awake moments later. When his chest expanded with his breath it caused the stone pillars to bite in on him simultaneously.

Daegan wept openly now that he was alone. He wept until there were no more tears. When his lungs would eventually protest at the lack of air filling them, he would cough violently. This action caused his body to spasm in his torture chamber and the sharp edges of the stone spikes would again bite into him. The pain of it overwhelmed Daegan and he passed out again.

This cycle continued and after the fourth time he passed out, Daegan stopped counting. He stopped caring to know how long he had been there. He stopped waiting for someone to come help him. He stopped hoping—pleading—for the aradium to work. For the pillars to simply dissolve at his command. He would go in circles like this.

At times, Daegan would try to feel for the vibrations—the thrumming sensations people claimed they could feel from rock and earth when they held aradium. He tried to will the stone to dissolve into his edir as he had been taught for so many years to do. At times, Daegan thought maybe he *could* feel it. But it was just his own limbs going numb with fatigue and strain.

The spikes didn't dissolve, they held fast and when his focus and effort fled him, Daegan would wheeze and cough. And the cycle would go again.

***

Daegan woke but it was not a harsh waking. The pillars were still crushing against his windpipe, but he could breath and his body wasn't spasming. For that he was grateful.

Light was beginning to creep in from the arched windows of the hall. This was the private royal training hall so only he and Landryn would train here. No other students would be coming to find or help him.

At first, Daegan had hoped that Landryn would find him. That his brother would rush to his aid and blast his stone prison to dust. But the bruises on his arms—now pinned by the pillar—made him think otherwise. Landryn would never betray their father.

Daegan wept as the sun rose. He wept because he knew it would be the last sunrise he would ever see.

***

Daegan was cold. He had soiled himself so many times through the rough spells of coughing and spasming. Pain flared everywhere in his body, and he was unable to control himself. During those moments he thought he wouldn't be able to draw enough breath to keep going. And then there were moments where he felt there was no point in *trying* to keep going. *It won't hurt so much,* Daegan tried to convince himself. He could just slip away and it would all be over. He could sleep without being jolted back awake in pain. *It won't hurt like this forever.*

As the early morning chill took him, Daegan began to shiver. His rattling caused the pillars of rock to stab at him. He blinked his bleary eyes open and was surprised to find Landryn standing in front of him. His brother looked at him with a horrified expression. Daegan, in his dazed state, couldn't tell if he was horrified to find that Daegan had been entombed like this or because he still hadn't yet figured out how to free himself.

And then, suddenly, there was a loud crack and sharp flaring of pain on his knees as Daegan fell hard against the floor. His elbows followed, cracking against the ground.

For the first time, in what felt like an eternity, Daegan took a full unrestrained breath, filling his lungs with air and dust.

He coughed and spluttered in a succession of heavy laboured breaths, kneeling on all fours. Through bleary eyes and a cloud of dust, Daegan could see Landryn kneeling in front of him. He was saying something but Daegan couldn't understand the words. He was so exhausted, he just wanted to lie down. To close his eyes and let sleep take the pain away. He collapsed onto the ground.

Absently, Daegan was aware that Landryn was carrying him. His head lolled as Landryn carried him down the hallway that led to their bed chambers.

Landryn gently lay him down in a bed, and Daegan felt warmth and comfort enveloping him. Unconsciousness hovered about him, waiting to claim any shreds of awareness he had left. Landryn stood to leave him and Daegan reached out a hand to him. *Please, Lan, stay.* He thought desperately. *Please, protect me.* His hand found Landryn's tunic and gripped onto it. The material in his fist the only tangible thing his mind could hold on to.

"Please, Lan," Daegan rasped.

"Let go of me," Landryn said, and then pulled himself forcefully out of Daegan's reach.

Don't go. Don't leave me.

Landryn walked away as unconsciousness finally grabbed hold and pulled Daegan under.

***

In the weeks that followed, Daegan's lessons in sword fighting and runewielding had come to an abrupt halt. During the brief moments that Daegan and his father crossed paths, Daegan would begin to choke and sputter, struggling to breathe from some imaginary hand choking him. His father did not even give him a cursory glance.

The King had never questioned how Daegan had been freed from the stone torture chamber, but Daegan suspected that he knew.

The King's son had no edir, that much was clear, and it was quickly becoming known throughout the palace. Somehow, a son of the Tredain family had been born without the ability to command the forces of the world to his will. It was not unheard of for a person to have a weak—almost indistinguishable—edir, but Daegan had none at all.

Daegan and Landryn did not speak much after that night. Landryn did not come to visit while Daegan was recovering. The palace healers and chirurgeons did their work to heal his wounds and injuries, as well as ease the pain.

Without an edir, the healers couldn't use bloodstone to accelerate the healing and so his physical injuries took time to heal. Most of the bruises and cuts were all superficial. He had suffered a broken arm and two ribs and, in time, those healed also. But something else was broken inside of Daegan, something that required more than just time to heal. Something that a twelve year old boy could never heal on his own.

Landryn was soon relocated to the main garrison in the city to complete his military training. In the years that followed, he and Daegan only had limited contact. For the most part, Daegan had become a shadow in the Tredain family.

His eldest brother Lukane would check in on him occasionally, he would feign interest in the boy's education. Lukane was inherently cruel like their father and would usually end up berating Daegan for his short-comings.

He was forbidden to spend time with his younger sister, Allyn, lest Daegan's affliction somehow also pass to her. But Allyn's edir was already growing. From what Daegan had heard, Allyn had a stronger edir than even Landryn or Lukane had at her age.

Daegan was a forgotten thing left to gather dust in the Reldoni palace. His education continued, he was still a Prince and would be required to serve the kingdom in some capacity, but he was a stain upon the Tredain bloodline—a cripple who would never live up to the legacy that all Tredains aspired to. Like a blunt training sword amongst razor sharp Reldoni blades.

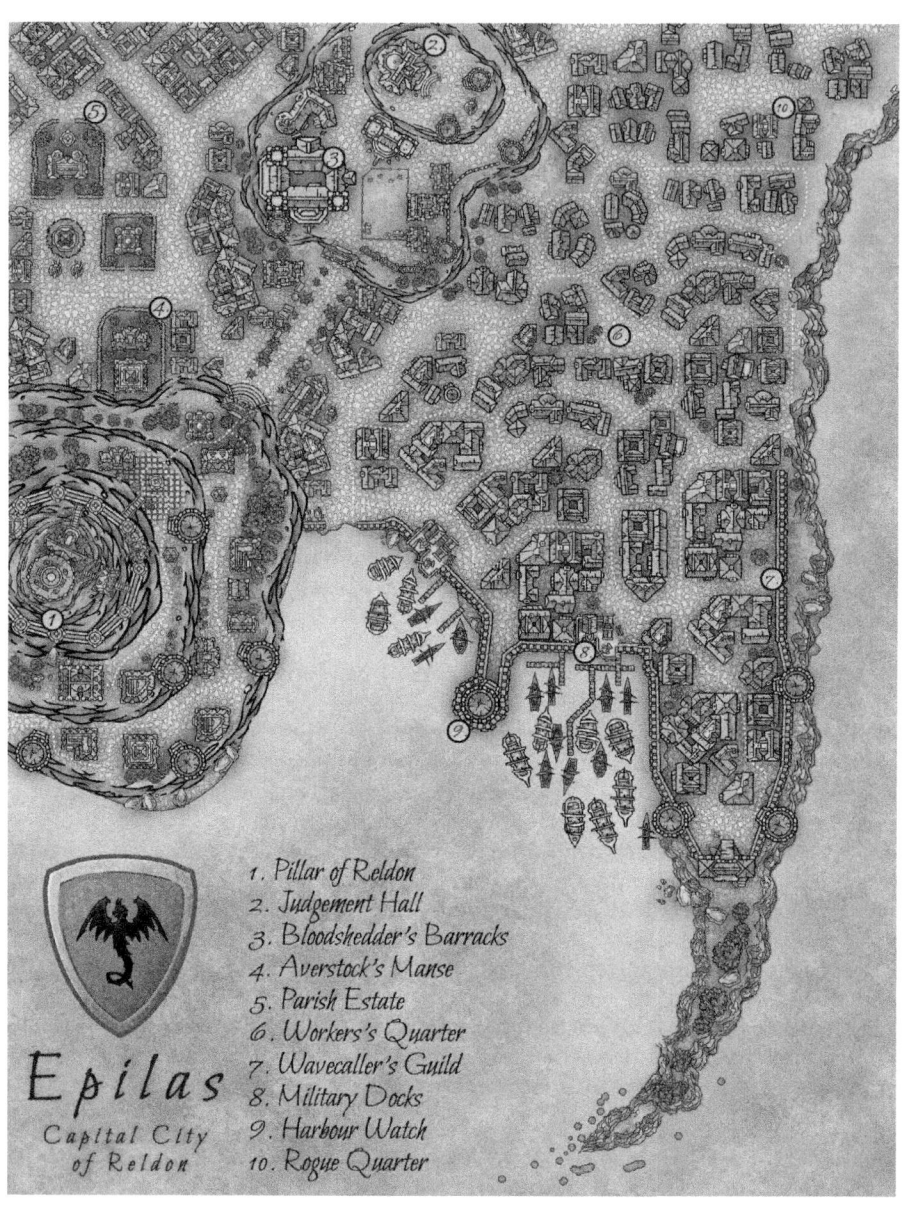

CHAPTER 5

Brutal Justice

Femira gritted her teeth. She leapt back as Loreli made another overhead swing at her with her wooden training sword. Of all the other students, Loreli moved the fastest. No matter what Femira did the younger girl always seemed to be ready to parry. She deftly evaded any attack Femira attempted with her own wooden duelling daggers.

The long weapon that Loreli wielded was reminiscent of traditional curved Reldoni blades and was the favoured choice for many of Garld's recruits. Femira had found them far too clunky. She had realised that once she was within close striking range, opponents struggled to block against her shorter duelling daggers. *But not Loreli.*

Femira managed to step into Loreli's range. With inhuman agility, the other girl somehow managed to launch herself away in another direction and swing her sword down in a painful whack against Femira's back.

"Another point to Loreli," Misandrei called from the edge of the duelling ring. The rest of the students watched from the sidelines.

Femira pushed herself back up from the dusty sparring ground. If she had been allowed the use of her earthstone, this spar would be going very differently. Femira would've whipped up a cloud of dirt and debris in her opponent's smug face and rushed her. But they weren't permitted runestones in this match.

Loreli had a conceited air about her that Femira found annoying. And she was that kind of beauty that men went to war for; light tan skin and distinct red gold hair which she kept tied back in a tight braid when fighting. It wasn't fair that someone as beautiful as her would be such a good fighter.

"Maybe next time you'll know not to challenge your betters, *vreth*," Loreli gloated, the last word delivered like an insult. In Keiran, vreth were a rare sight and seeing one in the wild meant bad luck, they were symbols of fear. It was the reason that Femira had chosen the name. She had learned since arriving in Epilas—almost four months before—that vreth were very common in Reldon. The creatures were seen more as vermin; flying pests that carried disease and lived on the waste of human society. But that fact had not dissuaded Femira from adopting the moniker as her own. If anything it made her more determined to use the name.

"Afraid to be knocked off your pedestal, Loreli?" Femira asked, shifting back into a fighting stance. Femira was still new to the structured forms and stances that all the other novices seemed to be intricately familiar with. Until recently the only stance Femira knew was: hold the blade with the sharp end pointing at your opponent.

Femira had quickly learned that the most effective way to get better was to spar with the more experienced fighters. This had meant taking a lot of smacks with wooden swords—and a lot of insults from the big-headed recruits that thought themselves too good to be training with a rookie.

Many of the other recruits couldn't understand why a highborn foreigner with no training in fighting—and even less in runewielding—was permitted to train with the bloodshedder recruits.

The recruits had been handpicked from the ranks of the Reldoni army for Garld's elite training. No amount of money or influence got a person here—only skill. Learning that had given Femira a sense of smug satisfaction.

Femira launched at Loreli in another attack, but the other girl's footwork was so unfathomably tricky. She moved so fast that it was as though she teleported from one side of Femira to the other. Loreli hit Femira with a hard jab to the midriff; if they had been using real blades the point would have gone right through her.

"Another point, Loreli."

The hit left Femira breathless. She doubled over, gasping for air. Loreli swung at her again, striking her shoulder. It's not just speed, Femira knew, it was years of practice and training that had given the other girl foresight that Femira simply didn't have. Loreli could anticipate what Femira would do next before *she* even knew it, it was a strategic game to the other girl. Femira knew she had to be less predictable, she needed to find a way to surprise Loreli. She *wouldn't* let the time of the match run without getting at least a single point.

On her next advance, Femira went to lunge for Loreli's chest—the same attempt she had made on a few occasions in the bout already. Loreli evaded as Femira expected she would, stepping back just enough to be out of range but still close enough that a strong push off her back leg would launch her back at Femira.

However, instead of facing Loreli as she sprang forward, Femira spun to the side. She lashed out with one of her daggers—catching Loreli in the shoulder—then allowed her momentum from the spin to carry her into a jab with her other dagger into Loreli's back.

Loreli fell forward on her face in the dusty earth. There was a collective gasp from the watching recruits, they had obviously not expected the newcomer to land any points against the best among them. Femira allowed herself a few seconds to revel in their surprise before readying herself. Loreli sprang back to her feet in a single motion. *Show off.*

The girl had a light covering of dust on the front of her black uniform and in her red hair. Although not nearly as much dirt that coated Femira's own uniform.

"Two points to Vreth," Misandrei called out. Loreli did not grimace or snarl, the girl's face was as cold and dead as stone.

Loreli surged at Femira with startling ferocity. All Femira could do was parry with both daggers against Loreli's unrelenting attack, driving her to the edge of the duelling ring.

Femira managed to sidestep and press her own attack. Femira was a quick learner but Loreli—it seemed—was faster for when Femira attempted another feint-and-spin attack, she responded with a drop to the knee leaving Femira slashing at air where Loreli's head had been. Pain flared in Femira's knee as Loreli struck hard against it, tripping Femira up and knocking the wind out of her—again.

Femira spluttered and struggled for breath. Shamefully, she felt her eyes watering as she finally managed to suck in short ragged breaths.

Loreli was already walking away from her to the edge of the ring.

"She's incapacitated, she can't continue," Loreli said to Misandrei. Femira tried to crawl to her feet. She tried to dispute but the words came out short and frazzled.

"Loreli: seventeen, Vreth: two," Misandrei announced, calling the bout. Loreli was already gone from the sparring yard by the time Femira had finally managed to pull herself together.

The other recruits were already petitioning Misandrei for their next bout. Femira's arms and legs burned from both exertion and the hits of Loreli's sword, she knew that she wouldn't be able to take another match. Instead she rested on the sidelines, and prepared to analyse the next match.

Loreli had bested her by fifteen points, but that didn't matter because if it had been a real duel—with real steel—Femira would have been dead on the first point.

"You did well," Garld said stepping next to her. As usual he was wearing his stiff black and silver uniform. He didn't often come to the sparring yard or oversee any part of her training personally but he would appear occasionally to check in on her. *His pet Keiran girl.*

"I lost," Femira grumbled.

"Loreli has been training with the sword since she was a young child. She has over a decade more experience than you."

"She's also the fastest of all the recruits—even the men," Femira added, as if trying to add justification of her loss.

"Did you enjoy the fight?" Garld often asked her strange questions like this.

"Yes," she answered truthfully. She might be battered and bruised now, but she could feel herself getting better with each match. Learning to time her attacks better, to make the right footing and timing strikes. Those seconds after she made that hit on Loreli left her with a sense of pride.

"Why did you challenge Loreli? Drawing the shortest grass meant you could have chosen anyone, why her?"

"*Because* she's the best. Everyone knows that," Femira replied. Garld simply nodded. He understood. Femira was beginning to suspect that the man was the first person to ever understand her desire to learn more. He understood that she needed to be the best, and true to his promise nothing had been held back.

"Prince Landryn returned yesterday," Garld said, shifting the conversation. Femira took a few seconds to sort through the ridiculously long list of highborn names she had learned over the past few months.

"The King's third son?" she asked.

"Second," he corrected her, "You've met him before... to an extent."

"He was in Altarea," Femira recalled, in all the chaos and confusion of that evening she couldn't remember exactly what he looked like.

"Landryn remained behind after the attack to oversee the occupation, and to establish the newly appointed Highlord's authority there." Femira hadn't known that Altarea was once part of Reldon and that the now dead King Armenia's grandfather had seceded from Reldoni rule half a century ago. Back then the stormguards were a militia that had overthrown their Highlord and seized power for themselves. All previous attempts to reclaim Altarea—and the highly lucrative Osiri mine—had been squashed against the walls of the palace, the stormguards raining death from above. *Until Landryn's assault.*

"You will attend the Prince's court today," Garld continued. "It is important that Lady Annali is seen to be supporting the Prince." Femira nodded, she still wasn't entirely certain why Garld had chosen her—of all people—for this facade. All that she and Annali had in common was the colour of their skin.

"What will I need to do?" Femira asked warily.

"For the most part, just be silent and be seen. You have had no appearances in court since our arrival here, the other highborn will be curious for a look at 'Lady Annali' so we should indulge them." The thought made Femira itch, she didn't particularly like the thought of being paraded about.

"Do you know how to reach Judgement Hall?"

"The big domed building at the top of the hill?" she asked, pointing toward it. Epilas was a large city and there were a lot of big fancy buildings on a lone hill rising up from the city. Impossibly thin towers and networks of arches connected the buildings on the hill and at its heart was a massive white domed structure.

The hill of lavish buildings and sprawling sets of barracks sat inside an inner wall made entirely of wood. The rest of the city was contained by a larger outer wall of stone. That wall didn't make any sense to Femira. *Why bother with a stone wall like that if a squad of stonebreakers could just come along and blow a big hole in it?* The answer, Femira guessed, was because wood was expensive, stone wasn't. *Meaning the people inside the wooden wall are all worth protecting, and the folk behind the stone wall are worth shit but we're going to pretend that the wall will protect you.*

"Good," Garld concluded, "you're finished here for the morning." He held up his hand when she opened her mouth to protest, "go clean up and make your way to Judgement Hall for court. Aden will take you." Femira nodded and turned to leave.

"And Vreth, remember to stay silent. I don't want your crass tongue giving you away."

"*Crass*, me?" she replied, "wouldn't fucking dream of it, sir." and performed an exaggerated soldier's salute.

"I mean it, Vreth," he said sternly, "I'll trust you to open your mouth when you've had more time to read over Annali's journals and get a feel for her voice. Until then I want you to keep your mouth shut. Now go and change into a clean uniform, it's widely known now that Annali is training with the bloodshedders, but even so, a highborn like her would sooner take fen-salt before stepping into court covered in dust."

Femira wouldn't have been surprised to learn that the real Annali took fen-salt—skaga as she called it. A major part of Lichtin's operation was getting skaga into the noses of highborn. *Nothing to be made in getting street dogs like you hooked on the stuff,* he'd say, *but those rich fuckers in the palace. Once they're on it, the gold keeps flowing.* But she didn't tell Garld that fact, he was military and from what Femira had learned, these military types disapproved of things like that. Instead she nodded, saluted again—for real this time—and left.

The duelling ring was one of four that occupied the main courtyard of the bloodshedder's barracks and Femira's room was in the large stone building that overlooked the courtyard. All bloodshedder recruits had their own private rooms. Unlike regular soldiers who had to sleep in rows of bunks in the other barracks. The bloodshedders got special treatment because they were superior; they were the elite force of runewielders. Many of the recruits owned their own runestones and were skilled in using them for combat. It was their skills in runewielding specifically that had gotten the recruits selected for the advanced training in the first place.

From what Femira had learned, there were less than a hundred fully trained bloodshedders in action. About three times that many were recruits like her.

Large groups of recruits watched their peers sparring in the duelling rings and would do so at all times of the day and late into the evenings, always learning and honing their skills. Femira herself had already spent many long evenings —exhausted and bruised from her daily matches—watching the other recruits fighting.

When she arrived at her room, Aden was already waiting for her. He was a classic Reldoni youth; light tan skin, dark hair and no beard. Aden was her assigned tutor and another bloodshedder recruit.

It was not known among the other recruits the extent of "Annali's" ignorance of Reldoni politics or culture. She couldn't even read Common Tongue. Aden was chosen personally by Garld to assist in Femira's rapid induction to everything that the real Annali should know. Why Garld trusted Aden with this task—and to keep discreet about it—she didn't know but his faith was well placed because it didn't seem that anyone else suspected her to be a fraud.

Aden was not alone today, accompanying him was Jazerah, another bloodshedder recruit. The pair were usually inseparable. The two boys were the closest thing to friends that Femira had come to since arriving, they reminded her a little of her brothers—and for that reason she resisted allowing herself to become too close to them.

Jaz was wickedly handsome, his long dark hair usually tied back and he had a tightly shaven face. Both of them were tall too, despite being a few years younger than Femira, they towered over her short Keiran stature.

"You see, told you she wouldn't be long," Aden said as she arrived. He was sitting on her bed while Jaz reclined on the desk chair. Having lived so long with nothing to call her own, Femira didn't consider these things to be *hers* exactly, this was just a space she slept and studied in. Seeing the two young men in her room didn't bother her no more than when people would walk past the shelter her brothers had made in the alleyway behind the fishmongers.

"You look like shit, Vreth," Jaz said, his gaze taking in her filthy uniform.
"I challenged Loreli," she grimaced, walking over to her trunk.
"Ouch," he whistled, "she's done me twice—and not the good way. I'm not in any rush to draw a listing against her any time soon. Can't see why anyone in their right mind would *choose* to challenge her."
"Annali likes to take the difficult path," Aden chimed in, his unusually high pitched voice always making him sound younger than his eighteen years. Femira unlocked the trunk and was already sifting through her meagre possessions for a clean uniform.

"I like to be the best, and to do that means *beating* the best," she corrected him, "and for the thousandth time—call me *Vreth*, Aden."
"I can't call you that," he fretted awkwardly with his spectacles as he spoke, "it's not right."
"It's what I choose to be called," Femira replied, taking out a uniform.

The women's bloodshedder jacket was longer than the mens and had clips to strap in shoulder pauldrons, she was going to court not battle so she wouldn't need those today. But then again, they did make her look stronger... more imposing. Considering most Reldoni loomed over her, it might make her look less like a child.

"Vreth isn't a good nickname," Aden continued, "they're vermin. They sneak around in the shadows and—" he shuddered, and cut himself off. Aden was a little more than afraid of vreth, "—not like you at all, Annali." *Oh Aden, if only you knew.*

"If she wants to be called a vreth then let her," Jaz chided him, then turning to Femira, "you can sneak into my room any night you like, Vreth." He winked as she stepped behind a partition to change.

Femira barked a laugh, "I think Loreli might be more your type, Jaz." She was no stranger to comments like that, she had lived in a crewhouse with a gang of thugs and criminals, these military types were a hundred times more respectful.

"I've tried," Jaz said with a smirk, "but I reckon she'd prefer a bit of you inside her than me, Vreth."

"You reckon she prefers girls?" Aden asked, his face fully flushed. Discussing sex made him uncomfortable, a fact that Jaz loved to torture him with.

"Oh absolutely," he said, "watch how she pines all doe-eyed for Captain Misandrei next time she does drills."

"So you don't *actually* know that she's into girls," Femira said, strapping in her shoulder pauldrons. They did make her look stronger.

"Not wanting to sleep with me is evidence enough, I would say," Jaz replied.

"That would include the vast majority of women in the barracks then," Femira sneered, adding the leather forearm guards for an extra intimidating appearance.

"Well yeah, obviously—we're soldiers, the job attracts that kind of woman."

"I think you're a bit off the mark there Jaz," Femira replied, moving to strap in her greaves also.

"I'm right about Loreli—ok, seriously, Vreth. What's the deal?" Jaz said, waving a hand over her uniform, "you're not going into battle."

"He's right," Aden piped in, eager to latch onto the change in conversation, "it's court—not war. I don't know how it's done in Altarea, but usually only the guards tend to be armoured."

"I've never been to court," Femira said curtly, "So I don't exactly know what the fucking dresscode is."

"Your uniform is fine," Jaz frowned, "just lose all the extra bits."

She reluctantly unfastened the greaves and bracers, but left the pauldrons, which had the bloodshedder's insignia on them—a stylised hawk clutching a sword. She wanted people to know that she was a bloodshedder recruit.

"You're coming too, Jaz?" she asked.

"My father wants me to start attending. I think he wants me as a contingency heir in case my moron of a brother gets himself killed in battle," Jaz sighed, "and when Aden told me you were making your first appearance today... well, I couldn't miss that. I've bet him a silver mark that you won't make it through the whole thing without saying 'shit' at least once."

"You might as well give him that silver mark now, Aden," Femira said. These highborn snobs got very offended by words. *Like they don't ever have to take a shit.*

Together the three made their way to Judgement Hall. There was a portcullis gate that separated the fancy hilltop buildings from the surrounding barracks. *Don't even trust your own soldiers.* Femira tutted.

Both Aden and Jaz were armed with long curved blades, sheathed at their hips. Femira had never owned any weapons herself, the closest thing was a set of climbing spikes she had once used to stab one of Lichtin's grunts who had tried to get a bit too friendly with her. She hadn't killed him, or even stabbed too deeply. *It was more of a warning jab,* like when a cat bites you when it doesn't want your affection.

Swords and daggers were far too expensive and she had spent most of her life more concerned with feeding herself. It amazed her how so many of the bloodshedder recruits scoffed at the meals in the mess halls. It was free food! *You don't even have to pretend to be interested in any weird gods or anything like that.* You just show up and eat, no questions asked. Not even checking if it was your second or third helping.

"You'll have to get yourself your own blades soon, Annali," Jaz commented when he caught her spying his. "My father says that you must find a weaponsmith that perfectly understands your needs."

"I'm fine with borrowing from the barracks armoury," she replied. Even if she had any money to spare on a set of her own daggers—or a flamboyant shiny blade like Jaz—why would she bother? The barracks had plenty that she could borrow any time she liked. *Well not exactly any time.* Strictly speaking she could only take them during training drills and duels. Femira had tried on a few occasions to slip the daggers back to her rooms unnoticed but the bloodshedder's quartermaster was a ruthless and beady eyed man, scribbling away on his ledger, always noting whenever she had them and for how long.

"That just won't do, Vreth," Jaz said, unsheathing his sword. It was a pretty thing but not worth the fifty silver marks it had likely cost him—or more accurately —his father. "You need to be so in tune with your blade that it moves as an extension of yourself. You need to be inherently familiar with its weight and balance," he slipped easily into a fighting stance and flourished the blade, "that's just not something you can do when you're changing weapons every day."

"And what happens if it breaks?" she asked, then badgered on before he could respond, "or gets stolen? You've built your whole form around only being able to use just one particular sword."

"Form is beginners stuff, Vreth," Jaz rebuffed and she felt herself feeling a bit hot in the face. She didn't like it being noted that she was still a beginner, especially not when she was finally starting to win duels.

"If you want to advance," Jaz continued. "If you want to beat Loreli, You're going to have to get your own blades. Train with them everyday until they move as part of you." Femira didn't respond. She was annoyed because deep down she knew he was right, she just didn't like to admit it because it didn't matter; she couldn't afford her own. *Not yet at least.*

Femira still had the chip of aeristone hidden away in her bunk. She just needed to suss out a suitable buyer for it. She wasn't sure what the going rate for aeristone was in Epilas; they were rare—even in Altarea where they were mined.

Lichtin could probably flog it for a gold mark there, so it only made sense she could make even more here. She was confident that any of the other recruits would happily pay that amount or more for the gemstone.

But something held her back, so far in her runewielding training, Misandrei had focused primarily on teaching her to use her earthstone, the others left neglected as she didn't have any of her own. Femira could come forward and tell them she had it, but something held her back. *The Reldoni had invaded Altarea for their aeristone. If they were willing to take down an entire city just for the stuff, then it's not crazy to think they wouldn't just take it from me.* So she kept quiet and hoped that an opportunity would arise to either sell it quietly—or better yet—learn how to use it herself.

***

Judgement Hall was an immense building with an incredible white dome ceiling. Inconceivably intricate pillars—the stone shaped in twisting, wrought vines like a rope—soared up to meet the edges of the dome. Everything was in glorious white marble with veins of black, gold and red that gave the hall an impressive atmosphere.

Femira suspected that every inch of the main hall had been created by a master stoneshaper. Regular tradesmen couldn't craft with this kind of dexterity or vision.

The court was filled with rows of benches, and raised tiers lined the walls to accommodate all the noble highborn folk who felt the need to be seen. Femira shifted uncomfortably on the smoothed stoneshaped bench of marble where she sat with Aden and Jaz near the back of the hall. At the head of the raised dais on the other side of the room was a throne made of the same ass-numbing marble.

"Epilas holds the prime garrison of Reldon," Aden informed her as he often took the liberty to do, "there are other citadels and barracks across the kingdom, but here is where our main army is trained and stationed."

"So that's why almost everyone here is in military uniform," Femira noted.

"Exactly—there is a smaller War Council where the Generals and Highlords meet, but this is the official military court of Reldon."

"And your King doesn't even show up for it?" she asked to which both Aden and Jaz gave her hard looks.

"He's *your* King too," Aden said firmly, "and no... the King doesn't precede over the military court, his throne and the royal court is the Pillar—"

"—that's the huge tower on the other side of the city?"

"That's the one. The King holds the royal court there but the military court is led by the Lord Commander here."

"And that's Prince Landryn?" She asked.

"That's right," Jaz put in, "Prince Landryn Tredain, Lord Commander and East Marshal of the Reldoni Army. My brother serves directly as his banner holder on the battlefield."—a weird honour Femira thought—"He's never had much to say about him, other than he's ruthless."

"They say he led the charge when the gate was breached at Altarea. Cut down dozens of stormguards himself," Aden chimed in.

"Did he train with the bloodshedders too?" Femira asked, her interest piqued.

"He *made* the bloodshedders," Jaz answered. "He and General Garld started recruiting all the highly skilled runewielders out of the ranks a few years ago."

"People still aren't really sure where we fit in the hierarchy either," Aden added, "we're seen as higher than regular soldiers and knights, and higher than some of the lower ranking officers but definitely lower than the Captains. We report to General Garld, as you know, but outside of our company, we don't really fit with the regular military."

Femira nodded, she'd been unsure about that. She'd already noted the special treatment the bloodshedders received compared to the rest of the army.

The afternoon laboured on, and Femira had discovered that court was incredibly boring. For hours, a procession of highborn nobles and military officers presented grievances against each other to the court.

Prince Landryn—another typical dark-haired Reldoni man—who she could barely see from her position, hadn't even spoken for the entirety of the afternoon so far. The other men and women in Reldoni officer uniforms—Femira had learned that the more frilly bits of silver or gold trim they had on their uniform was usually an indicator of how much of a higher rank they were to you—were speaking on behalf of the Prince. *Him being at the top, you'd think his entire jacket would just be made from golden knots.* But no, his uniform was surprisingly less decorated than most of the officers seated near the front.

The grievances weren't even interesting; Lord so-and-so hasn't paid stipends for months to whoever, and on and on and on.

Why do people attend this? She understood why Garld wanted her to attend. She was—as far as anyone was concerned—Lady Annali. He needed her to pretend like Annali supported the new Reldoni authority in Altarea. There were a few Altarean and Keiran officials in attendance but thankfully none had approached her. She wasn't even sure what she'd say if they did.

It was only when two dark-skinned Keiran men approached the raised dais that Femira's wandering mind snapped back to the court proceedings.

"Honorswords Azul Jahasa and Havran Karas," one of them announced. Both wore the ceremonial gilded armour of Keiran Honorswords with bright yellow cloaks and the red sun insignia of Keiran emblazoned at the center.

The yellow cloaks and gilded armour were a jolt of colour that caught the eye amongst the sea of black and red uniforms, it grabbed your attention like a sudden shout that breaks a long silence. It wasn't the armour of someone trying to sneak up on you.

Both men were darker than Femira, their skin a deep brown. Their long black hair and beards braided with golden clasps. They had the marked red eyes of men sworn as Honorswords.

Femira's brothers had often told her stories about the Honorswords of their homeland; both judges and executioners, they travelled the lands of Keiran administering the decisive—and often brutal—laws of the Keiran Emperor. The Honorswords were the voice of the Emperor, their word was the law of Keiran. Once sworn as Honorsword of the Emperor, they said you were no longer human, he took away your humanity and you became an embodiment of Keiran law.

"The Military Court of Reldon recognises you, Honorsword Jahasa, Honorsword Karas," one of the officers replied, "what matter do you wish to lay before the Lord Commander?"

"A crime against His Grand Excellency, the Emperor of Keiran," Honorsword Jahasa proclaimed, his melodic Keiran accent echoing against the white marble dome. "A crime committed by Prince Landryn, Lord Commander of Reldon."

The air in the hall grew tense. The room was filled almost entirely with high-ranking Reldoni military, it was a testament to the arrogance of the Honorswords that they would make a statement like that with such confidence in this place.

"Prince Landryn has taken control of the city-state of Altarea and its surrounding islands. He has murdered King Amenia Solodan and taken the royal family of Altarea as his hostages," Jahasa continued.

"His Grand Excellency demands that the Reldoni forces withdraw from the Altarean Islands. To allow Altarean allies to restore their original government and to return all that has been misappropriated from the Altarean Palace and Osiri Mines." Shouts of hostile protests rose throughout the hall as the Honorsword spoke.

It was only when a stocky soldier positioned on the dais, began to slam the base of his enormous axe against the floor did the crowd begin to settle.

"Silence," the axe-wielder roared, repeating the word in his bellowing voice, the word resounding through the acoustics of the hall. Femira guessed that this must have been the intended purpose of his long shafted axe.

She had not noticed throughout the afternoon's proceedings that Garld had also been seated on the dais, alongside the other high-ranking officers. *Well he is one of the Generals, so I guess that makes sense.*

Garld was now on his feet—along with three more of the high ranking officers—conferring quietly with the Prince on his throne. After a few moments, the Prince dismissed them and rose to stand himself.

"Your accusation has no merit, Honorsword Jahasa," Landryn announced loudly. While his voice did not boom as the soldier with the axe had; it still carried strongly throughout Judgement Hall. "The Altarean Islands are a part of Reldon, and have been since my ancestor, Queen Elyina, forged this kingdom from the ashes of the Sorcerer King's reign. It was King Amenia's grandfather who insurrected the city—whose militia of pirates seized power and *murdered* the rightful Highlord of the city. Our invasion of Altarea was an act of reclamation; to liberate our own citizens from the false King. A false King who had no right to the Highlord seat of Altarea. Who had no right to proclaim himself as a King, when Altarea is—and always has been—part of the Kingdom of Reldon!" Landryn's voice resounded through the hall.

"A false King whom I executed for his *treason* against Reldon," the Prince continued. "But I am not without mercy. I have not destroyed House Solodan utterly, I have spared the false King Amenia's heir from the misdeeds of his family. An infant should not be held to account for the crimes of his father. I can assure you that his wardship to the new Highlord of Altarea is a gift to House Solodan's continuity, and when he comes of age he will be offered a seat on the ruling council of Altarea. A generous offer for a House that stole the city in the first place."

"Your claim that Altarea is part of Reldon by right is ludicrous," Honorsword Karas rebutted, "If Reldon has any claim to the city, the crown should have enforced this right decades ago."

"Forty years of skirmishes and raids on our shores could not be ignored," one of the Reldoni Generals standing on the dais interjected. "Prince Landryn finally brought a decisive end to the Altarean rebellion." the General was a grey-haired man with a ridiculously pointed moustache, and a stocky frame that bulged in his decorated uniform.

"You call it a rebellion," Honorsword Karas said with reproach, "but Altarea is a nation in its own right, and has been for almost half a century, her people are *not* Reldoni citizens. Keiran will not stand by as her allied people are subjugated, and monarchies murdered."

"If Keiran will not stand for it," the moustached General rebuked and barked a bitter laugh, "where *was* Keiran when our warships sailed to Altarea. When we reclaimed the city and sieged the palace *for weeks*. Where were your armies when we raised the Reldoni flag from the palace towers. Where were the 'illustrious' Honorswords when we executed the false King!" His voice became even more heated. "Your Emperor sends his envoys *here*. You call our claim on Altarea to be ludicrous, well I call your alliance with Altarea to be ludicrous, it is *laughable* that your Emperor's cowardice—"

"—Lord-Marshal Mattice, that is enough," Prince Landryn interjected, silencing the now red-faced man. The tension had risen markedly in the hall. Despite there being only two of the Keiran Honorswords, many of the Reldoni soldiers in attendance were resting their hands on their weapons. Honorsword Karas himself was gripping the hilt of his oversized sword so intently that his entire body was shaking.

"Such insult to His Excellency will not be suffered," Karas snarled. "As Honorsword of Keiran, I challenge you Lord-Marshal Mattice to combat."

"Forgive my Lord-Marshal's guileless remarks," Landryn responded, "he speaks out of turn. I accept that insult has been made to your Emperor but the crown of Reldon does not share this conviction, I assure you. As Honorswords of Keiran, I understand that you speak with the voice of your Emperor, but I also understand that you listen with his ears. And so I give you this message for your Emperor; I refute your accusations. Reldoni forces will not withdraw from Altarea nor will the newly established Highlord be displaced. My father—King Abhran Tredain—will remain as the reinstated sovereign of Altarea. My father has always been an advocate for diplomacy between Reldon and Keiran. Under his guidance, I strive only for unity, my ardour for the peace and welfare of the Altarean people—Reldoni citizens *by right*—does not falter before your accusations. My message for your Emperor is this:

Together, let us embrace this new peace. We will welcome His Excellency—or any dignitaries he wishes to send in his place—to treat with us in agreeing terms to ensure this peace between us through diplomacy with my father, the King.

You knew this coming here, you didn't truly believe that I would accept your accusations, that I would offer myself to the judgement of your Emperor and withdraw our army from Altarea. If the Emperor wishes to discuss terms for peace between our nations then he is welcome to come and treat with my father."

The Honorswords did not immediately respond, instead conferring with each other quietly. Femira felt her heart pumping in her chest, the stories of Keiran Honorswords depicted them as monsters, administering the merciless law on whomever they saw fit. There had been stories of Honorswords slaughtering entire villages for the crimes committed by only a few.

"We will relay your message before the Court of the Sun and the Emperor," Jahasa—the calmer of the pair—responded, "But the insult made against His Excellency cannot be suffered. And so my comrade's challenge for combat remains."

"I accept your challenge," Lord-Marshal said, "and I name Sir Sadrian Graves as my champion."

"Honorswords have no need for champions," Karas replied coolly, "we place our own lives behind our words. Your tradition of naming champions lacks courage, and weakens the conviction of one's own word… but I will face your champion nonetheless." There was a stir of bitter comments in the hall but were hushed as Jahasa continued.

"Another matter is the abduction of Lady Annali Jahar," he said and Femira felt her bowels turn to ice water. "She is Keiran by blood and was married to the Altarean Prince Reselas—another of the many casualties of your invasion. The Court of the Sun, and House Jahar, are concerned for her wellbeing and safety." Femira shrank into her seat as many faces turned to her.

Oh shit, oh fuck, oh shit. Run!

"Lady Annali is a guest here in Epilas," Garld spoke for the first time, Prince Landryn giving him a pointed look. "She returned willingly with our forces to Epilas, and has been a proponent for the Reldoni occupation of Altarea," Garld said calmly.

Femira felt herself sinking further into her seat, desperately trying to make herself disappear from the eyes on her. The two Honorswords exchanged sceptical glances. Honorsword Jahasa spoke first, "we will require evidence for this claim."

"Your evidence sits right over there," Garld responded, pointing directly to where Femira sat. Her heart thudded loudly in her ears and chest. She felt the thrum of the earthstone's power throughout her entire body. She actively resisted the urge to turn the bench and ground below her to dust.

Both Honorswords turned to her, their eyes scanning the crowd in the direction Garld was pointing. It was Karas that spotted her first, his vibrant red eyes landing on her. Femira felt her stomach lurch under his gaze.

"Lady Annali Jahar," Karas called to her, "You will return with us to Keiran." Somehow she managed to hear him over the pounding of her heart and the overwhelming thrum of her earthstone's power. It resonated with her, responding to her fear. Unconsciously, she was sinking herself slightly into the stone bench.

"No," she whispered. Her head shaking.

"I don't think they can hear you," Aden murmured next to her. She couldn't speak up, not against Honorswords. *They'll kill me, they'll kill me if I speak against them... their word is law.* But they would also kill her if she went with them and discovered she was most definitely *not* Annali Jahar.

"No, please no," she found herself weakly whispering.

"Lady Annali has decided to remain here," Garld said. *Thank you Garld. Thank you, you wonderful man.* "Her marriage to Prince Reselas was simply a symbol of the alliance between Altarea and Keiran. But from that union, she was accepted by the Altarean people so she is now a Reldoni citizen, the same courtesy we offer to all Altareans. She has every right to remain here if she wishes to."

"We do not recognise your claim that Altareans are Reldoni citizens. She is Keiran, and she will return with us," Karas responded sharply, his red eyes finally pulling away from her, and back on Garld.

"If your Emperor decides to treaty with us," Landryn cut across decisively, "*then* we can negotiate Lady Annali's future, but for now she remains in our protection, if that is her wish." His dark eyes fell on her for the first time. *I can't go with them.* They'd kill her the second they realised that she was lying.

Honorsword Karas was shaking again, although Femira was unsure if that was just her own eyes shaking as her entire body thrummed with the earthstone's power.

"Bah," the Honorsword grimaced, and then announcing in the Keiran language, "*Annali Jahar, as Honorsword, I command you to return with us to the Court of the Sun.*"

"No!" Femira shouted in response, in Common Tongue so that the Reldoni would understand her.

Femira leapt to her feet, her whole body trembled.

"I'm not going anywhere with you," she called out, "I'm staying right here!"

***

Judgement Hall was the crown of Epilas with a ring of towers circling the domed building and a grandiose stairway leading to its arched doors. At the base of the steps sprawled a magnificent courtyard that overlooked the entirety of the city of Epilas and the sea beyond.

The red light of the setting sun touched every aspect of the city, from the white towers of Judgement Hall right down past the barracks buildings and training yards, to the sprawling city beyond, down to the wooden and steel warships docked at the harbour. The bay itself shimmered in orange and red.

You would expect at the center of the courtyard for there to have been some ostentatious fountain or a grand statue of Queen Elyina but this was Judgement Hall—the seat of the Reldoni military—and so at the center of the courtyard was a raised duelling ring. The steps curved around the ring like an amphitheatre, now filled with soldiers and court officials.

When the court fails, challenge by combat prevails. A Reldoni proverb Femira had learned. In Keiran, the law was the word of an Honorsword. She supposed it wasn't so different. *Either way the strongest make the rules.*

The two Keiran Honorswords clearly knew enough of Reldoni law that they could challenge any person to a duel, and the person challenged could fight themselves, or name a champion.

They could also just refuse, like any sane person should. But to refuse meant dishonour, especially when a high ranking military officer was challenged.

Lord-Marshal Mattice was not a young man. He had the arrogant bearing of a man who had once been a seasoned fighter, but most of his hair was grey and his weathered face showed that this was not a challenge he could rise to himself.

Being one of the highest ranking officials in the military, the Lord-Marshal would never have been expected to face the Honorword himself. And so he had chosen a champion—one of Garld's elite bloodshedders—a Foebreaker named Sadrian Graves. Garld seemed annoyed by the choice of champion, protesting at first. He insisted that Lord-Marshal Mattice choose from his own division, but the Lord-Marshal out-ranked Garld, and Prince Landryn allowed the decision.

At his request, Femira stood at Garld's side on the steps of Judgement Hall overlooking the duelling ring. Prince Landryn and other high-ranking officials were also around them. Femira tried her best to hide in Garld's shadow.

They were ringed by armed guardsmen, these might all be experienced fighting men and women but clearly no chances were being taken with the pair of Honorswords. Garld wore a concerned expression, he was evidently displeased that the life of one his bloodshedders was being thrown away.

It's a waste. Femira had been told that the bloodshedders were Reldon's best —their strongest and most skilled soldiers—but she knew the stories of the Honorswords. *Red eyes and no mercy... Entire villages slaughtered.* Her heart began thumping faster again.

Sadrian Graves wore the all black uniform of a fully trained bloodshedder. His armour and helm were also painted black, giving him a menacing demonic appearance. Sadrian stepped into the ring, his curved blade drawn, catching the light of the setting sun.

Honorsword Karas, in his golden armour, drew his own sword. It was straight and thick with both edges sharpened. To any normal person the blade would have seemed impossible to wield, far too heavy for use in a duel. It was the kind of weapon you could imagine a rak giant from children's stories wielding, cleaving scores of men in a single swing.

"I think you should reconsider this, Prince Landryn," Garld advised as the two combatants walked to the center of the ring, "you can still call this off."

"A challenge of combat is lawful, and a long standing tradition," Landryn responded. "I have long valued your opinions, General, but I cannot deny this request. Not when the challenge is made against one of our own Marshals."

"A formal apology would be more than enough—"

"—We *cannot* afford to appear weak, General," Landryn cut him off pointedly. "Graves is not ready to face a full—"

"—I will not argue this matter further with you," Landryn affirmed, silencing Garld with a hard look.

"We shall give these Keirans a taste of true Reldoni skill," Lord-Marshal Mattice boasted. "Your bloodshedders are unparalleled, Garld. I have heard reports of their effectiveness at Altarea… In fact, another matter I wish to discuss with you is redeploying some of your elites to my border skirmishes with the Rienish."

"That is for the Prince to decide—not me," Garld said although his tone made it clear that he did not approve of the suggestion. Garld shifted the conversation back to the matter at hand, "these men are here to make a show, we should be cautious of walking into whatever game they are playing."

"These *Honorswords* came to make a reprehensible claim against our Prince. We cannot stand for it," Mattice responded sharply, and Landryn nodded in agreement. Femira suspected that this Mattice guy had really just been saying what the Prince had wanted to but couldn't. *He's got to pretend to be gracious all the time, I suppose, being a Prince and all.*

"You shouldn't underestimate the Honorswords, Lord-Marshal," Garld warned, "I have heard reports that they fight with inhuman skill. I believe they may have discovered a Soulstone."

"Your belief in fables and myths grows tiresome, Garld," Mattice replied, "they're men—just like the rest of us, don't be fooled by those red eyes. A mere trick of bloodstone—besides, Sadrian Graves is one of your finest Foebreakers, I hear. I will assume that he is now in possession of our newly acquired Altarean aeristones too? He will make short work of this foreign bastard." Garld did not seem appeased.

Femira remained silent. As Garld had instructed her to be when his guardsmen had escorted her to him after her outburst in the hall. She wanted to add to Garld's statement; to express the danger of a single Honorsword, let alone two.

What was that he'd mentioned about a 'Soulstone'? That was what Garld had called the runestone that had been in the box in Altarea. *It sounds valuable.*

Reldoni tradition permitted the use of runewielding in duels, and so, the crowd that had gathered to watch the fight had given ample distance from the duelling ring. It was not uncommon for stray fragments of rock or ice to inadvertently strike a bystander. Honorsword Jahasa brazenly stood at the edge of the ring, clad in his matching gilded armour.

"Insult has been made against His Grand Excellency," Jahasa announced, "as Honorswords, we are duty-bound to defend his name." Honorsword Karas raised his hefty blade and assumed a strong footed fighting stance. The pair slowly circled each other weighing up the opposition.

Sadrian was notably taller, with greater reach, but Karas was powerfully built and his large sword made up the difference. Sadrian made the first assault; he moved with such lightning speed that Femira couldn't even follow the swing of his blade.

The swords clashed and Karas parried, pressing back. Femira had yet to face a Foebreaker in the sparring yards, but she had heard the other recruits mention them; a class of master duelists and—as the title suggested—specialised in breaking their opponent's morale.

She didn't know exactly *how* they did it but what she understood was that Foebreakers could wash their opponents with crippling fear so overwhelming that it left them unable to raise their weapon in defence. Evidently, Sadrian's abilities were ineffective against Karas' resolve as the man launched another aggressive swing of his blade. Sadrian leapt back deftly in an exaggerated jump. *Yes, this man certainly carries an aeristone.*

Airpushing with an aeristone could give you extra lift in a jump, or a more powerful swing, but it wasn't strong enough to actually hurt your opponent, Femira had learned. However, a well placed airpush could knock your opponent off balance and, in a duel, that could determine if you lived or died. Their effectiveness in battle is what had given Altarea an edge in resisting the Reldoni for so many years.

Karas was on him so quickly that Femira suspected that the Honorsword must surely also be carrying an aeristone. *But then again, maybe the stories are true. Maybe the Honorswords aren't human anymore. Maybe they were more like the draega demons that the priests in the temples always harped on about.*

Karas' blade crashed against one of Sadrian's pauldrons, obliterating it with a loud and terrifying crunch. The impact forced Sadrian back, blood now flowing from his shoulder and dripping on the stone.

It's over. Femira watched as Karas went in for another decisive swing. This wasn't a display of fancy footwork or swordskill, this was a demonstration of the Honorsword's raw strength. Sadrian dropped to a crouch, a defensive pillar of rock forming suddenly in front of him, bursting up from the pavement in front of him.

Femira gasped, she had heard that the bloodshedder stonebreakers could form stone quickly but a pillar of rock as thick as a person—and formed in a second's breadth—she would have thought it impossible.

So far Femira herself had only managed to form a few rocks, and even then it took her a few minutes to properly combine all the tiny grains of sand and compress them. To form a pillar this size would require more focus than Femira could imagine.

It didn't slow Karas' assault, his greatsword shattered the pillar in a cloud of dust and debris. Sadrian had used the rock shield to give him time to roll out of Karas' range. He slumped on the side he was bleeding from but still held onto his sword with his other arm.

Femira noted the dust and sand drawing towards Sadrian as he absorbed it into his concealed earthstone. A sharpened length of stone formed beside him. It was called a stonespear—a technique that Femira had seen diagrams of in a book Aden had lent her—the stonespear launched toward Karas as fast as a bolt loosed from a crossbow. The Honorsword's blade whirred and obliterated the projectile as it shot toward him.

Sadrian had obviously expected the Honorsword to dodge the projectile rather than deflect it, and had readied two more stonespears that now fired uselessly to either side of Karas.

The Honorsword didn't allow Sadrian to draw in more earth and rushed him again with his intimidating blade. Sadrian managed to sidestep but his movements were slowing with his wound.

Karas' blade struck the ground where Sadrian had been. Then, in a quick twisting manoeuvre, Karas dropped to a knee, swinging up at the Foebreaker, catching the man's breastplate. The twisting attack didn't have enough force to break the plate itself but it made a sharp ear-splitting screech as the blade slid against the steel.

While the strike hadn't been intended as fatal, it did push Sadrian off balance.

In the moment of lapse, Karas planted his feet and swung again with a murderous intent. The swing carried all of Karas' force and the blade struck against Sadrian's helm in a sickening thunderclap.

The steel edge cut down through the helm and then bone. It wasn't a clean strike, the kind that cut a man's head off as the stories often depicted. The enormous sword was wedged firmly in Sadrian's helm and likely the skull beneath. Sadrian's body crumpled and Karas let go of the blade, letting it fall with his opponent.

The crowd was left speechless at the display. It was not the practised sets of swings and parries that they expected from Reldoni duels. This had been a butcher taking strong and powerful cleaves. And the butcher had won, defeating one of their best duelists.

Keiran law is the judgement of the Honorsword.

Lord-Marshal Mattice had a face of open shock. Prince Landryn was impassive and wordlessly turned to walk back up the steps to Judgement Hall, the retinue of guards attending him. Garld remained beside Femira.

"Reckless," Garld muttered then turned darkly on Mattice. "A waste of a good soldier. Next time you let your temper rule your tongue, at least sacrifice one of your own soldiers—or better yet, step into the ring yourself!" He snapped and turned to leave the speechless Mattice on the steps.

Garld didn't give her any command to follow him, but what else would she do? She didn't want to be left in sight of the Honorswords. The Prince may have said she was under Reldoni protection but she wasn't about to linger around and let them threaten her into leaving with them.

Garld didn't protest as Femira accompanied him back to the barracks. She had spotted Aden and Jaz also watching the duel from the steps and decided she would catch up with them later. She had questions for Aden about the duel that she needed to ask him. *If Sadrian was a Foebreaker, why was Karas able to stand and fight against him?* If what she had heard about them was true, he shouldn't have even been able to move.

The deep shadows of the evening light were starting to claim the main thoroughfares. Some of the tall gaslamps were already lit giving the streets an orange glow.

"You were smart to fear the Honorswords," Femira said eventually as they walked.

"I don't fear them," Garld replied, "I simply disapprove of the thoughtless expenditure of good soldiers for a cause that achieves nothing."

"You're not afraid of that?" Femira asked incredulously. Had he not just witnessed the same display she had?

"Man-on-man I wouldn't want to face one but—from the reports of our agents in Keiran—there aren't that many Honorswords. They might be formidable opponents in a duel, but I would trust in any small strikeforce of bloodshedders to overwhelm one quickly enough on a battlefield."

"So that's the plan? Just recruiting more of us to throw against them?" Femira asked.

Garld stopped, his face stern. "At what point in this conversation did it sound like I thought of any of my bloodshedders like that?"

"Sorry," Femira said, and then hastily added, "but you *are* recruiting heavily. There's already a hundred new recruits since I got here. Are you preparing to fight the Keiran?"

"Since when did a thief care about world politics more than her next score?" Garld asked with suspicion.

"I'm not exactly sure *what* I am anymore," Femira countered indignantly. "You're having me trained like a soldier but I still don't know *why* I'm actually here? You said you had a job for me. One that only someone of my skills could achieve so why am I sitting in courtrooms pretending to be some highborn?"

They had arrived at the main barracks building where Garld's office was, he motioned for her to follow him inside.

"You're right," he acknowledged, "I have not been putting your talents to good use yet. Your training is still a necessity, your stonebreaking is impressive but that alone will not help you if you're caught during any of your assignments."

"I don't get caught," Femira boasted.

"*I* caught you."

"And you convinced me to work for you... if you hadn't," she shrugged, "I would have ran."

"You'd have been dead before you left the room." Femira opened her mouth to protest but Garld silenced her with a raised hand. His expression made it clear it wasn't a point he wished to discuss further.

"Today's events *have* worried me," Garld conceded. "The Honorswords I believe are not human... at least not anymore. I want your help in understanding what they are. How they *became* what they are." At the mention of the Honorswords, Femira tensed.

Blood flowing in gutters... an Honorsword's word is law.

"This has something to do with the soulstone?" Femira asked and Garld's eyes narrowed. He countered her with a question of his own, "What do you know of it?"

"It's what I found in Altarea," she answered truthfully. *And whatever it is, it's definitely worth more than what I'd thought.*

"I believe the Honorswords may have one of their own," Garld divulged.

"Is that why they're so strong?" She followed up, but he didn't answer her. *He still doesn't trust me yet. Well that's fine, I don't particularly trust you either.* Garld also had full right not to trust her, if she had the chance to skip out with the soulstone, she'd take it. *I wonder where I'd even sell something like that?*

A moment passed and Garld was still quiet in thought. The silence made Femira feel awkward and uncomfortable. She hoped whatever plan he had for her didn't include the Honorswords.

"You want me to spy on them?" Femira prodded, her voice cracking with apprehension. Garld was pulled from his concentration, and looked back at her.

"No..." he said with reassuring calm. "No. In fact, I want you to stay as far from those Honorswords as you can. Your Lady Annali identity is far more valuable to me and I don't want the Honorswords' presence in the city to threaten that. Your first assignment will not be so dangerous as that." Femira breathed out. The tension in her shoulders she hadn't even known she'd been holding was loosened.

"So what do you need?" she asked.

"I want you to do what you do best and steal something for me."

CHAPTER 6
People Change but Seldom for the Better

Femira crept along the shadowed corridor. It felt good to be back in her discreet stealth gear. The trousers and shirt hugged tightly on her legs and shoulders, inhibiting even the barest whisper of swishing cloth as she moved. Using Ecko's moonlight from the windows as her only guide through the dim, she lightly stepped around furniture.

When she had been new to creeping about in the dark in rich folks homes, Femira had been surprised at how much useless stuff they piled in their hallways. Suits of armour, randomly placed tables and plush chairs and the like. *As if you're just going to lounge around in your hallway all casual-like.*

Nothing highborn did with their money really surprised Femira these days. She'd once been paid for a job to break into a merchant's home and steal a single *flower* of all things. It wasn't even a pretty flower, just some regular blue flower that grows out in the desert in Keiran. And they paid her *five silver marks* for it, and that meant whoever had put out the job had paid Lichtin ten! For a single useless flower! Tonight though, she wasn't here to steal flowers or chairs that nobody ever sits in. She was here for paper—specifically a journal that Garld wanted.

Femira's socks brushed silently against the wooden floor—a much wiser choice than her clumsy soldier's boots. It was late, far past midnight but if she stopped and focused, she could faintly hear people moving about in other parts of the manse. Servants about their nightly duties and—more worryingly—guards.

Not to mention that highborn folk often have an annoying habit of staying up late to drink fancy wines. Femira had staked out the manse for the past few nights so she was reasonably confident this would be the quietest time in the night.

Her earthstone hung with a comfortable weight around her neck and was tucked into her shirt to not let off any light. It was strange that only a few months before she would have felt anxious if the earthstone had any substantial weight to it during a job.

Femira also had a pair of duelling daggers sheathed tightly on her belt. Garld had explicitly told her to avoid any violence, but if a guard stumbled across her, she would be glad to have them.

Femira approached a door. *Fourth on the right, top floor.* She checked the keyhole for any lamplight before taking out her picks and set to work on the lock. She felt confident enough in her new skills to dissolve the metal quickly and reform the latch when she was finished but this latching mechanism was made of wood. Lord Averstock was no fool it seemed. Regardless, any burglar worth their salt can pick a lock, and Femira had been one of the best lockpicks in Lichtin's crew.

After just a few minutes, she was in. As slowly as she could to avoid creaking hinges, Femira pushed the door open and slipped into Averstock's office.

Rich folk often thought themselves very clever. They would hide important things in books or secret drawers, but they were always painfully obvious places to Femira. Big fat hardback books were always the first checked. Then she ran her fingers along the seams of the brushed wood of Averstock's desk, looking for secret compartments.

She'd found two, and both had contained documents, but not the ones Garld was looking for. Femira pocketed them anyway in her satchel. *The pages will be old*, Garld had told her, *and handwritten, similar to these.* And then he'd shown her a tight scrawl of writing with diagrams she didn't understand.

Femira sat lightly in Averstock's chair, trying to think where he would hide something important enough that a General in the army would want to steal.

Ecko's light flowed in through the windows casting the room in a blue tinge. In Altarea, she would often wait for storm clouds to give her cover from the moonslight, but Reldoni nights were almost always clear. So she'd chosen tonight when Luna was the new moon, and she was left with only Ecko's dim blue to hide from. But that made it difficult for her now to get a good view of the room.

Tentatively, Femira pulled out her earthstone and let the yellow-orange light give her some extra illumination. She hoped it wouldn't be noticeable to the guards in the courtyard below. She felt a thrill being back in this setting, trying to outsmart sneaky highborn folk who thought themselves crafty enough to hide their valuables from her.

Femira double checked the lacquered desk for any hidden compartments but discovered nothing even with the additional light of the earthstone. It thrummed in her hand, resonating with nearby bits of metal.

An idea struck her. Femira gripped her earthstone harder. She could feel its eagerness for her to pull out the light from it and give it shape again. Femira ignored the pulsations from the stone and reached out with her free hand, running it again over the desk. As it was wood, it didn't pulse in response to her as stone or metal would have.

However, as she glided her hand over the brushed brass hinges she felt it beat in response, like the metal was calling out to her. Smiling, Femira ran her hands again over the desk and sure enough when she passed over the very center of the desk, she felt it.

The lightest whisper of a response.

There's something hidden in the center of the desk. Femira excitedly pressed at it, expecting a pressure mechanism that would pop up a secret latch but it held firm. *Rude!* She moved her hands along the desk looking for a release switch but came up with nothing.

"Hmm," Femira tapped her finger impatiently on the desk, trying to puzzle it out. She placed her hand back in the center of the desk. She could feel the metal just under the wood. It felt as if the metal was calling to her, beckoning her to absorb it into the earthstone.

Instead, Femira pushed out. She formed a thin thread of metal where she felt the hum. As with dissolving rock and metal, stoneshaping and metalshaping followed the same practise—only forming metal took a lot longer than stone.

When she first arrived in Epilas, Femira's attempts to form metal had taken her hours to even shape a ring to fit around her finger. Now after months of practice it only took her a few minutes to form this needle. She formed it *underneath* the wood, at the exact spot she felt the humming.

As the needle formed and grew, she felt it resist against the weight of the desk. Femira pushed against it, continuing to shape her needle. She strained against the weight of the table and found herself gripping at its edges, her muscles tightening as if she were using her own physical force to pull the needle up.

It popped!

A small compartment glided up smoothly at the very center of the table, moving up as she continued to form her needle. Femira marvelled at how well the compartment fit in the desk, considering her fingers hadn't been able to detect any seam. The compartment was no wider than her forearm, and inside she found scrolled pages.

Femira pressed them flat and felt a smirk pull at her lips. They matched the pages that Garld had shown her. Femira rolled them back up and tucked the pages safely into her pouch.

She drew the metal she'd used to form her needle back into her earthstone, and the hidden compartment slid neatly back into the table. Awed, Femira ran her hand back over the desk to see if she could feel the boundary. Now that she knew exactly where to look, she could feel it almost imperceptibly beneath her fingertip. Idly, she wondered how many times highborn had cheated her out of finding the really valuable stuff using concealed compartments like these. *Underhanded little crooks!*

A part of her felt a little sad that the game was now over, but the more practical part of her brain was eager to get moving. Linger too long in one place and you might as well scream for a guard to find you.

Femira peeked out into the hallway and after seeing no lights, she slipped out and reset the lock on the door. Something felt... off as she made her way back through the dark hallways of the manse. She couldn't pinpoint it, but it was the same feeling she got when she suspected a guard was just around the corner. A feeling that someone was nearby. She glanced over her shoulder and saw nothing.

She padded noiselessly along, ears straining for other sounds. Nothing but her own heartbeat, not even servants moving around anymore.

Femira continued on, trying to pass the feeling off as jitters. This was her first heist in a few months, after all. She slipped out the window, and edged her way along an exterior beam to an iron drainpipe.

She shimmied carefully down the pipe, keeping her eyes fixed on the backs of a pair of guards in the courtyard. Guards were the utmost peak of misplaced security in Femira's opinion—and the most costly. *Invest in wooden walls and more complicated locks would be my advice. If rich sods ever had the decency to ask. Don't waste your money on hiring men to look off mindlessly into space for hours. At best, they were no better than scarecrows to deter any amateur thieves. At worst, they were full on asleep. Get a scarecrow and put armour on him, it'll be cheaper.*

That opinion didn't make her reckless with guards however. All it took was for one of them to have a little unlucky glance over the house, and he'd spot a shadow moving along the wall. The whole night would be a colossal bust. Femira didn't doubt she'd get away, but the satisfaction of doing it completely undetected would be lost. Unsurprisingly, they didn't look in her direction, or any direction other than whatever spot outside the manse gateway that had taken their fancy.

The drainpipe ended on the roof of the stables, leading into a gutter that led away from the courtyard which Femira followed down off the roof. She felt the feeling again of someone being close by, and looked back up the way she came. There was nothing.

Femira took a calming breath and made her way through the garden, keeping to the shadowed hedges. She reached the palisade fence. The iron bars were cool against her touch. Her hands vibrated, ready to dissolve the metal. *Sorry bars, not today.*

Femira reached down and felt the familiar beat of the earth below her. In big sweeping gestures with her hands she pulled chunks of earth and rock into her earthstone, carving out a small hole beneath the palisade for her to wiggle through.

After climbing out the other side, she dusted herself off, then glanced up and down the street to see if anyone had spotted her. The gaslamps were lit and at the far end of the street, Femira could hear some drunks staggering along in the opposite direction.

She refilled the hole below the fence. It was messy and if anyone cared to look they would notice that the cobblestones of the pathway were missing next to the fence and had just been filled with dirt. She didn't have time to focus on reconstructing the cobblestones exactly as they had been and instead hurried off down in the opposite direction from the drunks.

It was a long walk back to the garrison and Femira kept to smaller streets and shadier alleyways. Epilas was primarily a military city, but every city has its crime regardless of how many soldiers were about. People often thought that they should keep to the main gaslamp lit streets at night, that they would be safer there. But all that did was make the roughs spot you easier. She had learned very young that it was better to stay hidden for as long as you could. Not that she really had anything to fear from street thugs, not with her earthstone and her daggers, but old habits and all that. So Femira kept to the shadows, trying to shake the feeling she was being followed still.

She was two streets away from the manse when she heard the scraping of a tile above her. Her eyes shot up to where a ribbon of stars split the alleyway.

She couldn't see anything so Femira continued on, rounded a corner, and broke into a full sprint down the gaslamp lit street.

She didn't look back and took a sharp turn into another alleyway. A couple of rats scurried away along the walls of the alley but otherwise there was silence. No indications of anyone following.

Femira waited, crouched in the shadows for any sounds. A few moments passed and she heard nothing. She waited for another few, then finally stepped back onto the main street. She cursed the gaslamps and the myriad of shadows they cast as she cautiously walked along the edges trying to remain unseen.

She kept her gaze on the rooftops. *Something* was off. She knew it. Then, a shadow moved.

Femira froze, keeping her gaze where the shadow had been. There was no doubt now that she was being followed. Her heart quickened. She resumed her cautious pace trying to devise a plan.

Fear won over and she broke into another sprint. *He won't be able to keep up on those rooftops.* She sprinted down the street aiming for the main thoroughfare that stretched from the port to the garrison.

The thoroughfare was only a few streets over and if she could make it, the wide street would be reasonably populated even at this hour. There would be duty soldiers patrolling at least. Femira cut through an alley and darted along onto a parallel street. She'd always been fast and the past months of endurance training with the bloodshedders had conditioned her so that her lungs didn't burn with the exertion. Adrenaline pumped through her as she ran. Femira stole a glance over her shoulder and she could see the shadow keeping pace along the rooftop. *Shit.*

"Eh love, where you running off to?" some drunk called as she ran past him. She ran into another alley, closing the distance to the main street.

She heard footsteps behind her. Panic gripped her, and she reached for her daggers. She spun, dropping into a crouch, and unsheathed them. The hooded figure pulled up a few feet away.

"Who are you?" Femira hissed.

"I could ask you the same thing," the person replied in an accent that Femira didn't recognise.

"You're the one following *me*," she spat.

"You have something... something that was not yours to take,"

"You were in Averstock's manse," Femira guessed, not exactly a question but wanting to validate her feelings of being watched.

"The journal pages," the person said. Femira couldn't tell with the accent whether the voice was even a man or a woman. "Give them to me and I won't hurt you."

"What right do you have to them?"

"More right than you," the person replied. "More than Averstock did."

Femira couldn't tell if they had any weapons. She remained in her crouched fighting stance, waiting for the other person to make the first move.

"Well, to me, you're just another thief," Femira said casually. "My right's about the same as yours as I see it, so you're going to have to do a whisp better than that."

"Who are you working with?" the shadow asked.

"Working alone," she said.

"Lying and thieving are often neighbours. If you're going to lie to me, at least make it a convincing one."

"I don't owe you nothing," she replied.

Her mind ran through the possibilities of what this person could be hiding in their cloak. Most likely daggers, similar to her own, or a shortsword, anything bigger would be showing.

Femira edged back closer to the street, hoping to lure the person into the light of the gaslamps.

"Just what you stole," they replied, and matched her steps, slowly advancing.

Closer to the entrance of the alley, lamplight broke through from the street. The person was hooded, but Femira was almost certain it was a boy. Not a man—a boy. *You've made a big mistake kid.*

Femira jumped at him, slashing out with her dagger. He took a quick step back, surprised at her sudden attack. His hood flopped back showing a young pale face. Her intent had not been to hurt him but to scare him off... but he didn't run.

"I'm giving you one more chance," the boy warned, a little shake in his voice. He was taller than her, to be sure, but still just a kid.

"I'm giving *you* one more chance, kiddo," Femira snarled. "Back off before I cut you from neck to balls." He didn't draw any weapon. *He's got nothing, foolish boy.*

But he didn't make any move to run from her. *Fine!* Femira took another swing at him. This one had more intent behind it—not a fatal wound, just a little warning cut. The boy sidestepped around her. Femira felt the rush of wind as her blade brushed the space he had been, and then she was falling.

The ground beneath her collapsed.

Her feet kicked wildly against dust and her torso slammed hard against the cobblestone. Her daggers clattered ahead of her, echoing in the quiet alley.

Arms outstretched, Femira grasped at the stones before she fell further into the ground. There was a sudden tightening on her legs, cold solid arms grabbed at her legs and waist.

Instinctively, she tried to kick, but the grip was impossibly firm. Panic rising, Femira tried to twist to see where the cloaked boy had gone. But she was pinned in place at the waist. She realised with sharp clarity that she was held by the *ground itself*. She felt her pouch containing the pages ripped from her back.

Femira reached for her earthstone, and felt the hum. She set to quickly dissolving the stone holding her, pushing her hand down with frenzied breaths.

In a few moments, she'd carved out enough space to wriggle her legs free and scramble up out of the hole. Without even getting to her feet, she launched herself forward, reaching for her daggers. Her hand clasped the hilt and she rolled on her back ready to stab the boy.

But he was... gone?

Cautiously, Femira rose to standing. Her braid swinging as she whipped her head about the alley looking for the boy.

Shit.

"Fuck! Shit! Shit! Prick!!" Femira shouted furiously at the empty alleyway. She darted onto the main street but didn't spot the boy anywhere.

"Ah!" she screamed bitterly, "get back here you little shit!" There were a few stragglers on the other side of the street and they hurriedly moved on.

***

Femira entered Garld's office. The General sat at his desk and was talking in hushed tones with a soldier in a bloodshedder's uniform.

The soldier was short for a Reldoni, which meant he was still a good head taller than Femira. He was bald and Femira recognised him as Loreli's mentor. He had a nose that looked like it had been broken many times. When Femira entered the room, Garld beckoned her forward.

"Come, you were successful then? You have the pages?" He asked. Femira shot a glance at the other man. "Endrin is one of my own. He can be trusted, Annali," Garld said. *Evidently not that trusted.*

"I don't have the papers, sir," Femira started awkwardly, "I—uh—well... I lost them."

"What do you mean you lost them?" Garld asked, his tone heavy with disapproval.

"Some guy in a cloak," Femira hurried to explain, "jumped in the alley and took them." She had little desire to admit that he had managed to follow her undetected from the manse itself—and even less to confess that it had been a *child* that had bested her. Not to Garld, and especially not with Endrin standing over his shoulder.

"You fought him?" Garld asked.

"Didn't even get the chance to," Femira grumbled. "He trapped me in the street, sir. I've no idea how he did it so quickly."

"*Trapped* you?"

"One second I was standing, next one I was falling," she explained. "Took me a moment to realise he had trapped me in the stone... but it was too late, he'd snatched the papers and was gone before I got myself out."

"What did he look like?"

"It was dark and he was wearing a hood... tall enough, not as big as you sir, but bigger than me. I couldn't get a good look at his face," and then more reluctantly, she added, "but he seemed young. Maybe a few years younger than me but it was hard to tell. Sir, I can't figure it out. How he managed to do it... no one in the garrison— Not even Misandrei or the other elites—can work runestones that quickly," Endrin bristled at that comment but Garld only nodded in understanding.

She continued, "he had me trapped in *seconds*, that shouldn't be possible."

"Did he say anything?" Garld prodded, breezing past her concerns, "was he Reldoni?"

"I couldn't tell his accent... he didn't sound Reldoni. His face looked far too pale. He asked who I was, who I worked for but I gave him nothing. He kept talking about how I didn't 'have any right' to the journal... he spoke like it was his."

"Journal?" Garld said, looking surprised. "He called it that? You're sure?"

"Yeah. Do you reckon it could have been his journal?"

"That's impossible. The writer is centuries dead," Garld said it so flippantly, as if she should have already known this, then added "Anything else?"

Femira shook her head, "he was no amateur. I don't doubt he was planning on breaking into Averstock's himself. I just beat him to it."

"But ultimately lost to him," Garld chided.

"You don't seem surprised," Femira said, suddenly feeling sceptical as to why he was so unphased by her account of the boy's abilities. "How he used his earthstone so quickly. You've seen it before, haven't you?" He didn't respond, instead he sat back in his chair looking at her appraisingly.

"What about all that trusting each other talk," Femira said with an accusatory edge to her tone. "You said nothing would be held back."

In her past few months at Epilas, Femira hadn't ever felt that Garld was hiding anything from her. Even now, a part of her felt uncomfortable questioning him.

"The Honorswords?" Femira mused, "they're like him aren't they? They move faster than even an aeristone would have allowed them to."

"I'm not sure," Garld answered. "In truth, I have no idea how the Honorswords do what they do. What you experienced tonight however—this accelerated form of runewielding—is known to me."

"How can I achieve this?" the words slipped out of her hungrily.

"You're not ready," he said. *Don't run before you can walk, girl,* Lichtin's words, Garld's voice.

She felt anger rise in her, "I am the fastest stonebre—"

"—you are addressing your commanding General, soldier," Endrin reprimanded, "you will show due respect."

"I wasn't talking to you," Femira shot at him, "and I'm no soldier!"

"No," he rebuffed, "you're not. You're just a spoiled little highborn lady who wants to play at being a bloodshedder!" His comment gave Femira a chuckle.

"You're really not the fastest rat in the gutter are you, Endrin?"

"That's enough," Garld interjected, cutting Endrin's response off and leaving the man with a confused look on his face. It looked natural on him, like his face was designed to fit in that expression.

"You are not ready, Annali," Garld reaffirmed, being clear to use her new name. "Believe me when I say that this is for your own good. I will tell a portion of it. We have had breakthroughs in how we use our runestones—advanced techniques we once believed to be myth. While these are powerful, the transformations are mostly unknown to us... and this makes them dangerous. I have invested both time and money in your training and education these past few months, I'm not so reckless with my vested resources."

"How can I prove that I *am* ready? I've done everything you've asked of me. You've seen the change yourself," Femira said. She'd already fought—and beaten, she might add—most of the other recruits in her division. Only Loreli and a few others remained on her list of unsurpassed rivals.

"To change, and to improve, are two very different things," Garld said. "You've advanced quickly in your training but you have a ways to go before you can be fully initiated into the bloodshedder ranks. I will consider this only once you've demonstrated that you are capable of completing the tasks that I've given you," he added curtly.

Endrin watched her with a satisfied grin. Reluctantly, Femira nodded.

"So... that's it," Femira said, "the initiation? This is what gives the bloodshedders their advanced skills?"

"Not strictly," Garld answered and she didn't miss Endrin's look of discomfort as Garld spoke, "but only the bloodshedders are resilient enough for it. I will speak no more on the subject, and you will continue in your tasks."

"Yes, sir," she responded even though it wasn't a question.

"Your next assignment will be something a bit different than you're accustomed to," Garld revealed and she piqued up, eager for a chance to demonstrate that she could move to the next stage of her training.

"The remaining lords of Altarea have signed a treaty with King Abhran, pledging fealty to the King and rightfully taking their place under Reldoni rule. As you are the sole living relative of the former King Amenia's infant son, your presence will be required at the treaty feast. You will attend and show support for Lord Ingel's inauguration as Highlord of Altarea; in addition to applauding the lords of Altarea in their own loyalty to the crown of Reldon."

"Yes, sir," Femira replied but there was an apprehensive quiver in her voice, "will the Honorswords be there?" Karas and Jahasa were still in the city so far as Femira could gather.

"Invitations to the envoys of Keiran have surely been made," Garld said simply. "Do not fret. You are still under the protection of Prince Landryn, Lady Annali. The Honorswords have no authority here." *That didn't stop one of them butchering one of your bloodshedders a few weeks ago though did it?*

"Sir... the Honorswords, what if they—" she glanced at Endrin, "—question me?" she asked, trying to get across the point she wanted to ask. *What if they figure out I'm not Annali-fucking-Jahar—that I'm the daughter of some nobody castaway who fled Keiran with everything she could carry.*

Even the Altarean nobles themselves would surely notice that she wasn't the real Annali—a woman who had married into their now dethroned royal family. In Femira's experience, the Altarean highborns were a prejudiced lot but even they weren't so blinded by it to be fooled into believing that any Keiran girl off the street was Annali Jahar.

Femira had ingenuously assumed the guise that Garld had given her had simply been a means to recruit her, naively assuming that all bloodshedders had to be highborn. She was beginning to realise that Garld had a lot more schemes for 'Annali' to be a part of.

Not that Femira minded all that much; she had a clean and safe place to sleep every night, full meals, *and* she was getting stronger and more skilled each day. A full belly, a bed and training tallied up however was not nearly payment enough to face an Honorsword's inquisition.

"To my knowledge, Annali," Gard began, "you've spent most of your childhood in your family's estates—far from the Emperor's Court. I can't imagine the Honorswords would have any matters of concern with you. Perhaps you should read over your journals. *Refresh your memory* for any Altarean connections you might have made in your year there." If Endrin found the conversation strange he didn't allude to it, in fact, he seemed to be quite bored.

"Of course, sir," Femira replied dutifully. "When is the feast?"
"In three weeks, plenty of time for you to prepare. There are certain highborn I wish for you to speak with and—more importantly—listen to."

She nodded in understanding, over the past weeks since Garld had started giving her assignments, many had involved simply listening to various lords conversations and relaying the discussions to him. It was easy work, the kind of tasks Lichtin had given her when she had first started working for his crew.

"I will have suitable clothing and a list of names sent to your room. You're dismissed."

Femira saluted and left. Almost immediately after leaving Garld's offices she felt a sudden wave of loathing for herself. *Yes, sir! Anything you want, sir! Empty your chamberpot? Yes please, sir!* When, over the last few months, had she become a pining pup, jumping at the chance to do her master's bidding? When had Garld even *become* her master? Until recently, she had seen him as just another employer. *An employer with an army of bloodshedders,* but still.

Over the past weeks, Femira found herself more and more eager to please him and—until tonight—it didn't seem like he was hiding anything from her. But he did hide things from others obviously—as far as she knew no one else knew that she wasn't Annali Jahar—had she been foolish to assume that he wasn't hiding things from her also?

Femira stepped out into the central courtyard of the garrison. The gaslamps were still lit but the sky was growing brighter, a muted predawn blue. There was an early morning chill and despite her lack of sleep Femira felt no fatigue. She was well accustomed to working through the night and into the morning. Scant windows in the garrison had any light in them, most of the other recruits would only be stirring in their beds.

"I suppose I shouldn't be surprised to find a vreth skulking about at this hour," Femira turned about to see Loreli behind her.
"I'm surprised to see you up," Femira replied, "training drills aren't for another few hours. Usually only *important* folk have tasks at this hour."

She'd learned that it was a bit of a pain point for Loreli that Garld had already started giving assignments to Femira. It was bad enough that Garld was showing a personal interest in her training. Now that Femira was advancing past most of the other recruits in the ranks, it hadn't improved Loreli's opinion of her. But that didn't bother Femira none.

"Actually, I'm meeting Endrin," Loreli said, a smug smile on her stupid pretty face, "I'm to join the bloodshedders officially. He's prepping me for the initiation. General Garld has decided that I'm the best of the recruits."
"That's bullshit," Femira spat, "I'm sure he's preppin' you for something alright, bet he's got—"

"—Recruit Jahar!" an angry voice called, "showing disrespect again!" Endrin was trotting over from the door to the garrison.

"She prefers Vreth, Endrin.... chose the name herself," Loreli chimed in.

"Fitting," Endrin replied, contempt plain on his face. Confusion suited it better. "Don't be so naive to be taken in by the General's words, girl. You're just Prince Landryn's bargaining chip for the Honorswords. You'll see, once the treaty's signed and all the Altareans are happy, we're going to pack you up and send you back where you belong."

"Are you really this intimidated by a girl half your size?" Femira shot at him, her anger getting the better of her. She knew she shouldn't be challenging the bloodshedders but her failure earlier in the night had her itching to recoup her pride.

"*Intimidated?* Your delusion is pitiful. You were bested by a *child* tonight."

"Really, a child?" Loreli laughed, "Vreth I told you to find opponents closer to your skill level, but we Reldoni have laws against duelling against children," a wide grin splitting that fucking face.

"I'm sure Garld would love to know you're discussing confidential operations out in the open," Femira retorted.

"It's *General* Garld," he corrected her, "and listen here, *Vreth*, you're here a wet fucking week and you think you're better than us just because you were married to some dead Prince? But the truth is, *you're the enemy*. We killed your Prince and now you're our *prisoner*. You're just too stupid to realise it."

"I *am* better than you," Femira growled. She cared nothing for the insults against Annali, Femira couldn't give two sinking shits for her but Endrin was insulting *her*, not Annali.

"I challenge you, Endrin whatever-your-fucking-family-name-is," she said drawing one of her daggers, "right now."

"I'm not going to kill you, haven't you been listening?" his voice rife with condescension, "you're our prisoner and the General wants you alive."

"Not a duel then! A bout, you vs me. First touch wins," she ran her hand over her dagger, her earthstone glowing as she pulled the metal blade's edge in, blunting it.

"You're not worth it."

"Draw your sword! Or I'll cut you," Femira shifted into a fighting stance.

He didn't pull his sword from its sheath, but his hand went to the hilt. *Good enough for me.*

She pushed off against her feet, her dagger whipping forward. Endrin didn't flinch or make any move to defend himself. She had expected to feel the blunted dagger bite into his chest, but as she rammed it against him, there was a puff of metallic dust and the hilt of her dagger smacked uselessly on his chest.

Femira staggered forward, losing balance. She was too dazed to move back. She remained frozen in awe, looking at the silvery-grey dust that glittered on Endrin's black uniform.

"Go home, girl," Endrin said coldly, "back to Keiran, or Altarea, or wherever you like but stop embarrassing yourself here." He casually stepped back from where she held the hilt against his chest. Femira just stood there agape as Endrin and Loreli walked away. They didn't laugh or taunt her, they just walked away wordlessly as if she were nothing to them.

It had never occurred to her that *Annali* was the true reason that Garld had wanted to hire her. Did she really look that similar to her? Was her past months training in Epilas all simply been a con? Garld's ruse to lure her into thinking she could become more than she was, that she could find real strength? Was her only purpose really just to pretend that Garld and Landryn hadn't simply locked the real Annali away... *If that's even what they did with her.*

The realisation that the real Annali was most likely dead suddenly seemed obvious to her. How had she been so blind? They killed Annali because she resisted them, and because they had me to pretend to be her if Keiran Honorswords came looking for justice.

CHAPTER 7

The Hunter's Son

Tanlor sat up in the bed. Danielle lay naked beside him on her side. For a time, he simply admired the shape of body; how her hips curved and how her chest lightly rose and fell with her breaths. Her blond hair caught the morning light that crept through the window, shining gold. Tanlor knew every aspect of her face, every blond hair on her head and the occasional red. He knew the dimples in her back and each of the small dark moles, the blemishes only added to her beauty in his mind. He ran his fingers lightly over her shoulder and along her back.

"Hmmm," she purred, "...you don't have to stop that."

"I'm sorry, my love, but I have to go."

"But I thought you were off duty today?" Danielle said, sitting up with a frown. Even with her face scrunched up at him, he was charmed by her and felt himself becoming erect again. *No time,* he thought wistfully, *I've already stayed longer than I should.* He glanced again at the rising sun. The more enamoured he became with Danielle, the more reckless he was becoming.

"I *was*," Tanlor grumbled, "but Keltin asked me to babysit the cripple today."

"Cripple?"

"The Reldoni Prince."

"Oh," Danielle sat up, propping herself against the bed frame and pulling the blankets up to cover herself, "... you shouldn't call him that."

"It's what all the other guards call him."

"*You* shouldn't though," she said pointedly. "It's not nice."

"But that's what he is," Tanlor replied as he climbed out of bed. He hurriedly pulled on his breeches before the morning chill got at him.

The hearth in the room had been reduced to a smouldering ash heap. He had left his topaz next to it the night before so that it would passively absorb some of the heat. It glowed with only a dim light. He picked it up instinctively drawing the heat from the gemstone and into his body. He immediately felt the flush of heat pulse through him.

"Ah," Tanlor sighed in pleasure, "Do you mind if I...?" He asked, nodding toward the dwindling fire.

"Go ahead," Danielle replied, "it's colder than usual today, you'll probably need it." Tanlor reached out his hand. Using the power of the topaz, he drew the remaining heat of the fire into his body. The heat prickled inside of him, there hadn't been enough embers left to give him the internal burning sensation he would normally feel when he pulled on a direct fire. He focused on moving all the new excess heat into the topaz. It flickered to life with an ambient glow. *Much better.*

"It's still not nice to use that word," Danielle said, pulling the conversation back.

"Well what should I call him then?"

"*Hindered* is a more polite term."

"Still basically the same meaning," Tanlor shrugged.

"Not exactly... 'cripple' is a vulgar and cruel word," she pointed out, "and you're not either of those things. Most people who use it, their intent is to be demeaning. 'Hindered' gets the meaning across, but it doesn't have any vicious intent."

"Oh you're just grumpy I have to leave. I promise you, I'll be back this evening, your father is dining with Arch-duke Edmund again tonight so I know he'll be distracted."

"I mean it," she said watching him put on his grey Dukes Guard uniform "please... for me, don't call him that... I've met him and he's actually very nice, and the people in court have been treating him like he's a fool."

Of course he was nice to you. You're a beautiful woman and he's a man. A man significantly higher ranked than Tanlor—and a more favourable match for that matter.

"Fine," he caved, "I'll be nice."

He began buckling his hand-and-half-sword to his back, and strapping on his armour. He had come directly from duty the night before. It had been past midnight when he finally managed to slip into her room, she had been awake and waiting for him, as she often did.

Not returning to his bunk in the guardhouse all week had meant that he had amassed a few belongings in her room. Things he should really take with him before any of her family's servants began to notice. Danielle had scooted to the edge of her bed and was organising his things; his coin pouch, a few reports that Keltin had wanted him to look over—an aspiring Captain of the Guard must always be aware of what's going in the palace—and a letter. And of course it was the letter—of all the papers she could have picked—that Danielle lingered on.

"What's this letter, Tan?" she asked.

"It's from my brother," Tanlor replied as he finished tightening the straps on his greaves.

"Oh," she said looking a little concerned, "it's a long way to send a letter from Garronforn, is everything alright?"

"All fine," he waved his hand dismissively, "in fact, Rowan is here... in Rubastre."

"Really?"

"Yeah... letter says he took a job escorting a merchant's caravan and they arrived here last week."

"Oh, how wonderful!" She exclaimed, "I'd love to meet him."

"No, you wouldn't. My brother acts like a commoner," Tanlor huffed, he knew there was a harsh edge to his words but he couldn't help it.

"He's staying at some tavern out past the Ironworks. I've told him before that he can stay closer to the palace if he likes. I'd happily put him up in a room at the White Foxes but he refuses... anyway, I'm sorry. I really have to go."

He walked back over to the bed and kissed her. It was a warm, deep kiss. He felt like melting back into the sheets with her. To ignore his duties for the day and just spend it nestled in her bed... but Tanlor couldn't disappoint Keltin, not when he had come so far... when he was *so* close to being the Captain's replacement.

Reluctantly, Tanlor pulled himself away.

"I love you," he said and she smiled. She had the kindest smile and it gave him a warm feeling in his chest. He left before his impulses took control and coerced him into staying.

Danielle's father—Duke Harfallow—had a permanent suite for his family in the Arch-duke's palace. Being a close friend of Arch-duke Edmund, the man spent a considerable amount of his time here in the capital than at his own keep at Hardhelm.

Having visited Hardhelm only once, Tanlor could see why Jared Harfallow spent so much time away from the place. The keep was built atop the cliffs on the very eastern edge of Rubane. As a result, the castle was perpetually buffeted by the fierce Altasjura winds.

When Danielle had told her father that she wanted to stay with him in Rubastre, the man had been more than pleased. Danielle being a part of the Arch-duke's court meant more opportunity for her to find a *suitable* husband, which was Duke Harfallow's paramount concern for his daughter. Unbeknownst to him, the girl's heart had long been given to Tanlor—ever since they were teenagers—since the moment they had met when Duke Harfallow and his family had visited Tanlor's family's keep in Garronforn.

Seven long years ago... We were different people then.

The Harfallow suite was a large complex of rooms and—lucky for him—Danielle's was conveniently situated right by a servants stairs that lead down to the palace kitchens... and it wouldn't draw *too* much attention for one of the Duke's personal guards to be moving about the palace. It was his duty to ensure that order was kept after all.

A few of the palace cooks gave him sharp looks as he made his way through. Maybe he had been a bit too obvious taking the same route each morning this week.

Stop being careless. You're so close.

Tanlor had quickened his pace, he knew that the Reldoni Prince had a habit of sleeping late in the morning but the sun was already risen and he worried that he had missed him. He made his way back from the lower levels of the palace, coming out in a hallway that led directly from the guard's quarters to the wing where the foreign dignitaries were located.

To Tanlor's relief there was still a pair of the Prince's soldiers standing guard at his chambers. Captain Ferath—a man that Tanlor came to like over the past month —was not present, at his usual station was another Reldoni soldier that Tanlor did not recognise and that woman bodyguard.

The crip—*hindered* Prince seemed completely blind to how inappropriate her position was. At first, Tanlor thought maybe the Prince was simply as dimwitted as the other highborn in the palace believed. But on further thought, maybe it was the apathetic regard to a woman's safety that was so inherent to his Reldoni upbringing that had created this blind spot in his judgement. Either way, Tanlor did not appreciate it when the Prince did finally emerge from his room and said that the woman—Kerala—would be part of his escort today.

The man has his own bloody bodyguards, he doesn't need any of the Duke's, wasting our time. But in conflict to that thought, Tanlor also suspected this had been Keltin's decision to have at least one Rubanian accompany the foreign Prince. *Always know what's going on in the palace.*

"Chanlan, correct?" Prince Daegan asked as they made their way to his first appointment.

"It's Tanlor, my lord," Tanlor corrected him.

"Oh, yes. You're that Hunter's son if I recall correctly?" *Well, here we go.*

"Yes, my lord," Tanlor replied bluntly, hoping to show he didn't care to discuss it, "Taran Shrydan was my father."

"I unfortunately didn't get the chance to hear the full story, I do wish to hear it." *Keep on wishing.*

"I'm not a good storyteller," Tanlor objected.

"Nonsense," The Prince waved a dismissive hand, "it's always better to hear the story straight from someone *in the story*." *That's what everybody bloody thinks, but trust me, cripple, you'll be just as disappointed as all the others who've asked.*

"Trust me, my lord. It's much better done by the bards, I'm sure you can have one of the Arch-duke's entertainers recite the tale for you."

"A *tale*, is it?" Prince Daegan asked with a sly smirk on his face. *No... not dimwitted.*

"My father saved my mother from some bandits... He married her and they had me and my brother... that's all there really is to the story." Prince Daegan didn't look satisfied but he didn't press Tanlor any further, finally taking the hint.

The Prince's first appointment was with the Merchant's Guild. The Reldoni consul had his own office in the palace so there wouldn't be much actual escorting today, just the mind numbing monotony of standing guard.

Tanlor had developed coping mechanisms for the boredom over his years serving in the Dukesguard. He would watch all the entry points of the room, envisage all the different types of assassins that could break in at any moment.

He would play it out in his mind; how the fight would go down. Sometimes he would duel with a swordsman like himself, other times it would be a more accomplished runewielder. A stonebreaker would hurl blades of obsidian at him, he would deflect them all, and in a clean swing, he would decapitate the assassin. And of course, for his valiant efforts, Keltin would award him with a promotion to Captain. So confident in Tanlor's ability to protect the Arch-duke, Keltin would even take an early retirement, naming Tanlor as his successor.

It was these scenarios that Tanlor played in his mind while Prince Daegan and the guildmaster discussed shipping tariffs on dragonshide or some such. It was a stark difference to Tanlor's early career as a knight. Back when he had taken contracts along the risky miner's paths further north in the Iron Hills; fighting—and killing—raiders and bandits. Tanlor had even taken a few contracts with his brother back then but always contracts close to Rubastre and Keltin's ears.

Get yourself a reputation as a fierce fighter and a good bodyguard.

That was the advice he'd been given when he was still a greenhorn, desperate to join the Arch-duke's personal guard. The unwelcome memory of Tanlor's first—and only—visit to Hardhelm forced its way into his mind

Being a fan of the story of Taran the Hunter, Duke Harfallow welcomed him as a guest and invited him to dine in his feasting hall and to tell the tale of his father. *As people always do.*

Tanlor had given Duke Harfallow and his guests the bard's rendition of the story. He didn't mind telling that version back then. The night had seemed promising; he and Danielle shared fond looks throughout the feast, her eyes would light up when he looked at her... and her father seemed to like him... unfortunately, that was not enough.

"You want to *what?!*" Duke Harfallow had roared, he had the attention of the entire hall. "My daughter?" Young Tanlor's face paled at the Duke's reaction... then the man let out the most wholehearted laugh that Tanlor had ever heard or had heard since.

"Oh lad," Duke Harfallow choked, wiping tears from his eyes, "for a moment I thought you were serious." His laughter continued, over and over. Inwardly, young Tanlor despaired, and the other highborn at the feast could see that Tanlor had been quite serious.

Duke Harfallow's mood didn't skip a beat that night, he continued to pound back the whitewhiskeys, telling stories of his glory days fighting rakmen. He would often come back to the 'side-splitter' that the young Sir Tanlor had made.

Tanlor could tell that Danielle was also devastated, their hopeful marriage laid to dust with each of the Duke's rancorous laughs. They didn't get to share any time —intimate time that is—during that stay in Hardhelm. Not with the watching eyes of the Hardhelm highborn... their knowing eyes.

After that first evening, Duke Harfallow had even offered Tanlor a place in his own personal guard—an excellent position for a fledgling knight—but it would have been far too torturous to have been so close to Danielle without being able to hold her. So Tanlor had declined, feigning that he wanted to explore more of the country; from the jagged eastern coastline to the wild untamed north and the Iron Hills.

"A hero from the stories, like your father," Duke Harfallow beamed. Tanlor faked a smile in response.

"Out of curiosity, my lord," Tanlor asked, "Have you chosen a suitor for Lady Danielle?"

"Other than you, lad," Harfallow guffawed... then after a moment he had composed himself. "Ah, I've had a few men that have come asking," he said lightly. "Most of the boys I turned away, but some of them are good matches; Lord Hembrook for one, Sir Dunsan too but he's a bit old I reckon. My Danielle would turn her nose up at him... I'm not the kind of man that will force his daughter to marry someone she doesn't want to." That single statement had been a shining beacon in the dark that lifted Tanlor's spirit. However those men he mentioned were all significantly higher nobility than he was.

"Sir Marshtan too... perhaps... if he becomes Captain."

"I'm sorry, my lord, Sir Marshtan? I can't say that I know of him."

"Not that you would, lad. He's a fairly low ranking nobility from Rubastre but he's a member of the Arch-duke's personal guard. He's too low to be suitable but if he were to become the Captain of the Guard, I would consider allowing it."

Tanlor's heart had lifted at that, Captain of the Arch-duke's guard... It would take work but that position wouldn't be impossible for him to reach. It had given Tanlor a target that he had pursued with relentless fervour over his career.

Tanlor had been so lost in his reverie, he had failed to notice when the guildmaster had left the Ambassador's office. *I really have to start being more attentive.* Keltin would of course ask him for a full report of the Prince's conversations throughout the day.

"Ugh, guildmasters," Prince Daegan sighed from his desk, "there's no bloody end to them in this city. Who's next?"

"A guildmaster from the Ironworks, my lord," Prince Daegan's manservant said.

Tanlor tensed, he recalled the curt conversation the Prince had had on his first night in the palace. But it was not Grimsworth that strode into the office, instead it was a strong-looking bearded man. He wore thin frame spectacles and carried with him a stack of loose documents and books.

"Guildmaster Arken," Prince Daegan said, offering him the seat at his desk, "you are undoubtedly here to discuss the *revoking* of the Reldoni contract with Rubastre Ironworks."

"Of sorts, my lord," Arken replied gruffly, "but possibly not in the way you might think."

"As I have already discussed with your superior Guildmaster Grimsworth," Prince Daegan said tiredly, "the contracts in Garronforn, Hardhelm and Edas are more than enough to fulfil our needs."

"That's not entirely true, my lord," Arken said, "if I may?" he said, opening up one of his ledgers.

"These records show the steel exports to Reldon over the past five years. As you can see, the demand has gone steadily up. Rubastre Ironworks is the *only* enterprise large enough to accommodate." He said and then turned more tactful.

"Not all of us in the guild agree with Master Grimsworth's methods," Arken said, "…or his leadership." Tanlor had seen enough of this type of underhanded scheming in his years serving as an armed statue. *Looking to usurp the Ironworks top seat.*

"No bribes," Prince Daegan said bluntly, "I don't work the same as Ormand." Prince Daegan it seemed was sharp enough to pick that up.

"Nor do I", the guildmaster replied. Although Tanlor suspected the man was lying. *Win back the Reldoni contract with the stipulation that Grimsworth must step down.*

It was a bold move, if it got back to Grimsworth that this man was working to oust him, he could have Arken removed from the guild altogether. Tanlor himself cared nothing for all of this nonsense but Keltin would ask him for a report and so he paid close attention.

"I'm just an engineer," Arken said, raising his open palms, "I just want to see right by my lads working in those factories out there" *Yes I'm sure you care ever so deeply for those soot-stained commoners, coughing up blood at night.*

"Obviously, Grimsworth must step down," Prince Daegan directed. *Not surprising considering the idiotic stunt the man tried to pull.*

"Of course," Arken agreed.

"And I mean it; no bribes, no *administration* fees or subsidies."

"I understand—however, I do have something else that your Generals might be very interested in…" Arken glanced at Tanlor, his eyes flicking to his grey tabard. *That's interesting… worried about this getting back to the Arch-duke?*

"The designs for the new model of handgun," Arken said, again looking through his ledger for the right documents.

"It is more or less the same as our Reldoni models," Prince Daegan replied casually, "I don't see why we would pay you for something that is just a slight adaptation on what our engineers originally designed."

"Forgive me, my lord, but in that you are wrong," Arken explained, laying out the technical diagrams of the weapon.

Tanlor had little interest in the new form of crossbow. From reports, they couldn't even break through armour. Like others in the guard, Tanlor saw these new weapons as a fad that would likely pass.

"The key is obviously in the gemstones, my lord… and how they work." Arken said, "and u-um forgive me for saying. But as you might have noticed being—er— hindered, my lord. You don't actually need to use one's own runewielding ability to use it."

"And that is important because…?" Prince Daegan asked, still seemingly unconvinced.

"The applications go so far beyond just this handgun, my lord... we are on the cusp of a *technological revolution*. We have discovered how to make gemstones work *without* needing a person to actually channel the energy."

"Does this not happen all the time?" Daegan asked rhetorically, "topazes will absorb heat when left close to a fire."

The Prince continued, "do these brass pipes in the palace not operate on the same principle? The heat from the inlaid topazes heats the oil in the pipes, do they not?" *Not a dimwit at all.*

Tanlor found himself quite surprised by the observations the Prince had made. They were simple truths, things that most people who had ever used a topaz would know... but he had merely expected the man to be oblivious to all of that. *Because he's hindered.*

"Indeed, my lord," Arken acknowledged. It appeared that he had not made the same preconceptions as Tanlor did, otherwise he wouldn't be here in the first place. "The importance is in the *type* of runes etched on the gemstones. For centuries we have been working only with the runes that would allow us to manipulate the stone's power using our own bodies. The idea that there were other *types* of runes in existence. It has astronomical implications!"

"And what have *you* to gain in sharing this knowledge with us?" Prince Daegan asked. Again, the guildmaster glanced towards Tanlor and hesitated for a second... then he smiled. *It's always gold.*

Tanlor had to admit that this man's absolute lack of candour was astounding. *He knows that I'll report this back...* but then, perhaps is that what Arken wanted? The Prince also seemed to be assessing the offer very carefully.

"As you know," Prince Daegan began thoughtfully, strangely rubbing at his throat, "my experience with runestones is... limited. Allow me some time to confer with my advisors."

"Of course, of course, here." Arken said, proffering the diagram to the Prince, "take this, share it with them to help them understand. There are more detailed research notes and guides that will be of much more value." Arken reached into his stack of ledgers and pulled out a small leatherbound notebook.

"This journal details just the *tip* of some of the discoveries my engineers have uncovered."

"Thank you, guildmaster," Daegan said, accepting the book, "I will think on this."

After the man had left, Daegan pondered a while in silence. He began flicking through the journal. After a few moments he turned to Tanlor.

"What are *your* thoughts, sir Tanlor?" Prince Daegan asked.

"Me? My lord?"

"Yes—The secrets that guildmaster Arken was wishing to sell could be dangerous in the wrong hands, would you agree?"

"Yes, my lord."

"And surely he knows that you will report this back to the Arch-duke."

"Most likely."

"And I would wager that I am certainly *not* the first foreign dignitary he has offered this to," Daegan considered, tapping the journal.

"He's not breaking any laws... from what I can tell," Tanlor reasoned, "sounds treasonous, yes... but the Ironworks are not part of Duke's military. They're a free organisation here, they pay their taxes to the Arch-duke, but they don't owe him anything."

Daegan smiled at Tanlor, "we both know that's not how Arch-duke Edmund would see it—or his High Court."

"I'm just a knight," Tanlor shrugged, trying to convey that this wasn't really something he would be expected to have much input on.

"Well, do what you must. Report it to Keltin… or whoever it is that pays you the most for information. I shall raise it with the Arch-duke myself also."

The Prince stood up from his desk, pocketing the small journal, and stretched. "My next appointment is on the other side of the palace" Daegan said. "Do you know how to get to Duke Garron's office?"

Tanlor felt his stomach sink. *Of all days you have to meet with Boern, it would have to be the day that I'm on duty.*

"Boern doesn't have an office here, my lord," Tanlor said tersely, "he tends to remain at Garronforn. Only comes to the capital when he must."

"*Boern?*" Daegan asked with an arched eyebrow.

"He's my cousin, my lord."

CHAPTER 8

The Hunter and the Lady

Daegan loped up the stairs. He had to admit it, if there was one single thing he liked about Rubastre; it was how *easy* it was to get around. The palace itself only had five floors to it, meaning you didn't spend your days with your legs burning. It was a welcome change to his father's palace, which was built right into the Pillar of Reldon itself. Daegan had spent his entire life arduously climbing the countless stairs in the place.

He was escorted by Kerala and Tanlor, and the two armed guards easily kept pace with him. Despite both being clad in armour; Tanlor in his brushed steel and Kerala in her black plate.

Being a Duke—the Rubanian equivalent of a Reldoni Highlord or Citylord— Boern Garron was residing in the upper eminent suites. Unlike Daegan's own set of rooms, the Duke's were much larger, having its own set of antechambers for various business dealings. When Daegan entered, he was greeted by the Duke's steward and then escorted to the lounge which wasn't that much different to Daegan's own.

"Duke Garron, I am Prince Daegan of Reldon, I'm pleased to finally make your acquaintance," Daegan introduced himself to the beast of a man. Boern looked much like Tanlor—it would be impossible to not see the familial resemblance— tall, broad shoulders, blond hair and a jaw that looked like a butcher's block. In traditional Rubanian fashion, Boern kept his hair long and tied back. The sides were shaved like a warrior and his build suggested that he fancied himself as one too.

"Prince Daegan," Boern inclined his head, "I am Duke Boern Garron, of Garronforn." He said, his eyes flicked to Tanlor but he did not make any acknowledgement of his cousin. Tanlor did not seem to take any offence but Daegan noted the man seemed even more stiff than he had been before. *Not a very congenial family, it would seem.*

"You wanted to meet with me?" Boern asked, taking a seat at his desk and offering the other to Daegan.

"I did," Daegan replied, "how was your journey from Garronforn? From what I've heard, the road east can be treacherous this time of year."

"It's always a dangerous road," Boern replied curtly, "almost impassable in winter with the snowfalls. And the bandits crawl out from Shrydan forest as soon as it thaws." Daegan did not miss Boern's glance at Tanlor at that comment.

"I won't be in the capital long," Boern continued, "so my time is in short supply. So let's get on with this. What did you want to meet with me about?" Boern had a certain dismissive air about him but that was something that Daegan was accustomed to.

"The Garronforn Ironworks," Daegan said, cutting right to his purpose, "the Reldoni army wishes to increase its shipments of steel."

"You're in the wrong place. Go discuss this with my guildmasters, I have no time to discuss such petty matters," Boern groused.

"I already did," Daegan replied, a little taken aback by Boern's abrasiveness, "they say our orders can't be fulfilled because of the increase in pirates along the Athlin coast."

"You don't seem to understand," Boern said condescendingly. "Dukes don't deal in mercantile matters… that's for the guilds to manage, it's *not* my concern."

"It *is* when it comes to policing your own coastlines," Daegan argued. "They need more protection for their merchant vessels," Daegan felt his irritation rising.

"Then send your own damn warships to protect them! The only reason there's so many pirates up here is because your brother's been running them all out of Altarea."

"Do you really want Reldoni warships patrolling *your* coastline?" Daegan admonished. "Besides, this is in *your* benefit, increased exports is good for your city," Daegan tried, opting for a change in tact, "the more gold that goes into your merchant's pockets, the more that goes into yours."

"Don't you patronise me," Boern said hotly, "do you think me a fool—that I don't understand how taxes work?!" The Duke got up from his desk, "I'm not wasting my time with a simpleton. It baffles me why the Arch-duke even entertains this farce."

He wasn't even talking to Daegan anymore, looking at his attendants. Daegan remained in his chair, the Duke's sudden outburst leaving him speechless. The anger and exasperation rising in him made his legs shake.

"We need a *capable* ambassador to work with," Boern continued, "until then, you can play at being the consul with my guildmasters and waste their time instead. Sevard," he stopped to indicate to one of his attendants, "give Guildmaster Urun's contact information to Prince Daegan so he can take up the matter with him." And then Boern proudly left the chamber, his other attendants trailing behind. Boern didn't even acknowledge Daegan as he left.

Daegan sat quietly fuming in his seat. He knew that other highborn would be difficult, particularly those with ranks close to his own. He knew they believed that because he was a cripple, he was also a fool. He had experienced it his entire life. But at least in Reldon, the other highborn were forced to be gracious. He was a Prince after all even if they thought he was a halfwit. He had not been prepared for the outright hostility he had received from some of the Rubanian highborn.

Sevard at least had the decorum to look awkwardly apologetic for his lord's behaviour. The attendant pulled a parchment from the stacks on the desk. "Forgive the Duke, my lord. He is very busy at the moment. Between the bandits and the pirates, we've now had reports of raids in the Balfold… even sightings of rakmen!" *Boern thinks me a halfwit yet he believes in stories of rakmen and trolls.*

"Just give me this Urun fellow's information," Daegan said with a resigned shake of his head.

"Of course, my lord, here," he offered a parchment to Daegan. "You can read, my lord?" Sevard's question was offensively innocuous that Daegan's jaw slackened. *He genuinely thinks that I cannot fucking read.*

Daegan fixed the man with a dark glare, mustering all his control not to slap him. The question did not even warrant a response. He snatched the parchment from Sevard's hand and stormed out of the room, Kerala and Tanlor dutifully tailing him.

Daegan's boots slammed against the hardwood floors. *Boern I'm-so-fucking-important Garron.* He crumpled the parchment in his hand and had been about to tear it up but restrained himself. He would need this.

I have to bend over for these Rubanian jackasses all because Landryn wants more fucking steel.

"Is everyone in your family as charming as him?" Daegan glared at Tanlor.

"Most of 'em, my lord," the man replied, evidently uncomfortable.

"You two seemed friendly."

"Last time Boern spoke any words to me was when I was knighted," Tanlor replied, "something along the lines of; 'you're a knight now, so fuck off out of this castle and provide for yourself.' That was about six years ago… so no, my lord, I can't say we've ever been close," Tanlor replied, his expression made it very clear how the man felt about Boern.

"My relatives are a pack of pricks too," Daegan replied, "come on, I need a drink."

***

It had taken some cajoling, but Daegan eventually coaxed Tanlor into telling him which of the taverns on the main thoroughfare he would be unlikely to run into any higher ranking nobles. He'd had enough of snide comments and—more offensively—condolences from the lords and ladies of Duke Edmund's court.

He knew he couldn't exactly go completely incognito here in Rubastre, unlike at home where he could just wear a hat and simply blend into the crowds. There weren't many Reldoni highborn in the city and someone would quickly recognise him as the Reldoni consul.

So instead, Daegan dismissed the idea of trying to blend into the crowds and opted for company who would simply be too afraid of him and—more importantly—his station to offend him. He found himself in a tavern frequented by lower ranking military officers, palace guards and wealthier merchants. The kind of place Tanlor undoubtedly felt comfortable bringing a foreign Prince to without fear of any trouble starting.

They sat with three other men. Friendly fellows, particularly after Daegan had bought them a few rounds of whitewhiskey. Kerala hung back near the door, preferring to keep a distance and have a better view of everyone in the tavern.

Two of the men were in Duke Edmund's own personal guard—both about Tanlor's age—the other was an older man named Gerold; a greasy dark haired man who smelled like he washed himself with ale. He wasn't a soldier and Daegan hadn't quite sussed him out or why he chose to spend his evenings drinking with palace guards specifically. But he was a friendly man and the others all seemed to know him. Gerold slammed back his whitewhiskeys faster than everyone else, taking the whole glass in one swig. Never a drop landing in his beard.

"We really should be going, my lord," Tanlor said to Daegan after he ordered the drink.

"What? The night is still young, Tanlor. Go on have a drink on me, you're off duty now, no?"

"I don't drink, my lord," Tanlor replied.

"Don't be ridiculous. Go on, I'm not in any danger here. These are all the Duke's men, no?"

"It's not that, my lord. I just prefer not to is all."

"Tanlor's usually too busy with his secret missus to be drinking with us," Gerold interjected, "almost midnight, lad. She's waiting for ye." Tanlor stiffened, even more so than usual.

"A secret lover," Daegan smiled, "what's her name?"

"Gerold is mistaken, my lord," Tanlor said, giving Gerold a pointed look.

"Tell you what," Daegan began, "if your lover is—" he cut off as Ferath strode into the tavern. Daegan shouldn't have been surprised, half the reason Daegan had been sent to this city had been to keep him out of trouble in the Reldoni vicedens, and he was beginning to suspect Ferath was told to keep an eye on him. To stop him slipping back into bad habits.

"Ah Ferath, come to join us?" Daegan asked as Ferath stepped up to their table.

"It's late," Ferath replied, his eyes scanning the tavern, "would you prefer I escort you back to the palace, my lord?"

"Nonsense, come have a drink—ale? Whitewhiskey? I think they might even have a Reinish red I spotted. Miss!" Daegan said, calling over the serving girl. "I'll take that bottle of Reinish wine you have behind the bar there for the table." The other men at the table cheered. If Ferath objected further to Daegan's protests he didn't show it but he also didn't pull up a chair either.

"Meetings didn't go well, my lord?" Ferath asked.

"Whatever makes you think that?" Daegan asked, and then took a long heavy slurp of a dark ale that was in front of him. It was cold, and delicious. The beers back home were too light, and just didn't have the same richness as a good wine, but these dark ales had a pleasantly satisfying weight to them. *It's like a meal in a glass, who needs food when you can just drink a tankard instead.*

"A letter from Epilas arrived," Ferath said, "Landryn isn't happy."

"Well, Landryn can deal with that ox-head Boern himself. The man's an ignorant cunt," Daegan said, "no offence to your family Tanlor," he added and then thought better of it, "actually no, I do mean offence to your family. That's exactly what I intended."

The other men at the table shifted uncomfortably. Tanlor didn't respond, "think I'll do some rounds," he said and then rose. "Oh come on, Tanlor," Daegan groaned. "You can admit it yourself, the man is a cunt."

"I'll go with you," Ferath offered, "Kerala can watch the Prince. She's one of my best swords. You can give me the guard report for the day while we walk."

"Fine then, go," Daegan said as they walked away, "I don't need your sobriety killing the mood."

"What was that about Tanlor's family?" One guard—Devon, if Daegan's recollection was accurate, which after a few whitewhiskeys wasn't very likely— asked once Tanlor and Ferath were out of earshot.

"Oh Boern Garron—his cousin. The man's an ass," Daegan said simply, and took another swig of his tankard.

"*Duke* Boern Garron?" Devon gaped, incredulous. "But Tanlor's just a guard, why isn't he off being a lord somewhere if he's cousin to a Duke?"

"You didn't know?" Gerold asked.

"Devon's only been in the guard a few weeks, he's just a greenboy," the other guard piped in.

"He's Taran Shrydan's son," Gerold divulged conspiratorially, leaning in closer to the table, as if he were letting them in on some scandal. *I've only been here four weeks and I know that, it's hardly a secret.*

Daegan was getting the feeling that Gerold was the kind of man who just liked to pretend he knew a lot of things that others didn't. Maybe Daegan should have held himself back in his comments on Boern, but then again did he really care if the remarks made their way back to the man?

"Taran Shrydan? Isn't that the hero from that story; the Hunter and the Lady?" Devon asked. "He's Tanlor's *father*?!"

"What is this story? I've heard it mentioned quite a bit," Daegan asked, his interest piqued.

"You never heard the story of the Hunter and the Lady?" Gerold asked. Daegan shook his head and Gerold leaned back in his chair, stroking his short beard, a grin splitting his face.

"Tis a fine story, m'lord, it begins in Garronforn," the others at the table groaned.

"What?" Gerold said, looking around at the other guards.

"You're awful at telling stories," the other guard said. Devon nodding in agreement, "It's true" he added, "I might only been here a few weeks but even I know that much. Let me tell it, I know that story."

"The Prince asked *me* so *I'm* telling it and that's that."

"It begins in Garronforn," Gerold started again. "It was late in the season, and as we all know the roads around Garronforn can be dangerous at the best of times, and this was back before they had chosen Duke Edmund in the moot to be Arch, before his men started the patrols. The Duke Garron and his family were on their way here to Rubastre to pay homage to the Arch-duke Tyron's passing. But the youngest daughter of the Duke Garron had fallen ill a few days before the trip so the family had proceeded on without her. When she suddenly started feeling better the young lady-in-waiting tried to catch up to her father's retinue. A foolish move by the silly girl, riding out alone on the road. It weren't long before she was kidnapped by raiders—"

"—It weren't raiders," Devon interjected, "it were rak!"

"How could bloody rakmen make it all the way to Garronforn, eh?!" *Especially considering rakmen don't exist.*

"I dunno, it's a story!"

"It's a *true* story, that's why we're telling it! And it were raiders. Anyways, the raiders kidnapped the youngest daughter of Lord Garron. His pride and joy. And these raiders, these were a trickier type, they were wildmen from the north. They disappeared into the deep forests north of Garronforn, beyond the Nortara Sheet. It was there they kept her as a prisoner in their camp while they worked on Duke Garron for the ransom.

The Hunter—he was a lone wolf, you see—he would spend months in the north; hunting great elk and wild mammanth across the frozen wastelands of Jok. Now, he stumbled across their camp and saw that they had a young woman as their prisoner. And being an honourable and courageous man, he devised a plan to save her. He snuck into the camp late at night, and as quietly as a fox, he slit the throats of the raiders in their sleep. Once he had done the gruesome task, he freed the lady from her bonds—"

"—No, no," Devon cut in again, "he didn't sneak in!"

"Yes, he did!"

"No, he didn't! The raiders were attacked by a dragon and he took advantage of the situation, you see, and managed to rescue her during the commotion."

"No, you're wrong. The dragon comes later, now let me tell it," Gerold said, giving Devon an exasperated look.

"So once they were safely away from the raider camp, the Hunter started asking her questions about who she was and how she ended up there. And now, you see—this girl was clever and educated. She knew better than to tell some stranger out in the wilderness that she was Duke Garron's daughter, so she lied about it. Said she was from a village not too far away and that the raiders had kidnapped her from there.

The Hunter may not have been educated but he knew the lands and he knew that there weren't no villages this far north of the frozen lake. But he played along. 'Alright, miss' he says, 'I'll take you back to your village'. And so, together they made their way through the wilderness. They follow the forest track for days and still no village appears. The Lady now, she starts getting worried that he's going to realize who she is and try to ransom her father himself so when the huntsman is sleeping she makes a run for it—"

"—Out on her own, in the wildlands. She hadn't a hope," Devon said.

"That's right," Gerold said, "she didn't. And *this* is where she runs into the dragon's nest."

"Dragon's *nest*?" Devon asked.

"Yeah a bloody dragon's nest. This is where the Hunter fights the dragon and saves her *again*."

"I thought it were trolls that she ran into."

"*Trolls*! There isn't even such a thing as trolls. It were a dragon's nest."

"I thought this was where the rakmen tribe took her," the other guard butted in.

"You're ruining the story!" Gerold said, "Either way the Hunter saves her. *Again!*"

"How does this story have anything to do with Tanlor?" Daegan said his interest in the story quickly diminishing with the haphazard telling.

"We'll get to that, m'lord, don't be worrying. So after the Hunter has saved her from dragons, trolls, rakmen and whatever else, she clearly starts to see this hunter as a hero and so she tells him the truth. Explains who she really is. Now the Hunter is devastated because he was beginning to fall for this lass who keeps running away and getting herself into trouble. But as he's an honourable man, he vows to bring her back home. It was on the journey *home* that they ran into the rakmen, you see. They'd attacked an outpost just north of the frozen lake and were holding it

With the rakmen holding the only passage south. They were holed up in a cave all winter. And as we know the winters up here can get awfully cold." Gerold said with a grin and the other men laughed.

"The two had made themselves a comfortable life in the wilds. He would hunt and she would prepare meals and the fire, they were happy. They stayed for months hidden in the forests.

But Lord Garron's army finally came north to take care of the rakmen. The Duke's men made quick work of the savages and when they were scouting the nearby forests, wouldn't you know who they found out in the wilderness; the lost daughter herself. And even though she resisted, even going so far as to lie to the Duke's men, claiming she wasn't the Duke's daughter, the soldiers bundled her up and took her back to the Duke.

They also took the Hunter too because they reckon he's the one that kidnapped her in the first place, you see. Now, Duke Garron's not seen his daughter in almost a year. He's overjoyed to see her but he's also thirsty for blood. He wants to punish the man who kept her from him. But the daughter threw herself at her father's feet and explained to him everything that had happened; that the Hunter had saved her life over and over. That she loved him and just wanted to be with him.

Duke Garron was so overcome with just having his daughter being found safe and unharmed and now he was realising that he had this man to thank for it. The Duke made the Hunter an honorary highborn of his court and even agreed for them to be married. And they all returned to Garron together, and on the following unionsday the pair were wed before the cliffs of Garron."

"Now, isn't that a lovely *well told* story," Gerold finished, taking a long satisfied gulp of his whitewhiskey.

"Em, yes lovely," Daegan lied and then said, "so I'm going to take a guess here that the Hunter and the Lady are Tanlor's parents then." Even without the more fanciful elements of the story, Daegan was suspect of how much truth was in it. If the Duke Garron that Daegan had met earlier was anything like his grandfather, he highly doubted the man would have so graciously allowed his daughter to marry the Hunter.

"Yes, they are," Gerold responded, "can't be too easy living in the shadow of a story like that, I can see why he never wants to talk about it. That and being the son of a hunter yet also being part of a highborn family."

The story certainly wasn't very captivating, perhaps Daegan should have taken Tanlor's advice and instead asked one of the Duke's bards to recite it for him. Likely would have been a great deal more poetic than listening to the butchered attempt by this amateur storyteller who'd had far too many whitewhiskeys and a very inflated opinion of his ability.

But still, he got the story across. Daegan had wanted to know and now he did. The tale of the Hunter and the Lady was the kind of classically dull Rubanian story of a hero and a damsel that Daegan was becoming familiar with. It jarred so starkly against his own culture. Had the story taken place in Reldon, the woman would likely have fought and killed her captors, or gotten herself killed, at the very start of the story, and that would've been the end of it. The story didn't teach him much about why Boern was such an ass or why he and Tanlor didn't speak, but it was another reminder for how Rubanian men saw women less as people and more as their property that needed to be protected.

It was a remarkable blindspot these men had and it made Daegan wonder why Rubanian women even put up with it. If she had been their captive for months then there surely had been multiple opportunities for an escape? Daegan dismissed the thought, he doubted there was much truth in the story and found that he didn't really care either way.

He was happy to just drink the Reinish red wine that the serving girl had brought to the table and enjoy the warmth of the tavern hearths and good company for a change.

CHAPTER 9

The Treaty Feast

Femira was not uncomfortable. She was not uncomfortable being restricted in her dress of tight red silk. She was not uncomfortable being so visible among so many people. She was not *uncomfortable* that she was a sacrificial lamb that was being paraded about before the slaughter.

She was not uncomfortable with all of this... she was *infuriated*. So when Jaz —leaning against a pillar outside the main feast hall—said to her, "You look a tad uncomfortable being here." her response was:

"No Jaz. I'm not *uncomfortable*," she said through gritted teeth.

"No need to be edgy," he smiled, offering her his arm, "I've barely seen you all week... come on, I'll be your escort. It'll be easier to have a guide."

Jaz was right, of course, and the part of her that didn't feel betrayed was grateful to see a familiar face. Without the barest hint of enthusiasm, Femira took his arm and they walked inside.

"Frankly, I'm surprised you haven't made appearances at these yet," Jaz shared.

"What do you mean? Does King Abhran do this regularly?—Invades a kingdom, captures its highborn and then forces them into a 'peace' treaty?"

"You're in a delightful mood this evening," Jaz countered, "I had meant *this*," he gestured toward the hall where highborn danced about in fancy colourful silks, "... feasts, galas, parties. You can't go a week in Epilas without some lord throwing a gaudy celebration because his cat had a birthday or some nonsense... I'm surprised that you've avoided them this far."

"Not my idea of fun," Femira said deadpan.

"And what is it that you like to do for fun, Annali? Lurk about in the shadows... train with your aradium?" Jaz nodded to the earthstone around her neck.

Along with the dress Femira wore, there had been a silver chain that she could replace her leather cord with waiting for her in her rooms. She had to admit that the silver chain looked a lot better, and smelled a lot better too. The leather cord for some reason had always smelled like potatoes to her.

Femira toyed with the chain, feeling the links in her fingers. In truth, the chain was the first frill she'd ever owned. Everything in her life had always had a practical use. But she couldn't bring herself to enjoy it, the chain was a noose—a pretty one— but a noose all the same.

"The Honorswords are here?" Femira asked with apprehension, her eyes scanning the colourful crowd.

"Haven't seen them. They're easy enough to spot with that gaudy gold armour and those unsettling eyes... is that common in your homeland, red eyes?"

"No," she replied, curtly. Femira knew Jaz was trying to coax her to relax and enjoy herself, but she couldn't shake her nerves.

Jaz wore a more decorative version of his soldier's uniform with silver and gold embroidered notches. A lot of the military types seemed to do that. She'd spotted Loreli wearing a black bloodshedder's uniform with gold trim, Femira hadn't seen her since the night in the courtyard. She hadn't seen much of anyone since then, she'd spent most of that time trying to figure out her plan of escape.

"You haven't been to the sparring yard lately," Jaz remarked, a playful tone in his voice, "I hope you haven't taken a secret lover."

"Thought you'd love to hear I'm spurning my training."

"I'd rather you spurned other men," he said with a smirk. She decided to ignore that comment.

She was having trouble thinking that Aden and Jaz both thought the same about her as Endrin... but then again, was that all part of the act? Aden must surely be suspicious that she wasn't Annali. He'd needed to teach her how to read Common Tongue! And he never once questioned why a highborn lady couldn't read or write in the most prevalent northern language. Or why she didn't understand politics or anything else that a good proper highborn lady should know.

"Is Aden here tonight?" Femira asked, looking through the crowds for him.

"Nah," Jaz said, waving casually to nobles he recognised. "Aden's family House isn't very influential. His mother and father might be here, but I highly doubt the invitation would have extended to him... don't get me wrong," he added when he caught her sidelong look, "the guy's a genius. Smartest in our rank without doubt —and some of us studied at Isoler before being enlisted—but being smart alone doesn't get you a place here, you need influence and we Reldoni care mostly about bloodlines."

Femira had known this already. The fact that most of the other bloodshedder recruits were all highborn—or close to it—made that pretty obvious.

"Better bloodlines make better warriors," Jaz continued, "and better leaders... Aden's not from the most prestigious of Houses. Nor does he have the grit to keep up with the rest of us in the sparring yard," Jaz wasn't being underhanded when he spoke about Aden like this. Femira had seen him do it to Aden's face many times. "But Aden will make it to Captain or even General on his brains alone," Jaz determined. "Until then, my dear, it'll be just us at these gatherings... care for a dance?" He bowed proffering his hand to her. Even bowing, he was still almost a head taller than her.

"I'm good," Femira snorted, "I've tasks from Garld for tonight." Not that she had any intention of fulfilling them. If Garld was going to use her as a bargaining chip then she wasn't going to let him squeeze anything extra than that use out of her. She was repulsed by the large part of her that resisted, that wanted to leap at the chance to prove herself to Garld, to prove herself worthy of knowledge of the bloodshedders.

"That can surely wait, come on, we're young and in love—"

"—I don't think you know what love is," Femira teased.

"I'll have you know I'm *quite* the expert... I've been in love three times this month."

"I think you're confusing love for lust," Femira smiled, enjoying the light conversation despite trying not to.

"What's the difference? At the end of the day aren't we all just bags of meat drifting through the world, slapping against one another," he slapped his hands limply against eachother to emphasise his analogy. "I didn't realise you were the authority on love."

"Hah," Femira barked, "I've never been in love."

"Not even Reselas?" Jaz asked, a cautious hint in his tone. She winced internally and hoped Jaz didn't notice—Reselas had been Annali's husband. She'd allowed herself to slip into her true self too much with Jaz and Aden.

Femira had skimmed over all of Annali's many—*many*—journal entries dedicated to Reselas. It detailed the slightest changes to his mood and the effect that he had on the woman, her entire life seemed to have revolved around her husband.

Not a chance the real Annali would have ever forgiven Landryn for killing her husband. She'd have fought the Reldoni with every breath she had in her. Which was why Femira was here, wearing her name with as much grace as a street dog.

"Sorry," Jaz fumbled a bit, "you never talk about him... I thought maybe at first it was because it was too painful for you," he said, his eyes showing genuine concern.

"I barely knew him," it was a small lie as Fermira didn't know him at all, she only knew the aggrandised version of him that Annali wrote about in her journals. "A purely diplomatic marriage then? I can't imagine that would be any easier... but I must admit I'm glad to hear it," he gave her a charming smile and the suggestion in it made Femira want to punch his teeth out.

Just as Femira was about to berate him, she noticed another woman approaching with an enthusiastic bounce to her step. The woman had brown curls and one of the biggest smiles Femira had ever seen—not as wide as Happy Jim, who Lichtin had cut a wider smile into his mouth after he'd been caught stealing skaga from the crew house. Femira doubted anyone could smile as wide or as horrifyingly as Happy Jim but this woman made a close second on both accounts.

"Annali!" The woman exclaimed and Femira found herself pulled into a tight embrace. The smell of strawberry and the silk of the woman's dress smashed against Femira's face. She hung her arms limply, her body rigid inside the arms of this mysterious, vivacious woman.

"Oh! How I've worried for you sweet girl," the arms clasping her eased but the other woman's face was still uncomfortably close to Femira's. The woman's eyes were watery, some might have described them as sparkly in the light of the braziers, but to Femira they were just watery. Soft hands still patted and rubbed at Femira's head, like a child affectionately stroking a doll.

"Have they been kind to you?" The woman asked with seemingly genuine concern, "the Reldoni have been saying you came here *willingly*?"

She glanced a suspicious look at Jaz who bowed politely.

"My Lady," he said and then to Femira, "I hope we can resume our conversation later, you clearly have old acquaintances to catch up with."

"Er—wait," Femira said, unfurling herself from the woman's embrace and grabbing Jaz's arm before he could leave.
"This is my friend, Sir Jazerah of House Beranth," Femira said, introducing him to the strange woman. Femira nodded to the woman encouragingly.

"Ah," she started, a bit confused, "a pleasure, Sir Jazerah. I am Meline Saredaan of Altarea."
"My Lady," Jaz said, inclining his head and giving the woman one his charming smiles, "you are most welcome tou our city. You are friends with Vreth?" Femira was still holding Jaz's arm, she gave it a subtle pinch, "—ah, uhm, Annali, I mean... you are friends?"

"Yes," the woman said, confusion and scepticism plain on her face, "I would very much like to speak to her privately if you please, sir?"

"Oh, uhm," he looked back at Femira and she nodded to him that he could go. *I've got what I need from you.*

"Thank you, Jaz," Femira said. He nodded awkwardly and moved away from them. Jaz's discomfort would've been entertaining if Femira hadn't felt mounting worry over Meline's arrival.

"Well is it true?" Meline asked as Jaz moved out of earshot, "did you *really* come here willingly?"

"Of course," Femira replied, her heart thudding in her chest. The woman looked at her expectantly, as if she wanted Femira to elaborate but she didn't trust yet in her ability to be Annali with people who had actually *known* her.

"You seem *different*," the woman's watery blue eyes bored into her. Femira looked away and took a step back.

"It's just... being here," Femira said, "I *am* different, I guess."

"Oh my poor sweet girl," the woman's face taking on a sickeningly pitiful expression, "I can only imagine what you've been going through. Reselas was such a dear friend, I think we've all had a lot of adjustments over the past few months. Can you believe the *audacity* of Karalan Ingel, jumping at the chance to be Highlady. It should have been you, my Lady. It is only right, you are rightful—"

"—I support the treaty," Femira interjected, not liking one bit where this woman was going. Meline's face dropped, "you *support*? H-how, why?" Meline stammered, "what have they *done* to you?"

"Like I said, I've changed," Femira said firmly. A plan began forming in her mind.

"Indeed," Meline's nose scrunched in distaste, "your voice even seems different. They told us you've been training with those foul bloodshedders, we couldn't believe them!"

"I have," Femira replied, carefully trying to make her accent more neutral. She doubted this woman would really notice that there were twangs of the Altarean streets in her accent. Femira's accent had always been heavily influenced by Keiran being her first language, she had hoped Annali's was the same.

"I've been learning from them," Femira continued. "Trying to understand where their strength comes from." She was relieved to see that Melinaewas nodding along with her.

"They overpowered our stormguards so easily," Meline said. "Father always said that the stormguards were the most elite force in the world. That the Reldoni never posed any real threat to us..."

"I need to understand how they are so powerful," Femira divulged.

"Oh my sweet girl," a look of painfully exaggerated sympathy crossed the woman's face, "you are so torn with grief... you shouldn't be here, not with *these*—these people." The woman's face looked like she'd dabbed bitter skaga on her tongue.

Femira didn't have the time to fully think through a plan here, but this woman could be a key to getting out of this place.

Is that really what I want?

Femira had already learned so much from the bloodshedders, she'd learned to fight, and to use her earthstone more effectively, but they still had so much more left to teach her. The memory of her dagger puffing to dust against Endrin's chest flashed in her mind.

"How many are with you?" Femira asked, dropping her tone conspiratorially.

"Over a hundred of us were invited to the feast," Meline said leaning in.

"How many fighters?" Femira asked. Meline raised her hand to mouth, her eyes widening. *Oh calm down, woman.*

"*Fighters?* Annali, we're highborn, not warriors!"

"Are there no stormguards with you? You all came alone?!"

"Well, of course, Lord Ingel sent a few dozen stormguards for protection... but our numbers I believe are desperately low after the attack."

"*Highlord* Ingel," Femira corrected her. She wasn't sure why she was still doing what Garld had instructed her to by feigning support for the Reldoni-Altarean treaty.

"I'm not sure the Reldoni will allow me to leave if I try to return with you," Femira rushed on, still in hushed tones.

"So you *are* a prisoner!"

"Not exactly... and they have treated me well. But I don't think that I can return to Altarea." Returning to Altarea would be a colossally stupid decision anyway. Femira he doubted she would last a day before someone figured out she wasn't Annali. *That's if Lichtin doesn't find me first.*

Femira was shocked that this woman still hadn't sussed it yet. She also doubted that Garld would just simply allow her to walk away... No, she needed to figure out a way out that didn't involve her pretending to be Annali.

"What about your homeland?" Meline asked, "I've heard there are Honorswords here, surely they can assist—"

"—No! Not them, I *cannot* return to Keiran. The Honorswords cannot be trusted," Meline recoiled from Femira's fierce expression.

"You always said that they were the warriors of justice in your home," Meline faltered. "Do you..."—she leaned in close again— "do you suspect they were somehow involved with the assault on Altarea?" Meline asked, horrified.

"It's possible," Femira replied, not really caring about the political implication she was making there.

"But *how*—why? The Keiran were our closest allies and they've never been overly diplomatic with the Reldoni." Femira found herself a little surprised by the woman's knowledge, her bouncy demeanor had led Femira to think that she was some idiotic highborn lady with no real experience in the world, parading through life going to fancy events like this one. Perhaps Femira had misjudged the woman too quickly on her appearance and initial demeanour.

"I don't know," Femira replied, desperate to make sure that Meline did not try to convince the Honorswords she needed their help, "but please—you must trust me. You cannot involve the Honorswords."

As if the mention of them had summoned the pair, Femira caught sight of the stark yellow cloaks. The pair of Honorswords stood amongst a mixed group of highborn. Femira felt herself tense, remembering the thunderclap of Honorsword Karas' massive blade smashing into Sadrian Graves' skull.

It was only then that Femira took note of how many non-Reldoni people were in attendance. A varied mix of highborn from all over filled the feasting hall, it made Femira think of the night market at Altarea. Where people from all walks of life poured in from the merchant vessels, only instead of foul-smelling merchants and foul-intented thieves in dirty clothes, these people were just foul people in general... but in fancy clothes.

A Keiran man, in orange silks approached them, a gaggle of Altarean nobles trailing him.

"My dear cousin, Annali," the man opened his hands and bowed his head, "what a delight to find you here," he said, oozing sincerity.

Femira's heart skipped.

Oh shit, I can't pretend to be Annali to her actual family. And all these people—all Altareans—surely knew Annali well also.

Femira's thoughts raced in panic. *I have to get away from here.*

"Dear cousin," Femira breathed. Her words felt strained. She bowed slightly, not even entirely sure how Keiran highborn addressed their own family.

Aden had done a wonderful job schooling her in Reldoni practises, and that was because he thought she knew nothing of Reldoni people. He never would have assumed she needed knowledge of how *Keiran* highborn acted.

"Your cousin?" Meline said, "how wonderful!"

"Daurond Jahar… a pleasure, my lady," he introduced himself with a large smile, his teeth were brilliantly white, stark against his coffee skin. Daurond's accent was thick with Keiran notes. Meline introduced herself courteously, and Daurond turned to address the group of Altareans with him.

"Annali and I have always been quite close, isn't that right, my dear?" *Oh shit, shit, shit.*

"Yes, of course," Femira replied, simply nodding, her eyes flicking around the nobles for any kind of recognition. None of them Reldoni… let alone other bloodshedders.

"I have been caring for my sweet cousin since she arrived here," Daurond went on, still smiling to the group of Altarean nobles. "It has been such a delight to have her close with me again. It was a sad, sad day when she left our home in Keiran to marry the honourable Reselas… but alas I knew that she was making the right choice for herself and for her family. I never would have thought it would be here in a Reldoni city that we would find eachother again." The Altareans seemed moved by the man's words and Femira tried to hide her surprise.

Caring for me since I arrived? Daurond gave her a wink. His enormous bright smile was unwavering but Femira spotted that he was sweating. *He's nervous?*

A thought struck her; was *he* another of Garld's other imposters? *Does Garld even have other imposters?* Of course he would, Femira realised. And then with a sense of bemused irony, she realised that this 'Daurond' probably didn't even know that *she* was an imposter. From what she could gather only Garld knew the truth.

"Thank you, dear cousin," Femira said in Keiran dialect, emphasising the word 'cousin'. She had been wary of speaking her native tongue—she hadn't lived in Keiran for long and wasn't sure how highborn folk talked—so she assumed her accent would be off.

Daurond's smile deepened, visibly reassured, "Lady Annali has quickly adapted to the Reldoni ways, she is already excelling in her bloodshedder training."

"You've been *training* with them?" one of the Altarean highborn asked, aghast.

"Yes," Femira replied, matching Daurond's wide welcoming smile, "The Reldoni have been very accommodating… Prince Landryn only strives for peace. My understanding is that more of the Altarean highborn will be offered the choice to join with the Reldoni forces." Again, she was unsure why she was reciting the words Garld had fed to her. A deep part of her was still desperate to prove her worthiness to him.

Some of the Altareans looked confused, others made poor attempts to conceal their disapproval.

"Prince Landryn *strives for peace*," an elderly Altarean gentleman in the group scoffed. He had a pointed grey beard and Femira did not recognise him, "a peaceful man does not send warships to claim a palace and pilfer their wealth… and now as further insult to this, our newly appointed 'Highlord' claims that our remaining stormguards will be *indoctrinated* into this warrior cult."

"The bloodshedders are a formidable force," Femira replied, "they rival even the Honorswords of my homeland in skill. The stormguards will be a welcome addition in their ranks, I am sure."

"My stormguards were the *most* elite force in the world," the man rebuffed.

"Exactly," Femira responded, remembering the fierce authority that Annali had spoken with when she had seen her in Altarea, she added that edge to her tone, "they *were*. I was there at the siege, or have you forgotten?"

"Of cou—"

"—I was *there* when they *killed* my husband… he was weak, and he failed to protect us," the group of Altareans gave her collectively appalled looks.

"We were lucky," Femira continued, a little off-script from what Garld had instructed her but she was enjoying the ride of Annali's anger in her, "…lucky that the Reldoni did not intend to crush us, to murder us all and enslave our children. They are offering us a *gift*, and you are too blind to see it."

"Annali!" Meline gasped, "you cannot mean this?" Even Daurond was looking at her dumbfounded, Garld's instructions had been to *gently* prod the Altarean highborn towards supporting the treaty, but Femira had never been very good at the gentle approach.

"You can all choose to resist the treaty," Femira said coolly, "but we have the chance to reach for real power, and it's foolish to ignore that."

"The Reldoni have certainly rubbed off on you," Daurond said, recovering his too-white smile, "I must say I *like* this change in you… this *fierceness*."

"What of the Keiran, Daurond?" The elderly Altarean asked. "We waited for weeks as the Reldoni sailed to our city for the Keirans to join us in fighting them off… where were your kin when our sons and daughters were being shot down from the sky?"

"Keiran does not wish to have open war against the Reldoni," Daurond replied, appeasingly, "and we cannot argue against King Abhran's claim on Altarea."

"Hogwash!" the man retorted. *Ooh pulling out the foul language, not very gentlemanly-like of you.*

"The Solodans have been ruling in Altarea for half a century!"

"And they will continue to do so," Femira chided, "when my nephew comes of age, he will be offered a seat on the ruling council of Altarea."

Despite enjoying the rise she was getting out of the Altareans, Femira did have an urge to separate herself from this discussion. However, she needed to find a way to pull Meline with her. The woman presented an opportunity to escape the Reldoni but at the same time, she didn't want to risk undermining Garld's objectives. If she was going to get away, she would need to do it discreetly, and make it difficult for Garld to track her.

But where will I even go?

"If you wish to discuss this directly with Prince Landryn, my lord," Daurond said, "he is right over there." He indicated towards the tall dark-haired man striding through the feasting hall. Femira hadn't noticed him amongst the crowds, he was dressed in a formal Reldoni military uniform with slight gold threaded trim. Command clung to him as tight as his form-fitted uniform. He bore a curved blade sheathed at his hip and his fine black armour complimented his uniform. If anyone thought it strange that the Prince was wearing armour, they didn't comment upon it.

"No," the elderly gentleman dismissed, stroking his pointed beard.

All the man's previous puffed up arrogance faded at the sight of the Prince. The other Altareans seemed to be hanging on to him, awaiting his reaction before committing to their own. His attire was militarian in style, blue like the stormguards of the Altarean palace. He was likely some former Commander or General in the last forgotten shred of the fallen Altarean government.

"I will take up the matter directly with King Abhran himself," he said haughtily, "do you know when he will be arriving?"

"I do not... but I am sure it will be soon," Daurond soothed, "come... allow me to introduce you to some more of Reldoni highborn that have been striving for an end to the conflict."

The Altareans bowed to Femira as they were shepherded away from her by Daurond. Only Meline and one of the other Altareans lingered behind.

"Annali, what is *happening* to you?" Meline asked once they'd left.

"Perhaps you should go with the others, Lady Melina," the other Altarean said, "I think it would be wise to stay with the group this evening."

The man was also an older military-styled gentleman but not nearly as decrepit as the man with the pointed beard. He looked familiar but Femira couldn't place him, he wore the blue stormguards uniform, tiny gilded wings decorating his shoulder pauldrons and an ornamental sword at his hip.

"Captain Darza," Meline said with distaste, "you're practically a Reldoni yourself at this stage."

"Please, my lady. I have some matters I wish to discuss with Lady Annali," he said.

"Anything you wish to say to me, Captain Darza, you can say to Meline," Femira said.

"Trust me, *Annali*. This is a private conversation regarding your family." His emphasis on the name gave Femira pause; she actively resisted the urge to run.

He knows.

Femira felt her eyes widen as she recalled how she knew the man. He had been there when the real Annali had been taken away... when she'd been caught inside the Altarean palace.

Femira nodded curtly to Meline, "it's fine, Meline. I will find you later." Meline reluctantly departed, rushing to catch up with Daurond's group.

"Your *cousin* Daurond does an even poorer attempt than you in pretending that this isn't all a farce to keep the Altarean highborn from resisting," Darza said, looking at the group being directed by the enigmatic man. "But at least he's actually the *real* Daurond Jahar."

Femira felt restricted in her dress. She had a dagger concealed in a leg sheath, could she reach for it before he drew his sword?

And do what? Attack him right here in the middle of the feast? Darza hadn't exposed her yet, he could have done so at any stage, so why hold off? Was he not fully sure yet?

"Captain Darza, was it?" Femira asked, trying to make herself sound haughty, "what is this family matter you wished to speak to me of?"

Darza gave her a pointed look, "You're not very good at this, Femira."

CHAPTER 10
Dishonourable Actions

Femira jumped. It was an involuntary response, it had been so many months since anyone had used her real name. It was this closely guarded secret, a tiny thing she kept inside, just for her. Hearing Darza say it made her feel exposed. A similar feeling to the few times she'd been caught thieving back in Altarea, back before Lichtin had first taken her under his wing.

"H-how," Femira stammered.

"You know the resemblance really is remarkable…" Darza mused looking her over, "not as noticeable when you were a dirty street dog, but I suppose… put you in a dress, and you do make for a good imitation of her."

"You *remember* me?" *Fuck!* She really hadn't anticipated running into someone who would've recognised her as Femira. *But how had Darza learned that name?*

"How do you know my name?" Femira hissed at him.

"It doesn't really matter how I know," Darza huffed.

"Eh, yeah—it kinda does," she replied through gritted teeth, "do you have any idea how much danger you're putting yourself in saying that name?"

Aggression was becoming her go-to response when she felt tense, she'd realised. Had that just started since she'd become more competent with fighting, or had it been going on longer?

"I do not fear Lichtin nor his crew of thugs," Darza snorted derisively, "you're all out of your depth here… flying before you can even call the wind," the man almost looked concerned. *He thinks I'm still working with Lichtin on this,* she thought with amusement.

"You have absolutely no idea what you're talking about," Femira scoffed.

"Be careful Femira, don't forget that I can expose you anytime I want."

"That would be the stupidest thing you could possibly do. Even *if* anyone were to believe you, there would be very bad consequences for you… what even makes you think it's Lichtin I'm working with on this?"

Darza took on a defensive expression and Femira pressed on, "well, you haven't done anything stupid yet so I'm guessing you want something?"

"But Lichtin… he said…" the gears in Darza's head seemed to be pretty slow movers. *How did this idiot become a captain?*

"He said that you were still on a job for him," Darza murmured, mostly to himself.

"Lichtin doesn't even know I'm here, does he?" *I will find you and you'll be fucking sorry you crossed me.* Lichtin had loved to remind her of that. Somehow now that she'd been training with the bloodshedders, Lichtin's words didn't sound so intimidating. What could he do to *her*? But then a small voice in her mind chided; *you're not a real bloodshedder. They've just been keeping you occupied so that they can parade you about as Annali Jahar.*

"What do you want, Darza?" Femira snapped. The Altareans weren't as ridiculously tall as the Reldoni so Femira only had to stretch herself up a little to be face-to-face with the man. He looked somewhat defeated, he likely had not expected Femira to be so dismissive of his threats.

"I don't know what you're doing here," Darza said eventually, his confidence evidently shaken, "but it's clear you're helping the Reldoni secure this treaty... for reasons I cannot grasp."

To be fair to Darza, Femira didn't fully grasp why she was doing either of those things too. What did she care if Altarea and Reldon slipped back into conflict.

"Ingel is a decent man," Darza continued, "he's unassuming and avoids confrontation, likely why the Reldoni chose him amongst the other highborn to be Highlord... but he's not right for the position, Altarea needs someone strong to lead them."

"And you think that should be you?" Femira asked with a laugh.

"And why not?" Darza replied, pompously puffing out his chest, "I'm one of the highest ranking stormguards in Altarea."

"Yeah, because most of them were killed in the assault."

"I'm of good birth and—more importantly—I too believe that the Reldoni are the way forward for Altarea."

"You don't care that they killed your King?"

"Do you?"

"Couldn't give six shits," Femira responded flippantly, "but I was a thief and you were a stormguard, aren't you supposed to have some kind of deluded sense of loyalty?"

"One King is not so different to another," Darza replied. "All I'm asking is that you... push the wind in a particular direction... *my* direction. You've somehow stolen your way into a position of power so perhaps you are a better thief than I gave you credit. Annali Jahar was very much loved by the Altarean highborn, and they've seen me as a coward ever since I surrendered the aeristone mines to the Reldoni. They fail to see that a wise leader knows when to surrender and when to fight... tell them that you support the actions I took that night, that you think that I should take over command of the remaining stormguards from that doddering fool Himsbrack."

Himsbrack, Femira guessed, was the elderly man that she had argued with earlier.

"Do that, and I won't expose you," Darza offered.

"And what's stopping me from letting my employer know that you're blackmailing me and leaving you to deal with him?" she countered matter-of-factly.

"I'm taking the risk that you won't want to admit that you've been caught," he said.

Fuck! He's right. It was a good bet, she had no desire to go to Garld with this. She didn't want him thinking that she had failed to keep her persona intact. But was there a way she could use this to her advantage? Could she somehow use this man as a means to escape Epilas?

"I will help you," Femira started carefully, "but I might ask for a favour in return."

"I don't think you're in much of a position to be asking *me* for a favour."

"As far as anyone is concerned, *I'm* the real Annali. The longer that stays the case... the better it will be for you," she shot, "but when the time comes, I might need your help in return."

"If you're exposed, you mean?"

"Not exactly..." at least that wasn't her biggest worry. "I can't go back to Keiran," she admitted, "I'd sooner go back to Altarea than there, so if the time comes and the Honorswords try to take me back, I will need your help to stop them taking me."

"And how am *I* supposed to stop an Honorsword?" Darza looked worriedly at the two yellow garbed warriors on the other side of the feasting hall.

"If we do this right, you should have command of the remaining stormguards."

She dared a glance over to the Honorswords herself and felt her breath catch at the combination of people they were speaking with.

Landryn and Garld. The pair of them speaking with Honorswords was enough to set a knot in Femira's stomach but also with them was a young Reldoni woman and a pale, white-haired boy.

Femira's mouth dropped a fraction. She recognised the soft, strange features immediately as the boy who had jumped her the night she had snuck into Averstock's manse.

What?! It didn't make any sense, why were they all casually talking to each other right in the middle of the feasting hall? Garld of all people, talking with the Honorswords and the boy who had stolen the documents he was after.

What is he doing?

"You fear them," Darza noted, watching her. Femira didn't bother denying it, her heart thumped every time she saw the yellow cloaks and red eyes.

"The Honorswords are not what you people think they are. They're executioners with the same authority as a judge… and they don't need a trial to dish out that justice."

She watched as the bizarre group broke apart, Garld heading off to join with a group of other military officers and the Honorswords moving towards Daurond and the Altareans. Landryn, the Reldoni woman and the white-haired boy left together for one of the exits leading out of the feast hall.

Where were they going? Femira couldn't help herself but take a step after them.

"So it's a deal?" Darza asked before she was too far away from him to be overheard by anyone nearby. Femira gave him a quick nod of agreement, and then discreetly followed after Landryn. As she made her way through the crowd, she'd noticed Jaz trying to make his way over to her. She curtly waved him off without breaking stride.

The red dress wasn't ideal for sneaking about, Femira would much prefer to be back in her dark stealth gear but when an opportunity arose, you make do with what you have. Garld would probably have said something along the lines of 'a soldier doesn't always pick his environment' or something like that.

As she entered the hallway, Femira gently kicked off her shoes, her bare feet touching against the cold stone. It felt good, having a piece of her skin touching against the stone. Her earthstone hummed to her in response to it. A pair of guards with black armour, watched her as she passed but said nothing, trailing after the Prince and his companions.

Femira tried to keep her pace without drawing too much attention but she couldn't get close enough to listen in without raising suspicion. Other nobles were walking along the hallway, coming and going from the feasting hall, so she didn't stick out too much. They turned down another walkway and then up a stairs and out onto a large balcony.

Balcony wasn't exactly the correct word here. It was large enough for decorative gardens to be cultivated along the wall with still enough room for a dozen people to walk abreast. The feast was taking place in one of the uppermost levels of the enormous Pillar of Reldon.

The Pillar was a seemingly natural tower of stone that thrust into the sky—although it was becoming increasingly difficult for Femira to determine what was natural and what wasn't. Ancient stoneshapers from what she'd read had managed feats that runewielders of today could only dream of.

The Reldoni royal palace was built around the pillar itself with many parts of the palace tunnelling into the stone. Femira didn't doubt that gardened balconies spread up and down the pillar. This one looked like it circled around the pillar in a full ring built out from the natural stone. Like Judgement Hall, the stonework was so impossibly smooth that it had to have been crafted by master stoneshapers.

The view was even more incredible, both Luna and Ecko's light working together to illuminate the bay in a dim swash of blue and red light. Unlike the stormy overcast skies of Altarea, Reldoni nights were often clear and bright. Even when only one moon hung in the sky, the combination of moon and starlight was enough to see well by. The gaslamps in the streets of Epilas lit the city aglow in orange light radiating up and into the night sky, blending with the blue and red light of the moons.

Femira didn't allow herself time to awe at the extravagant view, and continued after Landryn. They walked at a leisurely pace which meant Femira didn't have to rush to keep up with them. While the moons and gaslamps brought a lot of light, they also cast deep shadows by which Femira could sink herself into, allowing the darkness to envelop her.

It felt good to be hiding in the shadows again, it wasn't so different to when she would tail a mark for a few weeks to learn their habits so she would know when to best break into their house… except, instead of some merchant, she was tailing the Commander of the Reldoni army.

With having shadows to hide in, Femira was emboldened to move closer to listen in on their conversation. She grinned to herself, revelling in the rush she got from being able to sneak undetected.

The Prince and his companions found a secluded bench which had a spectacular vantage of the view. Conveniently for Femira, there was a manicured hedgerow behind the bench which she could discreetly linger behind. She was close enough that—with only a little straining—she could make out their conversation.

"He's not safe up there, you should speak with father," the young Reldoni woman said to Landryn, her tone implying she held every ounce of authority that Landryn did.

"Father has never listened to me on this matter… and likely never will. Perhaps *you* should try," Femira recognised Landryn's voice from the day in Judgement Hall.

"And you think he will be more likely to listen to *me*?" the woman replied, her voice was high and more girlish indicating she was younger than what Femira had assumed. *Those damn tall Reldoni.*

She had been walking with her arm linked with the white-haired boy. They were possibly about the same age. From the conversation, Femira figured she was Landryn's younger sister.

Femira suddenly realised the absurdity of what she was doing, it wasn't like they were going to just be casually talking about their secret plots out in the open. *Although Darza hadn't bothered with any subterfuge.*

Femira wasn't buying it. The presence of the white-haired boy had sparked in her a curiosity that she couldn't ignore. He had dissolved the road that night so quickly and effectively that Femira couldn't help herself wanting to know more about him.

"I'll send word to Captain Ferath," Landryn said, "tell him to increase the size of the guard on our brother, will that keep your mind at ease?"

"You think this is just me worrying?" the Princess asked with concern. "Lan, this is a real threat, I think he might be in danger… and he's so defenceless." Allyn was her name, if Femira recalled her lessons with Aden correctly. *Or was it Ellen?*

"I believe you," Landryn replied reassuringly, "and trust me, no one cares more for Daegan's safety than me. I was the one who argued against Lukane's decision to send him to Rubane in the first place… but Lukane is right, it's time for Daegan to start contributing to our family. Why else do you think we sent him there?"

"Because he's an embarrassment," Allyn retorted.

"I'm not having this conversation with you again… I've never been ashamed of Daegan… besides, your little project is of far greater concern to me right now," Landryn said, and through the obscured view of the hedge Femira saw Landryn waving his hand at the white-haired boy.

When the boy spoke, Femira was immediately reminded of his strange unplaceable accent, "oh me," he said with a casual flair, "I am not of any consequence to you, Prince Landryn."

"Vestyr is right," Allyn replied innocently, "the rumours of what we're doing have been grossly exaggerated."

"You're training a force of elite runewielders *without* the army's permission," Landryn said sternly. "Be very careful, Allyn, people are beginning to talk… they're worried you're planning on rivalling Lukane as heir."

"I'm within my right to do that," she said, sheepishly. "The firstborn son and firstborn daughter *both* have equal claim to the throne. The Royal Council would have the power to choose me if they wanted."

"I'm well aware of that… but you won't have the War Council on your side, Allyn."

"And why not? I already know that the Generals think that Lukane lacks conviction. If you support my claim, Landryn, the Generals *will* follow you. General Garld is like a father to you… more than ours ever was anyway, and the others respect you."

"You won't win them over—or me—if you continue training these secret runewielders," Landryn argued. Femira couldn't believe it, they really were just talking openly about betraying their older brother. This was full-blown treason from what Femira could guess—she wasn't entirely sure, but it sounded an awful lot like it. And they were just casually talking about it out on a balcony where anyone in a bright red dress barely hidden by a hedge could be listening in.

They weren't even the only ones on the balcony; there was a couple getting really cosy over by the palisade, another pair of highborn women that seemed to be having their own secretive—and potentially treasonous—conversation on another bench further down and…

A golden clad dark-skinned Keiran man striding in her direction.

Oh fuck! Her heart leapt. It was Honorsword Karas!

He was alone and walking directly towards *her!* In a sudden panic, Femira stepped out from the shadows. She strode past Landryn, Allyn and the white-haried boy nonchalantly. They barely gave her a glance as she walked past.

Femira made her way across the balcony, increasing her pace as she winded around the curvature of the pillar. She could hear Karas' boots thumping against the stone as he followed her. She didn't dare risk a look back. She resisted all urges to run, she needed to play this carefully. The real Annali would never have run at full pelt away from an Honorsword. Femira would have but that's because Femira was smart and why Annali was likely dead in some dungeon in Altarea. She needed to get back inside the pillar and lose him in the hallways.

Femira passed a row of neat hedges as she rounded the ring of the balcony. She could see that there was a stairs built into the wall that led up to a higher balcony above. She took the steps lightly in her bare feet, but notably increased her pace again.

"Annali," a deep voice called to her. It was Karas, the same voice that had challenged Landryn in Judgement Hall.

Femira froze.

This was it.

She should run. Why wasn't she running already? Her heart beat so heavily that she could hear it throbbing in her ears. It rang in beat to the pulsing of the earthstone around her neck. She was suddenly aware of the stone stairs beneath her feet, pulsing at her. The weight of the enormous stone pillar next to her, she felt as though she could feel the entire pillar itself pulsing. The weight of it, strong and defiant, as it struck up into air unsupported by anything but its own will.

Femira was aware of the dagger sheathed on her leg. It was a much more formidable weapon than her climbing spikes had ever been but Femira was in no rush to test her skills against an Honorsword.

She turned to face Karas.

"*Your family has commanded that you return home to Ka Pazar... you have been ignoring all communications from your family since your capture,*" Karas said in their native Keiran.

"My family was in Altarea... and they're dead now." Femira responded in Common Tongue, she didn't trust that she could pull off the right accent for Annali in her native language, but at least in Common she could rely on the generic Keiran accent, it was one of the reasons she had avoided all detection so far—well, almost all detection.

"*Your allegiance to the Altareans died the moment Reselas did, your true family will see you returned so that they may assign another duty to you,*" Karas said with a cold edge, as if Annali's choice in the matter was of no consequence.

Keiran women didn't enjoy the same independence as the women of Reldon or Altarea, their duty was to their family and often they were forced into marriages for the political or economical benefit of the family. A part of Femira seethed at the injustice even though they weren't really *her* family duties but the idea of it made her grit her teeth.

"My *duty* was to Reselas," Femira spat, allowing her anger to seep out in her tone but using Annali's words, "and the Emperor killed him just as much as the Reldoni soldier that stuck their sword in him. We waited for weeks for Keiran reinforcements. I stood watching the Reldoni warships sail closer and closer, *praying* that my kin would rescue us."

That part at least was true, Femira herself *had* knelt on the rooftops with Lichtin and the crew—along with half the city of Altarea—all watching with terror as the red sails crept closer.

The stories of Reldoni bloodshedders wreaking havoc on civilians had been perpetuated throughout the city in the weeks leading to that. Luckily for the citizens of Altarea, the stories were unfounded with the Reldoni accepting the city mayor's surrender with minimal bloodshed. It was the highborn locked away in the palace that had resisted and paid the price for it.

"*You dare to question the will of your Emperor?*" Karas snarled at her.

"He's not my Emperor anymore."

"*His Excellence is sovereign over all that sits under the sun and moons!*"

"Well, I think the Reldoni would disagree with you on that." Femira turned on her heel and made to leave.

"*Do not walk away from me, woman! Your time away from the Court of the Sun has made you insolent but I will humble you, and bring you to heel.*" Femira could hear the sliding of his weapon from its sheath. His great behemoth of a sword.

What had she been thinking? On instinct Femira reached out with her edir, the pulses of the stone steps reacted to her mind's touch. She rapidly drew the stone into her earthstone, smoothing the stairs into a ramp. Not that Femira expected that to stop him, she'd watched this man smash through a pillar of rock with his sword, shattering it as if it were glass. But she hoped to delay him while she sprinted up the stairs.

Femira felt a sudden wall of wind push against her. She could easily have lost her balance and fallen back down the ramp but her training fights against aeristone users had honed her responses to such manoeuvres. Femira allowed herself to flow with the force of the wind and fluidly moved into a crouched position, lowering her center of gravity, and retaining her balance. That was the trick to aeristone wielders, stay low and don't let them push you off balance. This set her eye level with Karas who was still at the foot of the ramp.

He stood with his greatsword casually held at one side in one hand as if it didn't weigh more than Femira herself.

"*The Reldoni might think it's acceptable for women to wield a runestone but you have broken the law of Keiran. You have forgotten your place, Annali of House Jahar. You have even forgotten the language of your own people it seems.*"

Femira noticed Landryn, Allyn and the white-haired boy standing not far behind him watching the exchange with curious expressions.

A bold plan formed in her mind.

"I'm not fucking Keiran anymore," she sneered at Karas, "so I'll runewield all I please. And your Emperor can go fuck himself!"

His eyes widened in suprise and outrage. "*You're not Annali Jahar!*" His face twisted into a wolf's snarl.

"*You're an imposter!*"

Still in a crouch, Femira easily drew the dagger from her leg sheath.

She wished she had insisted on wearing her military uniform instead of the silk dress but considering the way Karas had cut through Sadrian Graves' helmet, she doubted the uniform would have offered much more protection. She cut a long strip down the length of the skirt, to give her more manoeuvrability. There was no more doubt, it was coming down to a fight.

Jaz and Aden had poured over the details of Sadrian Graves' fight with the Honorsword. Sadrian had been one of the best bloodshedders in the ranks; how he fell so easily was a point of concern to many of them. The consensus had been that Karas was an exceptionally skilled aeristone wielder, attributing to the extra power in his attacks.

They also speculated that Karas was a Foebreaker himself, and that was how he had managed to withstand Havran's ability to crush an opponent's will. Becoming a master in the use of two disciplines of runestones was rare, but not impossible. This led Femira to the guess that he was unlikely to be skilled in the use of any other type of runestone. It gave her a *tiny* advantage in an otherwise heavily outmatched fight. *Although it didn't help Sadrian Graves.*

"You dare draw your sword on me!" Femira shouted at him, loud enough that she hoped it would carry across the balcony. She felt a sudden intense pressure on her mind, an overwhelming sense of fear causing her legs to quiver in their crouched position.

Femira felt like curling up, to hide her face. She knew that it was the aura of his Foebreaker ability. She didn't fully understand how it worked exactly, she was wholly unfamiliar with all of the ethereal runestones and mindstone was no exception. She did know that, similar to her own earthstone, there was a limit to its power. She had been told that most Foebreakers only used theirs when it was absolutely necessary.

The thought that Karas perceived Femira as enough of a threat to use his abilities on her did not ease the sense of terror paralysing her. She felt all the colour drain from her face, watching in panic as Karas performed an inhuman leap, clearing the ramp.

He grabbed her roughly by the neck and jerked her to her feet.

"You thought you could deceive an Honorsword?!" he growled at her. The intensity of his red eyes bore into her. This close she could see that the entirety of the eye was varying shades of red, the edges were vibrant as fresh blood, the iris was deeper, almost black. Somewhere in her mind, the part of her that was Femira tried to form a retort to his words but she couldn't think through the irrefutable panic taking her.

His eyes scanned the features of her face.

"Who are you?" His grip was iron on her neck holding her place, but he wasn't choking her.

There was a deafening crack.

In a blur, she fell from Karas' grip. Her vision swam and she felt her exposed legs and arms skinned against the smooth stone of the ramp as she slid down it. Her training kicked in and Femira rolled, coming up on her feet at the base of the ramp.

Looking up she saw Prince Landryn, his sister and the boy—Vestyr—stood in a row in front of her. Landryn had his sword drawn and levelled… but not at her. The blade was sleek, pointing above her. She glanced back and could see Karas recovering from having been knocked back by whatever had struck them.

Landryn carefully stepped forward, moving in between Femira and Karas.

"Help her," Landryn instructed Allyn and Vestyr. The two rushed forward to pull Femira back. The crushing sense of fear was retreating from her, she noted that she had the use of her legs again.

She pulled against Vestyr's grip but it held firm as he pulled her back. He was a lot stronger than she had expected from someone of his size. He pulled her back a short distance and released her. Femira, Vestyr and Allyn stood in a line, watching the pair on the stairs.

"You dare attack an Honorsword?" Karas snarled at the Prince.

"You assault a guest in my father's palace," Landryn scoffed. "You disrespect *every* courtesy given to you… tell me, *Honorsword* Karas, are you so deluded in your own sense of authority to think that your jurisdiction extends even here?!"

"All Keiran people answer to the Emperor of the Sun, that woman is the property of Emperor."

"As I have told you before," Landryn warned, "Lady Annali is under *my* protection. You have challenged that protection and now must suffer the consequences of that choice."

"And what can you throw at me, Prince of Reldon? I have already faced your best, your primitive runewielders cannot compare to the strength of the Honorswords."

"You haven't faced me," Landryn said with venom.

Quicker than Femira's eyes could follow, Landryn leapt at Karas, easily clearing the smoothed ramp. Karas swung his massive sword as Landryn landed. Landryn lithely evaded the swing, his sword flashed, landing a cut on Karas' cheek.

Karas jumped back, appalled. One hand reached up to touch the trickle of blood from the tiny wound.

Femira had seen aeristone wielders in action before, both in the training grounds and in the Altarean palace; she had seen first hand how they moved at inhuman speed. But they were sluggish compared to Karas and Landryn who danced about each other in such rapid movements that Femira couldn't even follow.

They exchanged a series of glancing blows and parries. Karas was evidently more powerful, but his weapon and golden armour were heavier—and imperceptibly slower—making it more difficult for him to land a hit on Landryn. Karas would likely only need one well placed strike of that sword to cleave the Prince in half. Landryn's black armour looked flimsy in comparison.

Landryn however, could move quicker. He easily dodged and parried Karas' attacks, which was a testament to just how fast Landryn was moving. The stairs itself was almost as wide as the balcony, giving the two enough room to fight, both trying to gain the advantage of the higher steps.

In other fights with aeristone wielders, Femira could feel the air itself warping and blowing indiscriminately as they fought. That was not the case here, both fighters using their powers so efficiently that there were no stray blasts of air.

Jaz had told her that an accomplished aeristone wielder could channel the air itself into their bodies, making them lighter and faster. While being lighter would make your strikes hit with less force, a practised push of air on your blade could drive it home with considerable power.

Landryn sidestepped a downward hit, causing Karas' sword to smash into the stone rails of the stairs. It obliterated the stone, raining debris onto the balcony below. Landryn reacted quickly to the mistake, striking quickly and landing another hit. The sound of metal on metal screeched as the blade slid ineffectively against Karas' armour.

Femira glanced to her sides, Allyn and Vestyr both stood watching with silent intensity. "Should we help him?" Femira asked them.

"Their ability is well above ours, Lady Annali," Allyn said but there was an edge of uncertainty in her expression. "Vestyr?" Allyn looked at the boy.

"Our assistance may be a hindrance, I wouldn't want to distract your brother," he said, his strange accent emphasising the "s" sounds sharply.

"You can sink him into the ground," Femira said without thinking, "trap him, that could give Landryn the advantage." Both Allyn and Vestyr looked at her with surprise. It was clear that he did not recognise her from that night a few weeks back. "You can do this," Femira nodded to him, and then stepped forward.

"Don't be foolish, Annali," Allyn warned, "you've only been training for a few months, this fight is far beyond you."

Femira didn't acknowledge her, instead attuning herself to the thrum of her earthstone. She pulled on it, forming two blades of sharpened stone. She was getting better at that but two was still all that she could manage at one time. They hovered in front of her, waiting for her command.

She waited.

Landryn and Karas continued their dance of swords, Karas' gauche but terrifyingly fast swings and Landryn's carefully timed strikes. Neither provided enough of an opening yet for a critical hit. They moved so quickly, but she just needed a second—just one second—where she could confidently push the stoneblades forward.

Landryn parried another attack, using his assured balance to deflect the attack, and allow Karas' sword to slide down against his own. They drew close in the exchange and Karas headbutted Landryn sending him stumbling backwards.

Femira pushed, forcing the stoneblades forward... but they didn't budge. She felt another beat vibrating against her. Vestyr took a step past her, laying a hand on her arm.

"It wasn't a clear shot," he chided.

She would have snapped at him, but the boy had bested her effortlessly and was clearly the more experienced stonebreaker. The vibrations from her stoneblades *changed* morphing into a new beat unresponsive to her as Vestyr forced control of them from her. She didn't even know that was possible!

Karas had pressed his advantage, and was now on higher steps taking powerful strikes down against Landryn. One of the stoneblades whipped forward, towards Karas who swiftly reacted by raising his armoured forearm to block the projectile. Landryn acted fast, lancing upward and slicing his blade deep into his opponent's armpit. Vestyr let fly the second projectile and it buried itself in Karas' eye.

The Honorsword let out a gasp of surprise and pain, his massive sword dropping from his hand and clattering down the steps, then sliding along the ramp before coming to stop. Karas himself staggered with a stunned expression on his face. His remaining red eye that seemed to shine before was now faded and dull.

"Allyn," Landryn called out, not turning from Karas but taking a step back as the man slumped. "Fetch General Garld and the palace healers. Do not draw alarm, we do not want to bring the attention to Honorsword Jahasa." Allyn didn't jump at the command, or seem at all disturbed by the scene she had just witnessed. The girl simply nodded agreement and walked purposefully back towards the feasting hall.

Vestyr remained by Femira, palace guards were now rushing from their posts. The fight had all happened so quickly, if the pair hadn't been such accomplished aeristone wielders they would likely still be throwing the initial attacks.

Femira hadn't noticed Landryn's approach; she was so fixated on Karas's twitching form on the stairs.

"Lady Annali," he inclined his head, "my sincerest apologies... I did not think that the Honorswords would be so rash in attacking you. In my experience, they are a very prideful organisation with a somewhat... *disconcerting* view on justice. I'm aware that they will often administer that impulsive justice at their own will... but I didn't think one would be so foolish to do that in a foreign palace."

Femira was still agape but she nodded to him. Blood was beginning to trickle down the ramp she'd created and was pooling at the base around Karas' sword.

"Vestyr, will you escort Lady Annali back to the feast?—or would you prefer to return to your rooms?" Landryn turned back to her. She looked to Vestyr who was inspecting the sword and the blood, he turned to look at her. His pale features giving him a ghostly appearance.

"No," Femira said, "it's ok—really—I'm fine."

Landryn didn't look convinced, "allow me, then," he turned back to Vestyr, "watch Karas until Garld arrives... I don't think he's likely to come back from that but it doesn't hurt to be cautious with his kind."

More palace guards were arriving, blocking off access to the balcony with quick commands from Landryn as he escorted Femira back the hallway they'd come.

It felt awkward now to be walking alongside him, instead of stalking behind. More palace guards were heading towards the balcony but there was no sense of panic. Allyn obviously had instructed them to be discreet.

Some highborn nobles gave her resentful looks as they passed. On her own they had mostly ignored her but walking with their Prince was too much for them to overlook.

Femira hadn't even noticed that Landryn was taking her along a different route than they had come until they reached a grand staircase leading down to a lower level of the palace. It led out onto another expansive balcony overlooking Epilas and the bay.

This balcony was much larger than the one above, with decorative water fountains positioned amongst the gardened areas on the walkway. Femira found herself captivated by the dancing waters of the fountains they passed, there was definitely some element of runewielding involved as the water flowed in the air in impressive arcing streams, the flow sometimes twisting in ways that flouted gravity.

"I had wanted to talk with you but I didn't know how to approach it... I'm sorry that it's under these circumstances that I finally did," Landryn said suddenly, and a little awkwardly.

"Why?"

"After everything that happened in Altarea, I... I didn't think you would want to speak with me."

"I meant why are you sorry?" Femira asked and then she realised abruptly that he didn't know she wasn't the real Annali.

Would Garld hide that even from him?

"You're my guest here... well Garld's guest really. I should have come to you immediately after I arrived back from Altarea. I have to admit I was surprised when he told me that you wanted to join our bloodshedder ranks."

"You didn't think a small Keiran girl like me would want to become a runewielder?"

"The only Keiran women I've met have been rather... *unenthusiastic* about runewielding."

"I'm not like most Keiran women."

"I think I'm starting to see that... how are you finding life in the barracks?" Landryn asked, "are you enjoying training with the other bloodshedders?"

"I'm not fully sure yet," she said with a bit of uncertainty, "I've only been doing it a few months now. It's not bad, I can stand it." She was surprised how quickly she was abandoning the feelings that her training was all some ruse from Garld and Landryn so that they could hand her over to the Honorswords. Landryn's actions tonight proved that was never their intention with her.

So why am I here?

"I've been told you're excelling in stonebreaking, have you started with a secondary runestone yet? A lot of us eventually learn to master two."

"I thought I was," she answered, truthfully.

"Not anymore?"

"Not lately no," she toyed with the idea of telling Landryn about her encounter with Vestyr but thought better of it. She doubted Garld would be hiding anything from his Commander but it felt wrong to tell him outside of Garld's instructions. And if Garld hadn't told Landryn about her true identity then it made her feel she shouldn't be so upfront with him.

When did I become a minion of Garld?

She already knew… it was the moment he had shown the promise of real power.

"Endrin and some of the others," Femira continued, "yourself included. You all runewield in ways I was told was impossible… ways I can't comprehend."

Landryn was quiet for a moment. Femira wondered if he was going to divulge the secrets to their advanced runewielding but was disappointed when he changed the subject. "And how do you find the other recruits?" he asked.

"I suppose it's a matter of mindset. You could let a lot of things bother you if you let it—the strict regulations and training drills,"—Endrin and Loreli's condescending faces—"but it's pretty much the same as… well, anywhere." She had been about to say 'same as when I was in Lichtin's crew but caught herself.

Landryn was nodding as if he understood, he seemed to be turning something over in his mind. Then looked straight into her eyes as if peering at some unusual object. She had never had occasion to look into his eyes before, not like this. It was the first time they had spent this much time together at all. His eyes were a dark brown… they suited his face.

"Why are you so interested?" she asked, feeling a bit uncomfortable under his gaze.

"I was just wondering what life is like for you here… " he seemed to be trying—and failing—to find exactly the right words. Then he sighed and looked down. "I don't know… nevermind."

He continued walking along the balcony making his way to one of the larger fountains and she followed.

"My brother and I used to try to divert the flow of these," Landryn said, "if you block the path of the water it always seems to right itself back on course. No matter how hard we tried we couldn't stop the inevitable."

He didn't continue and Femira wasn't sure how to respond.

"I miss my brothers sometimes," she offered honestly. The saddest part was they had both died so many years ago that she wasn't even sure if she recalled their faces correctly. The images she had in her mind slowly warped over time.

"You could return to them in Keiran, if you wanted to?"

"No," she said, firmly. He nodded and didn't press the topic. She absently wondered what Annali's brothers were like, in her mind she pictured her own brothers dressed as highborn.

"I'm glad we had the chance to talk, just the two of us," he said slowly. Femira struggled to remember what they had even spoken about.

"I wonder," he began, "if you wouldn't mind … I mean, if it wasn't any bother for you… do you think we could meet like this again? I know I don't have any right to be asking you this."

"Any *right*? What do you mean by that?" She realised her reaction might have been a bit strong but it was done.

"I don't know, I can't really explain it," he said, avoiding looking her in the eye. His gaze fell on the fountain in front of them. "I didn't mean to say 'right' exactly. I was looking for another way to put it. I know that this must all be very difficult. The assault on Altarea—being *here*. It all must be a lot for you."

Landryn leaned forward, resting his hands on the wall surrounding the fountain. He stared at it, almost as though he were hoping to find the proper expression in the flowing cascade of water. Failing, he sighed and closed his eyes.

"I think I know what you're getting at. I'm not sure how to put it either," Femira said.

"I never know what I want to say," Landryn continued, "It's been like this for a while. I try to say something but all I get are the wrong words—or sometimes the right words but they come out all in the wrong order. Sometimes it even comes off being the exact *opposite* of what I'm trying to say. I try to correct myself… and only make it worse. I lose track of what I was even saying to begin with. Most of the time, the Generals have already advised me on what to say and do. I don't…" he trailed off and went quiet.

"Everybody feels that way a little I think," she said looking to break the silence. "They're trying to express themselves and it's annoying when you can't get it right"

Landryn looked disappointed with the answer, "no that's not it either," he said without further explanation.

"Well yes, I would like to see you again," Femira said, attempting to move the conversation back to his original question. He smiled at her, but it was a sad smile, "I don't think I deserve this kindness from you, Annali."

It was only then that it clicked together for her. It was known throughout the Reldoni military that it had been Landryn himself that had fought—and killed—Prince Reselas in Altarea.

He thinks he killed my husband!

A lot of what he had been trying to say suddenly made sense… was he trying to apologise to her? Femira wasn't sure how to react, she knew what Annali would have done, she'd have screamed at him, hurled insults and accusations. Demanded the restoration of Altarea, but she wasn't Annali and she didn't care for any of that so she just stayed silent, unsure.

"Prince Landryn," Garld's voice said from behind them. Femira jumped at his presence, he was flanked by two other soldiers in bloodshedder uniforms. Femira didn't recognise them, but there were still many of the fully trained bloodshedders she'd yet to meet.

"Hello Garld," Landryn said, "Allyn found you, I assume?"

"Yes, what in the hells were you thinking? Attacking an Honorsword at a *treaty* feast!"

"Karas attacked me," Femira interjected, "I'm sorry, General. It was my fault." Garld gave her a considering look. *He's trying to figure out if I've been exposed.* She gave him the barest shake of her head. Karas was dead and it wasn't like Garld had any way to ever find out that he had figured out the truth.

"It was reckless," Garld scolded, "we were lucky we managed to distract Honorsword Jahasa and subdue him into our custody before he realised his colleague was missing. You should have—"

"—I will remind you, General, that I am your Commander," Landryn said firmly. There was no other highborn in earshot of their conversations and Femira didn't doubt the statement was for the two other bloodshedders… and possibly her?

Garld inclined his head, "of course, my Prince."

"Where is Jahasa?"

"Lukane's office. Your brother is not happy. We luckily got runebinding shackles on the man but we have a full guard on him also, as a precaution."

"Good, and Allyn?"

"With Lukane. As for her *friend,* I'm not sure."

"See if you can get someone to find him, I'll deal with Lukane." Landryn inclined his head to Femira and went to leave.

"I'll come with you," Garld said to Landryn but then leaned into Femira. "I'll want a full debrief tonight. Find Jazerah and make your way back to the barracks."

On that, Garld and the pair of bloodshedders left, leaving Femira alone next to the fountain. She turned back to it, the events of the evening swirling in her mind more erratically than the streams of water. Karas' blood pooling at the foot of stairs burned in her mind.

Red eyes and pools of blood.

CHAPTER 11
It's Nothing Personal

Tanlor dutifully followed the Prince and his guards. The Prince swayed as he walked, although not as much as Tanlor would have expected considering how much wine the man had drunk. Since arriving the Prince had put away as much alcohol than most men would drink in a year. And not cheap stuff either, these were all Reinish wines and whitewhiskeys from the more renowned distilleries. The man had even paid Tanlor's entire month's salary worth on a single glass of wine in the White Foxes earlier that night.

Prince Daegan was chatting nonsense to Captain Ferath—a good man, in Tanlor's opinion. He was friendly with the other Dukesguards and Tanlor had seen him in the sparring grounds a number of times although not faced him himself. The man's skill with a blade was certainly worthy of envy. Tanlor had little desire to ever be on the opposing side of the man in a battle.

However, Ferath's paramount skill was undoubtedly his ability to listen to the drivel this crip—*hindered*—Prince spat from his mouth each day. Even now, as the man blabbered on about the poker game he had with Duke Orland's son, Captain Ferath nodded along and seemed incredibly interested.

Intently interested.

Tanlor felt a tension rise in his shoulders, something seemed very *off* about the way Captain Ferath walked alongside his Prince. He was far *too* focused on the man, as a bodyguard he should be more focused on his surroundings and potential dangers… especially in a foreign land. His stride was purposeful and firm, Tanlor recognised his gait as a man that was readying to jump into a battle. Tanlor tried to dismiss the thought, but the more he watched, the more uncertain he became.

This is not a man on guard duty. This is a man who is ready to kill.

As the group strode into the eastern tower, they passed a pair of gate guards; he recognised both men. Tanlor hung back a little so as to be out of earshot of Ferath.

"Send for Captain Keltin," Tanlor whispered, hurriedly, "have him come to Prince Daegan's quarters with a squadron. Tell him something is amiss with the Prince's guard." The gate guards exchanged a confused looks with each other but they nodded and, without question, one of them dashed off back toward the main palace building. Tanlor trotted to catch back up with the Prince and his guards; there were three of them, including Ferath.

Ferath turned his head toward Tanlor as he caught up, his eyes narrowing. Tanlor also didn't miss that the man's hand moved slowly toward the hilt of his sword.

"Apologies." Tanlor said, off-handedly, "I thought I had spotted an old acquaintance."

"A girl?" Prince Daegan asked, a smirk on his mouth.

"No… unfortunately," Tanlor returned with a disarming smile, "but in either case, I was mistaken." Ferath's hand did not move away from the hilt of his sword and he eyed Tanlor suspiciously.

Tanlor nodded forward down the hallway, "should we be moving on?"

The group continued along the hallway and Prince Daegan launched back into his retelling of the poker game from earlier that evening. Tanlor took a steadying breath. *I'm probably overreacting.*

Keltin wouldn't be upset by Tanlor being overly cautious, and it wasn't as though Tanlor had a history of false alarms. Keltin had always encouraged the Dukesguard to trust their gut in any situation and there was certainly *something* in Ferath's demeanour that was making Tanlor uneasy. He just couldn't place exactly what it was. The man had always been a bit aloof but friendly enough, tonight he was acting very strange.

As the group climbed the steps that lead up to the apartments, the Prince prattled on. "Ugh, to think that at home there is a treaty feast happening tonight… and I'm stuck *here,* playing poker and retiring before the sun has even risen," he sighed, dejectedly.

They passed another pair of palace guardsmen at the top of the stairs, again they were men that Tanlor recognised.

"I bet my brother's entertaining some Keiran Honorsword right now," Daegan slurred, "probably some sexy red-eyed one… have you ever seen a woman Honorsword, Ferath?"

"Can't say I have, my lord," Ferath replied.

"Me neither, maybe the Keirans are all"—the Prince fumbled for his words—"you know—like you lot," he mumbled, waving a hand at Tanlor, "sexist and what-not."

The group proceeded on into the Prince's apartments and when Tanlor moved to follow them, the captain turned, blocking his path, "thank you for the escort, sir Tanlor," he said, firmly.

"You can come in for a whitewhiskey, Tanlor, if you wish?" the Prince offered, despite Tanlor on many previous occasions telling the man that he didn't drink.

"The Duke of Hardhelm sent over a casket of good twenty year," Daegan said, tossing his jacket over a chair, "almost as old as that daughter he keeps trying to push on me."

Tanlor hesitated with the offer, he had never shown any form of sociability to the Prince and to start now could possibly alert Ferath to Tanlor's suspicion. The Prince's words about Danielle's father trying to cajole Daegan into pursuing her, also gave him a bitter spark of jealousy. He didn't particularly *want* to spend any more time with the Prince.

"I'm sure you have other duties this evening," Ferath interjected, putting a hand on the door, barring Tanlor's path.

Why are you acting so strange?

"No, thank you, Prince Daegan," Tanlor said, "Captain Ferath is correct… I have rounds to make. Goodnight my lord." He bowed his head, turned and made his way back down the stairs.

Where he waited.

***

"Odd man, that Tanlor," Daegan said, undoing his vest and walking over to the whitewhiskey decanter. "Although I do enjoy his friends. That old terrible storyteller and that Davan fellow—I think that was his name anyway."

Daegan took a hearty gulp of whitewhiskey, it burned his throat and filled fire in his stomach. A new habit he'd picked up in the last few weeks here; it was so cold that he enjoyed having a glass of the stuff before getting between the frigid sheets. *The other highborn in this place keep a heated topaz by their beds to heat the sheets before getting in, no doubt.* Daegan himself could not avail of such a luxury so he made do with a glass or two of whitewhiskey. He poured himself out a glass, and turned to face Ferath.

"Do you want one?" Daegan offered. Ferath shook his head, and the solemn look on his face gave Daegan pause.

Ferath calmly drew his blade. The silver curved sword, sliding noiselessly out of its sheath.

"Ferath?" Daegan yelped, "w-what's happening?" instinctively, Daegan glanced about the living room, looking for the danger.

But there was nothing.

"What are you doing, Ferath?" he blustered.

"It's nothing personal," Ferath said sadly. He took a slow step towards Daegan, the other pair of guards standing by the door avoided looking at him or Ferath.

"Ferath, this is a weird joke," Daegan choked, but already he knew this wasn't a joke. The tension in the room was palpable as Ferath slowly walked towards him. Daegan took an instinctive step back and stumbled into the table with the decanter, it dropped and smashed. The noise startled Daegan into action and he darted for the balcony doors to his left. Ferath was quickly upon him.

"Guards!" Daegan roared. Ferath swung and Daegan leapt backwards, out onto the large balcony patio. He had no sword on him... why would he? The cold air rushed at him, fuelling his adrenaline.

"*Why*, Ferath?" Daegan shrilled, rounding to face the man.

"Like I said... it's nothing personal," Ferath replied evenly, taking another lunge at Daegan. He lept back and felt the palisade of the balcony at his back.

"Nothing personal? This seems very fucking personal!"

The training he had as a boy was kicking in, training he had done *with* Ferath. He quickly cast his eyes over the balcony for any kind of weapon. Daegan could hear now the Duke's guards in the main living room and the clanging of steel.

"Out here!" he shouted as Ferath took another swing. Daegan evaded again but Ferath's blade seared hot across his shoulder as he twisted away along the palisade. His heart was beating so fast, he could feel it throbbing in his shoulder. The pain was dulled by the adrenaline.

"This will be over quicker if you just stop," Ferath said, again lacking in any emotion.

"Yeah—I'll just *stop and let you fucking kill me!*" Daegan snapped and he jumped back before Ferath could strike again.

He reached for a plant pot, grabbing it and chucking with all his force at his former bodyguard. Ferath, sidestepped and lunged out again with his blade. Daegan attempted to sidestep towards the balcony doors but slipped and crashed down against the ground.

His shoulder was hot with his blood, a sharp contrast to the frost coated tiles. Daegan looked over to what he'd slipped on and saw the handgun in arms reach—the one gifted to him from Guildmaster Grimsworth right where he'd left it on the night of his arrival. Daegan launched himself, which was more of an awkward body shuffle, toward it. His fingers clasped the grip and he spun on Ferath.

In his fall, Daegan hadn't noticed one of the Dukesguards had made it to the balcony and was trying to jab Ferath with his spear. In close range like this, Ferath easily evaded and thrust his sword into the guardsman's neck. Blood sprayed across the tiles as the man slumped to the ground.

Daegan didn't hesitate and fired the pistol, missing the first shot. In a panic, and still lying on his back, he took a second shot without properly aiming. Missed again, followed by a quick succession of two more, none impeding Ferath's path. Through panic Daegan struggled to understand how he was missing at such close range.

I'm pointing it right at him! Work, damn you!

Ferath charged him, it was a reckless move in the small confines, and Daegan understood that he was now rushing to finish him. Daegan, still on his back, kicked himself backwards and took another shot; this one landed in Ferath's torso. The man grunted and faltered.

Tanlor burst from the balcony doors, his great bastard sword swinging in a large arc. Ferath didn't attempt a parry, and instead evaded the swing, and attempted to step into Tanlor's reach. Tanlor was evidently very well practised with a larger sword in small spaces, he fell into a low kneel with his swing, twisting his body around to take another swing at Ferath, who had to jump back to avoid being sliced in half.

Tanlor rose and fluidly placed himself between Daegan and Ferath. Both men were staring at each other, weighing the other man's abilities. Daegan had never seen Tanlor spar, but the other Dukesguards had claimed he was a formidable opponent.

"Drop your weapon," Tanlor said through gritted teeth.

"This doesn't concern you," Ferath said, calmly.

"This is the Duke's palace so it does concern me, now lower your weapon."

Six bullets, Daegan remembered. Six bullets he had fired that evening when testing the weapon. Ferath had refilled the barrel for him. And he had just shot four meaning he had two shots left. He stepped out from behind Tanlor and levelled the gun at Ferath, taking a moment to take a breath and aim at him.

"Tell me now, Ferath, why are you doing this?" He could feel the quiver in his own voice, breaking from fear and confusion.

Blood was dripping from Ferath's gunshot wound, and now faced against the two armed men, he hesitated. Daegan took a step closer, but Tanlor held out his arm.

"Don't go within his range, my lord. Captain Keltin and the rest of the guard are on their way."

"Speak Ferath!" Daegan shouted, his fear and fury untamed. "What orders are you acting on?"

Ferath looked at him and smiled.

And then he vanished in a cloud of dust.

Vanished! He didn't run or dive over the balcony. For a fraction of a second the man had appeared to be falling into the ground as the cloud of dust rose up and then he was simply *gone*.

Daegan gasped and Tanlor swiftly raised his sword into a counterstance position. Both men held their positions until the cloud of dust settled... revealing nothing. Slowly, Tanlor edged toward the spot where Ferath had been standing, glancing about the balcony for any sign of the man. After verifying Ferath had indeed disappeared, he kicked at the settled dust.

"The tiles are all gone," Tanlor mused in confusion, "but other than that it seems solid." He tapped the ground with his boot.

Daegan hesitantly stepped over, also looking about the balcony for any sign of Ferath. Inside the apartments, he saw his other two guards, Karsel and Timms both lying dead on the floor, along with another of the Dukesguard.

Daegan walked out to the balcony and peeked over the edge but saw nothing but the deep blackness of the sky and the few remaining lights of the city below. Tanlor was next to him, leaning far out over the balcony, trying to see into the balcony below.

"Is Ferath a talented stonebreaker?" Tanlor asked and Daegan shook his head. "I-I don't think so, at least he never mentioned it before."

But then again, Ferath *had* attacked him. There was obviously a lot the man was hiding from Daegan... Tanlor pulled back from the balcony, "I've heard of master stonebreakers who can disintegrate a stone wall and reform it in a few moments... but a regular soldier and in a few *seconds*? It doesn't add up. How long has he been in your service?"

Daegan was still shaking his head. *I need—I need to sit down.* His mind was racing, *I need to get home... I need to get out of here. Ferath, he—how could he? Why would he?*

"My other guards, we must wake them... Thalan also." Daegan said eventually, looking to Tanlor.

"I'm not sure they can be trusted right now," Tanlor replied. "You were just attacked by your own men. We should wait for Keltin. He will know what to do."

***

It was not long before Daegan found himself in Arch-duke Edmund's office. With both Tanlor and Sir Keltin. Despite the amount he had drunk earlier in the evening, Daegan felt very sober.

Painfully sober.

He was sweating, and despite the fire in the hearth next to him, he felt cold through to his bones.

"My men have been searching the palace, my lords," Sir Keltin said, "from what we could gather; Ferath was working only with two other guards on your duty this evening, we found the rest of your guards and servants dead, Prince Daegan."

"Dead? *All* of them?" Daegan breathed, *Thalan... Poor dutiful Thalan.*

"All but one, a woman named Kerala. We have not been able to locate her yet, but my guards noted that she had left the palace earlier this evening."

"Do you think she was involved?" Daegan would never before have dreamed to question Kerala's unbreaking loyalty. But he had never doubted Ferath either.

"Potentially... however we are more concerned with finding Ferath, he poses a much greater risk to your safety." Keltin said, "the woman is a lesser priority."

"She's a member of my guard, you shouldn't overlook her," Daegan said and then thought it was very likely that the sexism inherent in their culture had created a blind spot that they simply weren't capable of recognising such skills in a woman. The dismissive glances that Keltin and Edmund exchanged supported Daegan's suspicions.

"She is just as dangerous as Ferath," Daegan affirmed, "she's a skilled runewielder and warrior."

"We also have not been able to figure out how he managed to *disappear* as you both claim," Keltin responded, shifting the topic back to Ferath Vitares. He was decidedly uncomfortable talking about a woman with fighting ability.

"I don't understand it either, Captain, but I know what I saw," Tanlor replied. Daegan simply nodded along, deciding not to press the topic of Kerala at the moment. Ferath was still the primary concern. The reason for why was plaguing him most of all.

"For the Prince's own safety, Arch-duke," Keltin continued "I think it's best that we move him to a safehouse outside of the palace. With this assassin still loose inside the walls, we cannot ensure his safety."

"He's not an assassin," Daegan said, "h-he's Ferath... he's my friend. He..." Daegan trailed off.

"I understand your confusion, Prince Daegan," Edmund said calmly, almost comforting, "I too have had assassination attempts on my life in the past. And to have the attack from your own men. I cannot imagine."

"Why? Why would he do this?"

"I assure you, Prince Daegan. We *will* find Ferath Vitares and interrogate him. But for the moment, Sir Keltin is right. We can only assume that Ferath will make another attempt on your life. Someone wishes you dead, and there is the possibility that this is part of some scheme to sow distrust between our nations. We *cannot* allow that."

"I need to send word to my brother," Daegan nodded, "Lukane will know what to do, he can help me."

"We will release a statement that there has been an attempt on your life and that we have moved you into a secured area of the palace. This will hopefully lure Ferath into a trap by Keltin's men. You should write this story also to your brother, in case your attackers have spies in your brother's court. Meanwhile, we will do everything we can to keep you safe."

"You want me to lie to my brother?"

"No," Edmund said reassuringly, "not a lie. I simply want you to shroud the specifics of where you are being kept. The assassin will expect us to keep you hidden and protected here, so it is best you are kept outside of the palace. I assure, Prince Daegan, you will be kept safe. That is my primary concern."

"If you would follow me, my lord?" Keltin said to Daegan. "There are a dozen of my men outside. We will escort you to your rooms and help you pack what you might need."

Daegan nodded and allowed himself to be shepherded from the office. His mind still reeled from the events of the night, and it was easier to simply go along rather than trying to figure out what he should do himself.

***

Tanlor rose to follow Keltin and Daegan but Edmund caught his attention, indicating him to remain. Keltin nodded to him, and closed the office door leaving Tanlor alone with the Arch-duke.

"You did well tonight, Tanlor," Edmund began. His long grey moustaches were a whimsical choice for such an otherwise serious man but it was the fashion of the older gentlemen in the court. A close kept beard was the fashion of younger men, those that could grow them properly at least. Tanlor absently rubbed at his stubble.

"Thank you, my lord," Tanlor replied and then added bitterly, "but I couldn't stop Ferath from escaping, I should have been better. I *knew* something was off about him, I should have picked up on it sooner... alerted Keltin sooner."

"A man lives today who wouldn't have if it were not for you," Edmund granted. "I shouldn't have to explain to you how much of a disaster it would be for us to have a dead Reldoni Prince on our hands. Your actions in protecting the man could well have prevented a war, Tanlor."

"Surely it wouldn't have come to that?" Tanlor asked, aghast.

"Foreign relations with the Reldoni are good. This is in no small part because of our steel trade, but we must never forget that Reldon is a heavily militant nation, and King Abhran has been extending his territories aggressively over the past decade."

"Of course, my lord, I am not as… familiar with international politics as others," Tanlor confessed.

"No," Edmund agreed, "but you are observant. Keltin believes there is a lot of potential in you."

Tanlor felt a rise of pride and hope in him. It was no secret amongst the other Dukesguard that Keltin would soon be retiring.

Could this be it? He felt his shoulders twitch in excitement.

"I know that you want the promotion to Captain of the Dukesguard," Edmund continued, "but the truth is this; you are still new to the guard and there are others who have been serving ten years and longer. You have not yet proven yourself worthy to be Captain."

Tanlor nodded, "yes, sir. I understand," he lied through gritted teeth, resisting every urge in him to argue. He knew it would do no good, someone of his station didn't argue with the Arch-duke.

He thought he had been so close. *What if Harfallow forces her to marry Lord Hembook?* He felt Danielle, his dream, his love… his life, slipping away. He felt his shoulders slump with disappointment, and he didn't care.

Tanlor was about to ask to be dismissed but then the Arch-duke continued, "I know why you want it so badly," he disclosed. Tanlor felt his eyes narrow slightly, it was unlikely that Edmund knew the true reason. He couldn't know of his and Danielle's relationship. How could he possibly know, and why would he have even cared to know?

"My lord?" Tanlor prompted. Not wanting to give anything away.

"Lady Danielle Harfallow," Edmund offered, a smirk visible beneath the man's moustache. Tanlor did not attempt to hide his surprise. As if reading his thoughts, the Arch-duke's grin grew wider, "Not much happens in these walls without my knowledge, Tanlor."

"I want…" Tanlor started, "I hope to marry her, my lord," he admitted.

"I'm sure that you do," Edmund replied, "there's many men in my court that have been vying for both Duke Harfallow's and Lady Danielle's approval for years."

"I'm aware," Tanlor said, trying unsuccessfully to hide his frustration, "that doesn't change the truth."

"No, I doubt it does. My intent is not to discourage, Sir Tanlor," Edmund said, the ghost of a predatory smile crossing his face, "I daresay, it's entirely possible that you might marry her someday."

Tanlor's eyebrows rose. "But Lord Harfallow, he said that—"

The Arch-duke raised his hand.

"—Garret Harfallow will be very impressed when I send him this letter," Edmund interjected, picking up a sheet of paper from his desk. "It explains that one of my own personal guards—an honourable and dignified young man—wishes to marry his daughter. It explains that I will be *personally* grateful if he were to accept this man's request."

The Arch-duke said it all so matter-of-factly as if Tanlor's entire life and ambition were the simplest thing in the world. His dreams came rushing into his grasp. He was overcome and was at a loss for what to say.

"T-thank you, my lord."

"No need to thank me," Edmund's smile turned sickly-sweet, the moustaches curling around his grin. "There is something I need from you, however."

"Of course! Anything you ask of me, my lord," Tanlor implored.

"Prince Daegan needs to be taken away from the palace—and the city—tonight. You will be his bodyguard and his guide."

"Escort mission," Tanlor nodded, "no problem... where will I be taking him, sir?" Tanlor was still giddy with the thought of marrying Danielle.

The grin was gone from Edmund's face, his tone serious, "As far from here as you can get him," he instructed. "But still within our borders. His own men tried to kill him. I'm not sure what scheme is at play here and I'm sure you can understand why I want to keep a foreign Prince alive on our soil at all costs. I will soon release a statement that the Prince has been murdered by his own guard and we will await patiently for the reproach. Should this be some ploy to lay blame upon us, we produce the Prince and expose the orchestrators of this mess. It is vital for this plan, Tanlor, that you keep the Prince hidden—and most importantly—safe."

"A wise plan, sir, but why me?"

"Because you're a good bodyguard Tanlor; a strong fighter and runewielder. Do you recall the evening I learned that you were Taran the Hunter's son?" Tanlor winced. Of course he remembered. The Arch-duke, like so many before him, had insisted on Tanlor reciting the story with all the bells and lies that came with it.

"You said your father used to take you and your brother to the woods where he was born, if I recall correctly?" Edmund probed.

"Yes, my lord. He did."

"Perfect—that is where I want you to take Prince Daegan. The forests beyond the Nortara Sheet. You know the hidden trails, how to avoid the dangers beyond civilisation."

"Of course, my lord," Tanlor said with a great deal more confidence than he felt.

It had been nearly a decade since he had been up past the Nortara Sheet, but Tanlor would trek to the Black Sands barefoot if it meant he could get his hands on that letter.

"Most importantly of all, Tanlor," Edmund confided, "I trust you. Once this situation has been put to bed, I will send this letter to Harfallow." Tanlor was wise enough to know that he was using the letter to Harfallow as the security to that trust.

"You will not regret this decision, my lord," Tanlor vowed, earnestly.

"See to it that I do not," Edmund accepted, with a slightest edge of warning in his tone.

The Arch-duke then pulled out an iron strongbox with silver inlay from his desk. It was clearly stoneshaped, traditional ironcasting wouldn't have been able to weave in the silver flowing patterns on the box. Edmund brushed his hand over it lightly and the lid flipped open slowly on its own.

"I'm giving you ten gold marks. The Prince should have money of his own but if it comes to it, use this to fund the excursion. This—" he held up a small green stone that had the appearance of jade, "—is a signal stone, I'm sure you've heard of them.

I have the companion stone here. Both stones will change their colour to red if you press on either with your edir. Under no circumstance are you to do this with yours. *I* will activate the signal stone when I want you to return to Rubastre, understood?"

"Understood, sir," he affirmed, taking the gold and one of the stones.

The gold was more than he would make in a year and he didn't doubt that the value of the signal stone was more than he had ever made in his life both working in the Arch-duke's employ and from his early career taking contracts. From what he understood, signal stones were a specialised form of bondstone, a rare runestone as it was, let alone modified to be used as a signal stone.

"Show this," Edmund continued and offered a piece of paper, "to horsemaster Klyne and he will provide you with two horses. Do not wait for dawn, I want Prince Daegan out of this city *tonight*." He handed Tanlor the small unsealed writ for the horses.

Tanlor rose to leave. "I will not disappoint you, sir."

The Arch-duke began to pack away the iron and silver box, "also, Tanlor," he added, "I must urge you to be discreet." He nodded towards Tanlor's grey tabard with the Arch-duke's own crest—the Arctic Bear—emblazoned on it.

"For this mission, you are to be under the guise of a simple bodyguard; the Prince's identity *must* remain hidden."

Tanlor nodded with determination and left.

PART II

SOULFORGED

Interlude
Arken

Guildmaster Arken strode purposefully through the Ironworks Guild offices. As he walked, he admired the elaborate network of iron pipes decorating the walls, pumping heated water through the building. A true wonder of engineering, a beautiful example of the turning tide in the use of runestones. And Arken's ship was at the head of that tide.

It was a stark difference to the fanciful brass pipe system that adorned the Arch-duke's palace, an offensive display of the disparity of wealth in Rubane. Where the highborn control and squander wealth while the truly talented and innovative struggle to fund projects that could usher in a new world.

He approached the heavy doors of Grimsworth's office. He knocked loudly, and entered when beckoned. Grimsworth himself stood at the window, overlooking the labour yard where workers extracted and separated valuable metals from stone. Arken joined him and watched as master metalshapers and artificers work the metal into varying shapes. To Arken's ongoing disappointment, it was entirely weapons being produced, both modern and old.

"Such a waste," Arken said, shaking his head.
"Men will always want to kill other men," Grimsworth chided, "no matter how many new innovations we achieve."
"Steel makes blood, which makes gold."
"Indeed it does," Grimsworth turned to him. "There has been an interesting development in our plan," he confided, "it appears there has been an attempt made on the cripple's life."
"One of the Dukes?" Arken asked, his eyebrows rising in surprise.
"One of his own guards," Grimsworth scoffed, "Edmund is trying to keep it all under wraps but he won't be able to contain this for very long."
"And the Prince?"
"Rumours that he's dead. Others say that he's under the Arch-duke's protection. Nothing confirmed just yet." Grimsworth's unfathomable ability to always be aware of what was going on in the palace continued to astound Arken.

"Should we press ahead?" Arken asked worryingly. "Perhaps this is not the best time for you to be stepping down. We've already established you as an enemy of the Prince, were we too hasty?"
"No, no," Grimsworth dismissed, "for our plan to succeed the Dukes cannot suspect me of cavorting with the Reldoni. The stunt with the Prince will stand for that affirmation."

"But does this feud with the Prince make you culpable to the assisination?"
"Nobody would think to blame me for this," Grimsworth rebutted, "it's brazen—yes —but a stupid move. The Prince's death achieves nothing for me—no, we'll continue

with the plan. If the Prince is truly dead then it is indeed a setback. Make another copy of the schematics, we will have another Reldoni ambassador soon enough. A dead Prince won't change the fact that they will want their steel."

"The Reldoni might try to lay blame on Rubane for this," Arken noted.

"All the better," Grimsworth granted, "the pressure will push the Dukes into making rash decisions. They'll be too busy looking at the sword pointed at them to notice the knife at their back."

Arken grimaced, he didn't like the idea of such violence, but as Grimsworth had told him time and time again, for change—real tangible change—to happen in Rubane then the highborn would need to be taken down. Their bureaucracy and rules overthrown, their amassed wealth shared evenly and fairly across the guilds so that they might truly help the people of Rubane.

"I'll use my connections, try to uncover the one pulling the strings of this assassin," Grimsworth continued, "if their goal is to sow discord amongst the highborn, then we might have an ally."

Interlude
Baroc

The muzzle was downright uncomfortable. Baroc ground his teeth against the bitter iron pins that jutted between his molars. The roughshod leather tightened against his jowls in response, a truly unbearable sensation. He glowered and growled for all he was worth, but the rak didn't give a damn.

He never did.

The rak reached from the folds of his tattered robe and dangled a faded strip of cloth in front of Baroc's nose as though he were baiting a trout. If Baroc had glowered before, his eyes now shot crimson. The rak grinned, thinking Baroc had picked up the scent again. He was wrong. Baroc was simply deciding which limb he'd maul off the rak first. It was his favourite question these days. And when he broke free, it would be an immense satisfaction to decide in the spur of the moment.

Baroc twisted his snout, but the muzzle snapped him back in place, reminding him that day was far off. Right now, his was a life of humiliation. The muzzle was one thing, but the scent? Since when did he need the scent draped upon his snout to pick a trail?

Even among his kin of the Shadow Peak, Baroc had been the sharpest chaser. Naturally, he'd recognized the scent long before the rak had set his grubby feet in front of him. He first caught whiff when the rak had returned from scouting ahead. He'd been cavorting around the cooking fire, embalming himself in tinctures of salt, cayenne, and thyme, yet he could still smell it.

If there was one thing Baroc had learned this past year in captivity, it was *that* scent. The smell that dwelled on a certain torn cloth in the pocket of a certain rak chiefsman. The stench of another particular rak.

Baroc's snout flared, subconsciously retracing familiar ground as the rak gave the rag a final twirl. Baroc breathed it in deep, letting the stale taste settle within—iron, hunger... and fear. The scent twisted in Baroc's gut—entirely distasteful. It was a waste of his talents.

"Lead," the rak spat. Baroc instinctively growled—a deeper, lower grumble in his throat than his usual—at the command but that earned him a strong whack of the stick in the rak's hands.

"Stupid fucking dogman," the rak spat as he thrashed Baroc with his stick. Baroc tried to recoil but the stiff poles affixed to his collar locked him in place taking the brute of the attack. He hated how he whined each time the stick struck him. He was of the Shadow Peaks Pack, he was better than whining. But the noise came out regardless of his efforts to hold it in.

Satisfied that he had inflicted enough pain, the rak held out the cloth again. "Lead, dogman!" Baroc was unsure whether 'dogman' was just the name the rakmen had given him or if it was the name that they used for all of his kind.

Baroc wished to stay still in defiance, to refuse to submit to the rak and his stick. He wished that his clawed hands were unbound, so that he could pry the muzzle of his face. That he could tear the rak's head from his shoulders. He would feast on the rak's flesh as a mark of disrespect, even though he knew that meat would be coarse and salty. Instead, he grudgingly moved forward pulling the two other rakmen that held the poles connected to his collar in the direction of where the scent was strongest.

It always baffled Baroc that rakmen could not smell. *Why have noses if they can't smell?* It also baffled him how such a weak race could be so fearsome to his people. Their hideous furless bodies could not withstand the cold of the snow nor could their blunt soft claws inflict any damage on an enemy.

It was the lack of scent that stood foremost amongst all their shortcomings. How could they not tell that this rak they hunted had travelled south the previous day. The scent of his leather boots still hung on the stones he had trod on. It was fading—yes—but even in a few days time, Baroc would still be able to detect it.

He led the group of six rakmen further to the south, all the while resisting his urge to thrash wildly against the polearms. He knew what would follow if he did, the healing burn marks on his shoulders and arms were stinging reminders. The Flamefinder, the tall one who spoke little. He smelled far more of ash than the others... and confidence. The others deferred to him, you could tell it by the way they spoke to him. But Baroc could smell the subservience off them, like a cub scolded by its mother.

A scent that Baroc was beginning to smell of himself.

CHAPTER 12
The Broken Shield

The Broken Shield was an inn and tavern on the outer ring of Rubastre. The hanging sign was a depiction of a shield with a large crack down the middle. It was ironic that the sign itself was also broken, it dangled lopsided from one hinge, the other looked to have rusted and crumbled years ago. It squeaked an unharmonious song in the night along the quiet backstreet as the frigid breeze kissed it with each passing of the street.

The Broken Shield was a favourite of Rowan Shydran's and he would stay there each time his work forced him on the path to Rubastre. Being so far from the main thoroughfares meant that there were no crowds of highborn or similar wealthy folk cavorting late into the night.

The patronage of the Broken Shield were not unlike Rowan himself; travellers and caravan guards who typically spent most of their time on the road. Cities like Rubastre and Garronforn tended to be their destinations, but their lives were mostly spent between those places and it was where they were most comfortable.

The city was an unsettling place for people like him; far too many people for comfort, and most of them always wanted something. The poor wanted gold, and the rich wanted your time. Both were resources Rowan preferred to spend anywhere but Rubastre.

It was late—or early depending on how you looked at it. Mixing with the orange light of the gaslamps, the early morning sky was a murky purple. Frost was climbing at the window that Rowan looked out from. Two cloaked and hooded men on horseback were the only figures in the street.

"They say who they were?" Rowan asked, his voice croaky having just been woken.

"No, they didn't. Couldn't get a look at their faces neither. Real shady folk, if you ask me. Callin' in at this hour. What company you been keepin', Rowan?" Ger—the innkeeper—accused.

Rowan didn't respond, instead he pulled on his mail of interlocking metal rings over his linens and strapped on his large sword. He took his dark green cloak from the hook. *A good cloak that.* It was thick cloth and treated with dragon-oil to repel the wet. He'd known a runewielder once who had commissioned waterstones with specialised runes woven into the fabric of his cloak to repel moisture, the thing had cost him a small fortune. Rowan saw that same runewielder dead on the road a few days later, his cloak and coin pouch gone.

"There's not goin' be no trouble here, is there?" Ger asked worriedly as he watched Rowan clip on his cloak over the chainmail, pulling the hood up over his red braids.

"No trouble," Rowan grumbled, brushing past the man and making his way down to the inn's common room. The Broken Shield tended to close up not long after midnight which meant the place was eerily quiet but for wooden floorboards groaning under Rowan's boots, and Ger scuffling behind him.

Rowan opened the door to the street and was greeted by the pleasantly crisp and clear breath of early morning. One of the riders pulled back his hood to reveal a face almost identical to Rowan's own although his hair was blond and unbraided.

"I thought you didn't have the time to visit me," Rowan said to his brother.
"I need your help," Tan said without preamble.
"It's nice to see you too, little brother," Rowan started, "the journey was to be as expected, although there were bandits on the road—nothing new there, s'pose. Mother is well, as are Marie and the boys. I didn't see Bo—"
"—ok, I get it. I'm sorry," Tan apologised hurriedly, "It's good to see you but I'm on urgent business, I need to leave the city—tonight," he said, scratching the side of his neck.

Rowan suspected Tan was embarrassed with what he was about to ask, and then Tan grudgingly got to his point, "I need your help getting where I need to go."
"And where's that?" Rowan asked. Tan glanced at Ger who was still standing a foot back. The portly innkeeper had visibly relaxed once he realised that there wasn't going to be any fighting.

"Can we get some privacy?" Tan rudely asked Ger, who then looked at Rowan with insult.
"We'll speak outside," Rowan said.
"No," Tan replied, his gaze darting up and down the empty street, "I can't speak out in the open."
"This is Ger's inn and it's late," Rowan chastised Tan. "Pretty rude to just barge in here and tell him to bugger off, don't you think?"
"S'alright Rowan, I take no offence," Ger sassed, clearly offended.

Rowan nodded his thanks, and beckoned for Tan and his hooded companion to enter.

The pair dismounted and hurried inside. They were both twitchy and Rowan noted how Tan's companion held himself awkwardly. The companion's face was dark under his cowl, he was tall too, perhaps a bit taller than Rowan himself which was rare to see. They sat at a table and waited for Ger to move into the back room.

"I need to travel up past the Nortara Sheet," Tan said, steely determination in his blue eyes. "You've been up that way a lot more than I have the past few years."
"Ten years," Rowan corrected him.
"Ten years," Tan acknowledged.
"You're not with the Arch-duke anymore?" Rowan probed with concern. Knowing his little brother had a safe, reliable position in the Dukesguard was a comfort for Rowan, even if it was in Rubastre.

"This *is* a mission for the Arch-duke," Tan admitted, "but I can't give any more details than that. I need you to swear that you won't speak even that much of it."
"You've my word, of course. It'll be a hard passage over the Sheet this time of year. Most of the roads will be completely frozen over. And you'll have to go on foot in a lot of parts," Rowan advised, not that any of that would deter Rowan, but Tan had never really enjoyed the wilds as much.

"On foot?" the companion squawked, "in the snow?"
"Aye," Rowan said, "it'll be tough going, and there's not much past Twin Garde, where are you even headed?"
"Shrydan Forest, for now," Tan said, offering no more.

"Will you help us?" Tan asked, there was pleading in his eyes that Rowan was unsure he could refuse.

"I was headed back to Garronforn tomorrow," Rowan said. "Marie won't be happy if I take a contract headed all that way north. She was expecting me home for the season."

"I'll pay you two gold marks for the trip there," Tan explained, "and another for the journey back when it comes to that."

"Three gold marks!" Rowan choked, "where you getting that kind of money to be squandering?"

"Like I said, this is a mission for the Arch-duke," Tan said, looking nervously about the empty room. The other man still hadn't pulled back his cloak or said anything of note since arriving.

"And what's your deal?" Rowan asked the stranger, not bothering to hide his scrutiny.

"He's just a merchant, heading north—prospecting," Tan fumbled, clearly lying but Rowan let it go.

"And we leave tonight?... if you can still call it that," Rowan mused to which Tan nodded in response. Rowan remained silent for a few moments, considering the offer. He had to admit three gold marks was more than he would make across two seasons. Marie would be furious, but he could promise her the entire spring and summer at home. He enjoyed the road more in summer but spending the time with Marie and the boys would be a welcome change in pace for a while. And he had to admit, a deep part of him yearned to leap at the chance to head back up past the Sheet. He wasn't a young adventurer anymore but his days trekking along the mountain ridges with his father and brother forced their way into his mind with a powerful and overwhelming nostalgia.

He slapped both hands on the surface of the table, a grin breaking across his face. He pushed himself up.

"I guess, I'll go get my pack," Rowan accepted.

***

Daegan shuffled uncomfortably on the hard leather of the saddle. The sobering events of the previous night still played in his mind as he settled into his new reality. Ferath simply *couldn't* have betrayed him. Daegan hadn't had the mental capacity over the night to truly process that or to even start running through the list of potential reasons.

"Are we certain this is the right course of action?" Daegan asked Tanlor.

"I do not question Arch-duke Edmund's wisdom," Tanlor replied, simply.

"That's because you're in his guard..." Daegan's face scrunched as he spoke, "you're not supposed to question him. But this plan..." the harsh reality of being out in the wilderness in the snow did not sound like something Daegan would enjoy, "I'm not sure if it's the best thing to do... perhaps we should return to the palace and think it through?"

"I know men like Ferath," Tanlor replied, "he's determined... he will not stop hunting you if that is his goal." Daegan had trouble believing that. A part of him still refused to accept that Ferath had tried to kill him at all... *But he had*. He couldn't deny that cold, emotionless face.

"Ferath's resolve aside—" Daegan began to argue.

"—There is no putting Ferath aside," Tanlor cut him off, "not until he's captured or killed."

"I fail to think of a worse course of action than what we're currently taking," Daegan argued. "What's the worst that could happen if we were to head back to the palace?"

"Ferath would kill you—and me for being in the way."

Ah. That is worse, I do enjoy being alive.

Since becoming an adult, Daegan had always had the constant reassurance of his guard, any dangers he had faced had always been superficial; damages to his reputation or his political interests. There was a very tangible difference between damage to his family's prestige and his own person. He hadn't felt that sense of helplessness in a very long time. Not since he was a child. He rubbed consciously against his throat, frost had crusted the fingers of his leather gloves and the sharp sting of the ice distracted him from the phantom tightening at his larynx.

"Your neck cold?" Rowan asked him, astride his own horse. Tanlor and Rowan were unmistakably related. They had the same strong square features. The most obvious difference between them was their hair colour but Daegan noted that Rowan's face looked older. The face of a man who's weathered a lifetime of storms.

"It's fine," Daegan dismissed.

"It's going to get colder farther we go into the hills, if you need more layers we should stop in the next town," Rowan advised.

"I said I'm fine," Daegan replied, firmly.

The sun had risen a few hours before as they had ridden out of the city gates. They had moved quickly in the early morning through the outer villages. The sun hadn't brought much warmth with it.

The villages they'd passed through had been small clusters of wooden houses that looked like ships turned upside, nestled in the snow. Much like in Rubastre, Daegan was surprised with the amount of structures made of wood. A strong contrast to Reldon where almost everything was made of stone. Wood was harder to work with than stone so only the wealthy could afford both the material and the craftsmanship.

"Right so," Rowan said, not seeming like he was going to drop the subject, "we should make it to Edas in a few days. There's a few more villages along the way where we can pick up basic supplies. But if you need any new gear you'd be better off waiting until Edas. We'll get you proper gear for the northlands," Rowan informed, and then plucking at Daegan's cloak, "cotton kills," he made a *tsk*'ing sound.

"We're not going through Edas," Tanlor called up from the rear, bodyguards always liked hanging out behind you.

"The main road passes right through," Rowan argued, "we'd be just as quick going through Edas as we would taking the mining routes. The cliff road to Garronforn as far as the River Cress would be the safest road, and from there, we can follow the river north towards the Nortara Sheet."

"The backroads are a more direct route," Tanlor defended.

"But we'll be travelling slower on them," Rowan rebuked, "some of the roads are little more than farmer's trails."

"Backroads only," Tanlor insisted.

"Half of 'em will be impassable in the snow," Rowan scoffed, "doesn't make any sense."

"We *have* to keep off the main road," Tanlor emphasised, shooting glances at Daegan. Rowan didn't press the issue further, although it was clear he was disgruntled about it.

Rowan was a gruff man, his words crunched like horseshoes on frost. Like Tanlor, he had a heavy build and Daegan didn't doubt he was well capable of using the sword at his hip. Unlike Tanlor's ridiculous greatsword, Rowan's sword was smaller and more akin to the slender blades of his own people but without the gentle curve of the blade. Strapped to his horse was also a small armoury; he had a great double-axe, a bow and what looked to be at least a dozen knives and daggers in various hilts on his saddle. He had a round bronze shield with a green tree painted on it. By comparison, Daegan himself was only armed with his revolver, still empty from the previous night.

"I don't recognise that sigil," Daegan commented on the shield, assuming it to be the house crest of some lord. The paintwork had been heavily chipped with use, but it looked strong.

"House Shrydan," Rowan said, winking. He didn't say it with the smug pride that Daegan was accustomed to when highborn spoke of their Houses, but then again nothing about Rowan was very highborn.

He's not really highborn anyway. Daegan thought to himself but probably best to keep that remark to himself. Right now, the Shrydan brothers were his only protection, better to not belittle their family's significance.

"I suppose I've never seen you wear anything but the Arch-duke's colours, Tanlor," Daegan called back to him. Tanlor trotted his horse up in between Daegan and Rowan, his eyes darting about.

"We have to be careful, my lord," he said in a hushed tone so as to not be overheard by the wood pigeons, "I am not Tanlor of the Dukesguard, I'm just Tanlor —a simple bodyguard—and you are just Desmond, my employer."

"You know calling him 'my lord' doesn't help convince anyone he's just a merchant, Tan," Rowan contested.

"He has a point," Daegan agreed.

"Also—a prospecting merchant?" Rowan gave a raucous laugh, "what's there to prospect out past the Sheet, eh? It's against the law to trade with rakmen and besides they'd be more likely to skin you than trade with you. If you're going to lie about who you are, might as well make it a believable one, eh, Dessie?"

"And what would you suggest, Rowan?" Tanlor accused, "what else would someone like *him* be at up here?"

"What do you mean someone like *me*?" Daegan said defensively, pulling on his reins.

"I didn't mean it like that, my lo—Desmond," Tanlor stammered, awkwardly. "What I meant, not because you're—y-you know—it's just that you're not a northerner, you're not even *Rubanian*. Folk up these parts rarely go a few miles from their homes... half of them would think Reldon is some magical kingdom from the stories. Tales of Elyina the Earthmage and Ayden Lionheart are nothing more than faega tales to these people... and highborn folk, they don't go where we're going,"

"I've done a few escort contracts for Ironworks prospectors before but never past the Nortara Sheet—mind you—but close enough," Rowan offered, "it's a more believable story."

"No," Daegan growled, bitterly, "fuck the Ironworks guild." His hand touched against his revolver in a hilt at his hip, for him it wasn't a sign of aggression just a reminder of where it came from. Daegan kicked his heels into his horse, moving past the two, "I'll think of something else."

Rowan raised an eyebrow at Tanlor. "Don't ask," Tanlor said in response, and urged his horse to follow after Daegan.

CHAPTER 13

Soulforging

Femira found herself once again in Garld's office. This time she was flanked by both Jaz and Aden. She was still wearing her red dress, Jaz in his formal suit that he had been wearing to the feast. Aden was wearing his bloodshedder's recruits uniform.

"You're still not going to tell us why we're here?" Aden asked her.

"I'll wait for Garld to explain it," Femira told him. She was reluctant to part with any information on the events of the evening until Garld gave her the go ahead.

Endrin had caught her and Jaz on their return to the barracks and had directed them to the General's office for a debrief. For some reason, he had also sent for Aden. Endrin now stood stoic by the door, like a bouncer in a brothel. The bald man had a fixed glare and had told them nothing since they arrived. Before long, Misandrei arrived and took the space behind Garld's desk. She looked them up and down, appraisingly.

"You're dismissed," Misandrei said to Endrin.

"I'll wait for the General, if you don't mind, Captain," Endrin returned. Her mouth moved to a thin line but she didn't reprimand him. "Very well," she replied before turning her attention back to Femira and the others.

"Jazerah and Aden, your assignment is finished," she stated, Femira glanced between the pair at her sides. "What does she mean, what assignment?" she asked.

"Sorry, Annali," Aden winced.

"I hope you still feel that we're friends," Jaz added, a rare look of shame crossing his face.

"You were watching me," Femira realised.

"It wasn't like we are *always* on assignment hanging out with you," Jaz had been avoiding her eyes, but now fixed them on her, "we *are* your friends."

Femira mused quietly for a moment, she wasn't offended by the knowledge. It made sense when she thought about it, everyone but Garld thought she was a highborn Lady of a rival nation. She was trapped here—yes—but she also had a great deal of freedom in the barracks. For appearances it made sense for her to be watched. And Garld probably wanted her monitored in case she tried to steal something and make a break for it.

It was a better thought than the alternative; that Aden and Jaz had thought she was a bargaining chip for the Honorswords. She was beginning to worry that they were tasked in keeping her from running off so that she could be traded back to Keiran like a pound of skaga.

That idea—planted in her by Endrin—was quickly diminishing from her mind. If Landryn or Garld were planning on handing her over to the Honorswords, Landryn wouldn't have fought—and killed—one outright in her defence.

Outside of her training, all of Femira's time had been spent with Aden and Jaz.

Aden tasked with filling the gaps in her knowledge of her runewielding abilities and Jaz giving her insights on Reldoni high society. She hadn't really started to think of them as friends, but seeing how embarrassed the pair looked at being revealed for spying on her ironically made her appreciate them more.

"It's alright," Femira smiled, "I get it. Can't have a badass stonebreaker like me running about unchecked."

"Hah," Endrin barked from the corner, "where do you—"

"—hold your tongue, Endrin," Misandrei warned him, her face stern as always, "General Garld has deemed that Lady Annali no longer requires observation." Aden and Jaz had visibly relaxed at Femira's unfazed reaction.

"The three of you have all proven your loyalty to the bloodshedders in your own ways over the past months. I'm happy to be the one to tell you that are being promoted," Misandrei informed them. "Tomorrow you all officially join the ranks as full bloodshedders."

"Really?" Jaz's eyes widened, "are we going to... you know, become soulforged? Like the rest of you?"

Soulforged? She'd not heard anyone mention that yet. Was this something they'd been keeping from her?

"What's *Soulforged*?" Femira asked and as she did so the door behind them opened and Garld strode in.

He was also still dressed in his formal attire; black uniform, gold General knots on the shoulders. Garld had obviously caught the end of her question.

"The question that you've been trying to ask since you arrived here," Garld told her, stepping behind the desk.

"I'll take it from here, Captain," Garld said to Misandrei, dismissing her. "Aden, Jazerah; congratulations to you both. However, your training does not end here, this is just the beginning for you."

"Yes, sir," the boys replied in unison, "it's an honour, sir," Aden added.

"Endrin," Garld started, "take Aden and Jazerah to the advanced training halls and introduce them to their seniors. You will each be assigned a mentor to help guide you through the changes after your soulforging."

Jaz and Aden saluted and were escorted by Endrin out of the office, the man's face was impassive but Femira got the feeling that he was seething internally. *Why is he bitter about this?* Endrin, from the brief interactions she'd had with him, had come across as a man who enjoyed having authority over others; he had also demonstrated his superior ability on numerous occasions in the training yards on recruits.

Femira paused for a moment in consideration. "You're doing something to the recruits aren't you? It's how the bloodshedders are stronger than typical runewielders?"

"Indeed," Garld acknowledged, "it is called soulforging."

"Are all people able to become soulforged... what does that even mean?"

"All people can runewield," Garld replied. *Hadn't Landryn said that his brother couldn't?* she decided to not interrupt with that correction. "Some people are born with a natural affinity for it, people like you and I. But there is a threshold to how powerful our abilities can naturally grow."

"So I won't ever be as strong as Endrin?"

"Your edir is strong. You have a natural affinity for using aradium... but no, you would never be as strong as Endrin, not without soulforging."

"So soulforging can help people *learn* to have a stronger affinity for runewielding?"

"Not exactly," Garld replied, "it's a complicated process and it requires an extensive knowledge of how our bodies work." Femira's shoulders were slumped, if it couldn't be taught then how could she gain the power of becoming soulforged? And why were Jaz and Aden able to do it?

Misandrei's voice always had a commanding air about it, running training drills all day changed the way you spoke, "an adept runewielder can become a master of a particular type of runestone with decades of training and practice, building upon natural talent. But soulforging is something different, it is a *change* to a person's soul."

"Their *soul*?" Femira asked. There had been temples in Altarea where men in robes babbled about immortal souls inside people, but everyone knew those guys had a few blocks missing.

"Yes," Misandrei continued, "our bodies are the physical manifestation of the soul."

"I thought the Reldoni weren't very religious people?" Femira probed.

"We aren't," Misandrei affirmed. "When Queen Elyina killed the Sorcerer Kings, the temples lost much of their influence. But the soul has nothing to do with the temples or gods. It could be seen as a type of... map of a person's being. Or more like a series of instructions for our body to be."

"And *you* can change this?"

"There are... ways," Misandrei replied, looking at Garld.

"—with a soulstone," he confirmed.

"This is what I found in Altarea," Femira said, her voice rising in excitement. If Garld and Misandrei had both the knowledge and resources needed to make her soulforged, would that mean she would be as strong as Endrin?

"Indeed," Garld inclined his head.

"So, if you have the soulstone, why haven't you already turned the entire army into soulforged soldiers? Why restrict it only to those in the bloodshedders? Would doing this not make us the strongest force in the world?"

"There are a few reasons," Garld replied. "The cost of soulforging is... a *consideration* but also there are substantial gaps in our knowledge of how soulforging works. Much of the information had been destroyed during the fall of the Sorcerer Kings, when all of the known soulstones were hidden away. Our own founder—Queen Elyina—was a driving force behind that. But our scholars have confirmed that Elyina herself was a soulforged stonebreaker."

"The book," Femira mused, "the one in that room in Altarea."

"A guide on soulforging," Garld confirmed, "we have learned much from it, filling the holes in our knowledge. The existence of soulstone was little more than myth until only a few years ago. A cache of Elyina's journals was discovered buried within the Pillar of Reldon, confirming their existence. Along with crucial instruction on their usage."

"So the attack on Altarea... it was never about reclaiming the islands, it was about the soulstone?"

"Elyina's journals led us to believe that she had hidden her soulstone in Altarea, yes," Garld confirmed. "Altarea had been her seat of power for a time before she had claimed the Pillar of Reldon."

"So if the Altareans had the soulstone, why hadn't they created their own soulforged soldiers?"

"We believe they tried, but their knowledge was even more fragmented than our own. We discovered... evidence to suggest that they had made many attempts at doing this. The room where you discovered the soulstone we believe was a type of 'ritual room' where they were attempting to infuse aeristone affinity."

"I'm guessing they failed," Femira replied, "what makes you think that *you* have the knowledge to succeed where they did not?"

"From Elyina's notes, we have devised that there are multiple stages to soulforging. In the first stage, a person's soul can be bonded to a runestone. However once that is done, it closes off their edir to other runestones."

"So if you choose to become soulforged, you're limiting yourself to only using one type of runestone," she figured.

"Indeed, but the boost to your ability to use your chosen runestone is immeasurable. The book in the Altarean ritual room only had the instructions for extending this to include another runestone. The effects of this process on the body of a person who had not gone through the first stage is..." Garld's nose wrinkled, his otherwise handsome face curling in disgust. "It is unpleasant," he growled.

"And you had the knowledge from Elyina's journals on how to do the first stage, so you were able to succeed where they had failed?" Femira said.

Misandrei jumped in to take over the explanation. "Our understanding is still far from complete," she said, "Elyina's journals gave us the instructions for the first stages of infusion for aeristone, topaz and aradium. We needed only a soulstone to test it ourselves."

"Endrin..." Femira speculated, "he's been soulforged hasn't he?"

The new term still sounded strange, it was too close to the nonsense the lunatics in the temples blathered on about.

"That's why he can stonebreak so quickly," Femira didn't really need them to confirm it, her mind already working to connect to the dots. "He turned my dagger to dust."

"Many of us are," Misandrei confirmed, "there are one hundred in our ranks that have undergone the first infusion. Over the coming months, *all* of us will make the transition."

"Why are you telling me all of this now? You promised me nothing would be kept back," Femira directed to Garld.

"I didn't know if you could be trusted."

"You thought *I* was a spy?!" Femira laughed in surprise.

"It would've been foolish of me to not believe that," Garld defended, "I found a talented Keiran stonebreaker having just stolen a soulstone. The Keiran are among the other nations we believe to have uncovered a soulstone of their own."

"So you brought me here to keep an eye on me?"

"I saw your potential," Garld said with a touch of a smile, "and if you were indeed lying to me, then I saw you as a means to feed false information back to the Keiran Empire." Femira nodded in understanding, she looked to Misandrei.

"She knows?" Femira asked.

"I figured it out," Misandrei nodded, "Keiran women are sheltered from runewielding... but you. You were not sheltered, you had no knowledge at all of traditional runewielding. To be so accomplished in ability yet so uninformed in knowledge," her words weren't meant to be offensive but Femira felt herself grow a little hot in the face having her shortcomings highlighted.

"Aden and Jaz?" she asked, "do they know?"

"I assigned Aden to you to help in your training because he has an innate trust," Misandrei disclosed, "I don't think he questions even now that you are not Annali Jahar."

"Captain Misandrei and I are the only two who know the truth," Garld advised her, "and you must keep it that way. No one else is to know who you are." Femira immediately thought of Darza and whether she should bring his knowledge to their attention.

Karas had also known but had a stoneblade in his eye now, it wasn't likely he was going to be telling anybody anything. Folk in Keiran told stories that the Honorswords couldn't be killed, that the same magic that made them so strong stopped them from bleeding. Well Femira had seen a river of blood flowing from Karas so the stories couldn't all be true.

"Do you think the Honorswords are soulforged?" Femira asked curiously.

"I cannot think of any other reason they have the abilities they have," Garld responded.

"Sadrian Graves..." Femira considered. "He was too?"

"Graves was an excellent soldier and an exceptionally talented runewielder. I had him chosen to become soulforged but he was wasted on that spectacle."

"So the fight was a ruse to deceive the Honorswords into believing you hadn't discovered soulforging yet."

"A ruse that worked," Garld conceded, "that is until Landryn and Vestyr killed one of them tonight. Knowledge that we have soulforged soldiers will soon reach the Emperor, regardless of what happens. It's inevitable as our ranks grow and wasting Sadrian Graves in that deception was a mistake."

"Did you think I was working with Karas?" Femira's brain was working to connect all the pieces together.

"I thought it was a possibility," Garld said, "when Karas uncovered your guise and attacked, I could rule that out."

"I could *still* be a spy," Femira teased, then a thought surfaced to her mind. "That night I broke into Averstock's manse," she said with realisation dawning on her, "it was a test!"

"I had known for some time that Averstock had hidden some pages of Elyina's journal. It was a member of his House that discovered Elyina's journals in the first place. I had long suspected that he was keeping some information to himself for leverage."

"You had me tailed, to see if I would run off with Elyina's journal."

"I did."

"So Vestyr is working for you!"

"No," Garld grimaced, "Vestyr is not one of mine. I had Endrin follow you." Suddenly Endrin's distrust and aggression made sense to her. He believed she was a Keiran spy.

"Vestyr is working with Princess Allyn," Femira thought for a moment, "so she is working *against* the army's interests?"

"The Royal Council will deal with Princess Allyn. She is not my concern. From your description of Vestyr's ability, it confirmed my suspicion that she is also researching soulforging. The Aeth have always been secretive about their runewielding practices, perhaps she can garner valuable information from her relationship with the boy. Either way, she is inconsequential at this time."

"So, what does this all mean for me? By telling me all of this, does it mean that you're going to make me soulforged?"

"You have a natural affinity for stonebreaking," Garld smiled at her, "and your skills in stoneshaping have also progressed faster than I would have imagined. Your potential is great and Misandrei agrees with me on that point. Infusing you with an aradium runestone, I believe, will make you an invaluable asset to Reldon. My only concern is still your loyalty as you are not Reldoni, and beyond the training I have given you, you have no reason to pledge your life to our cause."

"I've done everything you've asked of me, without question!" Femira argued, anger rising in her, "I've passed your tests, what more can I do to prove my loyalty?"

Garld was silent in consideration, Femira couldn't hold herself back not with the promise of such power in her grasp.

"Make me one of the soulforged," she pleaded, "give me a chance and I can *prove* it to you!"

"There are few missions that could suit Femira's skills, sir," Misandrei added, "infusing her will open her stealth operations to a new level. And it won't take long before the Empire learns that Karas is dead."

"And figuring out we've unlocked the secrets to soulforging will soon follow," Garld agreed. "We need to start moving quickly to defend against retribution. Landryn killing the Honorsword has forced me to push carefully laid plans into action sooner than I'd hoped."

"Vestyr is also growing in his ability," Misandrei noted, "while we are busy looking to the Keiran, Allyn has been quietly moving her own pieces." Garld took a moment of consideration. Femira's heart fluttered in anticipation.

"We will do the first stage of soulforging," Garld said, and then solemnly to Femira, "prove yourself and we'll talk about the potential of moving to the second stage."

CHAPTER 14
Stoneskin and Rice Balls

Misandrei led Femira to the advanced training hall. They walked along the terraced mezzanine walkway that overlooked the central courtyard where recruits were running through training drills. In Epilas, the heat of the rising sun had a tendency to conjure a thick low hanging fog from the bay. The mist now hung over the courtyard. Coupled with the golden light of the morning, it cast a yellow haze over Femira's vision like she was inside a giant glowing earthstone.

"I hope you realise just how much of an opportunity Garld is offering you," Misandrei said, giving Femira a sidelong glance. Her dark red hair was shaved close at the sides, and the top was kept short. She was striking, and her ability in both the sword and runewielding had always set her as an intimidating presence.

"Are *you* soulforged?" Femira asked with genuine curiosity.

"I have been infused with aeristone," Misandrei replied.

"Is that how you move so fast?"

"Soulforging in and of itself does not make you any more skilled as a fighter. It does not grant the muscle memory that you've developed with your blades nor instil the knowledge of how to use them."

"But it makes you *faster*?" Femira pressed.

"You have yet to use any of the other elemental runestones," Misandrei continued, pointedly ignoring Femira's question to her annoyance. "You are becoming skilled with your aradium, but the others are still a mystery to you."

"What does that have to do—"

"—during the transference, when you draw material into your aradium, have you noticed the change in your body?"

"The change?" Femira didn't really consider it, she pulled in rock so quickly she didn't ever hold it in her for any length of time.

"For aradium," Misandrei replied without skipping a beat, "it toughens your skin. The rock or metal material literally strengthens your body's resistance… but it makes it heavier and slower," she then added with an arched eyebrow, "you've never noticed this?"

Femira shook her head, "No—I just move it right into the earthstone without thinking. With stoneshaping it's the same, I don't hold it in my body."

"You are quick," Misandrei nodded to herself, "in runewielding, we call this the '*hold*' ability. Each runestone has a *draw* ability, in the case of aradium it is pulling rock or metal into the stone. And finally the *push* ability, the push for aradium is stoneshaping, forming rock into a shape and putting force into it so that it can be used as a projectile. The *hold* ability is called 'stoneskin' by some. Many runewielders that favour aradium become guardians in battle, their enhanced resistance to attacks making them difficult to take down. These are the three types of ability that come with all elemental runestones; draw, hold and push."

"So for aeristone, this 'hold' ability makes you... lighter? And faster?"

"Exactly—Becoming soulforged hasn't affected my hold ability. I could move that fast using my aeristone as it was."

"So what did becoming soulforged do to you?" Femira implored.

Misandrei gave her a one-sided smile, it was an unsettling feature on her otherwise impassive face. She wasn't going to tell her. *Fine then, keep your secrets.* If Femira had secret abilities, she certainly wouldn't be rushing to tell everyone exactly how they worked. She could take an educated guess though as to what an aradium infusion would do to her if Vestyr and Endrin were anything to base off—assuming an aradium infusion was indeed what they had.

"Can a person be infused with multiple runestones?" Femira asked. As Misandrei had already noted, Femira didn't have any skill in the other runestones—not yet at least. Garld had mentioned that once she became soulforged with her earthstone, that she would be closed off from the other runestones. Was that permanent?

"Possibly, our knowledge with soulforging is still in its infancy. Becoming soulforged will make you significantly stronger in wielding the runestone you are bonded with, but it makes harnessing the others considerably more difficult. You're aware that a person can only truly master two runestones, yes?"

"Yeah—I thought that was just time though. The time it would take to become a true master of one would take years."

"That's true, but when you become soulforged, there's a change in *how* your edir works—it's difficult to explain. Garld described how it is a change to your very *being*. This is no exaggeration, my senses have changed, how I perceive the world has changed. This has all given me far superior command of aeristone, but at the cost of using *any* of the other runestones in a meaningful way. There might be a way to change this... but in the knowledge we've gathered, there isn't enough for us to go by just yet."

"Garld mentioned that the book in Altarea contained this information."

"*Fragmented* information," Misandrei corrected, "we want to be a lot more certain before we begin experimenting on people's souls."

Femira was quiet for a moment in consideration. She had made such minimal progress with any of the other runestones but by allowing herself to become soulforged, she could potentially be closing the door on those forever. Was that a path she really wanted to take? She thought of Landryn fighting Karas, the way his sword moved quicker than her eyes could follow. *He surely has the aeristone infusion too.* Loreli, always evading her attacks in training. Endrin puffing her dagger to dust. Vestyr trapping her in the ground.

Femira thought also about the small aeristone she had hidden away in her rooms, and its unused potential. She hadn't tried to sell it yet although that's what she'd always intended to do with it.

"Are you trying to talk me out of this?" Femira asked.

"Not at all," Misandrei replied, "we need people with your talents, Vreth," she used the name politely, not with spite the way that some of the recruits had. "We've been training soldiers," she continued, "but we need more like you. Agents that can move quietly in the shadows, and can make a hidden strike."

Despite all the training Femira had been given on learning to fight and using her runewielding abilities, she couldn't deny that stealth work was where she felt most alive.

"But I wanted you to be aware of what is to come," Misandrei went on, "the transition is... it can be *hard*. It's a very painful process and the aftermath... some find it difficult to adjust."

"Do I even have the choice?" Femira tossed out lightly. Misandrei pulled up, Femira also coming to a stop and looking back at her. Misandrei affixed her with an affronted glare.

"Do you think you're a prisoner here?" Misandrei demanded.

"Am I?"

"Perhaps Garld is right, maybe your loyalty is a concern."

"Are you serious?!" Femira contested, "an Honorsword almost killed me last night! Before that you can't blame me for thinking Garld might try to hand me over to them."

"Do you think we would invest this much time in you if we were going to just hand you off to Keiran?" Misandrei accused. "Do you think I would waste *my* time training you each day these past few months?"

Femira hadn't anticipated Misandrei's reaction, she hadn't really put much thought at all into the effort Misandrei had gone to on her behalf. Same with Jaz and Aden's lessons. She realised how temporary she'd been looking at all of this. She had been acting like this was just another job and that these people were all passing connections to her. But they were real people, people who saw what she could become.

"I'm sorry, Captain," Femira replied, looking at her feet, "I'm—I *am* grateful."

Misandrei was quiet for a time, her eyes still cold.

"Get some rest, Vreth," Misandrei said eventually, "you've had a long night and you'll need strength for tomorrow."

"But Garld wanted me to train for the infusion," she protested.

"I'm your Captain," Misandrei affirmed, "I decide when you need rest. Now return to your rooms." With that Misandrei strode past her.

***

It was only when Femira finally reached her rooms that she finally collapsed under the weight of the exhaustion she'd been carrying since the previous night.

She stripped off the dress and crawled into the sheets of her bed. The sheets were cool and welcoming. She hummed with satisfaction, closing her eyes and pressing face against the cold pillow.

The past week of unease over what Garld's intentions for her had been had made her sleep disturbed and restless. Knowledge that they wouldn't be giving her over to the Honorswords had released a tension in her shoulders that she hadn't even realised was there.

Despite the fatigue she felt in her body, Femira's mind was alight with the information Garld and Misandrei had given her. Knowledge that was initially hidden from her, but she could understand their rationale and hesitancy to tell her.

Couldn't she? She recognised the feeling she was having. It reminded her of when Lichtin would give her small nuggets of information on stonebreaking. She remembered with embarrassment the time Lichtin had told her that stonebreaking would only work at night, unless he adjusted her stone to work during the day. And she'd believed him, coming to him every time she needed to. She could recognise it all now as the different methods Lichtin had used to control her, to trick her into feeling that she *needed* him.

She grit her teeth thinking about Lichtin's lecherous face. She'd been so weak back then, not even six months ago. A part of her wanted to go back to Altarea, to stroll casually into the crewhouse with a pair of stoneblades floating about her. She'd make Lichtin kneel and kick him in the teeth. She would scream at him for everything he'd done to her. She'd force him to apologise for manipulating her, for controlling her.

For *betraying* her.

Her eyes watered thinking of her brothers. It was a simple job he'd promised them, they just needed to go rough up some lordling who owed a debt.

Femira wasn't sure why these memories were surfacing now. Maybe it was because of her conversation with Landryn that had brought them up. Once again, she wondered if she was remembering their faces correctly. It had been nearly six years since she'd last seen them.

Their bodies had been thrown off the cliff. Femira hadn't gone to the execution, but some of the thugs in the crewhouse had detailed how their bodies had bounced along the rocks. Femira clutched her eyes shut and thought about how she would drive the stoneblades into Lichtin's neck after he begged her for forgiveness.

***

Femira woke up to a gentle knocking at her door. She wasn't sure how long she'd been out for. The skin around her eyes felt cracked. She pulled herself up from the bed and hastily put on her bloodshedder uniform.

The door knocked again. "Just a second," she called out and splashed some water on her face from the washbasin and patted down her hair. Her stomach ached, reminding her that she hadn't eaten since the night before, she didn't have any food in her room and had been too tired to get any breakfast before crawling into bed earlier that morning.

She wasn't sure who she expected to be knocking at her door, but she sooner expected it to be Lichtin himself than the man who stood tall and imposing his fist raised for another knock.

"Prince Landryn," she breathed with genuine surprise, "w-what are you doing here?"

"I wanted to check on you," he replied, his face concerned.

"Why?" She didn't even think before the question was loose.

"I—uh," he struggled for a moment, "this was a mistake. I apologise."

"No," she insisted, "let's go for a walk." She closed her room door behind her and locked it although the metal lock was practically useless when so many in the barracks could stonebreak.

Femira's rooms were on the second floor, they were somewhat apart from the other recruits' dorms. She was Annali Jahar after all, and her illusory station gave her certain privileges.

"How are you, after last night?" Landryn asked.

"I'm fine," she lied. Truthfully, her head was still spinning from both the fight with Karas, and the revelations with Garld. "I'm made from tough stuff," she said with a smile.

They made their way up to the same terraced walkway that Femira and Misandrei had walked on early that day. The mess hall was on the other side of the barracks. A part of her doubted the Prince of Reldon would join her for a meal in the barrack's mess hall. She wondered longingly if they would even still be serving up breakfast at this hour.

The sun had risen fully, burning away the morning fog and beaming down on the marshalling yard. It looked like the recruits in the yard were still running through training exercises.

"There's more," Femira noted, counting the groups of recruits in the yard, "you've recruited more?"

"Garld brought them in, more hand-picked from the main army. The bloodshedders are poised to be the strongest arm of our military."

"Garld thought I was a spy," Femira wasn't entirely sure why she told Landryn that, but a part of her wanted to know if he thought that also.

"Can you blame him?" Landryn replied, "the other Generals thought he was insane bringing you here to train."

"I didn't think they even noticed me?"

"A member of the former Altarean royal family—a highborn woman from Keiran at that. It didn't go unnoticed."

"I don't blame you," Femira said. It felt uncomfortable pretending to be Annali with him when he seemed so pained to be talking with her. "For Reselas, I mean." He avoided meeting her eyes as she spoke. He stopped and leaned on the railing of the terrace.

"How could you not?" he sighed, "I… can't…. I don't know why you even tolerate speaking with me."

"I didn't know him," Femira said, "it was a political marriage. I'd only known him for a little more than a year…"

Femira paused thinking back to Annali's journals, "he was manipulative," she whispered. Landryn turned to her, his face unreadable. "He would control who I saw… who I could be friends with and who I couldn't." It was all true, the real Annali simply hadn't seen that as something wrong. She'd seen it as her new husband guiding her through the Altarean court. Femira saw it for what it was. Reselas and Lichtin had been one in the same; controlling and manipulative.

Femira had never seen Reselas' face. His image in her mind had Lichtin's face but wearing the same uniform Darza had; all pomp and self-importance. "He would lie to me," Femira seethed, "use my inexperience against me."

"I'm sorry," Landryn said, "that… sounds… he sounds like a terrible husband."

"I'm glad you killed him," Femira said with finality. She thought of driving her stoneblades into Lichtin's throat, of her faceless brothers and a young Femira forcing herself not to cry herself to sleep. Landryn looked at her with wide eyes, they looked yellow in the midday sun.

"Was he truly that awful?"

"My brothers are dead because of him," Femira said. She didn't even care if Annali's real brothers were still alive in Keiran. She didn't know if they were but they might as well be for all the good it did Femira. Landryn's face was stricken, confused, "I—I don't know what to say. I'm so sorry Annali."

"Don't be," she replied, "it's not your fault."

The pair remained silent for a time. Soldiers and officers were moving about the barracks, some saluted to Landryn as they passed, others moved on quickly with their duties. Femira idly wondered what it meant for someone of Annali's rank to be talking casually with the commander of the Reldoni army.

"What of your brother?" Femira asked, remembering the conversation they had had at the fountain, "where is he now?"

"Daegan is up north in Rubane. Allyn is worried about him. H-he's not like us," he admitted, and Femira gave him a speculative stare. "He's hindered," Landryn finished. Femira tilted her head to the side, she had never heard this term before.

She had lived in Altarea as long as she could remember and spoke Common Tongue as well as anyone. But her first language had been Keiran, so every now and then, a word she'd never heard stumped her. He looked a little uncomfortable but then again the Prince's stance always seemed a bit uncomfortable talking with her. "He can't use runestones," he added when he noticed her confused look.

"He never learned?" Femira replied, "I hadn't realised there was a word for that. Most people I've known prior to coming here never learned to runewield."

"It's not that... he *can't* learn."

"Well it's pretty hard," Femira replied lightly, "I still haven't figured out how to use anything but my earthstone. Maybe he just needs to be pushed harder?"

Landryn didn't respond, his posture becoming more stiff. He had an unfocused stare at the training yard below. Femira was finding her conversations with the Prince difficult. He didn't seem able to communicate properly, sometimes just trailing off or abruptly changing the conversation.

"Did you speak with Honorsword Jahasa?" Femira asked, deciding to move the conversation on, and she was curious if the other Honorsword was aware of Karas' demise. More importantly, she was concerned if he and Karas shared their suspicions about Annali's impersonation.

"Yes." was all that Landryn offered. His entire demeanour seemed off. *Was it something I said?*

Femira's stomach forced her mind back to the mess hall and what they had served for breakfast. A common dish in Reldon were these rice balls stuffed with some mystery concoction of spiced something. Her stomach growled at the thought of them. *Maybe I should head down, just to check if they're still serving.* She glanced down the walkway and saw that Garld was approaching them. He wasn't rushing to them but they were clearly his target.

"Commander," Garld inclined his head to Landryn.

"Hello Garld," Landryn said with a smile, he seemed a lot more relaxed than he had the previous night, "I hope you don't mind me distracting one of your recruits from her training."

"Annali has a lot to prepare for her next assignment," was Garld's response.

"I'm sorry, sir," Femira replied, "Captain Misandrei had instructed me to rest for tomorrow."

"Then I suggest you do that," Garld directed, "I have matters to discuss with the Commander."

"Yes, sir—of course," she replied quickly. She didn't want to offend Prince Landryn by leaping at the chance to remove herself from the conversation but her mind drifted back again to spicy rice balls.

"I'm glad to hear you're doing well, Lady Annali," Landryn said before she could leave and then he hastily added, "I wanted to say thank you."

"Ehm—I'm not sure why you're thanking me? Y*ou're* the one who took down Karas, sir," Femira said, narrowing her eyes.

"Oh, not that," Landryn replied, "your cousin, Daurond. He tells me that you supported us last night with the Altareans. He said you were quite *fierce* with Lord Himsbrack. He's been the spearhead of the group resisting Highlord Ingel's authority in Altarea."

"Himsbrack is a fool," Femira replied, at least he seemed to her in the brief interaction she'd had with him.

The conversation then reminded her of Darza and her promise to him in exchange for his silence, "Captain Darza on the other hand," Femira offered, "I think he's cleverer than he appears. He'll support Highlord Ingel too."

"Darza?" Landryn mused and then turned to Garld, "he's the stormguard Captain that assisted us during the take-over of the Altarean palace, wasn't he?"

"Indeed he was," Garld replied, giving Femira a curious glance. *I'm not entirely sure what I'm doing either, Garld.*

"Cowardly man, I thought," Garld continued, "… good self-preservation instincts."

"The other Altarean highborn think poorly of him," Femira noted, "but with the stormguard numbers decimated, you might not get much resistance appointing him as Lord Himsbrack's replacement."

"I'll suggest that to Highlord Ingel," Landryn replied. *Was that how easy it was to get someone promoted? A few flippant suggestions from some nobody.* But then again, Annali wasn't some nobody, as far as Landryn knew she had been an active player in the Altarean court.

"You spoke with Daurond?" Garld asked Femira, a small smile on his lips.

"I did—I was surprised to hear about how much he's been doting on me since I arrived. Especially considering that's the first time I've seen him *since* arriving."

"Indeed," Garld chuckled, "I had not had the chance to for you two to *catch up* prior to the feast." Did he find it amusing? Throwing her into a crowd and pretending to be Annali with minimal training seemed to be a game that Garld was enjoying.

"Daurond is a guest in my father's court," Landryn put in, "and from what I've seen the man loves to make a show, and tell a story… I'm not entirely sure how he ended up here after his exile from Keiran.."

"His lifestyle choices favour Reldoni courts rather than those of Altarea," Garld said.

Femira still suspected that Daurond was another of Garld's imposters. She wondered at the scale of many many frauds Garld had working for him. It was also a possibility that Garld was simply blackmailing Daurond, having him openly acknowledge Femira as Annali made it very hard for anyone to say that she wasn't. Femira still could hardly believe that people that had *actually known* Annali Jahar hadn't been able to see through her—they could tell something was off but they didn't seem to suspect she was an outright imposter.

"You don't need to thank me for that," Femira brushed off Landryn's initial sentiment and then remembered she was addressing the commander of the army and added a quick, "sir." She was finding that she was slipping out of her Annali persona more and more, but at the same time she wasn't being the same Femira she was before either. Maybe the two were slowly merging?

Nah, I'm just tired. And starving, her stomach growled at her, she'd gotten far too used to the feeling of not-being-hungry. Back in Altarea, she'd lived meal to meal, Lichtin paid her well enough after big jobs. But the big jobs were few and far between and most of that in-between time when her money would run low, she'd resort back to stealing food. Having all her meals for free in the barracks remained a luxury she was wholly unaccustomed to. *They might be setting up for lunch about now.*

"I best go," Femira said to Landryn and then saluted Garld. He nodded his approval and she made for the stairs leading down to the mess hall. She prayed to

gods she didn't know that they were serving those mystery spice rice balls today.
Was there a rice ball god?

CHAPTER 15

A Healer's Burden

"It really is a groundbreaking thing," Aden said. He was sitting on a crate watching Femira and Jaz run through a series of combat drills. At Femira's insistence, it had become a regular habit for the three to meet and spar in between other duties. She always wanted to improve her combat skills, and sparring was the most effective way she'd found to do that.

"But if people have been doing this since Queen Elyina's day, why is it only being used now?" Jaz asked, moving into a practised defence stance, readying to parry Femira's daggers.

"Yeah, wasn't that like a thousand years ago?" Femira added while gauging Jaz for a break in his defence.

"Hardly," Aden scoffed, "Queen Elyina only founded Reldon little over two hundred years ago." Aden chuckled as if that was something Femira should've known. *He should know better than that at this stage.*

She took a leap at Jaz's opened flank but his blunt training sword whirred and deflected her daggers.

"But still two hundred years! How have we not been using soulstones this entire time?" Jaz rebuked, taking a step back and evading another attack from Femira.

"After the fall of the Sorcerer Kings, a lot of their knowledge was either hidden or destroyed. From what I can gather, Elyina herself seemed to be behind that, maybe she didn't want an army of soulforged soldiers threatening her authority?"

"Leaving her open to attack from another nation?" Jaz countered.

"There's not a lot of information from that time," Aden replied, "perhaps Reldon was the only country that had discovered soulforging?—Annali, what are you *doing*?"

Getting past Jaz's defensive manoeuvres had proven difficult and she could feel her endurance waning. Instead of fighting clean she decided to use her earthstone to raise three mounds of rock from the dirt of the yard. She rolled behind one of them.

"Having stronger runewielders in your army doesn't have any drawbacks," Femira called out, leaning her back against the mound. She could feel the vibrations of the earth around her. She isolated the space where Jaz stood, sensing his slow approach to her mound. She could sense the pressure of his feet against the earth.

"She could have conquered more than just Reldon," Femira continued, "it was a wasted opportunity if you ask me."

As Jaz cautiously neared, she pulled at the earth at his feet—as much as she could draw in—and leapt up onto her mound. Jaz stumbled just a fraction as the earth at his feet shifted. She couldn't make a hole large enough for him to fall in like Vestyr had done to her, but it was enough to make him stagger which was all she needed.

Eager for the win, Femira batted away his sword with one of her daggers, and followed through with a kick to his torso using the higher vantage. The impact of her foot caused him to double over, dropping his sword.

"Yield!" Jaz spluttered, holding up a hand to her before she moved in for another kick. "Yield! Yield!"

Femira hopped off the mound, and then swept her hand over it and the other two nearby, pulling the material into her earthstone. Normally, she would immediately fill her earthstone with it, but she kept it in her body as Misandrei had told her. She felt it surging, the vibrations moving through her in tune with her heartbeat.

She'd never held so much in her body before. She felt heavy and rigid. Her skin didn't *look* any different but it felt tougher to the touch as she laboriously ran her hand over her forearm. Moving her arm felt like moving through water, like she was resisting against her own body to move.

"Hit me," Femira ordered, looking at Jaz with a wry smile.

"What?" he wheezed. "No—I yielded."

"I want to test something," she insisted.

"You're going to hurt me, aren't you?"

"You don't trust me?" She asked innocently.

"Not in the slightest."

"I just want to try my hold ability," she pleaded.

"Ah stoneskin," Aden chimed, "you've figured out how to do it?"

"I think so, I didn't even know it was a thing until yesterday," with difficulty, Femira raised her heavy fortified arms in a defensive block. "Come on, come at me, Jaz."

Jaz was hesitant at first, walking slowly towards her.

"Come on already, you wuss!"

He took a half-hearted swing at her block. She felt the impact but the attack felt more like a child swatting at her.

"Ah," Jaz recoiled, waving his hand limply in front of himself, "felt like punching a wall," he grumbled.

"Guess it works," Femira grinned, "thanks Jaz."

"Yeah—whatever," he replied walking over to pick up his discarded blade, "you want to try against this?" he offered.

"From what I've read," Aden warned, "stoneskin won't protect you much against an actual blade, it will still cut you."

"Yeah," Femira considered, "I think I'm good on that one Jaz, thanks for the offer though."

She pulled herself up onto the crate as Aden jumped off. He cracked his neck and worked his shoulder joints before drawing his own sword, readying for his round with Jaz.

"I assume you both are going for the topaz infusion?" Femira asked, knowing they both had a preference for that type of runestone.

"Traditionally, there wasn't many combat applications for topaz runestones," Aden began, "topaz specialists can use carbon pulled from their bodies to ignite external objects. However, this is an incredibly dangerous practice that has quite detrimental long term physical effects on the body. These days, however, grenadiers carry a host of incendiaries on hand and use their topaz to create bursts of flame with those."

"Grenadier?" Femira asked, she hadn't heard that term before.

"Combat topaz runestone users. Grenadiers throw incendiaries and ignite them across the battlefield," Aden informed.

"They're not considered particularly versatile soldiers," Jaz added, "I was a grenadier before being recruited into the bloodshedders. Enemy topaz users can quell the fires pretty quickly, and if there's a wavecaller in the opposing line, then you're useless."

"So if there isn't much use for grenadiers in the military, why are you even here?" Femira directed at Jaz.

"Someone needs to bring up the average attractiveness of division," he threw back, flashing a grin at her.

"I suppose we don't really know what grenadiers will be capable of with soulforging," Aden shrugged, "considering how powerful you've described Vestyr and Endrin's abilities are with the aradium infusion, it's possible that the ideas around the practical uses for topaz in warfare has changed. We do know that an adept topaz and aquamarine wielder can manipulate water and temperature and they can make pretty effective projectiles of ice."

"You still hung up on those iceblades?" Jaz jibed.

"I can *almost* get it," Aden rebuked, "I don't own my own aquamarine runestone though. The barracks will only let me train for a few hours a week with one. I don't know if you've noticed Annali but if you want to get skilled with a particular runestone, you kinda need to own one yourself."

Femira *had* noticed. She'd only been able to practise with her own aradium, and her repeated failed attempts to use the aeristone she'd stolen. *Is it really stolen if the guy was dead?* Looted was a more accurate term. It sure felt like stealing regardless of the technicality of it.

"You can use waterstones—aquamarine—too?" Femira cocked her head at Aden, from what she'd seen he was already an adept topaz and aradium runewielder.

"Aden is a bit of a prodigy if you hadn't copped on to that, Vreth," Jaz chuckled, and Aden blushed.

"I'm not a prodigy," he replied awkwardly, "I can just pick up runewielding a bit quicker than others is all. It's why I was recruited here."

"I'm surprised your family didn't try to push you into being a wavecaller, they're the most respected runewielders in the country," Jaz said.

"There's a reason for that," Aden replied, "wavecalling is an incredibly difficult thing to do, and there's a lot more at stake if you get it wrong."

"Yeah but you're all prodigy-like," Jaz grinned.

"There's a big difference between controlling a stream of water and diverting an entire ocean."

"Is that why the tides in Epilas aren't that big?" Femira said, "you use waterstone wielders to stop it?"

"Kind of... but not exactly," Aden replied, "there's the tidewall that takes the biggest brunt of it. The wavecallers though—they work the city's coastwall to guide the ocean currents away from Epilas. That prevents the bay from flooding, it's a monumental undertaking."

"So the main thing stopping Epilas from being smashed away by the tides is the wavecallers?"

"That's right," Aden replied, "wait until you see the harbour on Unionsday and Lua Nova, the uniontide is so massive that the wavecallers form an enormous wall of ocean to stop it." Femira shuddered, remembering the uniontides in Altarea. The waves often lapped up over the cliffs of the island, the stormguards had to keep it contained from flooding the city. She could imagine what would happen here with no cliffs along the shoreline to protect the city. *Without the wavecallers this city would be swept away, surely.*

"If you admire them so much, why *didn't* you try to join them?" Femira pointed out.

"My family," Aden sighed, finally resigned, "both my parents were in the military, and theirs before them. We're quite low nobility—my grandparents were commoners," he directed a glare at Jaz, "and I'm not ashamed of that." Jaz didn't respond but Femira sensed this was a topic they'd discussed before.

"My family is where we are *because* of the military. I can't turn my back on that." That response seemed to satisfy Jaz who just nodded in understanding but Femira wasn't sold.

Who cares what your parents did? You're not obligated to follow them. The last Femira had heard, her mother worked in one of the brothels in Altarea and Femira didn't feel any sense of familial duty to follow her into *that* vocation. Even if she'd known her father, she didn't think she'd be in any rush to follow in his footsteps either.

Annali—on the other hand—she'd moved to a different country, and married a total stranger because her family told her to. She'd just blindly gone along with it as if she'd had no choice in the matter.

She felt like telling Aden to stop being ridiculous, that if he wanted to be wavecaller, he should stop caring what others wanted of him, and to just do it. She restrained herself though, highborn had a strange way of looking at the world, and she'd already let herself slip back into Femira too much around Aden and Jaz.

The pair had started their bout and were moving through the rhythms of practised sword fighters. Jaz was considered one of the most skilled amongst the recruits, although he often restrained himself when training against Femira. Aden was one of those people that seemed to naturally excel in anything he was given, he wasn't the *best* sword fighter but he was certainly a great deal better than a lot of the other recruits.

"You didn't answer my question," Femira called out to them, interrupting their fight.

"What's that?" Aden asked, the moment of distraction was enough for Jaz to deftly disarm him. Jaz flicked Aden's sword into the air and snatched it.

"What infusion are you going for?" Femira repeated.

"Oh," Aden said, rubbing at his swordhand, "I don't know, yet."

"Did Misandrei warn you about not being able to use other runestones?"

"She did," Aden replied, "and that's a concern. I might take a little more time to decide—Jaz, you're going for the topaz infusion today, right?"

"Yep," Jaz replied, looking at Aden's sword in his hand appreciatively, "stick to what you know. This sword is actually pretty good workmanship," he noted with surprise.

"Just because my family isn't as wealthy as yours doesn't mean we can't afford quality weapons," Aden replied, defensively.

"Didn't mean any offence," Jaz said, and flippantly tossed the blade back to Aden. "I'll take a guess here, Vreth, that you're going for the aradium infusion?" Jaz asked, and Femira nodded.

"What was the deal with the three mounds?" Jaz probed, rubbing at his neck and giving her a confused look.

"What do you mean?"

"In our last fight, you made three mounds of earth. I watched you duck behind one of them, so what was the point of the other two?"

"You thought about them right?"

"Yeah," he conceded.

"So it distracted you?"

"Barely," he scoffed.

"That was all I needed," Femira shrugged, "you approached more cautiously because you weren't sure what I was planning."

"I'm not so sure about that," Jaz replied, uncertain.

"Well I won," she said, smugly, "so my three mound strategy worked."

"How—if it didn't distract me?"

"The outcome didn't change, I still won," she answered, jumping down off the crate, "I'm going to finish up and get some lunch. They haven't told us much about what's involved with the soulforging, but something tells me, I'd rather not do it on an empty stomach."

***

Misandrei and Garld guided Femira down to the lower underground levels of the barracks.

They'd taken a long flight of stairs that had brought them down, and passed through hallways and chambers of stoneshaped tunnels. Stoneshaped passages weren't considered very secure as a stealthy stonebreaker could easily forge a path in but it would be unlikely for someone to tunnel this deep below ground without knowing for certain there was something there. Gaslamps lined the walls and provided a flickering orange light, casting long dark shadows as they descended deeper into the tunnels.

"I didn't know any of this was here," Femira mused, "I bet you hide all kinds of goodies down here," she added with a smirk.

"The most secure rooms are shielded," Garld advised.

"Wood or metal?"

"Thinking of robbing us?" he asked with an arched eyebrow and small smile, "mostly wood. Although some have both steel and wooden shielding."

"Definitely hiding something good down here so," she replied, "dangerous game, giving that information to a known thief."

"I'm quite confident you're not going to take advantage of this information," Garld said, "especially considering we're planning to give you the most valuable thing we have to offer."

They arrived at a set of unadorned steel doors. Misandrei pushed them open, and held them for Garld and Femira to enter. The room inside reminded Femira of a chirurgeon's surgery that she'd once broken into. She'd stolen a bloodstone from that job. *Not that I got much of the cut out of that.*

There were six beds arrayed along the back wall. Along the walls were tables with stacks of notebooks and various surgical tools. Just like the hallways, the room was lit by gaslamps affixed to the walls.

Five of the beds were occupied already by unconscious men and women in Reldoni military uniforms. Not the black uniforms of the bloodshedders, these soldiers were from the general ranks. Femira had originally thought that the varying colours of soldier's uniforms in the main military was a ranking system but she had later learned from Jaz that the colours denoted which Highlord the soldier served. These soldier's uniforms were purple with black dragonhide elements. She didn't know which Highlord's colours they belonged to.

The sight of the unconscious soldiers gave Femira an apprehensive pause. "What is this place?" She faltered, reluctant to walk into the room.

"This," Garld disclosed, his arms outstretched as he entered the room, "is where we have been bringing humanity to its next stage."

"General Garld has performed over one hundred soulforging rituals since we first discovered the soulstone," Misandrei explained.

"You've been doing the infusions yourself?" Femira asked, taking a hesitant step into the room.

It smelled like a chirurgeon's surgery; the unnatural clean aroma of rubbing alcohol. The smell reminded Femira of the times when some of Lichtin's thugs would get wounded in knife fights with rival gangs. Lichtin had known a healer that smelled like he drank the stuff more than he used it. Lichtin had some kind of leverage over him because the man would stagger in at any hour at Lichtin's request to tend to any of the boys that needed stitching.

"You don't know much about where I come from," Garld replied, he went over to one of the desks and began unpacking some journals.

"You're Reldoni," Femira replied.

"Not the physical *where*," he said with a smile, "when I was a young man I had great ideals about saving people. I come from a highborn family—although not strictly a military family. But my mother and father were close friends of Landryn's grandfather. My mother was one of the finest surgeons in the King's employ and I took to her tutelage with a tenacious fervor."

"You're a *healer*?" Femira's head spun to him in surprise.

"I was," he clarified with a bitter chuckle, "I trained as both healer and surgeon. In fact, bloodstone remains to this day where I am most proficient. I had always trained in the sword, as many of my peers had, and my father had not neglected my training in this regard. My father had been King Abhran's swordmaster, a role that I later assumed myself for Prince Landryn."

"So it was your father that pushed you into joining the army?" Femira asked.

Garld gave her a strange smile, one she didn't recognise.

"No—my father approved of my choice of profession. I was a surgeon for many years and it was long after his death that I joined the military," his voice took on a bitter edge. "One of the sad truths I had learned was that the sword can save many more lives than the scalpel."

"General Garld is likely the most proficient wielder of soulstone in Reldon," Misandrei put in, taking up position beside the empty bed, "you are in good hands, Vreth."

Femira nodded. She felt a wave of calm wash over her, her resolve tempered. Had she really considered backing out now simply because Garld would be doing the soulforging ritual personally? Who else would she even trust to do it? Knowing that he was a skilled healer was comforting reassurance. She still had no idea what the soulforging ritual entailed other than it would hurt.

She glanced over at the unconscious soldiers. They were breathing, and looked to be sleeping peacefully.

"Who are they?"

"Potentials," Misandrei said quickly, "you need not concern yourself with them. They will be gone before you wake."

"I'll be asleep?" she asked, "like them?"

"Soulforging is... *taxing* on the body... and the soul," Garld informed her delicately. "We've advised you already that the process will be painful. Many fall unconscious from the exertion."

Femira nodded nervously but again, she felt oddly calm. *What is there to be nervous about?* This was what she wanted, wasn't it? Her emotions felt like they were swinging back and forth between irrational calm and very justified trepidation.

"Are you sure you want to continue?" Garld asked.

"Yes," she affirmed with resolution, another wave of calm certainty washing over her, "just got jitters is all." It was the same feeling she would get before a big job, she felt like she needed to pee. "Let's get started," she said, "what do I need to do?"

"Remove your shirt and jump on the bed," Misandrei instructed, nodding to the bed beside her.

Femira had never been embarrassed or ashamed of her body the way that highborn Altarean women seemed to be. Reldoni women were a lot more like her in that regard, she'd often seen women in the sparring yard stripping off to the waist with the men when it got hot in the midday sun. The setting here was a lot *creepier* though.

"This isn't some kind of weird sex slave dungeon is it?" Femira mocked as she pulled off her uniform tabard. The room wasn't cold but now that she was half naked, she felt the chill from being so far underground. She climbed up onto the raised bed. There were leather straps for restraining hands which she eyed sceptically.

"Sometimes the body can thrash involuntarily," Misandrei revealed, "I can hold you down if you prefer not to be restrained by those."

"Yeah, I'd really rather not be strapped half naked to a bed in a creepy dungeon, thanks."

"Your aradium too," Misandrei pointed to the earthstone on the silver chain around Femira's neck. "We'll need that for the infusion. Some people don't believe that a particular runestone can be attuned to a person's edir but I disagree. I think it will go better if we use your aradium for the ritual."

Garld was walking over to her as she undid the clasps on the chain and handed it Misandrei. She felt vulnerable without her earthstone. She hadn't parted with it once since before she'd broken into the Altarean palace. It had become part of her and having someone else handle it made her feel uncomfortable.

Misandrei had never given Femira any reason to not trust her. Not only had she figured out her secret, she'd kept quiet about it, and continued to train her diligently in runewielding. Femira appreciated that the woman pushed her to be a better fighter and runewielder.

Garld was carrying a notebook and a small runestone. It was clear, like a diamond, but Femira could see that there was a swirling pattern of rainbow colours inside the stone. She recognised the mesmerising stone immediately as the soulstone she'd found in Altarea.

"Are you ready to begin?" Garld asked.

"Of course," she plastered a half-hearted grin on her face, "Let's get to—"

—Pain erupted from her chest, cutting off her words. A searing hot sensation burned across her chest like a thousand needles digging into her. They burrowed into her and she gasped for air.

She was dimly aware of Misandrei pinning her to the bed as the pain built more and more. Garld stood over her impassively, holding the soulstone above her, a brilliant rainbow light emitting from it. As the light grew, so did the agonising sensation tearing through her chest.

She tried to scream, to beg him to stop but no sound would come out, only rasping breathless croaks. The world dimmed, everything fading to blackness but for the intense light of the soulstone in Garld's hands.

Once again, Femira felt a wave of calm flood over her, overpowering the pain. She could see Garld's face in the light of the soulstone. He looked sad but determined. A part of her understood that the calm was coming from Garld, that *he* was making her feel this way. She felt his *presence*—not just standing over her—but in her mind. She felt a connection to him she'd never experienced before, an unwavering sense of trust and certainty that she was going to be ok, that this pain was temporary.

Femira could *feel* Garld's fondness for her, it was a bizarre sensation that she couldn't akin to anything she'd felt before. She'd never had any children or younger siblings she'd needed to care for but she imagined that this is what that feeling was. The feelings of caring and devotion for another person that she felt flowed into her from Garld.

Femira felt his hand press against her head, and the calm washed over her. The pain was still there, growing in resonance with the light of the soulstone. It burned through her. It attacked her lungs and heart and caught the breath in her throat before it could leave. But she knew she was safe. She was going to be ok.

Her gaze was fixed on the rainbow light above her and everything seemed to fade away.

***

Garld rested a fatherly hand on Vreth's forehead. Her dark hair was slick with sweat, her head was hot under his touch, her breaths rapid and violent. She had fallen unconscious—thankfully—as this was often the most gruesome part of the task.

His hand still clutched the shining soulstone, and its power flowed through him. He looked down at Vreth's body, the flesh on her chest had been pulled away exposing her ribcage and the organs beneath.

The miraculous nature of the soulstone's power was keeping her alive, kept her heart beating and her lungs inhaling and exhaling as she breathed. It was a wonder; to see a body exposed yet working. In his time as a healer and surgeon, Garld had performed many surgeries, and was well used to seeing the inner workings of a person's body but that had been a pale comparison against this marvel. To have visibility on everything that was happening at once was impossible—or so he once believed.

Garld didn't allow himself time to awe at the majesty of the internal human form, and instead focused his efforts on the task at hand. He glanced down at his notebook, spread open on the operating table. It contained the runic formula that he had been tweaking and adapting since first uncovering Elyina's journals. He began to mutter to himself as he read, they weren't incantations or any such nonsense but it was hard not to see what he was doing as some kind of arcane ritual.

Garld's education had been extensive and human anatomy had been part of that. As a practising surgeon, he had learned that the knowledge and the application were two wildly different things. knowledge of how to repair a human heart was certainly a requirement to *doing* it, but the skill and practice of repairing a heart with the regenerative healing capabilities of a bloodstone was another thing entirely.

When Garld had first saved a man's life, he'd felt like a god. He had brought a man back from the brink of death with his skill and knowledge. That was but a faint shadow of what he was achieving now, what he could *see* now. Where the bloodstone had given him the ability to see into a person's body and repair it; the soulstone allowed him to look deeper. He could see down past the biological mechanics of the body, past the fibres of muscle and tissue, right down to the very threads of human existence.

As a healer, Garld had known of the existence of viruses and bacteria, how they both created and defended disease, and how the human body was utterly dependent on them. Now he could *see* them. Not only those, but all the miniscule particles that made up a person, how it all connected together in a beautiful matrix. Underpinning all of it, was a pattern of interlocking threads.

Garld had come to recognise this as the *soul*. It was like a woven tapestry, and it was the makeup of what a person was. The soulstone—while he held its power in him—allowed Garld to *see* the soul. But not only that, he could *change* it. His earliest attempts at this had been catastrophic failures, but now—with Elyina's journals and his own notes—he was close to perfecting it. He began to shift and adapt the pattern, directing his gaze between the notebook and Vreth. He didn't need to be looking at her, in fact, he could close his eyes and still be able to sense the threads of her soul.

Vreth's muscles began to undulate, the bones adjusting and the muscle fibres themselves disconnecting and reknitting. Her ribcage opened and her heart shifted into a more central position, her other organs refitting themselves.

"Now," Garld instructed Misandrei, "her aradium."

Misandrei raised her hand, and dropped the aradium onto Vreth's exposed heart. As the stone fell, its descent slowed in defiance of gravity. It slowed until ultimately the runestone remained still, hovering an inch above Vreth's heart.

Golden-red light began to emit from the stone and from Vreth's body, the light coalesced and merged, shining brightly. The light around the aradium grew more intense until it became difficult to look at before descending inside of Vreth's heart, merging with it.

Vreth's veins began to glow rhythmically in tune with her heartbeat. Her heart was now pumping the aradium-infused blood, carrying the power of the runestone throughout her body.

Through the soulstone, Garld could feel the shift in the fabric of Vreth's body. Subconsciously, she was trying to reject the infusion, and her body fought against it, as human bodies tended to when you introduced a foreign object into them.

Violently, Vreth's muscles began to spasm, her limbs jerking against the constraints. Ultimately, Vreth's own body would have pushed itself to death if it were not for the soulstone actively working to keep her alive and to merge the aradium with her soul.

The beauty of runestones was that they had their own threads of existence. They were both similar yet completely alien to the strands that made up a human but with instinctive knowledge Garld received from wielding the soulstone, he understood how the pattern worked and how it could be woven into Vreth's threads. He began to knit them together. Throughout Vreth's entire body, at the tiniest scale, each of the strands began to unfold and allow the aradium to lock in before reknitting together into a perfected form.

Garld was never aware of how much time passed when he performed the soulforging ritual, it felt like seconds to him but he had been often told that it took hours. Using the soulstone, he reformed Vreth's flesh over her chest exactly as it had been. Down to her core, Vreth was completely different. He had fundamentally changed the make-up of her soul.

The formula Garld used had been perfected over time to avoid creating abominations of flesh and power, so in appearance Vreth looked almost identical to how she had been. She would likely note the minute differences when she woke; her muscles and bones would be stronger than they had been, the power of the aradium flowing as part of her being rather than through it. Before, her body had been the conduit through which the power of the aradium was harnessed, but now she was *both* the power and instrument.

Garld felt the power and light of the soulstone begin to drain away, now fully spent... along with his own strength. His hand was still on her forehead and was wet with both his and her sweat. His legs felt weak and he struggled to keep himself standing. Garld smiled, stroking her hair, leaning against the bed frame for support.

"Another child of Reldon," he said softly through the exhaustion, "another shield with which we defend our home," he looked to Misandrei, "she did well."
"It is done?" Misandrei asked.
"Indeed," he replied, "her vitals are stabilising. Her body didn't resist as much as others."
"She had been using that aradium for years. It was already quite attuned to her—and she to it. Even when I tried to teach her how to use the other elemental runestones, her edir couldn't pick them up. I think this one had already ingrained itself too deeply in her."

"A lot of the King's scholars consider attuning to a runestone to be mere superstition," Garld knotted his eyebrows at her.
"Until proven," she scoffed, "those scholars in the Pillar have been reading books on runestone theory for decades but *I've* been the one training runewielders for years." Garld smiled, he himself had been one of those academics once, discounting the input of those who actually worked in the field. Assuming that all the knowledge in the world had already been discovered, documented and accounted for in the King's library. Extensive as those stacks were, they were woefully lacking.

"She had a lot of natural talent," Misandrei observed as she checked over Vreth's vitals, the girl's veins were still pumping a faded golden light under her dark skin. It would dull further over the next few minutes as the rest of the aradium diffused into her body. There was no further risk of her body rejecting it, not now that Garld had reshaped her soul. "I'm interested to see how she takes to the infusion," Misandrei continued, "she could be a powerful force on the battlefield."

"I had not envisaged a battlefield for this one," Garld replied and with effort, he staggered over to a chair by his desk, collapsing into it. He gave himself only a few seconds of respite before laboriously lifting his hand to begin writing notes in his notebook.

"She will be a tool for stealth operations," he determined.

"She's a novice in her combat skills, but she could be a formidable opponent," Misandrei argued.

"I will consider it... formula seventeen—" he said whilst making a mark against a ciphered equation, "—seems to be the most stable. Who else did I try this method with?" Garld asked, not looking up from his notes. Misandrei answered without checking her own notebooks, "Endrin Farit and Karylle Restores."

"Karylle is dead?"

"Yes."

"I don't think her body had fully taken the aradium," he noted that against the formula, "Endrin hasn't been showing any signs of degradation, has he?"

"Not that I could tell, although with some of the others it had come with increased runewielding. Endrin hasn't been reporting any signs though."

"Let's keep an eye on him," Garld judged, closing his notebook.

Straining against his aching muscles, Garld pushed himself up from the chair, and walked over to one of the desks where he placed his notebook in a locked drawer. It was a wooden mechanism, not overly complicated and he didn't doubt that Vreth could pick it given enough time. He didn't doubt her skills would keep her out of this room if she wanted to get in. The fact that so few knew of this place's existence was what made it so secure. The stacks of notebooks were written in his— or Misandrei's hand. All of his valuable formulae used his own personal cipher and would be near impossible for anyone to crack even should anyone happen across it.

He lingered for a while at the desk, he didn't put the soulstone in the desk, something of such unequivocal value would be kept on his person at all times.

"It won't be kept a secret for very long, will it?" Misandrei asked as if reading his thoughts.

"No," he replied, "Landryn made a foolish move killing the Honorsword. He has forced us to show our hand to the Keiran. They will soon put the pieces together and realise that we have rediscovered soulforging."

"He saved this one though," Misandrei said, nodding her head to Vreth.

"There were less violent means to secure her. Landryn opted to kill him because he wanted to. He was tired of pretending that his pride wasn't hurt each time the Honorswords claimed to be more powerful than him."

Vreth's breathing began to return to a normal pace, the pulsing light in her veins beginning to dissipate. Garld smiled, walking back over to her.

Perfection... she will be one of my greatest masterpieces. Risen from nothing, and placed amongst the highest nobility along with immeasurable runewielding ability... and irrefutably loyal to him.

Some might question a thief's loyalty... or their resolve. But despite what Vreth thought of herself, Garld saw so much more in her. There was a tenacity, a determination, and a thirst for power that she has yet to even realise in herself. And Garld was her benefactor, with him she would reach heights she could never have imagined.

In reciprocation of this, Garld would hold her unwavering loyalty. He had felt it through the connection, when his edir had merged with hers. Vreth craved for more, and so long as he held the soulstone and the knowledge of how to wield it, he had no doubt she would continue to serve.

The soulstone had returned to its drained state, its light was utterly spent. Once drained, its appearance looked like a cloud of rainbow colours swirling slowly, trapped inside of an uncut diamond.

Garld's gaze had pointedly avoided the other five bodies in the room. *The cost I must bear for this.* He looked upon them now, they deserved that respect from him. All that remained of them were withered husks in the shape of human bodies. The soulstone had sucked every shred of lifeforce from them in an unrelenting torrent as it powered the changes in Vreth. It was a fair exchange toward the cost of perfection.

"These men and women pledged their lives to the defence of Reldon," Garld intoned, "and today Reldon has claimed them."

"I'll ensure their stipends are paid to their families," Misandrei proposed, "Highlord Nallan's quartermaster is known to be... frugal."

"Highlord Nallan will also want a report on how his soldiers died, we'll need something to justify why their bodies couldn't be recovered."

"A fire? The Reinish have been deploying more grenadiers at the border at Adesh." Misandrei suggested.

"The skirmishes against the Reinish are too public, discrepancies might be noticed."

"Lost at sea then?" Misandrei offered, "there are reports of corsairs raiding the villages along the Tidewall."

"Hmm," Garld mused, "there are rumours that there are Altarean warships among them." He clenched his jaw for a moment and considered, "put a small team together and destroy the Altarean corsairs. We can claim we lost these on that mission."

"Of course, sir," Misandrei replied dutifully.

"I need to rest," Garld breathed. The strain of wielding the soulstone for even such a short time wore him out more than full days of healing with a bloodstone. But he couldn't argue with the results. *A small price for what we're achieving.*

He looked back over to the husks of the sacrificed soldiers. It was a cruel joke of the world that lives must be spent to prevent future deaths, and Garld would allow his own morality to be the barrier between them and a better world.

I will carry this burden so that others can be free of it.

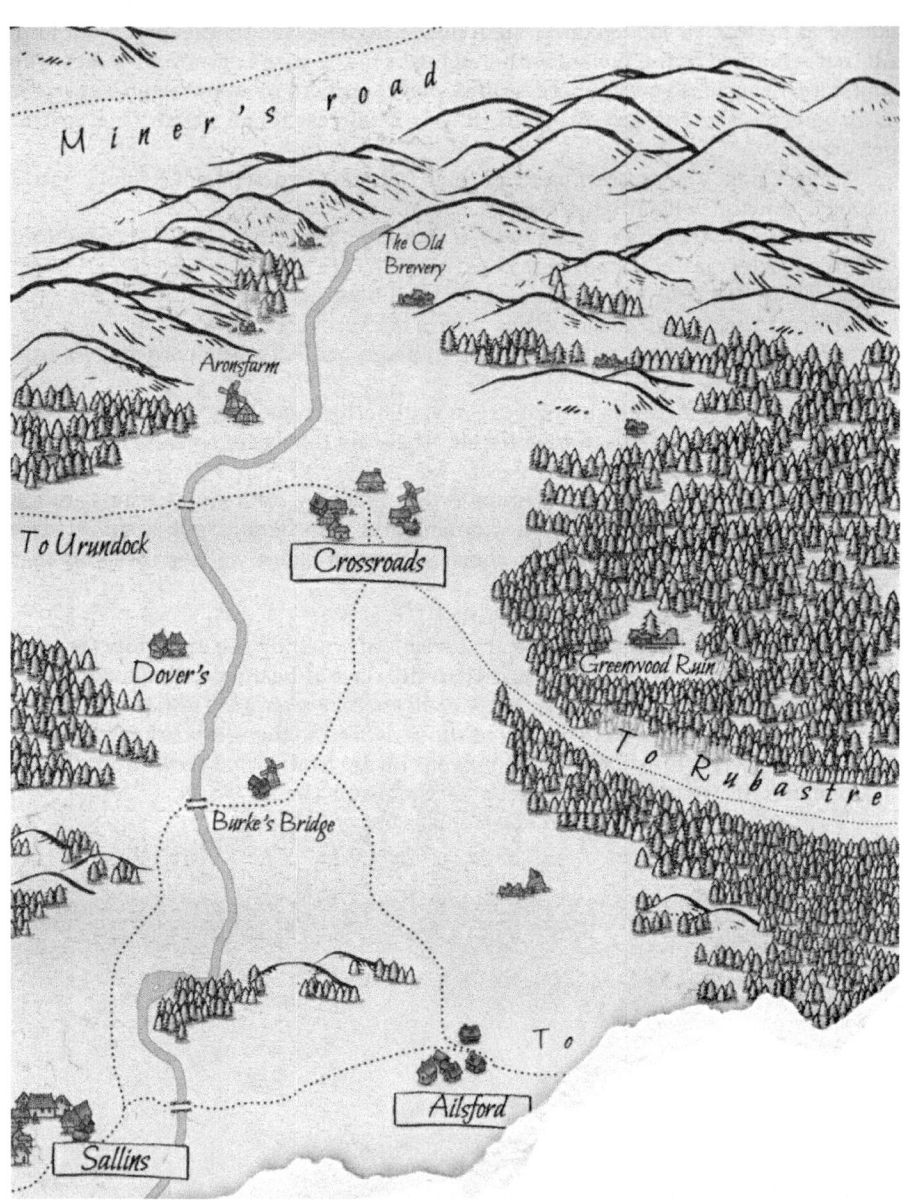

CHAPTER 16

The Greenwood

The wheels groaned in protest against the broken stone road. The cargo in the merchant's cart rattled and clanked. The cart was not a complex thing, it had no magic or specialised mechanics to it. It was a simple cart of greenwood and iron pulled by two shaggy oxen.

A round and soft man sat at the head of the cart, he was bald but he made up for it with an impressive white moustache. Alongside the cart, another man rode a large grey horse. This man could never be described as soft or round, he was stalwart and weathered, the kind of man you would expect to find in the iron mines to the north, or out logging in the surrounding woodlands, but this was no workman. The sword at his hip and round wooden shield at his back made it clear to any that he was a warrior, and any wise outlaw would avoid this merchant's cart but bandits are seldom wise men.

"If my memory serves me, there's an inn at a crossroads a few hours ahead, we should reach it before sunset," the round man said.

"If *my* memory serves me, the innkeeper is a cheat. Two copper marks for a night in a lumpy bed, I'll pass. I can sleep for free under the cart," the rider said, in truth he preferred to sleep outside, even this late into autumn. It was the best time for it when the air was sharp and fresh but not too damp.

"I thought your type were loose with their coin," the round man grinned.

"My type?"

"Hiresword—mercenary—or whatever it is you call yourself. Considering how much you lads cost, I'm surprised you're so stingy is all."

It was true, an experienced fighter and runewielder did not come cheap but people who can pay more for the best often do. This merchant was no exception, his cart may look like a simple thing but beneath the canopy there were dozens of ironcast caskets. Each one held a gold mark's worth of lamp-oil—not the expensive stuff that they farm lizards for in the south—the cheaper and fouler smelling stuff that rakmen traded up past the Nortara Sheet. His simple appearance was all a front to dissuade any unwelcome attention and the large bodyguard was extra security.

"So you've been up this way before then, Lenn?" The merchant asked.

"I've taken a few contracts to Rubastre before, usually I wouldn't take one so far from home but I've some family that live out near the city and I try to visit every few years," Lenn replied.

The two went on in silence, the surrounding woodlands became sparse patches of trees, and eventually only empty fields and farms could be seen. The small cluster of buildings at the crossroads was too small to even be called a village. It didn't even have a real name with locals just referring to the village as Crossroads. The inn was the only structure of stone. The inn had no name, just a hanging sign with a bed crudely carved into the wood. The round merchant—Baird was his name—was eager to get inside but like all meticulous merchants, he saw to his cart first.

"Hang on," Lenn advised, eyeing the surrounding structures suspiciously, his hand going to his sword.

"You mercenaries, I tell you, jumping at shadows at every—" a crossbow bolt burst through the merchant's neck.

"Fuck!" Lenn growled, drawing his sword. He whirled his horse about away from the inn and found that a small number of raiders had blocked each of the crossroad openings. He counted a half dozen and likely some more inside the inn. They were armed with rusted weapons. One big lad with a wiry mane of brown hair carried the crossbow.

"This doesn't have to get more bloody than it has," Lenn said to the big man, assuming him to be the leader.

"No, it don't," the big man barked, "just drop yer weapon and yer coin. Get off that horse and we'll let you walk outta here."

"Sure you will," Lenn replied. "Listen, I'll keep my horse, my sword and my money, and I won't come straight for you. How's that?" The big man lifted the crossbow.

Lenn didn't hesitate, kicking his heels. His horse launched forward. The raiders were quick to form into a line, but Lenn was a skilled fighter—and a runewielder to boot. He doubted any of these grunts had a runestone between them, let alone ever learned to use it. He drew on the power of his earthstone, forming a spear of rock that he propelled toward the leader.

As expected, they were an untrained bunch. As soon as they realised they were up against a runewielder, the more inexperienced broke formation, fleeing to the shelter of the houses. The rock spear was crude, not as sharp an edge that he'd seen more accomplished stonebreakers form but it was enough to crush the big man's chest as it smashed into him. Lenn barrelled past the remaining group. Some of the veteran thugs attempted to block his path. He cut down one of them as he passed at a gallop.

Shit. There goes my pay. Lenn thought bitterly as he tore away, the merchant had only paid him a silver penny upfront with the balance due when they arrived at Rubastre. *Fucking waste of my fucking time.* The rest of *his* money was now being plundered by the raiders. Although, did he really deserve it if the merchant died and had his wares stolen?—the answer of course was yes, he did still deserve it.

Pain erupted in his shoulder and his body lurched forward from impact.

"Ahh," he cried out, whipping his head back to see some of the raiders had run back onto the road, one of them carrying the former leader's crossbow.

You the leader now, eh, ye fucker?

The sight of the raiders mounting horses, spurred him to kick his heels in, urging his horse to more speed. The crossbow bolt bit further into his shoulder with each bound the horse made.

Lenn grit his teeth through the pain, and reached out his edir behind him. He pulled at the earth of the track, drawing it into his earthstone, leaving holes in the road behind that would impede his pursuers.

He then formed small projectiles—nothing fancy, just a few lumps of earth and rock—and launched them behind, not looking back to see if any hit a mark. Lenn didn't need to runewield often and as a result his edir wasn't as honed as other runewielders. He found himself tiring from the strain on it, and along with the wound, he was soon pushing through exhaustion. Only the surge of adrenaline was keeping him upright in his saddle.

Well this day has just gotten a lot worse.

***

"I don't think we'll make it to Crossroads," Rowan called back to Tanlor and Daegan. Daegan groaned, his entire body slumping back in the saddle of his wretched horse. The horse wicked its head in a sign of mutual disdain, steam puffing from its mouth as he protested.

"Does that mean we're sleeping out here?" Daegan asked, his eyes flicking apprehensively to the snowlined trees.

"There's a good clearing just off the road a bit further ahead," Rowan replied, "we can have a fire safely there."

"What about bandits or raiders?" Tanlor put in.

"They tend to stick to the main road," Rowan maintained, "a trail like this only gets used by goats and farmers. A band might come out this way if they're desperate, or running from something. I think we can take the risk. The alternative is pushing through the night and chance getting lost in the woods."

"We'll freeze sleeping out here," Daegan objected. Rowan pulled up his horse and turned to look back at him. It wasn't an intentionally patronising look, but Daegan couldn't help but feel like Rowan thought of him like a child despite them not being too far apart in age.

"Listen up, Dessie," Rowan started, "where we're going," he pointed towards the woods rather than the road ahead, "up past the Nortara Sheet. There'll be no comfy inns up there. So you best get used to sleeping out under the moons, or we can turn around and head back to Rubastre right now."

"No," Tanlor said quickly. "It'll be fine," he added, looking at Daegan.

Daegan nodded, this *was* better than the alternative, wasn't it? But maybe Ferath had given up searching in Rubastre and was now on his way back to Reldon. *Or to whoever had ordered him to kill me.* He dismissed the thought, Ferath wouldn't give up, not with the job left unfinished.

"Luna should be full tonight," Rowan said, looking up at the sky which was still bright and moonless, "a warm red moon and a cloudless night… we'll have a comfortable camp, trust me." Daegan didn't trust him. He'd trusted Ferath and he'd tried to stick his sword in him. Rowan was Tanlor's brother and that was the only reason Daegan had allowed the extra travelling companion at all. Tanlor had come to his rescue when he'd needed it most and for that the man had earned Daegan's trust.

It was a strange thought to have for a man he hardly knew but Daegan trusted him more than anyone he had before. But then again, Daegan had never had anyone try to kill him before and never thought this much about immediate threats to his life. Having Tanlor near gave him a slight reassurance, it was a far cry from any notion of safety but he latched on to that tiny shred of security.

They rode on for another hour through the forest trail. The sky above—visible between the breakings of the trees—was clear and fading to orange red.

"I miss the sunset," Daegan sighed.

"There's one every day," Rowan scoffed, "we'll be out of the woods tomorrow. The land is pretty open as far as the river. So you'll get a look at one."

"Not here," Daegan replied, "sunsets up here aren't as dramatic as back home. The sun becomes an orb of orange light, painting the whole sky in red. It's quite the spectacle."

"Sounds the exact same as here," Rowan rebuffed.

"It's not."

"Red sky, big shiny orange ball. I'm telling you, it's the same."

"It's too cloudy up here, obscures all of it," Daegan affirmed, wistfully wishing he was in the palace on the Pillar, watching the light of a setting sun reflect on the waters of the bay."

"How far to the camp?" Tanlor asked, diverting the conversation. He didn't talk much, Daegan had attempted to draw him into conversation a few times over the past few days on the road but other than discussing the route ahead, Daegan was met with one word answers.

"We can turn off here," Rowan replied, squinting into the trees, "there were a few paths to it back along the road but it's all overgrown. This will be as good as we'll get I think."

He urged his horse through the underbrush and into the woods. Daegan didn't even need to direct his own horse, the beast had already decided that Rowan was its master, and followed his lead regardless of Daegan's instruction.

The branches attacked Daegan, clawing at him as they made their way through. He lifted his hands to shield his face from them, in turn he tugged on the reins. But of course that didn't stop his horse who dutifully plodded along after Rowan. *How could he possibly know where he's going through this?* The fading light made the shadows of the woods grow deeper and more ominous as they trudged deeper in. Daegan couldn't see much beyond the dark mound of Rowan and his horse ahead of him. *Ugh, we're going to have camp right here.* He looked down at the uneven ground, laden in roots and undergrowth.

"Do you even know where..." Daegan trailed off as they emerged in a small clearing. There were remnants of a stone structure in the middle of the clearing, it had no roof which was made all the more evident by an enormous tree growing from the center of it. Daegan looked at it in astonishment, it was a beautiful tree. A gnarled trunk with huge heavy branches drooping out. It looked like an oak tree but on a much grander scale.

"A greenwood," Rowan said, dismounting from his horse, "you don't find many of them this far south."

"Huh, so they are real," Daegan chuckled, his horse following Rowan's until eventually stopping, indicating it was time for Daegan to dismount.

"What's that?" Rowan pried.

"Greenwoods, I thought they were a myth," Daegan shrugged.

"Think you'll find a lot of things you thought were myths are very much real up these parts," Rowan cautioned, "and on that point—Tan, you do a sweep of the perimeter. We're closing in on rakmen country now."

Rakmen! Daegan decided not to voice his opinion on the existence of rakmen, considering he was looking at something he believed to only exist in stories. Perhaps there was truth to the claims of rakmen although a part of him still believed they were likely just regular men. The stories claimed them to be more draega demon than man. Tanlor also dismounted, and pulled his greatsword from the saddle, strapping it to his back.

"I'll check for animal tracks too, make sure we're not encroaching on any bear or wolves' territory," Tanlor said, hitching his horse to one of the ruin's walls.

"Are there really bears and wolves out here? I've not seen any," Daegan put in, Rowan was unpacking supplies from his saddlebags and Daegan was unsure what was expected of him.

"You might not see the wildlife but trust me, lad, the wildlife will see you," Rowan said to him, and then turned to unsling his bow and quiver from his saddle, handing it to Tanlor.

"I'm not likely to catch anything with this light," Tanlor said but took the bow all the same.

"Better to have it and not need it, than need it and not have it," Rowan replied with a wink.

"Don't quote father to me," Tanlor shook his head, and then disappeared back into the trees.

"Looks like someone had a fire here recently enough," Rowan started, kicking at the remnants of a firepit, "few days by the look of it. You got a topaz, lad?"

"No," Daegan answered tightly.

"Right so," Rowan replied, oblivious to Daegan's shift in tone.

Rowan fished out a dimly glowing orange runestone from his pocket, "not much left in here. But might be enough to get it going." He tossed the runestone to Daegan who caught it—fumbling only a bit. It felt warm to the touch, like it had been sitting next to a fire.

"I..." Daegan croaked. Rowan was already walking past him back to the treeline. "I'll get more firewood for the night, there's enough dead wood around here to get you going though."

"Uhm, w-wait," Daegan stammered before Rowan could leave him.

The other man was about equal in height to Daegan which was unusual for a Rubanian. But with his wide shoulders, his bulky cloak and chainmail beneath, he looked a lot larger than he was. Daegan felt like a small child as he gripped the runestone, its uneven surface biting into his sweating palm. Rowan looked at him expectantly.

You're going to make me say it, aren't you? A moment passed and Rowan's expression fell further into confusion, his eyebrows knitting together.

He's going to think I'm a moron. The past few days, Daegan had been enjoying how refreshing it was, talking with a man who didn't think that he was broken. Rowan was condescending, yes, and he knew that Rowan knew nothing of the outdoors but at least Rowan didn't think he was incompetent. That he wasn't secretly measuring his worth with their every interaction, seeing if he could keep up with the conversation.

I'm not an idiot.

Rowan's eyes just watched him, a question in them. "I—I can't," Daegan admitted.

"What do you mean, you tired?" Rowan replied, flippantly.

"No," Daegan murmured, "I can't... I'm hindered."

"Ah," Rowan nodded casually, "right then. You can collect the firewood so," he said, clapping Daegan on the shoulder, and proffering an open palm. Daegan gave Rowan a bemused look before dropping the topaz in the man's hand. Rowan then strode back over to the old campfire and knelt, getting to work on re-igniting it.

***

Lenn slumped and weakly gripped the front of the saddle to keep himself steady in it. His muscles were strained from the ride and his shoulder ached where the crossbow bolt had got him. The bolt was still lodged in his shoulder, he knew it was keeping the blood staunched. The blood had run hot down his back and side at first, but had since cooled and now made him feel cold and sticky. He hadn't wanted to risk slowing his pace to remove it and bandage the wound. A decision he was now paying the price for.

The raiders—from what he could tell—had given up the chase an hour back on the road. For Lenn, tracking someone through the woods wasn't a daunting task but for the raiders, Lenn guessed, it was too much effort to bother with. *Even if I had killed their leader.* He doubted it was any sense of loyalty to him that had driven the raiders after him and more the fact that he clearly had a valuable runestone on him.

Lenn wanted to stop, to allow himself to collapse into the soft earth and sleep, but the rational part of his mind told him to continue on. He knew that he needed to find a safe place off the main track before he could rest. He also needed to get that fucker's bolt out of his back. He'd also need a fire to ward away any wolves or bears that caught the scent of his blood. *Probably some of the furry fucks on my tail already.*

He knew a good spot in these woods—an old abandoned lodge with a greenwood growing out of it—nestled a comfortable distance off the main track. The raiders would likely know of it—if they knew the area—but Lenn hoped they were blow-ins, pushed up north from the Duke's patrols and unfamiliar with the woods. He thought of the warm embrace of a nice fire to drift off next to.

The daylight was fading fast and he would be hard pressed to find that ruin in the dark. He leaned forward to his horse's ear.

"You're a good lad," he wheezed, "I know you can understand me." The horse flicked its head.

"You know the spot we need to go," Lenn continued, "the greenwood. Take me there." He let one hand go from the saddle and felt his whole body lean, his remaining hand strained to keep balance. He leaned further forward, his shoulder protesting at the movement. With his free hand, he weakly grabbed for the reins he'd long since dropped, dangling tantalisingly out of reach.

Come on, you useless shite. He leaned a little more forward.

The world spun, his head crashing into the ground. Pain lanced into his arm as the crossbow bolt dug deeper into him.

The frosty ground felt sharp against his head. It was a reassuring sting, the kind that let him know he was still alive. There was a warmth spreading down his back. That kind of seeping warmth meant death. Lenn coughed, his shoulder flaring in pain but he didn't spit up any blood. *That's good.* He tried to lift himself to his feet, but didn't have the strength and he collapsed back down on his face.

Maybe just... rest... a little. He deserved that much at least.

***

Daegan reclined back on his log. With a full belly of campfire-roasted beef strips, and the warmth of the fire on his face, he discovered that he quite liked camping.

They'd stopped on the first day in a small village for some provisions. Mostly grains and dried meat. At Rowan's recommendation, Daegan had purchased a sheeps-wool lined cloak that had been treated with oil to repel water, along with matching pairs of breeches, boots and gloves. His old fine stitched cloak had been reluctantly traded. *Cotton kills, apparently.* The quality was the best the village had to offer, but still far from the luxuries Daegan was accustomed to. His nicer fur-lined clothes that he'd worn in Rubastre were packed away in his saddlebag. *Best to keep clothes like that hidden away,* Rowan had cautioned, *no point making yourself a target for no good reason.* The cheaper clothes were far from roughspun, and were a good deal finer than anyone in the village had been wearing but to Daegan they might as well have been rags. *Warm rags,* he conceded appreciatively... *Very warm.*

"So you're the Hunter's eldest son?" Daegan asked Rowan who was still munching through his strip of dried meat. Tanlor sat further away, wiping a cloth on the blade of his greatsword for some reason. Daegan would have recalled if he'd killed someone with it, wouldn't he? Then again he had been pretty tired, hungover and reasonably distracted the first few days of their ride from Rubastre.

"Aye," Rowan answered, "so you know the story?"
"A version of it," Daegan replied, "but I bet you've heard all kinds of embellishments on the true story—dragons, rakmen, Arctic bears and the like."

"Oh there were rakmen," Rowan admitted, Tanlor was notably quiet—although he was always quiet—Daegan got a more tangible silence from him now.
"Up past the Sheet," Rowan continued. "There's a lot more of 'em."
"You've seen them?" Daegan asked curiously.
"Seen 'em, fought 'em, ran from 'em. Usually in that order. If you see 'em, you'll run too," Rowan promised.
"We'll stay well clear," Tanlor put in, not looking up from his wiping, "Rowan and I know how to cover our tracks. We also know the signs of rakmen."
"Let me guess," Daegan smiled, "the trees wither and die, cups of water start to boil."
"They're not storybook draega, Dessie," Rowan pointed a cautionary finger at him, "they're not too different from men... but they *are* dangerous." His tone was heavy with warning, "...very dangerous."
"What do they look like?"
"Like us," Rowan replied, "but also not like us. Their skin is black. Not tan like yours is, there's is as black as a moonless night. Got these blue marks all over their bodies too and pointy ears."

Pointy ears?! Daegan laughed, "are you talking about the Aeth?! Elves! They're nothing special, they might live a little longer than regular men and women but they're not any more dangerous."
"They're *not* like the Aeth," Rowan said darkly, "and it's not something you laugh about. I've had friends die on rakmen blades."
"Sorry," Daegan faltered, "I-I just... this is all very new to me." Rowan nodded and accepted the apology. The conversation slipped away and the three of them sat quietly eating their dinner to the sound of the crackling campfire.

"I've met your cousin, Boern," Daegan said after a few moments, looking to get the conversation going again.
"Most people call him the Duke, these days," Rowan grunted.
"Ah, I thought they were calling him the *Dick.* Seems more fitting." That earned him a choked laugh from Rowan as the man spluttered on his beef, "Ha! Where'd you find this one, Tan?" Tanlor didn't acknowledge the joke. Rowan thumped at his chest to clear the bit of food he was choking on. "So not just me then," Daegan smiled.

"Nah... not just you. Boern's always been an ass. Ever since we were boys. I remember one time, he knocked out half my teeth for no other reason than he wanted to."
"He's a good fighter, then?"
"Hardly," Tanlor scoffed, a grimace on his face, "Rowan was only a boy. What ten? Boern was almost twenty. Good fighters don't pick fights with boys half their age

and size."

"Is he the reason you like to pretend you're not highborn, then?" Daegan asked pointedly at Rowan, who leaned back on his rock.

"I'm not highborn," Rowan replied, casually.

"Your grandfather was Duke Garron, was he not?"

"Aye. Doesn't make me shit though. My father was a hunter, I'm not going to parade about pretending to be one of *them*."

"You're not pretending if it's in your blood," Daegan said, dismissively, "paint it any way you like but you're still highborn, despite pretending you're not."

"And what's your reason for pretending you're not highborn?" Rowan countered.

"Leave it be," Tanlor interjected, giving Rowan a levelled glare.

"Fine... you think of anything better than a merchant as a cover?" Rowan asked Daegan, "that story is fine down these parts but once we get to Urundock, people are going to start getting real curious about a merchant travelling up past the Sheet. Only men who go up that far are trading with the rakmen and that won't go down well with the locals." He was looking at Daegan expectantly.

Tanlor cleared his throat and sheathed his sword, "what about Iron pros—"

"—Cartographer," Daegan interrupted him.

"What... like a mapmaker?" Rowan questioned.

"Yeah, you said it yourself, no merchants go up that far north," Daegan replied, "and the map that we have from Arch-duke Edmund doesn't even have any trails marked past the Nortara Sheet. I'm guessing the region is mostly uncharted."

Tanlor was nodding along, "makes sense," he agreed.

"Also—who wants to kill and rob a man who only has pens and parchment," Daegan added.

"You'd be surprised what men would kill for," Rowan replied, "but you're right it's a good cover—if a bit unusual. Just keep things like that fancy revolver of yours hidden. I once knew this lad with a fancy cloak that—" Rowan cut off, his head whipping towards the forest.

Tanlor was on his feet in an instant, eyes locked in the same direction.

"What is—" Daegan began but was hushed by Rowan sharply throwing up his palm at him.

"You did a full perimeter check, Tan?" Rowan whispered, barely audible to Daegan.

Tanlor nodded, "half-mile around the camp, all clear," Tanlor replied in a similar hushed tone.

"You stay with the mapmaker," Rowan said, picking up his own sword and soundlessly disappearing into the blackness of the surrounding forest.

"What—" Daegan tried again, matching their hushed tones. Tanlor did the same sharp gesture as his brother and gave Daegan a firm look for silence. *I deserve to know what's happening!* He wanted to snap at Tanlor but Daegan restrained himself.

The Shrydan brothers were sometimes an overly cautious pair but the darkness of the woods gave Daegan the eerie feeling of being watched. A part of him doubted they were as jumpy as he was in the woods at night so this was not the reaction to a shadow.

Tanlor slowly—and soundlessly—drew his blade from its sheath. His eyes didn't leave the dark tree line. *How can he even see anything in there?* Was it some unknown runewielding ability Daegan didn't know about?

Luna's red-tinged moonlight gave ample light in the clearing, along with the bright orange glow of the fire but the trees themselves were a ring of impenetrable blackness.

They waited in silence but for the wind rippling through the trees, each apprehensive minute drawing out. Daegan wanted to speak, he wanted to know what was happening. Instead, he very slowly stood up from his position and reached into his cloak, drawing his revolver.

There was a rustle in the trees, the notable sound of cracking twigs. Daegan sensed a relaxation in Tanlor's posture, but the man didn't sheath his sword so Daegan kept his revolver up. The large dark shape of a horse loomed out of the trees, guided by Rowan into the light of the campfire. There was a man draped over the saddle like a corpse.

"You killed him?" Tanlor asked, surprised.

"No, someone else got him. There's a crossbow bolt in his shoulder. Still alive... barely."

"We should pack up, could be raiders or bandits," Tanlor said with concern, his eyes flicking from the newcomer to the treeline.

"Maybe he *was* the bandit?" Daegan offered.

"Not likely, cloak and weapons are good quality. A hiresword, maybe," Rowan replied, lifting the man off the saddle and moving him next to the fire.

The wounded man had wiry grey hair, slick against his face. He had a pallid look and Daegan would have guessed he was already dead. Rowan cut through the man's cloak and the leather jerkin underneath exposing the man's wound to the light. The bolt was broken, just a shard of black wood protruding from the man's back. Dark blood, caked and flaked around it.

"This happened a few hours ago," Rowan mused, cutting away more of the man's shirt, "all this is old blood."

"He must've been in a rush to get away if he didn't stop to pull that out," Tanlor said, he was kneeling over the man with a bottle of alcohol and a rag. Daegan watched in stunned silence as the pair efficiently pulled out the bolt, and pressed the rag against the wound. Rowan wrapped up the man's shoulder while Daegan just stood there like a useless idiot.

Rowan glanced up at him only now noticing Daegan staring dumbfounded.

"Go hitch this man's horse to ours, Dessie," Rowan instructed him, "check his saddlebags. See if there's anything that tells us who he is." Daegan jumped to the task, eager to be away from the bloody work.

The horse grunted and stamped at his approach, but Daegan held out his hands and hushed him. He slowed his approach and gently took the reins. He led the mount over to where their horses were hitched to the old ruin. Daegan shuddered, the chill getting into him now that he was away from the fire. He looked through the man's saddlebags but all he could find were some provisions, clothes and a few knives. He brought it all back over the fire to sort through.

"Anything?" Rowan asked as Daegan walked over, dumping the pile.

"Just these," Daegan held up the knives.

"Clothes look like decent quality... he probably works the road to Rubastre," Tanlor noted.

"Bodyguard," Rowan affirmed, "well, let's get him stitched and see if he wakes up —Dessie, why don't you try to get some sleep, eh? We might be in for a hard ride tomorrow."

"Sleep?" Daegan asked, incredulously, "you think I'll be able to sleep knowing there's some lunatic with a crossbow out there?"

"You can take guard duty if you want," Rowan offered calmly, "but frankly I don't trust you with the task so me and Tan will be doing that anyway in shifts. You'll just be awake for no real reason. The best thing you can do is to lie down near this fire and try to get some sleep, alright lad?"

Daegan was used to being patronised, he'd experienced it his entire life. But that had been different, it had been unjustified. People assumed he didn't know what he was doing because he was hindered. But out here, Daegan really didn't know what he was doing. He was lost in the dark and without Tanlor and Rowan, he'd very likely be dead already.

Despite wanting to argue further, Daegan grudgingly laid down on his sleeping roll. He couldn't shake the feeling that Rowan was treating him like this because he learned that Daegan was hindered. If he could use runestones, would he have been trusted with guard duty? Maybe runestones did give a person an enhanced ability to see in the dark?

Daegan tried to dismiss the pestering thoughts. His body ached from the days in the saddle and despite the bedroll only being an inch of material between him and the cold earth, his weight sunk into it with satisfaction. The nearby fire gave him a comfortable warmth but sleep eluded him. He couldn't relax knowing how useless he was while Tanlor and Rowan worked to save a man's life only a few feet away.

CHAPTER 17

Crossroads

"The inn at Crossroads is half-decent," Rowan said, "they'll have a bed for him, at least. The innkeeper's a good man. He'll make sure this lad's looked after."

Tanlor and Rowan gently lifted the wounded man into his saddle—his horse had the same light grey colouring as the man's hair. Rowan had started referring to both the man and his horse as 'the wolfhounds' for the way their shaggy grey hair resembled that of a wolfhound. They strapped the man's legs to the saddle so that he wouldn't fall.

"And what about when they ask how he got the wound?" Tanlor asked, picking back up the argument that they had been having all morning. "He's slowly regaining consciousness, I propose we leave him here with a fire, enough water and logs to keep him going for a few days. He has provisions on him for at least a week."

"I'll not leave a man to die out here," Rowan glowered at his little brother with obvious affront.

"He'll be fine," Tanlor insisted, "the wound's not going to get infected and if we leave now he'll not remember any of us."

Daegan understood the concern. Ultimately, Tanlor was trying to protect him as his primary objective. Daegan didn't doubt that under normal circumstances, Tanlor wouldn't hesitate to help the man but their mission depended on secrecy. A Reldoni man and two travelling companions saving a man's life on the road wouldn't go unnoticed. The story would make its way back to Rubastre which was still under a week's ride away.

So far, they'd done a good job of hiding Daegan's face under a hood when they stopped in villages and keeping a generally low profile as they passed through. Keeping your face hidden and riding into town with a dying man would give an entirely wrong message and could spread even quicker back to Rubastre. It was all in efforts to keep Ferath and anyone that he had been working with off the scent of their trail.

Daegan packed up his own bedroll into his saddlebag. He handed Rowan's green cloak to him and muttered a thanks. Rowan accepted it with a nod and said nothing else about it. Daegan had woken in the early hours of the morning to damp chill. He hadn't believed he'd ever been so cold in his life. The fire was still going and Rowan had been awake. Daegan had felt himself begin to shiver. Rowan calmly placed the cloak over him and patted his shoulder.

"This hour's always the worst," he'd said in a hushed tone, "just before the dawn breaks." Daegan in his half-asleep state didn't question or refuse the offer, gladly accepting the additional warmth and comforting weight of the man's cloak and had drifted off back to sleep.

"I'll not leave him," Rowan re-affirmed. "If you lads want to circle around

Crossroads, I'll catch up with you on the road tomorrow. But Wolfhound here is being brought to the inn and that's *that*."

"I'll keep my hood up," Daegan offered to Tanlor, "and I'll not speak to anyone."

Deep down, the main reason Daegan wanted to get to the inn was because he deeply desired a cooked meal, a glass or two of whitewhiskey and a warm bed. He didn't like the idea of skipping around Crossroads and spending a second night sleeping out.

"That settles it so," Rowan determined, swinging himself onto his own horse.

"No it doesn't!" Tanlor rebuked, also mounting. Rowan held onto the grey horse's reins and led him along. "Come on big Wolfhound, that's a good lad," he said, ignoring Tanlor's argument.

Daegan pulled himself up into his own saddle. His legs protested as they shifted back into the position they'd been forced into all week.

There was a misty chill to the morning and a heavy cloud had rolled in over the woods during the night. They rode on, Tanlor and Rowan still bickering over what to do with the wounded man. Wolfhound himself was starting to stir, mumbling things on occasion. They'd tried getting some details of what had happened during those spells of semi-consciousness but they couldn't even get a name out of him.

"He's trying to say 'Crossroads', I think" Rowan suggested and Daegan agreed. "He's probably *from* there. More reason to bring him back."

"We're not far from Crossroads now," Daegan offered to the man, unsure of whether he could hear him, let alone be comforted by it, "right Rowan?"

"Aye," Rowan added, "we'll have you home soon enough, Wolfhound." The man breathed an incoherent response, his eyelids fluttering, his head bobbing from his horse's movements.

They stopped for Rowan to check on Wolfhound's bandages and for the others to take a piss.

"His horse clearly knows where he's going," Tanlor said, "let's just send him on along the road. Then the three of us can circle the town and just be done with it."

"I don't want to spend a second night in the woods," Daegan groaned, "a night in an inn with some whitewhiskey. That's what I want."

"It's not wise, my lord."

"Not when you keep calling me that," Daegan reprimanded, "look where we are Tanlor. Nobody's going to recognise me out here. I'd guess half the people in Crossroads have never even *heard* of the Reldoni, let alone ever seen one... I think we'll be fine. Rowan doesn't seem worried." Tanlor looked at Daegan with frustration, Daegan could tell he wanted to argue further but was holding back.

Rowan was checking Wolfhound's stitching when the wounded man made a loud gasp, followed by a retching cough.

"You're alright, you're alright," Rowan soothed, pushing a water flask to the man's lips, "you coming back to the living yet?"

"Who?" Wolfhound managed to get out before another cough.

"Name's Rowan. That's Tanlor and Desmond. What happened?"

"What?... Where?"

"He's still pretty out of it, I think," Rowan said to the others, "let's just get him up again. We'll make it to Crossroads in less than an hour."

Wolfhound's eyes went wide and tried to speak before being hit by another series of choking coughs.

"Help me get him up," Rowan said to Tanlor.

"No!" Wolfhound managed to croak out, "not Crusruds... raiders." He let out a painful groan, letting his body slip back, easing the tension he'd put on it trying to speak.

"Did he say *raiders*?" Tanlor asked Rowan.

"Think so," he replied, his eyebrows drawn down, "you still with us, lad?" Wolfhound didn't respond.

"Shit," Tanlor spat, "if raiders have taken over Crossroads. They might be sending scouts out this far... we should loop back. The miner's roads are patrolled and will be safer."

"*You* didn't want to take those," Rowan accused, "we'd draw too much attention, you said."

"That was before I knew raiders had taken over a village on this road."

"The people of Crossroads are good folk," Rowan replied, "and like you said, the Duke's men don't patrol 'round here often. Who's going to help 'em?"

"*Us?!*" Tanlor shouted at him, "you can't be serious. Rowan, we've no idea how many there are."

"They're probably just some bandits come down from the hills, likely seeing Crossroads as a convenient place to attack travellers passing through."

"And we shouldn't be walking right into that. Word will get to the Duke's authorities eventually and they'll post a contract."

"You know what raiders do to people," Rowan said sternly, "those of them folk in Crossroads that are still alive. We can't let them suffer on like that."

"So you want to... what? The two of us ride into town and ask them nicely to leave?"

"By the time we get word out to any authorities, it could be days—even *weeks*—before anyone shows up here. You know how it goes, ain't no one but us to help these people. I've taken plenty of contracts like that in my time, and I can tell you what's left behind after a few weeks sometimes ain't worth saving. If these raiders have just rolled in then we have a chance to stop this."

Daegan watched the interaction between the brothers grow. All the while he couldn't shake the feeling that Tanlor wouldn't so callously abandon the people of Crossroads to their fate if it weren't for Daegan. *If he didn't have to babysit me, he'd probably already be halfway to Crossroads.*

"Look at Wolfhound," Tanlor pointed out, "he's a fighting man. He had a runestone on him and he almost *died* fighting them."

"He's just a hiresword, he's not trained like—"

"—I think we should help them," Daegan interjected. Both Tanlor and Rowan's heads spun to Daegan. Rowan gave an approving nod and Tanlor had an incredulous look.

"There is no *we* in this," Tanlor pointed at him, "*you're* not going to be helping anyone."

"I can help," Daegan spat back at him, "Rowan's right, we can't leave those people."

"Why do you even care? They're not your people!"

"Should it matter whose people they are? They're still people."

"I'm not arguing with you on this. I have orders to keep you safe and there's no chance in the nine hells I'm going to let you fight."

"You don't exactly have authority over me," Daegan replied snidely.

"Are you really going to pull rank on me?" Tanlor accused. Daegan hesitated, he didn't want to be arguing with Tanlor, he thought that once he'd offered his support that Tanlor would come around. He shouldn't have been so surprised that Tanlor wouldn't want him fighting, but the dismissal still stung.

"I'm not a fool," Daegan said quietly, "I can't runewield but that doesn't mean that I'm useless. I was still trained to fight."

"That's not what I meant," Tanlor sighed, "it's not because of that. I can't afford to have you dying on me, do you understand? I can't fail this mission—I *won't*." So that was it, this was just a mission for him. Daegan's safety was his objective. Tanlor was tasked with keeping him safe so why was he working against that, it was in his own best interest, wasn't it?

"I'll scout ahead," Rowan put forth, "get a count on the numbers. You lads hang back and watch over Wolfhound."

"Don't try to take them down yourself," Tanlor warned.

"Have you ever known me to be reckless?"

"The outlaw camp in the Balfold," Tanlor threw back quickly to which Rowan barked a laugh.

"Ho ho—I got lucky there, didn't I?"

"It wasn't luck," Tanlor replied, "it was Jarron's arrow in that thug's neck."

"We were barely more than boys then, Tan. That was your first contract, wasn't it? You didn't hang around long, you went off to Hardhelm to serve with Duke Harfallow, if I recall?"

"I never worked for Harfallow… but yes. Hardhelm is where I went," Tanlor conceded, "my point though. Don't get any stupid ideas about charging in there. Scout ahead, and even if there's only a handful of them, double back and we'll make a plan of action together."

"The Dukesguard really has changed you," Rowan chuckled, "where's my baby brother gone? The lad that broke Boern's arm in a duel?"

"You broke Duke Garron's arm?" Daegan laughed.

"Like you said," Tanlor said with a small smirk, "the man's a dick."

***

A few hours had passed while Daegan and Tanlor waited for Rowan to return from scouting. Initially, Daegan had been grateful for the extended break from riding. Tanlor had conjured a small fire that they'd cooked an early lunch on. It was pleasant to just take it easy but after a while, Daegan grew restless. Now that they'd finally stopped with no distance to be gained or camp to set up, he was left with his thoughts.

Daegan still couldn't fathom who had managed to turn Ferath against the Tredain family. The man was as loyal as they came, or so he'd thought. Now that he thought about it, Daegan actually didn't know much about the man despite him being in service to his family for years. Even as boys, he'd trained with Daegan and Landryn under Swordsmaster Garld. Ferath was from a reasonably wealthy highborn family and had been offered a place in the royal guard because of both his skill and his family connections. He'd served with Landryn, both alongside him in skirmishes along the Reinish border and then later as his subordinate.

From what Daegan could tell, Ferath had been a staunch supporter of Landryn's promotion to Commander. It baffled him how someone so patriotic could turn against the royal family.

Daegan spent much of his time actively trying not to think about his father, his imposing presence, or the way that he made Daegan's throat lock up anytime he was near. They hadn't spoken directly for years and King Abhran made no secret of his disdain for his crippled son, but he was still his blood and his son by right. An assault against his own blood would be an offence that the King would be swift to deal with harshly.

Ferath's own family will likely suffer greatly for his actions. *Unless, this is what father wanted?* The man's cold domineering eyes appeared in Daegan's memory. His throat felt tight and he began to sweat. Such anger and hatred. *Yes.* Father would kill him... dull aches in the scars around his body began to surface. They were phantom pains, he knew. The injuries he'd sustained at his father's hands had long since healed. But his father couldn't kill him, even the King couldn't openly murder his own his son for being a cripple. He wouldn't want the other highborn to think him so cruel.

But Daegan knew in his heart the truth; his father would have killed him if he'd been able to. But why now? He'd ignored Daegan for almost a decade, why now that he was out of the Pillar, and out of Reldon entirely, would his father decide to kill him? It didn't make any sense. Daegan had initially assumed when his brother Lukane had informed him he would be sent to Rubane to serve as the Reldoni consul that it was his father's goal to have Daegan finally sent away from his sight. Sent off to live and die in a frozen forgotten corner of the world. But why send Daegan here at all, if he was simply planning to have him killed?

Daegan couldn't entertain the prospect of any of his siblings being involved. Lukane, being almost ten years older than him, they'd never really had any bond. He wasn't that different from father, he'd been critical of Daegan during his training. Not abusive as their father had been but his disregard for Daegan's treatment back then was a cruelty that Daegan couldn't forgive. After his training had stopped, Lukane had mirrored their father's dismissal of Daegan until only a few years ago, he'd insisted on Daegan being given a purpose in the family and had him assigned to various positions in the palace until ultimately being sent here.

As for Landryn... the man was a stranger. He wasn't the boy he'd played games with in the Pillar, who'd sneak out of bed at night to play in the fountains on warm nights in summer. Landryn's training had intensified in their teen years and he was off being a war hero in Rein by the time they'd grown into men. Landryn probably didn't like him, but Daegan didn't think Landryn hated him, certainly not even enough to have him killed anyway.

And then there was Allyn, the only member of his family that actually brought joy. His fierce little sister, as gifted a runewielder as Landryn, but had taken a different path to him. Instead of training with the military, she trained and studied at Isoler. But she was kind, and her joyous smile gave Daegan comfort.

No, he didn't think any of his siblings could be part of this. Even his father being involved seemed a stretch, his father didn't care enough about him to waste the effort on planning this.

Do normal people ever have to worry if their family members were plotting to murder them? He glanced over at Tanlor who was cleaning a cookpot by the fire. He and Rowan didn't always seem to get along very well. But then again, he'd trusted him to come on this journey. Could Daegan say the same for his brothers? Yet here he was trusting two complete strangers on the journey. A journey that he wasn't even sure what the destination was.

"So where is it exactly that we're going?" Daegan asked Tanlor. He knew vaguely that they were going up past the Nortara Sheet. That Tanlor's father was originally from someplace up there."

"Up past the—"

"—Nortara Sheet, yes, yes," Daegan replied, "but *where* exactly? The map that we have doesn't note any towns up there. There's just a few outposts."

"That's because there aren't any towns up there. It's all wildlands."

"So how is that safe?"

"Safe from whatever's coming after you," Tanlor replied, "safer than waiting around Rubastre for Ferath to come at you again, or anyone else involved. Harder to kill you if people haven't a notion where you are. It's easy to hide up north. Lots of space up there, not much people."

"But what about these raiders, or outlaws," and then added, feeling a little silly, "rakmen or beastmen and such. Are those not just as dangerous?"

"You have us," Tanlor shrugged, "it's not so much a threat if you know how to avoid the danger."

"Is that what we're doing here," Daegan smiled and nodded to the still unconscious Wolfhound who was propped up against a log near the fire, "avoiding danger?"

"Rowan… sometimes he can't let things go," Tanlor said, "he's stubborn and if he doesn't like how someone's treated, he's going to try do something about it."

"What about these raiders, who are they?"

"Outlaws probably," Tanlor replied, "best to just put them down before they can do more damage." Daegan thought that was a bit callous. He was about to ask Tanlor if that's how he really felt but then was distracted by Rowan's appearance. He appeared further down the road. The pair waited quietly in anticipation while Rowan made his way to their makeshift camp by the road.

"Raider's have cleared out," Rowan said simply as he arrived, "watched from the outskirts for a while and didn't see any signs of 'em. A few folk moving about but none of 'em looked to be outlaws. They looked rough, beaten. I watched a while longer but it was clear they'd moved on. I went into the village briefly—" he held up a hand as Tanlor opened his mouth to speak, "—I know I said I'd report back first. But trust me, Tan. They were cleared out. Anyway, I went to the inn. Innkeeper's dead along with half the village. They're sending people out to nearby villages to try to get word to the authorities to get a contract out. The raiders didn't just take supplies, they'd taken a few people with 'em back into the hills. Ain't no fighting men left in the village, but they're hoping the Duke will put up a contract to get their people back."

"That's terrible," Daegan said, "what are we going to do?"

"Right now," Tanlor interjected before Rowan could speak, "we're going to bring Wolfhound to the inn. He can be their problem."

"And after that?" Rowan said pointedly.

"We'll talk about it."

They left the discussion there, and hurriedly packed up the camp. Gently, they got Wolfhound back onto his horse. Within minutes, they were back on the road to Crossroads. Daegan urged his horse up alongside Rowan's usual position at the front.

"You want to go after them?" Daegan asked.

"Aye," he grunted, "I've seen what raiders do to people they take with 'em. They're not going to live long enough for the Duke's contract to be any use to them."

"Who are these people?"

"The raiders?—Bandits, outlaws. Doesn't matter what you call 'em."

"They're still people though?"

"Some folk are born bad and some of 'em, some of 'em just go bad. Maybe something bad happens to 'em in their life. Makes them the way they are, maybe others just simply don't know any better. Doesn't really matter what got 'em there though, once they've got past a certain point there ain't no coming back."

"Probably a stupid question but what do you do with them?" Daegan asked, he didn't intend for it to come across as judgemental but he realised that as he spoke the words it might get picked up that way.

Who am I to judge what happens to these people, this isn't my country, these aren't my people. Even in his own country, Daegan didn't have a seat on any court rulings.

Rowan gave him a long, considering look, if he was offended by Daegan's line of questioning, he didn't show it.

"There's no stupid questions, only stupid people," Rowan replied and then a sad look crossed his face, "there's no prisons out here so what do you think we'll do to them?"

"Is there no judge? No trial? Are you going to execute them outright?"

"Sometimes you don't need a judge or a court to know what to do."

"What if someone is falsely accused?"

"All I can do is use my own intuition, if something isn't clear to me, I'll pass it over to the authorities to deal with," Rowan replied solemnly. "Although that's usually not the case. You'll see when we get to Crossroads that a lot of the time—out here—it's undeniable. We can't take every raider captive and bring them to a trial. A lot of the time, the trial is simply how good you can fight. I don't always like doing it, but that doesn't mean it doesn't need to be done."

Daegan let that sink in. It made him think of the Honorsword system in Keiran, where the Emperor's appointed judges were given authority to deal out execution as they saw fit. From what he'd heard, that led only to widespread corruption in Keiran. Their own system in Reldon was flawed, but Keiran and Rubane seemed very broken by comparison.

Reldon was ultimately a military country, their military was both the shield that defended the Kingdom and the sword that policed its people. It was something Daegan mentioned a few times to Lukane and other highborn in the Pillar but it had fallen on deaf ears, who was he to make comments on the law—he was the disgraced third son of the King.

Only his younger sister Allyn had been interested in his thoughts on how the courts should be separated from the military. She would likely have a lot of influence as she grew older. She was still a girl in Daegan's eyes although now at sixteen, she was showing a keen political mind. Being the eldest—and only—daughter of the King, Allyn had the right to contest Lukane for the throne like his great-grandmother had done.

Queen Freyna had challenged her older brother, claiming him to be an incompetent leader. Having lost the Altarean Isles to pirate militias and instigating the border troubles with the Reinish that still plagued them, Freyna's brother's support had been waning. When his sister rose as the potential heir, the highborn had flocked to her promises of regaining control. She'd reclaimed the lands taken by the Reinish invaders but Altarea had been well and truly lost. It was a defeat that only now Daegan's own brother Landryn had finally managed to undo, conquering the Altarean palace and deposing their false royal family.

That action of course would have a knock-on effect, Daegan guessed. The Altarean royal family had been supported by the Keiran Emperor. *Hadn't he married off one of his cousins or something like that to the Altareans?* But he doubted that Lukane and Landryn hadn't foreseen that and were actively working to ease any tensions with the Keiran.

It was a bold move; reclaiming Altarea. It was an announcement to the world that Reldon was once again establishing their control, that their military was strong and formidable. Daegan knew who the driver was behind it; King Abhran wanted nothing more than to be seen as powerful. His legacy as Queen Freyna's grandson and descendent of the great Queen Elyina herself was a shadow that he yearned to step out from. Daegan understood this, but that didn't allow him to forgive his father for the things he'd done, or for being a cunt in general.

Daegan wondered what his father would think of him now; in a sheep's wool lined jacket and at the complete and utter command of two Rubanian knights.

***

Crossroads was a lot smaller than Daegan had expected it to be. They'd broken out through the tree line to an open expanse of farm fields. They were dusted white with light snowfalls but hints of green underneath were still visible.

Horned and shaggy oxen in all shades of brown and grey dotted the fields. The line of trees spread to the north and climbed up into the snow tipped hills. Less than a mile in the distance was a small cluster of buildings. They looked like up-turned ships left out in the snow.

The village was just a handful of buildings and as they neared the cluster, the locals stared at them, some apprehensively, others with outright hostility.

Strangely, parts of the dirt road leading into the village had large chunks dug out of it. As if some giant had plucked up handfuls of the earth indiscriminately. Daegan attempted to manoeuvre his horse around the pits, the beast shook its head in disapproval but avoided the holes of its own volition anyway. Daegan decided to just let the horse make his own path.

"Remember, keep your hood up and don't speak to anyone unless you can't avoid it," Tanlor said to him in a hushed tone, riding up next to him.

"Yes, yes. Same as the last village, and the one before that. Just order me a whitewhiskey when we get to the inn," Daegan replied.

The inn was a crude building of stone brick. *I suppose it's hard to get a good stoneshaper out this far into nowhere.* The craftsmanship of Rubanian stoneshapers in general, Daegan found to be sorely lacking compared to masterful architecture of Epilas and the Pillar. But this one was the worst he'd seen, bricks of all manner of size and shape, haphazardly thrown together. There was a wooden sign with a bed carved into it. There was a patch of frozen blood in frost crusted ground where he dismounted from his horse. *Delightful.*

"Wasn't sure if you'd be back or not," a greying woman with a hard face said from the door of the inn.

"Just needed to go back and pick up this lot," Rowan replied walking up to her, "these are my companions; my brother, Tanlor and Desmond, a—er—mapmaker," he then pointed at Wolfhound who was unconscious again in his saddle, "you recognise him?" he asked.

"No," the woman shook her head, "but he's likely the one that got the bastards all jumpy last night." She looked to Tanlor and Daegan, taking both of them in with a face that looked like it had weathered a thousand storms. "I'm Mendy. This was my brother-in-law's inn before those fuckers cut his throat."

"I'm sorry for your loss, Mendy," Tanlor offered. Daegan dutifully said nothing, but he also wouldn't have known what to say in any case. Tanlor unbuckled the straps holding Wolfhound in place, "do you think he could be one of the raiders?" Tanlor asked, hoisting the fully grown man effortlessly into his arms.

"No," Mendy said bitterly, "I'll not forget the faces of any of 'em. I've not seen him before. But someone came through last night, a merchant and his hiresword. They did the merchant cold where the tall foreign fella is standing," she nodded to Daegan, "but his hiresword managed to make it off. He took down Dugg before he fled town though."

"Dugg?" Rowan questioned.

"Big fucker, he was their leader," Mendy answered, "without him, they started getting all angsty that the hiresword would get word to the Duke's men, so they left last night in a hurry. Come on, best get him inside. He'll need a bed and bandage change."

The inside of the inn was cramped. There were broken bottles and turned over chairs. A pair of young boys were moving about cleaning up, they eyed the newcomers suspiciously but after a few hard words from Mendy they kept to themselves. Another woman, similar in appearance to Mendy sat with an empty stare at one of the tables.

"Phyllis," Mendy said to her with a soft tone, "this man needs caring for. Will you put him in one of the rooms, I'll have one of the boys fetch Bod to check on his injuries." The woman just looked at her with a confused expression. After a few more gentle prompts from Mendy, Phyllis was escorting Tanlor—still carrying Wolfhound in his arms like a fully grown adult man-child—off into a backroom.

"So?" Mendy started turning back on Rowan and Daegan, "which of you is paying for his room? I wouldn't normally be so direct for funds upfront but we've just had every penny in this place dug out and robbed."

"Duke's men will post a contract for the raiders," Rowan replied. "We'll be long gone from here when they do, but we'll bring back the evidence that the raiders were put down. The village can take the reward for the contract."

"And why would you do that?" Mendy asked accusingly. "Ain't nobody work for free, least of all your type."

"We're not hireswords, miss," Rowan eased, "my brother and I are knights. Trained in Garronforn, Tanlor is in service to the Arch-duke himself." Her face seemed to break a little, small cracks in her hard visage. "Will you really get our girls back?" Daegan turned his head at her. What was she talking about? He looked at Rowan who didn't seem to need further explanation.

"I can't guarantee they're still alive, but if they're with 'em when I catch up to them, I'll bring 'em home. How many?"

"Three," she seethed. "Two are my nieces, another girl from the village. The blacksmith's son too, just a boy."

"And the blacksmith?"

"Dead, along with all the other men who tried fighting 'em."

"His son was training with him?"

"Aye, they took the village's earthstone and topaz too," she replied.

"They'll have the boy making weapons for them, I'd bet," Tanlor said from the corner. Daegan hadn't noticed him come back.

"My thoughts too," Rowan agreed, "there's hope for him at least. Which way did they go?"

"North to the woods… and the hills," she replied.

"There's a lot of hills," Rowan said.

"And a lot of woods," Tanlor added, walking over, "we should move quickly. If they only left last night, we might be able to catch up to them. Just the two of us riding hard, we could cover twice the distance they can with captives." Rowan gave his brother an approving nod, a small smile tugging at the corner of his mouth. *Just the two of them?*

"Do you know where the best camps are on the fringes?" Rowan asked Mendy, "old ruins, or a sheltered crag? Any place they might stop for the night?"

"There's an old abandoned brewery at the edge of the woods… some other ruins dotted in the woods, I wouldn't be too familiar further up into the hills though."

"How many are there?" Tanlor asked.

"Nine," she nodded, "there were eleven, but your friend killed two of them."

"They stole horses too?" Rowan probed to which she nodded again in response. "With the captives," Rowan mused, "they wouldn't be able to get further than twenty miles—thirty at the most."

"They also took the merchant's wagon," she pointed out, "a rusted, slow thing. But they got all excited about what they found in it. I don't think they'll be quick to abandon the thing," Mendy elaborated.

Rowan and Tanlor shared a look.

"Fifteen miles?" Tanlor asked.

"At best," Rowan agreed, and turned back to Mendy, "that brewery, how far is it?"

CHAPTER 18
Honest Work

Daegan sat sullenly in the corner of the inn. He fully intended to keep to himself but it was becoming increasingly difficult to ignore the stares of distrust and accusation that were being thrown at him from the people in the inn.

The place had been cleaned up and a few people had gathered near the bar to discuss what to do next. To take stock of what was left, and—more importantly—who was entitled to what inheritance. More than a fair share of the men in the village had been murdered by the raiders and most of what was valuable had been taken. But that truth hadn't meant the good people of Crossroads weren't going to argue over what belonged to who.

Daegan kept quiet through the discussions that were becoming more heated. He felt exposed being there alone. Tanlor and Rowan had departed earlier in the afternoon to hunt down the raiders. Daegan had been left with the strict instruction to not leave the inn.

Luckily, Mendy had disclosed that there had been a hidden trap in the cellar that the raiders hadn't managed to uncover. There had been a healthy amount of whitewhiskey casks and a few barrels of ale.

"Folks will be needing these over the coming weeks," Mendy had told Daegan, and he didn't doubt her. Most of the people that had come through the inn were completely downtrodden.

The raiders took from them all that they had and then took some more. Some had been killed and many had been beaten, or worse. Daegan let the fire of the whitewhiskey sting at the back of his throat. It had a satisfying burn to it.

One boy had come in, no older than ten, he had tear marks on his dirty cheeks. Daegan watched as Mendy and the other village folk tended to him, explained to the boy how his parent's store was now his, that it would be put in the care of his cousin until he was old enough to run it himself. Later in the evening, an argument broke out between that cousin and another elderly relative, the old man claiming *he* deserved it.

"It'll be five years 'afore the boy inherits it," the elderly man said, "I'll be good n'dead by then, I promise you that. Let me have it, and I'll pass it on to 'im when I'm gone."

"You've been itching to get your hands on that store for years, I'm not gonna let you steal it from under the poor lad!"

"Well the value of it, you said were three silver marks. If I sell my Bessy down at Ailsford, I'll make almost as much as 'at. How's about we make a—"

"—it was five silver marks," Daegan interjected from across the room, unable to restrain himself from correcting the man in his offensively belligerent attempts at stealing from an orphan.

"Wha's that, foreigner?" the old man spat.

"The store was valued by the group at five silver marks," Daegan corrected, "you're remembering it wrong."

"Rememberin' it wrong?! I've lived here my entire life, you! I think I'd know how much my bloody store is worth!"

"Well it's not *your* store, is it?" Daegan replied, snidely, "you're trying to snatch it away from a boy who's just lost his parents."

"How *dare* you! I've nothing but love for that—"

"—oh come off it," Mendy cut him off, "we all know that's what you were doing, Sham." The old man grumbled something but retreated back into his seat.

"You," Mendy called over to Daegan, "you got pen and papers?"

Surprisingly yes, he did. The night of his departure from Rubastre was a blur in his memory, he had been drinking that evening but also the traumatic experience of his most loyal bodyguard turning on him had turned his world upside down. When Daegan had taken stock of the things he'd packed into his saddlebags, he'd been surprised to see that he'd included a handful of notebooks, some charcoal pencils, an ink pen, amongst a few other clerical supplies. He'd spent all of his adult life working as varying forms of administrator so packing these things must have been a subconscious decision.

"I do," Daegan replied, "I am a cartographer after all."

"What's that, a cart maker?" one of the villagers asked.

"He don't look like no carpenter, his clothes are too nice," another added.

"I make maps," Daegan confirmed.

"Well tonight, you'll write up contracts," Mendy stated, "I'll assume a mapmaker knows how to spell?"

"I do," Daegan replied tightly, he knew that the comment wasn't an attack on him personally, not like the way people often assumed him to be incompetent because he was hindered.

"Right, over here, then" she beckoned him over to the group of villagers. "While your friends are chasing the raiders, you can help us clean up this mess, and make sure everything's documented proper."

Daegan could easily write up legal documents although he'd normally have given such tasks to his manservant. He had everything he needed to do it; parchment, pen and his ink stamp to seal them. The stamp had the sigil of the Reldoni royal family but it wasn't as though the people of this village would be able to recognise that for what it was.

"Sure, why not," Daegan grinned. "Just pour me another glass, will you," he added, nodding to his empty glass. The whitewhiskey away from the city had a sharper taste and stronger burn on the throat.

He liked it.

***

Luna was almost full, that meant that the night was warm, and would have been a bright one if it weren't for the heavy cloud cover. The warmer air meant that the snow had turned to wet sleet. The rain wasn't too heavy but enough to wash away the snow around the old brewery.

Convenient. Tanlor thought as he crept through the dark. Tracks in the snow were easier to spot, even in the dark. The noise of the rainfall also hid his approach.

His sword was sheathed, but his short dagger was drawn. It's edge black with blood in the poor light. The raiders had posted sentries, but they were amateurs. They weren't expecting to be caught up to only a day after fleeing from Crossroads. They likely expected a few days leeway before anyone had picked up the contract on them, giving them plenty of time to disappear into the hills. They certainly weren't expecting a pair of highly trained soldiers—who also knew how to move quietly in wild country.

The sentry that Tanlor had killed had been a young man who had been asleep by a fence that rimmed the perimeter of the abandoned building. Tanlor had stealthily crept up to him and grabbed his mouth to muffle any shouts and ran the edge of his dagger over his neck. The hot blood poured out, steaming and mixing with the slushy rainwater. Not a drop got on Tanlor's cloak.

The raiders had made a poor attempt at hiding their presence in the old brewery, the empty windows had been boarded up—likely long before these men arrived—but they hadn't bothered to cover the cracks in them so the light of the fires slipped out.

Plumes of black smoke that mixed with the clouds above were also a detrimental give-away. A Boreal owl hooted, four low distinct whistles. Though it was a rare enough owl, it wouldn't be uncommon to hear it in the woods north of Nortara but Tanlor knew that it was no owl that had made that sound. It was a big red haired man that had just taken down the other sentry.

That leaves seven more. Despite knowing that he and Rowan were castle-trained swordsmen, Tanlor still didn't like the odds of going up against seven armed opponents. The more that they could take down before the alarm was raised, the better.

The brewery was not much more than a large wooden barn. Big barn doors at the front, with likely a few smaller entry points on the sides. Tanlor kept to the shadows as he approached the building from the east side, Rowan would likely be synchronously approaching from the other side.

He pressed his back against the timber wall and edged along it, keeping himself concealed in its shadow. The Boreal owl hooted again. *Another one down.* Tanlor doubted there would be more than that on guard. Even three was a startling display of precaution from the raiders.

He could hear muffled sounds inside. Men talking, laughing. He didn't hear any sounds of distress from the captives, but that didn't mean they weren't inside. Suddenly, the wall behind him lurched. Instinctively he pushed his back against it as pressure came from behind. *Shit, it's a door!*

"It's fuckin' stuck," someone said on the other side.

"Aye, you, ye're just a weak piece of shit," another voice followed by a much stronger push on the door. Tanlor held firm, he could feel it pushing harder on his right side. Swiftly, he stepped left and ducked into a crouched position.

The door burst open with a shuddering crack, it bounced against the side of the wall—just next to where Tanlor was kneeling—and swung back on its hinges.

"There ye go, ye pansy. You need me to hold yer dick for ye while ye piss?" one of the voices taunted as a shape staggered out.

"Get fucked," the man grumbled, fumbling at his belt as he walked out away from the building.

"Here! Close that fucking door, you're letting all the cold in!" someone called from inside. Tanlor slowly stood and leaned forward, gently pushing the door closed. *There's worse waiting for you out here than the cold.* His dagger was still drawn, and he crept up behind the shadowed figure.

Steam puffed out from the man's piss stream.

"I'll just be a fuckin' second," the brigand shouted, turning his head to look back. Tanlor couldn't make out much of his face in the dark but he doubted it was a pretty one.

The raider cried out in alarm and terror; it was the kind of scream that catches in your throat before any sound comes out. Unfortunately, he did get a very loud scream out before Tanlor's dagger got him in the back.

As Tanlor pulled back his blade, the man spun around, his spray of piss splattering against Tanlor's cloak. *Ah gross!* In anger, Tanlor kicked the man away from him, and he stumbled back falling into the wet grass.

Orange light poured around him as the door opened. Tanlor spun about, pulling his greatsword from its sheath. It made a satisfying *shing* sound as he did so. He loved it when it did that. Chaos ensued inside the brewery as the remaining raiders jumped for their weapons.

Five left.

He liked those numbers a whole lot more. Two silhouetted figures moved out from the doorway, their steel swords glinting in the orange light. Their bulky forms in furs made them appear like bears in the poor light. He didn't reckon they were wearing armour underneath the furs. Probably just leathers, but he couldn't make the assumption that they didn't have chainmail underneath, however unlikely it was. *Limbs and heads it is.*

Both men hung back at first, and Tanlor shifted into an offensive stance, ready for large swinging manoeuvres with his sword. A well trained group of defenders would know to wait for their comrades, and to make a coordinated attack to take down a more skillful opponent. But these men weren't well trained, they likely weren't trained at all. Just men who were too poor and too foul to do anything else but take from others. They were the kind of men that ended up working for crime gangs in the cities, out here, they ended up as part of outlaw bands.

One of the men came at him with an axe in a clumsy, off-centered attack. Tanlor adeptly sidestepped, and then with a powerful swing of his sword, he separated the man's head from his body. The shadowing form crumpled to the ground, the head thudding as it landed heavily. Blood sprayed out in a fountain.

The other man faltered, having watched his comrade decapitated in an instant. Tanlor knew to capitalise on that hesitation. He let out a roar and charged at the man. This type of terror tactic worked well against untrained opponents, who usually reacted in one of three ways; they either fled, were too stunned to move, or they had a surge of adrenaline that triggered them to retaliate.

The latter of those was obviously the most dangerous and posed the biggest threat. Fleeing also gave them a chance to regroup with their companions and still posed a threat. Thankfully, this man was part of the group that were simply too startled that they stood still.

It was a quick and easy kill, Tanlor's attack cutting through him as he charged. His sword cut through the furs and leather and into the flesh beneath. The sharp edge, coupled with Tanlor's strength grinded through the rib bones and slid out as he passed. *Just three.*

Without hesitation, Tanlor stepped into the brewery. It looked like a barn on the inside too, everything of value having been long since taken out, giving the place the appearance of a big empty shed.

They'd made two fires in the middle of the brewery. His edir tingled in reaction to the flames, the topaz hidden beneath his shirt, eager to drink in the heat of it. It was smokey inside but weathered holes in the ceiling had prevented the space from becoming a smoke box.

Three young women were tied and gagged at the far fire along with a young boy, also bound. Two rough looking men were between him and the captives. Rowan was already on the other side of the brewery clashing with a man wielding a pair of woodcutter axes. He was the kind of ugly you'd expect to find working as a bouncer in a mining town brothel, with a big scar running along the side of his head.

Another was surprisingly overweight—typically outlaws were chronically hungry, one of the biggest reasons they were outlaws to begin with—his brown furs were belted tightly across his belly and he hefted a blacksmith's hammer. He had a brown beard that matched his furs and reminded Tanlor of the mammoths he'd seen as a boy with his father. The mammoth was hanging back from the fight between Rowan and the axeman. The third man had shifty eyes and was awkwardly trying to load a bolt into a crossbow

"Put that down and we might let you live," Tanlor advised him, "it doesn't have to go down this way."

"Piss on that," Crossbow said, "we both know this be the only way," he growled as he notched in the bolt and set the crank. *True, we probably wouldn't have let him live anyway.*

There was too much distance between Tanlor and Crossbow to rush him so instead, he pushed out his edir, pulling the heat from the fires. The sudden flush of heat over his body forced a hiss from his mouth.

It felt like a fire was erupting inside of him although he'd only pulled a small amount of heat. Any rise in your body's own temperature was considerable. It was dangerous to use topaz in a fight, your body had to be the conduit for the fire and if you pulled too much, you ran the risk of incinerating yourself. He focused on the metal handle of the crossbow, pushing out with his edir and forcing all the excess heat into it.

Just as the man levelled the weapon at Tanlor, the concentrated heat burned the man's bare hand. He yelped and flung the crossbow in dismay, pulling his burned hand close to his chest.

Tanlor quickly closed the distance between them, letting out a roar. This man was not a stander like the last one, he was a runner. He bolted away from Tanlor's charge but there was nowhere for him to run to in the building. Tanlor drove his sword into the man's back. He then kicked against the man, pushing him off the blade and whirling about in anticipation of the fat man's hammer. But he was nowhere to be seen. Rowan was still fighting with the axeman.

"*Really* Rowan?" He called over to his brother, "thought you said a castle-trained knight was worth a score of men like this." Rowan didn't reply, obviously too engaged in his confrontation with the scar-faced axeman.

Tanlor swiftly made his way to the discarded crossbow, still loaded and cranked. The handle had cooled already, not being able to maintain the heat without Tanlor's focused edir. He aimed it at the axeman, and took a few side steps to avoid the potential of accidentally missing and catching Rowan with the bolt.

The man wasn't even watching for Tanlor, he knew he was outmatched against Rowan and was giving him his complete attention. Rowan was avoiding glancing over but he was aware of Tanlor's position and jumped back as Tanlor loosed the bolt. The bolt caught the man in the neck, the force of it knocking him over on his side.

Tanlor let out a breath and took another glance about for the man with the hammer.
"The fat lad with the hammer?" Rowan called over.
"Gone."
"He won't make it far. We'll catch up to him,"
"Think you might have overestimated your abilities, brother," Tanlor said mockingly, nodding at the dead axeman.
"He was surprisingly skilled," Rowan said appraisingly, "definitely a former soldier. Maybe a deserter from one of the outposts?"
"Stop making excuses," Tanlor chided, "you're just getting old."
"Careful now," Rowan warned, then nodding to the bound captives, "you see to them, I'll go after the mammoth."
"Ha!" Tanlor barked a laugh, "he does look like one, doesn't he."
"These don't look like local outlaws," Rowan noted, nodding at the dead bodies, "they look like northerners."
"Maybe they got sick of the cold, or maybe just thought they'd find an easy village further south… which they did," Tanlor said grimly, then walked toward the captives.

His sword was still bloody and he didn't want to sheath it and let the blood crust in the scabbard, so he left it drawn as he approached the group.

All four of them looked at him with wild-eyed terror. He wouldn't ever be able to understand how they must feel, having been torn from their homes and dragged off by thugs. He didn't want to know—but could easily guess—what they'd likely already suffered through.

Tanlor knew how he must appear to them; his face and blond hair covered in blood, his greatsword still out and dripping with death. He didn't look like the heroes from the stories that these folk would have grown up on. Not like Balfol in his white armour or Valar the Bravest. *Not like Taran the Hunter; the courageous and kindhearted hero who saved people from raiders and ferrax and all sorts.* He didn't look like the lies that these kids knew… but he was all they had.

He gently laid down his sword, and showed his hands in a calming gesture. The effort did little to ease the panic in their eyes.

"My name is Tanlor," he said softly to them as he approached, "you're safe now. We're going to take you home to Crossroads." Two of the girls started weeping, choking on their gags between sobs. The young boy and the older girl were deadpan, as if in a trance by the bloodshed they'd seen. The girl's appearance reminded him of Danielle and the sight of her bound with matted hair made his stomach clench.

Tanlor unbound her first and cut her gag with his dagger. She worked her jaw but said nothing, her wary eyes frozen on him. The thought of Danielle being in this position; suffering the torment of raiders, filled him with a deep and sickened anger. His hands trembled as he freed the rest of them.

"I'm sorry," he said to them, "I'm sorry that this happened… that we couldn't get to you sooner." He knew that the apology was worthless to them. He also knew that he and Rowan had come as quickly as they could have. But he had argued it… he'd fought *against* Rowan's resolve to help them. It twisted inside of him, the thought that he would have *abandoned* them if Rowan hadn't been here.

The two crying girls continued on, inconsolable but the quiet girl watched him with a fierce glare. Then, she lunged for Tanlor's greatsword. She was young—eighteen years at most—and not nearly strong enough to wield the great blade but she tried. The blade wavered as she tried to hold it up.

"Stay back," she hissed at him, her face set in a stern and familiar way. Tanlor recognised the face.

"You're Mendy's niece?" Tanlor asked her delicately. She didn't answer but there was a crack in her expression. He still had his dagger, and he was fully confident he could easily disarm the girl if she tried to come at him, but he had zero intentions of doing that unless he needed to.

"She's waiting for you back at the inn," Tanlor continued, "your mother too."
"They killed pa," she breathed.
"I know," he replied, "I'm sorry."
"You're really going to take us home?" her voice was breaking.
"Yes," he stressed, "my brother's gone to get the last of the raiders. And once he's back, we'll get you all home."

***

The morning sun broke the mist. The rain from the previous night left the surrounding fields a vibrant green, clearing away all of the frost and snow. The hedges and trees were bare, having already shed their leaves for the winter. In the distance, the Iron Hills could be seen through the morning haze.

Daegan sat on a chair on the porch of the inn, his notebook in one hand and a charcoal pencil in the other, drawing out the shapes of the hills on the parchment.

The sight of Rowan leading a group of four—Tanlor bringing up the rear in his customary position—pulled him away from his drawing. Daegan had found it difficult to sleep through the night. He'd felt more vulnerable than when he'd slept in the greenwood clearing the night previous. So he'd taken to working through the night on the second of the tasks that Mendy had given him.

Tanlor's hair was tied back but Daegan noted that there was dried blood matted in it and on his cloak.

"You found them then," Daegan said as Tanlor took a seat next to him on the bench. Rowan was already guiding the fatigued youths into the inn.

"Yeah, they were at the brewery," Tanlor responded, he sounded exhausted. "All good here?"

"Some disputes between the locals on inheritance. But otherwise it was quiet," Daegan replied and Tanlor nodded in response. "Rowan and I will need to sleep. We'll get a few hours in but I'd like to be back on the road before midday."

"Neither of you have slept," Daegan accused. He'd also barely slept himself, "we should stay the night at least."

"We can't lose focus," Tanlor disputed, "we're still only a week's ride from Rubastre, we need to make more distance."

"Maybe we should discuss with Ro—"

"—I can't protect you from Ferath," Tanlor cut across bluntly, "I don't know why he fled when he did. Maybe he thought Keltin and the others were closer than they were," Daegan was taken aback by Tanlor's abruptness. "What Ferath did was *impossible*," Tanlor continued, "if he catches rumours of a Reldoni man out here, we're both dead."

With that Tanlor rose from the bench and walked to the door of the inn. "It isn't just your life on the line here."

Daegan didn't respond. He'd never really thought about it, all his life he'd had bodyguards. Members of the royal guard that had sworn their lives to protect Daegan's family—Ferath himself had taken those oaths. He'd never had to see the dangers of the occupation as there had never been any real threat to him personally. There'd been assassination attempts on his father and even Lukane before, but Daegan had only heard about them through the court and not been anywhere near the violence himself.

Daegan had never even thought of the lives of the royal guards that had died in those attempts. Or the countless others that died serving in Landryn's guard in his battles against the Reinish and Altareans. He'd never needed to think about it, how his careless decisions could have dire consequences for someone else. All the times he had pushed Kerala and his other escorts into more dangerous vicedens, he'd never thought of the danger it had posed to *them*. He had always felt safe and secure in *their* company, fully confident in their abilities to get him out if he strayed too far. But were they ever afraid? Did his guards that so diligently followed him day-in day-out worry that his recklessly childish behaviour was going to lead them to their deaths.

Not a glorious death on a battlefield either, but a pathetic one, dying to the blade of some thug because a self-centered fool wanted to drink himself into an oblivion. *Was that what had driven Ferath finally? I'd disregarded his safety on so many occasions. I brushed off his ambitions when he wanted to return home.*

Ferath had wanted to be back on the battlefield with Landryn, had he simply grown impatient being at the whims of a hindered moron? Daegan knew deep down that wasn't the truth. Logically, Ferath wouldn't have betrayed the royal family for such a mundane self-serving motive. But that didn't keep Daegan's mind from spiralling into that train of thought.

He looked back down at his drawing, the roughly sketched map of the area that Mendy had commissioned. Director of the Royal Cartographers had been the most recent on his tawdry list of meaningless sinecure positions he'd held in Reldon. Like the others before it, he'd taken to the role with as much enthusiasm as—well, anything he'd done in his life. Which was very little...

He'd enjoyed his time with the cartographers, it was a trivial position and an unimportant aspect in the running of their Kingdom meaning that Daegan could evade any real responsibility. But between the hangovers, he'd actually learned a bit about the craft which was why he'd decided on this guise.

The appointment as the Reldoni Consul to Rubane had been a considerable promotion on paper, but Daegan hadn't exactly cared for promotions. He'd have been happy to be left to toil away, spending his time and money in the less respectable taverns in Epilas. But no, he was here, swept up in an assassination attempt as far from Epilas and Pillar as he could be.

I need a drink.

***

Rowan yawned as he strode into the inn common room. It was early afternoon so the place was empty save for Dessie drinking a whitewhiskey in the corner. *Bit early for that.*

Rowan hoped the man hadn't put so much of the stuff into him that he would be a burden on the ride. They'd pushed the horses hard last night getting to the old brewery so they'd be taking it easy for a few days, but they'd be even slower if the lad was pissed drunk.

He didn't know the man well enough to judge if he liked him yet, normally Rowan reserved a judgement like that until he'd travelled with a person for a few weeks. People like Desmond tended to fall into the 'not liked' category; rich folk who didn't care much about those beneath them. They were a common type of employer, but Desmond didn't feel like an employer, he hadn't any inkling of a command about him. He actually seemed rather subservient to Tanlor which was strange as Tanlor was clearly his bodyguard. There was a lot more to the story here, but Rowan didn't prod. They'd tell him when they were ready.

Mendy was cleaning glasses at the bar. A common thing for innkeepers to do, Rowan had always noted, but it meant they were always there for a chat when he needed them. She would have her minions doing all the other work about the inn.

It was her inn now from what he could gather, with the old innkeeper dead and his wife still in a grief-stricken daze. Maybe the daughters might take over once they were recovered from the ordeal. They will need time though, he'd seen it enough times out in places like these. The people were hardy but this isn't something you can just move on from, it breaks you down and you have to pick yourself up from the pieces that were left behind, sometimes what you put back together is better than what you were before… and sometimes you just stay broken.

Rowan looked back over to Desmond who was immersed in writing something and hadn't noticed his arrival. *Could be that's what was happening to him, maybe something broke him and he's not sure where he fits anymore.* Rowan didn't think he'd been giving Desmond a hard time, but maybe he should make a little more effort with him.

"How much we owe you?" Rowan asked Mendy. She looked up at him with a curious expression.

"You joking?" she countered, her eyebrows raised "you and your brother got our girls back, you don't owe us nothing. You've also brought back most of what those bastards stole. I think it's this town that owes you, sir."

"Wolfhound's going to be needing a bed for a few weeks while he recovers."

"Thought you didn't know him?" She asked with playful scepticism.

"I don't, but I'd like to think if our roles were reversed, he'd have done the same for me."

"Right outta the stories, aren't you, Rowan?" she said with a teasing grin, "be careful, a lot of folk out there take advantage of good people like you." She stopped cleaning a glass and leaned against the bar.

"Doesn't matter either way, his bill's been paid too," Mendy nodded to Desmond, "had yer man there writing up legal papers all night."

"That so?" Rowan said with a grin. "You know he ain't a lawman." He had to give it to Mendy, she was a fair hand at keeping folk busy.

"Best we had," she shrugged, "what's a map maker doing out here anyway?"

"Making maps."

"It's a weird job," she noted.

"Aye," Rowan agreed.

"But I guess useful enough," she conceded, "folk always passing through here, looking for directions. He's drawing me up a map of the area that I can put on the wall."

"Not a bad idea," Rowan replied casually. Inwardly, he hoped that Desmond's imitation of map-making could mimic somewhat decently what a real map maker could do. But then again, what were the expectations of a map maker out here anyway.

"Where's he from anyway?" Mendy asked, her eyes were on the glass she was cleaning, trying to feign indifference.

"Not sure," Rowan lied, and then added a truth, "I've only been working for him less than a week." Lies felt easier when you surrounded them in a truth. Rowan had enough of them in his life to know what made a good lie.

"I've heard that men from Reldon look like him; tall and tan skin."

"Could be."

"You know there's a Reldoni Prince living in Rubastre?"

"I'd heard."

"You reckon he works for him?"

"Not sure. Why are you so interested?" Rowan narrowed his eyes. She gave him a grin with a glint in her eye, "you know how valuable information is."

"I'd appreciate it if you kept our passing through here to yourself," he said, earnestly.

"I won't be able to stop the story of what you did for us from spreading. Everyone in the village knows you brought the kids back."

"Maybe just don't mention *him* if anyone comes asking," Rowan didn't say it with any sense of threat, these people had been through enough. He knew he couldn't control the story spreading. Their names too being the sons of Taran the Hunter, the dots would get connected that they were out this way. Rowan just hoped that whatever mission his brother had wasn't compromised by it.

"Like I'd said, we owe you a lot," Mendy pledged, holding his gaze, "I'll keep quiet. And so will everyone that works here."

Rowan thanked her and walked over to the other side of the common room towards Desmond, "you'll be ready to leave in the hour?" Rowan asked as he approached.

"Should be... I'm almost done here," he replied, not looking up from his parchment.

"Not bad," Rowan noted, looking down at the map that the man was working on, "how'd you know about all these spots?" he asked, pointing at the locations outside of the areas they'd travelled.

"Mendy," Desmond replied, "she knows a good bit about the area. People tend to gauge distances wrong a lot of the time though. Some journeys might feel longer than others because of the road or nostalgia... all that skews it. Without going myself it'll be hard to judge accurately." Rowan gave him an assessing look, crossing his arms.

"Are you *actually* a map maker?" he asked incredulously.

"Of course," Desmond smiled up at him, "what else would I be?" This man was a fine liar. *Maybe he's a politician.*

The front door opened, letting in the chill damp air. Tan strode in, garbed in his dark grey travelling cloak, the blood stains already scrubbed out of it. *When had he gotten up?*

"Are you ready to leave?" Tan called over to them. "Horses are saddled and bridled. Let's have a quick lunch and be on our way," Tan said as he walked over.

"You're not finished yet?" Tan asked Desmond as he approached, "we've got to get on the road."

"Just a few more touches, I'll be done by the time you're through lunch." Rowan respected Desmond for the willingness to finish the job right, he hadn't pegged Dessie for a man like that.

"Looks good," Tan said leaning down, then made an angry *tsk* sound. He tore a tiny piece off the corner of the parchment.

"Hey!" Desmond shouted at him, "what are you doing?!"

"This," Tan waved the scrap of paper at him, bringing his voice down to a fierce whisper and glancing back at Mendy—who was back to cleaning glasses—pretending she wasn't listening to them, "is the kind of shit that gets us caught." He placed it down on the table. The small corner piece had a stamp mark on it. Rowan didn't catch the detail of it before Tan crumpled it and walked to the brazier and tossed it in.

"Who else saw this?" Tan asked with accusation. Desmond was quiet for a moment, he looked about ready to explode at Tanlor.

"Nobody," Desmond responded coldly.

"Be more careful," Tan said with a warning, which Rowan felt was a bit dramatic, it was just a stamp.

"Don't forget who I am," Desmond replied with a sharp edge to his voice. "I appreciate what you're doing for me. But there's only so far I'll allow you to push it, are we clear?" In an instant the Desmond that Rowan was familiar with—uncertain and a little nervous—was gone. What was left was a man who was wholly accustomed to others doing what he asked. *He was a politician alright.* Mendy was still listening from the bar. Rowan believed her when she said she'd keep quiet but that didn't mean they should be careless.

"I can't afford for you to make reckless mistakes," Tanlor said with reproach.

"Maybe ease off, eh?" Rowan put in, sensing the tension building, "we all make mistakes." Tan looked at him as if he'd forgotten Rowan was there, then swept off.

Rowan looked down at Desmond who was clenching his jaw as Tanlor walked off.

"Someone's following us?" Rowan asked with curiosity.

"Maybe."

"How dangerous we talking?"

"If what you and Tanlor say about what's ahead of us up north; rakmen and monsters and such," Desmond responded, "Tanlor believes what's behind us is more of a threat than those... I don't know if he's right."

Rowan had an evanescent feeling so fleeting that it was hard to determine if it was even his. It had been a long time since he'd felt fear. All of his training through his life and the trips taken with his father as a boy had exposed him to such dangers that fear rarely ever took hold of him now as an adult. And whenever he did feel it these days, his mental resilience training would kick in. Foebreakers were uncommon in Rubane—the extraordinarily expensive and precious mindstone made that runestone far too rare—which meant that there weren't many Rowan had faced in a fight.

His grandfather, Bodh, had been a foebreaker. He'd trained all of his grandsons personally in resisting the influence of a foebreaker's pressure. What had been left was a generation that was incapable of feeling fear, even when those emotions came from within. It was a mental reflex when fear would creep into his mind to acknowledge, release and then force it from his mind. It was something he now did instinctively.

Rowan nodded to Desmond, and left him to load up his horse while he made sure they had enough provisions for the road. While he went about these tasks, Rowan wondered at what danger was coming for them for it to have his brother so agitated.

CHAPTER 19
A Different Game

Femira clenched her fists. *Finally.* She gasped, revelling in the familiar sensation of vibrations in her hands. But it was different than before, she could feel the vibrations from the stone around her, the tiles of the floor beneath, resonating in alternating beats. Her senses could even perceive tremors beyond her sight. Giving her impressions of the hallways outside.

Grinning, Femira began to dissolve the training boulder in front of her without even taking a step toward it. The boulder instantly collapsed in on itself in a heap of sandy dust, most of its matter being sucked into her hand in fractions of a second. It was strange, not channelling the material into her earthstone. It was now *part* of her, ingrained into her being. She could feel the material of the boulder strengthening her skin as she absorbed it. She guided it to her heart where, in her mind, the earthstone still resided. Misandrei had explained to her that the earthstone was gone, that it had been diffused into every strand of her body. Despite knowing this, Femira couldn't help but think of the earthstone as a separate piece to her but simply contained inside of her.

Cracked lines of amber light showed under her skin, glowing with the new reserve of stone material as she guided it through her body. It was the same light that her earthstone used to radiate when it was filled. The light snaked up her exposed arms and faded as she drew it all towards her heart. Misandrei had told her that she didn't need to draw it there to fully absorb it, that she could do that instantly but the visualisation of bringing it to her heart helped her.

It also helped her sense the material of the boulder at her core. If she closed her eyes, and really focused, she could see it in her mind, swirling inside of an imaginary earthstone; golden red and brown with a silky lustre.

The boulder had been a hard grey rock pulled up from the earth. She could feel it *wanting* to return to its previous state. The material mixed with others that she had already absorbed. Sandy, coarse earth from the courtyard outside and tiny flecks of metal; steel, iron and bronze. She'd never before been able to sense this. The difference between them. She had been able to distinguish between metal and rock, been able to call and shape those respectively. But now she could detect the differences between the metal sources and various types of rock. She could sense it from them.

The grey boulder had been in this form for longer than Femira's mind could fathom. She could get a sense for its age, how it had been formed over thousands of millennia from pressure and heat.

It was different from the loose rocks in the courtyard. Those had been sand once, pressed and compacted until it had become something different. She could sense these differences, and could pick them apart. If she tried hard enough, Femira wagered that she could reform it as a different rock entirely.

Femira understood the concept of the edir. Both Aden and Misandrei had explained it to her. She never really thought of her edir as an extended part of her the way that they did. It had always felt to her as an additional piece of her senses. Those senses were now heightened, like when the morning sun cast the bay in vibrant light; enhancing the colours. The bay itself was no different than before, yet looked to the eye as a completely different place. One alive with shimmering colour as the sun rose. It was as though the sun had risen on her edir. Where before she had been fumbling in the dark, she could see it now with the vibrant glow of the morning light.

Misandrei had been correct; the soulforging had changed her completely and while her new enhanced senses were awe-inspiring, they were also impossible to escape from.

When Femira had first awoken after the soulforging ritual, it had been overwhelming. Her mind struggled to adapt to the senses her body could now perceive. The thrumming of all the stone, earth and metal around her. She had been familiar with it from her extended use of earthstone, but now it *invaded* every part of her.

Misandrei had been at her side, guiding her through the change. Teaching her how to channel this new energy and focus her senses so that they didn't overwhelm her. It had taken her two days before she had felt stable enough to even get out of her bed. And now, only a week later, she was standing in one of the elite training rooms, finally testing out the improvements to her abilities.

Femira wanted to push herself. She wanted to challenge someone. *Vestyr or Endrin.* She thought wickedly. She wanted to prove to them that, now that they were on equal footing, she was better than them.

Loreli, she thought with determination. Loreli would be her first challenge, she had been so close to finally beating her in the sparring yards. But then Loreli had been promoted and no longer trained with the recruits. Loreli had never confirmed which runestone she favoured, but Femira suspected at aeristone. The way she moved with such mind-bending speed was a dead giveaway. *Not as fast as Landryn is, but close.*

"I want to spar," Femira said with determination.

Misandrei smiled at her, "are you sure you're ready for that?"

"Yes," she replied resolutely, "I want to challenge Loreli."

"A healthy rivalry is a good thing," Misandrei noted, "but do not let that passion cloud who the enemy is."

Femira flinched at the accusation in Misandrei's tone. "You're a bloodshedder now. As is Loreli, there will be a day soon where you will need to trust one another. Your lives will depend on it."

Femira wasn't sure if she'd ever trust anyone with her life, least of all Loreli or Endrin. Although hadn't she already trusted Garld with it? The memory of the soulforging was a blur. She recalled getting on the bed. Garld's hand on her forehead... and pain... intense, overwhelming pain... but also safety. She had felt secure and protected. It was a strange, conflicting memory... but it was the first time in a long time she'd trusted someone.

"I'm sorry, Captain," Femira said.

"You are eager to prove yourself," Misandrei acknowledged, "I can understand that. I was once like you; I was a stronger runewielder than everyone in my rank. I strived for more. Bigger challenges, more chances to prove that I was worthy, that I was better than everyone else. I was accustomed to being the strongest, of having no equal," she held Femira's gaze as she spoke.

"My first real battle," Misandrei continued, "I faced a Reinish foebreaker... my comrades broke, many of them fleeing outright. The foebreaker and his men tore through them. Only myself and a few others in my squad held the line. It was then that I learned a crucial truth; you *cannot* do this alone. We were being overwhelmed, our muscles tiring, our resolve smashed to pieces. One by one, my comrades fell."

"What happened?"

"Salvation," she replied, "reinforcements arrived and the foebreaker was killed. His battalion broken—not by me... I was finished, I could barely lift my sword. Garld himself had been part of the reinforcements but he wasn't a General then. He healed my wounds and had me sent back to the rear lines. I fought him on that, I wanted to stay at the front, but he was right... I was of no use to anyone."

She paused and fixed Femira with an intense stare, "I couldn't fight as part of a team, and my comrades died because of that." Femira didn't respond. She wasn't sure what to say. She could see the lesson in Misandrei's story, but also didn't want to accept that she would have to trust Loreli and Endrin.

"I'm arranging a team for a mission," Misandrei disclosed after a few moments, "if you feel you are ready. I think you should join."

"What's the mission?" Femira asked, her curiosity piqued.

"Hunting corsairs," Misandrei replied.

"My abilities aren't exactly suitable for combat at sea," Femira said with concern.

"We won't be taking them down by ship," Misandrei replied, a smirk pulling at her mouth.

***

"That's amazing," Aden said as he watched Femira smugly form six rotating blades of glass. They weren't perfect glass formations, far from it. But she'd found that with the more material she gathered and extracted she could retain the tiny parts of quartz in the stone that could be made to form something that was almost like glass. Crystal blades would be more accurate, but they looked like glass so she settled on calling them glassblades.

Femira still had a limit to how much material she could hold. She wasn't sure exactly what the limit was but it was a few times her own body weight. And each day she trained her edir, that limit seemed to be increasing. Her own weight didn't seem affected when it was fully absorbed into her. If it was then it was negligible. But when she was moving the energy through her body; in shaping or using her stoneskin ability, she noticed her weight and movement were still massively affected.

Femira focused her edir on balancing the six blades around her, moving them in an intricate dance.

"How strong are they?" Jaz asked, reclining on his chair.

Jaz being from a wealthy family, didn't keep a room in the barracks. Instead, he rented a permanent room at an inn only a few blocks from the garrison. The inn was called the 'The Queen's Hand' and it was an obnoxiously patriotic place with tapestries of Queen Elyina and the founding of Reldon decorating the common room. It was a favoured establishment for highborn who didn't want to live in the barracks but wanted to stay nearby.

Jaz's room was exactly the kind of place that Femira used to spend her evenings trying to sneak into. She could already tell at a glance where Jaz likely kept his hidden valuables. The lounge area where they were now had a low coffee table in the center with two drawers. Both of those would be empty but the secret middle one would have gold hidden in it. Behind the mirror, Femira suspected that there would be a nook in the wall. This was a rented room, so the 'secret' spots were generic. Highborn folk had to be a lot cleverer at hiding their valuables in places like these. Femira doubted that Jaz gave it much consideration. He would keep his runestones on him, notably his topaz as he was a grenadier. *Well it's inside him now too, I suppose.* Jaz had also been promoted alongside her. His own soulforging having been done a few nights previously.

"Have you made a decision yet, Aden?" Femira asked.
"It's hard," he replied with frustration, "picking one runestone effectively means I'll be giving up all the others entirely. It's a massive sacrifice."
"You'll never master more than two anyway," Jaz said, "you're being an idiot if you think that you could."
"I'm not talking about mastery," Aden said defensively. "Right now, I can use all of the elemental runestones. I bet I could learn the ethereal stones too if they were available to me. I know soulforging would make me a significantly stronger runewielder—I know that! But I just can't decide!"
"You don't have to rush it," Femira said flippantly. "Jaz and I will just take all the good missions… and get all promotions and further soulforgings," she teased.
"What do you mean good mis—"
"—and when you've finally decided which runestone you're committing to," she cut him off with a menacing grin, "we'll be your superiors."
"Have you," Aden looked between the two of them, "have you both been put on the Altarean corsairs mission?" Femira glanced at Jaz, their eyes met in a knowing agreement and said nothing.
"They've been gathering only elites for that," Aden said with accusation. Femira shrugged, letting her glass blades dissolve, and absorbed the crystal dust back into her.

As before, it lit up the veins on her arms as it drew into her. *That's going to make sneaking around in the dark a lot harder.* She'd need to get new gear that covered her arms. She would normally leave them free as it allowed her more manoeuvrability while climbing.

She hadn't even tried climbing since becoming soulforged. *I could probably scale the barrack's wall in under a minute now,* she thought confidently. She would have to give that a go later. *Maybe not the barracks though.* She was supposed to be keeping her new abilities a secret so it was best not to show off to the other recruits. *The city wall is high enough.* Femira could try sneaking over it and back. She obviously wouldn't get caught by the cityguard… maybe she could try the Pillar; the palace guards would probably give her more of a challenge.

"Do you want to do a little demonstration?" Aden asked Jaz.
"Nah, my new abilities are a bit more… destructive," he replied, "wouldn't want to damage my rooms now would I?"
"How about a sparring session?" Femira proposed. "You against me. We can use the training rooms in the barracks." Aden had an eager look but Jaz was uncertain. *Come on, Jaz, don't wimp out on me.*
"Fine," he replied, reluctantly.

Femira, Aden and Jaz made their way to the barracks, passing through the busy streets of Epilas. When she'd first arrived, the wide thoroughfares had seemed ridiculous to her compared to the narrow streets of Altarea. She understood now after a few months why Epilas needed these. The sheer volume of people that thronged through each day from all walks of life demanded wider streets. This close to the barracks, the people were predominantly uniformed soldiers in black and red, along with other colours of noble Houses. They were part of a stream of other pedestrians, people on horseback, mule-drawn carts and more lavishly elegant carriages pulled by horses of equal elegance.

The thoroughfare had tall thin cypress trees lining the street, between them were old vendors with leathery skin that looked on with impassive faces behind mounds of fruits, or bags of aromatic spices. Some of the vendors sold cooked foods, the smells of which lured Femira in. A sharp, distinct smell of caramel drew her attention to a vendor peddling an array of candied nuts, their shells coated in some kind of sticky sweet syrup. Her mouth watered, the scents pulling her back in a nostalgic reverie to the shadows of memories of her childhood.

Images of sitting on a sunbaked clay wall while her brothers helped their mother in the market stall. *Is that even a real memory?* Femira didn't know what her mother had done for a living before bringing them to Altarea. She wondered idly whose market stall that had been, which seemed so tangible now as the image cemented its place in her memory.

Once they had passed into the grounds of the garrison, they made for the bloodshedder's barracks. The central courtyard was already teeming with hopeful recruits looking to hone their abilities in runewielding under the tutelage of senior bloodshedders. *Would we be expected to train recruits someday?*

Femira didn't particularly like the idea of having to stand about watching other people spar all day. She spotted Endrin who was instructing a group of ten recruits on stonebreaking. He had them lined up in pairs; one forming a projectile of stone and the other attempting to break it before it could be launched. It was an exercise she herself had been doing only three months before. He spotted her watching and frowned. *Ah shit.* Endrin stalked towards her, intercepting the path that the three were making.

"You've been promoted," Endrin said.

"Yes," she replied coolly. She wanted to prod him into an argument but her conversation earlier with Misandrei held her back. When she didn't offer anything further, he continued. "You're on my squad for the mission. Both of you," he looked to Jaz who didn't seem like he'd been listening at all.

"I thought Captain Misandrei was leading?" Femira said, trying not to let it come across as antagonising.

"She'll be leading the full party. But I'll be your squad leader. As your commanding officer, I will expect your full obedience, is that understood?" Inside she seethed. Under *his* command? Was that some kind of joke? She'd made her displeasure of the man known to Misandrei. Why would she place her in Endrin's squad?

"Yes, sir," Jaz replied with a salute, and then gave Femira a pointed look to do the same. *What are you doing?* She tried to convey her thoughts to him in a confused look. *You think he's an idiot too.* He just gave her a curt nod of the head to indicate that she should follow his lead.

"Of course, sir," she said reluctantly, and performed a half-hearted salute.

"Mission briefing will be at dawn, I suggest you both are rested," and with that he turned heel and returned back to instructing the recruits.

"What was that?!" Femira rounded on Jaz, "the man's incompetent, and we're supposed to follow orders from *him*?"

"He's a senior bloodshedder, Vreth," Jaz replied. "I might not like the man, but he *is* our superior."

"He also fought at Altarea," Aden put in, "and in numerous skirmishes with the Reinish. He's a seasoned soldier. You shouldn't dismiss him so quickly," Aden said to her.

What was wrong with them? Couldn't they see what Endrin was? He was a coward. He was clearly annoyed by Femira's accelerated progression through their ranks. He was probably jealous of her. He'd likely taken years to get to the level that Garld finally approved him for soulforging.

As they approached the training rooms. she shoved the thoughts of Endrin aside.

"Are we using full abilities?" Jaz asked her.

"Of course," she replied, "why else would I be here? I've been itching to test out my new senses in a fight."

"Should I fetch a healer to have on stand-by?" Aden asked with uncertainty.

"Yeah," Femira replied, while Jaz at the same time answered, "no."

"Might not be a bad idea," Femira offered, "I might accidentally break some bones."

"You're worried about me?" Jaz scoffed, "I was scared I was going to burn your pretty face."

She scowled at him and shifted into her fighting stance, drawing her daggers. Jaz mirrored her stance, unsheathing his sword. To her annoyance, it wasn't the shiny silver sword he usually kept on him. Instead it was a lacquered wooden imitation. *Clever.* She'd wanted to test out dusting a metal blade in a fight like Endrin had but Jaz had come prepared.

"First touch?" he asked with an arrogant flourish of the wooden sword.

"Only weapons count, a kick or punch won't win," she replied and then smugly added, "it'll still be over quickly."

"You're confident."

"Ehm—have you not *seen* my floating glassblades?"

As she spoke, Femira reached internally with her edir to the ever present thrum in her chest. Streams of golden light ran down her exposed arms as she guided the power out of her, and formed four of the glassblades that she kept hovering at her side. She could conjure and hold another two but she still found it hard to focus on all six at one time. She intentionally made their edges dulled. They'd still cut him, but not fatally.

Jaz grinned, "I was hoping you'd try those." He whipped forward with surprising agility. Faster than any of the other times she'd fought him. She shot a pair of her glassblades forward. Jaz's sword blurred, slashing at one of the glassblades as it neared him, then ducked below the other. She kept the last two hovering overhead.

Jaz had closed the distance between them so she had to focus on parrying his rapid attacks with her daggers. She backstepped from his onslaught. *He's gotten fast!* But the hold ability for a topaz was temperature control, it didn't make sense for him to suddenly gain such agility from his soulforging. As she parried another of his attacks she felt a sharp burning sensation on the palms of her hands.

"Ah" she gasped, dropping her daggers, the cloth wrappings on the hilts were singed black, small wisps of smoke twirling off them. *Dirty trick.* Jaz flicked his blade to the flat end as he went in for a strike against her shoulder.

She whipped a glassblade down, deflecting the attack. It shattered on impact but knocked Jaz's sword off target. She jumped back and brought the remaining blades about her in a protective shield, reaching out her edir to conjure another.

The pair of glassblades orbited about her like tiny murderous moons. She smiled to herself at that. *Murder moons was a good name for this skill.* The glassblades would shatter into fragments when Jaz struck them but they were extremely effective at keeping him away while she thought of a strategy.

Femira had never had a strong sense of other people's edir. Misandrei and Aden claimed that if she focused she would be able to sense them. She'd been able to sense Vestyr's only when he'd taken control of her projectiles the night that Honorsword Karas had attacked her. She'd hoped that now she was soulforged it would be easier to detect, and she thought *maybe* she could sense Jaz's.

She could certainly feel his attempts at manipulating the temperature in her body. Jaz wouldn't try to incinerate her, but he was definitely trying to increase her temperature to distract Femira. She felt intense flushes as her body temperature suddenly spiked. Her own edir instinctively worked to protect her from outside manipulation.

Even without a topaz, a person's own edir—even untrained—would be an effective shield to temperature manipulation. Prior to soulforging, it was one of the irrefutable rules of runewielding Femira had learned. It was supposed to be impossible to affect the internal workings of another person's body without physical touch. Physical touch formed a connection through which a person's edir could channel through.

It was a testament to how much stronger the soulforging had made Jaz's edir; that he could alter her body temperature—even moderately—without touching her.

Jaz dashed another of her glassblades but Femira quickly reformed it from the shards. Her edir was beginning to strain from the exertion of maintaining the murder moons but she hoped that Jaz's aggressive offence would exhaust him quicker.

Femira noticed that Jaz was pressing her towards the wall, she evaded his next attack by diving into a roll to the side. Coming to her feet, she felt Jaz's boot at her back, knocking her forward. She fell forward on her stomach, side-rolled and flipped back onto her feet.

A floor-to-feet backflip was the kind of flashy combat manoeuvre that would get you killed if you performed it wrong so Misandrei had drilled the move into Femira through constant repetition.

Femira's edir had dropped the glassblades when she'd been struck. She didn't have the time to pull them back to her before Jaz was on her again. She evaded his strikes as he pressed forward.

She realised with mounting concern that he was pushing her back to the wall again. He would be expecting her to side dodge again. There would be a fifty-fifty chance he'd land a hit on her if he guessed correctly which direction she'd go.

An idea struck her and with a firm push of her front foot, she leapt backwards toward the wall. Her edir exulted, finally unleashed to suck in the stone wall.

Dust engulfed her as the wall disappeared in a cloud of debris, most of the stone sucked into her, alighting her skin in gold. She was like a yellow sun, dimly visible through a thick cloud as she was launched backwards through the dust cloud.

Femira landed clean on her feet on the other side of the wall in the adjacent training room. She could vaguely make out Jaz's dark shape as the dust cloud cleared. He was tentatively moving forward, the tip of his wooden sword in front of him.

Femira smirked as he crept forward; Jaz was the mouse and she was the vreth about to strike from the shadows. The stone thrummed inside of her. The stone had been a wall for decades and *wanted* to be a wall again. She poured the rock out from her reforming the wall and within seconds, it was.

The debris coalesced, the bricks reforming into their original positions and locking back into place. All save for a tiny sliver where the tip of Jaz's sword was wedged firmly in the stone. She could picture Jaz's bemuddled expression on the other side, and his instinctive reaction to try to pull it out. But the sword would hold firm.

Femira could see in the corners of her vision; other soldiers in bloodshedder uniforms in the room but she paid them no heed. She ran a few feet down, readied herself, and sprinted full pelt at the wall.

Here we go!

She pushed out with her edir, pulling in the stone again and forming a hole that she jumped through. Femira erupted through the wall in a cloud of dust on the other side.

Jaz was where she expected him to be, his foot pressed against the wall, trying to pull his weapon out. His head twisted towards her, but she didn't give him time to react, moving forward for a punch. A crude cudgel of stone formed behind him as he moved to block her attack, she pulled the cudgel forward smashing it against his shoulder. He grunted as it struck him, and fell to one knee.

"I win," Femira breathed triumphantly through ragged breaths.

A bloodshedder soldier appeared at the hole she'd made in the wall, "keep your bouts in your own training room, will you?" the man called in angrily. Femira couldn't help the laugh that escaped her.

Exhausted, she collapsed to the ground, trying to suck in air through her laughter. Jaz also coughed out a laugh as he too fell to the ground to rest.

CHAPTER 20
Reining In

Femira had never ridden horseback. Annali Jahar likely would have but horses were a rare sight in Keiran. The beasts weren't well suited to the overbearing attention of the sun or the long expanses of desert. Horses needed water and most people in Keiran preferred to keep their water to themselves. Keiran travellers often favoured camels, garrifs or shari's.

Femira had no memories of riding on the backs of any of them, but she did have hazy images of sitting in the back of a cart being dragged along cracked and caked earth by a pair of slow-moving garrif, a rainbow tarp draped over the top of the cart to keep them cool.

This meant that when Femira was stood facing a massive white horse with brown patches, she hadn't the faintest idea of what to do. She watched as the rest in the group around her effortlessly jumped up into the saddles. *Ok, you got this. They're just sitting on them, it can't be that hard.* She took a step toward the creature and it stamped a hoof in the dusty ground. *Alright, stay calm you big lummox.*

"You've never ridden before, have you?" Jaz asked, already on the back of a sleek black horse, "I hear they don't keep them in Keiran."

"They ride camels and these strange horned cows," Loreli put in, also already mounted. Misandrei and Endrin were on the other side of the courtyard organising the remainder of the group. A dozen soldiers decked in black uniforms and a handful of regular soldiers.

"Gariff," Femira corrected her, "they're not cows."

"Here," Jaz said, effortlessly jumping down from his horse and walking over to her, "just pop your foot in here." He instructed and guided her leg into the stirrup. She felt a bit flush having him hold her leg like that. Jaz was attractive and her body reacted to his touch despite her wanting it not to.

"Careful Jaz, I think your edir might be leaking some heat into her," Loreli teased, Femira pointedly ignored her.

"You steady?" Jaz asked her once she was up in the saddle. She wobbled at first, but otherwise felt balanced. Years of walking along the rooftops of Altarea had given her an impeccable sense of balance.

"Whoa, whoa," escaped her as the horse took a few steps. *Ok, maybe not impeccable.*

"Just keep a tight rein on this one," Jaz said, patting the horse's neck, "he'll follow the group, but he'll veer to clumps of grass if you let him."

"Don't worry, Vreth," Loreli said with a grin, "I'm sure Jaz will rescue you if you get stuck." Femira sneered at her and had been about to give a smarmy retort but she noticed Misandrei approaching them and kept it to herself. *Show that you can work as part of a team and all that.*

"We're heading to the south dock, there's a ferry waiting to take us across the bay to Heraldport. From there we'll head north along the eastern side of the Tidewall," Misandrei informed them. "Keep to the group and don't fall behind. Endrin will be taking up the rear position today. Our mission is to patrol up along the coast of the Tidewall. The corsairs have been consistent in attacks specifically against Rubanian trading vessels."

"Steel shipments?" Jaz asked.

"Precisely," she confirmed, "and there's a ship bound for Heraldport this week from Rubastre. We've spread false information that there's a sizable shipment of weapons, ballistics and armour. The Altareans won't be able to resist such an opportunity. The Rubanian guildmasters have sent a decoy vessel which we have instructed to stop at a checkpoint along the Tidewall. There, we'll be setting up our ambush."

"How do we make sure the knowledge reaches the corsairs?" Jaz asked.

"Well there's a spy right there," Loreli nodded to Femira, "I'm sure she's already leaked the information back. I can take her into custody now, Captain, if you want to ensure the rest of the mission is kept a secret."

"That's enough, Loreli," Misandrei chastised, sternly looking Loreli down. "Annali is a bloodshedder now, I won't have you questioning her loyalty, are we clear?"

It felt strange to Femira having someone defend her like that. Loreli shot her a petulantly antagonistic look. Femira gave the girl a thin smile, proud of herself for not rising to Loreli's comments.

True to Jaz's word, her horse kept to the group once they'd departed from the barracks. Occasionally he would try to shift off course, but she heeded Jaz's advice and kept the reins tight.

"You have to let them know who's in control," Jaz said to her, "they'll walk all over you otherwise."

It was early morning, but the streets of Epilas were already bustling with activity. Street vendors setting up for the day, some already hawking their wares. An armourer touted that his steel was the finest Rubane had to offer as they passed.

"As strong as nythilium plate!" The armourer declared as Femira passed him.

"You really should purchase some of your own gear soon," Jaz recommended, "the barracks armoury is decent. But we're bloodshedders now, decent doesn't cut it."

Femira considered it, a few months ago she never would have thought of wasting money on such things. But now that she was a bloodshedder, she would soon be getting her first salary and it wasn't the pittance she'd been living on in Altarea. The look of shock had been mistaken for insult from the bloodshedder's quartermaster when he'd informed her that her salary would be three silver marks per month and bonuses for special assignments.

Three silver marks was more than she'd pull in half a year working for Lichtin. The quartermaster however had thought that Annali Jahar—who had been married to a Prince—had been deeply offended by the meagre stipend, and told her to take it up with her captain if she wanted it re-evaluated.

With that kind of money flowing in, Femira could easily afford a new set of daggers and her own armour. First on her list though was new stealth gear, something that could help hide her body's annoying new habit of glowing when she used her abilities. For someone who preferred to stay in the shadows, it made it pretty difficult to stay hidden.

A contingent of black-clad bloodshedders moving through the city didn't go unnoticed. Barefoot children playing on the street paused to gawk, soldiers garbed in the colours of varying highborn houses saluted respectfully. The part of her that was still Femira wanted to shrink away into the side alleys, but this new aspect growing inside of her was elated, commanding respect and honour. It was her adaptation of Annali Jahar. Not the stubborn, naive and foolish girl from Annali's journals, but the version of her that Femira had created, and morphed into.

She was realising with more and more awareness that the girl she had been; the one that preferred to hide, to back down, was fading away. She still clung to Femira. Her name that she'd held for most of her life. She didn't want to let her go. Vreth was who she had been becoming. Vreth wasn't afraid, she was the part of her that thrilled at the challenge of sneaking undetected into a mansion. This new Annali was like her, only her thrill was in being a runewielder—or more specifically; fighting as a runewielder. She enjoyed the challenge just as Vreth did, but the challenge was in fighting stronger and more skilled opponents. She revelled in the feeling of her heart thrumming in beat to the earthstone beside it.

Femira could feel it even now. It resonated in tune with her heartbeat. And with each pulse it sent out from her, she could feel the cobbles of the road beneath her horse, and the buildings lining the roads. She wasn't sure if her edir could draw in stone from those buildings, not from that far away. But then again, she hadn't fully tested out her new range yet.

"Control your edir, Annali," Misandrei said. She hadn't noticed the woman had fallen back from the front of the procession.

"What?"

"Others can sense your edir, and you're sending yours out in waves... broadcasting it. Your edir control has always been erratic and it's stronger now you've been soulforged. It's a lot more noticeable. If you do not master control of it, a skilled runewielder will be able to predict your next move." Femira reddened, both from frustration and embarrassment.

"I don't know how," Femira admitted quietly.

"You do," Misandrei chastised her, "rein it in, the same way you rein in that horse—with a hard grip."

"That doesn't make any sense, it's not as though I can touch it?"

"No?" She asked with a patronising expression of mock shock, "do you not touch it when you reach out your mind to the ground below you? The edir is *part* of you, Annali, it is your hand that clasps the rein. Remember that." Misandrei urged her horse back to the front.

Femira could sense the pulses, emitting from her in waves. She tried to focus on internalising them, to make the vibrations reverberate *inside* of her own body and not outside of it. Her sense of awareness of the ground and buildings around became weaker. She was still aware of them but she knew she wouldn't be able to disintegrate them, not internalising her edir as she was. In this state, Femira was far more aware of what was going on inside of her, it was like when she focused only on the material in her earthstone at her heart. Picking apart the tiny fragments of what the stone and metals had once been and focusing her attention there.

"That's better." Misandrei called back to her, "keep practising."

***

The docks at Epilas were miniscule compared to Altarea. A seawall shielded the city from the towering waves during the Uniontide and Lua Nova.

Wavecallers manned the towers along the walls, they worked to calm the waves so that they didn't break over the wall and flood the city. This meant that the city didn't have an expansive harbour.

South dock was a double wharf that sat within the confines of the seawall with an enormous gate that prevented the waves from destroying it. It was also small and could only hold less than a few dozen vessels at a time, and those were primarily made up of the barge-like ships that ferried people and cargo to the considerably larger harbour in the town of Heraldport.

Heraldport was less than two miles away, and built onto the very tip of the peninsula known as the Tidewall. It was named so because the peninsula was a long stretch of tall cliffs that sheltered the inner coastlines of Reldon from the brunt of the Altasjura sea's notoriously destructive tides.

"They say that ancient stonebreakers created it—before even the Sorcerer Kings," Jaz told her, the two of them leaning on the bow of the ferry, looking at the thin landmass on the horizon.

The scale of such a land mass being formed by a stonebreaker was such a ludicrous idea that Femira scoffed at him. "You expect me to believe that?"
"We don't know what ancient runewielders were able to achieve. Look at the Pillar of Reldon, that's pretty impressive."
"There's a difference between making a big tower and raising up an entire stretch of land from the sea."

Femira had been raised on stories of ancient heroes and gods that had created the world, but stories were all they were. She had seen the legacy of past stonebreakers in Epilas' architecture. The domes of Judgement Hall and the intricate structure of the Pillar were impressive, but they also weren't impossible. With enough time and resources, Femira was confident that she could build something just as impressive. But raising islands from the sea and pulling mountains out of the earth… those were just myths.

"I wouldn't have pegged you as one who believed in children's stories," she teased.
"Well when we're on the cliffs, and you're looking out at the uncontrolled wrath of the Altasjura, we'll see who believes or not."
"I lived in Altarea unless you've forgotten. They don't have any tidewalls created by made-up ancestors. There's just the cliffs and the sea."
"But the stormguards, they protected the city from the worst of it, no?"
"They could hold off the winds, but ain't no amount of aeristone is going to hold back the Altasjura." Femira responded. Looking down at the roiling current of the ocean, Femira could feel the tension knotting in her shoulders. She hated being on the water.

Hazy memories of the ship that had brought her family to Altarea, being battered and thrown about by the enormous and terrifying waves. Even when her brothers used to collect shellfish along the exposed coastline during lowtide, Femira couldn't resist the intruding thoughts of the crashing waves barrelling back to sweep them away. It was an understatement that being on the ship made her uneasy, but she masked it with a grin.

"Spar?" she asked Jaz, hoping to distract herself.
"Don't fancy setting the ship on fire," he said reluctantly and looked about the ship's deck.
"Come on," she pleaded, "you've got the advantage, there's no stone for me to pull on anywhere." It felt strange, when she sent out the pulses of her edir, to have them

resonate off so little.

The breeze around her and the current of the water below ebbed and shifted the pulses of her edir as they passed through but she felt no resonance from them. There was nothing from the wooden structure of the ship itself, only the isolated vibrations of nearby metals. The nails in the wood, her own daggers, Jaz's sword and the iron fittings of the bow.

Jaz seemed to consider for a moment. He'd lost to her in every sparring session they'd had since they'd become soulforged. He wasn't a particularly prideful man from what Femira had gathered, but after that many losses, it starts to hit at your morale.

Femira glanced over at Loreli who was in conversation with some other bloodshedders. Femira had yet to challenge her since becoming soulforged. *She's had three weeks to practise ahead of me.* Femira wanted to make sure she was at the top of her game before facing the other girl again. She also didn't want to face her with the disadvantage the ship presented to her abilities. She could tell Jaz was taking the bait but he might need a little more encouragement,

"No daggers?" She offered.

"Just fist and foot?"

"And runewielding," she added.

"Nah," he replied quickly, "not worth it. Too risky on the ship."

"Ok, how's this," she started, leaning in towards him, "you win and I'll stay in your room tonight."

"Oh really?" He smirked, turning and leaning against the rail, his back to the sea, "you know we can skip all the fighting part and just find a nice quiet place in the hull?" he suggested. She didn't really like Jaz in that way but she couldn't deny he was handsome. She'd also not had sex in months. Not since she'd left Altarea.

"Only if you win," she said.

"You've got a deal," he pushed himself forward, stepping into the middle of the deck. On standard passage over the bay there would have been upwards of a hundred passengers on a barge like this but due to the bloodshedder's request, only the contingent for the mission were on board, in addition to the ship's crew. This meant that big areas of the deck were left unoccupied, allowing plenty of space for small groups of soldiers to spar. The bloodshedders were constantly training, always honing their abilities at any opportunity.

Jaz walked into the middle of the deck and shifted into a combat position, fists raised. Femira smiled.

"First touch?" he asked.

"First takedown," she countered.

"You'll be on your back before you know it," he winked at her and in response she conjured up four glassblades, blunted edges but would still cut if they struck skin.

"Hey, you said no weapons!"

"I said I wouldn't use my daggers, the glassblades are part of my runewielding ability." He began to draw his sword in response, "you know I'm just going to turn that to dust right?" He grimaced and slid it back into the scabbard, "you've played me."

"Not my fault you're bad at the game."

***

After three rounds, Jaz was smashed once again onto his back with a kick from

Femira. He rose, spluttering and wheezing, "alright, I'm done."

"You don't want to try again?" she asked, innocently cocking her head to the side, "I could soothe out all those bruises for you…" she offered, "but you'll still have to get at least one win."

"I can't watch that pathetic display again," Endrin called over to them. Femira hadn't even noticed he'd been watching. She felt anger rise in her. *Who does he think he is?*

"Jaz is a far better fighter than you—" Femira started angrily.

"No he isn't," Endrin cut her off, "but I wasn't talking about him. I was talking about *you*."

"Excuse me?"

"You had weapons and he didn't. Jaz is also holding back so that he doesn't burn down the ship. You have a clear advantage so of course you would win. But that isn't the problem, your technique is painful to watch," he said scornfully, "it's an embarrassment. I can't fathom why the General thought it would be a good idea to promote you."

"Captain Misandrei trained me herself," Femira spat at him.

"And it shows," he replied, "she's an aeristone specialist. She is supposed to fight the way she does. You're a stonebreaker; finesse and quick movements aren't your strengths yet you rely on them as the cornerstone of your fighting style."

"Oh yeah? If you're so confident then why don't *you* face me?"

Endrin stepped towards her, she noticed now that the other bloodshedders were watching. Fine, she liked to have an audience when she beat someone down. The memory of Endrin turning her dagger to dust was a thorn in her mind. He'd made her question her place among the bloodshedders and her resolve had been thoroughly shaken for weeks. She wanted to beat him, *needed* to beat him. He couldn't surprise her, not now that she knew about soulforging and the boost to runewielding it gave. Not now that they were on equal footing.

Femira resummoned four glassblades. Orbiting two about her as murder moons and kept the other pair focused as potential projectiles. His face was impassive; she could feel his edir, similar to her own, sending out waves. She felt his edir passing over her glassblades. Endrin attempted to pull one from her control but Femira's edir held firmly onto it.

In response, she shot one forward which shattered on impact as it collided against his face.

He didn't even flinch?!

Endrin remained impassive as stone, his face glowing with amber light. There wasn't a cut or *any* mark at all from where the glassblade had struck him. His use of stoneskin wasn't surprising, but her glassblades should have at least made a shallow cut.

She schooled the surprise from her face. He calmly walked towards her, stepping into the orbit of the murder moons which also shattered on impact as he passed into their threshold. She swung at him and he didn't even blink as her fist crumpled against his face.

"Ah," she gasped, pulling her hand back to her chest in pain.

"We don't need finesse," Endrin said to her, "we are guardians. We are shields for our companions. You will *never* be fast enough to fight like them… but you don't *need* to, do you understand?"

"Stoneskin won't protect you from a sword or an arrow," Femira growled at him.

"You're right… but stoneskin doesn't have to be your last defence either. Incorporate it into your combat and you're unstoppable."

He turned his heel and walked away.

"We're not done," Femira called after him.

"Yes," he replied, not turning back, "we are."

CHAPTER 21
Hedgecliff

Femira spent the rest of the journey to Heraldport in a sullen reserve. She had been so confident, now she'd become soulforged, that she would be able to prove she was stronger than Endrin and to wipe that stupid smug expression of his face.

Endrin was rarely ever hostile towards her, mostly he ignored her. She wasn't sure which irked her more. Why did she even care what Endrin thought of her?

"Don't let it get to you," Jaz advised her as the ferry made its way into the harbour, "it's just his method. I think he's actually trying to help you."

"I don't want his help," Femira retorted, "I don't *need* his help."

"Are you sure about that?"

"What do you know? I've beaten you every time we've sparred," she said bitterly and then regretted it.

Femira had known that Jaz had been holding back with her, he didn't want to accidentally injure her with his abilities. Being a grenadier, Jaz's strengths were in fiery destructive blasts, they weren't the kind of skills you practised on your friends.

"He's been a stonebreaker a lot longer than you," Jaz said with slight reproach. "Don't be so arrogant to think that you know everything." He was right of course and she knew that.

But *why* did it have to be Endrin? There were plenty of skilled stonebreakers in the ranks, but so far she hadn't been able to get any time for training with them. Endrin was the only one out of them that had paid her any attention. She turned to apologise to Jaz but he was already walking away.

Heraldport was impressive, she'd seen it once before when she'd first arrived in Reldon. Back then she'd been in such a whirlwind of change with learning how to properly harness the power of the earthstone—and also trying to navigate what Garld and Misandrei's intentions were—that she hadn't acknowledged how impressive the town was.

The cliffs of the Tidewall were tall and imposing. Their rock faces had unnatural patterns that were distinctly different to the cliffs that the city of Altarea sat on. Dozens of long floating jetties snaked out from the leeward side of the Tidewall. The jetties heaved and bobbed with the swell of the currents. Hundreds of ships were docked along the jetties.

This was the closest major port to Epilas, it was the trading hub between Reldon and the rest of the world. The ships ranged from fishing dinghies to trading vessels of unrecognisable origins and large Reldoni warships. Femira even spotted the red rigged sails of a Yarji junk ship.

The group disembarked and were brought to the top of the cliffs by counterweighted lifts made of wood in groups of six.

Femira had struggled at first to understand how these worked without a stormguard pushing on the base of the lift as they did in Altarea. Her gaze followed the thick steel coils that strained as they lifted the platforms connected to a pulley and a counterweight; a huge lump of metal descended past them as they gradually rose.

Femira could feel it with her edir as it dropped further and further below them. *I could dissolve that in a few minutes now with my enhanced abilities. This platform and all of us on it would crash to the waters below.* It seemed like a monumental design flaw, couldn't they just counterweight with more wood? *Maybe it's not heavy enough.* Or maybe they just trusted that some lunatic stonebreaker wasn't going to just casually destroy the lift.

Either way the knowledge that someone could do that while she was riding it didn't make Femira feel at all comfortable. She edged towards the cliff face, which crawled past them as they rose. Femira had had a few slips while climbing before but she'd always managed to catch a grip, she wasn't entirely sure she could do that in a freefall, but it made her feel a little less apprehensive being closer to the cliff.

Once the full group and their horses had ascended, Misandrei led them through the bustling town. It reminded her of dockside in Altarea but with a much heavier military presence with soldiers and cannons lining the battlements. Bloodshedders were a rarer sight outside of Epilas and many looked at their black uniforms with deference; regular soldiers saluted, sailors and merchants avoided their path.

Jaz was riding further ahead on the line and Femira wanted to ask him about why there was such a strong martial presence, but she suspected he was still annoyed with her from their earlier conversation. Instead she kept to herself, Endrin was keeping up the rear of the column. She noticed Loreli pulling up beside her. The girls bright red-gold hair was tied back and braided.

"Hey," Loreli said as she pulled up. Femira simply nodded in response.
"We're both on Endrin's squad for the attack," Loreli started.
"You've made it pretty clear you don't trust me," Femira replied.
"And I still don't… but this will be the first time that our lives will be on the line," Loreli said with gravity, "and this is a warning; if you betray us, I'll kill you myself. Are we clear?" Femira bit her tongue, she wanted to lash out at her but her most recent embarrassment with Endrin still stung at her.

"You don't have to worry about me," Femira replied.
"We both know these aren't corsairs attacking ships," Loreli continued, "it's the Altareans. We know the stormguards are trying to build a resistance." Femira didn't respond, her horse following along after the one in front.

"You don't care that you'll be fighting your own people?" Loreli asked bitterly, "those stormguards once protected you."
"You don't know anything about me," Femira rounded on her with bared teeth, "you don't know a *fucking* thing. The stormguards never did shit for me." Femira gripped the reins tightly, and kicked into her horse. She still wasn't comfortable riding it but as Jaz had instructed her, keep a tight rein and show the beast who was in control.

Fucking stormguards protecting me. The most protection Femira had ever gotten from a stormguard had been when one had chosen to kick her in the stomach rather than in the face when she'd been caught stealing food. That had been before she and her brothers had been taken in by Lichtin, before she'd been taught how to avoid drawing their attention. Most of her childhood had been spent keeping an anxious watch for bluecloaks and bronze armour in the crowds. The bastards would make a judgement of her based on her raggy dirty clothes and assumed she'd been pickpocketing. *They were right, I usually was pickpocketing.* But that didn't mean she didn't have an instilled distaste for them. She would have no issue cutting one down.

***

The road north from Heraldport led along the top of the cliffs. To the east was the expansive and unstrained turbulence of the Altasjura. Deep blue and black waves swelled and crashed in a roaring mess. It was a familiar sight for her having spent most of her life living on a small island city.

There were other smaller ports and fishing villages dotted along the cliff tops, each with their own retractable floating jetties that could be taken in during particularly strong tides or storms. Femira couldn't understand how they lived here with the constant bellow of the wind crashing in from the east.

Large towns like Heraldport would have aeristone runewielders that would divert the strongest gales away but out here the locals were exposed to the brunt of it. Their own group was protected by those that had the aeristone on them. Inside of their bubble, the wind was quieted to a brisk breeze but Femira could still hear the whistling of the wind as it passed around them. Trees and hedges grew on the side of ridges in the cliffs but were bent and gnarled from years of wearing from the winds.

The group stayed in inns along the Tidewall and mostly kept to themselves. The locals were informed that they were patrolling the cliffs as a response to the recent corsair attacks. At one village—built in the shelter of Inish Head—they took a report from a group of fishermen who claimed that they had seen three warships flying unmarked sails.

"They didn't look like Reldoni ships," the eldest fisherman said, "They had the look of pirates, but they were too big and three of them sailing together… I've not seen that before."

"Thank you," Captain Misandrei said to him, "and you spotted them last week?"

"Aye," he replied, "they were heading back out east, not sure where they'd come from though." Misandrei paid them some copper coins for the information and dismissed them. Femira noted that Misandrei waited until they were well out of earshot of the locals before she spoke.

"It seems they've taken the bait," Misandrei informed them, "three Altarean warships which we can only assume will be fully armed and manned."

"Could be two-hundred soldiers on each of them," Endrin replied, "at best we would be outnumbered by forty-to-one. Even for us that would be a wildly arrogant move."

"We'll keep to the plan," Misandrei directed, "they won't have anywhere close to those numbers in runewielders. Most of their stormguards were killed in the assault on the Altarean palace. General Garld estimated they couldn't have much more than fifty remaining. We have an opportunity to potentially crush their resistance before it properly forms."

"Where do you think they've been hiding?" Loreli asked. "We still have warships occupying Altarea; they couldn't be sailing back and forth from there."

"We also have patrol ships to the south, they couldn't be taking refuge in Rein or Keiren," Endrin put in.

"Someone is helping the Altareans," Misandrei agreed, "hopefully we can take some of them alive. Get some answers."

Before the conversation could derail further into who might be sheltering the Altarean ships, Misandrei continued, "the decoy vessel will be docking here tomorrow. The Altareans will be lured close to the coastline by the Rubanian decoy, and we'll have our ambush ready on Inish Head," she informed them, "make any final preparations in town. We'll be camping on the headland tonight."

***

Femira had slept outside enough in her life that sleeping in a camp didn't bother her in the slightest. She had a military-grade tent and they had set their camp in the relative shelter of a rocky outcrop on the top of the cliffs. She'd spent many a night sleeping in nooks on roofs that the sleeping mat she had now was a welcome comfort.

It wasn't the camp that kept sleep at bay but the promise of what awaited them in the morning. Her first real battle. Femira had seen a battle before, in Altarea. She'd felt the rush of it but she hadn't been *part* of it, she'd merely capitalised on the opportunity the battle had presented to finally sneak into the inner depths of the Altarean palace. She hadn't had to fight for her life, she hadn't had to kill anyone.

People had died because of Femira before, but she'd never actually killed a person herself. She knew she could do it… she'd thought about it enough times. She'd thought of killing Lichtin for letting her brothers die. She'd thought of killing the stormguards that had been the ones to throw them off the cliffs.

She'd have killed Karas the night he attacked her in the Pillar… if she had been able to, and Landryn and Vestyr hadn't beaten her to it. But now that she was faced with the imminent prospect of it, she felt herself growing apprehensive.

"You're still up," Misandrei said to her. Femira sat on a rock above the camp, watching the coastline. The wind wasn't particularly strong and Femira suspected that Misandrei was diverting its flow to avoid the camp. "You are nervous."
"I'm not," Femira lied.
"It's ok to be scared," Misandrei told her, "I would worry if you weren't. You need a certain level of confidence to be a bloodshedder, but too much makes people foolish and reckless. I need all of you at the top of your game."
"I'll be fine," she replied. Reflections of the moons tossed about in broken shards on the sea, she hadn't realised how much she missed looking out at the sea at night.
"Pre-battle jitters are normal," Misandrei went on, "but don't let them keep you from —"

"—Why did Garld recruit me?" Femira asked her bluntly, turning to face the other woman, "you know that I'm not the real Annali. Was it really just because I look like her?" Misandrei didn't respond for a time, she didn't look offended at being interrupted, but then again she was always so stone faced it was hard to tell when the woman was offended or not.

"I don't know where or how Garld found you," Misandrei replied. "And I can't tell you for certain *why* he brought you in. This is simply what he does, he finds people that have unique skills and recruits them."
"I've never been in a battle," Femira admitted.
"I could guess that."
"I don't know—I'm not sure… if I'm strong enough."
"You're ready," Misandrei told her, "Garld thinks you are. You're here because he wants you to get combat experience."
"Is this what I am?" Femira asked, "…a soldier?"
"Is that what you *want* to be?"

"I…" she paused. *Was it?* She had been aware that ultimately that's where her training had been directed. But now faced with the realisation, it was a difficult thing to imagine herself as, "I don't know."

"You're a stealth operative," Misandrei replied, "that's what you've always been."

"You mean a thief," Femira said, a bitter smile tugging at her lips.

"The same skills really. You're an excellent runewielder and you have experience that no one else in the bloodshedders has. You can move unseen, we're not very good at doing that. Our combat styles and our training, it's all designed to be flashy and intimidating. Bloodshedders invoke fear, and break the morale of our opponents—even without a Foebreaker. Our enemies have lost the moment their swords hesitate… but with you," Misandrei put her hand on Femira's shoulder, "they've lost before they even *see* you."

"So you want me to be an assassin?"

"*You* decide who and what you are, Annali" Misandrei said, "and whatever your skills allow you to be." With that the woman rose and began to walk back towards the camp.

"Femira," Femira said, unable to restrain herself.

"What was that?" Misandrei asked, turning back to her.

"Femira," she repeated, getting to her feet, "my name is Femira."

Misandrei smiled at her, "thank you for sharing that with me," she said and then added pointedly, "but you still must be Annali."

"Is it really only yourself and Garld that know?" she asked.

"I don't know if anyone else has figured it out. I don't think they have. It's important that you continue to hold up the persona, Annali. Is anyone else suspicious?" Femira thought immediately of Darza and his attempts at blackmailing her. He was successful, she supposed, she *had* recommended him to be the newly appointed commander of the stormguards, after all.

"No one," Femira replied, deciding to keep that to herself. She hadn't heard if Darza had gotten that promotion or not. He hadn't attempted to contact her again, but then again, it had barely been two weeks since the events that night in the Pillar.

"Do you know what has happened to Honorsword Jahasa?" Femira asked, the last she'd heard was that he was still in custody. They couldn't detain him for much longer, not without the Keiran becoming alarmed on why their Honorsword delegates had gone silent.

"I don't," Misandrei replied, "but it is not our concern."

"But what if—"

"—focus only on the mission at hand, Annali," Misandrei advised her. "You can ask the General when we return. But for now, I need you to keep your mind on the mission ahead."

***

"I can see them," Jaz said just as she spotted the sails herself. They were white dots on the horizon. The Rubanian decoy ship had arrived earlier that morning, it had been hugging the coastline and had docked in at the fishing village just before the tide turned.

Their strategy was dependent on the Altareans leveraging the swell of high tide currents to propel them in when the trading vessel would be stuck at the pier. It was a classic manoeuvre that raiding ships took for smaller villages where there wouldn't be any tangible resistance from local authorities.

"Stay on the ridgeline," Endrin told them. They were organised into three squads of six. On Femira's team; herself, Endrin and another stonebreaker were tasked with ranged attacks. Loreli, Jaz and another grenadier were melee.

Misandrei's team was at the rear as a reserve, theirs was the only team with a Healer—a bloodstone specialist. Femira's team was on the higher ridge, with another offensive team further below. Both offence teams would be focused on targeting long-range destructive attacks to take down the enemy ships. Loreli, Jaz and the other short-range combatants were to defend the stonebreakers as they fired projectiles.

Resisting the urge to jump into the melee fighting around her would be a challenge for Femira. She knew that her instincts would be screaming at her to fight. But Femira needed to prove that she could be part of the team, that she could take orders. She waited in anticipation, watching as the ships crept closer along the horizon. She thought of the soldiers on those ships. They would be mostly men, if not all of them—she didn't remember ever seeing a female stormguard. She didn't know why that made it easier for her.

Her eyes spotted another white dot on the horizon... *Is that?*

"There's a fourth ship!" Femira called out, "is anyone else seeing that?!"

"What?" Endrin rose from his position. "Where?"

She pointed, but figured that was a useless gesture. It was always hard to follow a person's line of sight.

"Between the middle and the left ship," Femira said, "there's a fourth one in the distance."

Endrin squinted. "Shit," he said after a moment of scanning the horizon, "wait here," he instructed before heading off down the back of the ridge to Captain Misandrei's team position.

"Four warships," Jaz whistled, "there could be eight hundred soldiers in total manning them."

"Then it'll be a big win for us when we take them down," Loreli replied with a smirk.

"Why send four warships for just one merchant vessel? That doesn't make any sense," Jaz said, his gaze locked on the approaching ships.

The tide was carrying them in quickly. Beyond the cliff's edge was the broad expanse of coastline revealed by the low tide. The myriad of trenches and hollows in the exposed seabed were already being swashed with crashing white water as the oncoming tide surged in.

"Do you think they knew we were baiting them?" The other stonebreaker—Kerana was her name, she had a shock of blond in her black hair. She didn't seem much older than them, definitely still in her twenties. Loreli shot a glare at Femira at the woman's comment.

"Do you really think I warned them?" Femira snapped at her, exasperated, "I've been with you the whole fucking time." Kerana gave Femira a wary look. *Seriously, you too?*

"Both General Garld and Captain Misandrei trust her," Jaz scolded Loreli, "Annali is not our enemy. Stop letting your prejudice cloud your judgement."

"*Prejudice?*" Loreli's eyes widened, "she's Keiran! They *are* the enemy."

"I'm not Keiran," Femira said resolutely, "and I haven't been for a very long time."

Endrin was running back up the ridge towards them, bounding over rocks and clearing cracks with ease.

"Do you think we'll withdraw?" Jaz asked her. He sounded nervous. *Was this his first battle too?* She realised she'd never asked Jaz if he'd ever been in a battle before being recruited. He'd been a grenadier in the main army ranks, she knew that much.

"I don't know," she replied truthfully. The front three ships were fast approaching, the fourth fast on their tail. They wouldn't have long left to decide.

"We're to hold position," Endrin said as he arrived back.

"Hold position?" Kerana gasped, "has she gone mad?!"

"She's our commanding officer," Endrin reminded her with a stern tone, "get back into position. They'll be in range soon. Their numbers imply that they knew there would be some resistance waiting for them… but they're not expecting *us*. They have no idea the powers they're dealing with."

"Can we really take that many?" Jaz asked him.

"We're soulforged," Endrin said, "remember, most of these men won't even be runewielders. And those that are, well, they're nothing compared to the bloodshedders."

"How can we be sure they don't have any soulforged runewielders?" Femira asked, sceptically. She had found the soulstone *in* Altearea, after all. She also knew that the book had been one of the guiding texts on soulforging that Garld was using to infuse his soldiers. It was pretty obvious that the Altareans knew about soulforging and it wasn't a stretch to think that they might have had at least some success with it.

"We have the soulstone, remember?" Endrin said.

"You're not so foolish to think that's the only one?" she replied.

"It changes nothing," he growled at her. "We're not retreating. Get back into position."

They arrayed themselves in the agreed formation. The stonebreakers spread out, with Endrin in the middle. The melee fighters behind them, ready to jump into action when needed.

Femira could feel the pressure of the wind shift. It became wild and erratic, no longer billowing from the east, now twisting and undulating. She could sense the cliff beneath her, the weight of it, standing resolute against the wind and sea as the waves finally reached their feet.

The ground around her vibrated in response to her edir, she noticed that she could feel Endrin and Kerana's presence there too. Their edirs pulsing out from them, focused on the cliff. She directed her focus there.

The three of them began to form great spikes of stone out from the cliff face. It looked like the spines of a giant stone hedgehog were protracting out from the cliff.

Femira formed two, and could see below that the others had formed three each. She held the two and tried to focus on pulling a third out from the stone but it crumbled under the weight of itself, the rocks crashing into the surf below.

"Just two at a time," Endrin called over to her, "you don't have the strength for more than that." Angrily, Femira focused her edir on reforming the lost third spike, but then stopped herself. She was supposed to be learning to take orders.

She could feel her grip on the other two slipping, they strained and wobbled. She focused all of her attention back on supporting them.

Each spike was twenty feet in length and as thick as a horse, she'd never tried to hold that amount of weight before. She could feel it straining, and it thrilled her. She wasn't sure how long she could support it before she exhausted herself, she doubted she could hold on longer than a few minutes before needing a break to recover. She wouldn't need to hold it even that long.

"The first ship is almost in range," Endrin called out over the wind. "Hold!"

She could see tiny black specks on the deck of the ship. The Altareans undoubtedly had noticed their cliff hedgehog by now. *A cliffhog maybe? Hedgecliff?* She'd think of a better name for it later.

"Release!" Endrin roared. Femira felt the sudden swell of his and Kerana's edirs as they forced all their strength into their rock spikes. Six of hedgecliff's spikes exploded from the rock face, and hurtled towards the closest of the enemy ships. Femira's own pair followed a second later.

Femira grunted, her shoulders tensed and she had to adjust her stance to counter the sudden weight against her chest. She hadn't expected such a kickback from pushing on the heavy projectiles. The spikes tore through the air but as they neared she felt another force pushing against her edir to deflect them.

It was stormguards; using powerful gusts of wind to derail the trajectory. She pushed against the wind with her edir to steer them both back on course. But as the spikes neared the ship, a surge of wind blasted at them and they zipped past the ship. There was a fountain spray of white water as they crashed into the waves.

Endrin and Kerana's spikes had also been deflected. Although it appeared that one of them had managed to catch one of the masts as it was deflected, taking the top of the mast with it as it crashed into the sea with a massive splash. The ship itself was rocking wildly from the disturbed water, the sails billowing violently.

"Again!" Endrin roared, "before they regroup!"

Another set of rock spines grew out from hedgecliff, Femira tried to keep up but she couldn't form them as fast as the more experienced stonebreakers. They had already launched theirs before hers were even fully formed.

The winds had picked up even more violently than before, she could see now that tiny dark blue kites were gliding across the distance between them and the ships. She couldn't focus on counting how many there were but there was at least twenty.

"You see them?" Femira called back to Jaz.

"Don't worry," she heard in response over the wind, "I've got them."

"Focus on your own tasks, Vreth!" Endrin shouted over at her.

This time, she anticipated the pressure kickback and planted her back foot, pushing out with her edir and firing her pair of spikes forward.

A bundle of flames fell from the sky, it was close to her planned path but she didn't need to alter the course as the burning stormguard fell past. Her mind went to the horror that the stormguard must have felt realising that his stormsail had been set alight.

Femira remembered her own attempt at using one that night in the Altarean palace when she'd cleared the crevice. The panic-inducing terror of being completely unsupported and nothing between you and death below. Stormguards could manipulate the air but they couldn't fly, not without the aid of the stormsail and those didn't tend to work very well when they were on fire, Femira guessed.

She'd been distracted by the falling stormguard so when a blast of wind forced her spikes into the sea short of the mark, Femira cursed with frustration. She diverted her attention back to making another set.

"Reformation!" Endrin called out. *What? Shit, that meant—*

—Her breath caught and the world spun as a fist of air as big as her body slammed against her. Her vision spun wildly. Sky, land, sky, land, sky, land. A thud of pain erupted from her shoulder.

Disoriented, Femira looked up to see that she'd been knocked back against the rock formation. Three soldiers in blue cloaks and bronze armour landed in front of her on the ledge where she'd just been standing. A part of her mind was astonishingly grateful that whichever stormguard had blasted her had pushed her *away* from the cliff edge and not *over* it.

The three stormguards abandoned their stormsails and were drawing their curved swords. Suddenly, Femira was a child again fleeing through the market stalls in Altarea, swashes of blue cloak in the corners of her eyes. Instinct screamed at her to run but instead, she reached her edir into her chest and conjured all six of her glassblades. Four would have been a more manageable choice and meant she could summon another pair in case of emergency, but wasn't this *already* an emergency?

One of the stormguard's cloaks went ablaze and another bounded to the right, distracted by something. Femira didn't hesitate and leapt forward towards the remaining one, ignoring the pain in her shoulder.

She whipped out her steel daggers and kept the six glassblades in orbit as murder moons. She felt a tempest of wind as the stormguard attempted to hinder her with a gust but she drew in earth from below her, pulling it into her core as stoneskin. The action made her temporarily heavier, her skin stronger as the wind blast hit her. The murder moons were pushed out of orbit, but she reached out with her edir, catching them and firing them forward to the stormguard.

His face was masked by a bronze helm but Femira could see from his body language he was taken aback by her attack. The glassblades shattered against his armour, but she only needed them to be a distraction. She pulled at the earth at the man's feet drawing it in. He stumbled and she rapidly formed a mound of earth that she flung towards him. She had hoped there was enough force in the attack to push him over the cliff but his own wind manipulation skills protected him from that fate.

"Focus on the ships, Vreth!" Endrin's voice called out. *With a stormguard about to stick his sword in me I don't fucking think so.* She moved forward engaging the stormguard as she struck out with her daggers. He was quick in response with his sword, his fighting style similar to those she'd trained with.

He wasn't soulforged, Femira could tell that much already. However he was still faster than a normal person would have been, using his aeristone hold ability to enhance his speed.

Femira's forearm guard caught his sword as she failed a parry. His sword came back up quick as a snake, aiming for the vulnerable area under her arm. His sword was moving too quickly for her edir to catch it and attempt to dissolve the metal.

Instead, Femira focused on her stoneskin. She felt the sword cut through the material of her uniform and the blade striking into her armpit. With her focused stoneskin the blade tip felt blunt—like a punch—which was far more preferable to a blade slicing in there.

She needed to capitalise on the stormguard's confusion when his sword hit against something hard and immoveable rather than cutting up and out of her shoulder blade. The impact pushed her arm up—causing her to drop her dagger—she used that momentum to clamp her hand on the visor of the stormguard's helm. The vibrations of the bronze called to her and she pulled at it, the visor crumpling to dust under her hand. With her other hand, she buried the second dagger into his eye.

The blade slid sickeningly into the socket.

Femira felt the man's body go limp. The blade grinded against the bone and she gagged. Femira recoiled away and let go of the dagger. The man slumped away from her, her blade still lodged in his face. She trembled, feeling a sudden and intense nausea. She staggered back, her mind flashed to the feeling of blade edge grinding against the bone of his eye socket.

Then she vomited.

It was hot and acrid, and spurted out of her onto the man's body. *Oh fuck.* Her body erupted into a fit of shivers.

She looked around—more stormguards had landed. Loreli was engaged with three of them, her sword flashing and zipping. Jaz and the other grenadier were also embroiled in melee fights, their opponents' cloaks ablaze. She was aware of someone shouting but she couldn't focus on the words.

"ANNALI!" the words finally hit her. It was Endrin. *The ships!* The stormguards were just the vanguard; they were trying to take down the stonebreakers before they could sink the ships. If the ships landed then they would have a *lot* more soldiers to be dealing with.

A lot more blades in eye sockets. Her stomach clenched and Femira thought she might vomit again.

She took a stilling breath, calming her nerves. And then another, and refocused her edir on the cliff below her. She concentrated only on forming another set of rock spines, forcing the thoughts of eye sockets out of her mind. She looked out at the ships, gauging her target.

To her surprise there were only three ships remaining, with one now a jumble of broken wood being crushed and torn apart by the waves. She could see stone spears from the other team also being shot out from the cliff face. The other team had been focused on the ship closest to them but now all stonebreakers were directing their attacks at one of the ships that was streaming towards the headland.

The ship had made it within cannonfire range and bombshells were raining blasts against hedgecliff. They obliterated massive chunks of the rockface as Femira attempted to form her stone spikes. Some of the bombshells exploded in the air, having been intercepted by the grenadiers igniting them.

The ground beneath Femira shook as a blast hit close to them. They'd chosen this part of the cliff specifically because of its slope. It wasn't a sheer face so they would have stability without fear of pulling out too much rock from underfoot. Now with the additional blasts of cannonfire, chunks of the cliff rained down to the surf below. *Are they trying to take down the whole cliff?!*

It was the closest warship that was doing the most damage. And all attempts of stone spikes were being deflected. There were fewer spikes now as the endurance of the other stonebreakers began to wane.

Or maybe the stormguards had gotten to them?

She attempted to form another stone spike but it was blasted before fully forming. Femira tried to think of something else, she knew she was getting better at stoneshaping but it still wasn't her strong point. She'd always been better at dissolving rock than forming it.

The cannonballs would be metal, she could dissolve them? Try to give the others a better chance at forming their projectiles?

Femira tried to do that, and sent out her edir. But she couldn't reach them. If she were touching it, she could dissolve it seconds but the further away it was, the slower it dissolved.

Think of something! She looked over at Loreli, she'd taken down one of the stormguards but the other two were still on her, blue cloaks swishing as they fought. *Blue cloaks!* She realised. *All stormguards wear blue cloaks!* Their arrogant badge of honour.

Femira flicked her gaze back to the closest ship. It was close enough now that she could make out the people on the deck, soldiers milling about, loading cannons. The regular soldiers in dull grey uniforms and among them she could just about make out four men in deep blue cloaks. She could even catch glints of reddish light as their bronze armour caught the sunlight.

Femira kneeled down at the dead stormguard in front of her and placed her hand on his breastplate. She avoided looking at the dagger lodged in his eye socket.

The vibrations tingled Femira's hand as the metal poured into her. Her hands glowed with amber light and she reached out, forming a thin spear of bronze from it. She took aim at one of the stormguards and prayed that they would be too focused on the stone spikes that hedgecliff was launching at them to notice her spear.

With the full strength of her edir, Femira shot it forward. The spear tore through the air and she kept pushing. As it flew further away, her ability to hold on abated but she maintained her focus, holding on for as long as she could, guiding it with slight nudges.

The spear landed.

She could see the stormguard being knocked back across the deck from the impact. She couldn't really see if the spear had pierced the man's armour but she suspected it had. Her mind flashed to the eye socket and her dagger—only now she imagined it as a bronze spear. She shuddered and quelled the rise in her stomach.

The shards of Femira's glassblades were dotted about her. She reached out and pulled the shards into her and formed another spear, this one of glass. It possibly wouldn't have as fatal an impact as her last one, but it would still be enough to distract one of them long enough.

She rocketed the glass spear towards another of the bluecloaks on the ship. It whirred as it sailed through the air and struck him.

Femira had been so focused on her glass spear that she'd not noticed a stone spike crash into the hull of the ship at the same time. The stone spike tore through the ship and burst through onto the other side, crashing into the sea in a spray.

Soldiers on the ship scurried about but it was breached; the damage was done. Some had realised the inevitable and were diving over the sides before the ship eventually collapsed in on itself. The waves hammered at the breach, tearing it apart.

Femira felt the air sucked from her lungs as a vacuum pulled at the air around her. She recognised the sensation and drew as much stone from around her as she could hold. Her skin bursted with amber light as she did so. She held it in her core but didn't absorb it, using it instead to strengthen her skin and make her incredibly heavy in anticipation of a wind blast.

A second later—as expected—a blast of air smashed at her. This time from behind, an attempt at pushing her over the cliff but her additional weight of stoneskin held her firmly in place.

Femira looked to the top of a ridge where a stormguard was barreling towards her. She didn't have her daggers. Her glassblades were also gone. But she didn't need weapons.

She pulled the earth at his feet. Annoyingly, the man bound lightly over Femira's attempts to displace his footing. He was closing in on her. She attempted to pull up a mound of dirt as a barrier but a blast of air burst it apart.

Shit. Terror mounted in her as the man's sword was suddenly slashing at her. She focused stoneskin on her right shoulder where the sword collided. But then in an instant, he whipped his blade over to her left and landed a shallow cut. Her arm flared hot as the sword's edge cut into her just beneath her dragonhide pauldron.

Femira cried out in alarm, and barely had time to react as he stepped back and prepared to run her through.

The wind and light suddenly vanished and she was encased in a black void. She could still hear sounds but it was muffled, she stood frozen in complete darkness.

What? She reached out with her hand and her fingers brushed against stone. Her edir buzzed, and she was aware that she was encased inside a shell of rock. There was another presence there—someone else's edir—preventing her from dissolving it.

Endrin?

She pressed against the stone shell with her hands. She tested her edir against it but it remained resolute.

"Hey!" Femira called out, punching ineffectually against the rock. "Let me out!" She wasn't sure how much time had passed, it felt like seconds. Her heart was thrumming.

She could hear—and feel—the earth shaking as cannonfire blasts landed against the cliff. And then the edir was gone, leaving only the shell of stone. Femira reached out tentatively with her edir. It felt normal, vibrating in response to her touch. She drew it in and the shell around her dissolved instantly in a cloud of dust.

After her eyes adjusted to the light, she could see the body of the stormguard that had been attacking her. Blood stained his cloak and gave a vibrant red sheen on his armour. Loreli was standing near to her, looking out towards the sea. Nearby, she could see Jaz sitting on a rock and Endrin also walking towards them. She didn't see Kerana or the other grenadier.

"They're retreating?" Femira asked. Noticing that only one of the Altarean ships was still afloat and was hastily changing their direction away from the headland. The tide was still swelling in, it would be impossible for them to make it back out to sea against it. But they would surely have a wavecaller on board who would create a guiding current to channel them away from the bloodshedders.

"It's over?" Femira breathed.

"You're welcome," Loreli nodded to the dead stormguard in front of Femira. "I guess you're not a spy after all," Loreli took a step towards Femira and glanced at the man that Femira had killed, "dagger to the face..." she acknowledged with approval. "Nice."

Femira felt a lurch in her stomach, she buckled to her knees and found herself retching. There was no more vomit left in her, but that didn't stop her body trying.

"You alright?" Endrin asked as he made it to them. Loreli nodded, Femira tried to do the same but more bile hit her throat. Her eyes watered and she gasped and wheezed between retches. The wind felt cold against her sweat.

"Th—thank you," Femira managed to pant out, "for the stoneshell."

"Huh," Endrin considered, "stoneshell. Not a bad name for it."

"Better than hedgecliff anyway," she replied, leaning back and finally catching her breath.

"I have no idea what you're talking about," he replied.

"Nevermind."

"Where are the other two?" Femira asked, looking around. Loreli and Endrin shared a look. Jaz looked exhausted and didn't answer her. Femira nodded. *They didn't make it*. It didn't sting, she'd barely known them. So why then did thoughts of the stormguard with her dagger in his eye make her want to vomit?

CHAPTER 22

Rested is Rusted

When Femira had envisioned the aftermath of her first battle, she had imagined returning to Epilas in a victorious triumph. She'd pictured parades and cheering crowds like when Landryn had returned from Altarea. She hadn't really thought about the *immediate* aftermath and the grim duty of burying their dead.

Being stonebreakers the task would have been easily done with runewielding but proper burials were marks of respect for their fallen comrades. So they dug the graves by hand and their dead were placed ceremoniously in them.

Endrin called up a twisted spiral of stone as a marker for their graves and Misandrei spoke words of their commitment to Reldon and the bloodshedders.

Femira felt out of place standing amongst the other soldiers as they spoke about their fallen friends, she didn't really know any of the seven soldiers that had died. She knew their names and what runestones they had been soulforged with... she knew that Kerana enjoyed stout over ale.

And that Jaspar is afraid of being at sea. Was afraid. She corrected herself. *Past tense. He hadn't been afraid of the ship sinking but of giant crab monsters that his grandfather used to tell him stories about.*

Femira didn't know why she was thinking about these things, or why they made her sad. She didn't know these people, they weren't her friends. She'd travelled for a few days with them on the mission... so why then did this feel so much like real grief?

For the stormguards they'd killed, they used runewielding to dig out a pit where they dumped the bodies and filled it. She didn't know any of them either but had avoided looking at any of their faces for fear of seeing one with a dagger poking out of it. She still felt nauseous.

Femira was also surprised at how strong the smell of the blood was. The winds were trying to carry it away but it still filled the air, it was a thick smell of copper and iron. The last battle aftermath she'd seen had been at Altarea, and the scent of blood had been masked by the sulfuric smell of burning bodies. Either way, the smell after a battle wasn't a pleasant one.

"How are you doing?" Jaz asked her as the remainder of the contingent made its way back from the headland to the fishing village.

"I'm alright... I think," she responded with uncertainty.

"That was your first kill, wasn't it?" he asked and Femira nodded in response.

She thought it would be easier but every few minutes her mind would drift back to the dagger and her stomach would clench. She'd mugged people before at knifepoint, she'd even cut a few people—just a little—but never enough to actually kill someone. *Just enough to make them afraid that I would.*

Strangely, the two people she'd killed on the ship barely effected her. They had been so far away, she hadn't been able to make out what happened to them. But when she did think about them, it was just the face of the first stormguard except with either a bronze or glass spear in the face, those images made her feel ill.

"Do you get used to it?" Femira asked.

"Killing people *shouldn't* feel good," Jaz told her, "at least that's what my father taught me."

"They don't seem to mind," she nodded towards the other bloodshedders leading the way. For some reason she couldn't help but think of Landryn when he'd been fighting Karas. Karas had died with a stone blade in his eye. Why was it always in the eyes? Did Landryn feel this way after he killed people? Did Garld or Misandrei?

"They've been doing this a lot longer than us," Jaz admitted, "…I'm not sure what that does to a person." Jaz was younger than her by a few years. She didn't know exactly how old he was but she didn't think he was older than eighteen or nineteen. Should people that young know what this feels like? Should *anyone*?

The villagers cheered and clapped as they returned and settled into the only inn in the village. Femira was looking forward to a bath and some rest. She wanted to sleep for days. Even though the battle had only lasted a short time, the strain on her edir had left her exhausted. She could see that the others were in similar states. Misandrei would want a debrief however.

Three ships taken down.

Probably close to six hundred people manned those ships. Six hundred against two dozen soldiers. Two dozen bloodshedders. Their moniker now made sense to Femira. It was right there in the name, wasn't it?

We're bloodshedders. We create bloodshed.

They'd only lost seven of their number, not even a third of them. She knew that they had had a lot of advantages in the battle, but the crucial one was being soulforged. Loreli's count had been nine stormguards. Jaz had killed five.

The stormguards were experienced runewielders. In Altarea, they had been hailed as one of the strongest and most elite forces in the country. She'd not really thought of how the Reldoni had so easily swept over them in Altarea.

The Reldoni had larger numbers, they also had superior weapons and the Altareans weren't used to fighting against firearms. But it hadn't been either of those that had destroyed the stormguards. *It was us.*

She hadn't been listening to Misandrei's debrief and was shaken from her reverie when Misandrei addressed her directly.

"Did you hear me, Vreth?" she asked.

"Sorry, captain."

"You're scouting north in the morning," Misandrei informed her. "Reports from the locals claim that the Altareans had attacked some of the villages further up along the coast. Yourself and Endrin are to investigate any damage and report back. We do not anticipate that the escaped ship circled back to the north, but if you do encounter them. Do *not* engage."

"Yes, sir," Femira affirmed.

She looked over at Endrin who nodded to her in acknowledgement.

He'd shielded me. Why? She thought Endrin hated her. Loreli had also taken down the stormguard that had attacked her.

Femira had also learned that it had been *Loreli* that had blasted her initially when she'd been on the cliff, pushing her *away* from the edge. The girl didn't apologise for the forceful move or the bruised shoulder, she also didn't ask for any gratitude for coming to Femira's aid. The shoulder along with the shallow cut on her arm were her only injuries.

Femira paid mild attention to the tasks assigned to the others and her mind drifted towards the bath she would have. She was sweaty and bloody, that didn't really bother her... but she *felt* dirty. She let go a breath of relief when Misandrei finally dismissed them and made for her room without talking to anyone.

***

Bathed, fed, rested and fed again, Femira found herself back in the saddle as she and Endrin followed the cliff road north. It was awkward considering they'd never held any conversation where either of them weren't being antagonistic. Endrin's opinion of her hadn't seemed to have changed that much and he still treated her as if she didn't belong... but he *had* protected her during the battle.

"Why did you shield me?" she asked after a long spell of silence.

"What's that?" he grunted.

"Your stoneshell yesterday," she clarified.

"That stormguard was too fast for you, he was going to cut you down. Loreli was already on her way but she wasn't going to reach you in time."

"Why didn't you release me? I was in there for the rest of the battle," she said, accusingly.

"Safer for you in there."

"But *why*?" she pressed, "I thought you hated me." He pulled up, looking her up and down.

"I do," he said simply.

"So why save me?"

"'Cause you're a bloodshedder. You were on my team and you were my responsibility. The fact that you don't understand that is one of the reasons I don't like you," he continued. "That and you're friends with Jazerah..." his face moved into a scowl, an expression she was more familiar with on his face. "Not to mention that you didn't get here on merit like the rest of us. You're highborn. You and Jazerah expect everything to be handed to you."

"You're highborn too," she retorted and he barked a laugh in response, kicking his horse past her. "No... I'm not."

They continued with Endrin keeping a bit of distance between them, leading the way. The road meandered along the coastline keeping to the clifftops. Occasionally the road would split, leading down to coves or gulleys. They didn't bother going down any of them until they reached the point on the map that indicated a village nestled into one of the coves.

Femira wasn't sure how comfortable she would be living in a village so low to the shoreline. *Surely the uniontide came high enough to sweep the village away?* As they rode into the town, the remnants of an attack were evident. Stone buildings had been smashed to rubble. Broken timber planks littered the area. The village had only been a cluster of a few houses but now they were all in ruins. *Recently too. These aren't old ruins.* Clothes and other supplies were still scattered about so no scavengers had passed through yet.

"Doesn't look like there's anyone left," Endrin noted coming from behind one of the ruins, "you find any bodies?"

"Nothing," she said.

"Weird," he scratched at his bald head, "maybe they took them? Is that something you Altareans do?"

"I'm not Altarean," she spat at him, "and no... at least I don't think so."

"I've heard of Altarean pirates raiding villages and taking people captive."

"But *everyone*? Maybe the villagers spotted the ships, and fled before they arrived?"

"I don't think so," Endrin said, kicking at harpoons in the sand. "Looks like *someone* tried putting up a fight. And look there's old blood on that wall...and over there too."

"Blood but no bodies..." she mused, "do you think they buried them?" Endrin gave her a look that told her he didn't at all think that was a possibility.

Well maybe they're not as callous as you think they are.

The tide had washed away any indication of a ship being there along with any footprints but on the higher end of the village there were footprints and churned up clumps of earth. After another sweep for any survivors—or even any non-survivors—they made their way back up the valley to the cliff road. Femira took another glance back down at the village.

"Do you find it weird that they left most of the supplies?"

"Not much in the village... besides all the food was gone. Probably all they wanted."

"But all the fishing gear? Surely that's worth something?"

"Probably not worth their trouble... besides, they might not have even raided the village. Those houses look blown apart. They might have just used cannonfire from the ships," he responded. She shook her head in frustration. It was all so strange.

Why would they just blast them? It didn't make any sense. They were just fishermen. *Unless...* she rounded on her saddle looking back down at the village.

"Endrin," she said, "there's no burn marks or *any* indication of a fire. I don't think they used the cannons."

He twisted on his own saddle and squinted his eyes, "huh... weird."

They continued on north, there were two more villages that they were to scout to before returning back to Inish Head. There weren't many travellers on the road and when they did pass any, they would have brief conversations.

Endrin and Femira asked about the destroyed village but the travellers knew nothing of what happened. Even when they reached the next village, no one seemed able to tell them for certain what happened. Most suspected it to be the corsairs, everyone knew that there had been an increase in corsairs since Prince Landryn flushed them all out of Altarea.

"Cleared them out of Altarea and now they're here!"

"Maybe Prince Landryn should focus more on his people than out there at sea."

"Why hasn't the King sent anyone to deal with this!"

News would spread quickly that a team of bloodshedders had destroyed three Altarean ships on Inish Head but Femira and Endrin didn't mention it. Their mission was to simply investigate and report back.

No one could tell them anything of importance about the destroyed village in either of the two towns they passed through next. Similar to the people they passed on the road, most guessed that it was Altarean corsairs.

There were rumours of other villages further north that had also suffered the same fate in recent weeks. Femira could tell people were scared, some were packing up to leave, heading back to the mainland to find work on the dragonfarms or in the cities. They'd ask if the King was going to do anything about it. Some even claimed it was a sea monster, pulled in by the tides and stuck in the shallows, attacking the cove villages.

One fisherman even claimed that he'd seen a crab the size of a ship but that same fisherman had also gone on to tell Femira about the times in his youth when he'd seen—and bedded—a mermaid. She'd heard plenty of stories like that living on the island city of Altarea, and when she'd asked him how the logistics worked of having sex with a mermaid he'd just grinned at her and tapped his nose. She hadn't really known what he'd meant by the gesture and she was getting creeped out by the man so had given up trying to get anything useful out of him.

"Anything?" Endrin asked her.

"Nothing," she sighed, "just the same stories we've been hearing all day."

"We should head back. If we leave now we might make it back to Inish Head before nightfall."

They didn't bother to question any travellers on the road back and dusk was already falling when they passed the cove where the destroyed village was. Both of them were tired and simply wanted to return to the inn.

"I'm just not arsed," Endrin said, "nothing to be gained from checking the village again, and the sun's already set." Femira agreed, also not wanting to do a second sweep of the village. Although in truth, the place made her uneasy. *Where had the people gone?* There'd not been any graves or even any evidence to suggest the bodies had been taken away... just nothing.

Maybe it *was* mermaids and all the villagers had been cursed to be merfolk too. She'd heard stories that the nomadic seafaring Yarji people offered sacrifices to the mermaids so that they wouldn't turn their own daughters into mermaids. *They were also rumoured to eat people.*

"Do you reckon it could be Yarji people?" Femira mused, "I've heard stories of them being cannibals." Endrin barked a sour laugh, "Yarji," he snorted, "next you'll be suggesting mermaids or rakmen."

"I've *seen* Yarji," she snapped at him, "they're not myths. They'd trade with the Altareans. I'm pretty sure I saw a Yarji ship docked at Heraldport too." Their junk ships were fairly easy to distinguish. The rigged sails often made her think of dragonwings. Not that Femira had ever seen a real dragon but she'd seen drawings.

"Bullshit," he scoffed.

"How about this," she offered, "I'll prove to you the Yarji are real and you teach me that stoneshell skill." It wouldn't be hard, that Yarji ship was hopefully still docked at Heraldport.

"Fine," he grumbled and Femira thought she saw a hint of a grin on his face. *Was Endrin actually a decent person?*

Misandrei was collecting reports from other teams that she'd sent out to neighbouring villages when they arrived back, tired and hungry. After adding their own reports Misandrei informed them that they would be back on the road south in the morning, and that she intended to be back in Epilas before the week's end. That meant another few days in the saddle.

Femira groaned inwardly and spent the rest of the evening massaging out the cramps in her thighs from having spent so much time riding. For a person who'd never been on a horse in her life until a week before, she reckoned she was pretty good at riding. It beat walking for sure, but that didn't mean that she was filled with any measure of enthusiasm at the prospect of getting back onto that hard saddle.

It had been Jaz however that had finally voiced the complaint to Misandrei, "could we not take a day's rest here?" he hedged, optimistically.

"Rested is rusted," was her only response which Femira felt was conflicting considering the woman had often told her the opposite, that rest between training sessions was crucial to peak performance but she didn't add to the complaint. Her body was telling her she needed rest, but she wanted to be clear of Inish Head.

She felt like she could still smell the coppery blood. *Pouring out from an eye-socket...*

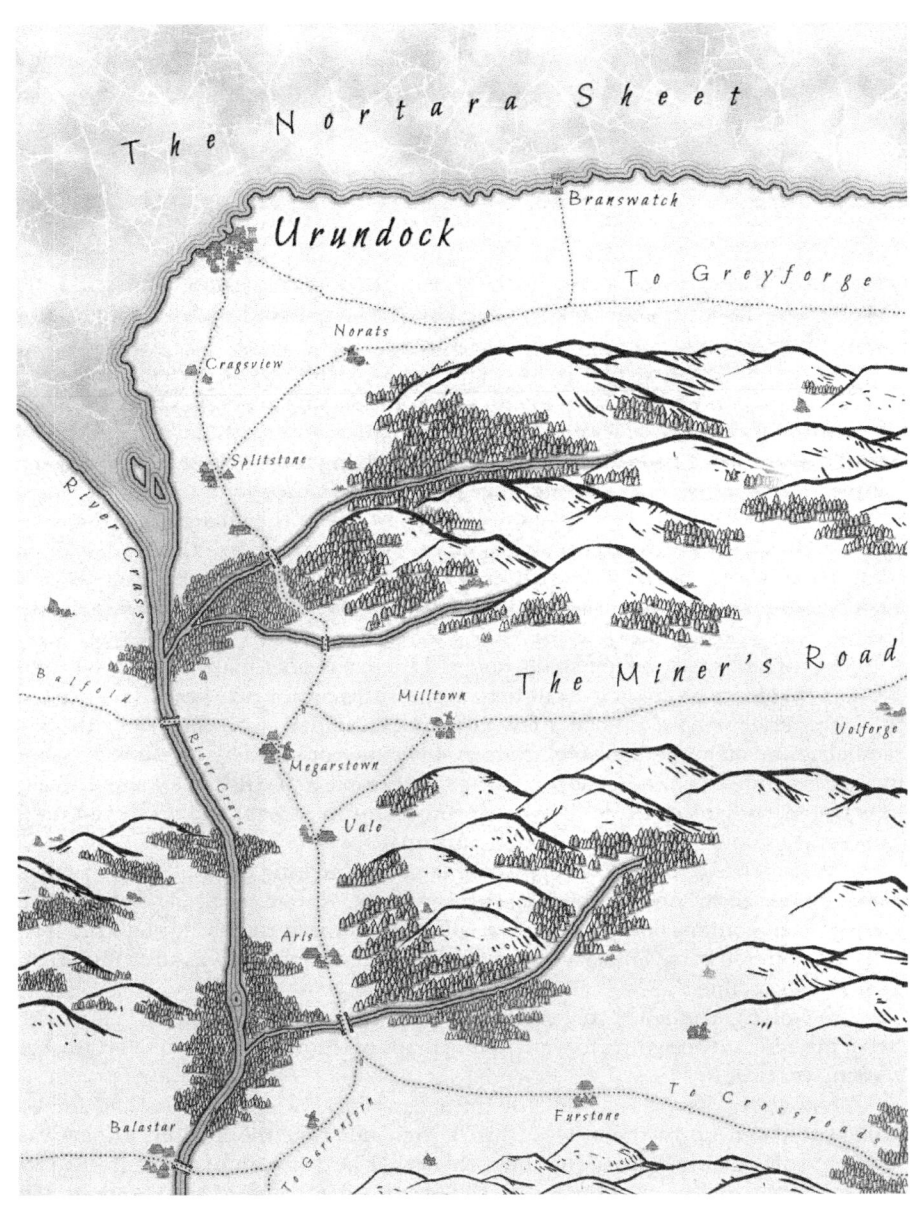

CHAPTER 23

Taking Shelter

The road to Urundock was much the same as the areas around Rubastre, only there was more snow and less villages. They'd had to sleep out six nights out of the ten since they'd left Crossroads.

Daegan was finding that he was settling into the routine of travelling; they would ride for a few hours, breaking for meals and setting up a small cookfire or—if they were close enough to a village—they would press on to get to whatever tavern or inn that the place had to offer. The food was getting progressively worse and the whitewhiskey progressively stronger the further north they went.

Daegan had purchased a dragonhide flask in one of the villages they'd passed through that he now kept topped up from every tavern they passed by. He'd paid ten copper marks for it. Rowan had said he was being cheated and that it likely wasn't even real dragonhide but Daegan didn't really care. What was ten copper marks to him?

The inns they stayed in usually charged them a copper mark each for bed and meal, at that price he could live out here in the outbacks for fifty years if he wanted to. *Longer even, maybe.* He had a few gold marks hidden in a secret pouch in his saddlebag and on his person. A lot more in silver and copper in his coin pouch—kept in a pocket in his cloak—his new flask fit snugly next to it. He had enough money, he wagered, to drink all the whitewhiskey these shithole towns had to offer and still have some left over for a plate of tough mutton.

The pretence of being a cartographer kept him making maps as they travelled which he traded to some of the inns they stayed at. At one village, the mayor had even tried to commission him to chart all of the mining routes through the Iron Hills. Had offered to pay him a whole silver mark for the job and was affronted when Daegan had declined.

"Ye won't get much better price than that 'round these parts, lad," he'd said, "trust me, ain't no one going to want to buy maps of the places north of Nortara. Yer wasting yer time."

They were a few days ride still from Urundock when rumours had finally started to catch up to them; word had gotten out that the Reldoni Prince was missing; some claimed assassination, others that he'd run afoul of the Ironworks Guild. Daegan had been surprised at the accuracy in some of the rumours and aghast at the ridiculousness of others.

There were claims that Daegan was working with his 'warmongering' brother Prince Landryn to sow discord between their nations.

That the Reldoni were plotting to invade.

That Altarea was only the first of Prince Landryn's conquests.

He'd been surprised to hear that his brother was getting an international reputation as a warmonger. Being a 'foreigner', Daegan was often asked his opinion on the alleged hostility of the Reldoni army. Some folk recognised him as actually *being* Reldoni and asked if he was a deserter from their military.

Daegan hadn't realised the extent that these people had thought of his people as being a military power. He supposed it made sense, they had been buying weapons from Rubane for decades and only increasing their demand during the war with Altarea and the rising tensions with Rein and Keiran.

"What do you think happened to the Reldoni Prince?" The innkeeper asked them as they settled their bill for the previous night.

"I don't think there's much truth to the rumours," Tanlor told the weasel of a man. Daegan could feel the tension in his shoulders. He glanced at Rowan who didn't seem overly interested in the conversation but when they met eyes, Daegan got the distinct impression that he was suspicious.

"You lads came from Rubastre? Did you see him?" The innkeeper's son asked, equally weasel-like in appearance.

"Can't say I had," Tanlor replied with a casual tone.

"I heard 'e was a cripple," the young man added, "that his brain didn't work right like Old Jim's lad. Got 'imself into trouble with the Ironworks." Daegan stiffened at that, his eyes snapping to the young man who seemed oblivious to the shift in his and Tanlor's postures.

"Aye, yeah. I'd heard he was a cripple alright," the innkeeper said, leaning across his filthy bar, "you sure you lads didn't see him? Jim's boy has trouble walking straight. Has a bit of limp, see. The Reldoni Prince is probably the same. You didn't see anyone with a limp like that?"

Daegan's throat locked up and he clenched his jaw so tight that he thought his teeth might crack. He wanted to throw the glass of shit ale into the innkeeper's face —no, he wanted to smash the glass right into it.

"No," Tanlor said, his voice now rife with condescension, "there's *tens* of *thousands* of people in Rubastre. More people than you can imagine so *no*... we didn't see him." He turned to Daegan and almost had to drag him out of the inn.

Daegan felt rigid with tension. The *audacity*, the outright disrespect! He could feel the anger scrunching up his face.

"Ignore them, my lord," Tanlor said gently to him before Rowan followed after them, "they're just ignorant fools and don't know anything beyond this pisshole of a town. Come on, let's get out of here."

They packed up their horses and were back on the road. Daegan didn't miss that Rowan was suspiciously quiet after the village, normally he would happily indulge Daegan in some conversation on the road. Stories of the contracts he'd taken and the like. Rowan had made a bit of a name for himself as a road-knight and tended to avoid the castle contracts if he could. Old acquaintances would often recognise him at the inns they passed through and he greeted them with friendly smiles and handshakes.

They followed the road along the river, heading north for a few hours and leaving the village behind them. Occasionally, the road would pass through thickets of woodland between the expanses of farms. The weather had been wetter which kept the snow from sticking—Rowan said it was normal for the area and that the snows wouldn't be coming strong there for another week or two. But it meant that instead of snowfalls to contend with, the group would often need to find shelter from downpours. Dark clouds loomed over the Iron Hills to the east bringing with them the threat of another rainfall.

"Looks like a heavy one," Tanlor guessed. "Let's take shelter under the crossing ahead. We'll camp there for the night if we have to."

"I don't fancy sleeping outside in wet clothes," Daegan agreed.

"Better to stay warm than get warm," Rowan added.

Daegan checked the weight of his flask, it wasn't even half empty yet. *Good.* The whitewhiskey kept him warm but only so much. *I'd really rather not be hungover and have pneumonia in the morning.* They pushed their horses hard as the clouds rolled down off the hills. They'd just made it to the stone crossing when the rain hit.

The bridge crossed a steep gully but there was a convenient flat area just at the base where they made camp. There were remnants of an old campfire. Just as they hitched up the horses, the rain came in strong, sheets of water pouring over the sides of the bridge.

There were a few logs left from the previous campers but not nearly enough for the night. Daegan looked out unenthusiastically at the torrents of rain. It had become one of his responsibilities to gather firewood while Tanlor and Rowan swept the area for any tracks that might allude to outlaws or anything else dangerous.

"So," Rowan started, pulling off his wet cloak and shaking it off. "I'm guessing the Prince of Reldon won't want to be collecting firewood anymore." Daegan froze and Tanlor turned on Rowan.

"You've no idea what you're talking about," Tanlor raised a warning finger at him.

"No?" Rowan chuckled, "your secret's safe with me, you should know that Tan and don't treat me like a fool."

Daegan eyed him. He'd enjoyed Rowan's company but he'd liked that the man didn't know who he was. He'd been friendly with him and hadn't judged him when he'd learned that Daegan was hindered. He didn't want that to change and he knew that Rowan wasn't overly fond of highborn and 'Prince of Reldon' was pretty much as highborn as you get.

Daegan looked back out at the rain and drew up his cloak around him, "it's true... I am a Prince of Reldon. My real name is Daegan Tredain," then he nodded to the campfire, "get that fire going, might be some driftwood along the bank. If I collect it now we can dry it with what we've got." He stepped out into the torrent and climbed—mostly slipped—down the gully to the river bank.

"Can I still call you Dessie?" He heard Rowan call after him.

"If you want," he shouted back up over the rain.

"Daegan's alright, I suppose."

He made a few trips back and forth gathering sodden branches. Rowan had the campfire going and was drying the haul that Daegan had lugged up. His cloak did an excellent job of keeping the rain off him. And his boots—"a pound on the feet is ten on the back," Rowan had told him when he insisted that Daegan buy the cheaper leather boots over the more expensive dragonhide. "Past Urundock, we're going to be on foot, the less weight on you the better." They were bulky, ugly boots but were lined on the inside with wool and Daegan's feet hadn't been warmer since he'd arrived in Rubane. However, the cloak and the boots could only do so much though, and the water did seep in.

"Dry them by the fire," Rowan advised him as Daegan pulled them off, "wet is —"

"—Wet is dead," Daegan interrupted, grinning at him.

Rowan gave an amused chuckle, "guess you have been listening." He handed

Daegan a bowl of stew that he'd been preparing over the fire. It was bland but hot. Daegan's hands stung pleasantly with the heat as he held it. He breathed in the warmth of the stew and let out a satisfied sigh.

"So," Rowan began, "what's chasing you?"

Tanlor was still off doing the perimeter sweep, making sure there were no bears or rakmen close by. Daegan eyed him over his steaming bowl, "an assassin," he breathed.

"I'd say you've had your fair share of those come after you, being a Prince and all. Why's my brother protecting you instead of your own men?" Daegan gave him a heavy stare but kept quiet. He had never said it out loud, it had been Tanlor that had given the report to Duke Edmund, Daegan had just dazedly nodded along in agreement.

He found now that it was difficult to voice what happened. Ferath, his own bodyguard—his *friend*!—had betrayed him. Had the man *ever* been his friend though? *He was Landryn's friend... not mine.* Ferath had always seemed so loyal... so trustworthy. He felt his eyebrows knot in anger.

"I see," Rowan granted despite Daegan not saying anything, "shit. You know why?"

Daegan shook his head.

"A stupid question but you got any enemies?"

"There's no stupid questions," Daegan replied a smirk at his lips. Rowan leaned back a grin breaking across his face, "walked into that one, I did."

"I've got enemies, but no one I can think of that would risk trying to have me killed... I can't make any sense of it." Talking about it, Daegan felt like a weight was being lifted off him. Like he'd been carrying it around with him since they'd left Rubastre. It felt good to talk about it openly, any time he'd tried bringing it up with Tanlor, the man would shut down the conversation with a hard look.

Daegan explained the events of that night to Rowan, not leaving anything out. How it seemed like a flame had gone out in Ferath's eyes and he was suddenly a different person. How they'd been friends before—at least Daegan had thought they were. And the impossible things that Ferath had done.

"I'm sorry," Rowan said with sympathy in his tone, "having your own companions turn on you," he shook his head. "I don't know if it helps at all, but I've felt a betrayal like that before. Someone very close to me," he trailed off, his brow deep and his eyes sad, "I've felt the pain you're feeling... the confusion, the anger."

"Thank you," Daegan replied, "that does help... actually," and surprisingly it did. Daegan *did* feel better, he felt understood. For the first time in weeks he felt that deep quiet anger starting to lessen.

"Who stands to gain from your death?" Rowan asked. It was a good question, one that Daegan had lain awake some nights trying to figure out.

"Honestly... your guess is as good as mine."

"Those rumours about you running afoul of the Ironworks Guild?"

"They're true," Daegan admitted, "but far too risky for them. They'd use other tactics, I think, conspire to have me sent back to Epilas. I don't reckon they'd try something so bold as to kill me. Other than that, I don't think I'd made any enemies in my time here."

"I've heard shady things about the Ironworks Guild," Rowan shook his head, "I wouldn't put murder past them if it's gold they're after."

"My father wouldn't allow the insult of having his son being murdered to go unpunished," Daegan replied, "he may hate me but I still reckon he'd burn Rubastre to the ground than let his reputation be wounded."

Rowan gave him a concerned look at that comment, "who do you think he'd come for first?" Daegan considered for a moment, scratching at his throat. He hadn't thought of that. Who *would* his father blame? *He likely wouldn't go directly after the Ironworks Guild, not with the dependency of our army's steel shipments.*

Then it struck him. *He'd go after the Duke. He wouldn't care if it was Edmund that did it or not, he would kill him just for the appearance of it.*

Would his father really wage a war against Rubane? They had stayed neutral throughout the war with Altarea and the centuries of border disputes with the Reinish. They were so far from Keiran that the Emperor wasn't concerned. Rubane had always been a bystander. *A bystander that sold arms to all the other countries at war with each other.*

Rubane's own military was incohesive, with each Duke having his own men that were loyal only to their Duchy. Each had their internal feuds to deal with and smaller scale skirmishes between unfriendly Duchies.

Rowan noted the realisation on Daegan's face, "he'd go for the Arch-duke," Daegan admitted.

"So," Rowan probed, "who would gain from a war between Rubane and Reldon?"

"Fuck," Daegan swore, he'd been coming at this all wrong. He never thought that his life would be used for such large scale schemes. Lukane and Landryn dealt with these kinds of things… *he* wasn't supposed to be involved with anything like this. He had to let his brothers and father know… and he *had*! He'd written a letter for his family and given it to the Arch-duke. Edmund had *asked* him to write that. He said he would make sure it made it to Reldon.

"Edmund had known," Daegan realised. "He knew my father would react with war. He had me write a letter to my family, explaining the situation."

"Why send you away in the first place?" Rowan asked, "surely it would be a safer option for the Arch-duke to send you home?"

"I don't think he trusted I would make it there." Within reason, Daegan's own men had tried to kill him and it's not as though Daegan could fend for himself.

A familiar frustration rose in him, it grabbed at his throat. He coughed to clear it.

"None of this would be happening if I were a runewielder," Daegan said bitterly, "I wouldn't even be here!" Rowan held eye contact and gave Daegan a sad look. The pity in it made Daegan angry, he was about to snap at him for that look but then Rowan spoke first, "how many runewielders has your father got in his army?" the question caught Daegan off guard.

"They're all runewielders," he replied with a dismissive hand wave. Rowan laughed, not his usual raucous laugh, but a low knowing laugh, "you've only as many runewielders as you've got runestones," he said, "so I guess a more appropriate question would be; how many *runestones* does your father have in his army?"

"I'm not sure," Daegan rubbed at his neck, "a few thousand maybe?" he answered. Rowan whistled at that.

"Rubane doesn't have that many?"

"Topaz is common enough so there's a few companies of grenadiers," Rowan answered. "Earthstone isn't as common here as your country, we have a few trained stonebreakers but most of them work in the mines or as smithies. I've got one,

I was castle-trained but I would be considered an amateur by any half-decent stonebreaker. Wouldn't be much use in a battle with it anyway."

"What about wavecallers? And aeristone?"

"Even less so. The runestones are too rare, and people who can use 'em, well they're even rarer. Up here, steel and the strength of your arm is what matters, not your edir. You won't find many folk outside of the highborn that can afford a runestone... I'd wager the same is true in your country too. Now don't get me wrong, up against a runewielder you're at quite a crucial disadvantage but I've seen a castle-trained knight with runestones taken down by a peasant with a bow and I've seen a farmer with a pitchfork defend his home from a rak chief with an aeristone."

"Rakmen can runewield?"

"They sure can. Runestones seem to be reserved for their chiefs. At least from the ones I've fought."

"I thought you don't see much of them south of Nortara?"

"Not usually, but every few years, a few bands of the bastards make a push south... but we're going off topic here."

Daegan had purposefully been pushing the conversation in a different way. He didn't want the same lesson he'd heard before that being hindered wasn't so bad, "I'm not some peasant with a pitchfork," Daegan said.

"No," Rowan acknowledged, "you're a Prince of Reldon. You're supposed to be a warrior—a General, even—like your ancestors before you. But you don't have to be a runewielder to be those things."

"Tell that to my father."

"I hope I never get the chance," he replied with a tight-lipped smile but then his eyebrow raised as Tanlor appeared, sliding down the wet grass of the gully to their camp. His cloak was almost black with the rain. Tanlor pulled back his hood, worry painted on his face.

"What is it?" Rowan asked, rising.

"Four men, heading this way from the north, and fast," he said.

"Probably the rain," Rowan guessed, "they'll likely want to shelter here too. Probably harmless." He still reached for his sword and buckled it to his belt.

"Doesn't look like you believe that," Daegan said, eying the sword. Rowan looked at Daegan and winked, "better to have it and not need it."

They didn't bother putting out the fire, the travellers were not far off and they would have already seen the smoke despite the rain. A large red-haired man with a warrior's braid, and shaved sides approached first. Despite the similar characteristics in build, hair colour and style, the man looked nothing like Rowan. The man had a thick neck and a jaw that could shape iron.

The man pulled up a few feet from their camp and called over, "we're just four travellers, looking for shelter from the rain... don't want no trouble."

"Keep your weapons sheathed and there'll be no trouble found here," Rowan called back to him, Tanlor gave him a wary look but didn't disagree.

The man waved up to his companions on the bridge and then walked his horse into the camp.

"Name's Owen—but most call me Ox," the red-haired man said, offering his ham of a hand to Rowan. *I bet they do.* Rowan introduced himself and the others, and invited Ox to join the fire.

Within a few moments, the man's three companions had hitched up their own horses and were airing out their cloaks, hanging them on the loose bricks in the bridge foundations. All four of the men were completely sodden, making them seem almost sickly. Their faces were pallid and their hair slick against their brows.

Geral was grey-haired and carried a longbow, he seemed to be the same age as Ox which was somewhere in the forties. The other two were young, barely men and could have been their sons; Shye and Jax. All of them had warrior's braids and carried weapons, a bit rusted and dented but still sharp enough to be a concern.

Daegan could feel the tangible tension around the camp as they settled in and started cooking. They spoke small, curt pleasantries about the road. The newcomers had come down from Urundock. They'd heard about the raiders in Crossroads and upon hearing the Shrydan brother's names, the other group visibly relaxed. Daegan took a swig from his whitewhiskey flask and felt the flush of heat filling him.

The sun was setting and the rain hadn't let up. It was looking increasingly likely that they would all be camping together under the bridge. Nobody had spoken more than a few words in over an hour and Daegan found himself growing incredibly bored with the additional campers and their lack of sociability.

"Here," Daegan said, tossing his flask over to their side of the fire, "whitewhiskey... not the best but it's strong." The four of them nodded their thanks, and took swigs in varying measures, the younger lads face's screwing up afterwards. Shye hacked and coughed and the others laughed.

"So... how's the road to Urundock?" Daegan asked in a friendly manner, hoping to get some kind of conversation going again with them.

"Ah, is what it is," Ox replied, he seemed to be the leader of the four, "what has ye lads on the way there?"

"Work," Tanlor replied, simply.

"What about yourselves," Rowan offered, "what has you on the road south?" The men all shared glances and it was Ox that spoke, "work," he replied and took another swig from Daegan's flask, not even a flinch out of him as he did so.

Oh, so manly. Daegan had always found humour in the bizarre custom of Rubanian men, the less you reacted to a strong drink, the stronger you were, apparently.

"More work to be found for fighting men up in Urundock, I'd have thought," Rowan probed, accepting the flask back and taking a small sip himself. Daegan noted tension in Rowan and Tanlor's postures. Even though they were all sitting casually around the fire, the two brothers had poised positions.

Ox didn't bother to deny that they were fighters, the warriors braids were evidence enough for that, if not the weapons. Daegan suspected that Rowan didn't even drink from the flask. *He wants to stay sober.*

"Grown sick of Urundock," Ox replied.

"Pisshole of a town," Geral chimed in, "too many people."

"There's more people, the further south you go," Rowan noted, "past Nortara is where you want to go if it's people you want to avoid."

"We're not going back there," Shye said, which earned him hard looks from Ox and Geral.

"You lads come down from Twin Garde then?" Rowan said, putting up a front of being more relaxed but Daegan could tell that he was still on edge.

"Aye," Ox said, "finished our contract up there. Looking to head home for a while."

"Commander Sheeth still up there?" Rowan asked.

"Aye," Ox replied at the same time Geral said, "no." They shared a look and Geral continued, "still up there, but he's not Commander anymore... got too old."

"Didn't think Sheeth would ever hang up his sword," Rowan said with a grin.

"Didn't have the choice," Ox replied, "got wounded bad."

"It were the rak that got 'im," Shye added quickly, he seemed fidgety to Daegan, like he couldn't stay still. "Whole bunch of 'em," Jax agreed, nodding.

The flask had made its way back to Daegan, he was shocked at how light it was. *Barely anything left in it.* He'd grown so used to travelling with Tanlor who didn't drink at all and Rowan who only had a small bit before bedding down.

He knocked back the last drops and opened his cloak to slip it back into his pocket but as he did so, the flask dislodged his coin pouch. It popped out of the pocket and dropped onto the grass with a heavy rattle, spilling out more than a handful of silver and gold marks.

Daegan's heart leapt and he instinctively grabbed for it and shoved the coins back inside. In a few hurried seconds he had it all back inside his pocket. *Stupid tiny pockets.* He looked up at the others, Tanlor and Rowan were eying the others, their hands not far from their weapons. Jax and Shye's eyes were wide and they gave uncertain looks to the older men, both of whom seemed disinterested in the coins.

"I thought you said that this Sheeth fellow was just wounded," Daegan said looking to shift the conversation back, "but you're saying now that the rakmen *killed* him?"

"Rak bowman got his leg," Ox said, "but he got back with his life." *Well these men are the worst liars I've ever come across.* He wasn't sure why they were lying but he supposed that didn't matter. If someone was lying, it usually meant they weren't up to anything good.

"Twin Garde is the outpost, correct?" Daegan asked, "apologies... I'm a cartographer, you see. I'll be mapping the area north of Nortara."

"My advice," Ox warned, "map someplace else... too many rakmen these days up in the forests," he turned to Rowan, "you're friends of Sheeth?"

"Met him a few times," Rowan replied, "haven't been up that way in about ten years though."

"Pretty different now, I'd wager," Geral said.

"Who's in charge now?" Tanlor asked.

"Hovis," Ox said.

"Krast," Geral said and the two locked eyes. The tension around the fire was as palpable as the heat radiating from it.

"Listen," Rowan started slowly, "we don't care if you're deserters... I know that Twin Garde's a rough hand to be dealt. If there's been a mutiny up there... well, I can understand why you lads are running down here." All of the men were slowly rising to their feet, eyeing each other.

Jax and Geral had hungry looks in their eyes and Shye just looked worried—scared even. *Oh shit... this isn't going to end well.* But Daegan had known that from the moment his coins had fallen from his pocket.

"Why don't we all just head our separate ways and pretend we didn't see each other, eh?" Rowan offered. Ox's face was impassive but the way his eyes flicked back and forth from Rowan to Daegan's cloak pocket was as much a give-away as Geral and Jax's eager expressions. Only Shye seemed to be uncomfortable, slightly backing up from the others.

Daegan's heart was pounding. Rowan's hand was resting on his sword hilt so Daegan also placed his hand on his revolver, holstered at his hip. Ox had a large axe leaning against the wall behind him, Geral and Jax had knives buckled to their belts.

"Not much honest work for deserters," Ox said, "and words going to start reaching soon that we killed Sheeth."

"That gold you've got will get us to Edas and we can take a ship," Geral added.

"Consider yourselves lucky we're letting you leave with your lives," Tanlor growled at them.

"You don't know what it's like up there," Geral spat. "Rakmen sightings almost every week. Was only going to be a matter of time 'afore they took Twin Garde."

"—So you killed your commanding officer!"

"Commander Sheeth was a fool, and we all would have died because of him," Ox rumbled. At least he out of all of them seemed a little remorseful, "I don't like this none," he said, "but hand over the coins and we'll be on our way and nobody needs to get hurt."

"You know that's not going to happen," Tanlor said.

Then the campfire dimmed, its flames dwindling to embers and sending them all into darkness. The camp erupted into commotion. Daegan was thrown on his back as Tanlor dove at him, the man's hand pushing hard against his chest and shoving him back from the fray. Tanlor's greatsword sang as he unsheathed it and swept out a protective perimeter around Daegan.

Struggling back to his feet, Daegan didn't see much in the darkness but the sounds of clashing steel and shouts were enough. He stumbled and slipped in the slick grass, pulling out his revolver.

The aradium and topaz worked into the barrel glowed dimly as he held it out in front of him. Daegan couldn't tell which of the moving black shapes were who so he held his fire. He could make out Ox's two handed axe swinging and a shadowy form that must have been Rowan stepping close into his range and driving his sword into the man's chest. Tanlor was engaged with both Geral and Jax, keeping them back with wide sweeps of his blade.

Daegan immediately scanned for Shye, assuming that the boy was planning to sneak around the fighting to attack them from behind but then he spied the boy backed up against the wall, a panic-stricken look on his face.

Daegan levelled his revolver at the boy, his finger trembled against the trigger. He gritted his teeth and then pointed it at Geral. He fired, it sounded like a crack of thunder. The bullet took Geral in the chest and the man let out a shout, dropping to his knees. Jax hesitated for just a second at the gunshot but it was all Tanlor needed, darting forward and slashing the youth across his chest.

Tanlor didn't waste any time and was moving toward the horrified Shye.

"No!" Daegan roared at the same time he heard Rowan shout, "don't!"

There was a clash of steel as Rowan's blade intercepted Tanlor's attack. The two shadowy forms struggled against one another, and then Rowan kicked Tanlor back.

"He's just a *boy*!" Rowan roared, and knocked Tanlor's sword to the ground.

"If we don't kill him, he'll be back to slit our throats in our sleep," Tanlor accused.

"We don't know that!" Rowan defended. Shye hadn't moved, his eyes still wide with shock, but Daegan kept his revolver aimed at him just in case he tried something while Rowan's back was to him.

"I won't suffer this Rowan!" Tanlor growled, "we need to put him down."

"You know the way to Crossroads, Shye?" Rowan called over his shoulder, not taking his eyes off Tanlor.

"N-no, sir," Shye stammered in response. Tanlor took a step towards his fallen sword but Rowan placed his boot on the blade. He turned his head to look at Shye. "Follow the river south towards Heronsbridge, then take the road east. You should make it to Crossroads in a few days."

The youth was edging along the wall away from them, towards where his horse was.

Rowan continued his instruction, "go to the inn at Crossroads and ask for Mendy. Tell her Rowan sent you, she'll have work for you. *Honest* work." Daegan could make out the dark splatters of Ox's blood on Rowan's face.

"You've got a second chance, lad," Rowan said with a threatening edge to his voice, "*don't* waste it. Go!" Shye didn't hesitate, he leapt at Rowan's word and ran for his horse. He hastily unhitched it and fled into the rain.

"Damn it, Rowan!" Tanlor shouted, "what if there's more deserters with them?! He could go back and tell them where we are." Tanlor was furious, more angry than Daegan had ever seen him.

"I don't think that he will," Rowan rebuked.

"They're not soldiers anymore, they're outlaws, Rowan!" Tanlor fumed, "they'll all turn to raiding, you know they will!"

"You *can't* know that."

"They're not all like him!" Tanlor said through gritted teeth, "they're murderers and they need to be *put down*."

"In another life that could have been us, Tan. Don't forget that!" Rowan replied coldly.

Tanlor's face was a mask of fury. Daegan watched as the man reached down for his sword, his knuckles white as they gripped the hilt.

They couldn't fight each other now. *Not over this.* Daegan held his revolver cautiously at his side, just in case. He wasn't even sure who he would point it at. Tanlor looked over at Daegan, only now realising that he was there, listening. He scowled and stormed towards his horse and began strapping up his saddle.

"Pack up," Tanlor shot at them, "we're leaving, *now!*"

CHAPTER 24

Parting Ways

It was a miserable ride. The wind whipped the rain against Daegan's face and he could barely see a few feet ahead through the darkness. He held onto the reins with one hand while using the other to keep the wind from pulling back his hood again.

"We could have at least waited until the rain stopped!" Daegan shouted back to Tanlor who was behind him. The other man didn't respond, but likely he didn't hear Daegan over the wind.

Daegan fell into a trance, the wet and cold had seeped in through all the cracks. He focused only on the left to right jostling of his horse.

"You don't want to be here any more than I do," he said to the horse.

The calm spells between the downpours were a welcome change. Daegan gave a sigh of relief when the road finally led into a thicket of trees, sheltering them from the wind and most of the rain. A thin sliver of purple blue was growing on the horizon above the mountains. Dawn was approaching and by the looks of it the clouds were thankfully clearing.

Daegan took the opportunity to ride up next to Rowan,

"What was that?" he croaked, he hadn't anticipated how rough his throat would feel after riding through the night in the rain. Rowan gave him a concerned look then leaned over, placing a clammy hand on Daegan's cheek. Warmth bled through the hand, filling Daegan with a satisfying heat—far more welcoming than a gulp of whitewhiskey and without the burning taste. Daegan gasped and staggered in his saddle, his shoulder and back tingling with goosebumps as the warmth passed into him.

"I forget you can't use a topaz lad... I'm sorry," Rowan said, and then added with a measure of concern, "you let me know if you ever start to feel warm when you should feel cold."

"Sure," Daegan breathed, revelling in finally feeling warm for the first time since they left the campfire.

"As far as I recall, there's a village just on the other side of this wood, in a few hours we'll get out of these wet clothes," Rowan said and glanced over his shoulder to Tanlor.

"It's better to stay warm than get warm," Rowan continued, "but sometimes we don't have a choice."

"What was all that?" Daegan asked, "Tanlor looked like he was ready to fight you."

"I couldn't let him kill that boy."

"What happened to 'doing what needs to be done'?"

"Like I said before Crossroads... sometimes all I have to rely on is my own judgement... and it told me to let the boy go."

"What if Tanlor's right?" Daegan asked, "what if there's more of them?"

"You saw that lad," Rowan shook his head, "you could have shot him dead if you'd wanted to... but you didn't."

Daegan couldn't deny that. He'd had ample time to shoot the boy but he had held back.

"The lad was terrified," Rowan continued, "he didn't want to be there no more than we did. I don't know how he ended up with that bunch but he wasn't so bad that he couldn't turn back, not yet... at least, that's what I reckon."

"I understand... I think. With Geral I didn't hesitate, he was attacking Tanlor and I just... shot. But Shye, he was so apart from it... it didn't feel right."

"Geral was your first kill?" Rowan asked. Daegan nodded, he wasn't ashamed of that, he'd often found it strange that some people thought that killing made you more of a man. His own father thought like that—his brothers too. *Do Rowan and Tanlor think that too?* Rowan with his weathered warrior's face certainly *looked* like a man that would. But his eyes looked concerned... not impressed.

"How do you feel?" Rowan asked.

"I'm not sure," Daegan answered truthfully. With the hard ride, he hadn't given much thought to it at all, "I don't think I feel anything." He said with an edge of uncertainty. He should feel guilty, shouldn't he? Geral would have killed him, but he should still feel something about killing another man.

"First time can be strange. Shouldn't ever feel good though," Rowan replied with a sombre note, "if you ever start enjoying it, it's time you should stop. Understand?" Daegan did, at least he felt like he did.

"What was that Tanlor said about 'not being like *him*', what was he talking about?" Daegan asked. Rowan let out a long breath, and looked back over his shoulder again. Tanlor was still further back and out of earshot.

After a few moments of silence, Daegan prodded further, "you already know my secrets," he offered.

"You know the story, don't you?" Rowan started, "Taran the Hunter."

"Your father," Daegan replied, nodding, "I've heard *a* telling of it."

"You've heard the lie... my father was no hunter," his eyebrows knitted, "he was a *raider*," he said the word with disgust. "He didn't save our mother from dragons and rakmen and the like... he was one of the raiders that kidnapped her."

Daegan's mind jumped to all the times he'd badgered Tanlor to tell him the story of his father, all the times that the man had politely—but firmly—refused to talk about him. He looked back at Tanlor now. The man was too shadowed in the early morning light to make out his expression. He looked back at Rowan whose jaw was clenched.

"How?" Was all Daegan managed to say, he wasn't even sure where to start. *Where did the false story come from? How does that even happen?!* From what Daegan knew, Rowan's father had lived in Garronforn castle and wed their mother. Rowan and Tanlor had both grown up in the castle as recognised members of the family.

How was that even allowed? Why wasn't he executed or imprisoned? He wanted to ask these questions but opted instead to let Rowan lead the story in the way he wanted to tell it.

"Father grew sick about ten years ago," Rowan replied, "told me and Tan the truth before he died. Tan didn't take it very well... he never spoke to father again."

I'm not surprised, my father is a psychopathic scumbag but at least he's been a consistent psychopathic scumbag.

"To be told a lie your whole life, believing your father was a hero from the stories…" Rowan's gaze drifted over the road.

"…And we *did* believe it," he continued, "I don't think it's something Tan can ever forgive him for."

"But *how*? How did the lie even come about?" Daegan probed.

"You remember what I told you about bears?" Rowan asked with an arched eyebrow. "Black, fight back. Brown, lay down—"

"—White, goodnight," Daegan finished.

"Arctic bears will tear through a full camp," Rowan said. "They're hard to take down… even for a runewielder… and that's what happened; an arctic bear killed half the raiders in the camp before they managed to take it down. Father said that only the worst of the lot were left, they wanted to kill my mother—cut their losses and flee deeper into the mountains. But my father, he… he wanted to protect her. He fought and killed the other raiders—his *friends*—to save her life. Then, he agreed to take her home."

"And it's true that they did fall in love," Rowan continued, nodding, "that part of the story was true." He looked over at Daegan. "I know this might be hard to believe but my mother *was* happy. She loved my father, I believe that… she still does."

Daegan didn't argue against that. He'd heard stories where people became attached to their captors, and began to identify and connect with them. *It was all kinds of wrong, of course, the captive's relief at the removal of the threat of death is transposed into feelings of gratitude toward the captor for giving him or her life.* But how do you explain that to someone whose parent's love was based on that unhealthy bond? Daegan just nodded sympathetically, unsure of what to say.

"The parts about rakmen taking over a village and my grandfather coming north with his army… that part was true too. Rakmen had come down as far as Balfold, not often they do that. My grandfather—Bodh Garron—had ridden with his army to run them back to the north. My parents were living in the woods then when the army found them. My mother lied to protect the man she loved, claiming that my father was a simple hunter, that he'd *saved* her from the raiders and the bear… I've heard versions of the story with dragons and trolls and fairies but they're all exaggerations… obviously."

They were quiet for a moment longer and Daegan didn't prod further, letting Rowan go at his own pace.

"My father was a good hunter, you know," Rowan added after a while, "he'd just gotten himself involved with a bad sort… It's hard to think of my father as being the same as the raiders I've come up against. I have to think that he was different, that he wasn't a bad person." The confession left Daegan feeling awkward and uncomfortable, he never had anyone confide in him before. A part of him wanted to shrink away at Rowan's vulnerability.

What do I even say to that?

Rowan didn't look like he was expecting a response. He looked relieved, as though saying it all out loud made it easier.

"I don't think he'd have turned against them to save your mother if he was a bad person," Daegan said after a few minutes of silence.

"That's what I tell myself too," Rowan admitted.

"So that's why you let Shye go?"

"Aye," he acknowledged, "there can't be badness in everyone, right? Sometimes people need a second chance to do things right."

Daegan thought about his own father and the night that he'd endured as a young boy, encased in the prison of spikes of his father's making. *Not everyone deserves a second chance.*

He thought about sharing the memory with Rowan. He had never told anyone about it, he didn't think he could if he'd wanted to. Sometimes, he would wake at night coughing and spluttering in a cold sweat, the nightmare already fading... but he would know from the tightness in his throat what he had dreamed of. He opened his mouth to start but wasn't sure how to begin.

"...He was a good father to you?" Daegan managed to ask, rubbing at his throat.
"Aye," Rowan said, his eyes glazing with what Daegan assumed to be nostalgia, "some of my best memories were when he'd take us past Nortara. We'd spend whole seasons up there; hunting and fishing... just the three of us—me, Tan and father."
"I suppose that's all that should matter then."
"I don't think Tan will ever forgive him," Rowan said sadly. "Not for lying to us for so long... for what he once was."
"Have you?" Daegan asked, and Rowan took on a distant expression, he'd likely never considered it. When he didn't respond, Daegan didn't press any further and they rode on in a comfortable silence.

The sun was cresting over the hills by the time they'd made it to the village.

As they rode up to the inn, Tanlor turned to Rowan, "this is as far as you come with us," Tan said with a bitter edge. "You can take the payment I've already given you and leave. Take the road we've come back to Rubastre or head south to Garronforn—I don't care, but you're not staying with us."
"You're overreacting, Tan," Rowan replied, the offence plain in his expression.
"You've jeopardised this whole mission. We *need* to keep a low profile and you're making that impossible. I should never have thought to bring you."
"If you're talking about Crossroads, I don't recall you complaining when we took down those raiders."
"Someone would've come to deal with that scum eventually," Tanlor waved off, angrily, "but at least then we were *thorough*... last night, you crossed the line."
"You crossed it the second you raised your sword to that boy," Rowan growled.

Both men were wet, tired and not at all in the right state of mind to be having this conversation.
"Let's discuss this after we've had some rest, eh?" Daegan offered, trying his best to ease the two brothers from brawling with each other right there on the porch.

"We'll rest here for the morning, and then we're hitting the road at midday," Tanlor responded, and then turning back to Rowan. "Like I said; I don't care where you go but don't follow us." And with that, he stormed off into the inn.

Daegan gave Rowan a sympathetic look. "I'll talk to him," Daegan offered.
"It's alright, lad," Rowan shook his head, "... it's alright."

Tanlor didn't speak with Rowan or Daegan for the rest of the morning. They slept until about noon and had hungrily accepted the innkeeper's offer of a late cooked breakfast. Without a word, Tanlor stepped out of the inn and started packing up his and Daegan's mounts.

Daegan and Rowan had sat uncomfortably in the silence with Tanlor and then continued the silence comfortably once he'd left.

It was evident that Tanlor wasn't going to be changing his mind anytime soon. *Who made him the boss anyway?* Daegan couldn't exactly argue against it though, he was utterly at Tanlor's mercy. Since leaving Rubastre, he'd been lost and guided only by Tanlor's decisive action.

Rowan had become an unexpected friend throughout their travels and he didn't doubt the man's ability nor his knowledge of how to survive past Nortara... but he also had never faced Ferath. Rowan himself admitted that Tanlor was the better warrior of the two of them. If it came down to a face-off with Ferath again, it would be Tanlor who had the best chance of standing against him.

"What will you do?" Daegan asked.

Rowan blew out a sigh and rested his back against his chair, "guess I'll head home."

"Marie'll be happy."

"Aye, and the boys too. I did promise them the winter after all." Then he added with a chuckle, "I don't know why she puts up with me. Disappearing off for months at a time."

"You don't like Garronforn?"

"Not much... can't say I like any cities though... but it's my home, ain't it."

"Is it?" Daegan probed, "seems like you're more at home out here." Not that Daegan had ever experienced Rowan for any notable time in a city. But it didn't take a genius to surmise that Rowan preferred the countryside.

"Suppose you might be right on that..." Rowan trailed off.

Daegan could feel the man's disappointment as palpable as the heat from the nearby stove. He wasn't sure whether Rowan was frustrated in not getting his full pay or at Tanlor's actions... or having to leave Daegan. He found resentment rising up in him. Would Rowan really just abandon them without at least a fight? Would he just walk away? Daegan looked up at the man, their eyes met. He could just ask him, couldn't he? He could ask him to stay...

"I'll pass through Crossroads on my way back," Rowan said after a while, "it's not far out of the way and I'll check in on Wolfhound... hopefully Shye takes my advice and heads there too."

That's awful decent of you, Rowan. Daegan thought bitterly, go help the strangers instead of him. But then again, Daegan and Rowan were little more than strangers too, weren't they? They'd barely known each other a few weeks. What right did Daegan have to claim this man's loyalty, his protection... his friendship? Why should he care for Daegan? No one else ever did.

...His own brother even abandoned him...

Tanlor and Daegan mounted their horses.

It was a small quiet village, as featureless as most of the ones they'd passed through. Being midday, there were a good number of farmers and other workers around to trade. It was likely as busy as the village ever got, and Daegan could still count the amount of people out on the street on two hands. Travellers weren't an uncommon sight, the road being the main route to Urundock so no one paid much mind to the outsiders.

"Remember to pick up warmer gear in Urundock, it gets a lot colder up past

Nortara," Rowan advised them from the inn porch. "You can take off what you have, can't put on what you don't."

"Goodbye, Rowan," Tanlor replied and then turned about, riding away from them.

Daegan couldn't bring himself to look at Rowan. He felt pressure at his throat, and tried to croak out a goodbye but he coughed instead. Rowan was running his hand through his red hair. He'd always seemed so wise to Daegan. He was only a few years older but his life experiences made him seem so much more knowledgeable but now he looked like a man-child caught doing something he shouldn't. This would likely be the last time they'd ever see each other. It wasn't like Daegan would ever want to visit Garronforn and he couldn't imagine Rowan in Reldon. Why did parting make him feel so frustrated? He barely knew this man.

"Good luck, lad," Rowan said.

Daegan clenched his teeth and rubbed at his throat, he nodded to Rowan in response, and pulled on the reins to follow Tanlor. He felt silly for caring so much. It wasn't like Rowan cared at all. Ferath hadn't… Landryn hadn't.

The horse wicked its head in protest, wanting to walk back towards Rowan. *Yeah, yeah I know you prefer him.* Daegan kept firm on the reins in the direction Tanlor went.

CHAPTER 25
No Horns, No Shells

"But they don't have any horns," Endrin grumbled.
"I never said they did!" Femira retorted.
"The Yarji have horns—like a stag. Everyone knows this," Endrin argued.
"He's right," Loreli added, "those just look like Keirans to me," nodding to the group of seafarers loading crates onto the Yarji junkship.
"What?!" Femira asked, incredulously, "you think they're *Keiran*?! The skin tone is way off, and look at the red tattoos."
"Anyone can get a red tattoo," Endrin replied, "doesn't make 'em a Yarji."
"No, obviously it doesn't—if I were to wear stilts and bleach my skin could I call myself Reldoni?"
"No horns. No deal," Endrin grunted and turned to leave.
"No way! You're teaching me how to do that stoneshell," Femira warned him, then strode purposefully towards the junkship.
She had a flutter in her stomach as she marched, the Yarji were known for being reclusive and aggressive towards outsiders but she was a bloodshedder now. She was soulforged! What did she have to fear from them?
"What are you doin—" Endrin started.
"—Hey!" Femira called over to the seafarers. One of them looked over at her—a handsome guy with hair the colour of burnt copper, "you're Yarji, right?"
"*Doveksji malesh,*" he replied in confusion.
"Yarji," she repeated, and pointed at him, nodding, "*you are Yarji*?" She tried in Keiran. The Yarji weren't part of the Keiran Empire technically, but the Empire claimed the mangrove forests where they lived even if it never enforced its rule there. Most Yarji wouldn't be able to speak any Keiran at all but these were traders so they might have picked up some.
"Yes, I am Yarji," the man replied in heavily accented Keiran, "*my name Hurok.*"
"My name Vreth," she replied, matching his style of speech and giving him a welcoming smile.
"Vreth," he mused, "*like the vreth?*" he flapped his hands in imitation of wings and bared his teeth in a mock snarl.
"Yes," she smiled again, "*like the vreth.*"
"Your mother cruel," he returned the smile but it looked wrong, like he was unaccustomed to the practice of it. *Not cruel, just selfish.*
"My friend," Femira said, pointing back to where Endrin and Loreli stood at the dock. She didn't like calling Endrin her friend but she was trying to use basic terms to help the Yarji man understand, "*can you tell him that you are Yarji?*"
"For the why?" the man replied.
"*He doesn't think you're real,*" she replied.
The man gave her a perplexed look, his nose wrinkling. "*I am here, how not real?*" he

said, patting his chest.

"*He doesn't think any Yarji are real... and he won't believe me because you don't have horns.*" The man barked a deep and resonating laugh. It sounded like an unnatural human laugh, more akin to the snorting of a seal.

"*No, no, no. No horns, I am hakrami.*"

"*Huk ranny?*" she asked, testing the word.

"*Hakrami,*" he smiled, it was a strange forced-looking smile on his handsome face, it looked like a grimace but Femira got the impression that he was trying to convey friendliness. *Why do people think they are aggressive? This man is so friendly.*

Hurok then repeated the word and did a swaying gesture with his hand on his chest that she didn't understand. He seemed to catch on that she was struggling and he pointed to the junkship, "*Hakrami,*" Hurok said firmly, then pointed at himself, "*Hakrami... No horns. Horns in Katvak.*"

"Wait! You're telling me that some Yarji really *do* have horns?"

"*Katvak, yes... horns.*" He opened both palms on his head to demonstrate the word.

"Endrin!" Femira called and waved him over.

"This is Hurok," she introduced with a triumphant air, "he's Yarji."

"Endrin," she said to Hurok, gesturing to the bald man, "*he's an idiot.*" Hurok made the low seal barking noise again.

"Nice meet, Endreen," Hurok said in common tongue, his gravelly voice making him sound like he was growling. *Maybe that's why people think they're so aggressive.* Endrin inclined his head to Hurok, his eyes narrowing.

"*No horns,*" Hurok said again, making the open palm gesture on his head and baring his teeth in that awkward smile. Endrin was stoic but Femira noticed his face reddening a bit. *Was he embarrassed?*

"You've made your point, Vreth," Endrin said to her, "I'm leaving."

"Did I just beat you at something?" Femira grinned but he was already walking away from them. She smiled back at the confused Hurok and thanked him before chasing after Endrin.

***

The trick to the stoneshell was so simple that Femira chastised herself for not realising it herself. She'd already noticed how rock was easier to shape when you were simply putting it back into its original form—meaning if you sucked in a wall then it was easier to reform it back to the exact shape it was before. It wasn't like the stone had memory, it was more like a primal will to *be* something. The rock wasn't conscious or sentient but it did have a distinct impression of self.

"That's your own projection," Endrin scolded her, "the stone doesn't *want* to be a shell any less than it wants to be a boulder... that's your own mind getting in the way."

"So you're saying I need to *believe* that the rock is a shell?"

"More than that, you need to *know* that it is," he continued, "as soulforged, we have an enhanced sense for the stone, that sense of *being* from it... but it's not alive."

"Obviously," Femira rolled her eyes and he snarled at her. "Do you want the lesson or not?" she shut her mouth and let him continue.

"I think it's because the aradium is now a part of us, we can feel more of the rock with our edirs. This allows more power and precision over it."

They were on the deck of the ferry crossing back to Epilas, Endrin instructed her to stand by the rail and then walked to the center of the deck.

"I'm going to fire a projectile at you, and you're going to summon the stoneshell," he instructed her. "You're going to *know* that it will be the shape of the shell."

"And if I don't shape it fast enough?"

"Then you're going to get a rock to the face."

Femira felt Endrin's edir whip into focus and conjure a small rock. It happened in an instant and he fired it towards her. She reached internally, guiding the material held inside to form the stoneshell around her.

Pain flared in her face and her vision swam.

Femira was on the ground, her nose throbbing from the clod of earth that had smacked into her face. She leapt back to her feet and shot Endrin a death gaze, her eyes stinging and her teeth bared.

"Getting angry won't help," he said, "again!"

She felt the rush of his edir concentrating again and she reacted faster, she willed the stoneshell around her and felt it beginning to form.

Pain. Coughing.

Blinded as another chunk of earth hurtled into Femira's face. Her eyes watering, she jumped back up again. She could feel blood trickling from her nose. He gave her no warning this time, his edir already whipping into action.

She grinned.

***

"You're lucky there's a healer with us," Jaz said, wincing as he looked at Femira. Her face felt like she'd taken a dozen punches... which wasn't far off. The healer was a hawk-nosed Reldoni man that looked more like an executioner than a healer.

"Reckless," the healer *tsk'd* and mumbled as he worked. It wasn't Femira's first time being healed and she reckoned it wouldn't be her last. It was a distasteful experience and not wholly unlike the sensations she'd felt when Garld had performed her soulforging ritual. Healers used bloodstone to repair injuries and minor wounds, more skilled healers could even tackle some diseases and viruses.

Bloodstone required touch. *The edir works as a preventative barrier to a bloodstone's influence,* Misandrei had taught her. It meant that someone with a bloodstone couldn't just stop your heart dead from across the room, they had to at least touch you. *And that means getting close enough to be jabbed in the face with a knife.*

Metal grinding against bone in an eye socket.

She felt vomit rise in her throat. *Shit.* Femira panicked and tried to turn away but it was too late, she spewed her lunch onto the healer's uniform.

"Ah," he recoiled in disgust, "I *asked* you if healing makes you nauseous!" He pointed an accusatory finger at her. He had been halfway through healing her broken nose and bruised eyes, it still felt itchy where the healing had been done but at least it wasn't throbbing anymore.

Jaz was cackling with laughter and Femira had to smother the sickness in her stomach. She actively tried not... to think about... she vomited again and the healer stormed off in a disgusted fury. *He shouldn't be surprised by a bit of vomit.* Wasn't that all part of his job?

"You feeling ok, Vreth?" Jaz asked with a touch of concern in his voice, "that's happened a few times since—"

"—I'm fine," she snapped, "just the ferry." She strode away from a now confused Jaz.

She wasn't angry with him. But she didn't want to talk about it. She didn't want to *think* about it... why was this happening to her? She'd cut people before. People had died because of her and she'd seen plenty of people die in front of her. Why was this stupid dead stormguard refusing to leave her alone?

Femira made her way back up to the deck of the ship in the hopes that the fresh sea breeze would settle her stomach and clear her head. *It's just sea sickness.* Although she'd never had sea sickness before in her life.

Endrin was now sparring with some of the other bloodshedders. She couldn't deny that he had impressive skill... and he wasn't *as* much of an ass as she'd thought. And true to his promise, he had taught her his stoneshell technique. Femira needed to practise it a lot more before she could summon it as quickly as Endrin could but the afternoon of having stones hurtled at her face had been a good incentive to learn quickly.

"Hey," Loreli said, approaching her with a purposeful stride.

"Don't start thinking that just because Endrin is mentoring you that we suddenly trust you," she said bluntly.

"Seriously, Loreli," Femira rounded on the girl, "what's your problem?!"

"You know what my problem is... you don't belong here," Loreli snarled.

"I'm not interested in your boyfriend if that's what this is about," Femira sighed, "he's just helping me with a skill."

"The fact that you think that's what my problem is just proves how naive you are," Loreli scoffed, "do you understand how hard some of us have worked to get here? The *years* of training it takes... and a silly girl who barely knows how to fight gets soulforged just like that because of who her parents were."

"You don't know a fucking thing about me!" Femira snapped, then growled through bared teeth, "you think your life has been hard? You know fucking *nothing*."

She felt her heart pounding in her chest, the waves of her edir pulsing from her. She forced it back, trying to contain it but Loreli had already felt her emotion. The other girl took a step back, her expression rigid. Loreli's mouth opened to retaliate but Femira cut her off, "I couldn't give two shits if you trust me or not, it makes no difference to me but I'm not going anywhere so you better get used to it."

Femira stormed off to the front part of the ferry, as far from the others as she could get. She wasn't in the mood to talk to anyone. She still felt nauseous but that was probably just the ship... not the dead stormguard... she forced down another lurch in her stomach. It definitely had nothing to do with stupid fucking Loreli. It didn't matter what the other bloodshedders thought of her. All that mattered was Garld and Missandrei's assessments, they would be the ones to decide if she got to proceed.

But does that even matter now?

She'd already become soulforged, along with more strength and knowledge that she could barely have imagined a few months before. So what was she still *doing* here? She should be looking for a way out, shouldn't she? But there was always the promise of more...

She watched the lapping waves in silence and was happy when she saw the city of Epilas looming on the horizon. The Pillar of Reldon standing tall on the skyline. She didn't owe any loyalty to the Reldoni. Not Missandrei, not Garld, not Landryn.

...Although they had protected her. And they'd given her what she wanted; power and promises of more of it... what was this she was feeling and why did Loreli's words sting like that? She shouldn't care what some highborn bitch thought of her. *Was Loreli even highborn?* She realised she didn't know.

***

The bloodshedders victory at Innish Head was already common knowledge upon their return to Epilas. Word had spread ahead of them that it hadn't been pirates but fully manned Altarean warships that had been raiding the villages along the Tidewall. The team's victory was adding to the bloodshedder's rising renown as the elite force in the Reldoni military. When they rode through the streets of Epilas, people cheered and applauded to their glory.

They'd killed hundreds of people. *Hundreds.* And people were *applauding* them. If a criminal killed one person, these same people would be shouting with anger and hatred. *But they cheer for us.* Femira's brothers hadn't meant to kill that man... but they'd been executed for it without question or trial. Now she'd killed three people with her own hands. And more died as a direct result of her runewielding. But the people applauded her for it. There was something wrong in that, she thought sadly as the group returned to the barracks.

Femira was happy to finally be back in her own room, her own bed. She thought about how funny it was that this room had begun to feel like home to her when it had only been a few months. She'd been in Lichtin's crewhouse for years and that place had never felt like home.

There was a letter waiting at her door when she arrived. Femira broke the wax seal and unfurled the scroll.

> *Lady Annali Jahar,*
> *Stonebreaker of the Reldoni Royal Army, Bloodshedder Division.*
>
> *Your involvement in the recent mission has received commemoration from the crown.*
> *King Abhran Tredain wishes to thank you for your exceptional service in his name. An invitation to a feast in the Pillar of Reldon is being extended to all members of the excursion party tasked with locating and destroying the Altarean corsairs.*
>
> *The efforts involved in this undertaking have been deemed as extraordinary and is a testament to the strength of the bloodshedders and the Reldoni Royal Army.*

The rest of the letter went on with the details of the feast the following evening along with outlining the bonus compensation that all members of the mission were receiving.

Fifty silver marks! It was more money than Femira had ever owned in her life. She wondered how much of a bonus Missandrei or Garld would be getting, or were they so rich, did they even care about such things?

Well if the promise of more power hadn't been enough to secure her loyalty to them then this payment certainly was. She couldn't help but smile looking at the paper. The name on it bothered her... would she always need to pretend? It was a silly question. She already knew she was too deep as Annali to turn back now. All of the nobility believed Femira was Annali, there wasn't any shaking that.

A feast at the Pillar would mean more nobility and more pretending... she thought idly if Landryn would be there too. The letter didn't mention him, it was signed by King Abhran's steward. Would the King himself be at the feast?

Her face was still bruised and cut from her training session with Endrin but that wouldn't matter. She was a returning soldier after all, a few injuries only made her look more battle-hardened. They didn't need to know it had been Endrin firing clumps of earth into her face. The healer had fixed her up mostly, but they always left a few of the superficial injuries. They claimed it was because they were conserving their energy for larger wounds but Femira suspected they left them as a lesson to be more careful in training and not to rely so heavily on being healed afterward.

Putting the thoughts of the feast and her face aside, Femira rested her head into her pillow and breathed a satisfied sigh, content with finally getting the chance to rest.

CHAPTER 26

Commemorations

The feast was much like the last one that Femira had attended although this time she was wearing her bloodshedder uniform instead of that wretched dress.

Once again, she had Jaz for company and the two were greeted and congratulated on their victory by various nobles as they moved through the feasting hall. There were even some Altarean highborn in attendance, proffering their over-zealous enthusiasm for the soldiers that killed their 'renegade countrymen'.

"The old commander Himsbrack has gone into hiding," one of the Altareans said. "We are all very approving of the new Stormguard Commander Darza... a good man... a trustworthy man... very loyal to the Reldoni, just like the rest of us... I for one welcome our Reldoni overlords." This statement was met with vigorous head nods from the flabby jowelled nobles. No doubt they had deluded themselves into thinking declaring such things aloud was bravery of the highest order.

Femira didn't care about the Altareans or their need to prove that they supported the Reldoni. She did idly wonder how many of them actually supported the rebelling stormguards in secret. Himsbrack had clearly been a stoic patriot. *Had he been on one of the ships we'd sunk?* How many relatives of these nobles had Femira and her companions killed? And they were here congratulating them for it.

Highborn are fucking weird.

Femira spotted Garld and Landryn speaking to General Mattice—whom she recognised as the man whose loose lips had gotten Sadrian Graves killed by the Honorsword—along with another highborn man that she didn't recognise. She'd wanted to speak with Landryn again, the conversation she'd had with the man before becoming soulforged had been strange but not unpleasant.

She found that she quite enjoyed his company and the way that his hand would sometimes rub at his jawline when he was thinking. He'd been reserved in her first meetings with the man but she still found him interesting.

She also hadn't gotten to speak with Garld since returning as Missandrei had given the report directly to him. She left Jaz with some fawning young women and made for the group of men.

Landryn inclined his head with a small smile as she approached. Femira saluted appropriately. He didn't seem annoyed by her interrupting their conversation.

"Captain Misandrei tells me you did well on the battlefield," Garld said, and Femira couldn't help the pitiful sense of pride she felt at his praise.

"Highlord Averstock," Garld addressed the other gentleman, a striking man with a tight beard and vibrantly blue eyes, "may I introduce Annali Jahar."

"Lady Jahar," Averstock inclined his head. Femira saluted respectfully and smothered a smirk, there was something very intoxicating about being in the presence of someone who's mansion she'd broken into. *Thought you were so clever with that hidden compartment in the desk.* She wondered if he even knew that the journal was missing. It still irked her that Vestyr had managed to steal it from her... and that Garld seemed to be completely aware of the fact. *It's all just a big game to these people isn't it?*

"A pleasure, my lord," she greeted with every ounce of Annali's formality.

"Lord Averstock is Highlord of the Tidewall," Landryn informed her.

"Although I do spend most of my time here in Epilas... very important business always in the capital," Averstock interjected with a haughty air.

"He and I both thank you for your efforts in keeping the Tidewall's shores safe," Landryn finished, without skipping a beat at Averstock's interruption.

"I don't like these mysterious reports of entire village populations disappearing, however," Averstock grumbled. It appeared they were already in an argument before Femira had arrived. "We need to bolster the patrols on the Tidewall," Averstock continued, his head angled so that his nose was always slightly in the air. *One of those types.* "The encounter the bloodshedders only proves the need," he declared.

"Mattice has ten thousand swords," Garld offered, "along with two companies of crossbowmen and three hundred runewielders... I think he can spare a few hundred men that can be re-deployed to the Tidewall," he suggested with arched eyebrows to the stout man.

"The Tidewall is not part of my domain," Mattice countered, offended by the very notion of it. "You should pull back some of the forces you have occupying Altarea, Prince Landryn. You still have a company of soldiers there."

"They're keeping the peace," Landryn said simply as if the matter was not up for discussion.

"Altarea is stable. Highlord Ingel's authority is undisputed in the city and this new stormguard Commander Darza I hear is quite competent..." Mattice rambled.

"Those soldiers were a contingency to hold the palace for when those missing Altarean warships came to reclaim it... but it appears those warships are now raiding the Tidewall instead. Send them to finish the job they were tasked with."

"You don't need the bulk of our army," Garld argued, "the Reinish border has been quiet for over a year. Our spies have reported that the Keiran Emperor has been mobilising his forces from his border provinces... he is demanding no less than twenty thousand spears. I believe the Keiran mean to make a push for Rein."

Femira didn't miss that both Mattice and Averstock had given her suspicious glances at the mention of the Keiran Empire's army. *Don't you think the Keiran girl would be a bit fucking obvious as a spy?!* Garld and Landryn didn't seem to take any concern of her being part of the conversation.

"If that's true, then all the more reason to keep our southern border strong," Mattice replied, his stubborn chin raised. "Heck, we should be making a push ourselves." *Careful Mattice, that kind of language is foul! You must be so very worked up.* "If the Reinish are preoccupied with the Keiran," Mattice went on, "then we can finally *take* the delta. The Reinish cannot fight wars at both ends, they'll withdraw from the delta and defend their capital from the Keiran."

"I'll not start an open war with Rein," Landryn replied. He appeared calm but Femira got the sense the conversation was irritating him.

"You had no problem doing so with Altarea," Mattice badgered, "or was that your father pushing you? Perhaps you're not as strong a leader as we thought!"

"Careful, Mattice," Garld said with no slight of warning, "you are speaking to your Lord Commander and Prince."

"He is our Commander because *we* chose him," Mattice said with affront and then raised a finger at Landryn, "the support of the Generals is *why* you are in the position you are, Prince Landryn. Do not forget that. Your bloodshedders may be making a name for themselves to the people, but do not forget that the bulk of our army still hold allegiance to myself and the other Generals." With that statement Mattice turned heel and left them.

"He should not have spoken to you like that," Garld scowled, "he's becoming too unruly."

"He's still annoyed that I was made Commander over him," Landryn conceded, "he'll come around." Femira didn't feel that he was convinced of that.

"And what of my shores?" Highlord Averstock asked, "I have enough soldiers for patrols but if there are more attacks… or more missing villages… and if Mattice will not release any of his soldiers… what can I do? Landryn, you simply *must* do something about this."

"Can you give us a moment?" Landryn asked Averstock, "and we'll discuss this." Averstock bowed his head and retreated leaving Landryn, Garld and Femira out of earshot of any of the nearby highborn. Again, they didn't seem to be bothered or concerned by Femira's presence so she stayed.

"The bloodshedders do not yet have the numbers for us to start filtering them into tasks like this," Garld said, "we need to focus on training… only deploying when *absolutely* necessary. We cannot afford *any* losses in their ranks." It was encouraging seeing how passionate Garld was about the safety of the bloodshedders.

"Mattice won't let us hand-pick any more of his runewielders either," Landryn noted, "we'll need to start recruiting elsewhere… what about the Altareans—Annali here seems to be doing well—Do you think there's any potential for the remaining stormguards to be assimilated into the ranks?—Those that aren't on those warships pretending to be corsairs."

"I'm not sure the bloodshedders will be so accepting," Femira said, feeling now that she was part of the conversation, "they're only now starting to come around to me… I don't think they'll warm to taking in recruits from people that were very recently their enemies."

"Even so, it could still be worth it…" Landryn mused, "there's surely talented runewielders left in their ranks."

"Darza seems to be the most aligned to our cause," Garld agreed, "he might have some potential recruits that we could trial."

"Good, let's do that… as for these destroyed villages," Landryn considered, "I want to investigate for myself."

"That isn't wise, my lord," Garld shook his head.

"I can't ignore this," Landryn replied, nodding over to Averstock, "you know I can't… and I need you here, you're the only one I trust to perform the soulforgings. We *need* more bloodshedders."

"You are Lord-Commander now," Garld said, sounding more like a frustrated teacher than a subordinate, "you can't simply assign yourself field duty because you're bored."

"Whatever happened to 'don't issue commands for tasks that you wouldn't do yourself'," Landryn said with a light grin and waved Averstock back over.

"My lord," Averstock said, his eyes expectant, "what was the outcome, will we have more patrols or not?"

"I will take a small team of bloodshedders personally to investigate the matter. We'll clear out whatever's been attacking the villages. I promise you that."

"Lord-Commander Landryn Tredain taking the task personally, I am honoured, my lord," Averstock bowed his head, "I'm glad to see that you have not forgotten your priorities."

"Of course not," Landryn replied, "family always comes first." *Family? Averstock is related to the Prince?*

"You were on one of the investigation teams that discovered the empty villages, correct?" Landryn asked, turning to Femira.

"That's right," she replied, "pretty spooky." *Probably not something Annali would've said but whatever.*

"You'll be part of my retinue then, I'll choose a few others and we'll leave tomorrow." *What?!*

"I'll choose a team for you, Prince Landryn," Garld offered but Landryn waved him off, "it's fine. I'll pick a team myself. I shall only need a handful." Femira was thrilled at the prospect of being on a mission with the Prince. Something about being around him made her excited. The way he'd taken down that Honorsword... he could teach her a lot.

"What is this you're scheming?" A woman's voice came from behind them.

"Precious daughter," Averstock smiled, opening his arms, "we are simply settling the issue of these disappearing villages along the Tidewall." The woman was in her late twenties, tall and dark-haired and impossibly beautiful.

"Oh, do tell," she said with an arched eyebrow at Landryn. *Wait, hang on.*

"Rhianne," Landryn said with surprise, Femira didn't miss the way that the woman placed a gentle hand on Landryn's arm. "I will be going myself to investigate."

"Leaving the city again so soon," she pouted, "but I suppose it is to help my father so I can hardly complain, can I?"

"I don't think we've met," Rhianne looked down at Femira, "you are... Annali Jahar... if I am not mistaken?"

Femira felt uncomfortable under the woman's gaze. She felt awkward... like she'd been caught doing something wrong. *Had* she been doing something wrong? Landryn was also avoiding her eye. She shouldn't give six shits if he was with this woman, what did it matter to her?

"That's correct," Femira replied. She'd been telling the same lie she'd been telling for months that it was easy for her now, "I'm Annali Jahar."

"I hear you've been made into a full bloodshedder now. *Quite* the achievement for someone so new to runeweilding... Keiran women—as I understand it—are prohibited from such practises?" The woman's way of speaking always sounded like it ended in a question. *It's annoying.*

"I'd had some experience," Femira replied, flatly. She couldn't shake the feeling that this woman was mocking her.

Garld and Averstock who were now separating into their own conversation drifted off. Femira wanted to follow them. She wanted to talk to Garld directly and discuss with him how she'd done in the battle against the stormguards. It irked her how much she craved his praise, it had started small, words of encouragement during her training and built from there. She also knew that the more he trusted in her skill, the more likely he would be to consider her for later advanced soulforgings.

"I had heard something very strange about you," Rhianne continued, "oh… the people in court can be so cruel." *I don't have time for your petty shit.* Femira knew what this woman was at. Friendly and polite demeanour veiling her insults.

"That people have been calling you *Vreth*," she scrunched her nose in disgust, "ugh such foul vermin… I'm so sorry if any—"

"—I like being called Vreth," Femira cut her off, "I've been called it a lot longer than I've been here… and I don't plan on dropping the name because Reldoni don't like them."

"It's a discredit for a…" Rhianne faltered, "a comely girl such as yourself?"

"Are you asking me that?" Femira replied, "or is that just the way you talk?"

"I think vreth are under appreciated," Landryn mused and Rhianne narrowed her eyes at him, "people fear them because they hide in shadows… because you can't see when they strike… and there's a *beauty* to their flight if you ever sit and watch them —"

—Landryn waved as a familiar pair approached them. Allyn Tredain walked with an arm linked affectionately with Vestyr. Femira still couldn't help but feel a rise of irritation at the sight of Vestyr. He never acknowledged the night that he'd stolen the journal from her in the alleyway. *Did he even recognise her?* She knew that Reldoni people sometimes had trouble telling Keiran apart. It was one of the reasons so few people questioned her about being Annali in the first place. The pale boy was still a mystery to her. His almost white hair fell in thick curls framing his boyish face. He made Allyn appear older by comparison than she likely was with his youthful appearance.

"Allyn," Landryn said affectionately as she approached. Rhianne also exchanged pleasantries. The girl cast a friendly smile at Femira despite the fact they'd never actually met properly. Eavesdropping on her conversation and watching her brother fight an Honorsword didn't exactly count.

"Have you heard from Daegan?" Allyn asked Landryn her eyes showing concern, "I've gotten nothing from him in two weeks!" *Daegan was the other brother… the one who somehow couldn't runewield.*

"He doesn't exactly keep regular correspondence even when he's sober," Landryn said off-handedly. "He's probably been holed up in some Rubanian viceden for the past two weeks. I swear… first, he ruins the contract with the Rubastre Ironworks and now this."

"I'm worried about him," Allyn affirmed, "I've tried sending word to Ferath even and I've gotten nothing back. Can you try to reach him, please?"

"I'll send a letter to Ferath," Landryn put a reassuring hand on his sister's shoulder, "I'm sure he's fine. I'd been meaning to talk to Lukane about him anyway, he's making a mess of our steel shipments up there."

"I don't know why Lukane sent him there in the first place," Allyn pondered, "he was happy with the Royal Cartographers… mostly… I think."

"Not exactly the most appropriate position for a Prince," Rhianne put in.

"Daegan isn't a normal Prince," Allyn replied, "he shouldn't be alone up there. He should be kept safe, here!"

"He's not alone, Allyn," Landryn argued, "Ferath is a loyal friend and an excellent soldier."

"Is he…" Allyn glanced around for anyone nearby, "*enhanced?*" she whispered.

Landryn narrowed his eyes at her, "I told you to drop that," he said.

"Soulforging won't be a secret for long, my lord," Vestyr put in, "my people are concerned with the *accelerated* rate with which affinity imbued runewielders are appearing."

"Stop meddling, Allyn," Landryn scolded her and then gave Vestyr a glare, "and *you*, if I find out that you've sabotaged another bloodshedder mission, your friendship with my sister will not protect you. Do you understand?"

Vestyr glanced at Femira, meeting her eye. *Yes, he does remember me.* Femira was surprised that they would talk about these things so openly with Rhianne present. Considering she was Averstock's daughter—the man from whom the journal was originally stolen from.

Also me? Did they no longer suspect her to be a spy? Landryn knew she was soulforged now, did that give him a level of trust in her?

"The journal was worthless anyway," Allyn said, fishing the small book from a pocket inside her dress.

Worth enough to you to keep it on your person.

"Here," she offered it to Landryn, "a peace offering," she said, brightly.

"You've made copies?" Landryn asked.

"Of course, I'm not stupid."

"Elyina's journals…" Landryn mused, flicking through the pages, "there's dangerous things in here, Allyn… be careful," he added with warning.

Landryn then looked to Femira, "I'll hang on to this for now," he said to her, "I'll give it to Garld soon enough."

He thinks I'll report this to Garld. He wasn't wrong as she likely would.

The group broke apart as Rhianne spotted some other people she wanted to speak with and all but dragged Landryn with her. Allyn also left to join another group, leaving Vestyr and Femira alone.

"You've been soulforged," Vestyr stated with a wry smile once everyone was out of earshot.

"What makes you think that?"

"Don't try to hide it," he said, "your edir is so much stronger than the last time we met… I don't think I would be able to force control of your stoneblades, if I tried."

"I wouldn't let you trap me in the ground either," she replied, "that was a cheap trick."

"You have to play to your advantages."

"You're not a bloodshedder," Femira said, "yet you are soulforged too?"

"You don't believe that Landryn and Garld are the only ones with their hands on a soulstone do you?" Femira didn't reply. She hadn't really thought about it much. Garld had been the only one who seemed to be up front with her… at least most of the time.

"The Aeth have been soulforging for centuries," Vestyr continued.

"You're one of the Aeth?" She asked, her eyebrows raising.

"I thought that would be obvious," Vestyr smiled, pulling back some of his curls to reveal long pointed ears.

Well fuck me sideways.

"And here was me making fun of people for not believing the Yarji were real," she scoffed.

"My people are a bit more… *reclusive* than others…" he conceded, "and generally we don't care much for the ocean. I would wager you wouldn't find a single Aeth anywhere in Alterea… but many of my kin do enjoy the Keiran sun… I am surprised you haven't met one of my kind before."

"Sheltered family," Femira replied. A handy lie she told to cover any obvious cultural mishaps she made. *I can't keep relying on it though.* "So you've been infused with an earthstone," she moved on quickly.

"Of sorts," he replied, cryptically. "The Aeth's ways of soulforging is a little different to yours… but the results are more or less the same from what I understand."

"So *mysterious*," she grinned, "I want you to spar with me."

"You what?"

"Training with those who can beat me is the only way I'm going to improve… so, I'm going to be on assignment for likely the next couple of days… maybe weeks, I'm not sure," she had no idea how long Landryn would need her help along the Tidewall coast, "but when I'm back we're going to spar."

"You're not concerned with me figuring out military secrets?" he asked with a hint of wariness.

"…you seem pretty close with the Tredains," Femira replied and nodded to where Allyn was charming a gaggle of haughty looking nobles, "especially, Princess Allyn," she noted. "I highly doubt there's anything I know that you haven't figured out already. I'm not interested in trading secrets. I don't really care what the Aeth have to do with all of this or what you and Allyn have been scheming. I just want to be a better runewielder and I think you can help me do that… so, when I'm back, you and I are having a rematch."

CHAPTER 27

Fight Back

Light snow topped the trees and covered the ground of the clearing. Daegan began sweeping it away with his boot, clearing a small patch where he carefully placed rocks in a circle. Tanlor was doing his customary search of the area for raiders, rakmen, bears and whatever else could be lurking in the woods.

It had been a painfully quiet three days since they'd left Rowan behind. Daegan had attempted to pull Tanlor into conversation on a few occasions but he'd have better luck trying to get words out of the snow.

The horses were given the freedom to roam the clearing and were trusted not to wander off too far. Daegan's own mount was busying himself by stripping the bark off a nearby tree.

"Weird habit that," Daegan said to the horse. The horse pulled a big chunk of the bark off and puffed loudly in celebration.

"Talking to my horse… this is how low I've fallen." The horse seemed to be warming to him now that Rowan wasn't around. Rowan had often talked to the horses like they were people, soothing them when they were skittish or patting them reassuringly after a long ride.

"You miss him?" Daegan asked and the horse continued stripping the bark, "yeah… me neither. We don't need him, eh?"

His horse didn't have a name. Rowan had chided him for not naming the beast. *A horse needs a name, you can't keep calling him 'horse'.* But Daegan had enjoyed calling him horse and he'd enjoyed how much Rowan had grumbled about it.

"Do you want a name?" The horse stamped a hoof in excitement, but that was because he'd finally gotten past the bark and was able to munch directly on the tree itself. "You are a strange one…" Daegan mused as the horse ferociously tore at the tree trunk, ripping splinters of wood out and chewing on them happily.

"My brother had a horse called Champion… how do you like that?" The horse ignored him.

"No…" he didn't look much like Champion anyway. He was a handsome beast but nowhere near as majestic as Landryn's silky black steed had been.

"How about Bark-biter?" The horse hacked as it tore off a piece too big for it and spat it out.

"Guess not… Woodcutter?" The horse snorted.

"No… you don't like that either… Termite?" The beast's tail flicked with glee as it ripped more chunks out, "yeah… I like Termite too. Let's go for that." Termite glanced at him for a moment then resumed his devoted work. Daegan took the gesture as approval.

Daegan looked up at the darkening sky. *Don't want to be collecting wood in the dark.* Although Tanlor would be upset if he left the camp before the man had done a thorough check. Daegan shivered. *Well I'm not just going to wait around to freeze.* He got up and began combing through the nearby underbrush for dead logs and tinder.

Dead wood was better for the fire and also tended to have mushrooms growing on it. Rowan could make a half-decent broth from elf-ear mushrooms. They were easy to recognise because they looked like elf ears poking out of dead trees.

"Not a hard one to get wrong," Rowan had told him, "unless they're black… then those are rak-ears and unless you want to be shitting buckets of swamp water for the next few days I'd recommend you stay clear of 'em." The ones Daegan had found were all white, some with patches of brown but nothing completely black so they should be safe. There was a plethora of other mushrooms but Daegan wasn't so confident in spotting which were edible so he avoided grabbing any.

"Elf-ears are easy not to kill yourself with and unless you're completely sure just leave 'em be. Some can even kill you just from touching. So don't even go near 'em if you're not sure." Daegan had been surprised when Rowan didn't have some child-like rhyme to help remember the differences but Rowan had simply laughed, "far too many to fit in a rhyme, you just got to know these things."

"White… dinner tonight… black, turn back…" Daegan muttered as he collected them. That was a good one. Rowan would like that. But Rowan wasn't coming back so it didn't matter.

There was a line of the white pointy mushrooms leading along some fallen branches that brought him further away from the camp. It was a good haul and he didn't overly fancy another night of dried meat. A nice elf-ear broth was exactly what he wanted.

Wash it down with a few sips of whitewhiskey too. Delightful. Daegan chuckled, amazed by his new standard of what he considered a good evening. Some dirty boiled mushrooms and cheap booze made from potatoes. If only his father could see him now.

A twig snapped ahead and Daegan's head shot up. He spied something large and black hulking in the gloom about two dozen feet away.

Oh shit! Daegan's heart lurched in panic and he dropped the bundle of kindling and mushrooms he'd collected. He staggered back and stumbled on the underbrush. The black mass made a throaty, guttural roar. It was a bear? *Oh no no no.* Instinct screamed at Daegan to run back to the camp. But what would that achieve?

"A bear will always outrun you," Rowan had said, "don't matter how fast you are, the bear's quicker." Daegan had never seen a bear, at least not a living one. There had been dead bears in the palace; hunted, stuffed and propped up for display. The teeth and claws on those dead bears hadn't been scary then but they certainly were now that they were attached to a very alive and angry bear.

"Ok, ok," Daegan breathed, slowly standing straight as the bear shuffled in his direction. He forced down the primal impulse to flee, knowing that turning his back on the bear would make the bear think he was prey.

Brown, lay down. Black, fight back. White, goodnight.

The bear looked pretty fucking black but it was hard to tell as all he could see was a massive lumbering shadow. *I am not your prey.* Daegan jumped up onto the log, trying to make himself appear the larger opponent. The bear stopped and raised himself onto his hind legs, his black form looming in the darkness. Familiar feelings of dread washed over Daegan, similar to the night that Ferath attacked him. That feeling of helplessness before an enemy.

The feeling sparked an anger in him.

"I am not your *fucking* prey," Daegan growled as the anger rose in him, smothering the terror. He reached for the revolver at his belt. The dim glow of the embedded runestones were stark in the dim light. He could feel the adrenaline rise in him. The bear slapped its paws together and made more unpleasant throaty noises.

"I'm not happy about this either, but you're the one that's approaching me," Daegan said, raising the revolver in the air. "Leave!" Daegan shouted.

The bear roared in defiance but didn't come closer.

"I said *leave!*" Daegan barked and fired a warning shot into the air. The bullet exploded out, the cracking noise of the gunshot resounding in the still woods. The feel of the trigger on his finger made him feel *alive!* The memory of killing the deserter-turned-bandit under the bridge a few nights before flashed in his mind. He'd felt strong… powerful. Like a runewielder.

"*Go!*" Daegan pointed the gun at the bear. The bear didn't retreat so he fired again. Another earsplitting reel echoed as he pulled the trigger. The bullet landed and the bear clamoured back in pain, stumbling off its haunches.

"Get out of here!" Daegan shouted again, summoning every shred of command he had in him. The shadowy mass of the bear rumbled and then retreated into the underbrush.

Daegan waited, his finger tentatively hovering over the trigger as the sounds of the bear moving through the growth faded into stillness. His breath was ragged with adrenaline. His fingers clasped tightly around the handle of the revolver, his palm was sweating.

I did it. No one had needed to come protect him, Daegan had faced a bear… and he'd *survived.* He hadn't run, he'd stood tall, defiant and strong. *Like a real Tredain… just like Landryn and father and all my ancestors back to Elyina the Defiant herself.* He was a warrior… he always had been.

Daegan heard rustled movement behind him and turned to see Tanlor rushing towards him.

"What is it?!" Tanlor hissed, his enormous blade already drawn, "I heard your gunfire!" His eyes scanned the trees.

"A bear…" Daegan replied, finally lowering his weapon, "do you mind?" he asked, nodding to the runestones which were now faded. His throat didn't tingle, he didn't feel any of the remnants of shame. *I am Tredain.* He didn't yield, he didn't cower, he didn't show weakness.

I am not weak.

***

"Next time wait until I've done my sweep," Tanlor grumbled, stirring the mushroom broth.

"I was fine… I don't need a babysitter," Daegan replied, hitching Termite to the tree that the horse had spent most of the evening butchering. He patted the horse's neck, "good lad," he whispered to it. Termite's ears flicked appreciatively and for once didn't try to bite Daegan's hand as he tied the rope.

"My job is to keep you alive," Tanlor continued.

"Well, you're doing a great job of it so far," Daegan smirked, widening his arms in an open gesture, "I'm still here, aren't I?"

"That bear could've torn you apart,"

"But he didn't," Daegan clarified, walking into the heat of the campfire, "I feel alive, Tanlor," he continued, unable to sit still, "that was… that was incredible."

"It was reckless, I can't—"
"—I want you to teach me how to fight like you," Daegan said with determination.
"I'm not sure if that's a good idea."

"It'll be a lot easier to keep me alive if I can defend myself when needed," Daegan tried appealing to Tanlor's rational way of thinking.

"I'm not against the idea…" Tanlor put his hand up in defence, "but we need to be level-headed about it," he postulated. "If you get injured in training… we don't have healers on hand to help. I can't recall the amount of broken bones and wounds I'd taken in my early years of training."

"Bloodstone doesn't work on me anyway," Daegan replied, waving his hand dismissively, "so having healers around wouldn't matter. You can bandage and stitch pretty well, I watched you work on Wolfhound back at the Greenwood camp." The fact that the healing effects of bloodstone didn't work on Daegan was just another frustration in a long list, but at least now it helped him with his argument.

Tanlor was quiet for a while as he gently stirred the boiling broth, his face bearing an expression of deep thought. Daegan was still too restless to sit down so he continued pacing around the camp.

"For how long did you train as a boy… before, you know…"
"Before I learned I was hindered," Daegan finished for him. His throat scratched at him as he spoke but he pushed on, forcing down the memory of the night his father had encased him with the stone spikes. "I was twelve when it was decided my training would end."
"So about two years?"

"Children in my family start young," Daegan revealed. "Runewielding from when we're old enough to sense edirs—which obviously never happened for me—my sister Allyn was runewielding before she could even fully form sentences," he'd not thought much about his little sister since fleeing Rubastre. He wondered in the back of his mind how his family had reacted from the Arch-duke's letter explaining the situation.

"Combat training starts when we're strong enough to hold a sword," Daegan continued, "Landryn and I had been sparring from as early as I can remember."
"Good," Tanlor nodded approvingly, "you'll have the basics down then… and muscle memory is a lot stronger than people give credit. I've seen veterans who've not held a sword in over a decade jump right into a fight as though they'd never even retired."
"So you'll do it?"
"Reldoni forms are different, so your combat style will be strange…" Tanlor mused, "you'll have to relearn some pieces to work with what I have to teach."
"I can do that."
"You'll have to do what I say," he said, giving Daegan a levelled stare.
"What do you think I've been doing since we left Rubastre!" Daegan countered.
"I mean it," Tanlor affirmed, "no arguments or pulling rank… just do what I say, when I say it. Even when we're not sparring."

Daegan crossed his arms in front of him. He didn't like the sound of completely submitting to Tanlor's charge. But at the same time… hadn't Tanlor already pulled authority over him multiple times on this excursion. It's not like much would change there.

"Agreed," Daegan conceded, and then picked two of the straightest sticks from the pile of firewood he'd collected. He tested the weight of one.

The bark of the stick was rough in Daegan's hand and wisps of dried moss fell from it as he swung it. It had been a long time since he'd held a training weapon. It didn't really pass for the weighted wooden training swords he'd used as a boy but the idea and intent he was putting into it was the same. Daegan tossed the other to Tanlor and watched him with expectant eyes.

"You want to start now?" Tanlor asked, incredulously. "The broth's almost ready."

"You don't always get to choose when to fight," Daegan grinned, remembering Swordmaster Garld's lessons.

He shifted into an offensive attack stance and lunged for Tanlor.

CHAPTER 28
Subterfuge

The hallways of the bloodshedders barracks were all made of stone brick. Femira had fallen into the habit of actively honing her edir as she walked through them. It had been a technique that Endrin had suggested to help enhance her edir control. Before, her edir would wash over the halls in waves, and she could sense each of the bricks resonate in response. She tried focusing on each individual brick so that she could only feel the vibration of just one. At first the action was slow, taking a few seconds for her edir to focus in, but now she didn't even need to slow her pace as she walked, making sure that her edir touched every single brick individually as she passed.

The edir—she'd learned—was like a muscle. The more you used it and trained it, the stronger and faster it became. This—in turn—made her runewielding stronger and faster. Although a normal person's edir had a natural limit to how strong it could become. Femira even before becoming soulforged had a naturally powerful edir but that didn't make her special here amongst the bloodshedders. All of them had been recruited because of their stronger edirs.

Becoming soulforged extended this natural limitation allowing her edir more strength and reach in runewielding, but this meant that she needed to actively train her edir to get to the same level as Endrin and the other bloodshedders who'd been soulforged longer than her. Even Jaz's edir seemed to be growing much more powerful after he had been infused with his topaz.

The only drawback to it—that she could see—was that an affinity to one particular runestone weakened the edir for using any other runestones. But considering Femira had never been able to use any other runestone in the first place, that didn't really matter to her.

Femira turned to the hall that led to Garld's office and reined in her edir. Her mind had often lingered in the early days of her training on how Garld had managed to detect her hiding in the treasure room in Altarea. Knowing now that adept runewielders could sense other people's edirs closeby, she figured that's how he'd done it. Femira hadn't even known what an edir was back then, let alone that she was broadcasting hers unintentionally.

It had become a game to Femira now to restrain her edir around Garld. In one part, to show to him the control she'd learned and in another—larger part—because she enjoyed trying to sneak up on him undetected. Garld's edir was always under immaculate control, other people had a tendency to flare out occasionally. For most people, it was like holding sand in your hands, it was impossible to ensure none slipped out, especially when you weren't focused on making sure you didn't lose any. But for Garld, it was like he had it all contained in glass, perfectly in control.

As Femira approached the door to his office, she pulled her edir in tightly, grasping to all the metaphorical grains of edir sand. She could hear voices within the office that made her pause. She could pretend that listening in was part of her edir training but Femira had long since accepted that she simply enjoyed stealing secrets as much as she enjoyed stealing gold. And Garld had plenty of secrets he was still holding on to.

" ...won't be long before it is common knowledge," Garld said. It was muffled through the door but Femira could still make out his voice.

"And we're certain he's still alive?" That was Misandrei.

"Yes," Garld replied, "I'm sending a small party to assist in the search. I want you to lead. You have full authority over the existing team... or what remains of them."

"When do we leave?"

"Tonight, I want you on a ship before word gets out. Bring a small team, four or five should suffice. A balance of specialists would be ideal."

"Loreli is capable," Misandrei noted, "I'll bring her amongst a few other trusted people. Will I take Annali or do you have another assignment for her?" Femira's heart skipped a beat at the mention of her.

"No. Landryn has requested her assistance," Garld responded, he sounded amused, "he wants her on the Tidewall mission with him... in fact, she's supposed to be here already to go over a briefing," he added with a note of frustration. *Well that's as good a cue as any.*

With a satisfied grin with remaining undiscovered, Femira slowly released her grip on her edir letting a small trickle out. It would seem that she was just walking towards the door to anyone who wasn't actively trying to sense for her. After a moment, she knocked on the door and walked through with a light bounce in her step.

"You're in a good mood," Garld noted.

"As anyone with a glass of sand would be," she grinned at him.

"Is that a Keiran saying?"

"Why not," she shrugged with a smile, then walked towards the desk. She saluted both Misandrei and Garld, respectfully.

"You wanted to speak with me, sir," Femira started.

"This mission on the Tidewall," Garld replied, "it will be just yourself and another bloodshedder—Selyn Caul—that will be accompanying the Prince. He will also have a pair from his own personal guard."

"Selyn's a wavecaller, right?"

"Indeed, she will be beneficial to your team if you happen across any remnants of the Altarean corsairs."

"You don't think it was Altareans that attacked those villages either?" Femira asked him.

"I believe the situation warrants further investigation."

"You're not telling me something here, sir," Femira prodded, trying to keep respect in her voice. Garld gave her allowances much of the time in her lack of decorum but she didn't want to push it.

Femira gritted her teeth when Garld and Misandrei exchanged glances. She hated how they seemed able to have full conversations with each other through glances alone.

"Landryn has suspicions that he wants confirmed," Garld offered, "I'm not convinced myself but I will trust his judgement on this."

"You're being really cryptic here," Femira narrowed her eyes, "is it something to do with soulforging?" Soulforging runestone affinities was the big secret that everyone was trying to keep hidden.

"What does it have to do with disappearing people?" Femira pushed.

"Soulforging can sometimes be…" Misandrei struggled with the words, "costly."

"What Misandrei means," Garld cut in, "is that those unfamiliar with soulforging… they make mistakes and lives can be lost."

"You think someone tried to soulforge the villagers? *Why?*"

"No," Garld replied, "no, I don't think so. But it might be related to the recent rise in the amount of soulforged runewielders. You might come up against foes stronger than we've anticipated."

"Landryn is a formidable runewielder, as is Selyn," Misandrei added, encouragingly.

"Your own ability also shouldn't be ignored," Garld offered and Femira felt a swell of pride, "I don't doubt that if you find the perpetrators of these crimes, your team will be able to handle it."

"So what is it that you wanted to speak to me about?" she prodded.

"At first, I didn't approve of the excursion," Garld said, honestly, "but Landryn being out of the city for a while will allow me to make some plans that would be easier made without him here.

"That sounds…" *very fucking suspicious,* Femira wanted to say, but settled on, "weird."

"The Prince has some blindspots in his judgement," Garld said with a look of genuine honesty on his face, "trust that everything I do is for his benefit… and for Reldon."

Femira did trust Garld. If he felt he needed to hide certain things from Landryn then who was she to question that?

"You've still not told me what you need me to do, sir," she said.

"It will take you two days to reach the villages past Inish Head. And two days to return, I need a little more time than that. I want you to prod the Prince towards continuing further north if you've not uncovered anything."

"Understood," Femira nodded, "how long do you need?"

"Ten days should be all I need to get everything in place."

"Easy," Femira shrugged, "what are these plans?"

"There's a small expedition team I need to send north to Rubane quietly, I don't want the Prince knowing about it just yet."

"Would he care about a small team heading there?" Femira asked. Rubane was an ally of Reldon, but she supposed it was pretty weird sending in a secret team of bloodshedders.

"Yes," Garld replied, sadly, "he will when he learns why… and I want you to make sure that this is kept from him as long as possible."

"What is it?"

"His brother—Prince Daegan—has been assassinated."

PART III

CREATURES LURK BELOW

Interlude
Arken

Arken sat in his office, lamenting over his disappointment. On his desk in front of him was an intricate device of wood and metal. He twisted a brass horn into place on the machine. His apprentice sat waiting dutifully opposite him.

"Many people overlook the practical uses for bondstone," Arken said, wistfully, "oh, it pains me to think how many are wasted as signal stones by the highborn." His assistant nodded along attentively, her eyes rapt and her ears hanging on every word he said. She was hopelessly in love with him, he knew. Arken had a strong build, immaculate bone structure and—most importantly—he was a genius. The girl would be a fool to not have taken a fancy for him. But she was his student and so he would respectfully decline her advances when she would eventually make them. She was much too young for him, and besides she was a cousin to Duke Garron. It would be very improper for him to entertain such a courtship.

"Did you know, my dear," Arken lectured, "that bondstone is the most powerful of all the runestones combined."

"What about soulstone?" she asked in her usual delicate voice.

"Oh come now child," he chided gently, "this place is for science and engineering. Not fables and legends... the soulstones of the Sorcerer Kings are but a lazy attempt to explain the feats those men had achieved. In truth, the Sorcerer Kings were artificers—engineers, just like you and I—they simply happened to have knowledge beyond what we could fathom. Centuries of research and knowledge... all lost thanks to Elyina and her *crusade* against the Sorcerer Kings."

He fished in one of his desk drawers for some shards of aradium. "Oh, but this wasn't supposed to be a history lesson now was it?" He indulged her with a smile, "although... evidence is plain throughout the realms that the Sorcerer Kings were artificers; The Red Throne of Athlin is a beautifully crafted work of runestone artificing. Oh, what I wouldn't give to study a relic of the Sorcerer Kings' era."

"Doesn't the Red Throne brutally kill anyone that touches it?" she asked. *Ugh, such savagery. Why does everyone focus on how runestones can be used for killing?*

"Indeed it does," Arken replied, "wouldn't it be marvellous to unravel how it works?"

"I'm sure that Grimsworth would certainly be interested in learning to replicate it," she noted.

"It pains me how much effort Grimsworth dedicates to weaponising our knowledge... and the Dukes are worse. Can't they see the wonders we could create if they would only give us the resources with which to create them."

Arken reached out with his edir to touch the bondstone, he pulled on its energy and held it inside of him. The tiny shards of aradium were arrayed in a tight line on his desk. He focused his attention and willed the energy of the bondstone to fuse them together into the shape of a needle. As he did so, his mind traced out the rune inscriptions he wanted on the newly formed aradium needle.

The standard runes for Draw, Hold and Shape were etched onto the face of the gemstone, so tiny that they were almost imperceptible to the naked eye. *Why do people think they're called runestones if not for the runes?*

He then added one of the newly discovered runes; Enhance which complimented and accented around the inscription for the Draw rune.

"You see this extra rune I've added here, Jesse?"

"Yes… I think," she cocked her head.

"This is Enhance. It will allow for additional draw… which the aradium should do naturally until reaching its balanced state. The funny thing about the Enhance rune is that it doesn't make the Draw rune any more effective when a *person* uses it. But the *natural* amount that the gemstone would draw in its active state is *considerably* increased. Isn't that fascinating?" He looked up at her over his spectacles. She looked lost, the gears in her mind trying to process what he was saying.

"This means," he tried another explanation, "that it will draw not only stone but also metal into itself *and* at an accelerated rate. *Without* the need for a runewielder, of course." Her mouth dropped ever so slightly at the revelation. *Yes, it is quite the discovery isn't it, my dear?*

"Now this," he took out a metal disc from another drawer in his desk. It was incredibly thin but about a half arm's length in diameter.

"This is the true reason you're here," he grinned at her and nodded to the violin Jesse had brought with her at his request. The girl could play the melody to the Hunter and the Lady with such beautiful delicacy that he could feel every morsel of love that the pair had for each other.

It was both a mystery and a blessing why Jesse had chosen artificing over her musical talents. But there was a genius to music that translated well to engineering and a keen mind needed to be challenged in order to be stimulated. And there was no better place for that than in his employ.

Arken placed the disc onto a plate on the device, then indicated to her that she should begin playing. Just as she touched the bow to the strings to play the first note, Arken held up his hand to pause her and gently turned the crank on the side of the device. A spring mechanism inside controlled the rotation of the plate perfectly. He lightly lowered the arm apparatus holding the aradium needle until it found its resting place on the top of the rotating disc.

He turned the opening of the brass horn towards her and nodded again. She played that first exquisite note of the song; slow and long. *Perfection.* Arken watched her as she played the song as he'd often requested her to since learning she could play it so skillfully. As Jesse played, the light of the aradium needle grew brighter and brighter. Arken held his breath as he watched the graceful manoeuvring of her fingers on the violin strings. Almost imperceptible rivets appeared in the needle's wake as the disc continued to rotate.

Arken sat silently, listening to the song and as she neared the end he felt tears in his eyes. *Oh such beauty.* Jesse concluded the song with a flourish, the resonance of the final notes slowly faded until the only sound was that of the quiet rotation of the disc. Arken carefully lifted the needle and plucked the disc from the plate.

Jesse—still unsure if she could speak—watched in confused silence as he moved it to an almost identical device on the table behind him, and placed the disc on the plate of the other device. The needle in this one was metal instead of aradium. He cranked it in the same manner as before and the plate and disc began to rotate. Just as meticulously as he had done with the last one, he lowered the arm holding the needle.

A crackle of sound came through the horn and then…

Music!

Wonderful, majestic, elegant, ingenious, *magical* music!

The sound of Jesse playing her violin echoed back at them, as if she had started playing it again from the beginning. A tear fell down Arken's face.

"You've created a machine to capture music?" she gasped.

"To capture all sound," he breathed. "Oh, to think of all the beautiful things we could create together… the art that we could bring to life…"

There was a knock at his office door. He knew who it was—and what they wanted—he sighed with relief that he hadn't knocked on the door a few moments earlier and ruined the capturing of the song.

"If only those with the coin weren't so concerned with killing and wanting more sophisticated ways to do it," Arken mourned, "then we could focus on making beauty."

He pulled on a smaller lever on the device, halting the music and called out to the visitor that they could enter. Grimsworth, in a well trimmed suit, strode into the office looking down at Jesse and taking in her violin on her lap.

"A private concert?" Grimsworth laughed, "oh Arken. The things you waste your time on. Come, we have a meeting with the representative."

Arken apologised to Jesse, and advised her that their lesson would resume in the morning. He followed Grimsworth out into the halls and out of the Ironworks Guild. The winter snows were arriving and Arken pulled on the heat of his topaz to keep from shivering as they stepped out into the light of the gaslamps.

"The Reldoni contacts we've made are keen to move forward with the plan," Grimsworth whispered to him as they walked.

"Are we sure this is the wisest course—"

"—We are not going over this again," Grimsworth hissed, "the Dukes *must* fall and the Reldoni are the best opportunity we have for this."

"But think of the amount of blood that will be shed."

"Do we not share the same dream, my friend?" Grimsworth implored, "the wonders we can create together."

"How do we know the Reldoni will hold to their end of the bargain?"

"We are giving them an open route into Rubane. With our help their invasion will be swift and effective. Why, think of all the lives we'll have *saved* by helping them reach that goal faster—and most importantly our *own* lives. The Reldoni *will* invade once it is known publicly that Prince Daegan has been killed. I have no doubt about this."

"You are certain that Prince Daegan was killed?"

"My spies are deep within the Archduke's palace. I am certain that he is not in the palace or any known safehouse this side of the Iron Hills. The man is dead. What of your information?" Grimsworth asked.

"Mine?" Arken replied, his nose wrinkling.

"Garronforn," Grimsworth insisted, "your contact is reliable? Duke Boern Garron means to send the bulk of his soldiers to the Balfold to deal with all of these rakmen reports, is that not correct?"

"Oh, yes… yes, of course," Arken replied. Jesse Garron was a lesser cousin to the Duke and he trusted his apprentice's knowledge in that regard. And what reason would she have to lie to him, she was besotted and would divulge to him any plans she knew of.

"I am very confident in that information," Arken affirmed.

"Good," Grimsworth smiled. "Good. Our entire plan hinges on that."

Interlude
Ferath

On the outskirts of Edas, there was a small village built around a large fir tree. The largest inn in the village was The Fir House. It was a squat building with a reasonably sized lounge area and bar. Inside the warm atmosphere, local men threw back ales and whitewhiskeys as if they were water.

The Fir House didn't often see travellers passing through as the village was a little too far north of Edas for anyone to bother taking that road. It was for this reason that the tall, dark haired man with light tan skin drew the attention of most in the room. He kept his face predominantly covered by a cowl and kept to himself in a corner of the tavern. He had a fine sword sheathed at his hip but he bore no shield nor insignia to denote which Duke he worked for. As the night drew on and the local men drank themselves beyond common sensibility, a pair worked up the courage to speak with the mysterious stranger.

Eric was the tallest man in the entire village. He was also one of the village's only fighting men. Solo mercenaries and contract knights were a rare sight in The Fir House so Eric and his companion Shayn felt it was their duty to question the man. Both men had thick beards—as was the style for warriors. Eric's long hair was tied back in a traditional warrior's braid with the sides shaved to boot. Shayn was completely bald on top but with his kept beard the man cut quite the handsome figure. They were exactly the kind of men Ferath had expected to find in an-out-of-the way village like this. Less than average fighters that never had any reason to go much farther from where they were born.

"So is it contract work you're looking for?" Shayn asked.
"I'm looking for a friend of mine," Ferath replied, truthfully, "he's one of my countrymen. Have you seen any others like me pass through here?"
"Another big tall lad like you, yeah, I'd have noticed him," Eric replied, "don't think your mate's been through. But then again, sometimes we're off on patrols, don't see everyone that passes through, you know."
"Where you from anyway?" Shayn asked, his eyes glancing down at Ferath's sword.
"Altarea," Ferath lied, it's not like these men would be able to tell. Ferath unbuckled his scabbard and placed the sword just at the edge of his reach on the bench to ease the man's concern.
"Nasty shit the Reldoni have been at in your country," Shayn replied, giving Ferath a sad smile. Ferath nodded in thanks and schooled his face into a matching expression.
"What about a Reldoni man? Have you heard anything about Reldoni passing through any of the villages around here?" Ferath tried to make his voice sound like an innocent, concerned friend.
"Sorry, mate. Can't say I have," Shayn replied.
"Where'd you get that sword?" Eric asked, nodding at the blade. Ferath had

considered discarding it in the river in Rubastre. The blade had an insignia of a hawk clutching a sword on the hilt. It was too identifiable as his sword to anyone looking for him, which he knew the Arch-duke's men were. He'd already left a trail of their bodies from the alleys of Rubastre and then along the road to Edas.

His contacts in Rubastre had taken a few days to verify that Daegan had fled the palace. They had also discovered an unlikely ally in the Ironworks guildmasters who helped him escape the city undetected from the guards. He likely could have done it easily on his own but with his still healing gunshot wound, he was happy for the assistance. The guildmasters had also helped with affirming that Daegan was no longer in Rubastre. Although they believed Daegan was dead so their spies weren't completely reliable. In either case, Ferath was confident that Daegan was no longer in Rubastre.

After his failed attempt at assassinating Daegan, Ferath had laid low in a safehouse in the city. The wound he'd taken from Daegan's revolver in his abdomen had taken a few days to heal—even with his bloodstone. His reckless mistake still galled him. How could he have failed such a simple task? The man was hindered! And drunk... completely defenceless.

He had not anticipated Tanlor Shrydan's prompt appearance and the man had proved to be a worthy adversary. But Ferath was supposed to be better than everyday soldiers. Tanlor was indeed a skilled fighter but he should have been *incomparable* to Ferath. It was his flawed runewielding that truly caused his failure. He could feel his accursed affinity now, pulsing in his chest and his ears. His edir was becoming increasingly uncontrollable and he had to actively focus on keeping it restrained.

His hand shook as he touched the blade. He couldn't bring himself to throw it away. It was Ferath's most prized possession and he'd be damned if he would discard it. Instead, he'd wrapped the ornate hilt and scabbard in rough leathers in an attempt to hide its appearance. But a long and slightly curved Reldoni blade was still an uncommon sight in Rubane.

"A friend gave it to me," Ferath eventually answered the man.
"The guy you're looking for?" Shayn prodded.
"No," Ferath replied, "a different man."

The men tried to pry more into Ferath's background. He figured they were looking for a good story to be entertained with but he kept quiet and after a while the pair grew bored and returned to the group of locals.

Ferath's lead in this direction was a bust, he'd managed to follow Daegan's trail south of Rubastre but as he neared Edas, the information was becoming less and less reliable. Ferath had assumed that Daegan would be making for Edas to try and find passage on a ship back to Reldon. However, once he'd arrived in Edas, Ferath had scoured through taverns and vicedens looking for any mention of a man matching Daegan's description but there were all empty leads. On a whim, he'd decided to head north to see if Daegan had been clever enough to take the backroads around Edas and make for the coast road to Garronforn. It appeared that Daegan hadn't passed through this way either.

Could he have gone East? The Prince had been friendly with Duke Harfallow, could the Duke have stepped in and taken Daegan to Hardhelm? All Ferath's instincts told him that Daegan would have fled home to Reldon, but perhaps the assasination attempt had shaken him and his decisions were being influenced by the Dukes?

Just as Ferath decided to retire to his room for the evening, a bard had begun playing on a painfully out of tune fiddle in another corner of the tavern. *Good timing,* he thought, grateful that he wouldn't have to listen to the countryside musician butcher any songs. The first long note of The Hunter and the Lady screeched out through the tavern and some of the locals jeered.

"Ah Pol! You're not playing that shit again tonight, are ye?" one of them called out.

"Will ye play something with a bit more soul," Shayn groaned.

"The Hunter and the Lady is a modern classic," Pol the Bard retorted, his jowl jiggling in offence, "if you all don't start appreciating me, I swear, I'll leave this town for good!"

"Do!" Eric called out.

"Yeah, would ye ever fuck off, will ye," another of the men shouted.

"Ruining the atmosphere in here every fuckin' night."

That was the last straw for Pol it seemed, who indignantly tossed his battered fiddle into its case. He puffed out his chest and strode out of the Fir House, "I'm sick of playing for backwater fools anyway," he declared, banging the door angrily behind him.

Ferath buckled his sword belt back on and made his way to the bar to settle his tab. "Pol will be back before the end of the night," the lanky barkeep told him, "if you were wanting music. Happens most nights, he'll grumble and groan and say he's too good for this place but he'll be back when he remembers that I'm the only one that'll let him play at all, let alone pay him."

"I'm good," Ferath replied, "not my taste in music anyway."

"You're not a fan of The Hunter and the Lady, friend?" Shayn called out from the end of the bar, "bit fuckin' dated if you ask me." The man answered his own question.

"Yeah, Pol's always playing those old songs. We want new songs, new stories," Eric added, "sure Taran the Hunter's boys are men grown already. Someone should be making songs about them."

"Aye, yeah, Rowan Shrydan's a good lad," Shayn added, "comes through this way every few seasons."

"You know, I heard the Shrydan brothers took care of some raiders up north not a week gone," the barman said, his lack of teeth slurring his speech, "Pol should write a song about that."

Shrydan brothers?

"Do you mean *Tanlor* Shrydan?" Ferath asked, leaning off-handedly on the bar in an attempt at appearing only casually interested.

"Is that the other one?" Shayn replied, "I've only met Rowan, but he mentioned his brother before. Works up in Rubastre for the Arch-duke... or was it Edas?"

"Tanlor and Rowan," Ferath said, looking to the barman to get the conversation back on topic, "they're up north?"

"Aye," the barkeep nodded, "some raiders had done some dirty business up in Crossroads."

"Would never happen down here," Eric added, "I promise you that. Not with me and Shayn here." *Of course.*

"And the Shrydans?" Ferath prodded.

"Caught up to 'em and butchered 'em all, I heard. Two against forty of the bastards, as I heard it told."

"*Forty?!*" Shayn exclaimed, "That's bullshit. Ain't no way, two men can take on twenty each in a fight. No matter how good."

"I heard it was a dozen rakmen, come down past Nortara," Eric said.

"The rakmen have been over in Balfold, ye donkey," Shayn retorted, "nah, it was just raiders. And no way it was forty of 'em."

"You're *sure* it was Tanlor Shrydan?" Ferath pressed.

"Aye, yeah. Sure as shit, my mate Dan's cousin was up in Ailsford," Shayn replied, "and well *his* wife's brother ran the store up in Crossroads. He got done bad by the raiders, I heard. His poor boy, had to take over the store and he's just a kid."

Shayn looked at him as if that answered the question.

"And?" Ferath prompted, looking for more.

"Well Dan's cousin himself went up to Crossroads to help once he heard, but the Shrydans had already taken care of it. Saw the pair himself, he says."

"Was there anyone else with them?"

"He didn't say," Shayn shrugged.

"Didn't he say somethin' about some foreign lawman or some shit, screwing him out of his inheritance?" Eric added.

"Don't know if he was *with* the Shrydans though, might've just been passing through."

"Did he get his name?" Ferath asked. He didn't think that Daegan would've been so stupid as to use his real name. But he had followed the trail south of a Reldoni man going by the name 'Desmond'.

"He didn't say, sorry, why you so interested anyways?" Shayn's eyes narrowed.

"Just curious…" Ferath said, waving his hand dismissively, "would make a good song, you're right," he added and grinned disarmingly to the barman.

Ferath paid for the drink that he hadn't touched and another round for Shayn and Eric before bidding them goodnight.

A part of him resisted the urge to run out of the bar and ride his horse north to Crossroads as fast the mount's legs could take him. But riding through the countryside on roads he didn't know in the dark was a guarantee to get lost.

He would rest first, have a letter sent to his contacts in Rubane and leave another for the team arriving. Then he would ride north to Crossroads.

CHAPTER 29
Salt the Earth Behind You

Urundock was the gateway to the lands beyond the Nortara Sheet—the enormous lake that stretched out across the horizon and was in a permanent frozen state. The town had originally been home to a community of fishermen who would travel out onto the ice and bore holes to fish. When the Arch-duke had decided to build outposts along the northern shore in efforts to reduce the number of rakmen coming south, Urundock had become the central hub for making the trip across. Over the years, the town had grown with traders often moving through.

That was the problem with towns that were grown out of necessity rather than any real desire for people to live there. What you end up with is people who are too poor to turn anywhere else. People with bad luck, bad choices—or both—all congregating together to carve out a tough life in a hard place.

Most of the inns were vicedens, catering for all the traders, soldiers and miners that passed through. Daegan didn't have any issue with that, but the quality certainly wasn't what he was used to, so he didn't argue much when Tanlor insisted that they stay at one of the very few respectable places. The Stag's Head had the skull of a Great Elk mounted above the fireplace, its antlers spanning almost the full breadth of the wall.

"You ever see one of those in the wild?" Daegan asked Tanlor as they walked inside.

"Once," Tanlor replied, not even looking over at the skull. Daegan waited for more and then sighed when Tanlor kept walking on to the innkeeper.

"Where? When? What were the *circumstances?...* Tanlor, you do know how conversations work, don't you?"

"The Balfold. When I was twelve. Father wouldn't let me or Rowan shoot it, then it ran off," Tanlor surmised quickly, and then with raised eyebrows back at Daegan, "happy?" Daegan wasn't sure why he even bothered.

"Whitewhiskey, please," Daegan asked the innkeeper as they approached the bar.

"You boys need a room too?" the broad woman asked.

"Aye," Tanlor replied, "and that yard out back, can we use it for some training?" The woman eyed Tanlor's greatsword and then scanned Daegan up and down.

"You boys mercs? Some of the inns down the docks might be more to your tastes."

"No," Tanlor grunted, "we're not mercs. Just travellers looking for passage across the sheet."

"You heading to Twin Garde? Some trouble up there the last few weeks I heard… you Duke's men?"

"No," Tanlor said firmly and left it at that. "Do you know any ice rafters that might take us across?"

"Snow's have been getting heavy," she replied. "You won't get many looking to risk their raft if a storm rolls in. You might be waiting a few weeks."

"Surely there's someone that will make the journey?" Tanlor prodded, prompting the woman's face to scrunch up in thought. She nodded after a moment, "Ardy might... the sod owes me twenty copper marks, along with half the taverns this side of Nortara. He might be desperate enough to take ye."

"He here?" Tanlor asked, scanning his eyes over the few men in the common room.

"Nah, he's not welcome until he has my coin. You might find him down the street at Miner's Rest though. Their ale's more water than drink but it's cheap, I've spotted him coming and going there." Tanlor thanked her and sorted the costs for their rooms. She eyed Daegan again, eventually asking, "and where ye lads say yer from?"

"We didn't," Tanlor cut her off, "thank you."

"You know I *can* speak without giving myself away, you know," Daegan said once they were out of earshot from the woman.

"Words spreading that the Reldoni Prince is missing, people might start putting the pieces together. Last thing we need is Ferath picking up any scent of our trail," he whispered to Daegan before heading out of the inn.

It was cold outside, as was to be expected. Daegan struggled to remember a time in the last few weeks he *hadn't* felt a sharp chill after stepping outside. He followed Tanlor through the street. Boots, cartwheels and hooves had packed the snow mixing it with the frozen crusty earth. As they walked down the street, Daegan spotted a store with a sword and an axe hanging over the door instead of a sign.

"A weaponsmith," he guessed, "I might see if I can pick up a sword. Might as well start training with real blades."

"Good idea," Tanlor conceded, "your form is improving. But your balance will be off if you keep training with sticks. Alright, we'll—"

"—No, no," Daegan waved dismissively, "you go look for the drunken ice rafter. I can handle this."

"I'm not sur—"

"—I'll be fine, Tanlor," Daegan insisted. In truth, he simply wanted to get some time away from Tanlor. The past few days had been filled mostly with awkward silences. Tanlor sighed but gave a resigned nod, "be careful."

"Well I'm hardly going to start a fight with some stranger now, am I?"

Daegan was a little surprised that the other man was allowing him out of his sight. He had been overbearingly diligent in his bodyguard duties and Daegan wanted just a few moments on his own. *I don't think I've been out of his immediate sight since Crossroads.* He breathed a sigh of relief when Tanlor kept on walking. Surely he needed a break from Daegan too.

The weaponsmith had the stock you'd expect to see of a remote trading hub; all strong steel with sharp edges. Swords, axes, spears, maces and crossbows amongst a plethora of other killing utensils along with varying armours to help prevent *being* killed. None of them were ornate or had intricate patterns along the blades. No gemstones inlaid in the pommel or dragons shaped along the hilt. Just simple plain steel swords in Rubanian style; long, straight and double edged.

Daegan hefted one from the rack and tested its weight in his hand. It had been a long time since he'd held a real sword.

Thirteen years. He coughed, clearing his throat of the scratch that came up. His free hand rubbing at it. The noise drew the attention of the weaponsmith.

"Bad cough there, lad. It's cold out," the blond man called over from where he was inspecting a helm with a broken visor. "A sword's good for making sure rakmen or raiders won't kill you, but the cold will kill you just as easily. You heading up north?"

"Yes," Daegan replied, his voice croaky. The door opened and a frosty chill swept in as a cloaked and hooded man entered the store.

"You got furs, yet?" the weaponsmith asked, ignoring the newcomer, "my brother sells furs down near the docks. He'll give you a good price. Bears, mammanth, wolves, ferrax, whatever you need."

"Ferrax?" Daegan asked, intrigued.

"Aye, a ferrax pelt's worth its weight in silver," the man winked, "ain't nothing better to keep you warm up past the sheet."

"Aidan don't have ferrax pelts no more than I do," the newcomer said, he had a strange accent. He drew back his hood to reveal long scraggly grey hair and a pale sunken face, like he'd had the life sucked right of him.

"He does," the weaponsmith countered with scowl, "trader brought 'em down three weeks ago. A whole raft-full. Didn't say where he'd traded 'em, mind you," he looked to Daegan, "ain't nobody willing to trade with those that make coin with the rakmen but if a lad comes through peddlin' ferrax furs well…" he shrugged. *Morals until those morals aren't good for business, I get you.* "I get it," Daegan replied, "I'll check it out."

"What you need anyway, Ardy?" The weaponsmith resumed his inspection of the helm without looking at the newcomer.

"Axle broke on my last run, I need someone to fix it."

"Plenty of metalshapers down the docks," the weaponsmith said, flatly, "I make axes and swords."

"I'll have better luck trying to fix the damn thing myself than convincing any of them to do it," Ardy grumbled, scratching at the side of his head. Daegan caught sight of a long pointed ear under the tangled grey hairs. *He's an Aeth!*

"Maybe you should start paying back some of yer debts and people might be willing to do work for you again," the weaponsmith sneered, "you still owe Aidan for that sail he mended for ye a few months back, ye know."

"Aye, I know, I know, you think I don't? I'll get to 'im."

The Aeth man had a gravelly voice that matched his dishevelled appearance. Daegan had seen—and smelled—men like him a lot around vicedens. The kind that didn't have the endless supply of gold needed to keep up with their habits, but he'd never seen an Aeth like that before.

"Come on, Ronan. I thought we were friends, we're friends aren't we?" the Aeth flashed a yellow stained smile, he was missing a few teeth.

"Ugh," Ronan the weaponsmith sighed, "I'm not doing no work for free… but if you can find some parts that might be of use to ye in the scrap over there you can take it. But that's all yer gettin'!"

Ardy mumbled a thanks under his breath before moving to sift through the pile of scrap metal. Daegan's curiosity was far too piqued to resist walking over to the Aeth.

"I would never have expected to see an Aeth out here in…" Daegan tried to come up with a suitable reference to the place.

"…the back arse of nowhere," Ardy offered, glancing up at him with his dark sunken eyes.

"Yeah. I thought you guys would turn to dust or something if you go too far from Evier."

"I'm still here, aren't I?" he gave a lazy flourish of his hand, "not many Reldoni out here either," he continued rummaging through the scrap, "aren't you lot supposed to be invading some kingdom somewhere."

"What's your name?"

"Ardy."

"Really?"

"Really."

"Most Aeth I've met, their names are, you know…" again Daegan was lost for the words he was looking for. Their names tended to be *grander.*

"Flowery?" Ardy offered.

"Kind of, yeah," Daegan grinned.

"Well… it's just Ardy, and yours?"

"Dessie," Daegan replied, a name he was getting used to introducing himself as. Desmond the Cartographer. Quite the renown Dessie was building for himself around these parts he might add.

"Why won't the metalshapers fix the axles on your… carriage?" He guessed.

"Ice raft," Ardy corrected.

"You're an ice rafter?" Daegan's eyebrows rose, "would you be able to take me and my friend across the Nortara Sheet?

"And why the fuck a man like you want to go up there," Ardy scoffed, "you know the rak will as soon as kill you as trade with you."

"I'm a cartographer, I'm going to map the region," Daegan said with such enthusiasm that he almost believed it himself.

"That's a fool's errand."

"All the same," Daegan shrugged, he'd gotten quite used to people having that opinion of the task. He enjoyed the optimistic persona of Desmond that he donned when chatting with the locals. "Can you do it?" Daegan asked.

"My last run," Ardy started with a bitter edge to his voice, "I was bringing some… let's call them soldiers… back from Twin Garde. Didn't spot this sneaky fucker of a boulder peeking up through the ice. A blasted *boulder!* Can you believe it? Anyway… the thing busted up my axle."

"… And that's why you need a metalshaper."

"Aye."

"And what? Folk around here racist or something?"

"Let's just say, I've got some bad credit with the metalshapers round here," He swayed slightly as he spoke. *Likely most of the taverns too.*

"How much do you usually charge for a run across the sheet?"

"For two people?—twenty copper marks before we leave. Twenty when we get there."

"And how much do you need to fix your axle?"

"Maybe about thirty copper."

This man didn't even have thirty copper marks!

"How about I front you the money and you take us across the sheet for thirty?"

The door banged again, followed by yet another cold breeze. This time it was Tanlor. He didn't look happy, but then again, Tanlor rarely did. His eyes quickly met Daegan's and he strode over to him.

"Couldn't find the ice rafter Ardy that the woman at Stag's Head told us about," Tanlor said with a note of frustration, "apparently the guy's a drunk anyway so probably not the best idea to trust him to get us across safely."

"Shelly's talking shit," Ardy looked Tanlor up and down, "I ain't no drunk."

"Tanlor," Daegan beamed, "this is Ardy, our ice rafter."

"He is?" Tanlor's eyes widened and Daegan couldn't help but enjoy the man's embarrassment. "You'll take us across?" Tanlor asked Ardy.

"Will take a few days to get my raft fixed," Ardy replied, "and it's really not the best season to be crossing... blizzards come in hard and fast between now and midwinter. Most rafters hold off until after Lua Nova."

"We can't wait until the new year to cross. We need to leave as soon as possible," Tanlor insisted.

"You lads running from something? Not that I care much, mind you."

"We're just looking to cross is all," Tanlor replied.

"Aye yeah... and salt the earth behind you. If my raft gets damaged in a storm, thirty copper marks ain't going to cover it."

"*If* that happens," Daegan interjected, "we'll cover the damages."

"Will ye now... how do I know you're not just going to run off the second I land you on the north shore?"

Daegan and Tanlor shared a look. Daegan wasn't sure how to move forward, he would normally rely on his name as a Tredain as a collateral for any deal. Even in vicedens, no one was going to argue against a Prince's ability to pay his debts.

"We're leaving our horses stabled at the Stag's Head," Tanlor told Ardy, "paid up for six months' board. I won't give you the writ for them but I will sign a contract that says if we're not back before the writ expires, they can be released to you," Tanlor offered.

"Two good horses are worth a whole hell of a lot," Daegan added.

Ardy scratched at the side of his head again. He looked back at the scrap metal he'd been rummaging through.

"You lads are desperate, aren't you?" A predatory grin appearing on the Aeth's face, "alright then, deal. Thirty copper marks up front and I'll take ye across." Ardy held out his hand and Tanlor shook it.

"You got the coin on you now? You're staying at the Stag's Head, you said? I'll come find you when the work's finished."

"No, no," Daegan shook his head, "we'll come with you now to find a metalshaper." He didn't trust Ardy to not take their thirty marks and bring it straight to the nearest tavern.

***

Daegan dodged a swing of Tanlor's blade, still sheathed in its scabbard. He rolled and came up quick enough to block another swing with his new sword—also sheathed. It made the weapons heavier sparring like this but it also meant that Daegan was unlikely to accidentally cut himself. Tanlor had puffed a laugh when Daegan had also turned the catch on his scabbard preventing the sword from being accidentally drawn, "you won't get a cut on me," he scoffed.

Daegan had made it his goal to make sure to get at least one hit on the man before the session was done.

"Good dodge," Tanlor conceded, but then twisted his sword down which pulled Daegan's with it. Tanlor then charged him with his shoulder, knocking Daegan to the ground and disarming him.

Sparring seemed to be the only times where Tanlor was actually enjoying himself and Daegan had taken to the activity vigorously. As a boy, his training had made him uneasy. He had been forever compared to his brother's advances in both swordplay and runewielding, and compared to how his father had been at his age. His brothers, his father, his grandfather and all of his bloody ancestors it seemed had all been far superior fighters than Daegan had been as a child.

Now, in the frost-crusted earth behind an inn in 'the back arse of nowhere' as Ardy described it, Daegan could finally just enjoy the heat of the activity. The clash of swords, and the excitement he felt when he'd almost land a hit on the other man. Tanlor was far—*far*—beyond his skill level, the man might be about the same age as him but Tanlor had spent the last thirteen years training and fighting. Daegan on the other hand had spent those same years drinking and wallowing in self-pity. He was done with the latter. The drinking however... well he didn't see any need to stop that.

His flask of whitewhiskey was replenished since arriving at Urundock. He took a hearty swig after getting to his feet. He felt it tingle in chest as it made its way down.

"Ah," Daegan gasped with pleasure, hopping back and forth on his feet and letting the alcohol fuel his adrenaline.

He took a lunge at Tanlor who easily sidestepped. Then, he attempted a manoeuvre that Tanlor had been teaching him, spinning around and bringing his blade up but Tanlor was waiting for it. *Of course he would be, he taught it to me.* Instead of bringing his blade up however, Daegan dropped to the ground and kicked out his leg against Tanlor's ankle. The man grunted and lost balance.

"What are you doing?" Tanlor growled.
"I got you," Daegan grinned up at him from the ground, "I got a hit."
"But you're dead," Tanlor replied dismissively, pointing the sword down at him, "you hit the ground like that and you're as good as."
"I still got a hit."
"This isn't a game," Tanlor rebuked, "I knew men who would drink like that before a battle, I can tell you not many of 'em survived long enough for a second or third."
"Rowan never cared about me drinking," Daegan objected, climbing to his feet.
"Well Rowan's not here anymore," Tanlor snapped, obviously annoyed at the mention of his brother.
"And who's fault is that?" Daegan threw back, equally agitated by Tanlor's tone.

"Look, you want to get yourself killed for reckless silly mistakes? I don't think so, not on my watch," Tanlor shot at him, "not when it's my life—my dreams—on the line!"
"Your *dreams*?"
"Doesn't matter... forget I said anything," Tanlor walked away from him, back towards the inn, "we're done for tonight."

"No, no—what was that, what's in all of this for you?" Daegan supposed he shouldn't be surprised that Tanlor had other reasons for accompanying him. The man so rarely ever spoke about himself that it was hard to figure out anything about his life.

"I said it doesn't matter," Tanlor replied, more firmly.
"Listen," Daegan said, his anger rising up in him, the alcohol and adrenaline

working in tandem to loosen his lips, "if you hadn't tried to kill that kid because he reminded you of your father or whatever—"

"—You have no idea what you're talking about!" Tanlor rounded on him, Daegan took a step back at the fury on the man's face.

"No?" Daegan retorted, "Rowan told me... it's alright,"

"Did he?" Tanlor glowered as if Daegan had slapped him.

"Listen, at least *your* father was a good man—"

"—You don't know anything about it."

"My father was enough of a bastard. Trust me, you had it easy, alright."

"You know what, *Desmond,* you're not the only person who's got problems. The whole fucking world doesn't revolve around *you*. We don't exist just for you and your problems," Tanlor advanced on him.

"You don't know shit," Tanlor said

"You think you're hard? I'm harder."

"You think you're tough? I'm tougher."

"You've been living your privileged life, getting whatever you want your whole damn life handed to you. Yeah, it's shit that someone's trying to kill you but guess what? People have tried to kill me a whole bunch of times. It doesn't make you special. It doesn't make you *better* than me."

"I never said I was," Daegan shot back.

"You think it though," Tanlor went on, "I'm not good enough for your halls, your parties, your daughters because my father was a hunter."

"I don't even have a daughter," Daegan defended. It was an odd thing to argue on but it was all that Daegan picked out.

Tanlor looked rattled. He breathed out a long breath, steadying himself and then turned away from Daegan.

"I don't need you," Daegan croaked, his throat burning.

"Yes, you do," Tanlor replied, coldly and without looking back, "you wouldn't last two days without me."

CHAPTER 30

Sea Monsters Aren't Real

Landryn and his two personal guards were dressed in black—although Femira noted that Landryn's was a finer cut, along with the dark metal of his armour he cast an impressive figure on the back of his horse. Femira and Selyn were dressed in their bloodshedder uniforms.

The group waited for the cliff-side lift to lower for them. Femira was admiring Landryn's horse while they waited. Majestic was the word that came to mind when she looked at the horse, it had a white mane, and fur around the hooves but otherwise was a deep black.

"His name is Champion," Landryn said when he caught her admiring the horse. "He definitely looks the part," she replied. She was riding a reddish horse this time, she liked the one she'd been given for the last mission but this one seemed a lot more attentive to her commands and didn't simply follow the group. *Or it could be that I'm just a better rider now. Yeah, that was likely it.*

"He matches your armour," Femira noted, her eyes running over the intricate plates of black metal. It looked expensive, but then again he was a Prince so of course it was. It was the kind of fancy armour that she wouldn't even bother stealing back when she was a thief. It was too identifiable and there'd be no pawner or shady merchant willing to take it off her hands.

Lichtin probably would've just melted down the metal and sold it but then it would've lost that impressive black effect. The armour didn't look to be painted but Femira didn't know any kind of metal that was completely black like that, it didn't even reflect any light. Tentatively, Femira extended out her edir and was surprised when there was no vibration of response from it. *Strange.* Metals generally had a duller—more reluctant—response to her edir, but this was completely silent. Almost as though it weren't metal at all. It was more like the empty response of a runestone—or something *organic*?

"What metal is that?" Femira probed, even more intrigued, "I don't recognise it."

"I don't think there's many who would know it to see," Landryn gave her an amused smile, "it's nythilium."

"Nythilium?" she echoed, cocking her head.

"You've not heard of it?" his eyes widened slightly in surprise, "I'd thought that there were some relics of nythilium in possession of the Keiran."

Shit, would Annali have known what this was? Femira racked through her memories of valuable items she'd stolen over the years. She recalled a disgraced highborn man that had wanted the crew to steal an old family heirloom from his father's home. It had been described as a very valuable and rare knife. *What had he called it?* A nightblade? It was definitely something that had made Femira roll her eyes.

"Do some people call it night metal?" Femira asked.

"Possibly," he conceded, "I've heard people refer to swords made from it as shadowblades." *That was it! The man had wanted us to steal his family shadowblade.*

"Ah," Femira replied, "yes. It's quite rare from what I know... it doesn't respond to my edir," she frowned.

"No, it doesn't," Landryn shook his head, "it's the only metal known that cannot be used in runewielding."

"Weird," she narrowed her eyes at the interconnecting plates, "why is that?"

"You've asked a question that has stumped metalshapers and runestone researchers for centuries," Landryn chuckled, "it can't be broken down by aradium. To shape it, you need to use traditional blacksmithing techniques. Heating it to an incredibly high temperature and hammering it into shape." *Traditional techniques.* She smiled inwardly, that was still the way that most people did it. Runestones were too expensive for most people to ever afford—let alone train with.

The lift was finally lowered, interrupting their conversation. The group dismounted their horses and boarded the wooden contraption.

Femira's eyes drifted over to the other bloodshedder—Selyn—who stood leaning against the rail of the platform watching the horizon as it rose up. Selyn was the wavecaller who had also been assigned to the trip and had hair as black as a Keiran woman. She was tall and lithe like almost all other Reldoni Femira had met. Beyond introducing herself to Femira earlier that morning, she hadn't spoken.

Femira had hoped to spar with the woman on the ferry across the bay as she'd not had the opportunity to train with a wavecaller yet. From what Aden and Jaz had told her, most wavecallers found employment working for shipping companies or along city coastwalls to protect against stronger tide surges. Very few enlisted to join the military and, from what Femira understood, Selyn was among only three wavecallers in the bloodshedder ranks. She was a strange addition to their party as wavecallers weren't seen as being very effective combatants and generally were only brought on missions that required extended periods at sea.

"Have you ever seen a Yarji junkship?" Femira asked the woman, hoping to spark up a conversation. Femira had spotted the red rigged sails of one in the bay and wondered if it was Hurok's ship.

"Of course," the woman replied, giving Femira a suffering look, "I worked merchant vessels for years before joining the bloodshedders," she said matter-of-factly as if Femira should have already known this and was ignorant for even asking.

"Did you know that Yarji have horns?" Femira continued, unfazed by the woman's attempt at pushing her away. All of the bloodshedders she'd met ranged from disinterest to outright hostility towards her at first. It irked her in the beginning, but Femira had realised that there was a lot to be gained from winning favour with them and she really wanted to test her skills against a wavecaller. Even Endrin had come around to her in the end.

"Don't be silly," Selyn scoffed, "everyone knows that's a myth."

"I'm not sure," Femira replied, "I met a Yarji last time I was here. He told me there are some that do." Femira still wasn't completely certain that Hurok had understood her correctly about the horns. She also wasn't certain why she was so intrigued by it. Landryn, who had been having a conversation with his pair of bodyguards, had moved over to them.

"That's foolish," Selyn said, dismissively, "it's as ridiculous as merfolk stories."

"The Yarji?" Landryn interjected, "it's true. Some of them do have horns, I've met one... I believe the leaders in their society all have them." Selyn's eyebrows rose at the comment.

"You've met one?!" Femira spun to face him, "what do their horns look like?"

"I was very young," Landryn replied, a thoughtful expression on his face, "there was a delegation of Yarji in the palace to discuss a trade agreement with my father... they were wearing these red masks," he covered part of his face with his hand to demonstrate. "My brother and I thought the horns were part of the masks. It was only when Daegan asked to try on the mask that we caught a look of his face without it," Landryn shuddered and grimaced. "It looked like an exposed animal skull with a stag's horns growing right up out of the bone," his hands stretched and strained, to convey the shape of the skull, "it was quite a horrifying sight for a young boy." And then he barked a laugh, his eyes lighting up for a moment, "Daegan ran... he was *so* terrified. You know, I don't think he left his room the entire time they were in Epilas after that."

"Was it his *actual* skull?" Femira asked.

"Yes... one of the strangest things I've ever seen."

"Do they still have eyes?" Selyn asked, her face knotted up in revulsion. Femira shuddered at the thought of a pair of living eyes inside the sockets of an exposed skull. *And a knife sliding in, grinding against the bone.* She felt her stomach lurch and she forced it down.

"They were quite like an Honorsword's eyes actually," Landryn mused, "but also... not like them. They were bright with a blue light, not red... it was like the light of a filled aquamarine runestone."

"You're fucking with us," Femira laughed. Seyln looked at her aghast. Femira supposed that she shouldn't be speaking like that in front of a Prince but Landryn didn't seem to care. In fact, he was chuckling to himself, "I swear it," he said, "you can choose to believe me or not."

Femira could stretch as far as Yarji having horns, but exposed skulls with magic glowing eyes like some kind of lich was a step too far for Femira to believe. She'd seen a *lot* of different kinds of folk passing through Altarea—she'd even pickpocketed and mugged a fair few strange looking people too—and none of them were undead skeleton people.

She opened her mouth to throw another disbelieving comment but then thought against it. She had scoffed at Endrin and called him a fool for not believing her that the Yarji existed in the first place. *Am I being just as foolish for not believing Landryn... but, seriously?! Blue glowing eyes inside a skull?* That was a bit too far into myths and monsters than she could take.

They passed through the same villages Femira had come through on her last expedition along the Tidewall. In most places they passed through, the Prince wasn't recognised. His uniform was unadorned and he kept his cloak up over his face most of the time. Femira wasn't sure why he bothered hiding his identity. It's not like anyone would risk robbing or attacking him, he was a renowned runewielder and would likely take care of any bandits or would-be assassins on his own, let alone with his bodyguards.

When they arrived at Inish Head, the town mayor did recognise Landryn. The mayor graciously pandered to their group and even offered his own home to the Prince and his companions to rest in. The annoying man continued to hover around them and Femira realised that Landryn hadn't been hiding his identity to avoid bandits.

Landryn politely declined, maintaining that the inn would be fine for them. Eventually the mayor realised that his company was not wanted by the group and left them alone.

The atmosphere in the inn was a lot different than the last time Femira had been there. The staff were better dressed, wearing what was likely the finest clothes they owned. Last time, they'd been served a watery fish stew for their dinner but now the inn had provided them with a plethora of dishes with grilled red trout, sea snails the size of her fist and Femira's favourite; spiced rice balls. The staff bowed every time they passed the table and Landryn had to insist that they stop. To which they bowed in apology.

Femira recalled the innkeeper being a timid person from the last time they'd been through. But that was to be expected when he had two dozen bloodshedders staying at his inn. Now, with the Prince, the man's voice was extra high and nervous.

Landryn attempted to engage in a conversation with the innkeeper, asking about the villages further to the north. The one's where the people had all completely vanished.

"Well, s-since the bloodshedders, milord, since they, you know, they took care of all them Altareans pirates. Everyone feels a lot safer."

"You believe that it was the pirates?"

"Oh well, milord, uhm, maybe... yes."

"You don't seem convinced."

"Well, it's just that, you know, travellers still passing through here from the north. They been bringing stories of missing people still along the coast. I-I'm not suggesting that the bloodshedders didn't do a good enough job or nothin'," he glanced nervously at Femira and Selyn's uniforms, "no, not at all. It's just that folk coming through saying, you know."

"What have they been saying?" Landryn asked, not at all irate at the man's painful awkwardness.

"Oh lots of wild things, milord. Some saying it's the Altareans, some say sea monsters coming up from the depths."

Selyn chuckled into her drink but Femira stayed quiet. She'd seen one of these barren villages for herself. The strange marks on the walls, the broken weapons... nothing stolen.

"What do *you* think?" Landryn pressed the innkeeper.

"Well, I-I've, you know," he began awkwardly, "I've lived here on the Tidewall for a very long time, see. City folk, they, uhm—" he glanced around the table—"I know they think that we're being foolish for believing in stories about monsters and merfolk and what-not. But I, ehm, I've seen a lot o' strange things o'er the years living out here."

"We're not judging," Landryn said, appeasingly, "we just want to get to the bottom of it."

"There's a reason people 'round here, we all head east to the bay for Unionsday, we have our weddings on the sands there, see. Nobody heads out east of the Tidewall..."

The Unionsday tide along with Lua Nova—when both moons were full—were when the tides were at their strongest. Miles of coastline were exposed for most of the day. Most people spent the day celebrating with weddings and festivities but there were still a lot of people desperate enough to risk heading out onto the exposed coastline, collecting pearls and waterstones. The east side of the Tidewall, Femira guessed, would be similar to Altarea, with miles of newly exposed crevices and gorges.

"Folk that head out east," the innkeeper continued, "those willing to take the risk—not many, mind you—and more often than not, they never come back... so no, milord, I don't think they're exaggerating claims... I think there's something dark hiding below the waters that's been attacking these villages. Don't know why they've started coming up to the surface now, what might be driving them up from their nests below the waves. The priests say it's demons; the spirits of the dead draega returned to sow death and destruction. I'm just thankful our town sits up on the cliffs and not closer to the water."

The innkeeper bowed and apologised stating that he needed to see to getting their rooms ready for the evening. Landryn thanked him for the information before the man scurried off.

"Sailors are always making crazy claims like that," Selyn shook her head, "working the ships, you hear nonsense like that all the time. The only real danger out there are Altarean pirates and storms. My guess is; it's the Altareans." The tone she used made Femira think that this woman had quite strong opinions on Altareans. Perhaps that was why she was still so standoffish with her.

"Could be," Femira offered "one of the warships did get away. But why attack random villages... killing civilians and stealing nothing? It makes no sense and not really what pirates do."

"'Cause they're scum," Selyn spat, "Altareans kill just because they enjoy it. I was working on a vessel two years back. We were attacked by this corsair ship... they managed to board us and kill half our crew before we finally pushed them back. I can tell you, those Altareans, they were killing just for the fun of it."

"There were a lot of corsair attacks around then," Landryn replied, sadly, "many trading ships had been disappearing. It was —along with my father's goal to reclaim the Altarean Isles—the driving reason for the assault on Altarea."

"I remember when you announced the invasion," Selyn said, "I enlisted that very day... I've no love for Altareans," she snorted, "pirates and cut-throats all of 'em. I wanted a chance to get some revenge on the bastards."

Femira never really thought about the amount of corsairs that operated out of Altarea. The city was rife with crime gangs—of which she was intricately familiar —and she knew a lot of them had some kind of pirating operations going on too. Lichtin himself had always planned to eventually get his hands on a corsair ship. Piracy was next level criminal activity, and was something that Lichtin's enterprise hadn't been able to break into.

"Not all Altareans," Landryn conceded, "but their navy has been splintered and most of their warships have unfortunately turned to piracy."

"Most of them actually *were* pirates to begin with," Femira countered, "King Amenia used to work with the pirates all the time." That fact was well known amongst the criminal gangs in Altarea.

Landryn looked at her with surprise. *Had he really not known this?*

"Amenia had a bounty on any Reldoni ships," Femira continued, "even before the war."

"We had suspected this in the months leading up to the invasion," Landryn replied, nodding, "but all the highborn we interrogated refuted the claims."

"Maybe they were ashamed they needed to resort to it," Femira shrugged.

"Forgive my forwardness, my lord," Selyn put in, "but are we really going to be recruiting former stormguards into the bloodshedders?" Selyn was visibly aggravated and lowered to a conspiratorial tone, "they can't be trusted. We can't really be considering making them soulforged like us... they're our *enemies*."

"Our goal is peace," Ladnryn replied, "Amenia is dead and the treaty we've signed with the remaining Altarean highborn has made Reldoni citizens of all Altareans. As Reldoni citizens they are welcome in our ranks. There are many amongst the Altarean highborn who held little love for Amenia, many of them have embraced Reldoni rule and the rest will soon follow as we build trust. Allowing the stormguards into our ranks will strengthen that trust."

Selyn inclined her head. She didn't look happy about it but the woman clearly wasn't going to disagree with someone so much higher ranked than her.

"What do you think, Annali?" Landryn asked Femira, "you lived amongst the Altareans for over a year." Femira had spent a lot longer than a year in Altarea.

"I didn't enjoy killing those bluecloaks," she admitted, "but that's not to say I like them much. I wouldn't want to be training with any."

"They are experienced aeristone users," Landryn said, "we could learn a lot from their techniques."

"You're an aeristone runwielder," she objected, "and you're far more skilled than they are."

"I am soulforged though," he countered, "my abilities are enhanced because of that. In terms of raw power, yes, I am superior... but in terms of skills and experience..." he trailed off, seemingly lost for what he was trying to say. "I believe that adding the stormguards into our ranks will be good for all of us," he eventually concluded.

Femira wasn't so sure. Despite Selyn's blatant apathy towards her, Femira agreed with the woman. The stormguards were still their enemies and inviting them into the bloodshedder barracks could be opening them up to danger. But also like Selyn, there was little *she* could do about it. Landryn was their Commander. If he and Garld wanted to do this, then they could hardly argue against it.

The next morning, the group headed north. Winter in Reldon was mild but the winds and rains still had a sharp sting to them.

Femira was thankful for Landryn's ability to deflect the power of the winds around them, creating a pleasantly still shell of air around them. The wind made a whistling sound above their heads as it slid over the invisible barrier. She could sense Landryn's edir maintaining the barrier but airshaping was so different to stoneshaping that Femira struggled to understand how it worked. Did he create a solid shell like the stoneshell she'd learned from Endrin or was he pushing on the opposing wind constantly, deflecting it around them? Femira watched Landryn as they rode trying to tell from his edir. He held solid control, but it would occasionally flare out similar to how hers did. Did Landryn struggle with the same edir control as she did? It was encouraging to think that someone with his experience and skill might still face the same issues she did.

Shortly before midday they reached the cove with the ruined village. The rains and tides had washed away all the blood stains. Evidently, people with no qualms with stealing from the dead had picked the village clean since Femira had last been. Not that she judged them, she'd looted many a dead body herself. It wasn't like she had any higher morals now that her job was making dead bodies instead of stealing from them.

As they rode into the village a small group of squatters who'd taken up residence emerged from the ruins. They were stragglers hoping to make something for themselves from the remnants of the village. Upon seeing their uniforms and weapons, the squatters quickly surmised that they were soldiers. They dropped to their knees and swore that they'd only just arrived two days before and were repairing the fishing boats, intending to use them. They had nothing to do with the missing villagers or even the looting. They looked like honest people, a group of five adults just wanting to feed their families. Small children in rags could be seen peeking out from the ruins.

Landryn told them there's no crime in trying to build a better life for yourself. He simply introduced himself as the leader of the group, omitting the fact he was the Prince. He told them that there were no families left to inherit the ruins from the missing villagers and that he would send a representative from Heraldport in a few weeks to formalise the new residents as owners, if they wished it. The squatters bowed and thanked him, profusely.

Landryn asked them if they'd noticed anything strange since they arrived. One of the squatters—a large man with hair poking out from the top of his shirt—spoke of noises at night coming from the north side of the cove. At first, they thought it was just the waves, but it sounded more like scraping. He went on to say how his wife had tried to convince him to give up the idea of repairing the fishing boats and continue on down to Heraldport to look for work. But he wouldn't be scared off by some noises. It was too promising an opportunity here to make a good life, he insisted.

Landryn began inspecting the damages to the buildings. The squatters had begun repairs on some of the buildings that had more than one remaining wall but most were still heaps of rubble.

"You were right," he said to Femira, "none of this looks like cannon damage. There's not a single scorch mark or any sign of explosives."

"A stonebreaker wouldn't have left this kind of mess either," Femira added, "if you were going to destroy a building it would be easier to just disintegrate the stone supports and let it collapse in on itself. The stone supports seem to be what held out in most cases here."

"Doesn't look to be the work of any type of runewielding..." he agreed, "an exceptionally powerful aeristone user perhaps but even then, there would be rubble strewn across the entire cove with airblasts strong enough to destroy these buildings..." he looked up at the surrounding cliffs, "a stonebreaker could have shot boulders out from the cliffs to destroy the buildings... that would explain how most seem to be crushed."

"Still seems like too much effort," Femira shook her head, "if the goal was to destroy all the buildings, it would be far more effective to just disintegrate them. Any runewielder that can manage to throw a boulder around would have the skills to dust this place easily."

Landryn kept his gaze on the cliff face, his eyes narrowing. Without a word, he started to stride purposefully across the beach. Selyn and Femira shared a confused look, Femira shrugged and started following after him. Landryn's two bodyguards;

Kendrik and Drad remained in the village, looking around the rubble. The pair understood that their Prince was more than capable of defending himself and their purpose was primarily for support and appearances.

The sandy beach gave way to rocky boulders that they stepped across towards the rockface.

"Does this area look strange to you?" Landryn asked Femira, pointing into a shallow cave. The walls of the cave looked jagged, the colour also slightly off compared with the rest of the cliff face.

One of Femira's jobs in Lichtin's crew had been to create hidden caches along the Altarean cliffs. She would hollow out small clefts in the rockface that the crew could use as discreet drop-offs for loot. She'd made hundreds of these over the years working with Lichtin, it was the first thing he'd shown her how to do with the earthstone. Something she'd always noticed was how flaky and crumbly the inside walls of the hallows she'd created were when compared to the smoothed sea-worn rockfaces.

"It hasn't been worn in by the sea," Femira surmised, chiding herself for not realising this the first time she'd been through. She'd never seen an earthstone-carved hollow this big before and she hadn't registered it.

"This whole cave looks like it was carved out by a stonebreaker... without being soulforged this would have taken days to make."

"I'm not so sure it was runewielding," Landryn contested, "look along the edges here," he pointed, "these look like impact marks... these rocks we climbed over I think they were dragged away from the cave when it was being hollowed out. A stonebreaker wouldn't bother. I think something tried to burrow into the cliff here... but then gave up when the earth above started to weaken." He indicated holes in the roof of the cave where chunks of rock had fallen.

They followed the cliff out towards where the surf met with the rocks, splashing up plumes of the white water against the shore. Landryn called out to his bodyguards in the village and they trotted over to join them.

"Can you forge us a path?" Landryn asked Selyn. She nodded and rolled up the sleeves of her uniform. An unnecessary step for a runewielder but Femira guessed that it was subconscious. Femira liked to have her arms free for using her hands to guide her edir in stoneshaping so Selyn must do the same with wavecalling. Her assumption was proven right when Selyn made pushing gestures with her outstretched hands at the surf.

The waves crashed against what looked to be an invisible barrier and roared upwards. Selyn's guiding hands directed the waves back into themselves creating a roiling, churning mass of water a few feet back from the cliff face, exposing a rocky path at the base.

"Whoa," Femira admired, blowing out a whistle, "that's impressive."

"This is nothing," Selyn gave her a sideways glance but Femira caught the hint of a smile. Compliments seemed to go a long way with Selyn. Femira noted that for when she'd later try convincing the woman to spar with her.

Landryn confidently strode out onto the slick stones of the newly exposed walkway, leading out of the cove. Femira and Selyn followed, the wavecaller maintaining a walking area of about two dozen feet around them. Femira watched in amazement at the force of the waves crashing against Selyn's edir. The woman tensed her shoulders but was otherwise unperturbed with the effort.

"What do you think is out here?" Femira called ahead to Landryn after a while of following him.

"I don't think that the claims the locals are making are that crazy," Landryn replied, "we know that strange creatures lurk in the simirwood to the east. The plains of Athlin and the Black Sands beyond are all said to have monstrous beasts roaming throughout. I think it would be naive of us to assume that there are none within our borders. There are stories of my ancestors fighting monsters and draega after the fall of the Sorcerer Kings... Elyina and her armies drove them from the lands."

Drad made some gesture with his hands that Femira recognised as some kind of prayer that the priests did to ward off demons.

"You think that they're returning, these monsters?" she asked Landryn, a little taken aback by his forthright conclusions.

"I think it's a possibility, yes."

Ahead of them, nestled between two jagged outcrops of rock was the large opening of a cave.

"This one's the same as before," Femira observed, indicating the edges of the cave that looked to have been carved out recently. Landryn turned to Kendrik and Drad who had been following along dutifully.

"You have torches?" he asked and Drad nodded in response. The stone-faced guard pulled out a vial of oil from his cloak along with a rag. There were some hardy bushes that grew out from nooks in the cliff face, Kendrick climbed up a few feet to tear a few branches out of one. The pair quickly fashioned sets of torches that were passed out to the group.

Selyn remained outside the cave, keeping her edir focused on repelling the waves. Kendrick had a topaz on him and ignited all of their torches. Landryn led the way forward, flanked by his guards, Femira trailing behind. She had little fear of the dark, but that was when the scary thing hiding in the shadows was her.

Their boots echoed against the roof of the cave. The walls were still slick, water trickling off them and forming pools that her feet would occasionally stumble into. They delved deeper into the darkness, the opening of the cave growing smaller behind them. None of them spoke as they made their way deeper inside.

The flickering light of the torches danced off the jagged edges of the cave and the ceiling stretched up into the darkness above. Femira sent out pulses of her edir, touching off the walls and roof of the cave as they moved. The walls resonated in response to her edir as she expected. As did the rock at her feet and the large boulders they passed—she froze.

A shadowy mound she'd mistaken for a boulder just ahead *didn't* resonate back. Her edir slid right over it and didn't react at all.

"Stop," Femira hissed. Landryn paused and glanced back at her, his face looking ominous in the light of the torches. "What is—" he began but then cut off when the shadowy mound began to rumble.

The sound of rocks grinding off one another echoed through the cave. More shapes just beyond the light of the torches began to shudder and rise. Landryn and his guards immediately drew their blades. Femira pulled out her own set of daggers.

She could summon her glassblades if she needed them and she'd also begun keeping a stock of steel material in her reserves if she needed to conjure up another set.

She felt Landryn's edir wash over her as he sucked the air around them into him. Long black insect legs began protruding out from the shadowed forms but in the flickering torch light it was difficult to really discern what was happening.

"Pull back to the entrance," Landryn commanded and the group edged backwards. Keeping their weapons raised.

The mounds were slow to rise but now that their many legs had been extended they scuttered about with shocking agility. Femira couldn't count how many there were as all she could see were dancing shadows. She pulsed out her edir but instead of seeking out resonances, she focused on the absence of it. Landryn, Drad and Kendrick's own edirs she could sense as she passed over them but the creatures had nothing. Her pulses detected that there were only three of them despite the amount of moving legs that the torchlight caught.

"There's three of them," Femira informed the men in front of her.

"You can sense them?" Landryn asked, his tone tense.

"More like the absence of them, if that makes sense?"

One of the spider-like forms shot towards them. A raspy hissing noise reverberating through the cave. Landryn blasted it with a condensed push of air, allowing the group a few more moments to make it back to the entrance. Selyn kept her position just outside, still holding back the wall of water.

"What's happening?" Selyn asked, her face masked with concern as the four of them backed out of the cave, their weapons drawn.

Before anyone could respond to her, a blue boulder the size of a horse was flung out of the cave entrance. Femira's instinct was to dust the boulder as it flew mid-air but when she pushed out with her edir, the boulder didn't pulse in response to it.

The thing's trajectory was aimed towards Landryn who dived out of the way before the creature uncoiled itself and smashed into the spot he had been. In the full light of the day, Femira could see that the monster was more like a giant crab than a spider. The blue material she'd mistaken for the boulder was its carapace. Long insect-like legs unfurled from the carapace with four enormous pincers at the front, protecting a toothy maw that reminded Femira of a bloodworm. Femira froze at the sight of it, her mouth agape.

Landryn spared not a single second, rolling to his feet and smashing the crab off balance with an airpush. Faster than Femira could follow, he darted in towards it and made a series of lightning fast blows with his blade.

His sword glanced off the carapace with minimum effect. He dodged out of the monster's range before a pincer could grab at him. He rounded to the creature's side and again danced his sword out in a flurry of attacks. *He's testing for the crab's weak points.*

"Vreth!" She heard Selyn shout at her. She glanced over at the woman who was pointing to where the other two crabs were emerging from the cave. They were both blue like the one Landryn was fighting; only this pair were a little smaller. Kendrick and Drad were embroiled with fighting one of them and the other was closing in around them.

Femira's edir whipped into action, repeated practice had trained her to immediately begin forming her murder moons but she reckoned that the glassblades would be useless against the hard shelled creatures. Instead she focused on the cliff face, pulling in the rock to her and reshaping it as a stonespear. She pushed with her edir, heaving the stonespear towards the third crab. The stonespear shattered on impact, crumbling against the crab's thick carapace but the force had been enough to hurl the creature backwards.

Femira immediately formed another stonespear above the creature, she balled her hand into a fist and pulled it down. The action guiding her edir, pushing more force into the falling stonespear.

The crab stumbled as the stonespear shattered against its back, the force pushing down on its legs. Wasting no time, she conjured another stonespear above it and crashed it down on the monster. Over and over, she pummelled the creature with repeated falling stonespears until there was an audible crack as the carapace was finally breached.

The crab made a pained hissing noise and launched itself at her. She dove out of the way but felt one of the massive pincers grab at her torso pulling her back. The pincer carapace felt like jagged rock biting into her core and lower back. Her version spun as the creature jerked her about like a ragdoll. She couldn't even scream as the tightening pincers forced the air out from her.

I didn't train every day to be killed by a crab! She gritted her teeth and focused her edir inwards, guiding the power of her earthstone to her core and strengthening it with stoneskin. The constricting pincers were still painful, but was more of a dull ache than the torture it had been. The creatures toothy maw writhed as it drew her close. She kicked at what she considered to be its face, refusing to allow the thing to eat her. *I'm not your fucking lunch!* The pincers tried to close tighter, but her stoneskin held strong against the vice grip.

She could see where the monster's carapace had been split on the top from her repeated barrage of stonespears. In the fracture, she could see soft grey flesh. Instinctively, she tried reaching for her daggers at her hips but the pincers around her torso made them impossible to reach. Instead she conjured a glassblade, her focus on her stoneskin waned as she did so but thankfully the crab didn't attempt to crush her in that moment.

Femira pushed her edir against the glassblade, flinging it into the gap in the carapace. A screeching hiss sounded, and she was falling, the pressure on her torso gone. She fell hard against the rocky ground but quickly regained her footing and rolled forward underneath the crab. Coming to a rise, she drew her daggers and could see that the underside of the beast had numerous gaps in the shell.

She thrust upwards in a quick succession of stabs. Each time she slid her blades in through the gaps the monster hissed and screamed. The legs of the creature buckled and twisted. Femira realised with a sudden panic that it was about to collapse on her.

She didn't have time to roll out from under it so instead Femira foolishly focused on a stoneskin as the crab fell on her, she cursed at herself for not thinking to create a stoneshell instead. Now she was pinned underneath it and needed to focus all of her attention on maintaining a full body stoneskin to prevent the body of the crab from crushing her.

Her breaths were ragged and she didn't dare shout out for help. She needed to retain all focus on keeping her stoneskin. Even with it, she could feel the weight of the creature's body pushing down on her, slowly forcing more air out of her lungs and putting more and more pressure on her bones.

I can't hold this! The thought flicked across her mind in a dazed panic. Her lungs were taking in less and less air with every breath and then suddenly she went completely cold, her vision going black. She was choking, and being spun about wildly. The weight of the crab was gone but her body was being thrown about. She coughed and sputtered and tried to gasp in a breath but only found water filling her mouth and lungs.

In a matter of seconds Femira was lying flat on her face on the rocks, soaking wet but with no giant crab monster on top of her. She choked up salty water, hot tears streaming against her cold skin. She struggled to her feet, still retching.

Glancing about, she could see through bleary eyes that Landryn had already dispatched the crab he'd been facing and was now finishing off the one that Kendrick and Drad had been fighting.

Selyn stood at the edge of the water; one hand still towards the waves, holding them back and the other was facing towards Femira.

Femira looked behind her and could see the crab that she'd been fighting was now rolling and spinning, being battered against the rock face by a torrent of water flowing in from a break in Selyn's invisible wave barrier.

Femira's breath eventually returned to her, her heart was still pumping with adrenaline as Landryn jumped in between the final crab's pincers and buried his sword into the maw. The creature had managed to clamp onto the armour at his torso but he didn't seem to be at all impeded by it. *Damn that armour is strong.*

The crab screeched in that horrible hissing sound before crumpling to the ground, Landryn pulling his blade from its face. Selyn had also put all of her attention back on keeping the waves at bay, the crab that Femira had killed was left in a heap by the cliff. Landryn was at her side in a moment.

"You're ok?" he asked, his eyes searching hers. She nodded. *Fucking hells.* They'd fought monsters! Genuine *monsters!*

"Those…" she breathed, "those were… *crabs*?!"

Landryn looked at her, and his face broke into a grin and he started laughing. Kendrick and Selyn followed with their own nervous and relieved laughter. Femira found herself laughing with them. Drad was stoic and making those reverent hand gestures again.

The joy of still being alive washed over her. She'd fought a crab monster the size of a fucking *horse* and survived!

Jaz and Aden are never going to believe this.

CHAPTER 31

Trying to get to Heaven

Femira winced as Drad placed a cold hand on her stomach. The bruises and scrapes inflicted by the giant crab pincers faded on her skin. She rubbed her hand over where the injuries had been and felt a tingly prickle. The wounds hadn't disappeared but appeared to be almost entirely healed, the healing process having dramatically accelerated her body's natural healing.
"Take it easy tonight," Drad said in his unusually high-pitched voice.
"Well, I've no plans to dance around the fire," she grinned at him and he sheepishly avoided her gaze as she pulled back on her shirt. *The royal bodyguards are so serious all the time.*
It had been a pleasant surprise to her that Drad was an accomplished healer and carried a bloodstone with him. *I suppose that's why Landryn brought him.* It's not like the Prince needed any assistance in taking down the crabs, but having a healer on hand was just good planning. The rest of the team were an assistance but Femira reckoned that Landryn could've taken all of the things solo if he'd needed to. He hadn't even taken a single hit in the whole fight and had felled two of the creatures.
Kendrick was holding a broken arm close to his chest, having taken a blow to it from a crab claw. The five of them sat around a fire on the beach a few minutes walk from the ruined village—out of earshot of the squatters. They'd decided to heal up and regroup on the beach for the evening rather than pushing to the nearest inn which was a three hour ride away.
"I won't be able to heal this," Drad blew out a long breath, tentatively looking over Kendrick's arm, "a few bruises and shallow cuts is fine... but this bone is broken."
"I thought it might be," Kendrick grimaced, pulling his arm back to his chest.
"There'll be healers with enough skill to fix it up in Heraldport," Drad reassured him, "or you could possibly wait until we get back to Epilas and leave it to the palace healers."
"You said that would risk the bone setting wrong by waiting," Kendrick grumbled.
"It's only a few more hours on the ferry," Drad shrugged, "you'll be fine."
"Getting back to Epilas with haste is our priority," Landryn put in, "we need to alert General Garld and the rest of the War Council on what we've found here."
Femira's ears perked up. *Oh shit, he wants to go right back to Epilas!* Garld had explicitly instructed her to keep the Prince occupied on the Tidewall for at least another week.
"Maybe we should reconsider that, sir. These crabs... I think it's pretty clear they destroyed the village, right?" Landryn nodded in consideration and she continued, "and one of them tried to *eat* me, so we can assume that they probably ate the villagers. And there's reports of *more* ruined villages up the coast..."

"That's why we should return to Epilas, we need to send a force to clear out what is evidently a growing infestation," Landryn replied.

"But *we* can take care of them," she said not even feigning her enthusiasm for the prospect, "we were *amazing!* We killed the three of them without taking any losses and we didn't even know what to expect. Now that we know what we're looking for, we can prepare and attack with a tactical advantage."

"It's reckless," Selyn scoffed, "and puts our Commander at risk."

"*He's* more capable of killing those things than any of us," Femira rebuked, "you saw him fight them. If we come up with a few strategies, we can clear out all of the nests ourselves. I'm sure of it."

"And if we die?" Selyn argued, "another group would be sent to look for us and face the same fate *and* without a forewarning."

"We could send Kendrick back with word on what we've found," Landryn pondered. *Yes! I have him.*

"We have a duty," Femira said, deciding to lean on Landryn's sense of obligation as a Prince of the realm. "How many innocent people could die if we waste days heading back to Epilas and then more waiting for reinforcements."

"The War Council would want to make it a local policing matter," Landryn grimaced.

"Local constables wouldn't stand a chance against those things," Drad piped in and Landryn nodded in agreement, "the War Council would waste weeks deciding the best course of action..." The lock was already picked, now she just had to make off with the goods.

"We don't know how fast these things reproduce," Femira pressed, "how many more could there be in that time?" Landryn was nodding along with her. He actually looked impressed, "you're really concerned for these people aren't you?" he asked. *I couldn't give six shits about 'em.*

"Yes," she replied, earnestly, "I do care."

Maybe she did care *a little* about them? She was mostly doing this because Garld had asked her to... but there was a part of her that felt bad for the people that had died. She'd been held by those pincers and she'd felt the terror when that crab had tried to eat her. It had been frightening but she had the skills to fight back. A lot of people couldn't do that, and it was that feeling that excited her most. *She* could fight them. She *wanted* to fight them, she'd revelled in it. And the best part of it was that it hadn't made her feel sick to her stomach killing them.

Landryn wore a thoughtful expression on his face, his hand rubbing at the short growth of stubble on his jawline. He was quiet for a moment and just when Femira had decided to press a little further he looked up at each of them around the camp.

"There's something I've been holding back," Landryn revealed, "I've seen these things before." Now that *was* a surprise. If any of the others were startled by that knowledge, they didn't show it. *They're all soldiers, I guess they're used to only being told what they need to know.* As a thief, not knowing all the information on a job could mean the difference between keeping your hand or not.

"What we fought are called kraglings. They're a type of draega," he said the word with a level of gravitas that was lost on Femira. Drad and Kendrick by contrast had furrowed brows in concern and Selyn was agape in outright disbelief.

"Draega?" Selyn choked, "but they—they were all destroyed?!"

"No," Landryn replied, "driven away, but not destroyed."

"Sorry," Femira spoke up, "but I'm a bit lost here, what's a draega again?"

"The temples in Keiran do not teach of the draega?" Landryn asked her in surprise. *Ah fuck.* She'd always thought it would be some religious crap that would catch her out.

Femira had little interest in the temples in Altarea, except for when they would occasionally hand out food to the children that lived on the street. It was always stale bread and mouldy cheese. *But when you'd not eaten in a few days, you don't tend to be picky.* The food wasn't free either, you had to listen to them prattle on about their weird gods and demons.

"Perhaps the temples in Keiran call them something different?" she shrugged nonchalantly. *Good ole reliable language barrier.* She could only fall back on it so much, but it had gotten her out of more than a few tight spots in her Annali guise.

"The draega are demons," Drad clarified for her, "they were all destroyed before the Age of the Sorcerer Kings." He spoke like a priest—and the man *was* also a healer. *Maybe there was some connection there?*

"In Reldon, this was true," Landryn said to Drad, "but they weren't eradicated entirely, only driven off our lands. I have read the journals of my ancestor, Queen Elyina. There were records of them even as recently as her time."

"So you've *seen* draega before?" Femira asked, she wasn't interested in a history lesson and wanted to drive the topic back.

"Yes," Landryn confessed, "it was before Garld and I formed the bloodshedders. I was not commander then. Border patrols to the north near Athlin had reported sightings of large spider-like creatures."—*All sounds pretty familiar*—"after a few days we found the carcass of one of them. We didn't know what managed to kill the thing but we weren't confident that any standard runewielder would be capable enough."

"Was it the same as the crabs?" Femira probed, "the *kraglings*?"

"Bigger," he admitted, "but yes. It was the same."

"How much bigger?" Kendrick followed up.

"Three—perhaps four—times as large," Landryn guessed.

"How did you know it was a draega?" Drad asked and there was definitive scepticism in his manner.

"The description in Elyina's journals fits... for the kraglings, at least," Landryn divulged freely, clearly unperturbed by their reluctance to accept his word on the matter. "There are many in the War Council that do not believe this... or at least, they do not believe it to be a threat."

"So what do we know about them?" Femira pressed, "how can we use this to our advantage?"

"For kraglings, we know that they are invasive with animal-like intelligence, driven more by instinct than design. They will likely have an alpha—a matriarch—that directs the spread. Possibly even creates the nests itself."

"So we find the alpha and we stop the spread?" Femira affirmed.

"In theory, yes."

"Then that's what we should do!" Femira could feel the excitement in her rising. The prospect of hunting and fighting more of the kraglings filled her with a passion. Pushing her skills and abilities to the limits and with no human collateral damage.

Landryn looked to Kendrick, "in the morning," he instructed, "you'll ride for Heraldport and take the ferry to Epilas. Make a report to General Garld and tell him that I am requesting reinforcements to clear out the infestation." Kendrick nodded dutifully in response.

"What if the other nests are larger?" Selyn asked Femira with distrust. Femira noticed how the woman purposefully didn't question Landryn, instead focusing her disagreement with Femira.

"As Annali said," Landryn interjected, "we know what we're dealing with now. We can strategise."

"I'm sorry, sir. I do not mean to question your authority or your foresight, but *you* were aware that we would be fighting these, no?"

"The kraglings have not been sighted in these lands in centuries. Frankly, I wasn't certain that we would actually find any. It was a hunch."

"So then *where* did they come from?" Selyn asked.

"That... I can't answer," he replied. *Can't or won't?*

"How were they driven from Reldon before?" Drad asked. Looks like Femira would get that history lesson after all.

"You all know of Queen Elyina, I'm sure?" Landryn asked the group, although the question was clearly meant for Femira who was the only non-Reldoni among them. All Reldoni knew of their founding Queen.

"Of course," Femira replied flippantly, "she conquered half the continent."

"Not as much as that," Landryn smirked, "but all that is now Reldon, Rien, Athlin, Altarea and parts of Rubane were all under her protection—"

"—I wouldn't consider being conquered being under someone's protection."

"She wasn't a conqueror," Landryn defended, "I know the histories they teach you in Keiran would likely paint her as a tyrant, subjugating all of the neighbouring kingdoms but it wasn't like that."

Femira didn't learn any of that in Keiran, in truth, she didn't remember much at all from her early years in Keiran. Her knowledge of Elyina had come from stories, and they'd always depicted her as a conqueror.

Landryn didn't seem offended by Femira's input and continued on, "Elyina was a liberator, the warring Sorcerer Kings had thrown the continent into centuries of darkness... famine, disease and death. Elyina was a saviour, one-by-one she challenged each of the Sorcerer Kings and defeated them in battle. Elyina forged our nation from the ashes of their reign." *Yeah, that's how the storytellers told it too. Doesn't make it any less a fanciful story.*

"What does this have to do with the kraglings?" Femira asked.

"The Sorcerer Kings were the original masters of the soulstones. They wielded that power for centuries, some led entire *armies* of monsters—the draega among them. Elyina and *her* army of runewielders destroyed them. They marched through the lands and drove off all the monsters into the far reaches of the world."

"Places like the Black Sands," Drad added and Landryn nodded.

"We know that the Black Sands is still infested. However, the northern lands of Athlin are the barrier between Reldon and there... I don't think these kraglings came from the Black Sands. I believe they came from the east... something out there drove them back to our shores for the first time in three hundred years."

"If Rien, Athlin and Altarea were all once part of Reldon," Femira mused, "what *happened*?"

"Greed, jealousy... war," Landryn admitted, "Athlin was the first to secede, they had never really accepted Elyina's rule and still held on to their true King's return... they still do. Altarea, as you know, went under a mutiny with the highborn living there joining with pirate factions and overthrowing the appointed Highlord. And Rien was a similar story to that. My great grandfather made a lot of mistakes in his rule. He ruled aggressively and made many enemies. Ultimately, it was his mistakes that caused Elyina's nation to splinter as it has."

"And your father is different?" Femira asked. She didn't know much about King Abhran but much of what she'd heard painted him in a similar light. The others shifted uncomfortably at the question and Landryn didn't answer, remaining silent and pensively looking into the fire.

Femira realised that she had stumbled into an awkward topic and after a few moments, Selyn informed them she was getting some rest and that she would take the later watch. Each of their horses had been packed with a sleeping roll and standard military issue tent. Femira had been surprised that Landryn's was the same as theirs, nothing fancy about it or that designated him as being any different. *That was likely the intention though.* He didn't want to be recognised on this mission.

Kendrick retired soon after, leaving Drad on first watch and Femira and Landryn still sitting around the fire.

"You did well today," Landryn told her, "not many would have faced such a creature with as much... enthusiasm."

"I won't lie," Femira admitted, "I enjoyed it." She felt a grin pulling at her face, after the battle with the Altareans at Inish Head, she'd been left rattled. She still felt queasy at the thought of her knife going into that stormguard's eye and she found herself disappointed by that. What was she training for if not to fight? By contrast the fight with the kraglings left her exhilarated.

This was what she was supposed to be doing with her skills—fighting and killing monsters. It was terrifying, yes, but it was also exciting and didn't come with any pesky guilt or nausea.

Landryn seemed to understand and was smiling at her, "so did I," he admitted, "I know it's part of my responsibility as a Prince to protect people... but I'm not supposed to be doing it like this. I'm supposed to be in command rooms and in court... out here, though," he looked over to the ruins of the village, "it's *tangible*... it's real. I feel like this is what I'm *supposed* to be doing. Does that make any sense?"

"It does... I've done a lot of shady shit in my life," she said earnestly, "might be nice to do something actually good." Landryn's eyes narrowed in mild suspicion and inwardly, she chastised herself for letting her true self slip out again.

"It's going to be dangerous," he continued, "I can't guarantee your safety."

"Don't worry about me, I'm just trying to get to heaven before they shut the door," she grinned at him. It was something her brother used to say to her before they did something reckless.

"You're not what I expected, you know," Landryn said, holding Femira's gaze. *Neither are you.* "Don't get me wrong," he rushed on, "it's not a bad thing, from what I've known of Keiran women, they've often been..." he trailed off.

"The word you're looking for is oppressed," she concluded for him, "Keiran women are not free people. They are slaves to their families."

"I didn't want to offend you... but yes," he said, "you're strong, like Reldoni women. More so even, and you don't hold back what's on your mind... or from doing what's right." She felt a little guilty when he said that. He genuinely believed that she wanted to help people, and Femira couldn't help but feel a pang of remorse for lying to him. If she was so caught up in doing the right thing, she would tell him about his brother. But what good would that do for her? Garld had given her power, and he had the skills and ability to give her more. She didn't like the way the conversation was making her feel so she decided to shift the topic.

"You suspected that these draega—the kraglings—were here… why? Does it have something to do with the soulstones?"

"What did you know about soulstone before joining us?"

"I didn't even know they existed," she answered, truthfully.

"Neither did we, until recently," he replied, "references to them existed in the histories but there were no records of them after the fall of the Sorcerer Kings. But then two years ago, a team of stoneshapers were tunnelling into the Pillar, extending the palace, and they came upon a hidden room. We didn't even know any of the passageways went that deep into the Pillar."

"What was inside?" The thief inside of her leaping at the prospect of hidden treasure rooms in the Reldoni palace.

"Runestones… lots of them. The rarer kinds too; aeristone, bloodstone and diamonds. Some had rune engravings that the scholars in the palace had never seen before. There were stacks and stacks of lost documents and knowledge from the Age of the Sorcerer Kings. Among them were Elyina's journals."

Femira's mind flicked back to the conversations she'd had with Garld and Misandrei before her soulforging ritual. *They told me that Elyina's journals had been discovered in the Pillar and it sparked the invasion of Altarea for the soulstone.* She didn't realise it at the time but now when her mind brushed over it, the night she'd sneaked into Averstock's mansion and Vestyr had got the jump on her. Vestyr had said that she had 'no right' to the journal. She'd foolishly assumed it was his. *They must have been Elyina's journals… or at least parts of them.* It was fairly obvious that Vestyr and Allyn were working together to try to piece together how soulforging worked. *Were they trying to create their own soulforged runewielders?* Vestyr himself was evidently soulforged—he'd all but admitted the fact to her—so why would they need to steal the journal? And more importantly, why had Garld needed to steal it from Averstock in the first place?

"It was quite the stir in both the Royal Council and War Council," Landryn continued on, "and with the ongoing feud with the Reinish, the increasing tension with Altarea and Keiran… it seemed a solution was dumped on our laps. We were already building our military for years and now with solid evidence on the existence of soulforging…"

"There wasn't any soulstone in the cache," Femira figured, "you needed one to test out soulforging. The invasion of Altarea was to capture the soulstone." She knew all of this already from Garld but she was curious whether Landryn would admit it to her.

"You knew it was there?" He looked at her with surprise, "we believed the Altarean highborn to be unaware of its existence. If not for Elyina's journals indicating she'd hidden one there, we would never have guessed."

Femira debated telling him the truth. He was being so forthcoming with his information, and the amount of lies she was telling were mounting so high she was beginning to lose track. Surely Garld wouldn't care if she told him the truth; that she wasn't really Annali. She could tell him *that* much, couldn't she? She could keep the knowledge of his brother's murder back for now but it would be nice to be able to talk to him as Femira—not Annali.

"I…" Femira faltered. He looked up at her, light from the flickering fire dancing across his face. "Garld told me," she lied, deciding to hold back. Drad was standing watch not far away, and Kendrick and Selyn were also close enough to hear if they were awake.

"Ah, I see," Landryn replied, "Garld trusts you... he is a good man and I trust him with my life, knowing he places such confidence in you gives me comfort." She felt herself smiling at that, it was good to know that Garld trusted her. She'd *felt* it when he'd done the soulforging ritual with her but it was reassuring to know that the feeling hadn't all been in her head.

"Did Garld do your soulforging ritual too?" she asked, curious.

"He did," Landryn winced, "it was..."

"... painful?"

"Putting it lightly but yes... also *enlightening*. I was a strong runewielder before, but now it's like my edir is an ocean and I'm a tidewall barely holding it back." She'd felt something similar after becoming soulforged, the waves of her edir pulsing out from her, far stronger than they'd ever been before.

"So if you only found the soulstone in Altarea," she thought aloud, "yourself and all the bloodshedders only recently became soulforged."

"Garld and I began recruiting for the bloodshedders after Elyina's journals were uncovered. We wanted to have a trained force of elite runewielders ready to be soulforged when we found it."

"And these monsters... the draega. They've only started appearing again since then?"

"Reports have been filtering in for months even before the invasion of Altarea. We know that it's not isolated to here, other creatures have been spotted on the fringes of the Simirwood too—not kraglings specifically—but creatures matching other descriptions of draega from Elyina's journals."

"So it might not be connected? The soulstones and the draega?"

"We aren't the only ones with a soulstone. The Honorswords are soulforged, I have no doubt in that. The Aeth have long held the secrets of their enhanced runewielding ability but I would wager there is soulforging at play there also."

"Do you think someone is *creating* monsters with a soulstone?" she asked, a chill running up her spine.

"I don't know... but it does seem like too much of a coincidence that the kraglings would appear here now."

"Is this why you've been recruiting so heavily for the bloodshedders? You wanted us to fight these draega?"

"My father sees the soulstone as a means to reclaim Reldon's former glory and many in the War Council agree with him," he replied. Femira got the distinct impression that it was not how Landryn felt about the matter.

"We should get some rest," he said abruptly and rose to his feet, "we have a long day ahead tomorrow." His eyes turned towards the cliffs where they'd discovered the kragling nest, and then over to the ruined village.

"We'll ride north to the other destroyed villages and uncover the other nests. Hunting down the alpha is our goal." Then, he turned back to look at her with an emphatic grin. There was a passion in Landryn's eyes that Femira couldn't help but feel excited by.

CHAPTER 32
Stolen Attention

There was a pleasant chill in the early afternoon breeze. Rowan loved the dry cold, he also didn't particularly mind wet cold either. That's not to say he didn't appreciate a warm campfire or pulling some warmth out of his topaz. He drew some heat now, giving him a flush in his cheeks, the boost of warmth in addition to the afternoon sun and he could pretend it was a summer's day.

Road contracts were always more enjoyable during the summer months, sleeping out under the moons and stars on pleasant evenings. What he really loved was a contract that would take him up far north for the summer. To walk along the old trails he'd taken with his father and brother so many years ago.

He wondered how his brother and Daegan would fare up past Nortara without him. Tanlor—for all his poor judgement—was still an exceptional swordsman. *Always had been.* And despite living in the city for so much of his life, he still remembered the skills that their father had taught them both. In truth, Tanlor hadn't ever really needed Rowan for the trip. Des—Daegan—on the hand, *he* was still learning. The lad had a good demeanour about him and Rowan found himself missing the man's company on the road.

In some ways, Daegan reminded him of Rowan's grandfather, Bodh. He too had enjoyed more than his share of whitewhiskeys, but he was a generous man and didn't care for the notions of pretentiousness that often came with highborn folk. How his cousin Boern could be so opposite to their grandfather, Rowan couldn't fathom.

Boern would be back in Garronforn by now, likely for the season. He'd undoubtedly have some skirmish he would want Rowan to assist on. His family believed he spent so much time on the road because he simply enjoyed the outdoors —which was true in part—but the main reason was Boern. His cousin wasn't blind to Rowan's skill and often tried to strongarm him into fighting skirmishes along the Balfold.

The Balfold had always been a contentious region; rich in resources but large portions of the land technically belonged to Duke Rivers of Nordock. This meant that Boern and Rivers often had skirmishes against one another to claim more of the land. It was usually done so under the pretence of patrols for rakmen and outlaws—both of which often attempted to stake claims on areas in the region. Rowan had little interest in being sent to kill other Rubanians to satiate his cousin's greed. He'd planned to spend the winter season at home anyway, he would just need to line up contracts for the spring to have a valid reason to decline his cousin's request... again.

As much as Tanlor always hated Boern, Rowan was disappointed in how alike his brother and his cousin were. Tanlor's rash and reckless attitude towards killing was playing on Rowan's mind. *He's not as bloodthirsty as Boern.* Perhaps he judged his brother too harshly. But then that boy's petrified face surfaced in his mind. *No, he'd have killed that lad in cold blood.* For no other reason than he'd fallen in with the wrong friends.

Shye had been a quiet lad. Rowan didn't know how he'd ended up with the deserters, and if he was a deserter himself then he couldn't have been a soldier very long. He wondered if Shye had taken his advice and headed to Crossroads. Rowan had taken his time on the road south, if the boy had kept on as fast as he'd fled the bridge that night, then he'd have reached Crossroads by now.

Rowan considered then if he should pass through Crossroads to check in. He wouldn't mind seeing how Wolfhound's injuries were doing and how Mendy and the village were recovering from the raiders. Mainly, he wanted to see if Shye had indeed gone there.

He was following the River Cress south until he reached the fork in the road at a large stone marker. To the north, was the road he'd just come, east to Crossroads and then Rubastre, and south to Garronforn. It would be a three to four days ride straight south to Garronforn... but he would add a few days to his trip if he took a detour through Crossroads, he could then loop back around south through Sallins.

With a nod, Rowan pulled the reins of his horse east towards Crossroads. Travellers on the road were always common in Rubane, sometimes people travelled alone but generally folk tended to travel in groups for safety from bandits and the like. Rowan didn't worry so much about travelling alone. He could handle himself well enough in a fight and he was also an accomplished runewielder in combat. So when he spotted another solo traveller further ahead, Rowan shifted his cloak to expose his sword belt. Rowan was a big man; he was tall and broad shouldered, and the sight of the sword might dissuade anyone foolish enough to attempt mugging him.

Rowan had honed his edir during his training to become a knight. While it wasn't as perceptive as others, he was confident enough that he could identify an opposing runewielder. The man was about one hundred feet up the road and Rowan felt something brush against his edir. The sensation made him turn his head about, thinking that there was runewielder riding up right next to him.

He saw nothing around but farmlands as far as the forests. He looked back up towards the man on the road. He was the only other person in Rowan's field of vision. How could Rowan have felt that man's edir long before he could even see his face? Normally, Rowan needed to be within a few *feet* of another runewielder before his edir would sense theirs. *Nobody has an edir that can stretch out that far.*

The man was riding quickly towards him, his horse moving in a sustainable trot. Rowan kept his going at a casual walk. As the distance between them closed, Rowan could feel the traveller's edir flare out erratically and then recoil back inwards. It had the uncontrolled feel of a novice learning to focus it. *Only it's got significantly longer reach than any novice.*

As he neared, Rowan had no doubt it was the man's edir he was sensing. It was... *frayed.* The man himself was hooded in a dark cloak. He was tall and had a long curved blade that Rowan could make out, poking out just under the cloak.

Rowan tensed as they approached each other. His right hand slowly moved to rest on the hilt of his sword. He could make out faintly the features of a man's face underneath the cloak.

"Evening," Rowan said in greeting. The man nodded in response, his horse not slowing as he passed. Rowan let out a breath as he felt the man's edir fade away behind him.

Who in the hells was that?

He'd heard plenty of stories throughout the years of warlocks and such things, he'd always passed them off as exaggerated stories of runewielding. But that man's edir felt... *wrong.* Erratic and uncontrolled, but someone with that much lack of control would never be able to use their edir to actually runewield in the first place. He glanced over his saddle behind him to see the man disappearing into the distance.

Very strange.

Rowan saw the clusters of wooden buildings as he crested a small hill that overlooked Crossroads. He'd slept rough for two nights and was eager for a hot meal and a warm bed. As he rode into town a few locals that recognised him called out and waved.

The entire road back he'd heard the story being told; Taran the Hunter's sons had cleared a band of raiders out of Crossroads—no it was the Hunter himself, hunted down a bunch of rakmen in the hills above the village. The storytellers obviously didn't care that Taran would have been an old man. Or the fact that he had passed away years ago.

Rowan was surprised how quickly the story was spreading. He'd fought outlaws and raiders before, sometimes under contracts, sometimes not. He reckoned it was the townsfolk of Crossroads, spreading the story. They seemed to be very grateful to Rowan and his brother for killing those raiders. Now with the reception he received riding back into town, he surmised that he was correct. Townsfolk waved and cheered him as he rode towards the inn. Rowan waved back and nodded with a grin.

He dismounted at the inn and hitched his horse. As he made his way to the door, Mendy appeared in it.

"Didn't think you'd be coming back this way so soon," she said with a look of surprise, "but if you think you're getting another free night in the inn you're mistaken. I've got enough freeloaders living here thanks to you."

"Shye found his way here then did he?"

"Sure did," she replied, "I have him round back chopping logs if you want to talk to him." *I had a feeling she'd put him straight to work if he showed up here.*

"Later," Rowan felt a grin on his face, "I'm starving."

"There's stew on, take a seat inside and I'll get one of the girls to bring you some," she said returning the smile, "glad you're back."

A warm, smoky interior welcomed him. It was still early in the evening so there were only a few patrons about. His eyes quickly found a grey scraggly haired man sitting on a stool behind the bar.

"She's got you working the bar already," Rowan laughed.

"Eh?" Wolfhound replied, his face scrunching up in confusion.

"Rowan Shrydan," Rowan introduced himself, holding out his hand for the other man to shake.

"By the gods," the man wheezed, "I owe you a lot from what I hear... I hope you're not here looking for payment," the expression of worry that crossed the man's face amused Rowan.

"Just passing through," Rowan reassured him, "I'm surprised to see you up and about already. You were in a bad way when we left you here."

"Don't have much choice, Mendy's a steely lass. Gotta earn my keep." Rowan barked a laugh, Mendy hadn't followed him in. He distinctly remembered Daegan had paid up front for a few weeks for Wolfhound's recovery with that map of his. It was hanging on the wall at the far end of the bar next to the contracts board.

"Aye," Rowan agreed, "she's a hardy one."

"Name's Lenn," Wolfhound scratched at his shaggy beard and avoided meeting Rowan's eye, "can't say anyone's done a kindness for me like you lads did. I didn't think I'd survive, if I'm being honest. What I'm trying to say is—er—well, thank you, sir. Yer a right fine man."

"I'd like to think you'd have done the same for me, if our places were switched."

"Not sure about that, but after what you've done for me... well, I won't soon forget it."

"What's your plan?" Rowan asked, deciding to change the subject and free the man from his awkward attempt at gratitude. "You were heading on the road to Rubastre?"

"I *was* on a road contract. The merchant's dead now though."

"The raiders?"

"Aye."

"Shame."

"At least you and your brother got the fuckers, eh?"

"That we did," Rowan said, grimly. "I guess you're not going anywhere soon anyway," Rowan nodded to the cane Wolfhound was using to prop himself up on the stool with.

"Nah, I reckon I'll be sticking around here for a while. These are good folk, and it'll be a long while before I can swing a sword again."

"This village could do with a few fighting men anyway," Rowan said. Rowan and Wolfhound shared a sad look. They both knew all too well how bad it could get when a group of outlaws passed through a defenceless town.

"I'm happy enough working the bar," Wolfhound replied, "but if I need to pick up a blade again, I'll do it."

"Good to know."

Wolfhound brought Rowan an ale and shared a drink with him at the bar. Soon enough, the serving girl brought him a bowl of stew that he tucked into. He shared another drink with Wolfhound and they slid into easy conversation. Wolfhound—like Rowan—worked the backroads, mostly bodyguard and escort jobs. He'd even been in a few skirmishes in the Balfold under Duke Rivers' banner. After exchanging some stories they surmised they weren't ever on the opposing side of a battle to each other. But that wouldn't have been the first time that Rowan shared a drink with a man he'd once been on the other side of a battlefield.

Rowan noticed Mendy's niece enter the inn. He couldn't recall her name but he recognised her as one of the kids he and Tan had rescued. She had a crude sword sheathed at her hip. Very uncharacteristic of a young woman. She nodded at Rowan as he eyed the sword. He nodded in response.

"She asked the blacksmith's boy to make that for her," Wolfhound told him when she moved on into one of the backrooms.

"Don't blame her, with everything she went through."

"Some don't think it's right for a girl to be carrying a sword."

"You going to say that to her?"

"Nope."

"You should give her some lessons. Make sure she doesn't hurt herself with it."

"Not a bad thought," Wolfhound mused, "might do just that... if she lets me."

After a time, Rowan's eyes moved over Daegan's map on the wall. He stood up and walked over to it. The man really did make for a good map maker. He ran his finger over the torn piece at the bottom. Tanlor had reacted poorly when he'd done that. His brother seemed more on edge than ever. Rowan thought that Tan's cushy job in the Dukesguard would make him less anxious. But there was something else to this whole situation that Tanlor wasn't telling him. *This is more than just a mission to him.*

"It's a good map, shame about the tear," Wolfhound said, slowly hobbling over with his cane.

"Aye."

"You know what happened to it?"

"Nope."

"Mendy said the lad was planning on mapping north of the Nortara?"

"Aye."

"Dangerous trails up that way. Reckon he'll be alright with just your brother?"

"Tanlor's the best fighter I know," Rowan said, truthfully, "he's in good hands." He turned to walk back to his seat at the bar.

"Either way, I'm glad his friend will be joining up with him. Hopefully he catches them in time"

Rowan froze.

"His friend?" Rowan asked, spinning quickly to face Wolfhound.

"Aye, another foreign fella," Wolfhound replied, a little taken aback by Rowan's reaction, "passed through yesterday." Rowan's mind flicked back to the man he saw on the road two days before. The strange man with unusual edir. Rowan attempted to school the concern on his face.

"What did he say?" Rowan asked, an urgent note in his voice. Wolfhound picked up on the shift in the tone of the conversation.

"He saw that map," he replied, "wanted to know about the tear in it. He was saying it's usually where the cartographer's stamp goes. Seemed pretty hung up on that stamp, actually. Anyways, that Desmond fellow, apparently he stamped a bunch of legal documents for the locals around here that night. Mendy told me he did the deeds for the inn for her too." Rowan felt his heart racing.

"You showed him these?!"

"I don't know where she keeps the deeds," Wolfhound said raising his hands, "but there's still a whole stack of his stamped papers over there," Wolfhound indicated to the end of the bar. "Locals are still waiting for someone to take them to the Duke's office to be stamped officially."

"He saw these?" Rowan asked, moving quickly to the stack of papers and rifling through them. Each was stamped with Daegan's stamp. The same one that Tanlor had gotten so upset about. *You stupid drunken idiot, Dessie!*

"From the look on your face, I'm guessing he wasn't no friend."

"I have to go." Rowan grabbed his cloak from where it hung on his chair.

"Fuck," Wolfhound breathed, "your friend and brother, they in trouble?"

"Aye."

"I'd help but I won't be much use in a fight right now but I owe you lads my life."

"I've got to ride fast. You'd only slow me down anyway."

Rowan stormed out of the inn, leaving Wolfhound dumbfounded by the bar. *Poor lad, how was he to know that Desmond was the Prince of Reldon being hunted by some monster assassin.* He prayed that Tan and Daegan had already secured passage across Nortara. They could lose the assassin in the wilds. Tan would know the trails well enough but Rowan couldn't just leave them.

He jumped up on his horse and leaned in close.

"Sorry, pal," Rowan said to his horse, "I know I promised you an easy ride but we need to be quick." His horse, bless him, didn't understand the words but sure as hell understood the urgency and tore out of the village at speed when Rowan kicked his heels.

CHAPTER 33
Bluebreast is Best

Daegan eyed the glass in his hand suspiciously. There was the slightest blue tinge to the otherwise clear liquid. "And the colour comes from *red* cabbage?" he asked.

"That's right," Ardy said and took a long satisfied gulp of the drink.

"I've never heard of alcohol made from cabbage," Daegan replied, his nose scrunching.

"I think it's mostly potatoes that the alcohol is distilled from."

"Cabbage and potatoes?" Daegan said incredulously looking at the blueish drink. The inventive ways in which remote areas conjured to get drunk certainly impressed him but he wasn't keen on trying it.

The pair were sitting at a table in a tavern near the docks. The place had plenty of grubby whitewhiskey bottles behind the bar but when Ardy had spotted one with a crudely drawn blue bird on the bottle, the Aeth man had practically whooped.

Daegan shrugged and tossed the contents of the glass down his throat. The incredibly strong alcohol burned at his throat and it had an ironically grainy flavour despite it being made from potatoes.

"Ugh," Daegan grimaced, "I like a strong drink but that's—ugh!" He retched involuntarily, the taste still lingering in his throat. "I can't imagine the Aeth at Evier drinking that," Daegan finished. He thought of the delicate and reserved Aeth men and women that sometimes visited his father's court.

"Those brainwashed cultists?" Ardy scoffed, "nah those idiots don't drink at all."

"Is that why you left?"

"I didn't even know what alcohol was when I left," he grumbled and shook his empty glass at the bartender. Ardy really was one of the most fascinating people Daegan had come across, the man defied everything he knew about the Aeth.

"Why *did* you leave then?" Daegan asked, "most Aeth I've met always seemed to long for their home."

"Love," Ardy sighed, "same blasted thing most young idiots do anything."

"I see, and that brought you... here?" Daegan looked around the shabby interior of the tavern.

"I suppose," Ardy grumbled, "...eventually... after about ninety years of poor decisions." *Ninety years!* Daegan supposed the scraggly grey-haired Aeth did have an aged look about him but he would place him in his sixties at best. *This man must be over a hundred years old!*

"How old *are* you?!"

"Left Evier when I was a young lad, maybe thirty?" His eyelids fluttered drunkenly, "twenty years in Durin... about forty years as a sailor... can't remember how long it's been since I came here," he looked up at the barman, "you remember how long I've been here, Pader?"

"You was 'ere before my young lad was born, so what fifteen years, at least?"

"Let's call it at that so," Ardy nodded, "one hundred and five," he said, swaying as he raised his empty glass in cheers.

"So the Aeth do have longer lifespans then," Daegan mused, "how long do your people usually last?"

"The elders in Evier, I think some of those hypocrites live to two, maybe three hundred years." Ardy looked like life had already sucked out as much as his lithe body had to offer. Daegan didn't want to think how decrepit he'd look in another two centuries. An old memory surfaced to his mind—one that was burned in Daegan's childhood—of a Yarji elder removing his mask to reveal a skeletal face with eyes like blue fire. Landryn had teased him for weeks for running straight out of the feast hall and hiding in their room.

"You'd look like dug up death if you lived that long," Daegan joked, pushing his glass of the blue liquid over to Ardy.

"You're implying that I don't already," Ardy plucked up the glass and downed it in one swig, "I won't live that long anyway. I'm not bonded."

"Bonded?" Daegan asked. *Like married? How does that impact your lifespan?* Ardy seemed to have grown disinterested in the direction of the conversation or perhaps was too drunk to realise Daegan had asked him about it. He spun around on his stool, surveying the other patrons in the tavern.

"What do you mean by bonded?" Daegan asked again. Ardy's head bobbled as he turned to face Daegan.

"What?" He grumbled.

"You said you won't live as long because you're not bonded."

"Ah" Ardy waved his hand dismissively, "cult nonsense. How do you feel about a game of cards? Feeling like luck's on my side tonight."

"Poker?" Daegan suggested also looking over the other patrons for potential players. He doubted they'd find any half-decent players of the game out in a remote town like Urundock but Daegan had no qualms about taking their money.

It was late in the evening and almost all of the twenty tables in the tavern were filled. *Surely some folk here wouldn't mind a game.* Daegan's eyes fell on a lonely figure sitting in the corner watching him. He felt his eyebrows heavy on his forehead and didn't bother to mask his displeasure. He had forgotten for a blessed few hours that Tanlor was sitting there. Daegan had spent the past week actively avoiding the man.

They'd not spoken since Tanlor's outburst in the yard behind the inn the week before. Daegan had spent that time drinking whitewhiskey and generally enjoying himself. He didn't know what Tanlor had been doing and didn't particularly care much either. He'd always found it awkward trying to talk with Tanlor compared to Rowan.

Maybe I should just leave, what do I care about going north? That was the Archduke's plan. Once again, Daegan found himself questioning why he was even going along with the plan. What did he owe the Arch-duke? What did he owe Tanlor? Sure the man had saved his life but wasn't that his job?

"You and your friend have a falling out?" Ardy asked, nodding towards Tanlor.

"Yeah," he replied in a tone that implied he didn't want to talk about it. The way Tanlor had spoken to him had been so utterly disrespectful. He'd experienced plenty of disrespect in his life, both subtle and aggravated. That didn't mean that he would just lie down and take it. He was sick of it. Sure, Daegan might have had a little too much to drink and pressed on a topic that Tanlor was touchy about but that didn't give the man any shred of right to explode at Daegan the way that he had.

No, Daegan figured he should finally tell Tanlor that he no longer required his service, and to head back to Rubastre. Daegan could then give up this ridiculous plan of heading north and make his own way home to Reldon. That's what he should have done from the beginning. Why had he allowed himself to be talked into this ludicrous idea in the first place? It made absolutely no sense to be heading up into the wilderness. He should be going home.

Tanlor seemed to take the pair of them looking over at him as an invitation to approach. He strode over to them and nodded to Daegan who returned the gesture with a glare.

"I thought the iceraft would be fixed today, shouldn't we be preparing for the journey tomorrow?" Tanlor directed the question at Ardy.

"Megar says it's fixed, aye," Ardy replied.

"So we can leave tomorrow?"

"Not if you're wanting us to freeze to death in the blizzard. It's rolling down off the hills tomorrow. A big one too, no icerafters doing runs this week."

"You promised to take us even if the conditions were poor. That was the deal!" Tanlor growled.

"Poor conditions is one thing," Ardy's words slurring slightly, "but a fucking *blizzard*? No way, that's not worth no measly thirty marks."

"And you're just going to keep paying for this cheat's drinks during that time?" Tanlor directed at Daegan.

"You don't control my money," Daegan grunted at him.

"He's playing you," Tanlor said, snidely, "the storm's probably not even that bad. He's just realised he's got you to cover his tab for a few extra days."

"At least Ardy knows how to have a good time," Daegan snapped.

"Yeah, looks like it," Tanlor snorted, looking at Ardy hiccup and slump in his stool, the Aeth no longer listening to the interaction.

I should tell him now. Daegan shook his head, "we're not crossing during the blizzard." *Or ever.* "No need," Daegan could feel his own head swaying. Maybe he'd drunk a little too much too. "Would be dangerous," he continued, "wouldn't want to jeopardise the mission now, would we?"

"You're drunk," Tanlor stated, and then leaned in, speaking barely above a whisper "come on, let's get back to the inn before you say anything that might give you away."

"Not fucking going nowhere," Daegan pushed Tanlor away from him. "You hear? Not the inn, not up to fucking nowhere, up there," he waved a hand dismissively trying—and failing—to get the meaning of crossing the Nortara Sheet. "So, just," Daegan made a shooing motion, "go away."

Tanlor's jaw tensed, his eyes darting around the tavern. *Likely looking for assassins and what-not.*

"There's no one here, Tanlor," Daegan scoffed. "There's no one chasing us. Just leave it be." *Ferath could be caught already for all we know.* It was more and more ridiculous the more he thought about it. Why would the Arch-duke concoct such a nonsensical plan? Simply hide Daegan in a dangerous and remote part of his country... to keep him *safe*? It made no sense. Was he really *that* afraid of Ferath? The man wasn't some mythical draega, he was just a man. A man that been Daegan's friend... and had betrayed him. A man who could rot in hell for all Daegan cared. *Tanlor can too.*

"I'll be over there," Tanlor sighed, nodding back to the corner he'd been lurking in.

"You know, Tanlor," Daegan badgered, "being all shady, *not* drinking—in a tavern—makes you stand out a lot more than me," Daegan raised an accusatory finger at the man. "Maybe *you're* the one who's the risk, eh? Ever think of that? Go on, get out of my face."

Tanlor shook his head and left them. *Finally.* Daegan turned back to Ardy who was busy trying to get the barman's attention for another round.

"I don't want another of that blue shit," Daegan said.

"Bluebreast is best," Ardy replied, flashing his stained teeth. The comment sounded like the type of thing Rowan would say.

"Fine, go on," Daegan sighed, "another one."

CHAPTER 34
A Man on the Road

Megarstown was a medium-sized town on the road to Urundock—meaning that it had about two dozen stone buildings and twice that in shacks and timber houses. This was Rowan's third time passing through it in the past few days. First, with Tan and Daegan, heading north. Then on his own returning south, and now he was back heading north again.

His horse was exhausted. *He* was exhausted. He'd made good progress on the road over the two days since riding out of Crossroads. He'd pressed hard through the night, sleeping in his saddle, only stopping briefly to allow respite for his dedicated and resilient horse. He felt a pang of guilt knowing that he would need to trade him today in order to continue the journey. Horses simply couldn't maintain that kind of distance for days and Red had given him more than he could have ever asked of the beast.

He approached the same inn he'd stayed in with Daegan and Tan a little over a week ago. He wouldn't be staying the full night, but even a few hours sleep in a real bed would give him a boost before hitting the road again. The innkeeper recognised him and asked about his companions. He told them he was temporarily separated from them and that he'd be catching back up with them soon.

Rowan inquired about a reputable horse trader in town so that he could switch his horse with a rested one.

"Jared's the man you're looking for. Busy man this week. You're the second lad in two days asking for a trade." Rowan didn't need to guess who the other man was so he said nothing.

"Foreign fellow, didn't look so different to your mate, either, where was he from again?"

"Not sure," Rowan replied, "don't know him all that long. This horse trader, he's trustworthy? I like my horse. I'd want assurances that he'll give me a few weeks to reclaim it before trading on."

"Aye, yeah," the innkeeper answered, "he's me brother-in-law. Most honest man this side of Nortara. He'll charge you a few extra coppers for the trouble but he'll give you six weeks at least."

"Good," Rowan said. He believed the man, horse traders in towns like these depended heavily on their reputation with travellers—as did the inns.

"That man yesterday," the innkeeper jumped back to the topic. He was clearly fishing for a bit of gossip. "He was looking for his kinsman, looked like he'd been riding hard, like yourself. Is that your mate he's looking for?" Rowan fixed him with a levelled stare. This man was sharp enough to see the connection and Rowan didn't want to bring any more trouble down on Daegan and Tan.

"I'd appreciate it if you kept quiet on this," Rowan said and slid a silver mark across the bar with his finger. It wasn't a particularly high bribe, worth maybe two or three week stay at the inn. "I'll be back in a few weeks to collect my horse," Rowan continued with the slightest edge of warning, "I'll have a lot more of this if no one else follows us." Rowan tapped the silver mark.

Wisely, the innkeeper nodded and pocketed the coin, flashing Rowan a pleasant grin. Rowan felt it was a particular talent of his being able to read innkeepers. This type liked to have rapport with his customers. He liked to buy and sell information and tried to gleam as much as he could for free. A lot of innkeepers did the same, it was an easy way to wrangle a few extra coins. Rowan had made efforts during his travels with Daegan and Tan to keep the innkeepers happy, build good relationships with them and make them less likely to sell them out to anyone who came asking about them. It was one of the things that Tan often overlooked. Tan had insisted on keeping low profiles but what he didn't understand is that trying to be discreet only made you more mysterious. And mysterious folk often *drew* the attention of people in small towns like these.

Rowan retired to a room to sleep a few hours. He was never the kind of man to lie awake worrying in a bed so as soon as his head touched the pillow he was out. Years of soldiering and working as a contract knight had taught him to welcome sleep wherever he could find it.

He awoke a few hours later and glanced out the window. The sun had set and Luna's reddish moonlight was breaking through the clouds. A blizzard was apparently on its way south from Nortara. Rowan hoped that Tan and Daegan had managed to cross the sheet before that blizzard came in. He pulled on his chainmail shirt and clipped on his green cloak.

His intent was still to catch Ferath on the road before the man reached Urundock. There was too much risk that Daegan hadn't yet crossed Nortara. Rowan still wasn't sure what he'd do when he did catch up to Ferath. Tan had claimed the assassin was a far superior runewielder to either of them and the story he'd been told of what Ferath had done the night of the attempted assassination had sounded impossible.

Tan should have been upfront with him from the beginning with how dangerous Ferath was. It did bother Rowan that his brother hadn't trusted him with the full extent of what was going on. A part of him had simply been happy that Tan had wanted him to come along. That his little brother still needed him. *He still should have told me what was following us.* They could have strategised a potential battle plan for facing Ferath. Rowan would just have to wing it when he did eventually catch up to the man.

Rowan had had to trade Red before. He was always happy to pay an extra few marks for a latency period to give him first right for the chance to trade back. Most reputable horse traders were happy enough to oblige. Having done it before didn't make the transaction any easier. Leaving Red behind always left him with a horrible sense of guilt. The beast's eyes watched him in confusion as he trotted away on another horse. Jared the horse trader said his new horse's name was Millie, she was a fine horse and she would do for the rest of the ride. If he pushed her he didn't doubt he'd make it to Urundock in under three days.

He came out onto the main street of Megarstown and had been about to pull on Millie's reins to head north when he spotted a group of four travellers arriving from the south. They immediately pulled Rowan's attention.

They were all Reldoni.

Two women and two men, each of them riding tired-looking horses. *This group has also been pressing hard.* Rowan understood that coincidences happen but he was no fool. He turned Millie towards the group and approached them. He could sense all of their edirs as he approached. His eyes flicked to a young man whose edir made him think of Ferath's. The edir flared erratically in pulses. The youth was trying to restrain it as if he were a novice. *He's at least seventeen, eighteen? At that age he should have much better control of that.*

The woman leading them had immaculate control of her edir. She had a stiff posture and the bearing of a soldier. Rowan didn't doubt she was one of the Reldoni warrior women that Daegan had told him about.

Rowan greeted the woman with a welcoming smile and introduced himself as Lenn Wolfhound. The woman didn't give her name but greeted him cordially in response.

"You folk look like you're heading north," Rowan said, looking them over, "you need a guide? I'm on a job for the next few days but I'll be back." Rowan wasn't a particularly good liar, but escort jobs were his bread and butter. It wasn't hard to simply pretend like this group was another potential contract.

"We are indeed heading north," the woman replied in an accent that matched Daegan's, "but we can't wait around, we'll be leaving tomorrow."

"Where are you headed?" This was what he really wanted to know. The woman glanced at her companions and deliberated internally for a moment before answering him.

"Not sure," she said coyly, "we're on the trail of one of our countrymen who we're trying to catch up to." Rowan felt his blood pumping in his neck and he resisted the urge to clench his jaw.

"This have anything to do with that murdered Prince in Rubastre?" Rowan asked pointedly. The woman's eyes flared but she recovered quickly. "Rumours have been coming this way the past few days," Rowan continued, "the whole town's been talking about it." This much was true, Rowan had heard the rumours for himself in this very town when he'd passed through with Daegan. He'd wanted to see her reaction to the mention of him and could confirm now without doubt that they were somehow involved.

"Our business is our own," she replied through tight lips.

"Well if you can describe the man you're after I might be able to help." There was always the chance that they were actually tailing Ferath and not Daegan. Surely, Daegan's family would have sent a party to find Ferath and bring him to justice.

Rowan noticed one of the younger men—a strikingly handsome man—with one of those wild edirs. He was sweating despite the chill. *Looks like the topaz flush of an amatuer runewielder.* Folk new to runewielding often didn't have enough control of their edir to prevent drawing in too much heat.

"You alright lad?" Rowan asked. The Reldoni youth shrugged in response.

"He's one of our kinsmen," the woman said finally answering his question, "have you seen another Reldoni pass through here lately?"

"Maybe. What set you on this route?" If he could figure out how they ended up here it might help determine if they're potential allies or not.

"We have contacts that informed us that our comrade is headed this way." *A frustratingly vague answer.*

"What's he after do you know?"

"You're asking a lot of questions," she replied, her eyes narrowing.

"Just looking to help," Rowan said, raising his hands in a disarming gesture and backing down, "listen, you need a guide or no?" Maybe he'd pushed a little too far. She was already suspicious of him so it was better if he disengaged. He'd gathered enough information.

"We believe our comrade is heading for a place called Urundock," the woman said, "do you know a faster route there or shall we stay on the main road?"

Rowan couldn't shake the mounting suspicion that this group was indeed working *with* Ferath, rather than against him. There was still the chance however they were reinforcements sent to retrieve Daegan and take him home. Surely the Arch-duke would have sent word of the mission to Daegan's family in Reldon? But Rowan couldn't take that risk. He and Tanlor might be able to take on Ferath alone, but not this entire group. *Not if they're all like him.* He glanced at the sweaty youth, again noting the erratic behaviour of the man's edir.

"There's a forest trail," Rowan said, as casually as he could manage, "the road north brings you to a bridge but the path through the forest meanders, it can be easy to get turned around in those woods." The woman nodded and pulled out a map of the area. The dotted line of the road clearly marked a direct route to Urundock.

"Ah yes," Rowan chuckled, "I've often seen this map and it's wrong you see." He ran his finger along to the west of the bridge below the treeline.

"Follow the river east for about half a day and you'll come upon *another* bridge that's not marked here," he lied, "cross there and there's a path that cuts straight through the woods to Splitstone—" he traced finger through the area of woodland to the village marked as Splitstone and tapped it, "—trust me, aye. Much better road that. You'll make it in half the time, I promise you."

The woman rolled up the map and nodded her thanks and Rowan inclined his head in acknowledgement.

"If, by chance, you're still here when I return, it would be my pleasure to act as your guide," Rowan said, driving home the act. The woman politely declined his offer again and the group made for the inn.

Good, that little detour should set them back a day at least... more if they get lost in the woods. It was a gamble he knew, but better to opt for the safer option. And give Rowan, Tanlor and Daegan a little more time to disappear into the North. He grinned to himself and patted Millie's neck.

"Ok, girl, let's see what you can do."

Further along the road Rowan approached the bridge where he and Tanlor had fought the deserters from Twin Garde. They'd left the bodies in their haste and when Rowan had passed back that way the following day they'd already been picked clean by bandits and thrown in the river. He didn't linger at the bridge and continued on.

He could see the dark clouds ahead. The blizzard was approaching. He didn't particularly want to be caught out in it but it was more important that he pressed on rather than seek shelter. He had his topaz that he could draw on for heat if he needed. He hoped that Ferath would elect to wait out the storm so that Rowan could pass him but he couldn't count on that.

As he neared the woods, Rowan spotted the remnants of a battle. *More like a massacre.* The bodies of over a dozen bandits lay strewn about the road. They were fresh, the blood mixing with the muddy path. One of the bandit's bodies was half submerged into the earth, buried below the torso. His upper half slumped and his head was missing. *What in the hells?* The bandit looked like he'd *sunk* into the earth. Many of the bodies had thin lengths of stone the size of spears protruding from them. A few appeared to have been cut down with a sword.

Rowan's mind moved with horror as he realised this was the work of a master stonebreaker. *Could one man have really done this?!* He'd fought alongside—and against—master stonebreakers during his career and *none* of them could have taken over a dozen bandits single-handedly. A part of him refused to accept that one man could have done this but then recalled the strength of Ferath's edir. How it flared and recoiled wildly over impossible distances. He's not a man... he's a demon. There were stories of rakmen and shamans from the Black Sands with powers that defied all laws of runewielding, but those were just stories.

One of the bandits was propped up on his knees, a blond man with a warrior's braid. He had been impaled with one of the rock spears, his weight slumped against it. A dented greatsword with flecks of rust on the blade lay dropped beside him. The man was certainly dead but Rowan checked him all the same. None of the bandits were left alive. Apart from the blond man, none of them looked like they were trained fighters. They likely relied on intimidation of numbers rather than actual fighting skills.

Rowan noted a few bows amongst the fallen, near the treeline. The bandits had likely barred the road to accost Ferath. A lone traveller was an easy target and faced against this many, even a highly skilled warrior would take the wiser choice and surrender. The bowmen would have been hidden in trees and emerged once the bandits on the road had threatened the man. The sight of the additional men would frighten and coerce most men out of resisting. *They were wrong.* And it gave their positions away.

He must've been quick. Six bowmen were impaled with the rock spears. *He would have had to conjure each of them simultaneously and strike.* He would've then drawn his sword and taken the bandits closer to him. *These ones here on the road.* They had deep cuts on the shoulders and neck. *Well placed strikes from horseback.*

The man sunken into the ground was further up, a crossbow lay next to him. *Would Ferath have been able to trap him in the earth like that whilst fighting the others?* No human man could have that kind of concentration. And then finally the blond man—likely the leader—had attempted to flee. His men being cut down so efficiently before him, he would have a strong enough sense of self-preservation to know when to run. And a final rock spear took him in the back and wedged him into the ground, pinning him to that kneeling position.

An effective swordsman that relies heavily on his enhanced stonebreaker abilities. Rowan would need to separate him from his aradium to have any hope of taking the man in a direct fight. That or face him in an environment that didn't suit stonebreaking. Ferath would have stored material as any trained stonebreaker would, but it was limited. *But then again, this demon regularly goes past the limits of a typical runewielder.*

He looked again at the blond man, blood congealing into the dirt around him. There was a twist in his stomach as the thought of Tan having to face this monster alone came to his mind.

Rowan swung back into Millie's saddle and kicked in his heels, whipping the reins.

CHAPTER 35

Disparity of the Soul

"Where did they go?" Tanlor asked with a sigh.
"Cedar's I think, down near the docks," Shelly replied, hefting a sack of vegetables onto her bar to inspect.
"How much have they drunk today?" Tanlor continued.
"I wouldn't serve 'em," she said sharply, "not after the trouble last night."
"Thank you," Tanlor nodded to her.
"Wasn't for your benefit," she sneered, "your mate might have some coin on him but he had half the bloody bar dancing on the tables last night. I don't mind if folk have a few drinks with their dinner but this ain't the place for that kind of carry on, y'hear?"
"I'm sorry," he inclined his head, "truly. We'll be out of your hair today. The blizzard's finally clearing up."
"If you want to be headin' today I'd get after 'em quick. I wouldn't wouldn't trust Ardy with a drink in him on the sheet no more'n I'd trust a wolf in with the chickens."
"Aye, thanks. Which one is Cedar's?"
"The one with the badly painted tree over the door."

Tanlor nodded his thanks and slung his and Daegan's rucksacks onto his back. He'd traded their saddlebags the day before and had spent the morning sorting and packing for the trip north. He didn't feel bad about going through Daegan's saddlebag and packing for him as the man had spent over a week doing nothing but drinking, smoking and gambling with that wretched Aeth.

To Tanlor's surprise, Daegan didn't have nearly as many useless belongings with him as he'd suspected. Other than the supplies they'd collected along the way, Daegan had only hung onto the finer clothes that Tanlor and Rowan had made him replace before Crossroads along with a few journals, parchment and pens. Tanlor packed the fine clothes into another bag, along with some of his own belongings that they wouldn't need up past the sheet. For a few coppers, Shelly would hang on to this one for a few months if needed and hopefully it wouldn't be that long before they came back this way.

He contemplated leaving Daegan's journals as well but then decided against it. Best not to push him too much, the man was already being testy with Tanlor after his outburst in the yard.

In his mind, Tanlor had assumed they would spend the winter—at most—in Shrydan forest. He resisted the urge to pull out the signal stone that the Archduke had given him to check its colour. Every evening before going to sleep, Tanlor would reach into the pocket in his cloak where he kept it, and each night the stone appeared as it always had—like smooth jade with no light emitting from it. The

Arch-duke had offered no timeline but surely with the rumours of Daegan's death propagating throughout the country, he would recall them soon. *He wouldn't want to deal with the fallout with Reldon for having a dead Prince on his hands.* The Arch-duke would *need* to have Daegan back in Rubastre soon enough... surely.

For Tanlor, that couldn't come soon enough. It had been over a month since he'd last seen Danielle. In the chaos of fleeing the city, he'd quickly penned a letter for her and left it with Keltin to give to her. He would have preferred to see her himself before departing but there simply hadn't been time. Fearing that Keltin would read the letter, he'd been careful to leave out any specifics for the mission in it, the words he'd hastily scrawled were still clear in his mind.

My apologies, my love. I must leave the city tonight on an imperative mission for the Arch-duke. I am unsure when I will be back however the Arch-duke has promised that he will bid your father for his approval of our marriage upon my return.

Please know that everything I do, I do for us... I love you.

Sincerely,
Tan

Tanlor, once again, chastised himself for the abrupt wording. He'd been in such a hurry that he hadn't taken the care and approach he'd normally indulge in when writing Danielle a letter. He didn't have any fears over her love for him. She'd proven her commitment to him time and time again over their years together. She'd waited patiently for him as he'd fought skirmishes in the Balfold, taken contracts in the Iron Hills, and while working his way up the ranks of the Arch-duke's guard.

The problem was her father. Duke Harfallow knew nothing of their relationship and would likely not react kindly if he discovered it. He was also heavily lobbying potential courters for her and was becoming increasingly persistent that she must choose a husband. *I just need to keep Daegan safe for a few more weeks.* And then he could return to her. A few more weeks and Tanlor would have everything he'd worked so hard for.

He strode out of the inn, his and Daegan's rucksacks over his shoulder. The tail ends of the blizzard swept at him, light snow fluttering at his face. Ankle-deep snow covered the streets. No one had cleared the streets yet—if they ever would—so walkways of compacted snow were forming as people resumed their daily activities.

He hurried towards the dock, praying that Daegan and Ardy hadn't decided to start the morning with that foul blue decoction that the Aeth man preferred. It had been years since Tanlor had drunk a drop of alcohol. The squad he'd been part of with Rowan during their time in the Balfold had been the only stretch of his life where he had drank regularly. He almost gagged thinking of the mornings when Rowan had convinced him to take a glass of whitewhiskey after long nights of drinking. *He used to have one of his sayings about it. Something about dog hairs or dragon scales or some shit.* It was clever—whatever it was—but it hadn't stopped Tanlor from vomiting the moment the drink touched the back of his throat.

Tanlor stepped out onto the main street that led down to the dock. Some of the smaller side-streets led the same direction. It was the only part of the town where the buildings clustered together and wooden shacks were wedged in the spaces between them, making narrow alleyways. He spotted two figures ahead through the light snow. They were ambling slowly down the street and Rowan recognised the

Prince's gait. He had a highborn's bearing that was easily recognisable among the beaten down postures of the locals.

He jogged to catch up to the pair. The tin pots attached to his rucksack rattled and his boots made heavy prints in the snow. Daegan looked behind at the sound of his approach, the glower he gave Tanlor made him wince internally. It was rare that Tanlor let his temper loose like he had, and it had been years since he'd been foolish enough to do so at another highborn. Tanlor might be a cousin to Duke Garron but his father's blood still pushed him to the bottom rungs of the hierarchy and that meant he needed to have a firm hold on his tongue.

Tanlor inclined his head to Daegan, and then looked to the Aeth. "The blizzard's passed. We leave today," Tanlor stated.

"You can try to make the journey on foot if you want," Ardy scoffed, "some fools try it every few months. But me and Dessie are heading to Cedar's for the day. Hear he's got a half decent lute player up from Heronsbridge for the night." *Another night of debauchery.* Tanlor couldn't stand to watch the pair spend another day drinking and wasting gold in a tavern, and then shambling into the vicedens for the evening for more.

"No," Tanlor said, firmly, "you're taking us *today.*"

"Tanlor, listen—" Daegan began but Tanlor cut him off before the man could dismiss him.

"—I've packed your bag," Tanlor insisted, turning to show Daegan the rucksacks, "I've left most of your clothes with Shelly but I've packed everything you need for the journey."

"You went through my things?" Daegan growled at him. *Oh spare me.*

"I'm hardly going to rob you," Tanlor retorted.

"I've had enough Tanlor," Daegan sighed, "it's time to end this charade."

"We *have* to cross the shee—"

"No," Daegan replied with severity, "we don't! Go back to Rubastre, I don't need you. I'll make my own way to Garron and head home from there."

"You can't be serious?!" Tanlor shot at him, incredulous. *What is he thinking?* "Is this all because of the day in the yard? I *apologised* for that." Daegan's eyes flashed with anger. No, he hadn't forgiven him yet.

"I should have done this *weeks* ago," Daegan replied, rubbing furiously at his throat, "there is absolutely no reason for me to be going north. I should be going home! I don't belong here."

No, no, NO! Tanlor felt his heart beating with rage. He wasn't about to let his one opportunity to marry Danielle ride off to his death.

"I'm not letting you," Tanlor said through gritted teeth, he felt the heat of his anger begin to rise in his shoulders.

"What are you going to do?" Daegan's brow furrowed, "you can hardly force me."

"You are going north, even if I have to drag you kicking and screaming the whole way." He could recognise his fury growing. *Don't get angry with him.* He thought, his arms tensing.

He reached his edir to his topaz to dispel the rising heat from his anger. It was a trick he'd been taught years ago to help control his temper. To his surprise, Daegan stepped forward and *shoved* him.

"I," Daegan said with a raised finger, "am not *going!*"

Tanlor forced more of his growing heat into his topaz. It rushed to his topaz like a fire towards kindling. He took a calming breath, steadying himself.

Then his eyes widened as he felt another edir wash over him. He could feel its presence behind him and recognised it instantly. He dived toward Daegan and tackled him to the ground, the two men falling to the snow. He felt the whoosh of a projectile passing just above his head.

"Get off!" Daegan shouted but Tanlor ignored him, looking back the way he'd come.

A figure stood in the middle of the street. A long curved blade drawn in his hand. *Ferath!* He couldn't make out any details of the man's face but he knew with certainty it was him.

"He's here," Tanlor growled and pulled Daegan to his feet.

Ferath was sprinting towards them, fragments of rock appearing in the air around him. The bits of rock swirled and coalesced, forming a length of rock the size of a spear. Tanlor drew his own sword from its sheath. The rock spear flew towards him, it moved slower than an arrow shaft and Tanlor managed to deflect it. He'd spent years training, honing his reflexes to such precision. The rock spear crumbled as Tanlor's massive blade knocked it aside.

His edir still burned and he was unconsciously still feeding all of his excess heat into the topaz. Tanlor reversed it, drawing heat as quickly as he could without burning himself. He glanced up at the snow covered rooftops and reached out with his edir, pushing the heat into it. A wall of slushy snow tumbled from the roof of the building. Tanlor wasn't certain if he'd timed it right to fall on top of Ferath but at worst, it would bar his path for a few moments.

Tanlor grabbed Daegan's arm and darted for a nearby alley. Ardy followed them, screeching like a moron.

"Ardy, is the ice raft prepped to leave?" Tanlor said, glancing over his shoulder as he ran.

"W-w-what the fuck was that?" Ardy replied.

"Ardy! The iceraft!"

"What trouble are you—"

"—*Is it ready to go*?!" Tanlor roared at him, letting go of Daegan's arm and grabbing Ardy by the shoulders. They were at the end of the alley, leading out onto a parallel street.

"U-ugh, y-yes," Ardy stammered, "repairs were finished days ago n' I—".

"—You have your pistol?" Tanlor turned back to Daegan, dismissing Ardy.

"Yes," Daegan replied and drew it from his cloak.

"Good."

"Tanlor, I won't ask you to—" Daegan began.

"—Stop that," Tanlor cut him off, "I'm not going to abandon you to him." *This is not the time for some foolish heroics.*

Ferath appeared at the mouth of the alley—soaking wet—his blade raised. The sounds of people screaming echoed in the street as townsfolk fled the commotion. Tanlor raised his own greatsword.

"Go," Tanlor told them, his eyes not leaving Ferath's, "I'll meet you at the docks." Tanlor heard Daegan draw his own sword next to him. Tanlor glanced at him, he held the sword in his offhand, his main hand levelling the revolver at Ferath. *That's why he insisted on training with his off-hand so much.* Handguns were such a new invention in warfare that Tanlor hadn't even considered people would be attempting to incorporate their use into a fighting style.

Tanlor expected Daegan to attempt to talk with Ferath, to warn the man not to come any closer, or to demand answers for why he was relentlessly hunting him.

But to Tanlor's astonishment, Daegan opened fire without any preamble, firing off two shots that blasted through the alleyway.

The wall of stone that appeared in front of Ferath was instantaneous. *He's not going to make the same mistake twice.* Ferath had fallen victim to the speed of the revolver's bullets before. The wall of earth appeared in the blink of an eye, and was immediately followed by another spear of rock that formed in the air and was sent hurtling towards them. Again, Tanlor deflected it with his sword, knocking it towards the wall of the building where it smashed apart.

Faced against a master stonebreaker that could conjure and fire projectiles it made tactical sense to remain in the alley. The stonebreaker would be forced to work within the confines of the passage and limit the possibility of firing a projectile at Tanlor's flank but Ferath was no ordinary stonebreaker. Their best hope was to lure him out onto the ice sheet where Tanlor's topaz-wielding ability would be superior.

"To the dock," Tanlor pushed Daegan and Ardy ahead of him. The three of them raced down the street in the direction of the docks. After a few moments, a voice boomed from behind them.

"Daegan!" Ferath roared, "you know this is foolish. You cannot outrun me!" Daegan responded by turning over his shoulder and firing another shot of his revolver. *Good man.* Tanlor had to admit that he was impressed by Daegan's calm resolve. Again, a wall of stone appeared in front of Ferath, the bullet biting a chunk of it off.

Daegan didn't falter and was already sprinting ahead, Ardy was furthest down the street, the Aeth man moving with far more speed than Tanlor would have assumed the decrepit drunk could muster. Tanlor was at the rear, moving slower with the two rucksacks and also wanting to remain as the first line of defence between Daegan and Ferath.

Tanlor was pleased with Daegan's level-headed demeanour. The first time they'd faced Ferath, he'd been a shrieking, useless mess. He was like a different man now and Tanlor didn't feel the fight would be completely reliant on Tanlor's skill.

He felt an edir slam against his. He shot a glance back at Ferath who had dismissed his protective wall in a cloud of dust and was barreling after them. It was his edir! *He's at least twenty yards behind us!*

Tanlor felt the snow at his feet rumble. He immediately recognised the trick that stonebreaker's often used to knock their opponents off balance by dissolving the earth at their feet. He leapt to his right before the place where he'd been running collapsed in on itself, snow falling into the hole.

"Jump!" Tanlor shouted ahead at Daegan but he was too late, the Prince staggered and stumbled into the snow. Tanlor swung around to see another projectile barreling towards Daegan. Tanlor leapt out and slammed down with his sword, knocking it to the ground. Another came flying towards Tanlor and he dodged to the side, its trajectory was off for it to be a danger to Daegan so Tanlor let that one fly off towards the end of the street.

Ferath was quickly closing the distance towards them, sprinting down the middle of the street. The snow on this street was packed hard on the ground and Tanlor reached out his edir as far he could towards the man and pushed out all the residual heat in his topaz. A chill swept over him as most of his own body heat rushed out of him along with the runestone's stored heat. A cloud of steam erupted between them, the snow rapidly melted and evaporated in fractions of a second as Tanlor fuelled heat into it.

Tanlor didn't waste any time, rushing to Daegan and dragging him to his feet. More projectiles of stone flew through the air. They were wildly off target as Ferath shot blind through the steam cloud.

They were in sight of the docks, Tanlor could see that Ardy was already racing ahead of them and had reached the wooden jetty that jutted out into the ice. Tanlor and Daegan bolted after him. The snow rumbled again, this time Daegan rolled to the side alongside Tanlor. The rucksacks on Tanlor's back rattled as they were flung about. He was satisfied that he'd opted for smaller ones in anticipation of a scenario just like this. His balance was off though when he regained his feet. His leg muscles burned with exertion, he fuelled that heat back into his topaz, feeling a flush of cold over his legs. *I'll need that.*

Another spear of rock crashed into the jetty ahead, obliterating a portion of it. Fortunately, it was further ahead from where Ardy was currently untying the rope of his icecraft. They were a few feet away from the wooden boardwalk of the jetty when once again the ground below grumbled. Tanlor shifted his weight, preparing to dodge to the side but instead of the ground below disappearing, it *rose*. Giant fragments of earth and rock burst up from the ground in front of them, compacting together into a wall barring the path to the jetty.

Tanlor glanced to the sides of the wall where the snow covered ground gave way to the sleek ice of the Nortara Sheet. It was too risky slipping on the ice, Ferath would quickly finish them with one of his rock spears if they fell.

He turned about to face the street. Daegan was already levelling his revolver towards Ferath who was emerging cautiously from the steam cloud. He held his sword in front of him. *He's not going to make the same mistakes as last time.* Tanlor's interference and the practicality of Daegan's revolver had caught Ferath unaware before. Ferath's strategy was different this time, he'd attacked aggressively initially, attempting to dispatch them quickly from a distance but now that he was less than ten yards from them, it was clear this would come to a direct fight.

Tanlor's heart raced. *If only Daegan could runewield then he could get to work on dissolving the wall while I keep Ferath distracted.* And Daegan couldn't hold Ferath for the minutes that Tanlor would need to dissolve it himself. Stonebreaking was never his specialty so he'd need a while to clear it.

"I'm going to have to fight him," Tanlor said to Daegan, dropping the rucksacks off his shoulders.

"I can help," Daegan responded.

"Try to flank him," Tanlor instructed Daegan, not taking his eyes off Ferath, "if you get a clean shot, take it."

Amber light—like that of aradium—began to emit from Ferath's chest. *What is he?* The light spread into his hands. The ground trembled again and Tanlor and Daegan both dodged in different directions. A pair of rock spears hurtled towards each of them. Tanlor managed to deflect the one aimed at him but Daegan cried out as the sharpened rock caught him in the shoulder.

Tanlor darted towards Ferath. The man's edir whipped about wildly, the strange amber light flaring. Tanlor noticed that the light seemed to *follow* his edir, like a trailing after-image of where it had been. *What kind of runewielding is this?!* He needed to separate Ferath from his aradium, it was the only way he could finish him. The light had emitted from the man's chest initially so Tanlor guessed that was where Ferath kept his runestone.

As he approached, Tanlor saw Ferath's face twist into a wolf's snarl. His veins were dark and popping, his eyes glowing with a bright amber light. Tanlor dodged a rock spear, then deflected another, and leapt as the earth shook below him again. Ferath seemed to have simple stonebreaker tricks, there was no finesse or skill to them, just raw power and reach.

Tanlor was just about in range and Ferath bounded forward, his sword arced overhead. Their blades clashed and the pair became embroiled in a series of parries and deflections. Ferath's form was perfect, his precision was on point but his movements were slow and sluggish. He pressed aggressively at first, trying to dispose of Tanlor quickly.

Tanlor back-stepped, parrying the attacks, and looked for an opening. He noticed that Ferath's movements were becoming quicker and the light was draining from his arms in conjunction. *Runewielding makes him slow,* Tanlor realised. How could he use that to his advantage?

Tanlor kept his calm and dissipated all of the adrenaline fuelled heat into his topaz. He'd realised long ago that by doing that, he could fight longer. His muscles would still tire but he had fought through exasperation before and had no qualms doing so again.

Ferath lunged at him and Tanlor just about managed to deflect the curved blade, it brought them close together and Tanlor realised with horror that it had been a feint as light surged into Ferath's chest.

The ground beneath Tanlor shook. He reacted quickly—but not quick enough—and the world spun as he fell into the ground. He jerked as cold snow constricted and compacted around him. He could feel Ferath attempting to reform the ground around him to pinch him in place, but there was a cushion of snow preventing it. He was, however, half buried to the waist in snow. Tanlor looked up in panic as he saw Ferath bring his sword down.

A blast sounded and Ferath staggered back, dropping his blade. *Bless you, Daegan,* Tanlor thought as he clawed and struggled out of the snow and kicked himself back. He'd dropped his sword but had time to retrieve it while Ferath recovered from the shock of being shot.

Ferath was in a kneeling position, light coalesced at the man's torso. *He's focusing his edir there.* Bright red blood dripped on the white snow below him. The man's face was a mask of anger and determination but he made no move towards Tanlor. *Could he be dissolving the bullet inside of him?*

Another shot fired but this time Ferath was prepared and a wall of rock formed around him, this time it completely encapsulated him. Tanlor couldn't fathom the speed at which he did that. It was impossible, aradium simply didn't work that fast. *I have to re-assess what is and isn't possible with this man.*

"Hey!" Tanlor's head whipped about to the shout and saw Ardy waving his arms from his icecraft. Tanlor and Daegan shared a look and Daegan nodded in understanding. Both men sprinted back towards the dock.

There was still a wall about twice Tanlor's height of rock blocking the entrance of the jetty. With Ferath recovering from his wound, they had a few precious moments to scale it. Tanlor cupped his hands to give Daegan a boost over it.

As Daegan scrambled up, Tanlor tossed the two rucksacks over, glancing back to Ferath's stone cocoon of which he still hadn't emerged. The bullet looked to have taken him in the chest, a shot to the chest would kill a regular man. But Ferath was not a regular man.

Tanlor looked up at the top of the wall. Daegan's head and shoulders were poking out, his arm reaching down for Tanlor's.

"Grab it," Daegan said and Tanlor leapt up, grasped his wrist and felt Daegan's hand clamp around his arm, pulling him up.

Both of them over the wall, they raced towards the iceraft. Daegan slipped a few times on the ice and Tanlor steadied him with a firm grasp on his shoulder.

Ardy was pulling on a rope as they approached the iceraft.

"Quickly, quickly!" the Aeth man said, a frantic air about him, "get in, tie yourselves to—" he cut off, a look of terror crossing his face. Tanlor's head whipped back to see the rock wall vanishing in a cloud of dust and Ferath barreling towards them with two spears of rock forming at his sides.

"Take him across, I will follow," Tanlor instructed Ardy.

"No," Daegan cut across, "I can help."

"Your safety is paramount," Tanlor replied, tossing the rucksacks into the iceraft.

Tanlor assumed a defensive stance with his greatsword, preparing to deflect the rock spears. He didn't want to move towards Ferath and expose the iceraft.

The iceraft was only slightly larger than a dinghy, with a mast that extended about fifteen feet. If Ferath targeted the mast, Tanlor likely wouldn't be able to do anything to defend it. As Ferath approached, Tanlor could see amber light radiating from the man's eyes. Parts of his skin even looked to be *made of* stone. In truth, Ferath looked more like a stone golem from the stories than a man. The man's face twisted in a pained expression as he charged towards them.

Two of the stone spears were let loose; one directed towards Tanlor, the other angling towards the iceraft. Ignoring the projectile coming for him, Tanlor performed a sweeping swing of his blade catching the one aimed at the iceraft. It connected and sent the spear of rock spiralling toward the ice. He felt a whoosh of air as the one aimed for him narrowly flew past his ear.

Tanlor felt a sharp, searing pain on his leg. He spun in response and saw the blur of Ferath moving past him, his blade slicing Tanlor's thigh as he did so. Tanlor didn't cry out, he was too much of a seasoned fighter for that, instead choosing to throw all of his weight against Ferath and tackling the man to the wooden boards of the jetty.

The two of them fell in a heap. He felt Ferath's hand grab at his face and force him on to his back. The man was incredibly strong and surprisingly heavy. Tanlor felt his head being crushed against the wood, Ferath's weight bearing down on him.

The physical touch was exactly what Tanlor needed. Syphoning the heat directly from a person's body temperature was a quick way to make them panic. Tanlor tried to focus his edir, but Ferath slammed his head against the boardwalk.

There was an overpowering ringing in Tanlor's ears and he could barely make out Ferath's frenzied snarl through the fingers that gripped at his face. He could feel the heat of Ferath's hand... he just needed to pull on that heat. His topaz beckoned for the heat and Tanlor started to draw on it, directing the heat into the gemstone.

His head was smashed again and his vision turned dark. He could still feel Ferath's hand but his head was burning with the impact. He reached up, his hand grappling desperately to pry Ferath off. Ferath's grip was as firm as stone itself. Tanlor swung his free hand in a punch at Ferath. He felt it connect against the man's head but his grip was unrelenting. Tanlor felt his head being pulled forward again. He struggled, knowing that another slam was coming.

Tanlor braced for the impact but it didn't come, a second passed and he was suddenly free. Ferath's weight suddenly gone. Dazed and disoriented, Tanlor staggered to his feet. There was red in his vision. His head was bleeding.

He felt hands grab at his cloak and pull him. He was shoved and sent falling. He hit hard against a wooden surface... dazed, he could see a sail mast above him... he was on a boat?

It was getting hard to think through the delirium. His thoughts felt sluggish. He tried to stand but stumbled, and gripped the railing of the boat for balance.

He blinked away the blurriness in his vision and saw ice over the railing. *I'm on Ardy's iceraft.* A few feet away, on the jetty, he saw two men duelling. Swords clashing against one another, faster than Tanlor's disorientated mind could follow. *Daegan?* Surely not. Then he realised Daegan was standing next to him, his revolver out and aiming at the two swordsmen.

He felt the floor beneath him lurch forward.

"Brakes are off," he heard Ardy call out. There was a deafening crack as Daegan fired a shot of his revolver. Tanlor lost his footing as the iceraft jerked away from the jetty. He glanced at Ardy who was pulling on a rope and opening up the sail. Wind rippled against it and he felt the iceraft shudder and groan as it was pulled by the winds.

Who's fighting? Tanlor looked back at the jetty and saw a red haired man in a green cloak running alongside the jetty in line with them.

"Jump!" Daegan shouted, and the man leapt out towards them, clearing the short distance and falling into the raft. There was a clatter of metal as the man landed in a jumble.

"Rowan?" Tanlor breathed, dumbstruck. He felt dizzy and more of his vision began to turn red. He could vaguely make out his brother getting to his feet and pointing. Tanlor tried to follow his line of sight, spinning his head back towards the town. Tanlor couldn't make out anything. All he could discern was that the iceraft was pulling them away from Urundock... and fast.

"Tanlor, you're bleeding," Tanlor heard Rowan's voice just before his vision turned dark.

"We need to bandage your wounds..."

"I'm fine," Tanlor tried to say but it came out as a murmured breath.

He could hear Daegan and Rowan's voices but couldn't understand their words. He just needed to sit down. Blindly, he tried to sit back but his grip on consciousness was slipping away from him. The sounds of the rushing wind and voices faded away as Tanlor's mind finally surrendered.

CHAPTER 36
Sweeten it With Whiskey

"What's your name?" Rowan asked, crouching down next to his brother.

"Tanlor," he mumbled in response, his eyelids heavy.

"How many fingers am I holding up?" Daegan only half listened to Rowan as he continued the series of questions he'd been asking Tanlor every hour since the man had regained consciousness.

Tanlor was propped up on one of the fitted seats on the raft, his head dressed with a blood stained bandage. Another strip of linen was wrapped tightly around the gash on his leg.

"You'll be fine," Rowan patted his shoulder, "you can rest a little more, brother, I'll wake you in an hour." Tanlor's head bobbed in response and he was soon slipping back into sleep.

"You lads get head injuries a lot?" Daegan asked Rowan.

"A few... it's the line of work, I guess," Rowan responded, looking out at the horizon.

It was a strangely disquieting sight, in all directions there was nothing but pure whiteness. The ice that the iceraft glided along was dusted in pure white snow. The low hanging cloud made the distinction between land and sky impossible. The raft could've been soaring through an empty void.

Once the sail had caught the winds in full, Ardy had pulled on a mechanical lever that retracted the wheels that were fixed along the runners. The wheels pulled up allowing the runners to glide easily along the ice. Daegan felt the contraption was more like a giant sled than a raft.

Ardy moved about the iceraft with surprising grace. Hopping up onto the mast to adjust the sail, walking along the edges of the runners to the rear to work the rudder. He was like a one man sailing crew, always moving about and tinkering with something on the raft.

The Aeth man had a sour tone in his voice when he curtly responded to their comments. *He's not used to fleeing for his life from a murderous runewielder.* Daegan himself had acted like a sullen child in the days after the assassination attempt. It was strange thinking that was only a few weeks before. He'd felt that he'd been on the road with Tanlor and Rowan for far longer than that.

He looked to Rowan who'd taken the seat next to Tanlor. *He came back.* And at just the right moment. Daegan's hand still trembled with the memory. The impending horror that Ferath was going to kill them all. Ferath had reacted quickly when Rowan appeared, sprinting down the jetty. He'd rolled off Tanlor and jumped into action. Daegan had taken the chance to pull Tanlor onto the iceraft and given Ardy the push to put up the sail. He hadn't had a clear shot of Ferath when he was fighting Rowan but Daegan had taken it anyway. It had given Rowan the precious time he'd needed to catch up to the iceraft and jump aboard as they'd made their escape.

Rowan explained how he'd returned to Crossroads, how he'd seen Ferath on the road without realising it was him and how he'd spent the past five days in a relentless pursuit. Daegan found himself grinning despite the recent attack and Tanlor's injuries. He was happy to see Rowan again. He was happy that he'd saved their lives. That he cared enough about them to risk his own in saving them. Tanlor *was* his brother, and Daegan couldn't ignore that the man surely had a sense of familial duty, but he liked to think that Rowan had come back for him also.

"There were some Reldoni in Megarstown too," Rowan said after a while, "small group of 'em. Trying to pretend they weren't fighters but," he shrugged, indicating they weren't very good at pretending."

"What did they look like?" Daegan asked, his interest piqued.

Daegan had given the letter for Lukane to the Arch-duke to send for him. He'd been expecting a team of royal guards to come looking for him eventually. He'd outlined the plan to head north in the letter to his brother, he hadn't known then the specifics of the journey, only that the Arch-duke believed he'd be safer there than remaining in Rubastre.

The descriptions Rowan gave him didn't match any of the royal guards Daegan had known in the palace.

"Their leader—well she acted like it—a tall woman, dark red hair, kept short, shaved at the sides like a warriors." The description could've matched many women in the Reldoni military. All Reldoni were tall compared to Rubanians and dark red hair was common enough.

"She had a scar though," Rowan went on, "just over her eyebrow." *Misandrei.* Daegan thought immediately but he could be wrong, it wouldn't exactly be strange for soldiers to have scars. But the description was a bit too perfect.

"Misandrei," Daegan voiced his suspicion, "she's a bloodshedder."

"That don't sound pleasant."

"Elite runewielders," Daegan clarified, "it's a class my brother formed a few years back." Not that Daegan had been paying that much attention to his brother's deeds as Lord Commander but it was impossible to ignore sometimes.

Misandrei had been a decade older than Daegan, maybe more? They'd never trained together but he knew that she'd trained under Swordmaster Garld's tutelage —like himself. *Like Ferath had.* The woman had also served alongside Ferath during the war with the Reinish. *They'd both been part of Landryn's retinue.* There were too many coincidences.

"Elite runewielders," Rowan whistled, "you think this Ferath fellow was part of 'em?" *It makes sense.* The man had runewielding abilities far beyond anything Daegan knew was possible. Was this what Landryn had been up to? Training a legion of super soldiers? *If they're working for Landryn then why the fuck are they trying to kill me?!*

"I think you did the right thing," Daegan said, looking at Rowan, "not telling them about me."

"You think you know who sent 'em?"

"I've my suspicions," Daegan replied, a large part of him was disgusted and confused by the thought of it. "These are my brother's soldiers. Ferath himself... he... he was staunchly loyal to Landryn."

"Shit," Rowan shook his head, "you said your family was ruthless but..."

"I just don't understand it," Daegan said with a bitter edge to his voice, "*why*?" They'd barely spoken since they were youths. *Not since...* he shoved down the memory but it was too late. His throat caught and before he knew it he was coughing violently, phantom stoneblades pushing against his larynx.

"You alright, lad?" Rowan asked, moving to him, his face heavy with concern. Daegan nodded and tried to say he was fine but he coughed more. Rowan patted his back and eased him into one of the seats. Daegan felt a familiar warmth seeping through Rowan's hand.

"My family," Daegan started quietly, stealing a glance at Ardy who was at the head of the iceraft. He couldn't hear them over the wind. "They disdain me," he said, "they always have... maybe not all of them." He thought of his little sister. Her joyous laugh and her charming demeanour. She was also an exceptional runewielder and he knew that even she was ashamed of him. *They couldn't all want to kill me?* Could they? He'd suspected it before and he felt it mounting now, stronger than ever. His father. His father *hated* him. For no other reason than being what he was.

Inadequate. Weak. An *embarrassment*.

His eldest brother Lukane was cut from the same cloth as their father, but he'd never shown any outright hostility to Daegan. The man had simply ignored Daegan's existence. Did they all conspire to do this? Had Lukane, Landryn and his father all wanted him dead so as to no longer be a stain on their precious family name? He refused to believe that Allyn had any part of it.

There was also still the possibility that Ferath was acting alone or had been compromised. Misandrei's team could still indeed be a search and rescue party.

"Maybe I shouldn't return to Reldon," Daegan thought aloud, "but I don't know what I'd do otherwise." He rubbed the balls of his palms into his forehead.

"You want to continue with the Arch-duke's plan?" Rowan asked.

"What is there up north for me?" Daegan sighed, "I'm not like you and Tanlor... I can't survive on my own."

"You seem to be doing alright," Rowan granted, "I mean you've got some lunatic chasing you down, if not for that you'd be fine." Rowan's words sounded genuine but Daegan couldn't shake the feeling he was just humouring him.

"Getting Tanlor to a healer should be our priority," Rowan continued, "I'm not worried about his head, he's had worse hits. The leg too will heal up quickly enough but I've no doubt Ferath will be soon across after us. We need Tanlor back to his full game if we're to make any distance from him."

"Where will we find a healer?"

"What's our skippy's name again?" Rowan nodded towards Ardy, still adjusting ropes on one of the runners.

"Ardy," Daegan answered.

"Ardy!" Rowan called over, "you reckon you could swing this rig east to Twin Garde?"

"'S'pose," Ardy considered, making his way lithely atop the runner back to the main body of the iceraft, "wind's are angling that way. If they keep up, we could make it there in two days but it'll cost you."

"Another thirty coppers fair?" Daegan offered. Ardy made a face as though he'd taken a bite of a sour apple.

"Hardly," the Aeth scowled, "ain't no one say there was a deranged murderer chasing after you. I ain't 'bout to risk my life for a measly thirty coppers. I ain't taking you anywhere unless you tell me what's going on."

Daegan and Rowan shared a considering look. Daegan might have spent the past week drinking with the Aeth but that hardly made him a trusty confidant. In fact, from what Daegan had seen; Ardy was incredibly unreliable and fickle. Daegan could admit that—at times—he enjoyed alcohol a little too much, maybe even relied on it. But Ardy was on another level, he was the 'sell out your own mother' type of drunk. He shook his head slightly at Rowan, Daegan didn't trust him with any measure of his secrets. Ardy would betray them in a heartbeat for a few bottles of that nasty blue drink he loved.

Then, Daegan remembered his flask—recently topped up—still in his cloak.

"It's better you don't know," Daegan said, taking out the flask and popping the lid, "but how's this. I'll pay you two silver marks if you take us as far as Twin Garde, another two if we need to travel on from there."

To sweeten the deal, Daegan proffered the flask to Ardy. With the prices of drinks around these parts, a single silver mark could keep the man intoxicated for a month, assuming he didn't gamble it all away on the first night.

Ardy's eyes fixed on the flask, Daegan could see the hunger in them. It didn't matter what Daegan offered him, all he wanted was the contents of that flask. *And that is why Ardy can't be trusted.*

"Duke's men will hopefully arrest the fucker," Ardy said leaning forward and taking the flask. He took a long, hearty swig. After he finished, the Aeth grinned from ear to ear, "aye, fine. I'll take you to Twin Garde and wherever the fuck else after that. But listen here, that madman catches up to us, you're on your own, y'hear?" He pointed the flask at them both as he spoke.

"Deal," Daegan smiled and winked at Rowan.

"Let me see the silver," Ardy grumbled. Daegan reached into his coin pouch and pulled out four silver marks. When Ardy reached for them, he pulled his hand back. "Two when we get to Twin Garde," Daegan warned, "two when we get to our next destination."

"And where'll that be?" Ardy probed.

Daegan and Rowan shared another look—a moment of understanding passed between them.

"I'm with you," Rowan avowed, "whichever way you decide, Des, if you want to head home, the quickest route will be getting a ship from Nordock." Daegan felt a knot release in his shoulders.

"West, then," Daegan said confidently, "to Nordock."

CHAPTER 37

A Sea Painted Black

To Femira's relief, Landryn's wind breaking ability sheltered them from the gales that blew in from the Altasjura sea. As they crested a rise that overlooked a scenic beach, she could simply enjoy the view without the relentless wind blasting in her face. The sparse trees and shrubs on the cliff tops grew at angles away from the shoreline.

The stretch of golden sand was nestled between two headlands. The cliffs surrounding the beach were dark in contrast and pockets black rock jutted up closer to where the surf broke. An impressive natural arch stretched out across a portion of the beach. It was still early morning and the sun was behind them illuminating the dark green of the ocean like a sheet of rippling jade.

Their guides—two fishermen from the nearby harbour town of Idrisport—hung back. They shuffled their feet in apprehension, refusing to come any closer to the edge of the cliff. It wasn't the fear of falling that had them spooked, it was what they knew lurked in the caves at the rim of the beach. As the group had travelled further north, kragling sightings had grown more common. Word had also spread that there was a team of bloodshedders hunting them.

They'd passed through more ruined villages, many with survivors that were able to give details of the monsters. Most stories were consistent with what they'd already discovered. The larger towns were all left unmolested, it appeared the kraglings were clever enough to only target smaller human settlements. Survivors told horror stories of watching their loved ones being consumed by the kraglings. Landryn would make assurances that they would clear out all of the nests. Some would pledge their blades in assistance but Landryn would politely decline and tell them that the group of bloodshedders were more effective combatants on their own.

But that didn't mean the locals weren't useful. Having the locals guide them to the nest locations had proved an effective strategy for discovering the nests quickly. In the first six days, they'd scouted out two more nests along the coast. The further north they went, more folk were willing to lead them to the nests. Over the next four days they'd found and exterminated three more nests.

"This one is the main nest," Landryn said with a confident step, looking out over the beach. They'd passed through two ruined fishing villages that morning and a small farm further inland that was completely destroyed. The kragling tracks all looked recent, at least a dozen of them, leading up from the gaps in the cliffs that led down to the beach. The last nest they'd found had fourteen kraglings holed up and it had been a chaotic fight. With that victory, the team had been left with a feeling of exhilarating inexorability in their duty.

"I can feel it," Landryn continued, "the kragal is here." The kragal was the name they'd given to the alpha. More and more reports claimed a much larger creature was moving north. This alpha was what Landryn believed to be the true draega. That it was spawning its lesser monsters to sow death and destruction. He surmised that the alpha would create a nest and then move on after a few days.

They weren't sure how big the kragal would be but the men leading them claimed they'd seen a shadow the size of a house moving in the dark a few nights before. They'd wisely fled for the safety of Idrisport—which was where Landryn's team had been gathering information on nearby kragling nests.

"We should plan an ambush," Drad suggested. The man was a lot sharper than Femira had earlier given him credit. She'd foolishly assumed that because the man wasn't a bloodshedder, he wouldn't be as skilled as the rest of them. She'd been proven very wrong on that. In addition to being an invaluable healer on the team, Drad's spear fighting skills were an integral part to many of their team tactics; placing well timed strikes at vulnerable points while Landryn occupied the kragling's attention.

"We should draw them from the nest, lead them over there," Landryn pointed to a narrow gulley cutting into the cliffs.

"What about the arch?" Drad suggested, "they wouldn't be able to flank us in there either."

"A good thought, but the gulley is better and we'd have the high ground," Landryn said, not dismissively but with an air of authority.

"Annali and Selyn should stay up on the cliffs for support"—they'd learned from previous fights with the kraglings that they were deathly fast and could easily jump short distances—"Selyn can your edir reach the water from that distance?"

"So long as we don't do it at low tide, I should be fine."

"Important thing is to keep them off the sand," Landryn continued on. On sand, the kraglings fought best, they could bury themselves quickly underneath and move with shocking agility *underneath* the sand. Femira could clear massive sections of sand to expose them quickly but it was best to keep that advantage away from the monsters altogether.

"If we can funnel them through the gap in the cliffs there," Landryn continued, "Drad and I can take them one at a time—Annali," he turned his attention to Femira, "could you keep the attention of those that manage to break through the surf?" She nodded, holding his gaze confidently. They'd taken a similar approach in the last fight, Femira had remained up on the cliffs, firing projectiles. The kraglings weren't the best climbers and those that did manage to scale the rock face she sent crashing down by dissolving the rock.

"What if the kragal *is* here?" Selyn asked, chewing her lip, "how do we take it down?"

"Important thing is to isolate it from the rest," Landryn once again, he turned his gaze on Femira. "If the kragal is here we're going to be even more dependent on you, Annali. You need to keep its attention until Drad and I dispatch the smaller ones."

"I'll try to keep as many as I can caught in the surf," Selyn added, "but the kragal might be too big for me to hold."

"I can keep it occupied," Femira grinned, "let's just hope it's not bigger than the cliff."

Overall, the team had an air of tenacity about them. They'd not taken any injuries in the last two encounters and there was an assured synergy emerging from their teamwork. This was what Loreli and Endrin had with the other bloodshedders. Something that Femira hadn't put much value in before. She'd needed rescuing during the battle with the Altareans because she didn't know how to fight as part of the team. She could claim that she'd simply not had the same time and training as the other bloodshedders to work as part of a team but she would be lying to herself. She'd *chosen* not to work as part of a team. She'd focused primarily on sparring and increasing her skills in a solo combat style. She'd actively avoided training drills with other teams. Now she was experiencing just how effective team strategies were.

"If the kragal gets up on the cliff, we fall back," Landryn moved his gaze over the three of them, "we'll leave the horses saddled and ready by the road, we break back to Idrisport and formulate a new plan of attack. If we need to wait for reinforcements from Epilas then we'll wait."

"If Selyn and I break, then you and Drad are left unsupported."

"We'll hold our own. Drad's our healer so he should fall back before me, I can keep them occupied while you three gain some distance."

There was a bizarre irony in many of their strategies in that they often left Landryn as the most vulnerable on the team. As the head of the Reldoni military and a Prince, Femira assumed the priority would always be his safety. But as he was the most skilled among them and—with his soulforged aeristone affinity—he could move faster than any of them. Landryn was so fast that no one felt he was ever in any real danger. He hadn't taken a single hit during *any* of the previous encounters with the kraglings.

The team had a few hours before the tide would be high enough for their strategy to work. This gave the group time to prepare. The kragling's only ever hunted at night, so the group figured that they must be nocturnal. Attacking during the day had proved to be advantageous but this also meant that the kraglings had to be drawn out from their caves.

Femira began forming a host of stonespears. Her edir could form them quickly enough, but if she had them prepared, her edir could propel them one after another. The kragling's carapace could weather five or six strikes of stonespears before it began to weaken, ten were usually enough to take one down. She wanted well over a hundred stonespears at hand if they were facing a dozen or more of them.

They assumed the kragal would have significantly stronger carapace than its smaller offspring so she planned to form ten more spears made of steel. The strikes with steel spears would need to be more precise hits. Generally, the kraglings were weak at the joints and the undersides. The maw was also another weak point but the pincers made it a tricky shot. Their best tactics involved targeting the legs, maiming and then going in for the finish. Their strategy for the kragal was much the same, assuming its weak points matched that of its spawn.

"You should eat something," Landryn approached her. She glanced over at the small cookfire where Drad was frying some dried meat strips. "I'm almost finished here," she replied, forming a length of steel with a deathly point. Landryn had bought her the ingots of steel back at Idrisport once they realised that the kragal might be too big for her stonespears to be effective.

Femira always kept a small reserve of the steel and some rock in her earthstone heart in case she needed it. She could always pull on the materials around her but it was wiser to have a reserve, if she needed it quickly.

"There's a thrill to this, isn't there?" Landryn said, his eyes scanning the beach below.

"Yes." She couldn't deny it, the past few days had been incredible. Her abilities were finally being pushed to their extremes. There was an insurmountable surge of satisfaction when they took one down. Femira craved it, she hungered for the adrenaline and the exhilaration of the fight. She was like a skaga addict, revelling in the thrill of a hit and spending the time between seeking another. She didn't want to admit the extent of how much she enjoyed it to Landryn but knowing he was feeling the same gave her encouragement.

"Feels like I've taken fen-salt," he gave her a savage grin, "I feel *alive*."

"That's exactly how I feel," Femira replied, amazed that he would describe it so similarly to how she felt, "I feel like I was made for this."

"This *is* what we were made for," Landryn caught her eyes and a fire ignited inside of her, "the soulforgings... I don't believe in the gods," he admitted, "I don't believe in any divine powers guiding our actions but I cannot help but feel that the threads of fate have brought us to this."

Femira felt a pang of guilt as he spoke. It hadn't been fate that brought them here. It had been her deception. He still didn't know that his brother was dead and Femira's regret for withholding it from him was growing with each day they spent together.

Would this all end when he found out? The rhythm of their days were invigorating. Once they'd found a nest and dealt with it they'd move further north and start tracking the next. Days that they didn't find one, the group would close each evening with training exercises. Landryn had proved to be an invaluable sparring partner. He moved with such lithe grace and precision that Femira could see tangible improvement in her form and style to match his.

"Is it terrible that I *want* there to be more of them out there?" Landryn said, his eye contact breaking as he looked to the ground.

"I want to keep hunting them too," she admitted.

"We can," he looked back at her, his eyes alive with intensity, "there *are* more. To the north; the Simirwoord... the Black Sands. The borders of Reldon once extended as far as the Northern Towers. My father has grand ambitions to return Reldon to its glory; that includes the wildlands of Athlin and the Black Sands. In Elyina's time, monsters like the kraglings have prevented any war parties mobilising there but the bloodshedders could be the sword that forges a path forward. We could finally reclaim those regions."

"Your father would support that?" she asked hungrily.

"Maybe," Landryn scowled then, "he's still too bitter with the skirmishes against the Reinish, and the rising tensions with Altarea and Keiran. His attention is focused on the south when we should be setting our sights north. That is where the true danger facing us lies."

Having seen first hand the destruction that these monsters cause, Femira was inclined to believe him. If the creatures of the north were as invasive as the kraglings, it wouldn't be long until they were roaming the lands of Reldon.

Femira understood that she was not considered a Reldoni—nor would she ever be fully accepted as one—but she was still part of this country. She'd trained with their soldiers, lived amongst their highborn, and despite often feeling like an outsider, she could feel Reldon becoming her home. More so than the streets of Altarea had ever been... and she had hardly any memories of her Keiran homeland. If the purpose of the bloodshedders was to defend the borders of Reldon from creatures like the kraglings then it was a duty Femira was eager to be called to.

"I want to go with you. To the north, to the plains of Athlin and the Black Sands," she said, holding his gaze with determination. He nodded and Femira didn't miss the hint of a smile on his lips.

"When we return to Epilas, I'm going to propose the expedition to my father. The War Council is eager to expand our borders. They're all too concerned with the Reinish but I'm going to propose we head north to the untamed lands," he said with determination.

There was something else that Femira wasn't ready to admit out loud. Something that festered inside and whispered to her. She had no desire to fight in real battles against other people again. The thought of it turned her stomach. *Knives sliding into eye sockets.* She shuddered. But she had no qualms with killing *these* creatures. This way, she was *protecting* people, not killing them.

"I'm going to check on Selyn's progress, don't forget to eat something," Landryn finished. Selyn was below them in the gulley that led to the beach. She was pulling out moisture from the earth, drawing it into herself and discarding it further down the beach. The kragling's insect-like legs would churn up that ground to mud, making it far harder for Landryn and Drad to fight. The kraglings by contrast could move just as effectively in the mud as they could on sand. Another lesson they'd hard learned over the past few days.

Despite their initial unsympathetic relationship, Femira and Selyn had fallen into an amicable familiarity. They were both primarily range support for the battles against the kraglings, and the more they discussed tactics and put them to use, the more each had come to trust on the other's ability. They'd even discussed potential compounding of their abilities; Femira could control sand, but its practical application was limited mainly to cover and blinding tactics. Grains of sand on their own—even when whipped into a sandstorm—could do little real damage but when combined with Selyn's watershaping skills, the two could potentially work together to make large coordinated attacks.

Femira resumed her task of forming the lances. Dissolving and shaping metal was still a lot slower than rock, but she could create the lance in under a few minutes now. The metal felt different inside of her. It had a different resonance to it. Rock mostly all felt the same with minute differences between the various types. Solid stone, glass, metal and sand all had distinct impressions she could sense.

The metal had been dissolved from ingots and the impression of that shape was still there. She could reform an ingot much faster than changing it into something new. The same rules applied to the other materials. Once shaped however, the impression began to change. With each dissolving and reforming, the metal's previous impressions would fade. She was becoming more and more aware of these impressions as she used her abilities and as a result the speed of her shaping was improving drastically. Even the limit of material she could store inside of her was growing each day. Femira didn't doubt that it was another effect of being soulforged. Would it continue to increase? Surely there would eventually be a limit to how much her body could handle. She pushed the idea to the side of her mind and continued the task at hand.

Once she had ten steel lances formed and in position at the top of the cliff, she joined the others at Drad's cookfire to eat and run over some last minute battle plans.

The tide was approaching and with it the promise of their next battle.

***

Femira watched as Landryn loped along the sands like a panther. His black armour of nythilium barely hindered his speed. Scuttling after him were—as they'd guessed—a dozen kraglings. It was a testament to how quickly Landryn could move that he easily outpaced them.

This had been their tried and tested tactic. Landryn would draw them out of their nest caves with wind blasts and then lure them back to the waiting ambush on the cliffs. On their first two attempts, they'd tried fighting in the cave but they found that the kraglings moved more erratically in daylight, their vision evidently impaired by the brightness.

None of the kraglings seemed much larger than the ones they'd already faced. The largest was about the size of a horse, the smallest being no bigger than a dog.

No kragal then. As if in response to her thought; a deep rumbling sound echoed from the other side of the beach, the noises that followed sounded like a crashing waterfall.

Landryn cleared a large split boulder—the first marker on the beach. Femira raised her hand and three of her stonespears rose to her command. She focused her attention on the kraglings closest to Landryn and waited for them to enter her range.

When the first kraglings entered the periphery of her range, Femira targeted one and shot the three stonespears in quick succession. The first struck, exploding in a cloud of debris against the blue carapace. The second smashed against it immediately after, staggering the creature's movement. Femira deftly adjusted the trajectory of the third, she hadn't expected the first two to cripple it. The third stonespear landed with a satisfying crunch.

Femira immediately shifted her focus, raising another three and targeting another kragling. The eleven remaining were all still chasing after Landryn, who had now made it to the gully. Landryn turned to face the oncoming creatures, his blade extended before him. *Gods, he really does look like some fucking hero when he does that.*

Femira maimed two of the larger ones with well placed stonespears to the legs. She didn't bother wasting effort on killing those, they were as good as dead once they reached Landryn and Drad. Her objective was to maim the bigger ones, if possible, but primarily to draw the monsters' attention. Already a cluster of kraglings were splitting off from the group, shifting direction towards Femira and Selyn's position on the cliffs. They weren't very intelligent creatures and rather than follow Landryn's route up the gully, they attempted to climb the cliff directly.

Atop the cliff, Femira and Selyn had an excellent vantage point to assess the progress of the battle. Landryn and Drad were engaging with the first kraglings to reach the crevice. They leaned on their tried and tested tactic; Landryn occupying attention with glancing blows and staying in the kragling's field of vision, while Drad struck against the weak points with his spear.

Selyn surged into action as more of the creatures hastened towards Landryn and Drad. A thick stream of water barrelled out from the shoreline, it burst up from the surf like a river and rushed towards the approaching kraglings. Four of the monsters were swept up in her torrent. She used her hands to guide the surging waters in an arc, creating a twisting whirlpool in the middle of the beach.

The three remaining kraglings not caught up in Selyn's whirlpool—or facing off against Landryn—were attempting to climb the cliff face below Femira. She grinned as one made an impressive leap, digging its enormous claws into the rockface and using its many legs to scuttle up the cliff.

Femira reached out with her edir and felt the vibrations of the cliff face. She could sense when kragling's claws dug into it. She sucked on the rock, pulling as much into her as she could in a single draw. The kragling made a hissing sound as it crashed back against the rocks below, landing on its back. Femira followed up with volleying three of her stonespears on its exposed underside, tearing the creature apart.

This is too easy.

Just as she was about to repeat the same tactic for the second kragling when the entire ground shook. Bursting out from the mouth of the cave was a *titan*—a moving mountain of blue and red carapace.

Femira felt her jaw go slack at the sight of it. Spines along its outer shell jutted upwards like spired towers. Its colossal foreclaws were as big as fishing dinghies. Its six legs were wider than the biggest tree trunks she'd ever seen. The legs groaned and strained under the weight of the creature's enormous carapace body. The kragal shambled towards them, each leg stomping down with such incredible weight that it sent tremors reverberating across the beach.

The priests in the temples had always squawked about primordial monsters. They'd been described as behemoth creatures large enough to destroy entire cities in a rampage. Young Femira had listened to the ramblings of the priests when they would hand out food to the streetdogs like her. Femira had never believed in their gods or their primordials but at that moment, she could think of no other way to describe this creature. The cliff that she and Selyn were perched on was easily a hundred and fifty feet high, and this creature easily came up to half of that. If ever there was something to be described as a draega, it was this.

Femira worried the claws fully extended might reach her. Then, with dawning horror, she thought of how high the kraglings could jump, flinging themselves five or six times their height in the air. Could the titan kragal do the same? Could it easily clear the height of the cliff if it wanted to? She dreaded to think of the aftershock that would follow from its landing.

Their strategy for the kragal hinged on Femira being able to incapacitate the thing. But how could she take down something that *big!* She glanced over worryingly at Selyn whose face was pale and drawn back in horror. They had assumed the kragal would be three or four times the size of standard kragling. *Not this!* This thing was a behemoth.

Femira clenched her jaw.

This is what she'd wanted, wasn't it? *This* is what she'd trained for.

This is my calling.

The two remaining kraglings climbing the cliff were nearing the top. Femira crumbled the rocks they clung to, sending them plummeting to the rocks below. She then rained stonespears down on them, brutally smashing apart their carapace.

Her gaze whipped back to the kragal as it laboured towards them. It had just passed within range of her stonespears. She stole a glance down to Landryn and Drad, they'd killed three more, and Selyn had released another from her whirlpool for them to tackle.

Femira fixed her sight on one of the kragal's monstrous legs. The muscle was blackish brown and wrought like a twisted tree trunk. Parts were shielded in carapace, but like the monster's smaller counterparts, the joints were exposed flesh. That flesh however looked *stronger* than a tree trunk and Femira was hesitant to waste one of her steel lances. She wanted to be sure it would pierce before using one and she still had dozens of stonespears.

Femira raised her hand, using it to guide her edir in her mind. Three of the stonespears rose and she shot them forward. She focused her edir on keeping them on target, adjusting pressure to counteract the force of the winds. Each of the stonespears hit their intended targets but shattered ineffectually against the thick twisted flesh.

The thing didn't even notice.

She might as well have been throwing pebbles at it for all the damage they did. *Shit.* Their entire tactic was dependent on Femira bringing it down.

"Selyn," Femira shouted, "that thing's a lot fucking bigger than we thought."
"There's no way I can make a whirlpool big enough for *that*," the woman replied, her voice edging near panic. "Maybe if we could lead to the water, I could leverage the force of the swell, hold it under a while."
"That won't help us kill the fucker though," Femira said through gritted teeth.
"If it's as strong a swimmer as the kraglings, I'm not sure any amount of swell would hold that thing back anyway."

Femira didn't want to give up. She didn't want to admit to defeat, but how were they supposed to fight something like this?

"Annali! Selyn!" She heard Landryn's voice shouting up, "pull back! This foe is beyond us!" There were three remaining kraglings in Selyn's whirlpool. She had been making circular motions with her arms to maintain it but now she shot her hands forwards and the flow of water straightened, barrelling the kraglings caught in it towards the shoreline.

Drad lanced forward, his spear driving home into the maw of the kragling they'd been facing. They had a clean run back to the horses. Femira and Selyn set off, the giant black shape of the kragal still looming in the periphery of her vision.

Femira heard a thunderous cracking, she turned her head to see the kragal had plucked a boulder the size of a cart from the beach with its pincer. *No, it couldn't...* it flung the boulder towards them as easily as skipping a stone.

"Selyn!" Femira shouted, pointing at it. The woman's head turned and they both watched as the boulder arced towards them. They tried to gauge where it would land, judging the right moment to dodge out of the way. The kragal's aim was shockingly accurate, the boulder landing with a deafening crash ahead of them. Had they kept running that boulder would have crushed them.

This thing is a lot smarter than its offspring too.

The kragal was already throwing more boulders at them. Femira reached out with her edir and turned one to dust, and then another... and another. She couldn't keep up and started flinging her stonespears at the boulders trying to knock them off course.

"Annali!" Selyn pointed and Femira followed her line of direction towards the horses.

No! It was too late but she shot her edir out anyway. It was a panicked, pulsing wave as she desperately attempted to dissolve the flying boulder before it... she winced.

Her chest felt like it was caught in a kragling's pincer from the pained cries of the horses as the boulder landed. More boulders flew towards them and Femira jumped back into action, firing stonespears to deflect them.

It had felt like only seconds but Landryn was already at her side, Drad following up behind. Both men wore faces of calm determination as if their only means of escape hadn't just been left in a bloodied heap of broken bones and stone. The kragal had cleared all of the nearby boulders and was now resuming its ominous approach.

"We can't outrun that, once it's over the cliffs it'll be on us," Landryn determined. It wasn't entirely true. *Landryn* could outrun it, the others couldn't.

"It has to have a weak point," Drad put in, "I'd make a bet on the maw."

"You want to get close enough to that thing's mouth?!" Selyn contested.

"Those cavities in the shell near the mouth," Landryn pointed out two cavities, "those are the eyes—just like on the kraglings. If we can blind it, it'll make the job a lot easier."

"I don't have the precision to shoot them," Femira admitted, even if she managed to get her projectile past the front pincers.

"We have to find a way to restrain it," Landryn continued, "if I can climb onto its shell, I can take out the eyes. Those claws will crush us if we get close but if we can somehow hold them down."

"I've an idea," Femira put in, jumping to Landryn's beat. "But we're going to need to lead it over towards the arch," she said, pointing at the arch on the other side of the beach.

"You're not strong enough to bring down that arch," Selyn challenged, "nobody is."

"If we can drive it under the arch though," Landryn considered, "its movements will be restricted."

"It'll be stuck," Femira grinned, "and we can focus on taking it down."

"I don't think it'll allow itself to get boxed in like that," Drad said.

"That's why we'll have to blind it first," Femira replied, the rest of the group turned to look at her and she locked eyes with Selyn, "I'm going to need your help with that."

***

Femira darted across the sand, her three lances trailing after her. The wind pushed at her back, propelling her faster than she could normally run. The enormous body of the kragal loomed to her right and the ground shook as it took another step.

Femira passed into its rear shadow, the sea arch ahead of her. The wind behind her curved with her path, still pushing her. She reached out her arms and pulled at the sand supporting the kragal's tree trunk legs. The sand dissolved in massive clumps, evaporating to nothing as it was sucked into her. She could feel the weight of all the additional material slowing her muscles but she was unrelenting with the momentum of the wind behind her. *That is a very useful trick.* If they found a way to soulforge another runestone, Femira decided that aeristone would definitely be the way to go.

The sand at her feet shuddered as the kragal lost balance, stumbling backwards into the pit that Femira had created. The pit itself was huge but to a creature the size of the kragal it was a mere pothole.

Femira sprinted as fast she could, rounding the creature. She flung the sand out from her, away from the kragal, as she would need the space. The additional weight gone, she felt a burst of speed as she approached the front of the creature. Its front four legs were already clambering forward, pulling itself out of the pit and adjusting its focus on her. *Good, that got its attention.*

Femira smirked and pushed off on her back leg, launching herself into the air.

Another gust of wind rushed up underneath her and gave a considerable boost to her jump.

Soaring through the air, she launched her steel lances in a succession at the kragal's face—or rather the breaks in the carapace that she assumed was its face. She aimed for the two crevices at the front. Its eyes were large black orbs of emptiness floating in those crevices.

The first lance glanced off the carapace right next to the eye. The second was too far off and batted uselessly against the harder shell further up its back. The third bit into black flesh at the crevice but didn't pierce the eye itself.

So close! She'd figured her aim wasn't good enough to land. But that wasn't her objective. She landed, her boots thudding against the sand and she rolled so that her legs didn't take the full impact of her wind-enhanced jump.

She heard the kragal groaning. Glancing over her shoulder, Femira saw the creature shifting to face her head on.

This was what she'd wanted.

Its mouth pincers shuddered, and its behemoth claw rose laboriously into the air. The sun was blocked out as it dominated the space above her.

Femira bared her teeth in a malevolent expression halfway between a grin and a snarl. She sent out a pulsing wave of her edir and dissolved all of the sand around her in a powerful blast of her edir, absorbing as much as she could hold. Just before the sand beneath her feet vanished, she kicked off backwards and felt a mighty surge of air lift her up, flying her back out of the kragal's range. She couldn't see Landryn but she could sense his edir pushing the air around her, throwing her out of the strike zone.

The spot where Femira had been standing was now a crater twenty feet in diameter and depth. She dropped ungraciously just outside of the perimeter. The kragal's claw—easily the size of a fishing boat—crashed down into the crater. Femira staggered as the ground shook violently.

"Now!" Femira roared, regaining her balance.

Her skin was alight with the amber power of the earthstone inside of her, holding the mountain of sand she'd just absorbed. She thrust her hands forward and felt the sand explode out of her in a storm. She looked to her side and saw Selyn sprinting towards the crater—right on cue—with a river of crashing white water flowing around her. Selyn glowed with an azure light as she came to the edge and shot her hands forward.

The torrent of water cascaded into the crater like a breaking dam. The deluge of water mixed with Femira's own flow of sand. At first it flowed brown and wild until blending further, forming a heavy roiling clay on top of the kragal's claw.

Femira pressed down with the force of her edir on the clay. Selyn to her right also strained with the effort. She could feel the creature attempting to pull itself out from the clay. Her muscles tensed as she poured every ounce of strength she had in holding down the massive claw. The clay began to solidify as Femira exerted more and more pressure.

The kragal made a roaring sound that reverberated in the air. It's six legs pressing hard against the sand in an attempt to pull free its trapped claw. Femira didn't relent. She poured all of her focus and will into maintaining the pressure.

A black shape blurred past her. Landryn moved with such grace and speed that he seemed more like a shadow than a man. He dashed along the top of the cracking clay towards where the claw arm was submerged. In a series of elegant bounds, he leapt up onto the creature's arm and climbed up the carapace.

Landryn didn't climb the way that Femira did, hoisting herself up to the next handhold. Landryn *launched* himself from one grip point to the next and within moments he was on the kragal's flat top shell, weaving his way around the sharp spines.

The kragal either didn't notice or didn't care that the man was scaling up it. In the same way that a man didn't bear much mind to an ant crawling up his leg. But some ants carried a deadly bite.

The kragal's shell shifted and staggered as it continued to fight against Femira and Selyn's combined effort. Landryn deftly stepped his way closer to one of the eye sockets. To Femira, he looked so small on the kragal, like a tiny black-clad insect. The silver of his sword caught the sunlight in Femira's eye as he drew it back. It was working, their plan was working!

The sudden burst of force against her edir caused Femira to lurch back. The ground trembled violently underfoot and the kragal let loose a deep and hateful roar. Femira could see Landryn's body being tossed by the kragal's jerking movements, clinging fiercely to his blade now buried in the creature's eye crevice.

A large fracture appeared on the surface of the clay, then a network of cracks forked out from it like streaks of lightning in a storm. Femira tried to push down against them but it was useless, it was like trying to hold back a landslide with your bare hands. The claw burst up from the ground in an explosion of clay.

Femira turned her heel and ran, hoping to outrun the falling chunks. The sand beneath her was still shaking and she lost her balance tipping forward into a roll. As she came up, she glanced over her shoulder and watched in horror as the kragal swung its claw to the side in a sweep. Selyn was also running but she was right within the kragal's range.

Femira opened her mouth to scream at her but no noise came out. It wouldn't have mattered if she had. The claw swatted Selyn as if she were nothing. The woman was flung across the beach like a ragdoll, the azure light of her soulforged waterstone ability winking out like someone had blown out a candle.

Her lifeless body hit the sand in a heap.

Chunks of debris rained down where the crater had been. The kragal's body moved with the weight of its claw, the powerful legs stepping forward with the momentum. Femira saw Drad running towards where Selyn had landed.

She felt her chest tighten. She could feel it all falling apart. This had been *her* plan. She had gotten them all killed with her recklessness.

Femira watched, frozen, as the kragal took a step forward, its other claw coming down on Drad.

It crashed down with a deafening boom. The sand around where it had dropped dancing up into the air around it.

They were dying and it was her fault. *Selyn, Drad... Landryn!*

She looked up at the creature's head. Somehow Landryn had managed to climb his way across to the kragal's other eye crevice, despite the thing's erratic movements. His sword flashed and he drove it into the crevice.

The kragal reeled backwards, its legs twisting and crumpling in pain. It tripped into the first pit Femira had made, falling and stumbling under the cliff arch. The monster shook it's body violently, the sides of the shell carapace grinding against the leg of the sea arch. Chunks of rock rained onto the sand below.

Landryn had somehow managed to hold on to the shell during the collision.

A boulder bounced off the chestplate of his nythilium armour—not even making a dent in the thing. But the force threw him from the creature, falling directly into the danger zone between its claws.

Landryn fell in a bundle, a small black mound in the sand, the enormous creature looming above. The Prince of Reldon, Lord Commander of the Reldoni military, was going to die... and it was Femira's fault.

She thought she could hold it, but she'd been wrong.

The kragal still thrashed blindly inside of the arch. It's claws and shell grinding against the rock.

Femira was on her knees, her teeth gritted. The image of Selyn being thrown across the beach flashed in her mind.

She was on her feet. *Drad being crushed under the creature's claw.*

She was running towards the sea arch. *Her blade puffing to dust against Endrin's chest.*

Her edir stretched out before her and her chest burned, amber light filled her vision. The pain of her soulforging ritual now thrummed in her chest.

Her brother's bodies bouncing against the cliffs.

The kragal's claw raised up above her.

She was *so* close.

Landryn lay just a few feet ahead. She passed under the shadow of the sea arch, the claw directly above her. She leapt forward, her stoneshell forming around her.

Femira landed on top of Landryn and everything went dark. For a single moment there was nothing. She could feel the cold metal of his armour beneath her. The two of them existed in a space of pure silence and nothingness.

A second passed and the entire world shuddered around her. The impact was so deafening that her ears rang in the hollow darkness. Then light appeared in cracks around them and in the fractions of a second the stoneshell was crumbling. Femira felt the dust debris fall against her back.

She was on top of Landryn. Her face inches away from his. He looked up at her through dazed eyes. She could feel his breath on her face. She heard crashing and cracking as the kragal tried to move within the sea arch.

She looked up. The toothy maw was above them.

Femira clenched her jaw. Her hands came together in fists. Crumbling rocks fell around them. Each of them resonated with her edir. She ignored them.

She ignored the kragal's approaching maw.

Her mind darted between forming another stoneshell to dissolving the sand below them. They could sink into a pit... and then what? She could feel the sand below her resonating in response to her edir. It begged her to be pulled in... then she felt something *else* below her.

It was a distinct and inharmonious pulse. A cacophony of oscillating senses touched against her edir, radiating from her clenched fists. She looked down. Her fists were planted on Landryn's armour.

The mystic metal of Landryn's armour was giving its own distinct impression on her edir. The nythilium did not beat in a regular cadence like regular metal. It was wild and erratic, like it didn't *understand* what she wanted. *Like it's alive?*

On instinct, Femira tried to absorb it. The metal resisted her and a dissonant blast of bizarre senses invaded her mind. There were flashes of concepts her brain couldn't understand. Rolling fields of stars. An alien woman's face laughing. A roiling sea, painted black. And a hand holding a blade.

The image of the blade formed and took root in her mind.

She opened her palm and slammed it down onto the breastplate, clenching her eyes shut. With every ounce of strength in her will, she commanded the nythilium to obey. The armour exploded into a cloud of scintillating dust and flowed into her.

She could see in her mind's eye the amber light coursing through her. She was the vessel, the conduit and the conductor all in one. She channelled it above her and reformed the metal into a long black sword. It was unlike anything her mind had ever grasped before. A thick sword so large that no human could ever wield it. Its blade was twisted in a paradoxical helix, knotting together at the tip into a deathly point.

Femira's eyes snapped open and she looked up. The mouth loomed just above them. The creatures jagged teeth mere inches above the tip of the blade.

Every muscle inside of Femira tensed and she pushed up with all of her mental and physical force, shooting the sword forward. It sunk into the mouth of the monster as easily as if through butter.

Femira pushed forward with her edir and felt the blade tear through the kragal's fleshy interior. The creature recoiled, its pincers flashing forward protectively and crashed against the walls of the sea arch.

Femira kept pushing, the pulse of her edir washed over everything. She could feel the sand below, the rock of the arch around her. And the weakening pillar of rock. The arch itself was losing its stability.

She rose to her feet and focused her edir on the rock above her and *pulled*.

Dust and debris began to fall.

Chunks of rock tumbled down from the underside of the arch.

The kragal was thrashing against the arch walls, trying to back up. The nythilium blade still forced its way through the monster's insides like an enormous crossbow bolt. Her hands shot heavensward.

She pulled with all of her strength.

The arch groaned.

More rocks fell.

There was a sound like the rumble of thunder.

Femira grabbed Landryn's tunic and dragged him back out of the shadow of the crumbling arch. Her boots dug into the wet sand as she pulled him back, desperately trying to get out from under her own destruction. Within moments, the arch collapsed in on itself in an inexorable cascade of falling boulders and debris.

The rock rained down on the kragal's shell. The carapace was too strong to break but its tree trunk legs buckled, crushed beneath the weight of the falling arch. Femira watched as the creature seized. Its wrought muscles tensed, then went slack, succumbing to the inevitable.

It was all over in moments. A few smaller rocks continued to tumble down the mound of the now buried kragal.

Femira let out a breath.

She'd *killed* it.

The exertion of what she'd just done slammed against her. Her vision blurred and she stumbled. She looked around and saw the remaining kraglings—the ones that Selyn had originally swept up into the ocean—scurrying across the beach. *Oh.* She tried to think through the haze of exhaustion.

Shit. She didn't have the energy to fight them. She could barely keep her eyes open.

She took a step towards them but her legs buckled. She felt hands catching her before she hit the sand. She looked up and saw Landryn's face... then everything went dark.

CHAPTER 38

Follow Your Light

Femira felt the warmth of a campfire on her face and her nose was filled with the sharp scent of the smoke. Her eyes twitched and her body stirred, pulling her from sleep.

Her muscles ached as though she'd spent the day running up the steps of the Pillar. Stiffly, she rose up from her sleeping roll. It was twilight. The sun had already disappeared behind the hills but its light was still casting shades of red and purple on the clouds. The small campfire blazed unhindered by the winds, despite the branches on nearby trees flipping about wildly. *Landryn must be close.*

Femira's mind flashed to her most recent memory; passing out on the beach after she'd killed the kragal. And the kraglings scurrying across the beach.

She laboured to her feet. She was still wearing her black uniform. The camp was set up on the cliffs overlooking the beach and she could see the dark mass of the collapsed sea arch in the gloom of the twilight.

A short distance from the camp, a lone silhouette of a man was shovelling dirt into a hole. Femira approached, the air was so still inside of Landryn's bubble, a direct contrast to the howling wind that passed overhead.

"You're awake," Landryn said as she approached, "I wasn't sure how long you'd be out for." There was a sombre tone in his voice.

There was a cairn of rocks above another patch of freshly churned earth. Wordlessly, Femira took the shovel from him and began filling the rest of the dirt into the pit. *You don't use runewielding when burying your comrades.* In Keiran, they burned their dead, too many scavengers in the desert would dig you up. The Altareans had been like the Reldoni, they buried those that deserved respect, those that didn't were thrown from the cliffs to the crashing waters. Like her brothers had been.

Femira didn't feel any joy over killing the kragal. There was an emptiness to the achievement that Drad and Selyn weren't here to enjoy it with her. It had been just under two weeks, but an indescribable kinship had been built with them in that short time. They'd fought together, camped and shared meals together. The thought of returning home to Epilas without them made her stomach clench.

It had been different before, in the aftermath of the battle against the stormguards at Innish Head. They'd buried their fallen comrades and headed home but Femira had barely known the people that had died. Selyn and Drad hadn't been her friends, but they *had* been a team. She found that her eyes were watering.

"Drad served with me against the Reinish," Landryn said, sadly, "his cousin Ferath and I trained together as boys... he'd always wanted to be a soldier. Even when his father was pushing him to train with the palace surgeons, he wanted to serve in the military..."

"He was a good healer," Femira added. Some healers only healed your wounds just enough that your body would recover easily on its own. Drad would spend the extra effort making sure the wound was completely healed, the skin smooth again.

"I didn't really know Selyn," Femira said, "she was kind of... distant... at first... but I thought, maybe, we were becoming friends." The hole was filled, and Femira began arranging the stones in a small cairn.

"The dead with the dead," Landryn said, his tone turning impassive, "the living with the living."

He turned his heel and returned to the camp.

They shared a silent meal from the provisions in Drad's pack. It was bland compared to the spicy dishes that the man had used to prepare for them. Landryn volunteered for the first watch so that Femira could rest some more.

She didn't feel like sleeping but Landryn insisted. He claimed that the exertion she'd placed on her edir alone would be enough to be assigned bedrest for a week. She reluctantly agreed and the moment she laid her head against her bedroll she was immediately asleep.

Landryn woke her gently as the dawn was beginning to crack.

"You've been up all night," she rubbed at her bleary eyes, noting the pale blue on the horizon. The campfire had long since burned down to embers.

"You needed the rest." He wasn't wrong, her body felt like she'd been showered with rocks... which she had, she realised.

"It was incredible what you did," he said, "I... I don't know how to thank you for saving me. I'm not used to others coming to *my* rescue."

"I don't feel like I saved anyone..." Femira replied, "it was *my* plan... it's my fault that —"

"—Stop," there was a gentle forcefulness in his tone, "there's nothing to be gained from that path, trust me. The dead with the dead."

"If I hadn't been so cocky, if—"

"—Then it wouldn't be just Drad and Selyn's bodies buried. It would be mine in the dirt too and *yours*, and gods know how many more that would've fallen victim to that monstrosity. What you did was heroic, Annali, *never* doubt that."

The flare to her ego momentarily overshadowed the guilt she'd been feeling, Landryn's praise igniting in her a fevered hunger. He held her gaze with his beautiful dark eyes. Misandrei and Garld's praise was like a drug; doses of gratification that she craved and sought out. But Landryn's compliments made her feel different. It felt like fireworks going off inside of her. She could feel a flush rising in her cheeks. She jumped up from her sleeping mat before he could notice.

How could she feel proud of what she'd done? When the cost had been the lives of two people that had trusted her. They'd believed that she could hold the creature down—*she'd* believed it. But she'd been wrong... and now Drad and Selyn were dead.

Landryn didn't seem to think it was her fault. But he was a Prince—and a military commander—he was used to playing with the consequences of life and death. People died because of *his* decisions all the time. Not *hers*... she looked down at her hands. She wasn't *supposed* to be here... she wasn't supposed to be thinking like this. Her breaths came in short. The flush didn't leave her face and she felt herself growing hotter despite the morning chill.

"Annali?" Landryn looked at her with concern.

"It's hot," she gasped.

"Breathe," he said, soothingly and placed a hand on her shoulder. She felt her body tremble underneath it. People weren't supposed to die because of *her*.

A knife sliding into an eye socket.

"Sit back," Landryn instructed her.

She could barely hear him. Her vision swam, Landryn's face blurring. A myriad of faces flashed in her mind. Drad and Selyn listening to her plan on the cliff tops. Her mother scowling at her on a ship. Her brothers' bodies bouncing off the cliffs. *I hadn't even been there.* Femira hadn't been the one to get caught, she hadn't even been on that job... *Had I?* She hadn't seen the stormguards throw her brothers off the cliff, but then why did she have such a vivid image of it in her mind? Had she been there and somehow blocked out the memories surrounding it?

She was dimly aware of Landryn's arms around her shoulder, rocking her back and forth. The image of blood flowing in gutters forced its way into her mind. And she was crying... she'd cried then too.

"Breathe... listen to my voice," she heard Landryn's voice from far away. Blood was being soaked up by the desert clay and there were bright red eyes searching for her. So many people slaughtered... because of *her*. Because she *existed*. Shadows of memories danced on the edge of her mind. She realised her hands were shaking. *No, no, no.* A deep part of her mind stirred, memories she'd shoved into the far away recess of her psyche long ago.

Her brother—much younger than Femira remembered him—dragged her by the hand, running towards a river. Blood ran down the gutters and their mother was ahead of them. "*They've come for you,*" her brother's voice was high, "*come, Fimi, run!*"

"Fimi," Femira breathed. That was what Rashav used to call her. *Fimi and Rashi.* She was choking back sobs now as Rashav's face came into clear definition in her vision. But he was gone... he was dead. Both of them were. Rashav and Kamal... her brothers who'd always protected her.

Her mother was screaming at Kamal to untie the boat but he pretended to fumble at the ropes... he was waiting for Rashav and Femira. He refused to leave without them. Behind her, an ochre-skinned man in golden armour and red eyes, callously cut down every person Femira had ever known.

"Leave her!" her mother had wailed, "he will kill us all!"

"Fimi! Rashi! Run!" Kamal screamed to them. She remembered Rashav lifting her over his shoulder and being thrown into the boat. She remembered watching the smoking huts of their village disappear behind them. She'd been too young to understand what was happening then.

She'd known what *karasi*—a bastard—was. She knew it was a loathsome thing and she knew that her mother was punished because Femira was one. But she was far too young to understand why. The way that Femira's mother looked at her when they were on that boat floating away from their village was a manifestation of the contempt the woman felt for her. Femira was the physical evidence of her mother's sins and she'd hated her for it. From that day onward, Femira was no longer her daughter. She'd been orphaned, and Rashav and Kamal had been tasked with raising her.

Femira didn't know how long she'd been crying for. When she finally felt reality returning to her, she felt Landryn's arms around her, rocking her gently back and forth.

"I... I'm sorry," she choked.

"Everything will be ok," he said reassuringly, "you are new to this. But it does get easier, I promise."

"*Should* it?"

"Death is the only certainty in our work," he spoke with such solemnity that she couldn't help but be drawn into him. "We must overcome death and it's hold on us so that we can protect our people. Only then, can we truly be the shield that holds back the darkness." She nodded along with him. She wanted to be the shield. She wanted to be the reason people *lived*. She didn't want anyone else to die because of her.

"We have a duty," Landryn continued, "we are the chosen; the soulforged. It is our purpose to fight where others cannot." She knew at that moment that she would follow Landryn wherever he would go. That he was her commander, her Prince and her leader. His mission was her life. This was her purpose. This was what Rashav and Kamal would have wanted for her.

***

The days passed by in a blur. Femira and Landryn couldn't press on with just the two of them. They were confident they could handle a couple of kraglings but they both mutually agreed it would be foolish to seek them out. From the knowledge Landryn had on the kraglings, there should have been only the one alpha —the kragal. The kragal was the head of the colony and without it, the creatures wouldn't be able to expand any further. There were still smaller nests that needed to be dealt with but Landryn decided it was best if they returned to Epilas. The reinforcement parties should already be on their way out this direction.

They left the corpse of the dead kragal on the beach. Femira had used her edir senses to locate the sword of nythilium she'd formed from Landryn's armour. As it had when fighting the kragal, the metal of the blade responded to her edir in that bizarre—almost confused—resonance. She could sense it buried deep beneath the fallen rocks of the sea arch, embedded within the body of the kragal itself.

She attempted to recall the metal but it wouldn't respond. Not at this distance and with so much material between her and the sword. Landryn assured her that no looters would be capable enough to dig it out and dissect the creature to claim the metal, not before a team sent from the palace arrived, that is. The scholars at the palace would want to study the kragal and they could recover the precious metal.

Landryn told her that he had vague and hazy memories of the battle. He remembered the darkness of her stoneshell. He recalled the looming maw of the kragal above them. He had felt his armour dissolving around him as she did the impossible. She explained to him the dissonance of the metal when she reached out to it and the flashes of images she'd felt through the edir. He'd never heard of anything like it before.

For four days they travelled back the road they'd come. Femira did her best to shove the surfaced memories of her brothers back into the corners of her mind. She wasn't ready to unpack any of that right now. She wasn't sure if she ever would be.

Lucky for her, there was plenty of distraction on the journey south. People *cheered* as they passed through towns and villages. Prince Landryn Tredain and Annali Jahar were collecting renown as the 'Saviours of the Tidewall'.

Before, when they'd passed through, mayors and innkeepers would bow and scrape out of duty and respect for their Prince. Now, they did so out of reverence for both of them.

The kragal's slain body was left visible under the broken sea arch. Locals used to call the place Temple Beach, for the way the rock formations resembled the spires of a temple. Considering the arch was now gone and the enormous shell of a mythological beast now decorated the place, people had started referring to it as Kragalsbane Beach.

All across the Tidewall, towns and villages spoke of the shattered shells of kraglings strewn across the beaches that Landryn's team had left in their wake. Landryn was quick to decorate the achievement of taking down the kragal as Femira's—or rather Annali's.

In the barracks, soldiers had been taught to withhold any information to local authorities until a debrief could be had with a senior officer. Landryn was as senior as it got in the military and he seemed to have little regard for hiding what had happened from the mayors and town lords that they met on their journey back south. It was clear that he was trying to ease them into believing the threat had been dealt with, that their towns and villages were now safe from sea monsters. But there was another element to what he was doing. He spoke about how the bloodshedders had been trained for this and how exceptional a fighting force they were. How the crown valued the lives of their people, and that they would be protected.

The story of how Femira had killed the kragal was a mantra that he repeated at each new place they arrived. Then he would lead into the rest. Femira couldn't help the pride she felt as Landryn spoke but each time he called her Annali, it was like a spike in her chest. It was a constant reminder of the lies she was telling him. And coupled with it was the lie for why she'd pushed him to continue this far north in the first place. His brother was dead… and she was still hiding it from him.

Femira wondered if would Landryn would think so highly of her if he knew she was lying to him. If he knew that she was *karasi*? The Reldoni didn't seem to look upon sexual promiscuity with as much disdain as the Keiran did. Aden had told her that many Reldoni highborn had bastards. They were usually well looked after by the noble houses. Often given lower-ranking but respectable military positions, or married off to wealthy associates. They weren't highborn, like their siblings, but they weren't hated either. Not like *karasi*. To be *karasi* in Keiran was a crime. Especially if you are the *karasi* of a noble house.

As they left one town, Femira awkwardly worked up the courage to ask him to stop calling her Annali.

"You wish for me to call you Vreth, like the other bloodshedders?" He asked, incredulous. The nickname was one she'd held for so long in Altarea that it was synonymous to her actual name.

"I don't want to be called Annali," she replied. *Not by you.*

"What would you prefer I call you?" he asked, a playful smile on his lips. *Femira.*

"I…" she faltered, "Vreth is fine."

"I can't introduce you as that in these towns," he laughed, "they'll think I'm mocking you." How bad would it really be if she told him the truth? He would understand why she'd kept it from him, wouldn't he? Garld had *asked* her to. She'd be betraying Garld's instruction if she did… and she owed Garld everything. He'd given her the power she now held. He'd taken her from nothing in Altarea and given her prestige and purpose… she couldn't just throw that away.

"Nevermind," Femira sighed. What did it matter if Landryn thought her name was Annali? It wasn't as though he'd ever meet the real Annali. She was dead... probably. Femira tried to recall what the woman had looked like. She remembered her from the night in Altarea when Garld had found her. Had he seen the resemblance then? Was it so obvious? She'd foolishly assumed the Reldoni were all blind to the difference between them. But maybe those had just been superficial differences. Annali had been beautiful; she'd had long black hair that fell in waves whereas Femira's was shorter and usually scraggly when not tied up in a braid. Like most female highborn, Annali's face had been coated in a mask of makeup. Perhaps underneath it, Femira and Annali did look alike. Annali's own cousin had said so.

"What became of Honorsword Jahasa?" Femira asked after a few moments. Landryn seemed surprised by the question. The two were walking, guiding their newly acquired horses by the reins along a cliff path. Femira had learned that the best way to keep your horse from tiring was to give it regular breaks from your weight on its back.

"My father decided he was too dangerous to keep as a prisoner."
"He was released?" Femira's head spun in surprise.
"No," Landyn replied, flatly.
"Oh."
"The Honorswords were never here for peace. The Emperor doesn't *want* peace, he might entertain the idea for a time but he will never be content with it." He gave her a thoughtful look, "have you ever met him?"

"The *Emperor*?" Femira couldn't help but laugh. She knew it wasn't an unrealistic idea for a highborn woman like Annali to have met the Emperor of Keiran but the way in which Landryn so innocently asked her that was just too amusing.

"I'll take that as a no."
"Women aren't permitted in the Emperor's Court," Femira replied, she knew that much at least. If there was one thing that could be relied on for Keiran culture; it was the inherent sexism.

"Do you think he will retaliate?" Femira followed up, "for killing his Honorswords?"

"Potentially," Landryn speculated, "The Emperor, I believe, wants to make a move for Rien. But from what our spies tell us, his warlords are too busy fighting each other for him to be able to make any substantial moves against us. His Honorswords —while overzealous in their devotion to the Emperor—are too busy maintaining order in Keiran than to be mobilised as a true invading force. If the Emperor was going to go to war with Reldon, he would have done so when we reclaimed Altarea. The Keiran showed they don't have the unity—or strength—to rally to the aid of their so-called ally. The Honorswords were sent to bluster and intimidate. They were sent as a show of Keiran's power. I think that the Emperor may truly believe that his elite are unique—that only *they* hold the secrets of soulforging. I would have allowed them to return home, thinking that they'd demonstrated their prowess and frightening us out of any kind of military manoeuvres against them. But then..." he looked at her apologetically.

"But then one of them tried to kill me," she surmised. *Fuck, she really threw a spanner in the gears there.*

"My father chastised me for defending you. He thinks I should have let the Keiran deal with their own... but how could I? When I spoke out against them at

Judgement Hall, I said that you were under my protection. What message would that send to our people?" *Is that the only reason you did it?*

"The Emperor's pride will take a hit, but his grip on power in his own country is too weak to risk war with us."

"Is that what you told your father?"

"I reminded him that we are Reldoni. That we do not yield. We do not bend nor cower before our enemies. We show strength and we cut down our enemies or we die in the effort," Landryn took on a coldly distant expression as he spoke. Those didn't sound like his words.

Later that evening, they reached Innish Head and it was there that they finally met up with the reinforcement contingent that had been sent after them. When Kendrick had arrived at Epilas a week before; injured and with the news of the kraglings. Garld had dispatched another team of six bloodshedders along with the support of thirty infantry soldiers from Mattice's division.

Femira recognised some of the bloodshedders. Some were recently soulforged —like her. Landryn gave them an account of the events over the previous weeks. They looked at her with a mixture of respect and disbelief after Landryn had told them of the battle against the kragal.

Landryn and Femira then went over battle strategies with the new team along with how to find and expose the nests.

"We're not staying with them?" Femira asked Landryn after the bloodshedders had left to set up their camp outside the town.

"No," he replied, "we're returning to Epilas. The kragal was more… destructive… than I thought it would be. I don't know how it managed to infest such a significant part of our country so quickly. Yours and Endrin's accounts were some of the first reports and that was barely a month ago. If the draega can spread that quickly, then we need to increase the patrols on our other borders. The plains of Athlin are mostly ignored by our military. Athlin is a wild land, with no king… no unity. As a result we've mostly ignored that border, but if there are draega in the plains, growing and spreading…" he shook his head. "The War Council needs to make a decision with what we do. If there's more of these things out there then we *need* to make a plan."

CHAPTER 39

Out of the Frying Pan and into the Freezer

The two spires of Twin Garde appeared first, looming up from the fog like a pair of grey spirits in the sky. The icraft glided along the flat stretch of ice, the wind filling the sail. Daegan could make out the outlines of the surrounding pine trees on the horizon. In the misty haze, the whole area looked washed out like a faded painting.

"Place has seen better days," Rowan commented as the battered battlements of the keep came into view.

"Been a lot of trouble up in Twin Garde the last few months," Ardy put in.

"I'd heard," Rowan replied and left it at that. Daegan leaned back on the bench, Tanlor rested beside him. The man had been coming in and out of consciousness for hours.

Twin Garde was built on a rocky outcrop on the north shore of Nortara. It was the largest military post that the Dukedom had on this side of the frozen lake. There was a small dock with a handful of icerafts already docked.

Ardy pulled on a series of levers and the wheels of the raft clunked out to lift the runners off the ice. Daegan watched the man's actions with interest.

They hadn't needed to stop at any stage of their journey across the ice. *It wasn't like there was anywhere to stop at.* When it had gotten too dark to continue, Ardy had simply taken down the sail and let them slowly glide to a rest and they'd slept cramped together under blankets on the raft floor.

Ardy retracted the sail and allowed the momentum of the iceraft to carry them closer to the docks. Neither Rowan or Ardy seemed concerned with the rapid speed of their approach and Daegan suppressed his worry.

"Hold on," Ardy called out. Daegan saw Rowan grab the side rail firmly with one hand and planted a strong palm on Tanlor's chest to hold the man in place. Daegan gripped the edges of the bench just before Ardy pulled on a wooden lever. There was a loud screech as the brakes clamped onto the wheels. Locked in place, the wheels still glided over the ice and Ardy pulled another lever which angled the raft, controlling the swerve and maintaining course. Then, in a fluid motion, the Aeth man stood up and kicked at a metal box at the edge of the raft. The box tumbled off the edge of the rail and made a loud thump as it fell heavily onto the hard ice.

Daegan's mind flashed with the image of the box cracking through the ice and the raft sinking into the frigid waters. A metal chain affixing the box to the raft, rattled as it was pulled out of the raft. *An anchor!* The solution was so mind-bogglingly simple.

Daegan gripped hard onto the bench and braced for the...

He lurched forward, his head whipping as the raft was abruptly pulled into a

355

swerve. It glided around the anchor in a dizzying spin until eventually coming to a stop. Daegan felt like he was going to vomit. He'd lost count of how many times the raft had circled about the anchor.

"Is that the *only* way to stop this thing?" Daegan mumbled.

"Only way that doesn't involve tipping the raft over," Ardy replied jovially.

"Surely you could just pull in the sail earlier?"

"Nah," Ardy pulled out a long stick, "too hard to time it right, we'd end up too far away," the stick had a flat end like a hammer which was wrapped in cloth. Ardy pushed it against the ice and the raft was slowly pushed forward.

"You, muscles," Ardy said to Rowan, "you can probably get us into dock quicker than me."

"We all have our roles to play," Rowan replied and made no move to take the stick from the Aeth. Ardy mumbled something under his breath and continued working, slowly directing the raft into the dock. It was an arduously slow process. *Ok, I get the reason for the anchor now.* It would've taken them hours to push this rig to the dock if they'd been left any further out on the ice.

There were four soldiers already waiting on the docks for them, their tabards were blue with two light grey towers for the insignia. Each of the four had the Rubanian style warriors cut, shaved at the side with a braid on top, similar to Rowan and Tanlor's. The man at the front had a red beard and face so weathered that Daegen thought it unlikely the man had ever been indoors.

Daegan thought apprehensively back to the group of deserters that they'd killed only two weeks before. *They'd come from Twin Garde.* They'd spoken of mutiny in the place.

"Twin Garde welcomes you," redbeard said, "state your names and business."

"Name's Rowan," Rowan stood up on the raft, "this my brother, Tanlor, and our employer, Desmond," he pointed to Daegan, "Des is a mapmaker, he's charting the area." Daegan waited in anticipation for the ridicule on his task like he'd been greeted with in other towns. To his surprise, the man didn't make any comment on it, just a simple nod.

"Rowan and Tanlor..." the man mused, "are you Taran Shrydan's boys?"

"That we are," Rowan beamed back.

"Name's Mika, from Heronsbridge. I was in Duke Buran's contingent in the Balfold, six years ago. You boys were there then, if I'm not mistaken."

"Aye," Rowan replied.

"Showed up in good time then. Can't say we'd have held on much longer."

"It was a good fight," Rowan nodded, then his eyes drifted up to the damaged walls of the keep. "I'd heard there was trouble up here the past few weeks," Rowan commented, "I'd heard Commander Sheeth was killed?" Mika's gaze followed Rowan's over the keep and he sighed.

"Aye," Mika replied sadly, "he's dead."

"What happened?"

"There's been a lot going on up here."

"Rakmen?" Those deserters had said they'd been involved with Sheeth's death. Daegan kept his mouth shut and let Rowan continue to lead the conversation. He was likely trying to figure out who was now in control before making the man aware that they'd killed some deserters on the road.

"More than ever before," Mika spat, "been coming down further too. Sheeth sent out a big hunting party, trying to route out their camps and push them back to the hills..."

"Some didn't agree?"

"Aye, *some*... cowards. Most of 'em here because they've no place else to go. Not real soldiers. Krast, Hovis and Ox, they'd not been happy with how Sheeth had been running the place, and they'd collected a few of the others that wanted a change. Waited until we were all gone a week and they killed him... took the keep and killed those still loyal to Sheeth... it was a fucking mess."

"Who's in control now?" Rowan asked with concern.

"Captain Crann was leading the expedition to root out the Rak. He was... not happy when we came back... ten days trying to take back our castle from our own fucking men. Crann though, he wouldn't give in, not after what them bastards did to Sheeth. On the tenth day we finally got through the gate. He'd had Hovis hanged but Karst and Ox had managed to slip out with some others before we'd come back. All those that'd supported Hovis—well, Crann had no sympathy for 'em and had each one of 'em beheaded, those that didn't run before we got back that is... rest of us left were all loyal to Sheeth and we're happy to follow Crann now."

"A waste," Rowan shook his head.

"Aye, we should be fighting the Rakmen, not killing each other."

"There's still some of the deserters out in the woods?"

"Aye," Mika replied, his eyes looking over the surrounding woodlands, "not found Karst or Ox yet but Crann's got lads out scouting. Messengers sent south to Rubastre as well, we're hoping the Duke will send more men to help hold the keep from the next rak assault."

"Ox is dead," Rowan said levelly and Mika's head whipped to him, his eyes narrowing in suspicion.

"We met him along the road, big guy? Red hair and warrior's beard?" Rowan indicated his own as similar. "Thick neck. Maybe forty-odd?"

"Sounds like him."

"Was travelling with a grey haired fellow with a bow—Geral and a younger lad, Jax."

"Aye, Geral wouldn't have been far from Ox. And Jax—well—he's just a pup who'd made some bad choices in friends."

"They attacked me and my companions not too far south from Urundock, and tried to rob us."

"I didn't think they'd fall so low so quick," Mika grimaced, "Crann'll be relieved to hear you took care of 'em."

Daegan noted how Rowan specifically excluded mentioning Shye but again decided it was best to continue allowing Rowan to lead. Rowan went on to explain how his brother had been injured in the fighting—opting to allude that it was the fight with Ox and the other deserters that had led to Tanlor's injury—and explained how he needed healing.

Not long later, Mika was leading the three of them through the keep's courtyard and up one of the round towers. Rowan and Daegan each supported Tanlor's weight. The man's eyes had a dazed cast over them. Ardy was left at the docks to tie up his raft and check over it. The man would likely be quick to find his way to the only tavern in the outpost soon enough.

They carried Tanlor up to the infirmary where they laid him down on a bed and explained the head injury to the healer. The healer was a tired-looking, bespeckled and grey-haired man, who asked direct questions in quick succession.

"When did this happen?"

"Have you let him sleep?"

"Is he drinking?"

"Can he speak?"

"What hit him in the head? A hammer, a mace, a fist?..." *Well technically it was a dock that hit his head...* but that was hard to explain. "His head was hit a few times against the ground," Daegan explained.

"He's lucky," the healer sucked a breath through his teeth, "ok, I will work on his wounds but it will take some time." They left Tanlor in the care of the healer, sprawled out on one of the beds.

Mika then led them up to the Commander's office where they were introduced to Commander Crann. The man had long hair that was more grey than black, tied back in a braid. He had a scar that went right down the side of his face, leaving a bald patch in his eyebrow and beard. Similar to Mika, the man did not look like he'd spent much of his life working in a command office.

"So..." Crann greeted as they entered, "I have you to thank for killing that traitor, Ox, and his weasel friend, Geral. Two less men for me to worry about."

"Commander Crann," Rowan inclined his head respectfully and then introduced Daegan as Desmond the Cartographer.

"No offence, lad, but we don't need map makers," Crann said, "we need more soldiers."

"Has there been any response back from Rubastre?" Rowan asked.

"Not yet," Crann sighed, "truth be told, when we spotted your raft, we were hoping you were carrying news. I've sent requests for reinforcements to Urundock, Garron, Rubastre, Nordock... anyone who'd listen... but so far we've gotten nothing."

"They like to forget about us up here," Mika put in, "but every season there's more and more of the rak fuckers coming south. And more of the men are getting worried."

"Aye," Crann added, "ones that killed Commander Sheeth were cowards, to be sure, but there's a reason they were so scared... strange stories coming from the uplanders, stories of monsters roaming the hills and rakmen crossing the snowfields in the droves beyond the mountains. One of my own men *swears* he saw a fuckin' dogman out in the woods a few weeks back. A dogman!"

"People will always tell wild stories," Rowan commented.

"Aye, suppose there's stories of your old fella fighting dogmen and dragons and gods know what else... I was sad to hear about Taran's passing, he was a good man. Very different to how the stories painted him."

"You knew him well?" Rowan asked, his eyebrows going up.

"He'd stop by here each time he'd go north. I remember him bringing you and your brother when you were wee boys a few times. I'd heard the pair of you had grown to be good soldiers."

"We do alright," Rowan replied, likely knowing where Crann was leading to.

"We need good men, Rowan. We need numbers or the rak are going to take these towers... and once they're in, it's going to take a lot more men to take it back. Duke's don't seem to realise that... or maybe they just don't care."

"I don't doubt you, but I'm already on a contract," Rowan shook his head, then nodded to Daegan.

"Aye," Crann grunted, eying Daegan suspiciously, "not much point mapping the area if it's going to be all rak land soon enough. I hope you lads aren't planning on heading north."

"West," Daegan replied, speaking for the first time since arriving and finding his voice breaking as he did, "to Nordock. The maps for those areas are shockingly outdated." He hadn't a clue what the maps were like for that region but in Daegan's experience, cartographers always wanted more up-to-date maps and could be quite pedantic about it.

"That's dangerous territory," Crann warned, "we've gotten no reports from Thuris Keep in almost a month. Last we heard there were sightings of large groups of rakmen coming south from Shadowpeaks Pass. They've broken down as far as the Balfold before, my guess is they've done it again. You lads would be better off going straight south; to Urundock and then on to Garron, and taking the cliff road."
"Too long," Rowan replied, "we've got to be there in a week."
"That'll be a hard run," Crann grunted, "you sure there's nothing I can't do to convince you to stay here and fight with us?" He directed the question to Rowan.

Daegan couldn't help himself from feeling pity for the man. He was stranded and abandoned in a remote outpost in a frozen, forgotten part of the world—not unlike Daegan himself—struggling with external threats as well as fighting from within his own men, and the Duke's couldn't give two shits for this region.

Daegan made a mental note to question Rowan on why the Duke's even bothered to man outposts this side of the Notara Sheet in the first place. *And why in the hells did Arch-duke Edmund think it would be a good idea to send me out here?* The more and more Daegan thought about it, he just could not understand the man's rationale.

"I feel for your men," Rowan said, "I really do. I don't envy the charge you've got up here. My brother is in the personal guard for Arch-duke Edmund. I promise you, when we return to Rubastre, we will inform the Duke of your plight here."
"I thank you for that," Crann nodded his head, "and your cousin, Duke Boern, would he sympathise with our situation? Would he send reinforcements, do you think?"
"Boern despises the rak… but he's also not concerned with lands outside of his domain. He'll rally men if the rak break into the Balfold. But he'd not likely send any further north than that."
"Will you speak with him?"
"I'll do my best," Rowan said carefully. Daegan knew that Rowan's relationship with Boern was tenuous. He guessed that Rowan was lying, trying to placate Crann.

"I would appreciate that," Crann replied, "Our healer—Yaref—might be past his prime but he knows his business and has been fixing up wounds here since before either of us were born. He'll do what he can for your brother. His injuries, as I understand, are minimal. Way I see it, we owe you that much for taking care of that traitor Ox. We're not lacking in provisions, so feel free to head down to the mess hall for a meal… also plenty of spare beds now in the barracks too," he added while shaking his head, "make yourselves at home, lads."
"Your hospitality is a welcome change," Rowan grinned.
"Can't say it's from the goodness of my heart," Crann replied, "I need men, Rowan. Even if you're only here for a few days, you've a sword and an arm to wield it."

***

"Pleasure doing business," Ardy grinned a yellow toothed smile, pocketing the coins that Daegan handed him.
"When are we off out'a this dive?" Ardy asked, knocking back a tankard of ale. The

mess hall was filled with old dented tables occupied by soldiers in light blue tabards. Occasionally, some would drift over and offer thanks and respect to Rowan for putting down Ox. Some gave him dark looks as they passed. It was evident that this place was still reeling from mutiny.

"As soon as Tanlors recovered," Daegan replied.

"They reckon he should be good to travel again in the next two days," Rowan added, "but I'm not sure I want to hang around that long. Ferath will be swift on our heels."

"We should leave in the morning then," Ardy responded, a slight shrill in his voice.

"If Tanlor's alright to move then we will," Daegan concluded. He didn't like the idea of rushing Tanlor back onto the raft. He'd rather the man have a few days recovery under the watch and attention of a bloodstone healer. But he also felt the mounting shadow of Ferath's pursuit.

"I do have half a mind to suggest we stay here," Rowan put in, "Crann seems a decent man. Having more fighting men around might not be a bad idea for when Ferath catches up to us again. Maybe we should consider setting a trap for him here."

"These men have enough on their plate," Daegan shook his head, "I don't want to add to their troubles." It was only a small lie. Daegan *did* feel somewhat remorseful for bringing more danger to these people, but he would be lying to himself if he didn't acknowledge that it was his own desire to go home that drove his decision to continue.

"Tanlor won't like the plan," Rowan directed towards Daegan. *No, he probably won't.*

"I can convince him," Daegan replied half-heartedly, "we know Ferath will never give up. Getting back to Epilas is the best thing we can do. Surely now, he'll be able to see that too."

***

Tanlor was already sitting up in his bed when Daegan entered the infirmary. A bandage wrapped around his head with a dark stain where he had bled from. The dressings that Rowan had applied to his wounded leg were already changed with clean linens.

"Tell this man that I'm fine," Tanlor said to Daegan as he entered, nodding to the grey-haired healer from earlier—Yaref.

"Yes, because *I* healed your wounds," Yaref scolded. "But this healing comes with a price, yes? Surely a soldier such as yourself knows this. You are experiencing the adrenaline rush? Of course you are! This is not your body, I can assure, no, no. This is your *edir*. It is surging, you see? To accelerate the natural healing process of your body. It is a famous error to mistake this feeling for being completely fine but I assure you this; once your edir has finished the job, it will crash... this energy you have will flee from you faster than the winds." Yaref then laid a gentle but firm hand on Tanlor's chest pressing him back into the bed. "Rest," he instructed. "Allow your edir to continue its work, and then your body to rest."

"We'll leave in the morning," Daegan said reassuringly to Tanlor.

"No, no," Yaref's head whipped towards Daegan, "are you the healer here? No? You have a bloodstone on you? I didn't think so. This man will stay here for two days, no less than this. He needs sleep. You young men are always all the same. Rush, rush, rush, but this will kill you if you continue this way. Allow your body to rest."

Tanlor was rolling his eyes as the healer walked away from them, continuing to mutter to himself about the recklessness of younger men.

"So not tomorrow then," Daegan said with a smirk. The two men's eyes met awkwardly and Daegan shifted his step uncomfortably, "I wanted to thank you," Daegan said.

"There's no need," Tanlor replied, "just doing my job."

"Still," Daegan insisted, "I was... being..." he fumbled.

"Really, it's fine," Tanlor breathed, laying his head back onto the pillow.

"Where's Rowan?" Tanlor asked, his eyes closing, "I want to run over the plan with him for heading north. He remembers the trails around here better than me."

Daegan felt an anxious knot form in his stomach.

"We, uh," Daegan started, "we're not going north." Tanlor's eyes snapped back open.

"What?"

"I'm heading home—"

"—You can't be serious!" Tanlor pushed himself back up on the bed, his brow furrowing. "You've *seen* Ferath fight and you want to just offer yourself on a platter to him?!"

"I *need* to get back to Reldon," Daegan maintained, "Rowan's agreed to escort me to Nordock. I would have you too if you want to join us."

Tanlor's expression turned dark.

"No," he growled, "you're staying up here until Edmund calls us back to Rubastre."

"I'm sorry, Tanlor, but no," Daegan defended, "I *need* to return home... I need to figure out who is trying to have me killed and I can't do that if I'm running off into the hills from assassins."

"You *owe* me," Tanlor rebuffed.

"You're right... I do," he granted, "and that's why I'm *asking* you to stay with me... let me repay you when we get to Epilas."

"I'm not going to abandon my duty," Tanlor said with resolution.

"What is Edmund offering you that I cannot?"

Tanlor was quiet for a moment while they held each other's gaze. Daegan admired Tanlor's adamant loyalty to the Arch-duke, but there was a part of him that felt there was more to it than that. Daegan had spent the past two weeks seething at Tanlor for the way that he'd spoken to him. People had been rude to him his entire life, sometimes outright hostile but it had stung when he'd been on the receiving end from Tanlor. However, throughout his anger he never put any thoughts to the words Tanlor had actually said.

Tanlor's jaw was tensing now, the way it had that day in the yard. *You're not better than me. I'm not good enough for your halls, your parties... your daughters.* The man clearly had issues when it came to nobility. He was a bodyguard to rich and powerful people but his own grandfather had been the Duke of Garronforn.

Yaref seemed to take the gap in their conversation as an opportunity to walk over to them, "you're Taran the Hunter's son if I'm not mistaken?" Tanlor shot the man daggers with his eyes but the bespectacled man didn't even look up from a notebook he was reading over.

"Yes, yes... you are. Your brother, the red haired brute. I thought it was you two. I healed your father's broken arm once before, you know." Tanlor didn't take his eyes off Daegan as the healer spoke, nor did he respond to the man.

"Such a humble man, your father, a good honest man. I was so sorry to hear about his passing." Daegan felt the fire in Tanlor's eyes.

"Now is not the best time," Daegan directed to Yaref who didn't seem to take the hint at all.

"Did your father tell you the story?" Yaref continued, "he was hunting a ferrax, can you believe it?! Normally, I would scoff at such endeavours, but a hero like your father... well, yes, yes, if anyone was going to take down one of those, it would–"

"–He didn't tell me about it," Tanlor scowled at the man, his tone had a sharp edge to it and Yaref finally seemed to catch that he was pushing a sensitive topic.

"Ah, well, um, another time, so, yes," and then he was ambling back to the other side of the infirmary.

Tanlor's jaw was tense and Daegan sat down on the bed next to him.

"You hate him?" Daegan tried, "your father? For lying to you?" Tanlor glared at Daegan, his face curled in anger. He reached forward and Daegan jumped embarrassingly in surprise. Tanlor grabbed for his grey travelling cloak hanging by his bed and fished inside it roughly.

Daegan did his best to hold a face of understanding compassion. *I'm your friend.* He tried to convey in it, *you can talk to me.* Tanlor pulled out a topaz of all things. It was dim but Tanlor closed his eyes and breathed out a sigh.

"It's ok to hate him," Daegan said. *Gods know that I hate mine.* The anger seemed to melt away from Tanlor's face, and he looked down.

"I don't..." Tanlor faltered, "I never hated him... I *idolised* him."

"And he lied to you."

"No one ever asks about *me*. I've been in more battles than my father ever was. *I've* been the hero. All I've wanted..." he sighed, "Taran the Hunter, that's all people ever want to hear about. Nobody cares about the things *I've* done."

"I'm not so sure about that," Daegan offered, optimistically, "rescuing the kids at Crossroads. That story was being told in every town we passed through..." then he mused for a moment, "you've saved the life of a Reldoni prince... twice actually."

"No one will ever hear of this story though."

"Maybe... maybe not... come with me to Epilas. Let your story be known." Tanlor met Daegan's eye again. There was no awkwardness in it this time. No distrust or hostility. "I'm asking you as my friend," Daegan implored, "I need you."

Tanlor's head bowed, his expression softening, turning thoughtful. Then his head twisted back to his cloak, he swung his legs out from the bed and reached for it again.

"Hey, hey," Daegan started to protest. He didn't want another scolding from Yaref but Tanlor waved him off. He reached into an inner pocket in the cloak and pulled out a small piece of smooth jade and stuffed away his topaz. Daegan watched in confusion as Tanlor slumped back on to the bed, staring at the small green rock.

"That's...?" Daegan started.

"A signal stone," Tanlor replied quietly.

"Ah," Daegan replied in understanding. *Bondstone.* A rare and expensive runestone, more valuable than bloodstone—or even a Foebreaker's diamond.

"The Arch-duke has its pair?" Daegan guessed and Tanlor nodded, not taking his eyes off the stone.

"It should turn red," Tanlor said, "when its companion stone is activated."

"What happens then?"

"I take you back to Rubastre."

"And then?"

"...And then Edmund gives me everything I've ever wanted."

"And what is that?" Daegan asked carefully. Tanlor looked up from the stone.

"Danielle," he said softly.

Danielle? Daegan's mind flicked through the names and faces of the nobility he'd met in Rubastre. He'd met a lot of women in the months that he'd been there, but his mind rested on one. "Duke Harfallow's daughter?" Daegan recalled her blond hair, her alabaster skin, her kind words. He'd met her on a few occasions. She had been cordial, but Daegan could tell she had only been meeting with him to appease a request from her father.

"We've been in love for years," Tanlor spoke lightly now, his eyes sparking with a joy that Daegan had never seen in them before.

"Harfallow doesn't approve?"

"He doesn't know… he would never…"

"I understand."

"If you understand then you know why I can't let you go…"

A horn sounded outside and both men's heads whipped around at the sound. Yaref was on his feet again rushing to the door, his face a mask of alarm.

"What is it?" Daegan asked but the man had already disappeared through the doorway. Tanlor was getting up out of the bed and Daegan met his eyes, "what's happening?"

"That's a war horn… someone is attacking Twin Garde."

CHAPTER 40

The Deepest Blues are Black

Moments after the horn sounded, Rowan was taking steps two at a time to the battlements. The sky was utterly black, neither ecko nor luna's light breaking through the overcast.

Soldiers in armour that glinted in the torchlight milled about, rushing to their posts. Rowan spotted a man with a captain's plume sticking up from his helm and pressed towards him.

"Captain! Do you need another sword?" The captain's face was mostly obscured by his helm but Rowan could see the man looking him up and down, taking in his warrior's cut, his chainmail and sword.

"You're one of the lads who arrived today?" the Captain asked.

"Rowan Shrydan," he nodded.

"Grest," the man replied, "the night scouts have reported a rak war party on their way here."

"How many?"

"Scouts claim they saw a score of 'em but you know how it is, they're good at keepin' themselves hidden. 'Specially at night."

"And how many on the towers?" Rowan asked, his eyes scanning over the soldiers. Their armour was dented and their swords chipped. These weren't the markers of novice fighters. These were men who'd seen and fought rakmen regularly.

"We barely had over seventy before the trouble with Ox, Hovis and Karst..." he shook his head in frustration. "Now, we're forty... at best." *Not terrible odds*. They had superior numbers and they had the battlements. However rakmen were a different breed to ordinary men. They were larger, stronger and if they had a runewielder...

"I have a topaz," Rowan confided, "as does my brother. Tanlor also has aradium. We're battle trained with them."

"Good," Grest nodded, and pointed to a group of soldiers arrayed above the tower closest the gate, "we've split the grenadiers and stonebreakers between the towers but this one could do with another."

Rowan saluted—thumping a fist on his chest—and Grest responded in kind.

Not long after, Rowan was atop the tower amongst the other runewielders. There were two grenadiers, each had a collection of powder explosives in iron boxes close at hand. Another three stonebreakers were dotted along the tower battlement, closer to the gate, mixed in with the archers and a few riflemen. Only one of the stonebreakers was battle-trained, the other two were smithies. When the number of fighting men was low, you enlisted everyone who could deal some damage. Rowan even spotted the grey-haired healer who'd taken care of Tanlor, decked in chainmail, a mace in one hand and a shield in the other, taking up position at the rear.

Crann and Mika were on the other tower, directing the rangers into formation. Twin Garde wasn't a large outpost. The barracks were housed within the two stone towers and a high wooden wall surrounded the towers. It wasn't a town, although a few non-military folk did reside there. Those people retreated into the safety of the towers when the horns were sounded. A low windowless building connected the two towers. The doors to it were sealed and barred in preparation.

There were a dozen men atop each tower, with another five on the battlements roof of the connecting building. It was a strong defensive position to be holding, the fact that the towers sat atop a rocky outcrop not-withstanding. Rowan didn't envy the task of trying to take the towers.

Rowan spotted Tanlor's blond head appear on the other tower, accompanied by Daegan—his revolver and sword in hand. *Good lad.* The Daegan he'd met a month ago would've been hiding inside the tower with that cowardly Aeth. Rowan had seen it happen before, young lads thrown into the deep end. Highborn youth often had dreams of becoming renowned knights, a lot of them carried aspirations of following in the footsteps of their ancestor's glory. But reality is quick to set in. Long hard rides in the cold, the fear of having your life on the line, a lot of them just can't hack it and give up after a few months. Occasionally, you'd get one that grows into a harder man. One who adapts and changes with the snowfalls. He wouldn't have thought Daegan would be one of the latter but here he was; sword-in-hand and about to fight an unknown enemy.

Tanlor had the gait of a man recently healed. He was fidgety. His greatsword drawn. It was the adrenaline, working with his edir to heal his wounds. That rush was a powerful thing, but it was also dangerous. Rowan had been healed more times than he could remember. In battle, he'd had to be restrained from returning to the fray after a field healer had fixed him up. The healing gave you a temporary boost but your body would crash with exhaustion soon after. You did not want to be facing an enemy when that happened. If Rowan was on that tower he would have scolded Tanlor for being there, but his brother was a grown man, and this was his decision. Hopefully, the need for melee fighting wouldn't arise.

Any man who's fought against the rak knew it was better to take them down before it came to one-on-one. In single combat, rak always had the advantage. They were larger, stronger and faster. Their flaw was that they rarely fought as a team and almost never worked in co-ordinated attacks, taking them down was achievable if you had the superior numbers.

Rowan recalled the first time he'd faced a rak. He'd heard they were large, but being a big guy himself, Rowan had anticipated facing someone roughly his own height. The rak had *towered* above him, his thick curved blade coming in fast, brutal sweeps. The rak had wielded a weapon larger and heavier than Tanlor's like it was a rapier.

"You need some?" The grenadier next to Rowan asked, he knelt measuring pouches of gunpowder out of his iron strongbox.

"If you've any to spare."

"If you use it to kill some rak, I won't complain none," he gestured to the mound of pouches leaning up against the battlement.

"Name's Puck, you're Rowan?"

"Yup."

"Taran the Hunter's son?"

"That's me."

"Well I'm glad you're here," Puck cast a worrying glance at the surrounding trees, "you fought 'em before?"
"Aye, at Balfold. Every now and then, some get spotted south of Nortara, too."
"So you know, then,"
"I know… they're not easy to kill."

***

Ardy scowled when the fat cook asked for a swig of his flask. The man's face was blotchy and held an expectant expression. Like Ardy would really just *hand over* his flask to this stranger. But then again, this man controlled the kitchens. Always a clever move to be on the good side of the kitchen staff. He'd learned that when working on old Alron's ship.

He flashed the man a grin and handed the flask over. A generous offering today could mean a few extra tankards of ale with his dinner tomorrow. *That's assuming we live.* Another blast sounded outside and Ardy felt his heart lurch in his chest. *Oh how I hate grenadiers… soot-stained and stinking of sulphur.* The grenadiers that worked the cannons on Alron's ship had always insisted on an extra store of spirits for themselves. They claimed it was for the machines but Ardy would catch them taking sips throughout the day. *The bastards.*

He watched as the cook took a hearty gulp, and then *another!* Ardy reached his hand back out to the man and clicked his fingers before the man emptied the blasted thing. The cook gave him an apologetic look, handing it back.
"Uh," he stammered, wiping spittle from his chin, "just need to settle the nerves, y'know yerself."
"Yeah, yeah," Ardy grumbled, then took a swig himself. The whitewhiskey tickled as it went down and he felt a comforting warmth spreading in his belly. He closed his eyes and tried to remember the calming lapping waves of the sea once again. Another blast hit outside, pulling him from his tranquillity.

"How'd an Aeth end up here anyways?" the cook asked and Ardy sighed. *Oh yes, the usual series of questions.* He normally tolerated them if there was a promise of a friendly drink to be awarded throughout the telling. Desmond's company had been endured initially for this reason, and then because he was a friendly enough fellow… doubly because he was rich and didn't seem to care how much of his money was spent on friendly drinks. He was the kind of man that Ardy would latch onto for as long as he could.

That is if the man wasn't a magnet for disaster. First, that lunatic stonebreaker in Urundock, and now this—a bloody *rak* assault! If he survived this, he would be jumping back on his raft and heading straight back to Urundock. After Desmond paid him what he owed him, of course.

When Ardy didn't answer, the cook tried another tact, "you ever see a rak?"
"Course I have," Ardy replied. He had in his shit, Ardy had never been anywhere *close* to a rak before.
"Rak, bandits, raiders, they're all the same," Ardy grumbled, "…trouble." Not worth the hassle and certainly not worth his life. He'd ferried smugglers before across the lake—traders who risked dealings with the rak. He knew enough about them to know he wanted no dealings with them.
"You're an icerafter, right?"
"Aye,"
"I heard some traders've been selling the fuckers weapons and runestones. They've

got gold y'see, the rak. There's lots a gold up in the Black Sands, they say."

"Maniacs," Ardy replied, "or liars. Rak would soon as cut your throat as trade with you."

"You think that we'll have to fight?" he asked nervously, sweat glistening on his brow. *I fuckin' hope not.* There was another explosion outside and Ardy took a comforting swig of his flask. *I should've left the second I dropped them boys off. Never hang around on the north shore.* It was his only rule.

Another blast sounded, this time followed by a shuddering of the walls, dust falling from the timber rafters above him. *Nope. That's it. I am* not *dying here!* He leapt to his feet and the cook looked at him with fear. "You're going to fight?" he asked.

"Not a chance," Ardy spat, and made for the door.

***

Daegan watched as dark figures moved in the shadows beyond the perimeter of the wooden wall. Every few moments, a grenadier would hurl a gunpowder pouch off the battlements and a second later it would explode in a bright and deafening blast. In that moment of illumination, Daegan caught glimpses of lithe figures moving about like draega demons.

The archers sent a volley of arrows into the darkness, to Daegan it was a mystery how they could have any idea of where to shoot. He held out his own revolver and tried firing a few shots into the darkness but it was useless. There was no point in shooting blindly. Even if he *could* see them clearly, the revolver's aim wasn't nearly as accurate as a bow. His weapon was more suited to closer range.

One of the stonebreakers looked at him confused when he asked the man to fill the aradium in his revolver with metal. The runestone powered weapon was very much a luxury item than a practical one so the concept was lost on the man.

"It's the size of the aradium," Tanlor noted when Daegan returned to their position, "I think if we replace it with a bigger runestone it'll have much better capacity. It's quick to fill, the runes they've made on it look different to standard aradium. They must help it fill faster. The thing's probably meant to be wielded by a runewielder." There was no insult in Tanlor's remark and Daegan found that his throat didn't close up at the comment.

"Wouldn't someone with an aradium be able to just make their own projectiles, why would they need a gun?"

"Shaping's hard," Tanlor shrugged. "Learning to dissolve and fill aradium is a relatively easy thing to pick up... but shaping a projectile, firing it and keeping it on course. Not a lot of people master that, even with years of training."

"So it's a lazy runewielders weapon, then?"

"Suppose it is," Tanlor laughed. An actual laugh. Daegan wasn't exactly sure what caused the change in Tanlor's demeanour. *Maybe he still has a concussion.* But Daegan was grateful for the change in him.

"Anyway they probably didn't anticipate someone like you using it," Tanlor continued, "that's only a fleck of aradium in there. I reckon if we add a decent sized one," he held out his finger and thumb demonstrating the size of a coin, "about this big maybe. We can increase the hold on that thing to a hundred shots... maybe more."

"That would be decent," Daegan replied, looking at the revolver in his hand. *A hundred bullets in such a tiny thing.*

"I didn't realise most stonebreakers never learned shaping," Daegan said, partly because he was nervous and wanted a distraction and partly because he was curious. He'd always assumed that runewielding came easy to everyone else. He'd thought that it was gaps in wealth and access to runestones that kept most people from being master runewielders. *Probably that too.*

"I can shape… but it's slow," Tanlor replied, "far too slow to be of any use in battle. Rowan's the same. Takes a lot of discipline and a good measure of natural talent from what I understand. We're trained enough to hold our own against an enemy runewielder but our expertise lies more in our sword skills."

"I've noticed."

"'I suppose you've had plenty of opportunity the past few weeks. There's been no shortage of fighting," Tanlor didn't take his eyes off the moving shadows, the conversation with Daegan was simply an aside to his main focus.

"I'm sorry for that," Daegan confessed. And he truly was, he'd spent so much of his life without any regard for the safety of those around him.

"Don't be," Tanlor fixed him then with a thoughtful look, "honestly… the past few weeks. *This* is what I'd always imagined my work would be like. Working for the Arch-duke… my days aren't particularly exciting."

"Sentinel duty," Daegan nodded. That's what his own guards referred to it as.

"Aye," Tanlor grinned, "fucking boring listening to you lot talk nonsense in meetings all day."

"Us lot?"

"Highborn… and Keltin wants daily reports on who discusses what. Always with the schemes and politics between nobles," Tanlor shook his head, "I don't know what kind of people enjoy that kind of thing but I don't want it to be my story."

"What *do* you want it to be?"

"I…" Tanlor looked out across the battlements, his shoulders squared as dark figures started appearing over the tops of the outer wooden wall. "*This*," he said, resolutely. "They're within range."

Tanlor hefted a crossbow and took aim at one of the shadowy forms. At this distance they didn't seem that large to Daegan but he remembered standing by that wall and looking up at the height of it, twice his size. Some of those figures looked like they could reach the top with an extended arm. *They really are giants.*

Tanlor let loose a bolt that fired towards a rak just beyond the wall. Daegan didn't see if it landed and was busy aiming his revolver at another that had already cleared the wall and was dashing across the keep yard.

Daegan was just about to pull on the trigger when the rak threw a hand up into the air. A peel of crashing thunder sounded as a projectile thrown by a grenadier exploded mid-flight in a flash of bright light. *A runewielder!* Even with the illuminating flare of the blast, the rak still appeared to be completely black, like he was made of darkness.

"Tanlor," Daegan said, hurriedly pointing to the approaching rak, "he's got a topaz." Tanlor's gaze—and the direction of his crossbow—whipped towards the rak Daegan indicated. A bolt was loosed towards him and again the rak threw up an outstretched arm and the bolt erupted in flame and turned to ash in fractions of a second.

"Impossible!" Tanlor gasped.

More of the dark shapes were clearing the walls now and Daegan felt fear mounting in him. He'd foolishly presumed that their superior numbers and the advantage of the battlements gave them an assured victory.

"Stonebreaker!" Tanlor called out across to the other side of the tower, catching the attention of a helmed man that was forming lengths of stone projectiles. "Take him down!" Tanlor pointed at the runewielder rak. The man looked to Tanlor and then to Commander Crann who was busy directing the archers and grenadiers at another set of oncoming rakmen. The stonebreaker nodded and then fired his projectile towards the rak.

The lithe black figure leapt aside and the stonespear crashed into the earth. The rak cleared a set of stakes in the ground and was fast approaching the main building. The stonebreaker began forming another stonespear and Tanlor kept on firing crossbow bolts in succession. Each bolt erupted in flames and ash before hitting their mark. Daegan tried to fire a few shots too but the accuracy of the revolver even at this distance was too poor. The riflemen on the battlements also didn't seem to be having much luck taking down any of the oncoming rak. *This isn't working.*

"This is *useless*," Tanlor spat, then cursed as the rak launched himself at the wall of the connecting building. He landed against it and he scaled up with astonishing speed. He was followed a second later by another pair of rakmen. *He must have an aradium too,* Daegan realised. The rak was forming handholds in the stone and his comrades were following in his wake.

Commander Crann was shouting for attention on the other side of the tower and Daegan realised with horror that on the other side there was *another* rak runewielder following the same path-forging tactic.

"Shit, this is too co-ordinated for rakmen," Tanlor said, then aimed his crossbow at one of the trailing rakmen climbing the wall. He fired and bolt took the rak in back. The rak didn't cry out, falling soundlessly off the wall, and hitting the ground in a heap.

"Finally," Tanlor grunted, "got one of the bastards." Daegan counted five in total that made it to the lower battlement. The front rak—the runewielder—was making quick work of the defenders on the roof. He moved through them, efficiently cutting down one after another. The defenders looked like children fighting against him and those that weren't killed as he passed were taken down by the rakmen that followed in his wake.

Targeting the central roof was a bizarre tactic as it left the attackers pincered by the two towers that would rain down projectiles. In spite of this, the leading rak didn't seem at all deterred. Arrows and crossbow bolts turned to ash soon after being loosed towards him, it was as though the rakman had a protective bubble around him. This close to the towers, the grenadiers didn't risk throwing any more explosives at him and were now redirecting their efforts to the straggling attackers that hadn't yet made it to the roof.

Now that the leading rak runewielder was within the range of his revolver, Daegan took aim and fired again. Bullets were a *lot* faster than a crossbow bolt and —hit! The rakman staggered. His sword was raised for a strike as Daegan's bullet caught him in the shoulder.

It was only then that Daegan caught a good look at the creature's face. Up to this point, he'd thought that the rak weren't much different to ordinary men—or maybe the Aeth—but the face that glared up at him was as alien to him as anything he'd seen before. There were definitely some human-like features; eyes, nose and a mouth, all in the places they should be. But the mouth—curled in a snarl—showed a row of pointed teeth like a wolf's. His nose was broad and flat and his eyes glistened with a striking blue, stark against the jet black of his skin.

Daegan and the rak held eye contact for a whisper of a moment and then the rak was darting towards the tower. In an incomprehensibly quick series of motions the rakman launched himself at the tower and disappeared within.

"Shit!" Tanlor cursed.

"Crann! They've breached the tower barricades!" Daegan heard the stonebreaker call out. Daegan knew there were a few soldiers stationed inside the tower for such a possibility but he did *not* like that all that separated him from the rak runewielder was a few flights of stairs and a handful of guards.

Daegan glanced over to the other tower and saw now that the rakmen had also broken through its barricaded door and had split the attack force into taking both towers simultaneously. At a quick count, Daegan could see bodies of only three rakmen amongst the armoured corpses of the Rubanians on the lower battlement. Another handful of dead rakmen were strewn about the yard, caught by either crossbow bolts or the runewielders.

"We descend into the tower!" Crann announced to the other men, "the rak are big fuckers and they'll be constrained fighting in the tower walkways. They've two runewielders leading this charge. Take them down and the rest will follow."

"Sir!" one of the grenadiers spoke up, "what that rak's doing, he's burning arrows right out of the air… dozens of 'em. That's not possible!"

"You'd be surprised what some runewielders are capable of," Tanlor said to the man, "he's just a rak like all the others. A sword will kill him just the same."

"The newcomer's right," Crann nodded, "we've still the advantage of numbers. Don't let—"

He cut off as a blast sounded by the other tower. The top of it burst alight in an explosion of fire. Chunks of the battlement rained off into the yard below. *Rowan!*

***

Rowan watched with mounting disapproval as the defenders continued to focus their efforts on the leading rak chief. All crossbow bolts and arrows fired uselessly towards him and even the stonebreakers were getting reckless in attempting to bring him down.

"Take down the others!" Rowan roared after it seemed no one was going to. They needed to thin the rak's numbers first before focusing on the chief. Their chiefs were the most trained, and often were the only ones carrying runestones. This one was clearly *trying* to hold the attention of all the ranged attacks.

From this distance, Rowan could sense the rak's edir. It was iron-strong and shot up decisively at arrows and crossbow bolts when let loose. There was a crack of gunfire and the rak chief halted for a brief moment before charging for the door to the other tower. He burst through it and disappeared within. The other rak cleared the remaining defenders and split; some breaking into Rowan's tower, others following the chief.

"We hold here!" Grest called out to the other soldiers. *Stupid fucking idea.* They'd be better off trying face off against the rakmen inside the tower where their movements were limited by their size. Rowan knew better than to challenge the Captain, he was an officer to these men and Rowan understood that the chain of command needed to be upheld. Especially in a crisis. To contest him now would risk their entire defence. Rowan was an outsider, so he didn't *need* to obey Grest but sometimes it was better to go with the tide than against it.

Within moments, the dozen men on the tower were positioned for an assault. They waited, an apprehensive air hanging over them. The sounds of fighting inside the tower below echoed up. Then Rowan felt... *something*. It was subtle, but had the distinct feel of an edir. It was a strange edir, and not unlike the Reldoni he'd met before Urundock. His eyes met the other grenadier—Puck—who was looking about with a bewildered expression. He felt the edir probe stronger now, pulsing from below and Rowan's eyes snapped to the pile of gunpowder-filled pouches bundled next to Puck.

"RU—" Rowan started to shout but it was too late.

The edir flooded over him. Rowan leapt out and a blinding white light covered his vision. He felt a surge of heat and pressure push him forward, flinging him off the battlement. He was blinded by the flash and deafened by the sound of the explosion. Wind rushed at him from all angles and for a moment he felt like he was soaring through the air like a bird.

But then something hard hit Rowan in the back knocking the air out of his lungs. He was falling again. The ground and sky flashed in his vision and spun about. Then another hit and he was rolling on the ground. The taste of earth filled Rowan's mouth as he tried to gasp for breaths. After a few moments, he eventually came to a stop.

The ringing in Rowan's ears didn't subside and his vision swam with glaringly bright after-images. He was lying on his back, and instinctively tried to roll onto his side. He hacked and spluttered as he attempted to draw breath. The taste of coppery blood filled his mouth. *That's not good.* The thought drifted over Rowan's mind as his vision faded to black.

***

Despite being tall and having the distinctive features of an Aeth, Ardy had always had the uncanny ability to slink away from detection when needed. Part of that was attributed to the Aeth's natural ability to move lightly on their feet but it was also in the way that Ardy had mastered a slouched, unassuming posture that caused most people's eyes to simply slide over him.

This wasn't the first battle that Ardy had managed to slip past both defenders and attackers and flee, although he certainly hoped it was the last. That's what he'd told himself in the Balfold six years ago, and in Nordock two decades before that. And, of course, there was the Altarean rebellion fifty years ago. That had been a really nasty one, but he had still managed to sneak onto a ship and flee the city before half of it burned to the ground.

The rak however had pretty good eyesight—even in the dark. They also moved faster than his people so he wasn't sure if he could outrun one—even if he was in good shape and not half-drunk. He could try to feign a lack of allegiance to the humans if he was discovered by one. Ardy didn't know what services he could possibly offer the rak, but it was better than being slaughtered.

Thankfully, most of the invading rakmen had already stormed the roof of the building and were breaking into the towers, fighting their way up. This had provided Ardy with a chance to make a dash for the jetty where his icecraft was still docked. Ardy didn't have any major obstacles between him and the dock, he just needed to be quick and avoid detection. He scurried from one row of spiked blockades to the next, stopping to take a breath and survey the next patch of ground he needed to clear.

He was almost at the jetty when a light flared, followed half a second later with a loud blast. His head spun to the source and saw one of the towers erupting in a shell of fire. Debris rained down. He saw a man fall near him and roll down the slope before coming to a stop.

The top of the tower was a bonfire throwing light into the area and casting dancing shadows about the scene. Ardy froze at the sudden explosion. The light of the fire exposed the clear path to the jetty in plain view for anyone watching. *Fuck, fuck, fuck!*

Ardy's attention was drawn back to the man who'd fallen from the tower. He could make out the red hair of the man. Ardy watched as he stirred slightly, coughed and then passed out. Ardy shuffled to the man. As he approached, he recognised the man's face and confirmed that it was one of Desmond's bodyguards.

Robert if Ardy recalled it right... or maybe it was Robin? He was still breathing which was a surprise considering the man had just been thrown from an exploding tower. Ardy glanced up at the distance to the jetty and back down at the man. It was a long way to drag him. *But I don't get paid if they're dead...* but then again, he couldn't get paid if *he* was dead.

Ardy then reached for the man's neck and fished his hand down the chainmail. Robin's skin was clammy but in a few moments, Ardy's hand clasped around a small warm stone hanging from a leather cord. *Jackpot.* Classic place to keep a runestone. Ardy pulled it off the man and stuffed it into his cloak pocket. *That's at least thirty silver.* He thought happily. Should cover the cost of this fiasco. *Always collect payment.* It was his one rule.

Ardy then glanced around again for any nearby rakmen—which there were none as they had all stormed inside the towers and were busy killing the Rubanians. Once he was sure it was clear, Ardy sprinted for the jetty, not giving Robin or the burning tower a second look. He threw himself onto the iceraft and began furiously working on untying the ropes.

This was the second time in three days that he'd had to do this in a rush. *Blasted Reldoni, always bringing trouble.* Even though Desmond hadn't seemed like a typical war-hungry Reldoni, he was certainly a magnet for trouble. Ardy didn't feel an ounce of remorse as he pulled on levers and whipped the sail of the iceraft up. The sail caught the winds and began pulling the raft away from the damned place. The thought of waiting to see if Dessie or the blond prick were alive was never a consideration.

Not for all the gold in the world.

CHAPTER 41

Scattered & Shattered

The rak chief's sword severed Crann's head from his body.

Daegan had never seen a man decapitated before. He'd seen executions of course, but no one had been beheaded in his lifetime. It was gruesome, the man's head hurled across the corridor. His body crumpled to the floor, a spray of red blood shooting up to the ceiling. Daegan's jaw went slack as he dumbly watched the rak chief advance through the corridor of defenders.

The rak seemed impossibly large in the narrow corridor. His long black hair almost brushed the rafters. The creature's thick curved sword was as large as a greatsword and he wielded it in one hand. The other clasped a dagger that looked to be made of blood red crystal. The rak's armour wasn't steel but instead a thick hide of some kind, it reminded Daegan of the dragonhide armour that Reldoni soldiers wore, only this kind was more crudely fashioned.

Daegan was at the very rear, being the last to descend into the lower hallways. Tanlor stood guard in front of him. Only six of the remaining Twin Garde soldiers stood between them and the rak chief. Of all the ways Daegan thought he'd die, fighting a rak chief, in a cramped corridor, in a Rubanian outpost miles from any civilisation would have been very—*very*—low down that list. There was no escaping the fact that death was coming. He might not be a seasoned fighter like Tanlor or Rowan but he was competent enough to see they were losing.

Tanlor had stood his ground against Ferath—twice, in fact. Ferath was able to do things beyond what was considered normal runewielding. He was somehow *enhanced* and from what Daegan had just seen this rak chief do, he had no doubt that he was the same. Unlike Ferath, the rak was not alone. Daegan couldn't count how many of the hulking forms were trailing behind their chief, their oversized swords catching the torchlight.

Daegan met Tanlor's eye. Surely he also knew that this was the end. Tanlor glanced back at the chief who was now fighting the next pair of soldiers in line. Tanlor's hand reached towards a torch on the wall and Daegan noted that the man's face went suddenly flush. Tanlor's other hand then extended towards the wooden rafters above the rak's head. Wispy tendrils of smoke began to crawl along the rafters. Plumes of smoke seeped out of the woodwork, conjured by invisible flames.

Then in a burst of bright light, flames burst out of the wooden beams.

The rak chief's offhand—the one wielding the dagger—shot up and the flames disappeared in seconds. Then with his main sword-hand he cut down another soldier.

"He's got nowhere to dissipate that heat," Tanlor grunted, "he can't risk throwing fire around or everyone in here will burn."

"What does that mean?" Daegan asked, he could feel the panic in his own tone. It made his voice shrill and breathless.

"It means we might still have a chance," Tanlor retreated back up the stairs to the rooftop. Daegan followed after him. No way he was just going to wait around to be butchered.

"Cowards!" He heard one of the soldiers cursing up after them.

At the rooftop doorway they still had a view of the full corridor below and could just about see the chief cutting down another of the soldiers. The other tower top was alight. *Like an enormous candle.*

Daegan's chest tightened wondering if Rowan had survived the explosion. *He could have jumped.* He glanced over the edge of the tower. It wasn't *that* high of a drop. The towers weren't much higher than fifty feet, he could survive that, what were the odds? Daegan then considered jumping over the side of the tower himself. It was surely better than the absolute certainty of death by a rak's blade.

"We're jumping?" Daegan asked with a hint of hope.

"What?" Tanlor looked at him, his face scrunching in confusion, "no," he scowled in revulsion, "of course, we're not jumping."

Tanlor then pointed an open palm to the burning tower. He dropped his sword and directed the other hand down the stairs. The man's face knotted in concentration and Daegan realised what he was planning to do. *You're going to flood the corridor with fire. The chief won't be able to absorb all of it or he'll be incinerated. He'll have to withdraw.* It wasn't a perfect plan but it at least gave them a few minutes to plan for an escape. *Oh Tanlor, you genius!*

***

Tanlor hated that this was the only course of action he could think of. He hated that he was dooming the soldiers facing the rak chief to their fate. It was a sloppy and dangerous use of runewielding that his grandfather would have been utterly disappointed in.

Within seconds, the flames began to climb along the rafters and every other burnable object in the corridor. The defending soldiers began to back up the stairs as the corridor filled with smoke. But the rak chief didn't relent, pushing forward in defiance of the flames. The fires seemed to fuel him onward.

Tanlor could feel the fire scourge his veins as his edir pulled the heat of the flames from the other tower, drew it into his body and expelled it back into the corridor. His mind remained focused on directing the flames onto the rafters above the rak's head. If he could burn enough of those supports, the ceiling might just collapse on him. But the creature was moving too fast, he cut down another of the defenders, pressing forward.

Tanlor redirected his efforts now to the rak's sword. His skin prickled with the heat and he knew that he was pulling far beyond what his body could handle, he'd likely already caused himself serious internal burns. *Pull too much and you'll be ash, boy.* His grandfather had told him. But if he didn't, they'd all be killed soon enough anyway.

He focused on the blade, pouring all the heat he could manage into it. The near constant blaze of the twin tower was the only reason this tactic was even working. He channelled more, and the blade began to glow with an orange hue. The light grew and grew, until it was almost incandescent.

At first the rak chief didn't seem to care about the heated blade, and why would he? A super-heated blade was a foreboding sight to an enemy and could burn an opponent with a light touch. But when the blade gets too hot, the metal starts to soften and—the blade *dripped*. Red molten blobs of metal began to fall from the blade and the rak dropped the sword and back stepped realising the thing was melting.

Tanlor looked down at his hands and could see smoke rising from charred and blackened skin. *Oh shit*. Tanlor felt like he'd just swallowed an entire bottle of whitewhiskey. The heat pulsed inside of him. He turned his head to see Daegan looking at him with a horrified expression. Tanlor felt as though he had pushed his face into a brazier. His vision grew hazy. He could see Daegan reaching for him before all the colours of the world began to merge together.

A part of his mind knew that he never should've overexerted himself after the healing. His body was still surging with adrenaline from that. He also knew that he should never have pulled so much fire so quickly. Tanlor knew all of this, and the thoughts drifted across his mind as he slumped into Daegan's arms. He could smell sulphur. It smelled like a funeral pyre. *Is this my pyre?* The thought brushed across his fading consciousness.

He could hear the crackling of flames, and an instinctive part of his mind tried to summon his edir, to force all the excess heat out of his body. Bright after-images of flames danced across his vision.

He heard a roar from below but couldn't distinguish if it was a shout of anger or fear before the darkness and the flames claimed him.

***

Daegan held Tanlor in his arms. Misty trails of smoke wafted from the man like he was a smouldering fire. Parts of his skin were bright red with cracks of black. The acrid stink of burning flesh overpowered the smell of smoke. Daegan had even thought for a moment that Tanlor's eyes had been shining red like an Honorswords.

"*Undak Savura'an!*" the words came as a low grumble from the murky corridor.
"Flame finder..." the same undulating voice said in deeply accented common-tongue. An accent that Daegan couldn't place even if he tried to.
"Surrender the flame and live," the voice growled.

Daegan awed that the rak could even speak. He knew that was a silly thing to be surprised about, but speech was such a human thing that it seemed bizarre that these *creatures* could.

There were only two other soldiers left, separating Daegan from the rak chief. The pair backed up the stairs and exchanged worried glances. Whether it was because the rak was speaking or because they were next to be butchered, Daegan did not know.

"How do we know that you'll let us live?" Daegan called out, he lowered his tone in an effort to make himself sound stronger. He was proud that his voice didn't break as he did so. The rak gave a considering pause.
"Khandamos has need of blood... surrender the flame," the rak chief replied, stepping forward out of the smoky haze, appearing as a massive black silhouette against the flames.
"If we give you the flame... you'll let us live?" Daegan wasn't entirely sure what the rak meant by 'the flame'. *He could be referring to the topaz.* It was the only sense he could make of it and from what Daegan understood, runestones were extremely

valuable to the rak.

"Weak," the rak spat the word like an insult. "Men always weak... Always bargain... Always talk out of death."

"We have something you want—the flame," Daegan replied, "if we give it to you, you'll let us go?"

"Him," the chief gestured at Tanlor with the red dagger, "he is flame finder." *Yes, I suppose that's what a primitive cult-like society would likely call a runewielder with a topaz.*

"He is," Daegan replied, cautiously.

The pair of soldiers kept their weapons raised but their faces were hopeful now that Daegan had somehow managed to converse with the creature.

"Weak men," said a different voice—still deep and terrifying but different—came from behind the chief, "Khandamos has no desire for the weak."

"Khandamos needs blood, strong blood of flame finder," the rak chief snapped in a chastising manner. Daegan only now noticed how when the rak moved his head, the faintest of blue light moved along the muscle of his neck. *What are these things?*

"The flame finder goes to Khandamos... the others die," the chief said and Daegan felt his stomach drop.

"Wait! I'm a flame finder too!" One of the soldiers said—the grenadier that had been atop the tower. "I can go, I'll join this *can-demons* thing!" The man had clearly come to the same conclusion as Daegan had about the topaz and saw a way to save his own hide. *Coward,* Daegan thought, but then doubted he would've done anything different.

An idea struck him.

"Me too!" Daegan called out, "we're all runewielders here." The last soldier started nodding emphatically too, jumping onto the chance at surviving the situation.

The chief stepped forward—within striking distance of the two soldiers. Both looked up with terrified faces as the chief stepped within range. He held up the blood red dagger and spoke, *"kuled maz akraz."*

A light grew from within the crystal of the dagger, casting the faces of the soldiers in an ominous red hue. It was not unlike the red light that filled a bloodstone that healers used.

Daegan watched in mounting horror as both men fell to their knees in agony. Their faces became gaunt, their throats shrivelling as they gasped for breaths. In a matter of seconds, their skin began to char and flake as though invisible flames were licking at their faces.

"No Undak," the rak growled, teeth baring in revulsion as the two soldiers perished at his feet.

Daegan's heart pounded in his ears. He was suddenly aware of Tanlor's weight in his arms. He could still run. He could push Tanlor down the stairs and take his chances jumping off the tower. The thought lingered shamefully and it wasn't any sense of morality that prevented Daegan from moving.

It was fear that paralyzed him.

Daegan wasn't sure if he'd ever felt the emotion manipulating effects of a mindstone runewielder, but he was sure in that instant that this was what it felt like; sheer terror locked his muscles in place and they refused to budge despite his mind screaming at him to flee. The chief loomed above him, like a shadowed and sinister father standing over a child.

The rak looked down at Daegan, his blue eyes were radiant, striking against the blackness of his alien face. Daegan had spent his entire adult life in the belief that monsters or draega didn't exist but in that moment he knew that he had been wrong. They were very much real and they were *here*. This was a draega—this was a demon.

The rak raised the dagger towards Daegan and he thought he saw a question in the creature's expression. *He's giving me the choice… he's asking me if I want to die the same way that these two men did.* Daegan supposed the alternative would be to die in a more traditional stabbing manner.

The timber steps of the stairs groaned as the rak took another slow step towards him. Tanlor stirred in Daegan's arms and he shifted his grip, propping Tanlor up. Tanlor was still very much unconscious. To Daegan's shame, he slightly repositioned his friend so that he acted as a bodyshield between him and the rak.

"You are *Undak*?" The rak nodded back towards the two husks that had been the bodies of the other soldiers. Daegan figured that whatever *Undak* was, it meant that the red crystal dagger wouldn't turn you into a charred, shrivelled corpse… it would be quite a major gamble on his part to agree. But then again, something about the dagger gave Daegan pause. The colour was remarkably like garnet gemstone —bloodstone. Daegan had never studied bloodstone, his training in runewielding stopping long before reaching such advanced practices. Daegan by his very nature as hindered couldn't use bloodstone, but another notable disadvantage was that he also couldn't be *healed* by one either.

Daegan looked at the dagger and the dim red light still glowing inside with apprehension. The other rak behind were now advancing, their large black swords glinting in the light of the flames. He locked eyes with the chief and nodded, "I am *Undak*."

Daegan still clutched both his revolver and sword in each hand. The chief took another step towards him and Daegan considered taking a shot. He could shoot him. He had six bullets, he could attempt to fight… but… he couldn't. Beneath the gaze of the rak chief he felt like a child again. Though their faces looked nothing alike, Daegan saw his father in the rak's hateful eyes.

The dagger was raised slowly towards him, light building inside of it. Daegan became mesmerised by its light and his vision turned red. He felt the air being pulled out of his lungs. Daegan's chest locked up and he lost his grip on Tanlor. The two of them went down; Tanlor dropping in a heap and Daegan falling to his knees. His muscles seized up and he was overcome by a sudden and intense prickling sensation—like thousands of insects with tiny blades for legs were crawling all over his body.

Daegan's hands tightened around the hilts of his revolver and sword. He looked down at them, white knuckles clenching. The skin on the back of his hands began to crack with black rivets.

He'd been wrong.

He'd been so hopelessly wrong.

He looked up at the rak, the blue eyes looking down at him. It was the same cold disinterested look that his father had given him when he'd trapped Daegan in the prison of stone. He felt now the tips of the stone spikes pressing into his shoulders, his back, his torso.

He tried to suck in a breath but his throat felt like there were hands of stone crushing around it. His vision blurred and the face of the rak warped, only the pair of bright blue eyes remained constant. Daegan's mind filled in the blurring spaces with the image of his father.

He was back in the training room in Epilas.

Daegan didn't deserve this. He didn't deserve to be hated for just being what he was! His father loomed over him, lifting him by the chain of runestones around his neck. Pain racked his body.

"We have coddled you long enough," his father said. Daegan clenched his eyes shut but the image remained clear in his mind.

"Tredains do not yield!" his father roared in Daegan's face. "We do not bend. We do not cower. We cut down the enemies before us or we die in the effort!" Daegan's hands clenched tightly around his sword and revolver. "We do not have *weakness* in our family," his father snarled. "Now get up, Daegan," his words were thick with disdain.

Daegan coughed.

You're a monster. Daegan growled the words in his mind. He wasn't sure if any sound came out. *I was just a child!* He clenched his teeth as the pressure closed around his throat. Phantom spikes of stone digging their way into his flesh.

Daegan's eyes snapped up. He strained against the pain, he raised his hand holding the revolver. His father's expression remained devoid of any emotion beyond contempt. To him, Daegan was no threat. Daegan was useless. Daegan was an embarrassment. Daegan was *broken*.

"I am not broken," Daegan seethed, "*you* are."

He pulled his finger down on the trigger.

PART IV

A CRACKED MASK

Interlude
Ranjen

The smell of smoke had always made Ranjen feel nauseous. It reminded him of Nazakar, the city in the heart of the Black Sands.

Smoke was oppressive and it invaded his lungs. He wanted to push forwards, past Chief Yakra up to the roof of the tower and be free of the smoke. But he waited, patiently. *Yakra commands obedience, you do not disobey Yakra.* If Yakra wishes to condemn the pale ones to *Vasrak* then that is what he will do. *He is almost finished.* The last remaining pale one was already on his knees, his eyes glazed over and his flesh rotting.

There was a sound of lightning crashing and then Yakra's blood was spraying out from the back of his head. Their chief fell backward, revealing the kneeling pale one. His hand raised holding what looked to be a small contraption of metal, two bright *kazas* shining on the sides of it. Ranjen was not *Undak*—was not an immortal or even one of the chosen. He had little understanding of how the *kazas* worked but he knew that only a very powerful *Undak* could have taken down Yakra. Ranjen did not feel fear, but he was practical enough to understand when it was best to flee before a stronger opponent.

The human *Undak* however did not immediately turn his wrath upon the remaining rak. He remained kneeling then tipped forward, an unreadable expression on his pale alien face. Ranjen clenched his fist around his blade in anticipation of an attack from the enemy *Undak* but none came. The human fell forward on his face and remained there, unmoving.

Smoke continued to swirl around Ranjen's face, stinging at his eyes and filling his nose with its oppression. *Yakra is dead.* He had never liked Yakra so he was not upset by this but Yakra was their leader and the strongest among them. His death would throw their clan into chaos as the strongest fought for the right to be chief. Ranjen himself would likely have to kill some of the men in this smokey corridor in the coming days.

"Take the *Undak*," Sakas commanded and Ranjen turned around and walked away from the scene. He wouldn't take orders from Sakas of all people.

"Yakra has fallen," Ranjen growled, "I'm going back to Joku'ur." He hadn't wanted to invade the pale one's lands in the first place. He'd done it because Yakra had commanded him to. But he'd be damned if Sakas thought he was strong enough to force Ranjen into continuing this foolish attempt.

"The *Khandamos* will want more blood," Sakas said. That gave Ranjen pause. He'd never crossed paths with the *Khandamos* directly. Nor did he ever want to. He glanced back at the humans. The *Undak* was unconscious now. He could see the rise and fall of his breath along with the other—the *Undak Savura'an*, the flame finder.

Those who could wield fire were rare amongst his people. *He could be sold as a slave.* But captured humans always made poor slaves. They clung to their will like frost on the sands.

He glanced back at Sakas who gripped his blade in his hand. The bloodlust was still on him, Ranjen could smell it. He glanced about at the others in the corridor. Like him, they were all of Yakra's bloodsworn. It would be one of them that would come out as the new chief.

Ranjen was faced with a choice. Fight Sakas here and now and claim the title of chief as his own—or submit. The *Khandamos* would want the blood of these *Undak*. Sakas would deliver them to him. Or Ranjen could kill Sakas, take these *Undak* as slaves and sell them to another chief and be done with it. Be done with this absurdity of invading the lands of men.

Razef's clan would be arriving in a few days, so he could sell the prisoners to him. Razef was a strong *Undak* and Ranjen figured he could sell both Yakra's dagger and the slaves to him for a tidy sum.

"The *Khandamos* can fuck himself," Ranjen growled and lunged at Sakas.

Interlude
Edmund

Arch-duke Edmund Dal'Regan sat on the Eagle Throne.
The Eagle Throne had been the highest seat of power in Rubane for over a hundred years. There had been many Arch-dukes in the past that had sat upon it, even in Edmund's time. But he had been elected as Arch-duke by the Dukesmoot three times in succession. His eyes moved to the Artic Bear emblazoned on grey banners that decorated the hall. He remembered his inauguration when those banners had first been unfurled here. How proud he'd felt to see them decorating these halls once again. For almost thirty years he had dedicated his life to serving all the peoples of Rubane as their leader; from the wealthiest merchant to the poorest beggar, he cared for each individual Rubanian as if they were his own blood.

So it galled him—*boiled his blood*. To know that they were betraying him. His *own* people. The people he worked so diligently to protect, were committing treason against him. He glanced about at the gathered attendants in the throne room. This Assembly consisted of six of the seven Dukes from across the country, along with dozens of their Barons, and scores of representatives from the major guilds and trade houses in Rubastre. Edmund pondered how many in this very room were conspiring against him. He resisted the urge to grind his teeth. To scream at them for their treachery.

"The Reldoni Army contract is our most lucrative arrangement," Guildmaster Arken of the Ironworks argued, "you cannot be proposing that we break it."

"The very steel you supply those devils with will be used to cut out your heart," Knight-Marshall Karvel bellowed. *A staunch patriot... but perhaps that was a well-played front, could this deception have roots in our army?* Of course, the Ironworks would hope to retain their contract, it would be suspicious if they did not. But then again, the Guildmasters were clever enough to know that too. His head spun and he found he had no desire to let this farce continue as it was.

"My Lords, Guildmasters and honoured guests," Edmund announced, "as it stands, the threat of a Reldoni invasion is still all rumour and hear-say"—although the spies that Edmund had in the Reldoni palace had confirmed that the threats were very much real—"we have sent an envoy to Epilas in the hopes of putting this matter to rest."

"Your Grace," Duke Boern spoke up from his position at the front of the Assembly, "King Abhran is known for his aggression. His son was killed here in your palace, do you truly believe that he will not seek retribution for this?"

"We have discussed this at length, Duke Boern," in both the Duke's Assembly and in smaller councils, meaning that Boern's insistence at re-surging the topic here was a political move. "King Abhran will not take bold action against us, not when it was Prince Daegan's own guard that were the assassins. Once Ferath

Vitares is found, this can be settled." He searched Boern's face for any hint of acknowledgement at the lie.

Boern was at the top of Edmund's list of potential conspirators. A young man—for a Duke—not yet in his forties and prone to bold and impulsive action. Edmund's own spies had confirmed that Boern had planned to contest him at the next Dukesmoot. *He thinks he can oust me from this throne… he can pry my dead body from it.* But so far, Boern had not given any indication that he was aware Daegan Tredain was still alive.

Frustratingly, none of the people in this room seemed to have implied knowledge of this. He needed someone to slip on the dangerously thin ice that they'd strayed onto.

"How has the City Watch not found this man yet?" Duke Harfallow directed his disapproval towards Lord Essing, Knight-Captain of the Watch.

"I have a hundred men combing the city for any trace of the man, my Lord Duke, he has fled," Essing replied in his usual whining tone, he then turned to Edmund's throne. "There have been sightings of powerful Reldoni runewielders in Urundock, your Grace. Perhaps it may be best to focus efforts on the northern regions?"

"*Urundock?!*" Harfallow cut across. "Lies! Nothing happens up in that backwater town. Even this morning, runners from Urundock came claiming rakmen had taken outposts along the Nortara." It was true, Edmund himself received the runners as they relayed the claims. He'd sent scouts to the outposts to confirm before issuing orders for a contingent to be sent to the north. He didn't want any portion of his army caught up in the north by some blizzard when this conspiracy was finally uncovered—or if the Reldoni really did decide to invade.

"Should this not be our top concern?!" Lord Fetters spoke up, the slimy representative for Duke Rivers of Nordock—who had inauspiciously not been able to make the trip to Rubane on Edmund's request. "Rakmen taking outposts should not be ignored, many here were in the Balfold not twenty years ago when they'd last come south." Of course, he would be fearful of that… or was there something more?

"The scouts will confirm the legitimacy of these attacks. At this moment, the Eagle Throne will reserve any hasty actions. Our priority remains. Lord Essing, you have my approval to dispatch a score from the City Watch to Urundock to investigate, they are not to indulge any response to claims of rakmen, I do not want this rumour to be given any merit until proven. Their purpose is to search for Ferath Vitares."

Edmund was beyond exasperated with this Assembly. He loathed open room discussions between Dukes and Guildmasters, it always descended into petty bickering. His objective in this Assembly had been to weedle out who might be responsible for this whole fiasco. He could envisage more than half the men in the room scheming for Edmund's downfall. He'd climbed to his position by breaking some of them down and stepping on their backs, or the backs of their fathers. It was always the same as it neared the Dukesmoot every eleven years. Months of ensuring the loyalty of his most trusted with political favours and gifts, and subtle sabotage for any would-be rivals.

The assassination of a foreign prince under his protection was precisely the kind of short-thought manouvre that one of these half-wits would attempt. War was an excellent mechanism for jumping to power. Edmund himself had leveraged war—or threats of it—in the past to his political benefit. He had no doubt that there were co-conspirators within the Reldoni royal palace in Epilas, they would be stirring the broth of war on the other side. He needed to see who would be most in favour of war with the Reldoni. Those he would watch like an eagle-hawk.

"This matter of the Reldoni is not settled," Karvel spoke up again, "to continue feeding them weapons and armour is stupidity beyond comprehension."

"All shipments have been halted since Edmund's order a week past," Arken sneered at Karvel, "my request is that we begin fulfilling this once again. The taxes on the contract is what sustains your men's salaries, Knight-Marshall."

"Who are you to demand anything?! You're nothing but a commoner," Karvel huffed as if having delivered the most offensive remark he could. Arken, to his credit, inclined his head, "Indeed, I am not of noble blood such as the majority of men in this room. I understand that my place here is by the grace and generosity that the nobility have provided the Ironworks, amongst all other Guilds. But I must insist that I *demand* nothing... what I *request* is for the Assembly to consider the Ironwork's quite considerable ongoing contract with the Reldoni."

"*Consider?*" Duke Boern barked, "filling the Ironworks coffers is very low on my considerations." Many of the other Dukes professed similar vehement statements and Arken despite his large size seemed to shrink beneath them. The man fussed with his optics and cast his eyes to the ground like a chastised child.

"We shall give the Reldoni steel," Boern spoke up above the rising voices, "we shall let them taste the icy sting of Rubanian steel! Right in the heart!" His booming voice reverberated against the walls and many in the room cheered to the patriotic valiance of the statement.

A smile tugged at Edmund's lips, the curls of his moustache brushed his cheeks. *So... it was you after all Boern.* He should have known. His spies in Boern's household staff had been telling him of Boern's comments of Edmund's 'gutless' and 'ineffective' leadership. Edmund watched with outwardly-apparent reservation as Boern stirred the attended nobility's chauvinistic Rubanian pride. The Dukes of Undanskill, Easkey and Edas, along with a host of Barons attested to the strength of their men. Many of the Guildmasters and representatives of workers unions joined in the fanaticism, leaping at the opportunity to join the nobility in a unified ideal.

"The strength of Rubane will prevail, as it has for over a hundred years," Edmund announced over the growing clamour of patriotism. His own voice gravelled as it rose. A lifetime of whitewhiskey, cigars and shouting had left him with a larynx that felt like he was gargling rocks.

"The Reldoni rely on their women to fight for them!" The young Baron of Heronsbridge quipped. Some of the others laughed, but many of the older Dukes and Barons' faces knotted into snarls. These were true Rubanians. They were respectful of women and the thought of giving one a blade was so offensive it didn't warrant thought nor comment.

"I suggest, Arch-duke," Boern began, now with the raucous approval of the Assembly, "that we spit in the face of the Reldoni accusations! They claim that their Prince's death was our responsibility and disgrace our honour! Let us show them that Rubane is not Altarea, their runewielders will fall upon our blades, our bolts and our bullets."

All eyes now turned to the Arch-duke. Edmund felt the weight of their expectation. Many in the room were swept up in the din of sanguine ardour, but equally as many knew the cost of war.

A price in both gold and blood.

"The Assembly has given me much to deliberate upon. I will reflect on what has been discussed here," he saw some faces drop with disappointment. A few without the decency to cover their anger, but there was also a relief on many. Boern had a smirk. Edmund's reservation played right into his advantage. It portrayed Boern as the true exemplification of Rubane, strong and proud.

Edmund dismissed the Assembly and took the door to the rear of the throne. Boern would use the aftermath of the Assembly to gather more to his cause but that didn't matter. Boern was not nearly as clever as he thought he was.

He could see it all now, Boern's master plan unfolded in Edmund's mind. He strode purposefully along the corridor towards his office, flanked by four of his loyal Dukesguard. With the cripple prince murdered, Boern simply had to wait for the rumours of a Reldoni invasion to propagate. Then capitalise on the strong sense of Rubanian patriotism to bat the flames of war, all with Boern regarded as the spearhead.

The Reldoni would strike at Rubastre first, their thirst for vengeance as fresh and sharp as the first ice on the Jakuss River. Boern would flee to his own fortress and hold out for the initial waves of the invasion. *And hoping that my walls were breached and the Reldoni would take care of me.* After a few weeks of siege, Boern and his army would come to the salvation of the poor capital. *'The Saviour of Rubastre' the bards would call the bastard.* Edmund could hear the ballads now. A strong warrior of a leader, who else would be more suited to lead this mighty nation through times of war?

But there is a fatal flaw in Boern's plan. Edmund's smirk deepened. *Daegan Tredain was still alive.* And the irony was that Boern's own blood would return him to Edmund and prevent this war from ever starting. A careless man would think that Tanlor would be loyal to his cousin but Edmund had many spies in his own household and amongst his guards. He knew his own people better than they knew themselves.

He entered his office and made his way to his desk.

Tanlor's hatred for Boern was no act. Tanlor had but one secret: Danielle Harfallow. He took out a ring of small brass keys and slotted one into the lock of his desk drawer. Edmund would, of course, indulge Tanlor upon his return. What kind of Arch-duke would he be if he did not fulfil his promises? Duke Harfallow was a good and loyal friend, and Edmund's spies in the man's keep attested to that. Harfallow would agree upon Edmund's request, he had no doubts. He opened the drawer and took out a stone with the appearance of smooth green jade. *Tanlor would have his prize at the end of all of this. And his cousin Boern will receive exactly what he deserves.*

Edmund had always admired the appearance of a signal stone before being activated. It was the murky green of a summer sea, frozen and preserved. He ran his hand over its smoothed surface. Traced his finger along delicate runes that linked this stone to its pair. *Over a hundred miles from here.*

It really was a marvellous thing. To be able to send a message over any threshold of distance. He reached out with his edir and felt the signal stone vibrate in response. It was always a strange experience, drawing on the power of a signal stone. All runestones filled you with the power of control. But the energy of the signal stone simply dissipated once drawn upon, vanishing to nothing.

The change was almost instantaneous. A tiny pinprick of red, bleeding out from the heart of the signal stone, soaking up the green like blood seeping from a wound. The sea-like appearance of the stone was now painted with the colours of a sunset. Up past the Nortara sheet, the paired stone in Tanlor's possession would be undergoing the same transition.

Now that Edmund was certain it was Boern who had concocted this fiasco, it was time for Tanlor to return with Daegan Tredain.

CHAPTER 42
To be a Shield

The story of Femira and Landryn's battle against the kragal had spread back to Epilas, along with the efforts the team had taken to clear out the kragling nests along the Tidewall. Waiting at the docks was a fanfare of cheering townsfolk as the pair stepped off the ferry. Also waiting at the dock was a sleek black lacquered carriage.

Garld stood by the carriage amongst a few other soldiers in bloodshedder uniforms. There were a few nobles also in the vicinity, applauding Landryn's victory against the monsters of the Tidewall region. Notably present was Lady Rhianne—Averstock's daughter—that Femira recognised. She was waiting alongside Garld for their arrival.

Landryn frowned as they approached. Femira hadn't liked Rhianne the last time she'd met her. The woman had been openly flirtatious with Landryn that night at the feast and Femira wasn't sure what the relationship between the two was. She and Landryn hadn't spoken about it at all. Their conversations tended to revolve around the kraglings—particularly on how to hunt and kill them, theorising where they were coming from and how to stop the spread.

They'd spoken at length of Landryn's plans to propose an excursion party to the north to the War Council. An excursion party that he would lead and Femira would be part of. Together they'd made plans to cleanse the lands of the monsters that threatened the people who couldn't defend themselves. It was grand ideals and Femira exalted at the prospect of using her abilities for such a magnanimous cause.

Femira recognised in her the emotion she was feeling when she spotted Rhianne. It was jealousy. She was emotionally mature enough to call a spade a spade on this one. While she and Landryn had never had any kind of romantic relationship thus far, she couldn't help but feel drawn to him in that way. The man was undeniably handsome but her attraction went beyond appearances. It was in the way that he carried himself, his confidence in his skills yet his almost awkward tendencies in conversation. It was the way that he held her gaze as he spoke. How he'd held her on the cliffs after the battle with the kragal, reassuring and comforting her. That wasn't compassion between comrades. There was something more there, she could feel it.

"Landryn," Rhianne beamed when she saw him. She did not rush to him, but took steps towards an embrace that Landryn took her in. Femira smothered the flare of resentment in her at the sight and instead saluted Garld. The man responded with an approving nod and a kindly smile.

"The stories of your deeds have preceded you both," Garld praised, "tales of Landryn Tredain and Annali Jahar fighting monsters and draega have been fast spreading through the city." Femira detected an element of teasing in Garld's words. She knew that the relationship between Garld and Landryn was a strange one. There was a strict formality at times with Landryn being Garld's commander. But Garld had been Landryn's swordsmaster and tutor for most of the Prince's life and there was an aura of fatherly appraise in Garld's manner towards Landryn.

"The work is not yet done," Landryn said, removing himself from Rhianne's embrace, "there is much that we need to discuss with the War Council."

"Surely that can wait?" Rhianne said softly, "you're just home." As it often was in situations like this, Femira felt like a spectator, hanging on the fringe of the conversation. But she was more than just Vreth now. She had fought alongside Landryn Tredain as an equal. She'd battled—and defeated—monsters. She was a fucking hero.

"I don't think we have time to wait," Femira spoke up, pulling the attention of both Rhianne and Garld. Rhianne looked at her with disapproval evident on her face and Garld's laced with surprise. She knew that Garld was her General but surely Landryn's authority was more important. If Landryn wanted her with him on his hunting parties, then Garld wouldn't refuse it.

"We believe there may be more of them," Femira said, "we need to act quickly." It was what she and Landryn had discussed on the ferry. They knew that together they would need to convince the War Council of the importance of this task. It wasn't as though Femira had any sway with the Generals, she barely knew most of their names. But she was one of the few people in Reldon who had actually fought against the draega. And she was soulforged—that had to count for something.

"You would deny your wife's request, my love?" Rhianne looked back at Landryn, stroking his face with a tender hand. The statement crashed into Femira like a rock to the face. *His what?*

"Of course not," Landryn replied, gently removing her hand from his cheek, "we will have time together before I meet with the War Council." *His fucking wife?!*

"We should return to the palace," she heard Garld say but Femira's mind started rushing through all the conversations that she and Landryn had had. *He never once mentioned that he was married! Not once!*

"There are many other matters to discuss," Garld continued, "Annali, I will get a debrief from you on the way."

She recounted Aden's lessons on the Reldoni highborn and royalty. All those long lists of names, along with who was married to whom. How had she missed that Landryn was married? It was his older brother, Lukane that was married. Daegan, the younger one was too—wasn't he? *Shit.* Had she gotten them mixed up on the list? Those lessons had been before she'd met Landryn so she couldn't put any faces to those names. How had she been so oblivious to miss that?

"Annali?" Garld prodded her, his face looking concerned. *Shit, what had he asked?*

"S-sorry, sir," she shook her head to clear away the rambling thoughts, "what was that?"

"Selyn Caul," Garld said, evidently repeating himself, "I'll need an account of how she died. You can tell me on the way."

Selyn and Drad. Their faces shoved their way into her mind and she felt her visage crack, her stomach tightening.

"Perhaps," Landryn interjected, "I will do that," he stepped up beside Femira, placing a comforting hand on her shoulder. She didn't want his hand there. It wasn't his place to comfort her. But she also didn't make any move to remove it.

"I will write up an account," Landryn explained, "for the bloodshedders' records. As for Selyn and Drad's families… I will arrange to visit them personally. They deserve that respect."

"Of course, my lord," Garld nodded, decorously.

"Drad was Ferath's cousin," Landryn mused sadly, "I must write a letter for him also."

There was an abrupt shift in the body language of both Garld and Rhianne. Garld's face stiffened and Rhianne's expression broke into anguish.

"What is it?" Landryn asked, his gaze flicking between the pair.

"Oh, my dear," Rhianne started, her eyes becoming glassy, "I wasn't going to bring this up here but—"

"—We should talk about this back at the palace, my lord," Garld interjected, his face showing concern.

"I'm so sorry," Rhianne continued on as if Garld hadn't cut over her. "It's *so* tragic," she choked back a painfully fake sob. Femira felt her chest tighten. This was it, Rhianne was going to tell him. A part of her was terrified that she would be outed for knowing about it the entire time and hiding the truth from Landryn. But then again, he'd been lying to her too.

"What is it?" Landryn asked, maintaining his composure but his eyes betraying his concern, "is it Allyn?"

"It's your brother," Rhianne whimpered.

"Let us discuss this away from here," Garld leaned forward, his gaze flicking to the surrounding highborn.

"What's happened? Is it Daegan?!"

"Oh my love," Rhianne's tears were now flowing freely, "I'm so sorry that I have to be the one to tell you this. Daegan has been murdered."

The breeze vanished and all sound hushed.

Femira could feel the stillness that dropped over the docks as tangible as if she could touch it. Femira could recognise Landryn's air bubble now by familiarity, but it was different this time. It was eerily still, like he was forcing the air to stagnate around him. She could feel his edir lock into place. Outwardly, he showed no signs of anguish but his edir wasn't so easily masked. Femira could tell from the averted eyes of the highborn, the awkward shuffling and bated breaths that they all knew already.

Rhianne watched her husband with expectant eyes. She *knew* that information would hurt him. And she'd *chosen* to deliver it here, she'd wanted him to have an audience for his grief.

Garld's face was a mask of pained concern, he reached forward and placed a reassuring grip on Landryn's shoulder. "Come, let us go to the palace," Garld urged.

"Who?" Landryn asked, there was an icy edge to his tone.

"It was—" Rhianne started.

"—That is *enough*!" Garld growled to the woman, who recoiled at the vehemence in his tone, then turned to Landryn. "My lord," Garld said in a quick yet controlled manner, "this is not the place to discuss this. Please, I will tell you everything back at the palace."

He gestured to the open carriage door. Landryn looked at it, then back at Garld. His eyes didn't shift to Femira or Rhianne, or any of the watching nobles and soldiers. Wordlessly, he stepped up into the carriage and was followed swiftly by

Rhianne behind him. Garld stepped towards it and placed a hand on the cabin door before Rhianne could close it after her. "I will be accompanying you. The Prince will need military counsel at this time."

"My *husband* needs time to process this," Rhianne seethed, "he needs *me*."

"He does not have the luxury of time," Garld affirmed, then turned his head back to Femira.

"Follow us to the palace," he told her, "there is a lot we need to discuss," then pulled himself into the carriage, pulling the door shut behind him.

Femira watched, her mouth agape as the horses pulled the carriage off towards the Pillar. There was a murmur spreading through the highborn and Femira fixed them with a glare. She recognised some of the soldiers that had been accompanying Garld. Some she knew were soulforged. They looked at her now with... *deference*? She'd take that over the borderline hostility they'd shown her prior to becoming soulforged.

"Is it true?" One of the soldiers—Tobias was his name, if she recalled correctly—worked up the courage to approach her, "people are saying you fought a draega, like a *real* one?" Tobias had been on the corsair hunting mission with her a few weeks back. She'd not talked much to him as he'd been on one of the other teams. He was a soulforged stonebreaker like her.

Femira had never thought the Reldoni to be particularly religious people. They had temples and there would be people passing through them, but they didn't blather on about the gods and demons the way that some other nations did. A lot of them did seem to put a lot of stock into the stories of the draega however.

"I can't say I know exactly what a draega is," she shrugged in response, "but it was a monster... and it was big."

"People are saying it was as big as a trading ship," Tobias said, with a hint of reverence.

"I suppose yeah," Femira looked back at the ferry that had taken her and Landryn across the bay, "not as big as that one," she pointed, "but almost."

"How?" the man gaped, "that's enormous, how do you defeat something like that?"

"I dropped a cliff on it," she said nonchalantly, "say, you wouldn't know where Aden is?"

"I've not seen him since his soulforging ritual," Tobias replied, "but—hang on—you dropped an actual cliff on it?!" he asked incredulously.

"Well it was more like an arch, but back to Aden. His ritual should've been weeks ago, surely he's recovered by now?"

"This happens sometimes," Tobias said, "General Garld will send newly soulforged on assignment immediately after the change."

"That doesn't make any sense," Femira scrunched up her nose, "you need at least a few days to recover, and then a few more to adjust to your new edir senses." She also didn't think that Aden would leave on assignment without leaving any message for her.

She thought about checking in with Jaz or Misandrei to see if they knew anything about it but then remembered that they too were on assignment. *Where is everyone?* Misandrei and Jaz were in Rubane she was quite sure. *Endrin and Loreli too.* There were other bloodshedders that she could spar with in their absence, but a part of her really just wanted a distraction from thinking about Landryn and Rhianne. *Don't fool yourself. You're avoiding thinking about Selyn and Drad.* She shoved those thoughts aside. *Nope.* Now was *not* the time for that. Garld had wanted her to follow to the palace so that's what she'd do.

As Femira made her way through the cypress-lined streets towards the Pillar, she thought about how much Epilas had begun to feel like home to her although she'd spent most of her time in the barracks on the hill, aside from the occasional times that Jaz would drag her and Aden down into the city. She found herself missing the pair. Jaz with his charming, overconfident aura and Aden so introverted by contrast. They were unusual friends, and now that she thought about it, she had never even asked how the two had met.

She wondered if Aden had been sent to Rubane as well. She didn't know much about the place—other than it snowed a lot. The women in the bloodshedders didn't have much respect for Rubanians and she gathered it was yet another backwards patriarchy like her own homeland. Reldon was definitely different in that regard. It was likely inherent to their culture considering their founding monarch had been a woman. But then again, their current leader was a man—King Abhran and his successor, his son, Prince Lukane. Landryn's sister, Princess Allyn had spoken about having the right to challenge him as the female heir. Femira had learned that it was written into Reldoni law that the eldest daughter could challenge the eldest son to the right to rule.

As she made her way to the palace, Femira wondered how many times that law had been enforced over the centuries. Beyond Queen Elyina herself, all of the notable Reldoni monarchs had been men. And now that she thought about it, almost all of the Generals in the War Council were too. *Perhaps Reldon isn't the pinnacle of gender equality as much as they think it is.* While there were still women in positions of authority in the military—Misandrei's position as one of the few bloodshedder captains as an example—there did seem to be a general lack of this across the board. There was definitely not an even split of men and women in the military. The general ranks were seemingly dominated by men. It was primarily in the ranks of runewielders where the numbers started to become equal. She would need to ask Misandrei about that when the woman finally returned from Rubane.

She arrived at the steps to the Pillar and was cleared for entry by the guards manning the gate. From there it was a long climb of steps up to the lower levels of the palace, and then even further up to where Garld would meet her. *No wonder most of the Reldoni highborn are in good shape.* Life in the palace was a constant workout with these steps. Almost a year of training with the bloodshedders—and then climbing and running around on rooftops for years before that—had strengthened her body so that the hundreds of steps left her only a little out of breath when she reached the higher levels.

The Reldoni palace was a thief's nightmare. The Palace was built around—and inside—a giant natural stone pillar that rose up from the ground. The only access to it was via the guarded stairways. Even with her aradium runestone, Femira would have trouble sneaking into this place. The Pillar itself was said to be nine-hundred feet tall; she guessed that the palace balconies started at maybe four hundred feet. *It would be a tough climb.*

To date, the highest climb she'd achieved was the cliff that the Alterean palace had sat atop. *That was at least half this height.* But she was also an infinitely more efficient runewielder now. She toyed with the idea of trying to sneak into the palace sometime as a test for her new skills. Being soulforged, she could now dissolve and reform entire walls in seconds, that kind of skill was like cheating for most break-ins. The palace would make for a good challenge.

She passed by the fountain where she and Landryn had had their first conversation. As it had that night, the waters flowed up into the air and curled in defiance of gravity in complex circular patterns. She understood that there were intricately sophisticated devices that made this work, it involved the use of waterstone gems and rune patterns but she'd never had much interest in understanding how they work. She much preferred using a runestone personally than sticking it into a device.

She thought about how awkward he'd been with her that first night. Landryn had been tiptoeing around her because he thought she resented him for killing her husband. *Which was all bullshit, of course.* She wasn't the one that was married. That realisation was a surprise, and she could admit to herself that it stung. Although he'd never actually alluded to anything romantic with her. Besides, he was a Prince and she was... well, less than a year ago she'd been stealing food just to survive.

It's not as though she wanted to *marry* Landryn. But Femira couldn't deny that getting to know him a little more intimately hadn't crossed her mind. None of this changed the fact that she wanted to be part of what he was planning. Pushing aside any feelings she might've had for him in that way, she still wanted to be part of his team fighting the draega.

"Ah, the draega-slayer returns," a familiar accented voice came from behind her, pulling her attention from the fountain.

"Vestyr," Femira turned in surprise as she hadn't sensed his edir at his approach.

"The palace is whirring with two notable topics today," he smiled indulgently, the adult expression looking alien on his child-like face. "The first," he held up a finger, "and most concerning is that Prince Landryn has learned of his brother's demise. The King and many of the highborn lords in the city have known this for days but how *Landryn* will react is stirring some disquiet within the palace." *Can't you all just leave the man to grieve in peace?*

"The second," Vestyr continued without skipping a beat, flicking up a second finger and pointing at her, "is Annali Jahar. I don't know how you've managed to stay out of the attention of the noble houses these past few months but people are rapt by your actions of late. Many of them believed you were simply a coerced hostage taken from Altarea, but now that you've risen so swiftly through the ranks of the bloodshedders and the stories of you fighting draega alongside our valiant Prince Landryn... well, you've garnered their attention."

"I don't want their attention," she brushed past him.

"You've got it whether you want it or not."

"It's worthless to me."

"I doubt that, but regardless, some of the factions in the palace will seek to sway you to their causes."

"Is that what you're doing right now?" she turned back to him, "you want to bring me into whatever you and Allyn are planning?"

"I wouldn't be so forward," Vestyr chuckled, holding up his hands in a disarming gesture, "I have no doubts as to your loyalties to Garld... or Prince Landryn for that matter."

"So what do you want?"

"To take you up on that offer you made before leaving for the Tidewall," he grinned, "to train with the draega-slayer herself."

Femira had forgotten about that and she couldn't deny that she was still very intrigued by the Aeth boy's abilities. He was undeniably soulforged but yet seemed ignorant of the bloodshedders methods. Despite Femira's attempts at it, she still hadn't managed to trap anyone in the ground as efficiently as Vestyr had done.

"Ok," she said with a measure of consideration, "I can't right now but I'll let you know when suits me."

"Excellent," he beamed, "I have a permanent residence in the city but more often I stay in the guest levels of the palace. You should be familiar with it, your cousin Daurond's quarters are there too and as I understand it, you two are very close," he flashed her a wicked grin and winked before turning to leave. *What did he mean by that?* She'd not visited her fake cousin once since arriving. In fact, she'd only ever spoken with him that night Honorsword Karas had attacked her. Could Vestyr have been alluding that he was aware of Femira's lie? She wanted to shrug it off as nothing but she felt a knot of apprehension at the thought. Would Garld still want to keep her employ if her cover was blown? Did he have use for Femira as she was, or did he still only see the value in Annali?

***

All members of the War Council had a personal office in the palace. Being a General in the army meant that Garld had a seat at the War Council and—as such—an office. Femira had never visited his office in the palace and was taken aback at the opulence of it compared to the pragmatic office he kept in the barracks.

Seeing Garld now in that office standing by the window overlooking the city, there was a lot she still didn't know about him. There was so much that he was still hiding from her. Landryn seemed to trust Garld as much as she did—more so even—yet Garld had hidden the truth about Daegan's death from him. He had asked Femira *specifically* to keep Landryn from discovering it. She wanted to understand why. She also wanted know what he was keeping from *her*. Landryn wanted to use the bloodshedders to fight against the draega but did Garld hold the same aspirations for them?

"Vreth," he smiled warmly as she approached, "you did well. Both in your tasks with Landryn and the draega."

"Did you know about them? The kraglings?" She could feel an element of accusation in her tone.

"Ah," he gave her a pained look, "truthfully... no, I did not."

"Landryn said that you and he started the bloodshedders to fight them. If that's true, then you *did* know that they existed."

"Yes," he agreed, "I was aware of their existence. But I never believed that we would find any in our own borders. The draega have been sighted in the Simirwood—yes. And along the Athlin border but *never* this close to Epilas. I thought we would have years before it became an issue for us."

"Why didn't you tell us?" Femira shot, she was surprised with her own anger, "why keep this from us?"

"There are many reasons," he replied, calmly, "but the first thing to remember is that you are soldiers. Your role is not to question the authority of your senior officers. We kept this from the bloodshedders because we didn't feel it was the time to tell you." She didn't like that one bit. It sounded too much like what Lichtin used to say. *I'll tell you only what you need to know.* And almost always it was the more dangerous parts of the job he kept from them. *Was that it?*

"Are you worried they'll be afraid... that they won't fight?"

"Of course not," Garld shook his head, "I have faith in the bloodshedders—no, the reason we have kept this secret is far more complex than that."

"Then tell me! Landryn told me *everything*; about the dead draega you found, about Elyina's journals and why you invaded Altarea. Why have you been hiding all of this? Do you not trust us? *We're* the ones fighting out there. Selyn and Drad *died* fighting that thing…" Femira trailed off.

This was why she was angry. She wasn't mad at Garld at all. Femira felt a wash of regret flow over her, dispelling her anger. *Remorse*. She deflated realising that she was just looking for someone to blame for her own recklessness.

"It's alright, Vreth," Garld walked around the desk and placed a reassuring hand on her shoulder.

"I thought I could kill it," she broke.

"You did," he held her gaze, "you *did* kill it, Vreth." She'd never told him her real name. Did a small part of her always hold back from trusting him entirely? She'd told Misandrei once, on the cliffs at Innish Head. *I thought she would have told Garld.* But maybe not. Maybe they weren't so concerned with what her real name was.

"Why did you want me to hide Daegan's death from Landryn?" Femira asked, the memory of Landryn's impassive face when receiving the news drifted across her mind. The cracks of his grief that she could feel through his edir.

"Landryn is an exceptional runewielder," Garld replied, taking a seat at his desk and indicating for her to do the same. "He is a good tactician and knows when to heed the advice of his elders. A thing you that must understand is that Landryn has been raised and molded to be a military leader from birth… his upbringing was more difficult than you would think for a person of his position. He did not face the same struggles that you must have… his hardships were of a different breed. As a result of this, Landryn's greatest ability is to mask and suppress his emotions. This is a valuable asset in a commander who needs to think rationally and make pragmatic decisions with people's lives… however, with Daegan, he has acted… *rashly* in the past. Landryn cared deeply for his brother. I worry that he will make some poor and hasty decisions in these revelations."

"You think he'll seek revenge?" Femira couldn't deny that she had desired the same when her own brothers had been killed.

"Landryn's blade will find vengeance, I have no doubt on that. But where that is directed will have consequences for us all."

"Do you know who killed Daegan Tredain?" Femira probed. Garld didn't answer at first, instead his gaze drifted. *He definitely knows more about this.* "Yes," he replied eventually, "I know who killed Daegan and I know why." Femira leaned forward expectantly.

"He was killed by one of our own," Garld admitted, a troubled look crossing his face, "a soulforged bloodshedder named Ferath Vitares."

Ferath? Had she heard that name before?

"Did I train with him?" she asked.

"No," Garld replied, "he was sent to Rubane not long after you first arrived in Epilas. Landryn had placed him as the Captain of Daegan's guard. I'd argued against it at the time, Ferath was one of the first soulforged and I wanted to keep him close for monitoring but Landryn insisted."

"He and Landryn were friends," Femira nodded in remembrance, "he's Drad's cousin, right?"

"You are always a lot sharper than I give you credit," Garld surmised, smiling at her, "indeed... Ferath trained with both Landryn and Daegan when they were boys. Ferath was one of my finest students when I was swordsmaster. It was one of the reasons I'd chosen him to be among the first soulforged."

"So then *why*?" Femira shook her head, "why would he betray Landryn like that?"

"I believe that Ferath and Daegan are both pawns in a larger game," Garld intoned, "*someone* wishes to sow discord amongst the Reldoni military leadership. They want to turn Landryn and the Royal Family *against* the bloodshedders... I believe that it is the Dukes of Rubane that have orchestrated this. They have long been growing apprehensive with Reldon's growing military strength... we have already reclaimed Altarea and I believe they fear we will target Athlin and then Rubane next, with the ultimate goal of restoring Reldon's former glory." From what Femira had heard of King Abhran that wasn't an unrealistic judgement to make.

"So they turn the Commander of the army against his own elites," Femira speculated.

"Along with the rest of the Royal Family," Garld nodded. "It is a widely known truth that King Abhran had little love for Daegan, but he will not stand the insult of his own blood being murdered. Abhran's retribution will be swift and brutal on those responsible." Femira felt a knot of worry grow in her stomach.

"And the King thinks *we* had something to do with this?"

"That is the story the Arch-duke of Rubane is attempting to perpetrate. I do not believe that Ferath turned against his own people. Every man has his price but Ferath is loyal to a fault."

"Misandrei and the others," Femira guessed, "their mission to Rubane... they're looking for Ferath Vitares," she concluded.

"Indeed," Garld nodded, "our first priority is to find Ferath and to apprehend the true assassin and question him. Arch-duke Edmund claims that Ferath escaped in the aftermath of the assassination. His statement claims that Ferath demonstrated 'inhuman' runewielding ability, he even goes as far to label him as a potential draega! It appears that they are as ignorant of soulforging as we recently were... I believe the Dukes' have attempted to frame Ferath and seek to place the blame on us as means to undercut the Royal Family's trust in us. Their full plans ultimately foiled by Ferath's superior runewielding."

As always, Femira was encouraged to see Garld's passion in his trust and confidence in the bloodshedders. *Even now he trusts that Ferath didn't betray them.* She wondered if everyone who had been soulforged by Garld had shared the same sense of compassion from him during the ritual as she did.

"Does the team have a lead?" Femira asked.

"I have agents in the city of Rubastre, contacts that I can rely on," Garld said vaguely, "and I have received word from Ferath directly and understand that he is attempting to lie low and avoid capture from the Rubanians. They expected him to attempt to flee to Reldon, which I am glad that he did not. The last correspondence I received from him was that he had instructed Misandrei's team to meet him at a town beyond the Iron Hills called Urundock. This is where he believes Daegan's murderer was last seen."

"So we find Daegan's killer, and then we figure out who orchestrated all of this."

"Precisely."

"And you've told Landryn this?"

"Of course. Like me—Landryn has difficulty believing that Ferath would turn against us so easily. Ferath served Landryn directly for many years. But Landryn's judgement at this time is irrational, we must not let him make make reckless decisions in his grief."

"How is he doing?" Femira asked, concerned.

"He is... in shock, I believe. But we must use these events to our advantage. Vreth, I need you to sneak into Landryn's office and recover Elyina's journals along with anything that might give us insight into what Landryn intends to do."

"You want me to *spy* on him?" she asked, incredulous. She'd have had no qualms about the request before. Sure, he was their commander, but when had she ever let authority stop her. But it felt *distasteful* to her now. Now that she and Landryn were... friends? *Are we?* He'd hidden the fact that he was married from her. That wasn't something friends did.

"For his own protection, you see," Garld concluded, "we must *shield* him from his own grief, you understand." Femira felt her reluctance falter. She opened her mouth to respond but then thought for a moment. *Maybe Garld was right?* Femira herself had made a lot of poor decisions in the wake of her brothers' deaths. *Being taken in by Lichtin's lies had been the biggest one.*

"What will I be looking for?" She asked tentatively.

"Anything that indicates Landryn suspects the bloodshedders' involvement with Daegan's murder. He will likely have many letters of condolences from the Highlords, along with their subtle and not-so-subtle advice on what he should do. Read through them, and note which ones seek to paint the bloodshedders in poor light. Averstock in particular." *Highlord Averstock.* He was Rhianne's father. How does he play into all of this?

"What would Averstock have to gain from that?"

"Averstock is far more cunning than he would seem. Make no mistake, Rhianne is a representative of the Highlords and they do not like how much power the bloodshedders are gaining. They want our ranks dispersed and integrated with their own armies. And she is undoubtedly swaying Landryn towards their way of thinking."

They want their own soulforged soldiers. The Reldoni army was nuanced with large divisions reporting into Generals. The Generals then reported to the Highlords of their region. The bloodshedders sat outside of this with General Garld as their leader who reported directly to Landryn and, by extension, the Tredain family. This meant that the Tredains now had sole control of the most elite runewielders.

"If they play him against the bloodshedders," Femira guessed, "they'll undercut his trust in us and the bloodshedders will be absorbed into their armies. They're trying to make it seem like they're protecting him but in truth, they're working *against* him."

"You see it," Garld nodded, "*we* must be the ones to ensure that he is protected."

CHAPTER 43
Held Tight

Femira crept silently through the palace halls. If she weren't so swept up in the concern for Landryn she would have been disappointed in how *easy* it was to infiltrate. *Seriously, the flaws in the Pillar security needs to be addressed.*

Although she did have some *slight* advantages over an everyday burglar. Firstly, Annali Jahar had clearance for most parts of the palace giving her a very favourable safety net so when she did stumble across some guards they didn't question her. In fact, one had even *saluted* her.

And secondly—possibly more emminently—she had the exceptionally convenient ability to *walk through fucking walls*! And this wasn't dissolving a wall, stepping through and then crudely reforming it as a smoothed piece, no, no. *That would be* far *too obvious.* She could recreate the wall *exactly* as it had been before.

Femira stepped up to the wall, glanced down the hall to see if there was anyone coming. It was clear. She placed a hand on the wall, and felt the vibrations of the stone underneath. She could feel the depth of the wall through to the other side.

This was where her skill came into play. She pushed her face forward, dissolving the rock and absorbing it until her nose poked out on the other side, followed closely by the rest of her face.

The hallway on the other side was illuminated by decorative gaslamps. Her eyes quickly scanned the hallway and landed on a pair of guards further down. She pulled her face back and reformed the wall perfectly. Most of the palace had originally been stoneshaped so it wasn't hard to reform it back into its original appearance. She did have to avoid the more opulent parts of the walls where the original stoneshaper had taken a more *artistic* approach to their construction.

Femira tested a few areas like this, teasing the easiest place. She had clearance to be in the parts of the palace where the War Council was held along with the offices of the various Generals and military Highlords. Landryn's office however was not in this area. The uppermost floors of the Pillar were reserved for the Royal Family and the most important dignitaries. It added a mildly additional difficulty to sneak into it.

Femira just had to be wary of the Royal guards—all of whom would be skilled runewielders and could likely sense her edir if she didn't contain it carefully. *Some of them will be soulforged too.* She knew that some of the bloodshedders had been reallocated into the King's personal guard. *Would it not have made more sense to get one of them to spy on Landryn?* Maybe Garld simply trusted her more than any of them. That thought gave her a small swell of pride.

Getting to the upper levels was easy but the Royal chambers and offices were all behind a few layers of security. She'd done a round of the hallways surrounding these, testing the other side at various points. Each time she quickly pulled back as there was someone on the other side. She was averse to doing another round as the guards on *this* side might start getting suspicious of her lurking around.

Garld had instructed her that Landryn's office was on the outer edge of the Pillar and had a balcony that overlooked the city. She'd wanted to avoid climbing out and along the side of the Pillar as the larger walkways that ringed the Palace on the lower levels would have a clear view of her. In general, guards tended to be oblivious but it was a substantial risk doing it in broad daylight.

Femira followed a hallway down towards a window and looked out. It was still a few hours from sunset but she decided that waiting until nightfall and then climbing out and around was the best path to take to avoid any detection.

Resolved to wait it out, Femira returned to the lower levels. She decided to loiter in an inculpable area on one of the gardened balconies. *Just a girl wandering the palace gardens. Nothing suspicious in that, nope. Purely innocent, my friend.*

She let her mind drift back to her conversation with Garld earlier that day. Now that she was out of his office, she felt the unsavoury taste of guilt at spying on Landryn rise up in her. She'd noticed this happen before when speaking with Garld, where her emotions would slip away from her. Once again, she suspected him of using a mindstone. But maybe he just made very convincing arguments.

Misandrei had given her some basic training in resisting mindstone runewielders. She said that they couldn't read your thoughts or change them, but they could manipulate your emotions. She said the most important thing to remember was that if your emotion was to abruptly shift, it was likely a mindstone user trying to make you feel that way.

The biggest defence against mindstone manipulation was simply identifying it happening, in most cases that knowledge was a defence that crumbled any mindstone effects.

"The edir is a lot stronger inside your own body," Misandrei had taught her, "even the strongest mindstone user would have difficulty manipulating a person's emotions if they're aware of it happening. Their edir would instinctively work against it."

"So the edir is like a natural defence to this?" Femira had probed.

"Not exactly," Misandrei had replied, "in truth, the mindstone works by manipulating one's *own* edir against them. It's confusing, I know. But it's the same with bloodstone, it's almost impossible to use runewielding inside of another person's body. You need to physically touch them to break that barrier. Mindstone and bloodstone work by manipulating your target's edir and guiding it to your will. With bloodstone it is the physical body, manipulating your own edir to the will of another and then using the power of the bloodstone to make changes to the body. When healing is done, it's your *own* edir doing the healing but guided by the healer with the bloodstone. The same applies to mindstone, it's your own edir manipulating your emotions, only your edir is being controlled by an external force. This is why recognising this is happening is so important. Your edir will instinctively resist that control if you're aware that it's happening."

Femira didn't like the idea that Garld could be manipulating her emotions. It was illogical too, the man was already a specialist in both bloodstone and soulstone so he would need to be some kind of prodigy to be skilled in the three. Even so, she decided that she should be a bit more wary around the man.

"I don't see *you* in the gardens often," Femira heard Daurond's voice. Her fake cousin was dressed in orange silks and was interlinking his arm with a young handsome man. Daurond let go of the man and politely shooed him away, leaving him and Femira alone in the gardens.

"I'm not usually in the palace," she replied, "but I had business here so decided to look around."

"Well, it is a delight to see you, dear cousin," he flashed her one of his bright smiles, "I would love to linger for a chat but I do however have an engagement I must attend to. I insist that you come by my quarters this week. There are some things I would like to discuss with you." And with that comment, Daurond was gone as quickly as he appeared, linking back in with the man waiting nearby.

Things I need to discuss with you. The comment left her feeling apprehensive. Did someone suspect her of being an imposter? Or perhaps, this was what Vestyr had warned her of. He'd told her that the various nobles in the palace would begin to seek her out now that she was becoming a person of importance. Either way she didn't particularly like it.

She missed Jaz and Aden. She missed her training sessions with Misandrei—even the sessions with Endrin and Loreli. But they were all off on assignment. She admonished herself for forgetting to press Garld about where Aden had been sent to —and more importantly—when he would return. Aden was a wealth of knowledge for her. And she didn't doubt he would have some insights into the draega.

She would have to make do with sparring with Vestyr for now—and whoever else amongst the bloodshedders might be willing. She realised that lingering around the gardens was a perfect opportunity for more highborn to approach her and she didn't particularly feel like speaking with any of them. Not while she was on an assignment. She found a reclusive bench hidden away behind some trees and waited for nightfall in peace, watching the wind rustle through the leaves and listening to the birds.

***

Femira leapt lightly onto the balcony. She left the handholds on the exterior of the Pillar in place, deciding not to bother reforming them until she climbed back that way when she was done. There was a chill to the breeze this high up the Pillar that reminded Femira of the cold winter winds in Alterea.

Landryn's office balcony was long and wrapped around a significant portion of the Pillar, she could envisage Landryn sitting out here in a meditative position and honing his windshaping abilities. The door to the office was glass with a lacquered wooden frame. It was also locked which was no surprise. The lock, she could sense with her edir, was entirely wood. It was decent security, but was ultimately all useless as the walls were stone.

Peeking through the glass she could see that the office was empty. *Unless someone was sitting in the dark waiting for a spy.* She was confident that there wasn't. She sidestepped and reached out her edir to the stone wall. Much of the palace was carved right into the Pillar itself but the uppermost portion was too narrow so many of the higher floors were constructed around it. Her edir senses told her that the wall was about fifteen inches thick. Without breaking stride, Femira stepped through the wall, dissolving it to nothing. The stone material rushed around Femira in a wave of dust and debris and then reformed immaculately behind her. She grinned. *Far too easy.* She'd been hoping that the upper levels were all constructed with wood. *That would've at least been a little bit of a challenge.*

The room inside was unlit. Underneath her black uniform, her chest was glowing with the light of runewielding. She thought back fondly to the days she would use the dim light of her earthstone to navigate through dark rooms she'd broken into. She focused her edir inward, guiding the power of the earthstone inside of her to her hands. They began to glow with a soft amber light. *I suppose this works too. Powers to reshape the earth and defeat ancient demons are good but also make for a very useful lamp.*

Her instructions had been to simply sift through Landryn's letters to look for anything incriminating from the various highborn houses. Femira made for the desk and began rummaging through the drawers. *Anything that looks like it's trying to blame Daegan Tredain's murder on the bloodshedders.* She found Averstock's seal easily enough on an opened letter.

Prince Landryn,

My deepest condolences for the loss of your brother, Daegan. Although I did not know him well personally, I am aware that he was a fine gentleman and he will be greatly missed amongst the noble houses, I am sure. I am grateful that Rhianne can be at your side during this incredibly difficult time, House Averstock will always and forever be House Tredain's closest ally. I treat this loss as painfully as I would a member of my own house. Rest assured, that any and all resources you require are at your disposal to bring the culprits of this crime against Reldon to justice.

I would also like to offer my sincerest gratitude for your valiant efforts in eradicating the draega threat from the shores of my lands. The Tidewall is often overlooked as a vulnerability in our nation's defence and I am eternally grateful for your commitment. It will not be forgotten.

Faithfully,
Edwin of House Averstock, Highlord of the Tidewall.

Femira scoffed. Who signs off like that with their official title to their son-in-law? The whole letter read to Femira as faff. *Sorry your brother's dead. Didn't know him and didn't really care to. A reminder that we have an alliance and thanks for sorting out my pest problem.* There didn't look to be anything incriminating in the letter but Femira memorised the wording all the same to report back to Garld. Perhaps there was something in the words that gave a more subtle indication of subterfuge.

She sifted through more letters of condolences from the noble houses. Houses Darine, Loale, Worthe and Lamgan were all similarly written. The letter from the Highlord of House Mattice—the very same General Mattice that got Sadrian Graves killed in that duel with the Honorsword all those months ago—had a suspicious note in it:

I trust that you agree we must take a firm hand with our justice. The Dukes of Rubane must pay the cost for this insult to our crown in blood.

That was the most aggressive statement she'd found, however as she read through more she could see that almost all of them were under the belief that it was the Dukes of Rubane that were responsible. Some expressed shock at Ferath Vitare's betrayal but not a single one seemed to call out the bloodshedders as potential culprits. *Perhaps Garld was mistaken?* Or could it be that Garld is being paranoid and overly-cautious in sending her?

Finally at the bottom of the stack she found a letter from Landryn's brother. Landryn's mother had passed away soon after giving birth to Allyn and with Daegan deceased that left only his sister, Allyn, his elder brother Lukane and their father, King Abhran. There was no letter from Allyn or the King but there was one from Lukane;

Landryn,

Now is not the time for foolishness. We must act decisively. Father has summoned us to his chambers before we meet with the War Council.

Lukane.

A bit blunt. Lukane didn't seem that cut up about the death of their brother or perhaps he just wasn't that poetic a man. *He sounds like an ass.* She'd only ever seen Lukane and the King once, at the feast celebrating the bloodshedder's victory at Innish Head. Even then, Femira had not spoken directly with either the King or his heir.

The other thing that Garld had wanted her to do was to recover Elyina's journal. *I wonder why Landryn didn't give it to him straight away?* From what Femira knew, Elyina's journals were the only reliable source of information they had on how soulforging worked. *You'd think Landryn would want the man actually doing the soulforgings to have this.* Considering the lengths Averstock had taken to keep the journal he had hidden, she suspected that Landryn would keep it similarly secured.

She checked over the desk and a number of hidden pressure release compartments. Some were empty and others had various documents that she left untouched. One had a store of runestones that she had to actively resist the urge to pocket. *No journals.*

She checked over the bookshelves. There were stacks of books on military tactics, and advanced runewielding. Her eyes scanned over all of them looking for anything out of place. *Rich people don't actually read as much as they want people to believe they do.* And Landryn—as much as she liked the man—was as rich as they come. She smirked as she noted which books didn't have a layer of dust on them. *The Founding of Reldon* and *Elyina's Crusade* didn't seem to have anything hidden inside. Both were topics that Landryn would have an interest in if he'd been researching the draega before their mission to the Tidewall. She also noticed that *Myths & Legends: The Draega of the Black Sands* looked to be heavily worn from multiple readings.

The only suspicious book that wasn't covered in dust was *Military Logistics: Calculating Cost Estimates.* That was the winner. *Not a hope in hells anyone would casually pick this up for some light reading.* Unsurprisingly, when she tried to open it she found that it was, in fact, a fake. *Shocker!*

It was a rudimentary puzzle lock and Femira found herself disappointed in Landryn's lack of ingenuity here. She pressed the last bit into place and... nothing? *Hmmm.* Maybe not so disappointing. She tried a few other patterns but nothing. Then she tried reaching out with her edir and *still* nothing. What kind of lock was this thing?

A part of her wanted to just smash the thing apart but it was also too risky without knowing what was inside. Besides, that would be too clear of an indicator of a break-in for Femira's tastes. *The best part is waiting to see how long it is before anyone even realises they've been robbed.*

She was about to try again at the box when she felt Landryn's familiar edir approach the door. Her eyes snapped open up and she pushed the fake book back into place and prepared to bolt for the balcony door. She didn't have time, the door swung open and Femira panicked and instead backed up to the stone wall. *Fuck, fuck.* Wait. She could just... she extended out her edir behind her.

Landryn stormed into the room followed closely by Rhianne. He ignited the gaslamps which illuminated the office but also—thankfully—cast the area Femira was in into a deeper shadow. Femira sunk into the stone wall behind her. She didn't want to risk backing into another room so instead of reforming the wall exactly as it had been, she shaped the stone around her body. She enclosed herself entirely in the stone—well, almost entirely. She faced her head slightly to the side so that one eye was still poking out from the wall and hoped that the shadows would keep her from being discovered. She then restrained her edir, containing it completely inside of her.

It was an uncomfortable feeling being completely restrained by the stone wall, the rock pressing against her muscles. When she breathed in, her chest pushed against the immovable stone. She found it peculiar that she didn't feel in any way claustrophobic by being confined. Perhaps it was because deep down her body knew that she could dissolve the stone whenever she wished to. She'd only been runewielding a few years, she wouldn't have thought that it was long enough for her instincts to completely re-adjust but maybe that was simply part of what soulforging did to you.

"I won't stand for it, Rhianne!" Landryn snarled. His words sounded muffled to Femira's trapped ears. She watched as another two highborn women followed in after Rhianne.

"Leave us," Rhianne said to the newcomers and waved them off. They all but leapt at her command.

"Now is the time to act, my dear," Rhianne said appeasingly but didn't approach Landryn. He had changed out of his travel garb and was now dressed in a pressed black military suit. The calm demeanour he'd held onto earlier was falling apart, his anger and rage evident on his face.

"And do as your father wishes?" he said accusingly, "*invade* Rubane?!"

"The Highlords are angry, just as you are. We are all grieving."

"*No!*" Landryn shouted. "No, you're not! *None* of you are! None of you even knew him. The Highlords are greedy and want to exploit the invasion for their own profit under the cover of loyalist vengeance. Do not play me for a fool, Rhianne!" Femira could feel the vehement sting in his words. She did not envy Rhianne's position.

"Be careful how you speak with me, *husband*," Rhianne said with an icy tone. Femira didn't need to extend her edir to feel the swath of Landryn's edir pour over the room, drawing in the air around him.

"Go," Landryn growled. "Get out!" Rhianne must've been able to feel the change in the atmosphere of the room because she quickly fled, slamming the door after her.

With Landryn's edir now pulling erratically at the air, Femira felt a sudden spike of panic that he might sense her presence. But he was too distracted by his own emotion to notice her.

The wind picked up, swirling loose papers as it did so, and began building rapidly. Books were lifted up from the shelves, and then the chairs and the desk itself were all swept up in the tempest. Even muffled, Femira could hear the rushing of the wind and the clattering crashes of objects being thrown about the room.

Landryn paced about, trembling, as the gusts grew stronger and stronger. The winds circled about Landryn in a frenzy, wreaking havoc on the office until eventually the force of the gales shattered the windows.

The room went still, the air rushing out of it in an instant. Books and furniture all dropped abruptly in haphazard heaps, loose bits of paper fell slowly like confetti.

Femira remained frozen, watching with dismay as Landryn collapsed to his knees. The man bent over onto his hands and began shaking with the intensity of a person vomiting.

The stone holding Femira in place turned to dust at her command. She tentatively stepped out from the wall. Landryn didn't notice her. He simply remained where was, his entire body trembling with emotion.

Slowly, Femira stepped over the books and papers, making her way towards him. As she approached, Landryn looked up and their eyes met. There was so much pain in them. Femira felt her own visage crack at the sight of him, her chest tightening. She hated it. She hated seeing him suffer like this.

Landryn looked down at his hands, and he continued to cry without a sound. She remembered only a week before when their roles had been reversed. It had been Femira who had been unable to control the pain of her memory.

Just as Landryn had done for her, Femira knelt beside him and took him in her arms. The weight of him pressed against her, and his whole body trembled. She pulled his head to her chest and felt the cloth of her shirt grow damp with his tears and hot breath. Holding him in her arms, she swayed gently back and forth.

She took deep steadying breaths. Holding him in that position, Femira waited for Landryn to stop, to say something... but he didn't. So she kept on waiting. Femira continued to take calming, reassuring breaths, reminding Landryn that he wasn't alone.

His body felt so strong in her arms yet he was so vulnerable. The heat of him against her was a contrast to the chill breeze flowing in from the broken windows. She took comfort in his warmth and found herself hoping that he felt the same.

She rested her head on top of his. The smell of his hair filled her nose. She was intoxicated by it but she didn't dare to move. He was like a bird with a broken wing and she feared that any movement would send him in a stumbling flight from her.

Eventually, Landryn's body stopped trembling and she realised that he was sleeping, his head heavy against her chest. As gently as she could, Femira lay him on his side on the carpeted floor. Then kneeling on all fours next to him, she leaned down and kissed his cheek. The bristle of his hair growth tickled her lips.

It felt wrong to leave him there like that after everything he'd just been through. Femira looked about the destroyed room, rose to her feet and turned the knobs on the gaslamps plunging it into darkness. Her eyes adjusted a moment later to the soft light of the moons streaming in from the empty window panes.

She lightly stepped back to where Landryn was sleeping and lay down next to him. Femira wrapped her arms around his shoulders and tucked her face into his back. The soft fabric of his shirt and the warmth of his skin beneath lulling her into sleep.

**

Femira stirred at one stage in the night and felt arms around her. Her face resting against the soft carpet. In a half-dazed state, she glanced over her shoulder and could see Landryn's face in a deep sleep. The warmth of his body covered her back and encompassed her. She allowed herself to be pulled back into her slumber.

***

Femira woke a few hours later to Landryn slowly rising to an upright position. The murky blue light of an approaching dawn was visible through the windows. Femira opened her mouth to speak but then found she couldn't find the words for what to say.

"Thank you," Landryn whispered to her, "I… " he trailed off.

"It's alright," she wasn't sure how she would explain what she was doing in his office but he never asked. Landryn was quiet then for a moment.

"What was he like?" Femira eventually asked, "your brother?"

"He was… " a sad smile crossed his face, "a lot smarter than people gave him credit for." Landryn's smile was genuine, "he'd convince you to bet everything you had in a game that he'd just made up the rules to… he could also hold his drink better than anyone I know…" his words trailed off.

"What would you say to him now, if you could?"

"I'd say that I'm sorry," his word's broke again, "I'd say that I wish I had done more for him. That I should have *been* there for him… that I should never have left him alone."

Landryn went on to tell her more of what Daegan had been like. The games they'd played as children. They'd been so close as boys and had been separated when Daegan's affliction had become known.

He told her of the tortuous methods his father had employed in Daegan's training. Landryn said that he'd always thought it was to spark a response in Daegan's edir, but as he got older he could see that it was simply his father's cruelty and malice that had driven the man to it.

Landryn was convinced that Abhran saw his own failings as a father and as a King reflected in Daegan's inability and had punished the boy for it. Femira was surprised at how much reflection Landryn had already given the topic. One of the things he seemed to regret most was never speaking to Daegan about it. Never confiding in him or allowing his brother a safe place to talk about it.

Landryn then spoke of his sister, Allyn. How she had tried to mend the bridge between Landryn and Daegan. Then he spoke of his mother, how caring and kind she'd been in the hazy memories of his early life.

Femira continued to let him speak and after a while, Landryn had burned himself out.

"Thank you, Annali," he said, placing a hand on hers. Femira frowned and he had taken the expression as an offence and tried to pull his hand back. She gripped it with her other hand.

"It's Femira," she said, watching his face as it scrunched in confusion.

"My name is Femira."

Understanding was slow to cross his face as the realisation of what she was telling him sunk in. After a moment he was nodding. "That… that makes sense."

"I'm sorry for lying to you." *About who I was. About Daegan… about everything.*

"So… who are *you*, Femira?" His hand felt warm cupped in hers and she felt his other hand resting on top. The two of them knelt in the middle of the destroyed room, their hands interlocked. He didn't hate her. He didn't blame her.

"I... I don't know," she answered truthfully and shrugged, "I'm just... me?"
Bright rays of the morning sun crept into the room. They touched his face and accentuated the contours of it.

"I would like to get to know you better, Femira," Landryn said, his smile reaching his eyes for the first time.

Swept up in a rush of passion, Femira grabbed Landryn's head and pulled him towards her. Their lips met and she melted into him. Their faces pressed against one another, she wrapped her arms around his neck and pushed her body against his. She felt heat rush through her.

After a few moments they broke apart, faces less than an inch apart, their breaths heavy. Awkwardly, she laughed, her smile genuine. He was laughing now too and she could feel the warmth of his breath on her face again.

Then there was a knock at the door.

The sharp noise wrenched them both from their moment of passion. Landryn gently stepped back from her, she stood straight and adjusted her uniform and patted her hair flat. It was obvious that she had slept there.

"I should go," she said looking back to the balcony.
"Who is it?" Landryn called out.
"Ceren, my lord," a man's voice called through the door.
"Come in," Landryn replied, and then surveyed the damage he'd done to his office the night before.

The door opened and a broad shouldered man stepped in, he was garbed in the uniform of the Royal guard. *The same uniform that Drad used to wear.* Similar to Femira's but his was both red and black whereas hers was all black. Ceren's eyes landed suspiciously on her, and then realising she was not a threat, his eyes quickly took in the ruined office with alarm.

"Is everything alright, my lord?" he asked with urgency, his eyes darting about looking for intruders.

"Nothing that you can assist with. This was my own doing," Landryn replied, "what is the matter?"

"Uh, the Prince-heir has summoned you, my lord" he responded nervously, not entirely sure what he'd intruded into, "he says you are to join him and the King in the Throne Room."

"Tell them I will be there shortly," Landryn responded.

"Um, apologies, my lord. Prince Lukane was quite adamant that I escort you there personally, you understand?"

"I do, Ceren. Not to worry, I will come, allow me first to change," Landryn walked towards the door, "you can escort me first to my chambers."

Landryn then looked back at Femira and gave her a warm smile, "we can continue our conversation later?" He posed it as a question for her but he didn't need to, Femira had every intention of resuming what they'd started. She nodded, a smirk pulling at her mouth. Landryn departed and Ceren gave her one last curious look, then another confused glance over the room before nodding to her and following after the Prince.

Left alone, Femira let out a long breath and looked about the ruined office. *I suppose I can just use the door now?* It didn't seem like Landryn had any intention of hiding the fact that she had stayed the night there. *Maybe I should still climb out... just in case.* She made her way towards the balcony and her foot stepped on a fallen book.

She looked down and realised that the bindings were familiar. Leaning down she hefted it into her arms and inspected the cover. It was an unusual blue leather with a strange pattern emblazoned on the front.

She recognised it. But she wasn't sure from where... *the colour.* She realised. The first time she'd seen it, the book had been bathed in the ambient purple light of the aeristone cache in Altarea. This was the book that she'd found all those months ago that night she'd broken into the Altarean Palace. The night where this had all started. It felt oddly strange seeing it here now. She opened up the first page, she could read it now that she'd been taught Reldoni letters from Aden.

The Art of Soulforging

A memoir of King Ediňar, First Khandāmos of Reldôn

King Edinar? She'd never heard of him before. Queen Elyina had been the founding monarch of Reldon. She also had no idea what a *Khandamos* was.

She glanced around the room and considered for a moment. She *was* still a thief after all. She held onto the tome and made her way back to the balcony.

She hadn't planned on stealing anything larger than Elyina's journal which would have fit inside her shirt. This book however was too bulky for that. Climbing along her handholds with it might prove a little too difficult. *Leave the book and climb back?* Or take the front door? She hefted it up, deciding her curiosity was too great, and strode towards the door.

CHAPTER 44
Here to Stay

Femira fought back a yawn as she neared the door to her room in the barracks. It had been a long early morning walk back from the palace. She had practised the exercise of touching her edir off each individual brick in the hallway so much that she now did it instinctively as she passed through it.

Femira still held the book she'd stolen from Landryn's office under one arm. It was yet another piece in the ever growing puzzle that she'd been swept up into. How had she gone so far as this? She'd only ever intended to stay in Epilas for a few weeks.

When Femira had accepted Garld's proposal, she'd done so out of fear that he probably would have imprisoned her as a thief if she hadn't. Then she'd begun to learn the secrets of runewielding, and as her skills had grown she'd come to rely on the training methods of the bloodshedders for further advancement.

Femira had become intoxicated by the prospect of getting stronger and now where was she? She was so embroiled in their schemes that she wasn't even sure if she could get out anymore.

She wasn't even sure if she wanted to. *This was supposed to be temporary.* But now Epilas was her home. There were people that relied on her. That *needed* her. All the people of Reldon needed her. They needed her and Landryn and the rest of the soulforged to fight the draega.

She looked down at the book in her arms. Landryn and Garld had invaded Altarea to retrieve the soulstone because Elyina's journals had implied it was hidden there. They'd used King Abhran's ambitions for reclaiming Reldon's lost territories as the justification for the invasion to the noble houses.

Femira had little love for the stormguards of Altarea but she wasn't sure how she felt about all the lives that were lost in the efforts in claiming the soulstone. She remembered the fires burning in the city. The bodies of the stormguards strewn about the battlements. She remembered the sulfuric smell of the burning bodies the morning after the assault. *Was the cost of all that bloodshed worth it?*

Upon returning to Epilas, Garld began soulforging bloodshedders. So in those early days when Femira was beginning her training, the first soulforged were discovering their new abilities. *Ferath Vitares is soulforged.* He must have been one of the very first to undergo the process before Daegan Tredain had been sent to Rubastre. Her first days and weeks in Epilas had been a blur and she couldn't recall any mention of Daegan Tredain back then. That had been before her tutoring sessions with Aden, so she hadn't known anything about the Reldoni royal family or the various highborn houses.

Femira trusted that Landryn and Garld had ultimately created the bloodshedders to fight the draega. They wanted powerful runewielders to defend people from the creatures. But now that their skills and prowess were known throughout the nobility, their objectives were being diverted from that cause.

Femira and Landryn had discussed all of this before returning to Epilas. Now he would need to convince his father and the members of the War Council to direct the efforts of the bloodshedders back to the reason they were originally created. But the news of Daegan's death had thrown a wrench into that plan. Femira didn't know what Landryn would do. He was still hurting and all she wanted was to be back with him again.

Her mind kept drifting back to the feel of his lips on hers and his arms gripped around her. She took a steadying breath. That was a distraction. Their goal was to convince the War Council that the draega threat took precedence. She couldn't allow her growing relationship with Landryn to interfere with that.

When Femira reached her room, she saw that there was a plethora of letters that had been slipped under her door. She recognised the seals of the various noble houses on the letters. These would be the invites to dinners and gatherings that Vestyr had mentioned. He'd mentioned that the highborn factions would seek to embroil her in their own schemes and objectives. She stacked them all to the side and ignored them for now.

Garld had instructed Femira to debrief him in the morning so she didn't see any point in delaying. She splashed water on her face and forced away her weariness. She rebraided her hair, changed into a fresh uniform before leaving for Garld's barracks office.

***

Femira didn't want to tell Garld about her night with Landryn. *It's none of his business anyway.* So she told him that she'd fled through the balcony when he'd returned and that she hadn't discovered Elyina's journals prior to that. She had also kept the book she'd found a secret too. *He'd not asked for that specifically.* Considering it had been in Garld's possession after Altarea, he surely knew that Landryn had it?

Femira *did* inform him of all the letters she'd memorised, recounting as much of the details as she could. Garld listened with his usual stone-faced patience for her to finish and then—as was expected—gave her nothing as to what any of it meant to him.

Femira then questioned Garld about Aden and when he would return. The mission that Jaz, Misandrei and the others had been sent on would likely continue for months so she didn't expect them back anytime soon. Garld was tight-lipped about Aden's location, only that he was off on assignment and that was all she needed to know, to which she quietly bristled.

Garld was pleased to learn that there was little suspicion pointing towards the bloodshedders being involved with Daegan Tredain's murder, despite Ferath's role in it. It was clear the highborn were mostly all of the opinion that the Dukes of Rubane were responsible. The theory that the Dukes wanted to sow discord amongst the Reldoni military factions was a narrative that Garld himself was perpetuating strongly throughout the members of the War Council.

"The Highlords are hungry for Rubanian blood," Garld spoke as he sorted through parchments on his desk, "they will not be so easily dissuaded from that cause."

"It's Landryn's decision though, isn't it?"

"Landryn has sway within the War Council, his opinions will not be ignored.

Ultimately, this decision rests with our King. And Abhran will not lightly go against the wishes of his council. Particularly when their wishes align with his own vengeance."

"Will that lead to war with the Rubanians?"

"Potentially," Garld intoned, "yes."

"What will that mean for the bloodshedders?"

"We are a small but effective arm of the Reldoni military, I don't doubt we will be called to join the invasion."

"But what about the draega? They are the real threat."

"Landryn believes this too," Garld replied, "it was his fear of these creatures that brought him to me with the plans to form the bloodshedders."

"He approached you?"

"Indeed," Garld replied, "I had already transitioned from my role as Landryn's swordsmaster. It had been my responsibility to train him not only in the blade but as a tactician and strategist. He had tutors from across our military but he trusted me with this undertaking."

Femira could understand that. Even *she* trusted Garld and she'd only known him a little under a year. Despite his secrets, Garld had a way of making you feel safe. She could only imagine how Landryn felt having had Garld as his teacher and mentor for most of his life. *I suppose if you're going to trust anyone to make you an army of soulforged, it may as well be the person who taught you everything you know.* Garld's background as a healer prior to that was an obvious benefit to soulforging.

"Why did you give up being a healer?" Femira asked bluntly. Garld's eyebrows rose at the sudden shift in conversation but Femira was curious what the drive had been for the man.

"Ah, that is a rather long and meandering story," Garld replied, "but I will indulge you with the short of it. Something you must understand is that I was always skilled in the sword. My father had trained me to be a soldier, you see, this is where my own knowledge of warfare came from. My mother was a chirurgeon and I followed her path more diligently... however, as I grew older, I learned that the best way that I could prevent death and suffering was to prevent the very wars causing them, and I couldn't do that as a healer. How I became Landryn's swordsmaster... well, that too is a long story. My family and the Tredains have long been allies but it was Landryn's mother who convinced me. We were friends, you see, we trained together in the Healer's palace before she wed Abhran... and suffice it to say, it was at *her* request that I chose to train Landryn."

"But," Garld diverted, "that is enough for my story. We must discuss your own rising notoriety." Femira shifted uncomfortably.

"It was inevitable," he continued. "You are an exceptional runewielder and the story of your battle with the draega will only perpetuate and grow. It's not what I envisioned when I recruited you... but we can still lean into this."

"You wanted a thief."

"I wanted a stealth operative," Garld smirked, "but what I obtained is something far more valuable. With prestige comes passage. It's a lot easier to steal information when you've already been invited through the door." Femira couldn't deny that logic but the thrill of the whole breaking-and-entering bit was the part she enjoyed the most.

"The invites have already started," Femira revealed.

"I have no doubt," Garld said, "but a drawback to the spotlight is that it makes it quite difficult for you to slip into the shadows. There will be more eyes on your comings and goings.

You were a novelty before; a Keiran highborn girl in the Reldoni military is an oddity that garnered some attention… now, however, you are a draega slayer and an elite runewielder, people are more curious.

You must be careful with whom you choose to be seen in public with. Alliances form and crumble in moments in Epilas. You are my agent, and your actions reflect upon me. Your *company* reflects upon me." Femira couldn't shake the feeling that he knew about her and Landryn. *But how could he possibly know that?*

"Is there anyone in particular I should avoid, sir?" Femira asked, innocently.

"The Aeth, Vestyr, is not your friend," Garld said, bluntly.

"I never considered him one," she replied, surprise taking her aback.

"No, but he's taken an interest in you. You must be cautious with him, Allyn Tredain may only be a child, but she has within her power, the ability to throw the entire nation into turmoil."

"The Succession Law," Femira noted.

"Indeed, the first born-daughter may contest the first-born son for the right to rule. It is a handover from Elyina's time. A contingency for ensuring that this country did not slip back to its former patriarchy."

"Like King Edinar, before her?" Femira asked and Garld's eyes widened as she said the name.

"So," he said with amusement, "either you *could* read common tongue that night I found you… *or* you saw the book in Landryn's office."

"The latter," she grinned.

"Edinar was one of the last Sorcerer Kings; the last true masters of soulforging. Elyina's progeny worked diligently to eradicate Edinar's name… along with his work," he added the last bit bitterly.

"So Elyina wasn't the first monarch of Reldon?"

"Gods no," Garld chuckled. "There have been Kings, Queens, Chiefs and Overlords in these lands since time immemorial. The people have always been here, and there have always been people with the strength to command them since the dawn of man. Elyina's dynasty is simply the latest in that long line of subjugation… alas we are digressing. Vestyr will attempt to befriend you. He will have aspirations to lure you to Allyn's cause."

"And what *is* Allyn's cause?"

"To destroy what we have built. There are many within the nobility that still hold to the belief that soulforging is a crime against nature, and they seek to undo us."

"But Vestyr is soulforged himself."

"Indeed he is. And I believe many of the Aeth are—much like the Honorswords of Keiran. Vestyr is ardently working against the blooshedders' progress, and will continue to do so. What his ultimate end is, I can only speculate."

"So why is he tolerated in the palace?"

"Despite his youthful appearance, Vestyr is the representative of the Aeth here in Reldon—he is an ambassador. Reldon's western border is hazy; Isoler is our westernmost city and has many ties with the Aeth of Evier.

The Aeth hold no significant territory themselves however their homeland is a stronghold that we would never entertain the idea of capturing. The Aeth are the barrier between our lands and the Black Sands to the west so keeping good political relations with them is in our interest."

"I see," Femira deliberated, and then added with a dejected sigh, "I had hoped to train with him. With Misandrei and Endrin in Rubane, I am without a senior sparring partner. Landryn will train with me when he has the time, but I was hoping to glean some skills from Vestyr."

Garld considered this quietly for a time, rubbing at his jawline in thought. It was a habit that he and Landryn both shared. There were quite a few mannerisms that the two had in common now that Femira thought about it. The way they carried themselves and how they would hold your gaze when you spoke with them. There was a passionate intensity to the pair.

"This is not a bad idea," Garld granted after a long moment, "and he will attempt to make acquaintance with you regardless so perhaps you *should* get something out of this. But be mindful of his words, he is a poison to our objective. Already he has swayed Princess Allyn to his distaste for soulforging and I do not want him gaining any more influence. The King and Prince-heir are wise enough to see the military advantage that soulforging provides, but if enough of the Highborn begin voicing complaint, even the King's support might wane."

"I understand, sir," Femira replied, "I will be cautious."
"Good, get some rest today," Garld said, "I have more assignments for you tonight."
"Of the sneaking variety?"
"Indeed," he smirked, "you're going to have a busy week. The War Council is meeting in seven days to decide on what to do regarding the Rubanians, I want to know what all of the Council members' objectives are before that meeting."
"Leave it to me, sir."

Garld scrawled out a short list of names on a piece of parchment and slid it over to her. "Start with these tonight," he tapped the paper. "All of them currently keep residence in the palace although, as you know, Averstock and Mattice have their own mansions in the eastern quarter. If you can spy on any meetings all the better, otherwise you know what to look for."

"Notes, letters... anything suspicious," Femira nodded.

"Also it would be wise to accept some of the invitations you've received," Garld instructed, "it will give you good reason to be seen about the palace. I'll arrange for you to be provided with accommodations on the guest level to make your operations less suspicious."

Femira didn't particularly want to entertain any nobles that just wanted to use her, but she couldn't argue that it was a good cover. A small part of her was excited to be staying in the palace as it would mean being closer to Landryn.

"You're dismissed, soldier," Garld said. Femira saluted and left.

**

When Femira finally returned to her room, she found a new letter had arrived. Her breath caught with excitement when she noted that it had a red wax seal with Landryn's personal crest; the same hawk clutching a curved blade that had decorated his nythilium armour.

She snatched up the letter quickly and closed the door behind her. She sat on the bed holding it, her eyes darting from it to the door. Even though no one had ever entered her room unannounced before, she couldn't help feeling paranoid that someone would discover her with it.

Femira cracked the wax seal and unfurled the letter. She couldn't resist the smirk that pulled at her mouth as she read.

Interlude
Jaz & Ardy

Jaz swayed as he walked, sweating profusely. He tried to dissipate the excess heat into the snow around him but it flooded out in a pulse. The snow evaporated in an instant causing a puff of steam to billow up.

"What part of discreet did you not understand?" Endrin hissed at him, dragging him by the shoulder to a nearby alley. Loreli was quick on their heels, glancing about the dimly lit street to see if there was anyone that noticed.
"The Watch are on lookout for Ferath after his brawl with Daegan and his bodyguard. We're already suspicious enough as it is without you and your erratic runewielding."

They'd arrived into Urundock the very same day that Ferath had attacked Daegan on the street. There'd been plenty of eye-witnesses that had seen Ferath chasing the two men down the street and the Watchmen had warrants out for his arrest. *Not like they had any cell that could hold him... or any of us for that matter.*

"I'm sorry," Jaz panted, "it's getting harder to control. I don't know what's happening."
"What's happening is," Endrin chided, "you were too arrogant. You thought you were ready to be soulforged and now your body is rejecting the process. It's happened to others already."
"How do I stop it?" Jaz asked, Endrin and Loreli shared a worried look then Loreli shook her head, "we'll help you, ok?"
"We just have to finish the mission and get you back to Garld," Endrin added, "He can fix this."
"He's done it before?" Jaz probed, and was ashamed of the pleading in his tone. Endrin nodded, "it happened to me... and a lot of the others that were first to undergo the change. For some of us, our bodies simply couldn't handle it. It kept accelerating and we couldn't control it. But Garld *can* fix it, you understand? You just have to hold out." Jaz nodded, his resolve strengthening. But then another dizzying flash of heat radiated out from his heart.

Jaz wanted to discard all of the clothes he was wearing. He already looked strange, dressed in nothing but linen trousers and a light tunic on the snow covered streets. This was Urundock, one of the most northern human settlements in the world and he was wearing a fucking tunic and sweating like a pig. What was happening to him?

He breathed through the wave, knowing that it would pass. The heat pulses had started a few weeks after his soulforging, and had grown in frequency. They had been sporadic, at first, but now Jaz had come to expect one every few hours.

It felt as though the topaz in his chest was trying to burn its way out of him. Sometimes, when Jaz slept, he dreamt of waking up in a bed of flames. *This can't go on.* He had considered asking Misandrei for permission to abandon the mission, to ride out of this shithole of a town, to the nearest port, and sail straight back to Epilas. He knew that she wouldn't allow it. Not now they were so close.

"Captain said the Aeth was spotted in a tavern just down the street," Endrin noted.

"How did an Aeth end up in a forsaken place like this, running an icraft of all things?" Loreli scoffed.

"Haven't a fucking clue," Endrin snorted, "but he took Daegan across the ice sheet and he's going to bring us right after him if he wants to keep his head attached to his body."

***

"Ain't no way you came across that honestly, Ardy," Shelly gave the Aeth man a hard look from behind the bar.

"Was payment from that pair you sent my way," he gave her his most charming grin.

"Thought you said they was caught up in that rak assault in Twin Garde," Juri—a fellow bar fly—chimed in from the end of the bar.

"They was," Ardy pulled up in offence, "doesn't mean they didn't pay me 'afore it all kicked off."

"I call bullshit," Juri threw back, "if Twin Garde was attacked by rakmen, why isn't there no reinforcements coming through? No runners or nothing."

"It was only two days ago," Ardy spat, "weren't you listening? I only got out by the skin of me teeth."

"That makes no sense, skin don't have no teeth," Juri's face scrunched up.

"It's a saying."

"I ain't never heard it said."

"That's because you've never been five feet outside of Urundock," Shelly cracked at Juri.

"Now," Shelly turned back to Ardy, wiping down a dirty glass with an even dirtier rag. "You're telling me that foreign fella and his bodyguard paid you with a *runestone* for a trip to Twin Garde." Her tone and eyes made it very clear what she thought of that.

"C'mon, please, Shelly," Ardy leaned against the bar, "ain't nobody willing to buy it off me. They're all scared because of that maniac Reldoni runewielder that was running through the streets the other day."

"Rightly so," Juri piped in again, "killed half-dozen of the Watch after *you* left with the people he was fighting. You know the Watch are looking to speak with you too over all o' that mess."

"Aye," Shelly agreed. "Mayor's put out a contract for the man's head. And from what I hear, the Arch-duke himself has been looking for that same man."

"Have you tried Darel?" Juri asked, leaning in the direction of Ardy, "she'd buy cuts of my fat arse if I was selling 'em." He was leaning so far off his seat, Ardy was surprised the man was still in it.

"Tried," Ardy grimaced, of course he had, everyone in town knew Darel was where to go if you needed something pawned fast. "She offered me a measly one silver-ten. This is worth twenty times that, at least."

"That's what you get for trying to pawn stolen shit," Shelly snorted.

"It weren't stolen," Ardy shot back. *It was looted from a corpse... well, an almost-corpse.* He sighed and pushed himself from the bar. There was no other way about it. He'd take the one silver and ten coppers. It would still be enough to get him plenty of drinks for the next few days.

Ardy stepped out into the dimly lit street, tasting the fresh chill of the air. He liked the cold of Urundock. It reminded him of the frigid sting of the ocean winds. Not for the first time over the past few months, Ardy considered if he should give it up out here. Perhaps it was time to head back to Edas and find work on a trading ship. He missed the salty air of the sea and the rocking movement of a ship at night.

"I'll take that runestone off your hands." Ardy jumped at the male voice. He hadn't thought anyone else was on the wooden porch of the bar. A dark figure loomed from the corner. Ardy had been in enough precarious situations over the past few days and was not at all impressed with being blindsided in the dark.

"Thirty silver," Ardy snapped, "coin only."

"We'll pay, but we also want you to take us to its previous owner." The figure stepped closer into the light and Ardy caught sight of bald man with a nose that looked like it had been broken many times over. Even in the dim light, Ardy could tell the man's nationality.

"No dealings with Reldoni, thank you very much," Ardy sneered and stepped off the porch.

"I'm not asking," the man grumbled.

"You'd be smart to listen to him," two more figures appeared from around the side of the building. Ardy felt the all too familiar feeling of dread looming over him. *No!* How was this *still* happening to him? Why did he have to accept Desmond's stupid fucking offer.

"L-Listen, I don't want no trouble."

"And we don't want to cause you any," it was a woman's voice but Ardy couldn't make out the faces of either of the two newcomers. "All we're asking for is a ride." Both of the newcomers had the silhouette of swords, sheathed at the belt. He knew well enough how formidable a Reldoni woman with a sword was.

He could try to outrun them. One of the newcomers was swaying as if drunk and Ardy could be quick when needed.

"The man's up in Twin Garde. I-I can't... I mean the place was swarming with rakmen, I can't advise you go there."

"We can handle ourselves well enough," the man on the porch said.

"I'm not going back."

"You don't have the choice," the man replied with the grim solemnity of a man whose business was death. It was a voice that carried a threat and Ardy had experienced it many times in the past.

Some people have heard threats so many times that they begin to sound hackneyed and meaningless. Ardy was not one of those people. Ardy had survived this long by staying exactly where the trouble wasn't. By avoiding threats and fleeing when faced with them.

He'd fled Altarea when Lord-whatever-his-name-was had declared himself King and annexed from Reldon some fifty years ago. He'd fled when Nordock had been faced with their own rakmen problem two decades ago. And he'd fled three nights past when there'd been grenadiers throwing around explosives and rakmen jumping over battlements. He had absolutely zero intent of going back to exactly where the danger was.

But then again if there was a very *immediate* risk to his life if he didn't play along… Ardy straightened his back and turned to face broken-nose. "Fifty silver."

Interlude
Baroc

The aroma of burning meat filled Baroc's nostrils. The rak feasted a victory tonight. The sharp, ever-present taste of the iron pins sticking into his mouth was heightened by his own salivating.

Baroc would have preferred the meat raw, but he couldn't deny the smell of cooked deer had an instinctive response in his body. It couldn't mask the scents of the battle, however. It was a combination that Baroc was becoming very familiar with.

Rak blood was heavy with zinc and it lingered on rock and in the soil for months. There was a lot of rak blood on the ground in this place. The blood of the smaller pale raks was more coppery but Baroc's senses were sensitive enough to notice the difference.

White-grey smoke drifted up and around the false-peaks. These southern rak had the peculiar habit of building these. It was a strange amount of effort, cutting rocks into squares and stacking them atop each other over and over. Both of the false-peaks were blackened with fire but the rak were busy repairing the tops.

Baroc could smell the residual ash of the wood that had been burned. *Three days.* He didn't guess, he knew. It had been three days since those fires and the blood of the rak had seeped into the ground.

The thick chains affixed to his collar rattled as Baroc rose to his feet. The chains and collar were covered in chinks from Baroc's previous attempts at clawing them off. It had been weeks since his last attempt to escape. That complacency had given Baroc some measures of freedom. He was still forced to wear a muzzle, he was still chained but at least he now had the liberty of his hands to be unbound.

Baroc watched as a set of the small rakmen—now slaves like him—were led through the encampment. There were a dozen of them in total, collars similar to his clipped around their necks and heavy chains linking them together. These were fighting rak. Those that had been injured but not killed in the battle. They would be sold to other rak chieftains or sent back to the rak chief-of-chiefs. They had a word for him but Baroc had forgotten it. It was a strange concept to him. A chief above other chiefs. How could that even work?

One of the pale rakmen stank of infection. There was dark blood crusted into his red fur. Baroc could smell the infected wound under his cloth robes. Rakmen bodies were different to his own clan, their wounds festered easily, especially the pale ones.

The shamans of his own people would insist that the wound be cleaned with boiled water every few hours until the rot was stemmed. But this rak would not have that privilege. Baroc could smell the delirium fogging his brain. *He won't last.* None of the rak being marched out of the encampment seemed like they would.

The only two that seemed in good condition were a pair caged at the foot of the false-peaks. Baroc could detect the charcoal-like smell of skin that had been touched by flames along with the sulphurous odour of burnt hairs; it was fading but still lingered on the yellow-furred one.

The other looked a bit more like the rak he was used to although not as dark and still quite small. In appearances, the small rakmen didn't look much like the rak of the north, but they had the same scent signature and the same play of emotions on their scent. These two did not hold the same fear that he'd seen of captured rak. He knew the scent of defiance. He used to smell it on himself.

CHAPTER 45
Looking Down the Barrel

Daegan blew warmth into his hands. The cold sting of the north was seeping into every part of him. The rak had left him with his cloak but he had that draped over Tanlor while the man slept. Tanlor had been stripped of his battle leathers and light armour and was left with only an under tunic and breeches. The man needed the cloak more than Daegan did.

The chill breeze blew in unimpeded through the frost-coated iron bars of their cage. The cage was—thankfully—nestled up against the wooden wall. It gave Daegan a full view of Twin Garde's keep yard. Both towers had been blackened by the fires, along with some of the outer buildings that were damaged by grenadier blasts.

Tanlor and Daegan were in the same cage, barely large enough for both men to lay flat. More cages flanked theirs. A trio of Twin Garde soldiers were housed in a cage a few down from theirs. Daegan had spotted the healer—Yaref—among them.

The rak seemed to have some measure of concern for their care as they were fed broth twice a day and given water to drink. But that concern didn't stretch as far as blankets, or linens for Tanlor's wounds. Daegan checked on those wounds now. Angry red blisters still covered Tanlor's arms, hands and chest. There were also a few up along his neck that would likely scar. Tanlor had spent four days since the rak assault drifting in and out of sleep. Daegan had fed him the broth and cleaned his blisters with shreds of his cloak.

Tanlor stirred, shivered, then coughed.

"Easy," Daegan offered a hand to help as Tanlor struggled to rise up to a sitting position.

"Every time I wake in this cage," Tanlor mumbled, "I think I've woken up in hell."

"Perhaps it is, maybe we did die up in that tower."

Daegan recalled the final moments in the tower. He remembered firing his revolver, watching as the rak chief's head snapped back from the bullet. But nothing distinctive beyond that. He remembered feeling pain. And then waking up in this cage next to Tanlor.

Daegan's own injuries were minor next to Tanlor's. Daegan's wounds were similar to burns, although they did not feel hot to the touch. Rivets of angry, swollen scratches snaked up Daegan's arms but they were mostly scabbed over now. The skin felt tight around the wounds and stung whenever he bent his arms. He had no idea what the rak chief's bloodstone dagger had done to him. *Whatever it was, it had been working.* Daegan didn't doubt that if he hadn't shot the chief, he'd be amongst the dead.

"Where is Rowan?" Tanlor wheezed, looking out to the area where Rowan and a dozen other Twin Garde survivors had been chained.

"They moved them out yesterday," Daegan recounted, "I tried to call out to him but he couldn't hear me."

"How did he look?"

"Not good," Daegan choked. Rowan had looked like a walking corpse. The man's eyes were sunken and dazed, his skin pallid. Rowan had been chained and dragged along by the others.

"Did you find out where they were taken?" Tanlor breathed. Daegan shook his head.

"That one," Daegan pointed at a rak with two long blades sheathed on his back and a red scar on his eye. "Seems to be the one left in charge. Another of their leaders took the rest out, it looked like a disagreement between the two but I couldn't hear them properly. Their language is… strange. There's a lot of Old Esterin in there though so I can pick out parts."

"You speak Old Esterin?" Tanlor asked in surprise.

"My education was quite extensive," was all Daegan said on it.

The language had been widely in use prior to the fall of the Sorcerer Kings. Esterin had been a domain covering Rubane, Athlin and parts of current Reldon. After Elyina's rise to power, she had spread Common Tongue as the dominating language. The reason for why Daegan could speak it was because almost all texts preceding the Kingdom of Reldon had been written in Old Esterin. It had been part of his tutoring as a child to learn the language despite its use being mostly defunct in everyday use.

Daegan felt apprehension growing in him as it neared sunset. When the sun went down it got *very* cold. Each morning he worried that he would wake up to find Tanlor frozen next to him. But Tanlor was more talkative today, that was a good sign that he was recovering. Daegan didn't want to think about wherever Rowan had been taken. Marching through the woods to gods knew where.

A smaller rak came with wooden bowls of broth for them as he did every evening. The broth was bland but considering it was the only food they were given in days, it was the most wonderful thing Daegan had ever tasted. Most importantly it was *warm*. The heat flowed through him as he gulped it down from the bowl. The wood itself was also warm and Daegan held it in his hands, savouring it.

"I think the smaller ones are just children," Tanlor commented after they finished.

"They're still as big as us," Daegan remarked. "You think they'd bring children in war parties?"

"Yeah," Tanlor nodded, "maybe adolescents… like squires? Youths to run errands and do all the jobs in camp that the older ones don't want to. You see it often enough in war camps."

"That's a very human thing," Daegan noted, "I don't think we can make that mistake with these creatures."

"Good point," Tanlor said, his gaze drifting over to a dark figure chained to the opposite wall—the dogman.

Daegan often found his own gaze being pulled to the creature. The dogman wasn't as large as the rakmen but it was still taller than a regular man. He was covered in grey and black fur reminiscent of a wolf, but he stood upright on two strong legs. He hulked as he walked, whether that was due to his captivity or his body shape, Daegan couldn't guess. The creature was usually chained and had a metal collar with a muzzle contraption worked into it.

One of the Twin Garde survivors—a heavier man that Daegan was almost certain he remembered as the cook—had gotten lucky on the second day. A rak youth hadn't locked the cook's shackles properly and he'd managed to sneak away during the night. Somehow the man had managed to avoid the sentries on guard. The next morning, a pair of rak had taken the dogman out with them. They'd returned in a few hours. The dogman's forearms and claws had been stained red. When the handlers re-affixed the chain securing the beast to the wall, the dogman growled at them. Daegan had watched as the rak handlers beat the dogman with sticks for that.

A stick was the tool of choice for rak that wanted your attention. Daegan and Tanlor had not been let out of their cage yet, and so far the stick only came as far as rattling their bars. Daegan had watched Rowan and the dozen soldiers whacked a few times on their march out of the keep.

"We'll have to do something about that dogman when we make our escape," Daegan nodded to the beast. Remaining in captivity was never even a consideration. "We should just kill it," Tanlor whispered. They spoke in hushed tones as many of the rak could understand bits of Common Tongue.

"I'm not sure I'm comfortable with that," Daegan disagreed, "he's clearly a prisoner, like us."

"Better than him hunting us down."

"We should focus on *how* we're even going to escape first."

"You have any ideas yet?"

"Getting out of the cage is the first hurdle. After that, my plan had been to free Rowan and the other soldiers. But now..." Daegan sighed.

"We'll figure something out for Rowan. At least we know he's alive," Tanlor took on a distant expression. "I thought he was gone. I thought we all were, truth be told."

"So did I," Daegan replied, then remembered the shameful thoughts he'd had in the final moments before the rak chief tried to kill him.

"I wanted to leave you," Daegan admitted, "I'm sorry... I tried to be brave but... I wanted to jump off that tower and run."

"But you didn't," Tanlor said, he put a hand on Daegan's shoulder, "you didn't. You stood your ground and by some fucking luck of the gods we're both alive."

"I wouldn't call this living," Daegan felt the corner of his mouth turn up in a sly grin.

"Breathing then," Tanlor smirked. "Don't worry princeling, we'll have you back to destroying your liver in a viceden soon enough."

"So, what do you reckon about the dogman?" Daegan asked, bringing the topic back.

"If we're not going to kill the thing, I reckon we set it loose, see how much damage he can cause to the camp and we slip away while he's chewing on the rak."

"Risky move, what if he turns on us?"

"We're not the ones torturing the wretched thing," Tanlor nodded to where some of the rak youths were banging the sticks near the dogman, making him flinch.

"Fucking scum," Daegan scowled.

The warrior rak sat on sentry posts watching from the battlements. They were focused on the outside more than what was happening inside the walls. *They're expecting retaliation.* There was another pair of warriors near a cookfire on the other side of the yard.

One of them was toying with Daegan's revolver, trying to figure out how it worked. He tried prying off the runestones with a knife but they were too integrated into the contraption. The revolver's metal had likely been shaped around the stones themselves.

"How long before the Arch-duke sends men to take this place back, you reckon?" Daegan asked.
"You said that Crann had sent for reinforcements already?"
"Yeah," Daegan replied, "he said he'd sent runners out to Heronsbridge, Garronforn and Rubastre. Hoping that any of the Dukes would listen."
"Baron Greyson of Heronsbridge is a good man," Tanlor said. "And he'll not want any rak coming south of Nortara. He'll send men, I'm sure. We could be looking at a few weeks though. I don't reckon they'll keep us here that long."
"You think they'll send us to wherever Rowan's gone?"
"Rak usually just kill everyone. They don't take prisoners so this is unchartered territory."

"The rak chief said something about a 'Khandamos', you ever heard of that?" Daegan asked and Tanlor shook his head.
"'Khan' is Old Esterin for chief. 'Damos' is similar enough to *Damas*—which means death," Daegan mused.
"You think they're speaking Old Esterin then?"
"I think their language has parts of Common Tongue and Old Esterin in it. The histories prior to the Fall of the Sorcerer Kings is sketchy... but I think the rak and humans might have once co-existed. Would make sense if we've got a similar language."

"So a 'Chief of Death'... maybe the rak have a new leader? One that's pushing them south," Tanlor considered.
"And taking slaves rather than just killing everyone," Daegan suggested.
"Not what you'd expect of the Chief of Death though."
"Guess not... they did mention something about Khandamos demanding blood," Daegan offered, "maybe it's a sacrificial thing?"
"I don't fancy being sacrificed to some Death Chief."
"Nor do I," Daegan affirmed, "guess we better start figuring out a way out of this cage then."

"If we could get our hands on an aradium runestone, I could dissolve these bars," Tanlor rapped his knuckle against one of the bars. "Even with a topaz, I could melt one."
"You almost burnt yourself to a crisp last time you used one of those," Daegan nudged Tanlor with an elbow.
"Saved our asses though."
"No you didn't," Daegan rebuffed, "*I* did... by blowing chunks out of that rak's head."
"Well why didn't you think of doing that earlier," Tanlor gave him a sidelong look.
"If I had that revolver now it would sort out all our problems," Daegan grumbled. "It's got both aradium and topaz inlaid in it."
"You see where they're keeping our weapons?" Tanlor asked.
"I think their warriors requisitioned them for their own use," Daegan scowled, "I saw a rak with your greatsword sheathed at his hip. And my revolver is over there," Daegan pointed out the rak by the cookfire playing with it. "He's been trying to pry out the runestones for over an hour."

"And what's happening over there?" Tanlor asked and pointed to where a pair of rak youths had started brawling. One had drawn a knife and the other larger one was deftly avoiding wild swings of the blade. The larger one sidestepped then brought an open palm slap to the smaller one's hand, knocking the blade to the ground. In seconds, the bigger lad was grappling the smaller one into submission.

"I think they fight like that over chores," Daegan noted, "whoever loses ends up doing more work. The lad that's been emptying our shit bucket is the small one over there." Daegan pointed to a rak that was no taller than a human adolescent. He was digging a hole to empty the buckets. The youth had quite a few shallow knife cuts covering his arms.

"Shit-digger is the bottom rung on the rak hierarchy then," Tanlor noted.

"Sometimes they get a little bloody, but I've not seen any of them kill each other... yet," Daegan continued.

"Pretty intense way to assert dominance," Tanlor shook his head as he spoke.

"Likely how their tribal society works," Daegan guessed, "I've noticed some of the grown warriors doing the same."

"I guess it's not much different to how we do it, whoever's got the bigger army and the best weapons gets to tell everyone else what to do," Tanlor replied.

Daegan dreaded to think what a large scale rak army could do. *Fully armed with the latest weapons; crossbows, rifles and revolvers.* Daegan shuddered but then an idea struck him. He rubbed at the hair growth on his chin, playing out the scenario in his mind. *This could work.*

"What is it?" Tanlor asked, noticing Daegan's concentration.

"I've got an idea," Daegan disclosed in a hushed tone, "I think if we convin—"

—There was a resounding crack like the sound of thunder.

Daegan and Tanlor's heads spun to the sound. The rak that had been playing with the revolver crumpled to the ground. Blue blood sprayed on the wall behind him and covered his rawhide armour. There was a dark blue pit where his eye had once been that was pouring out blood like a hole in a keg. The revolver was still clutched in his hands, pointed towards him, thumb curled around the trigger.

"I guess they haven't figured out how revolvers work," Tanlor said bluntly.

"Seems instinctual to look down the barrel," Daegan replied. Both men watched as the rak gathered around their dead comrade. They seemed reluctant to touch the weapon as though touching it might somehow make their eyes blow up too.

The youths hung around the back of the crowd trying to get a look at the dead body, elbowing and shoving each other for better vantage spots. Shit-digger hovered at a distance from the other youths, standing on a crate to try to peek over the crowd. Daegan's grin once again pulled at the corner of his mouth.

"Didn't think you were so bloodthirsty," Tanlor remarked, glancing at Daegan.

"It's not that... I think this helps my plan quite a bit. Do you think you'll be ok to run if we do this tonight?"

"If it means getting out of here," Tanlor nodded.

"We may need to fight. You sure you don't need another few days?"

"I don't think we should risk it, if you've got a way out of this now then let's do it."

***

"Hey, you," Daegan hissed in a hushed tone when shit-digger came to change their waste bucket. Night had fallen but it was uncharacteristically clear with the light of both moons shining in full. *It must be Lua Nova tonight.* Funny how time goes by quickly like that.

Most of the rak were gathered around various cookfires. Daegan thought it was strange that they preferred to cook and eat outside rather than using the mess hall. Those not around fires were at sentry posts.

"Yeah, you," Daegan followed up when shit-digger met his eye, "the other lads always beat you?" Shit-digger cocked his head.

"Can you understand me?" Daegan tried speaking slower and in a lower tone to match how the rak spoke. "*Kavek nim tur?*" Daegan tried the same question in Old Esterin.

"*Yes,*" shit-digger responded in the same language. *Right, so it is Old Esterin they speak.*

"*You want to fight the boys?*" Daegan asked and shit-digger glanced wearily back to the campfires.

"*You need to fight back or they'll keep treating you like...*" Daegan couldn't remember the Old Esterin word for 'shit' so he said it in Common and spat, hoping the youth would get the meaning from context.

"Human know not of strong," the youth replied in accented Common. His voice was surprisingly deep. His voice and size were a potent contradiction to the assumption the smaller ones were youths. But his behaviour seemed a lot more boyish than that of the larger warriors.

"*We are Undak,*" Daegan replied, thumping his fist against his chest. He was betting that *Undak* was the term for runewielder. It was something the rak chief had repeated a few times. Shit-digger glanced back nervously at the fires. In the dark light, the faint luminescent blue glow along the veins of his neck and exposed forearms was more apparent. Daegan wondered absently what caused that.

"*Undak strong,*" Daegan continued, "*Undak most strong.*" He gripped his fist and tensed it at the rak. "*You become Undak and fight back.*" Shit-digger looked at him with suspicion, but there was eagerness in his blue eyes.

"*How?*" Shit-digger asked.

"*I teach you,*" Daegan replied, then nudged Tanlor, "*we teach.*" He nodded at Tanlor who also nodded along, holding Daegan's determined expression.

"*No one gives water freely,*" the rak responded with narrowed eyes, "*What you get?*"

Daegan and Tanlor shared a look, and Daegan made a show of looking sheepish. "*My friend needs bandages and salve,*" Daegan answered, indicating the blisters on Tanlor's hands and neck. "*This is all we ask.*"

"*And you teach Undak? You teach Savara'an?*"

"*Yes, yes all of this,*" Daegan lied. He would have felt guilty about leading on the naive boy if he weren't locked in a cage about to be sacrificed to some Death Chief.

"*You teach first. Then bandages,*" shit-digger insisted, excitement growing on his expression. It was strange how human those expressions looked on his alien face. Daegan glanced at Tanlor again. Tanlor of course couldn't understand a word of what was being said, but Daegan just needed the look to help sell the illusion.

"*Fine,*" Daegan answered. "*But you will need runestones for us to teach you. You know these?*" Shit-digger's head turned in confusion, his brow knotted trying to understand the word.

"*Stone that glows,*" Daegan demonstrated a small circle with his fingers, "*runestone.*"

"*Yes, yes. Vastek*" shit-digger nodded emphatically, but then frowned looking about the camp, "*vastek valuable. I have none of these. Only Undak have them.*"

"*My weapon has them.*" Daegan maintained. There was no Old Esterin word for pistol or revolver so weapon would have to do. He pointed to where the rak had blown his brains out earlier that day. *"My weapon,"* Daegan mimed the bang with his hands and blew through pursed lips to make the sound. Shit-diggers eyes took on a hungry look.

"This weapon kill Yakra and Sojin," shit-digger said with unrestrained craving. *"Yakra most strong chief. You teach me to use weapon?"*

Daegan grinned, *"yes I can."*

CHAPTER 46
Life in the Palace

Not for the first time that week, Femira strode through the hallways of the palace. As always, she was dressed in her uniform but that was mainly because she didn't own any other clothes than these and her stealth gear. There was that infuriating red dress she had worn to the feast—the one where she'd first spoken to Landryn—but that could sit collecting dust in her trunk at the end of her bed for the rest of eternity. *The bed that I've not used all week,* she realised with mild amusement. Since that night in Landryn's office, the pair had spent every night with each other.

As a result of her recent notoriety from killing the kragal, Femira's presence in the palace was welcomed by the highborn. And true to his word, Garld had arranged rooms for her on the guest level. Rooms that Landryn frequented each night.

Femira was not on her way to those accommodations at the moment however. She had tasks today and Landryn had a busy day preparing for the War Council. The draega threat had unfortunately taken a secondary priority against what they would do with the news of Daegan's death. The King was still deliberating on which course of action the army should take with regard to that.

Femira arrived at a door and knocked. A moment later a familiar handsome blond man opened it.

"Lady Annali," he bowed, "please come in, please." She followed him inside to an ornate living room with doors leading off to a bedchamber. It was similar to her own rooms in the palace, but had a more permanent "lived in" feel to them.

Decorating the walls were drapes of Keiran silk tapestries and ornamental urns in the style of her homeland. The man hurried about the room with agitated movements.

"My apologies for the state of this place, my lady," the man flustered, "Daurond hadn't warned me that you'd be arriving today." He began collecting empty bottles of red wine and glasses from the table.

"You don't need to bother with the 'my lady' stuff with me," Femira teased lightly.

"You see, Ovis," Daurond said walking out from the bed chambers. Annali's cousin wore a purple silk lounge robe that complimented his dark skin. His eyes were bloodshot with dark circles around them. "My cousin has grown quite relaxed with propriety since arriving in Reldon, I told you she wouldn't care if the place was a mess or not. Now hurry on to your appointments, I will see you later tonight." Daurond smiled at the man, guiding him to the door. Ovis grinned sheepishly at Daurond and then apologetically again to Femira before departing.

"You look like you had a fun night," Femira said, cheerfully.

"Epilas is quite a fun place, if you would ever do anything other than hide in that barracks... one would think you're hiding a secret lover." He spoke in their native Keiran so Femira responded in the same tongue.

"Plenty of ways to keep yourself entertained in the barracks," she replied and then regretted it when Daurand's eyes lit up with the potential gossip.

"That friend of yours... Jazerah? He is a fine specimen wouldn't you say?" The man wasn't wrong, Jaz was incredibly handsome but Femira didn't think that way about him... at least not enough to do anything about it. Although the mention of him now dampened her spirits.

"He's been on duty out of Epilas," she said and didn't bother to mask her disappointment. Femira then decided to embellish her display by sighing emphatically. She didn't care if Daurond spread a false truth about her having a thing for Jaz. It was better than the truth, and Jaz wouldn't ever think anything of it, if he ever heard the rumour. It's not as if Jaz didn't proposition her half the times they sparred anyway.

"Well, when he returns you should invite him to one of my little parties sometime," Daurand smiled as he spoke, picking up a decanter of wine and pouring himself a glass. He then lounged onto a cushioned sofa and offered her to do the same. She did but refused the glass of wine he subsequently offered.

"You're becoming quite a person of interest around the palace lately. I swear, the way people talk about you it's as though I really am back in the same city as my cousin."

"Is that a compliment?" Femira teased.

"If you choose to see it that way," he smirked.

"And what do they say?" Femira asked, her interest piqued. She didn't really care if the highborn were gossiping about her as she had the veil of Annali to hide behind. What did it matter to her if she ruined the woman's reputation?

"Oh most of it is all very boring," Daurond sighed, "how *exceptional* a runewielder you are. The stories people are telling of you fighting monsters," he waved away the word flippantly, "dragons, demons and giant crabs... I swear some of it is just ridiculous. The *most* shocking thing is that no one here even seems to *suspect* that you are an imposter," he chuckled and Femira smiled inwardly.

"Although," Daurond trailed a finger around the rim of his glass. "I did hear one particularly juicy tidbit," he continued and Femira eyed him warily, "about you and Landryn Tredain." He eyed her with a mischievous glint as he spoke, waiting for her reaction to the name. She maintained composure but inside her chest tightened.

"He's my Commander," she replied evenly, "that's all... he's also married."

"That wouldn't have stopped the real Annali," Daurond smiled with his too-white teeth.

"Is this really what you brought me here to talk about?" she made a point of showing her boredom on the topic. Daurond sighed and reached for the crystal decanter, topping himself up.

"No," he said, disappointed, "I do like to partake in a bit of gossip though. Can't blame me for being intrigued by the rumours."

"Our mutual friend Garld has invested much in you," Daurond said, shifting on to the main topic, "he wishes for me to tutor you. He is quite eager for you to quickly acquaint yourself with the all particular intricacies of the Keiran Emperor's Court."

"Do you know why?" Femira prodded.

"I can speculate," he had a glint in his eye, "I imagine that he wants you to be able to hold up to an Honorswords questioning if you are to meet one again."

"I don't intend to be facing off against any Honorswords again anytime soon. And if I do, I think I can handle them without words."

"Oh I'm quite sure the great Annali Jahar, slayer of draega and monsters, is more than capable of fending off some Honorswords. All the same, you may find yourself in a situation that you cannot kill your way out of.

I'm sure that Karas saw right through your brutish Keiran accent. I don't know where you came from but you've obviously had some training in pretending to be a noblewoman. However, there are some very obvious flaws in your accent. We must work to rectify this."

"Why would you do that?"

"Because Garld has instructed me to."

"I didn't realise you were a bloodshedder," Femira replied in a mocking tone.

"No, no," Daurond scoffed, "I'll leave all that violent work to you lot. However, Garld has helped me much in the past. He keeps my presence and standing here in Epilas in good order, and I help convince the Altareans that the Reldoni aren't so bad. Along with adding some weightable credence to your Annali impersonation. In return... well... he pays me. What more do I need to say beyond that."

"And what is it exactly that Garld wants me to improve on?" Femira questioned.

"I am to teach you how to properly conduct yourself as a Keiran highborn lady. Frankly, he should've done this from the start."

"Hasn't seemed to be much of a problem so far," Femira shrugged.

"Not to these Reldoni barbarians but to other Keiran, your speech is that of a streetdog and your manners are worse."

"If the Reldoni are so backwards, why are you here?"

"I didn't say that I don't like barbarians. In fact, I *quite* like some of them, especially when they're shirtless," Daurond said with a playful grin. His melodic voice made the suggestive comment dance lightly rather than perverted, as it would have sounded in a regular accent. "There are certain choices in my lifestyle that are quite frowned upon in Keiran."

"Our family doesn't approve of your lifestyle?" Femira probed.

"Surely you know enough of our people's culture to know the answer to that question."

"A bit... I left Keiran when I was very small. I might need a lot of tutoring," Femira let out a brief groan of annoyance, "this is going to seriously impact my runewielding training, isn't it?"

"We have plenty of time," Daurond expressed. "You might not be aware that many of the things that you and I do here are considered *crimes* in Keiran. We are very much *karasi* in the eyes of our kin."

Karasi. The word sparked recognition inside of her. Her mind flashed with the memory of her mother spitting the word at her with such vehemence that it made young Femira cry without knowing what it meant.

"*Karasi* is a bastard?" Femira asked casually.

"*Karasi* is anyone that brings shame to a noble house," Daurond corrected, "a son who turns his back on the wishes of his father is *karasi*, a wife who lifts a weapon is *karasi*. But yes... bastards are the highest form of *karasi*. Their existence itself is the shame of their parents' actions." Femira was pensively quiet for a time, trying to understand what that meant about her.

"You really do look shockingly like her," Daurond noted after a while, his eyes sharp, like a hawk watching a mouse. "Who were your parents?" Femira didn't know her mother's name. She'd always called her Mami up until the woman had disowned her, after that she was just another nameless stranger. And her father... well.

"My parents were Nurak and Azela Jahar," Femira said with a playful smile.

"Ha," Daurond chuckled, "I suppose they are. You know," he flashed her one of his brilliant white grins, "I prefer *you* to *her*. You're much more fun... Annali was such a brat. Always doing what the family wanted; the perfect, dutiful daughter... she was a bitch."

"What makes you think I'm not?"

"You're the better kind. The kind that will punch you when they're angry. Annali was the sort to spread rumours and sow distrust."

"Is that what happened to you?" Femira asked pointedly.

"Ha!" He barked a joyful laugh, "no, no. The stories Annali would tell about me were always true," he said with a mischievous grin.

"So that's how you ended up here?" Femira decided to pry into Daurond a bit more.

"Ah, not exactly," Daurond's eyes twinkled and he began running his finger around his glass once again, "I fell in love with the wrong man but that is a tale for another day perhaps."

They spoke more throughout the afternoon and Femira found herself enjoying the man's company. He was incredibly witty in a charmingly vulgar way and despite her best efforts to remain elusive to him, Daurond had managed to pry out of her some of her past living on the streets of Altarea.

"Oh," he cackled, "how Annali would simply *seethe* if she knew that a thief off the street was pretending to be her. You'd better hope that Garld has indeed killed her. If he hasn't, she will spend all of her energy in making you suffer for this ruse."

"You think that he did?" Femira jumped at this, something she'd suspected for a very long time but hadn't worked up the courage to ask Garld directly. She also wasn't entirely sure she wanted to know the answer.

"It would seem likely, unless he has her locked away in some dungeon somewhere. All he ever needed Annali for was to help cement the takeover of Altarea. If a former princess was seen to be supporting the new Highlord then the lesser nobles would fall in line. You being such an eager—and effective—little killer was a bonus." That comment stung more than she liked.

Femira knew that when she'd been training to become a bloodshedder that she'd be expected to kill people. She just hadn't anticipated finding the act so distasteful. Not like killing the kraglings. Killing monsters hadn't left her feeling as sick as a fish in a wine bottle. It had left her with a sense of pride. A stronger pride than when she'd successfully steal something. For the first time in her life, Femira truly felt like she'd been doing the right thing. Like she had a purpose.

Femira and Daurond agreed that every morning she would come to his rooms in the palace where he would tutor her on Keiran highborn etiquette so that she wouldn't trigger any obvious suspicions. Since returning from the Tidewall, Femira's training regime had been sporadic anyway so she didn't mind dedicating the extra time to Daurond's lessons.

Aden still hadn't returned from whatever assignment he'd been sent on and Femira normally went to him for tutoring in the late morning anyway. Some of the other bloodshedders had agreed to spar with her so she could continue to hone her combat runewielding skills but it was a long trek from the barracks to the palace and back.

She had permission from Garld to seek out Vestyr for training sessions. Which she had been meaning to do but all of the meetings throughout the week with various noble families had occupied a lot of her time. And the evenings she spent sneaking into the War Council member's offices to collect information for Garld. Well... that was how she spent a *portion* of her night. After midnight was her time with Landryn.

Femira's afternoon consisted of entertaining Lord and Lady Arteste, both of whom were not-so-subtly talking up their youngest son, a Knight-Captain rising through the ranks of Lord-Marshal Mattice's division. She feigned interest in meeting him, and kept her discussion polite but inwardly she was bored out of her mind.

Lord Arteste had been on Garld's list of nobles he wanted her to build rapport with. She couldn't fathom why, but she trusted Garld's judgement on these things. She'd had a few meetings like this one all week and she figured this was Garld wanting to give more credibility to her Annali disguise. *Maybe he'd wanted to do this earlier but didn't trust I wouldn't blow it?* She was certainly better at holding her tongue and maintaining composure than when she'd first arrived.

"Thank you for having me, my Lord, my Lady," Femira inclined her head in respect to the pair as she left their palace accommodations.

"You're sure you can't stay for dinner?" Lady Arteste pressed, "our son, Jerome will be joining us."

"Thank you but no, I am needed in the barracks this evening. Late night training sessions," Femira lied but she needed a cover in case she was seen leaving the palace. Her duties would take her to the West Quarter of the city tonight.

"A dedicated soldier," Lord Arteste said with admiration, "Jerome is much the same." She found it ironic how much they were pushing their son on her. She wondered what their reactions would be if they ever learned that she was just some lowborn thief.

The whole situation reminded her of the cons that she and her brothers had done when they'd first arrived in Altarea. Femira and Rashav would pretend to be visiting Keiran highborn children that had been separated from their parents. They were the distraction for Kamal to pick pockets. They'd stopped pulling those tricks once Femira had gotten too old to pass for a lost child but by then she was agile enough to pick pockets herself without being caught. They'd also been taken in by Lichtin and his crew by then so were usually working on bigger scores.

The sun was setting as Femira made her way down the palace steps. Tonight, she planned to infiltrate Lord-Marshal Mattice's manse. He was Highlord of Dagero to the south but as with most of the wealthier nobles, Mattice had a considerable estate in Epilas. Even lesser Houses from remote parts of Reldon would still own a property in the West Quarter. Epilas was the center of government and the military heart of Reldon, so anyone with any measure of influence wanted a piece of the city.

Femira made her way on foot. Underneath her uniform, she had her stealth gear. She stuffed the uniform into an alley once she neared the West Quarter. The military uniform stood out too much and with her growing notoriety, it was becoming harder to move about incognito. She'd even picked up a black cloak of light material to help avoid being recognised on the street. She pulled the black cowl over her head.

The streets were reasonably busy and she was more than effective at dodging any patrols. Garld had been strict on her remaining undetected for these missions. Femira did not want it getting back to him that she'd been spotted in the West

Quarter. Frankly, it was all so frustratingly easy with her enhanced stonebreaking abilities. If she needed to evade sight all she needed to do was side-step into a quiet alley where she could literally walk through walls if she wanted to.

Femira felt like it was cheating. Not for the first time over the week, she thought about how easy it would be to steal away from Epilas and the responsibilities of Annali. Femira already had the skills to be the greatest thief in history. She could pass through stone walls as if they were curtains, she could climb any tower, bypass any lock. There was nowhere in the entire world that was closed off to her. But she knew she was in too deep now. She couldn't leave Epilas. She couldn't leave Landryn.

By the time Femira made it to Mattice's mansion the sun had set, casting the city into twilight. Neither moon had risen yet and the gaslamps lining the streets were in the process of being lit.

Like many of the other mansions in the West Quarter, Mattice had a steel palisade surrounding his gardens. Metal was too slow to disintegrate for those that weren't soulforged so the patrolling guards would catch any would-be intruders. Mattice had quite few physical defences around his mansion but he had a considerable amount of household guards which posed a slight challenge. The gardens themselves were well-lit and Femira had to employ her stealthiest manoeuvres to stay in the shadows, rolling under bushes and diving for cover behind flowerbeds. However once she neared the building itself, the hard part was over.

"You see that?" Femira heard the male voice of a guard say as she rolled towards the wall of the manse. She pressed her back up against the wall.

"Nah, what was it?"

"Looked like a shadow."

"Probably just a bird…" The conversation muffled and died away as Femira sank herself into the wall. Her edir senses told her the wall was thick, more than wide enough for her to step in and not come through on the other side. She pushed her face through and was greeted by an unlit storage room.

Femira knew that Mattice's study was on the second floor in this corner of the manse. She was surprised that the building seemed to be made entirely of stone. It was clear that Mattice was happy to rely more on guard patrols. *Makes it easier for me.*

Mattice himself was in the building, likely making his way to his study right now. She heard the temple bells toll for the eighth hour. Femira had overheard—while eavesdropping on his conversation—that Mattice was meeting another War Council member in his study at this time. Her goal was to simply listen in on the conversation and glean a little insight for Garld on how Mattice intended to push the council.

She needed to find a stairway. The floorboards were timber and likely would be on the second floor too so climbing up through the roof was impossible.

She moved quietly through the hallways. Fire sconces lined the walls providing illumination but Femira noticed the light growing stronger at the end of the hallway and ducked into a shaded space. Lamplight glinted off the steel pauldrons and breastplates of the patrolling guards that rounded the corner. *He really does have a lot of guards.*

Femira faded into the wall before they could spot her. She could hear the muffled sounds of their boots thudding on the floor, moving past her position and disappearing. *This is the problem with guards. Most of the time there's no intruders, so they're not really paying attention.* Guards were only useful when the alarm was already raised.

Femira continued on, peeking around the corner of hallways and ducking away from two more patrols as well as some passing servants. *A busy house.* Mattice's immediate family all lived at his estate in Dagero but that didn't mean that Mattice's house was quiet. Other relations, mistresses and staff all kept the manse alive with activity.

She found a servants' stairs that led up to the second floor and continued along back to the south corner of the manse where she would find Mattice's study. Garld had visited on a number of occasions and had been able to describe to her the rough layout of the building.

Edging along the side of a wall to a corner, Femira crouched down and formed a flat piece of steel from within her reserve. The beauty of runewielding meant that she could summon and dismiss any tool she needed at a moment's notice. She'd perfected the art of metalshaping to get a flawless mirror-like appearance.

She carefully pushed the mirror along the floor to get a look at the hallway around the corner. There was a single guard stood watch outside a door. *That's the study.* It was two rooms down on the opposite side of the hallway. *Too easy.*

She judged the width of the hallway to be about six strides. *Give another two in case the wall is thick.* She walked up to the opposite wall. Turned until she was lined up along it and side-stepped into the wall, dissolving the stone around her and reforming the hole she'd stepped through.

Enclosed completely in darkness, Femira felt the stone all around her hum in response to her edir. She took one stride forward, slowly and carefully. The stone in front of her dissolved and reformed behind her. Another step. Then another. It took so much focus to keep the pocket within the wall intact as she stepped that she almost lost count of her steps. *Was that eight?* It didn't really matter if she overshot it anyway.

She pushed her face through slowly and was again greeted by a dim room. She stepped through and quickly realised she was not alone. She was in what looked to be an office. Not the luxurious office of a nobleman but the reserved practical offices of an administrator. *Probably Mattice's head of staff.*

There was a man sat the desk, shrouded in shadow. He was also snoring. The noise was akin to a gutted boar, gasping its final breaths. Delicately, Femira made her way silent-footed across the room to the opposite wall. Without a glance back at the snoring man, she stepped through again.

The next room was also unlit and—after a more thorough check than the last one—was assuredly empty. *Ok, Mattice is in the next room.* This one would have to be done very carefully. She didn't want her face appearing in a well-lit part of the room in plain view of the Lord-Marhsall or his guest.

Ideally, she would have arrived before the meeting started but that would have meant trying to make her way past Mattice's patrols in the half-light of twilight. *Too risky.* Even with a normal person's level of guard staff. *Well, normal for someone who was ridiculously rich.*

The fortunate thing about a study was that people like to show off. They tended to decorate the walls with bookshelves, tapestries and paintings. They were also quite predictable with *where* they chose to put these things. Right in the center, there would likely be a giant painting. *Of a battle, probably.*

Femira didn't want her face pushing any painting off it's hanging and dropping right there and then with her face sticking through. The corner was the best bet, although he'd likely have a bookcase pushed right up along the wall to the corner.

She stepped through the wall at the corner and slowly pressed her head through, angling it so that her eye would be the first through. As expected her brow pushed against something solid. *Bookcase, I knew it. Highborn are so fucking predictable.*

This worked to her advantage however. As there was a half an inch gap between the stone wall and wood. She angled her head again, pushing her ear out against the timber.

"...with you on this matter," Femira heard Mattice's voice, muffled by the bookcase in her way but clear enough to discern his words.

"Then it's settled," said Prince Lukane, "we push for war with Rubane." *Just in time.* Femira had worried that she'd already missed the bulk of the conversation on the matter. She grinned within her hole in the wall. In the first second, she'd already gathered enough to bring back to Garld.

"My father will not entertain any other options," Lukane continued. "The insult against the Royal Family is too great. Any Houses that go against it will be inviting themselves to falling out of favour with the crown."

Femira felt her ego inflate. Eavesdropping on a private conversation between the military's most prominent leader and the heir to the Reldoni crown was new ground in her career.

"I can't imagine that many Houses will oppose," Mattice replied. "Rubane is rich in untapped resources. The Iron Hills, the forests, all of it."

"The northern lands have issues with local tribes of wildmen from what I understand."

"Nothing that our military cannot bring to heel."

"I agree," Lukane conceded, "we have dawdled with Altarea for too long. My father's ambition to reclaim all of Reldon hinges upon claiming Rubane. Athlin will soon follow."

"And then with the might of the entire north, the bastards of Rien will finally be crushed beneath our heel."

"Once and for all."

"Quite convenient wouldn't you say, Prince Lukane. That your brother was killed in Rubane of all places. I believe it was you yourself that pushed for his appointment to Ambassador. You must be absolutely awash with guilt." Femira could detect the playful tone, even obscured through the bookcase.

"I am, of course... *devastated* by this news," Lukane replied, "Daegan and I may have had our differences, but he was my brother and I miss him dearly. It is my wish and the desire of my entire family to see him avenged."

"I am sure you are. This may well be the first time that Prince Landryn and I will agree on a course of action," Mattice remarked.

"My father is not blind to the difficulties between you and my brother."

"Yet he appointed him as my Commander."

"You understand Mattice, that we Tredains must always align with our blood."

"Of course, of course... but perhaps it is time, the King... *reconsiders* my proposal. Divide the military. Let Landryn and Garld continue killing good soldiers in their little *experiment*. Set the bloodshedders apart on their own, with Landryn as their Commander. He wants that. Allow *me* to assume command of the rest."

"You have no desire for soulforged soldiers among your ranks?" Lukane asked.
"It's not worth the expense to me. They never live long enough to be worth the cost."
"Their process seems close to perfection," Lukane mused.
"Would you risk undergoing it yourself?" Mattice asked.
"Perhaps, with a few more test subjects. Landryn himself has been faring well."
"Indeed, yet dozens of mine were sacrificed for it. Garld believes the lives of his bloodshedders are worth a hundred of mine," Mattice said bitterly.
"Perhaps he's right," Lukane considered, "I thank you again, for your time and your support, General Mattice."

The pair exchanged pleasantries and Lukane departed. His carriage and personal guard were waiting for him in the central courtyard. Femira wasn't entirely sure what to make of that conversation. *Had Mattice been implying that Lukane had been somehow involved in Daegan's murder?* It seemed the kind of thing she should refrain from telling Landryn until she'd first had the chance to debrief with Garld on it.

What was all of that about sacrifices? The bloodshedders were instrumental in operations along the Tidewall. If anything, they'd *saved* the lives of many of the regular soldiers. Femira knew that many of the bloodshedders had been recruited by Garld and Landryn from Mattice's and other divisions. They'd handpicked the best runewielders and those they thought would take to being soulforged most effectively. Mattice was likely still bitter about that. It also seemed like he was openly trying to wrangle a stronger hold on the military leadership from Landryn. She would need to relay all of this to Garld.

Femira decided that any further prying into Mattice likely wouldn't bear more fruit than she'd already gathered. She had more than enough to report to Garld on and it would be close to midnight by the time she could make it back to the palace tonight.

Femira made her way back the way she'd come in, bypassing the security with as much ease as before. She found it quite frustrating, if she was being honest. *No challenge at all.* She'd been hoping that Mattice being a self-important jackass would have at least been a little more challenging then the other places she'd broken into this week.

***

"I have something for you," Landryn said.
"You've already given it," Femira wrapped the linen sheet around her body and rose from the bed.
"Not that," Landryn said coyly, a sheepish grin pulling at his handsome face. It was a smile that warmed Femira's heart.

She walked to an ornate desk by the wall and picked up a polished brass jug of water. She didn't bother pouring a glass and simply gulped directly from the jug. She liked the tingle of the brass on her lips and the coolness of the liquid when drinking from metal over glass. She panted after taking a long drink. The linen clung to her clammy skin. She hadn't realised how vigorous their love making had been.

Landryn was draped on the bed and she took a moment to admire the shape of his naked body. He was lithe, every part of him was wrought iron from years of steady training. But his skin was surprisingly soft despite the hardness of his muscle. She lingered, leaning against the desk, the jug still in her hand.

"It's outside, by the door," Landryn said with a playful grin, and made no move to get up from the bed.

"You want me to get it?" She asked with mock incredulity.

"You're already up."

"You really are a Prince, aren't you," she pointed an accusing finger at him.

Femira put down the jug, bundled the sheet closer around herself, and moved into the antechamber of her palace accommodation. It was the finest room Femira had ever stayed in and she was finding herself enjoying the luxuries more and more. She could see how people overstayed their welcome in the palace.

Next to the door was a long object about the size of a spear wrapped in fine gold-threaded cloth. The cloth itself was probably worth more than anything she'd ever stolen in Altarea.

She vaguely recalled Landryn holding it when Femira had opened the door for him. But it was quickly discarded in their frenzied passion. The rush of kissing him again after not seeing him all day gave her a flutter in her stomach. Even now the memory of that feeling made her want to run back to the bed and jump on him.

Femira picked up the object and found it surprisingly light. Carrying it under her arm back into the room, she felt an unusual but familiar resonance beneath the cloth.

What is this? It was metal surely or her edir wouldn't have responded to it. But it was too light. *Maybe glass?* If he'd gotten her an ornamental glass spear, then he really did not know her very well. She could also fashion herself anything she liked out of metal or glass.

Back in the bedchamber Femira held out the bundle with an arched eyebrow.

"That's it," Landryn nodded.

"What is it?"

"Open it and see."

"I'm not like the women at court, I don't expect to be given trinkets because we're sleeping together," Femira teased but began unwrapping the cloth anyway.

"Does that look like a trinket?" he pouted with the hint of a smile.

"It's light," Femira replied, "but a weird shape. Is it a paddle?!" she guessed while working at unwrapping the cloth. "I know! You've got me a boa..." Femira trailed off as the sight of the smooth black metal was uncovered, the familiar edir sense abruptly registering in her memory.

"Landryn," she breathed, "...this."

"You like it?"

"I-I'm not sure if I can accept this." But she already knew that was out of the question.

Femira pulled back the rest of the cloth, revealing the complex shape of metal. It looked exactly as it had the last time she'd seen the nythilium. A large sword with two blades intertwining in a bizarre helix. She could see it in more detail now, the fine sharpened edges of the blades. The pommel and hilt in the same smoothed black finish. It was like no other sword she'd seen before. And she was the one who'd created it.

"Your armour," Femira started. Although it wasn't armour anymore.

"Nythilium."

"You're the only person known who's been able to shape it," Landryn revealed. "It feels right that you should be the one to have it," he insisted. She could see her own reflection perfectly in the metal although shaded dark. Like a demon version of herself. When it was armour the metal hadn't given any reflection at all, she wondered why it gave off a slight one now.

"My father's scholars have been studying the kragal's body at Temple Beach. The nythilium was delivered to the palace this morning, they found it buried within the shell."

Femira ran her hand along the surface of the metal and her edir thrummed gently against it. As before, she felt an unmistakable resonance from the nythilium. It was different from regular metals. *Very different.* She got the distinct impression that the sword *remembered* her.

"The scholars are attributing your accomplishment to the fact that you're soulforged."

"It would make sense," Femira replied without taking her eyes from the sword. She could feel an almost sentient presence within it. Like it *knew* her.

Femira reached out with her edir and felt the sword evaporate to dust in her hands. The black cloud flowed into her hands and chest, and within seconds was completely gone. Only the gold threaded cloth dangling limp in her arms remained. She heard Landryn suck in a breath from across the room and she looked up meeting his eyes.

"Incredible," he breathed.

"It's strange," Femira said, cocking her head to the side.

"It's so different from other metal and rock. I can feel it inside…" she placed a tentative hand against her chest. "But it still feels… separate from me. It's hard to explain. The aradium inside me feels like it's part of me. When I draw in rock and metal, it's like an extension of me. I can control it and it flows to my will. But this… I feel like it's trying to tell me that I do not command it. That it flows in me because it has *chosen* to."

"Can you shape it again?"

Femira pursed her lips in concentration and stretched out an arm before her, guiding the nythilium from her chest. It flowed down through her arms and golden light appeared along the lines of her veins. It flowed out of her, turning into a stream of black dust. In her mind, Femira called forth an image of a spear. The same shape she'd made a thousand times before in training. The nythilium resisted. It swirled and coalesced… but did nothing. She impressed the image of the spear harder and the black cloud thrummed in frustration.

There was a petulance in the impressions she felt on her edir. As before, she was imprinted with a series of outlandish and bizarre images, most of which she couldn't even discern what they were. She imagined the shape of the helix blade and in an instant the black cloud rushed inwards on itself, consolidating back into the shape of the large sword.

"I've never seen a sword like that before," Landryn remarked.

"Neither have I."

"But then how?"

"I don't know…" Femira shook her head, "it's like the nythilium is telling me that this is the shape it wants to take."

"Pity it won't go back to being armour… nythilium plate is all but indestructible. It also has some very interesting affects. You probably never noticed but every time Drad healed me, I needed to take it off. Something about the metal interferes with bloodstone and mindstone. When wearing it, neither has any effect. Quite useful when you're faced against an enemy foebreaker."

"That's a good benefit. I didn't know that."

"One of the reasons it's so sought after. Father's crown is made from the same stuff. To prevent any mindstone manipulation."

"Your family has a lot of it?"

"A few relics that we've hung onto over generations. That armour had been in my family for centuries."

"I'm sorry for breaking it."

"I've told you before, you need not apologise for saving my life."

"Will your father be angry that you've given this to me?"

"Well…" Landryn unabashedly ran his fingers through his hair, "my father doesn't know."

"Will he not be furious?"

"I will handle him. You're the first person we've known to ever runewield with nythilium. I think we'd be foolish not to explore that. I can convince my father of the tactical advantage of it in the fighting to come." Femira's chest tightened at the last comment.

Since returning to Epilas, Femira and Landryn had scarcely discussed what the next move would be. The War Council was tomorrow and she didn't know which direction Landryn would push. Prior to their return, he had been adamant that hunting the draega was their priority. But the news of Daegan's death had changed everything.

They spoke about Daegan a lot and Femira felt she was helping Landryn through his grief. She was more than just a friend and confidant to him. She was… what was she? She was his lover.

But not his wife. Rhianne Averstock—or rather Rhianne *Tredain*—was a thorn in her gut whenever she thought of her future with Landryn. Every time Femira shoved aside thoughts of the woman, Rhianne always seemed to claw her way back into her mind eventually.

Femira raised her hand again and breathed out. The blade dissolved once again and was absorbed into her. She could feel it there, thrumming inside of her. Landryn was still smiling at her and she felt compelled to rush towards him. She leapt up onto the bed and he grabbed her as she fell, pulling her in to an embrace. She kissed him, wrapping the linen sheet around them. She could feel him becoming aroused again and it stirred a warmth in her.

"So you like it?" he asked.

"I love it, thank you. It's the nicest gift anyone's given me." It was the only gift anyone had given her in a long time. Not since her brothers had been killed.

Femira wanted to ask him what all of this was to him. What was she to him? She found that she didn't have the courage to ask. She was enjoying their time together too much to spoil it with whatever the truth was. Instead she buried her face into his neck and kissed his skin.

CHAPTER 47

The Belly of the Beast

The next morning, Landryn left early to prepare for the War Council. Femira had to debrief with Garld in advance of it to relay the conversation between Prince Lukane and Lord-Marshal Mattice.

It didn't bother her to hide the information from Landryn. She trusted that Garld was doing what was best for Landryn… and for her. Garld wanted the information first so she would bring it to him for the decision on what to do with it.

Landryn didn't seem to have much concern about who saw him coming and going from Femira's rooms. The subject of his wife was a topic the pair actively avoided in conversation. However he was always gone from her rooms before the servants arrived in the morning.

Femira could get very accustomed to having servants. Unlike in the barracks, people brought breakfast straight to her door. They set the table for her, took away her worn uniforms and used linens to be washed. They even lit the fire in the hearth with the mornings getting colder as they approached winter's heart.

A pretty female servant in the red livery of the Tredain household held out a note for her. This was also a custom in the Pillar. People didn't slip letters under the door, they had servants hand-deliver them. She recognised Garld's signet on the wax seal and cracked it open. Garld wrote that he would be in his office in the Pillar for the day, and that she should report to him after her morning session with Daurond.

Annali's cousin had a tendency to sleep in late so Femira usually met with him in the late morning. As a result, she resumed her training in the early morning. Running the steps of the Pillar from base to top and then practising runewielding in the sparring yards. Finding sparring partners hadn't been that difficult, many of the highborn were eager to spar with the 'infamous' draega-slayer and Landryn himself often took the time to train with her. Today, however, she was hoping to get some time with a specific training partner.

"Will that be all, my lady?" the servant asked.
"Actually, do you know where Vestyr's rooms are?" Femira inquired.
"Vestyr the Aeth?" The girl had an innocent tilt to her head.
"Yeah," Femira decided not to mock her by pointing out how many other people named 'Vestyr' were in the palace.
"The eastern side of the Pillar, my lady. On the twelfth." Femira was on the tenth floor.
"Can you run a message to him?"
"Of course, my lady," the girl pulled out a scribing pen and parchment and moved to hand them to Femira who waved her off.
"Just tell him that I want to meet him in the sparring yards in an hour?"

"The sparring yards. In an hour," the girl nodded determinedly as she spoke. *Something tells me you've forgotten messages in the past.*

The servant departed and Femira finished her breakfast of spiced eggs and cheese. *A weird combination but it works. Although it's no spicy rice ball.* The food in the palace was remarkable. Sometimes Landryn would send for a servant in the middle of the night and freshly cooked food would be brought straight to them. It was ludicrously indulgent. A year ago, Femira had to steal from market stalls just to keep from starving.

There was something she wanted to attempt before leaving. The task required a bit of open space, and her rooms didn't have a balcony, so she pushed the furniture to the walls. This left just the plush rug in the middle of the room. Femira stood in the center of the rug, taking deep calming breaths.

"Alright, let's try this again," she muttered.

It didn't take Femira long to get into a focused state. She pulled her edir inward, ignoring the reverberations of the stone walls, the tiles and ceiling. It was a state of mind that she found easily these days and was crucial for her runewielding. She listened to the beat of her heart and the hum of the aradium inside of her. They worked in harmony with each other since she had become soulforged.

There was a new sensation in there too, however, something she could only sense when she focused on it. It was the erratic discord of the nythilium metal. She had other material inside of her too; a few ingots of steel which she always kept inside for emergencies. Stone was easy to come by so she never bothered to store any. The steel resonated with her edir, eager to obey her will. The nythilium, however, was aloof.

"What *are* you?" Femira whispered. The dissonant humming continued. She focused her edir on it and guided the nythilium through her body. It was an exercise that Misandrei that taught her in the early days to help learn to focus her edir, cycling metal and stone through her body. The nythilium flowed where she directed it, first down to her feet, then back up again to chest and to her hand. *Ok... so you're happy to do that.*

She tried to impress the image of a simple dagger. She was immediately flooded with images in response. The images were just as perplexing as before. Shifting sands of scenes that whirled about but never took full focus. One moment there was a ship unlike any she'd ever seen upon a sea of silver. Then next, creatures of shapes and sizes that defied all reason and logic moved about in bizarre landscapes. She stayed resolute on the image of the dagger but the nythilium stubbornly resisted.

"Ok, let's try something different," Femira said and envisaged a simple fork for eating. The response she received was far angrier than before; a chaotic chorus of images flashing with red lightning

"Ok, ok," Femira held up her hands even though there was nobody actually there. She hoped that the meaning of the gesture might convey to the nythilium. *What am I doing here?* Was she really trying to communicate with a piece of metal?

She remembered the details of Landryn's armour. The hawk grasping a sword emblem on the breastplate. The shape of the interlocking parts on the pauldrons. She pushed the images forward and the vibrations of the nythilium quieted to almost a whisper.

You didn't like being armour?

She sent forward more images of armour; hte gilded plate of the stormguards and then the dragonhide jerkin that she'd worn when fighting the kraglings. She tried to convey the images as questions, not commands. *I'm asking you to be something like this... I'm not forcing you.*

The nythilium buzzed inside of her. Again, the images Femira received back didn't make much sense to her. And then, suddenly, the nythilium burst out from her in a cloud of dark sparkling mist, the flecks of metal catching the morning sun through the window.

The cloud swirled around her and Femira was unsure if it was even *her* edir guiding the nythilium or if it was deciding itself what shape to take. It was like dough telling the hand how to knead it.

Femira felt the metal compact on top of her uniform, coiling around her arms and legs to form armour. She felt it wrap around her neck like a noose and her heart quickened.

"Uhm," she started, "maybe... let's rethink this." The coiling continued and then solidified, the last remaining whisps locking into place.

What she was left with was the most bizarre armour Femira had ever seen. Impossibly thin braids of metal wrapped around her. It allowed for surprisingly easy movement as she tested a few steps and swung her arms around. A thick coil protected her neck but also made it hard to turn her head. A major flaw was that all of her vital organs were exposed, as was her head.

"Ok, this is... progress?" Femira said, carefully. She could feel what almost felt like satisfaction from the nythilium.

"You *are* alive aren't you?" she wasn't sure how to convey that in images to the nythilium but tried anyway. She portrayed the images of children running, fish swimming, birds flying in her mind.

The nythilium responded with grass and trees, clouds and water. *Ok, those things are alive too right?* Well maybe not water and clouds. *But we're getting closer.*

"What are you called?" Femira tried sending images of her own name written on paper and then of herself. Shifting black sands were sent back, the sea of silver and then a field of blue stars.

"Humans call you nythilium, do you like that?" Again there were indiscernible images sent in response.

"How about Nyth? Do you like that?" *That's a stupid name. It would be like calling me Hume.* Well she liked Nyth and until it learned how to tell her it's name it could stay that way. Nyth resonated in response and Femira took that for agreement.

She tried again to create a breastplate, sending Nyth the image of Landryn's armour but the metal sent back the image of Femira wearing the coiled armour.

"No, this won't work," she said, "all my vitals are exposed." Nyth sent her images of a bird soaring on the wind, of a tortoise shell perfectly in shape. *Are you trying to tell me this is the most efficient? I can assure you it's not.* She sent the mental image of a blade cutting into her heart.

"Armour," she stated, "to protect me."

The shifting sands of images coalesced into an alien figure. It was a spindly form that reminded Femira of an insect. *Or an insect in the shape of a person.* The arms and legs were wrapped in the coiled armour, a thick gorget protecting the neck. The chest and torso were exposed as hers was now but the creature was impossibly thin, it's central body being little more than a spine. The spine itself seemed to be able to rotate completely.

"Well I don't know what the fuck that is but humans have some pretty important bits around there," Femira said. Nyth dissolved back to dust and reformed again, this time with the coils looping around her waist and chest. There was a sense of disgruntled compromise in its resonance. There were still key parts of her exposed but it was definitely a start.

"Maybe let's try a weapon again," Femira sent the image of a dagger and the Nyth armour burst to dust and formed a smaller version of the double helix blade. A smaller version still being larger than a longsword.

"You're really sold on this helix shape aren't you?" Nyth sent the image of the helix blade tearing through the maw of the kragal.

"I suppose I can't argue with you there," she chuckled.

The image that Nyth sent next gave Femira pause. She could recognise a silhouette of herself, holding the helix blade. The sky was painted red. Enormous shards of stone were rising from the earth all around her. The image of herself looked strange, and when she tried to focus more on it, it turned completely black, her eyes shining with a blue light. There was almost a question to the image Nyth was portraying to her but she couldn't figure it out.

The tolling of the bells marking the hour pulled Femira from her concentration and she jumped. She couldn't believe how much time she'd spent at this without realising. Hopefully the servant girl had remembered to pass on the message to Vestyr.

***

Femira hurled boulder after boulder at Vestyr who was being pressed to the rear of the duelling ring. Vestyr disintegrated them in the air but he was sweating with the effort. Femira had manoeuvred so that Vestyr's back was to the Pillar and she had the open air of the balcony at her rear.

The palace sparring yards were on the lower levels of the Pillar on an extensive balcony. It was reserved for highborn runewielders and all of the duelling rings had a pair of combatants. It looked more like a grand outdoor gallery than a training yard with its shaped columns and arches of marble stretching out from the walls of the Pillar.

Femira and Vestyr were the only soulforged training today and they had gathered a small crowd of onlookers. Soulforging was no longer just a rumour in the palace halls with many nobles discussing it outright, however the King had yet to make any official statements on soulforged individuals in the military.

Vestyr had to roll to the side as Femira's barrage continued, her boulders smashing against the wall of the Pillar. He dashed towards her, a cloud of silvery dust burst out from him and he formed a steel quarterstaff in his hand as he ran. Femira responded by forming a pair of blunted duelling daggers.

She parried his attacks in quick deflections, dodging and rolling when needed. Vestyr was incredibly agile although not as fast as Landryn or Loreli—both of whom Femira set the bar for in terms of speed.

Femira knew how to manage a faster opponent, shifting her edir inside of her to concentrate stoneskin on the areas that Vestyr would strike next. Stoneskin slowed her but at least she didn't suffer any damage, and could quickly dismiss it and perform followup attacks.

All-in-all, it was a fairly well matched fight and Femira found herself panting, having only made a handful of hits on the Aeth. She had chosen not to bring out Nyth even though she was sure it would have given her a distinct advantage. But she didn't want to expose all of her cards to Vestyr, not while the possibility of them fighting him for real someday was a reality. There was also the crowd watching to consider. Any of them could be a potential opponent someday in the future. No, she would keep Nyth to herself unless she found herself in a real fight to the death.

Vestyr twirled his quarterstaff and leapt at her in an offensive. She braced herself in a block with her daggers raised but then his staff burst to dust just before striking. Vestyr then rolled past her, the silver cloud rushing around him and reforming. He swung hard at her back and she felt the reformed staff whack against her shoulder blades sending her sprawling forward. She held onto her daggers and fell forward onto her elbows, rolling to the side to avoid a follow-up.

Vestyr was already on his feet and Femira swung her leg out in a sweeping kick, catching the back of his ankle. Vestyr fell hard on his back and Femira launched herself on top of him, the blunted tip of her dagger pressed against his throat.

"You've gotten better," Vestyr wheezed, still winded from his fall.

"I've not spent this whole time lounging around the palace." Femira got to her feet and offered him a hand. He was taller than her but she still easily hoisted him up from the ground.

"Your abilities are getting stronger?" Vestyr probed as he dusted himself off.

"Doesn't everything with training?" she replied with a wink.

"You know what I mean," he said pointedly, "soulforging has heightened your abilities. And they're still growing each day, no?"

"Of course, you should know that already."

"It's not the same for me," Vestyr replied. "My progress is... limited."

"I think there's a limit for me too," Femira conceded, "although that limit keeps stretching as I train. A month ago I could only hold three stonespears at a time. I reckon I can manage five or six now... maybe you're not pushing yourself hard enough."

"It's not that," Vestyr shook his head, "my umbra power is but a trickle next to yours. My soulbond enhances this but not nearly as much as to what yours is."

"Umbra?" Femira's brows knotted and her head tilted slightly.

"The strength of my soul. It is what powers our runewielding," he replied matter-of-factly as if this was all information she should know. "The umbra you absorbed when becoming soulforged has strengthened yours far more than mine ever will be on its own."

"I've no idea what you're talking about," Femira replied. It sounded like the kind of stuff the priests in the temples used to try preach at her.

"When you became—" Vestyr began but then the palace bells rang the eleventh hour of morning in the background and Femira's eyes widened.

"Shit, I'm late," she cut across him, leaving the boy with a startled expression. "These bells are controlling my life these days. I've to go. This was fun though," she was already trotting away from him, "we should make this a regular session!" She meant it. It was hard to come by good sparring partners.

Femira felt bad cutting him off and leaving him but she was late for her session with Daurond which they normally started by now. She made for the steps and back into the halls of the palace. She was familiar enough by now with the many halls, galleries and stairways to make her way to Daurond's apartments without getting lost.

Femira had been so distracted by her duels with Vestyr that she'd completely missed the tenth hour bell toll. As it was, she and Daurond would barely have any time for his tutoring before she'd need to leave to meet with Garld.

Daurond, as it transpired, wasn't even *in* his rooms. He'd spent the entire night in the city and had been far past the point of coherence to stagger up the steps of the Pillar. There were a few inns close to the Pillar that were well accustomed to catering to palace residents that found themselves looking up at the thousands of steps in the late evening and deciding… not tonight. Daurond had made quite a habit of this.

Femira made herself comfortable in the lounge of Daurond's rooms. She was slowly becoming familiar with Nyth inside of her, humming its unusual beat. It became background noise to her in the same way that the constant vibrations of the stone around her could be pushed out of her attention.

Femira felt that she'd made great progress with the… well, whatever Nyth was. She wanted to talk to Aden about it. He was clever and always had insight into things like this. He was also very resourceful with books. Surely he could help her find some information on nythilium. But that would have to wait until he was back.

She was also eager for Jaz and Misandrei to return. She missed their company and was eager to test out Nyth in her fighting style. She even missed Endrin and Loreli too. They weren't so bad and she felt they were almost becoming friends before they'd been sent to Rubane. She hoped that they were all still alive up there. And that they could make it out before any of Reldon's warships started sailing. *Rubane won't be kind to any Reldoni within their borders in the coming weeks.* She made a mental note to ask Garld about them again.

Daurond eventually shuffled into the room looking like a dug-up corpse wearing crumpled silks. He groaned as he noticed her waiting for him.

"Ugh, I'd forgotten you'd be here" Daurond lamented, "why did I agree to this." He fell into a lounge chair and rubbed at his forehead.

"Can we skip today?" he asked, "I feel like a garrif has been dancing on my head."

"We don't really have much time before I've to meet with Garld anyway," Femira pointed out.

"Oh lucky me. Would you be a dear and get me some water?" he had such a pathetic pleading in his eyes that Femira indulged him, rising to fetch the brass jug of water. She took a gulp herself, then offered it to him.

"Right from the jug, how ladylike. We really do have a lot of work to do before we arrive in Keiran."

"What?!" Femira snatched back the jug.

"Oh," he whimpered, weakly reaching for it, "please, my dear… the water."

"What do you mean *when we arrive in Keiran*?" Daurond didn't respond, just continued reaching feebly for the jug. *Fine.* She shoved it towards him and he took a tiny sip. Smacking his lips with the liquid.

"I thought Garld had told you already," Daurond curled up his feet on the lounger, clearly preparing to fall asleep right there. "He's sending us to Kerian. This is why he's had me tutoring you. Don't worry, little cousin," he closed his eyes and nuzzled his face into a cushion, "we'll have plenty of time on the ship to correct all of your little discourtesies. You'll be the very heart of Annali's dignity by the time we arrive."

"I am *not* going back to Keiran," Femira hissed. The image of an Honorsword's yellow cloak stained with blood flashed in her mind. *Blood caking into the dry earth.* She felt her heart quicken.

"Well that's between you and Garld," Daurond mumbled, "if you wouldn't mind." He waved his hand towards the window, indicating he wanted the curtains drawn closed.

Femira stood up and stormed for the door. She could feel her breaths coming in shallow, and she paced back and forth for a time. *I can't go back. I won't!* She could talk to Garld, maybe Daurond had misunderstood. She was *needed* here. She was supposed to fight the draega. The Reldoni needed her here. *Landryn* needed her here.

"Annali, the drapes," Daurond groaned.

"Close your own fucking drapes," Femira snapped at him, then swung open the door and made her way purposefully in the direction of Garld's office.

Femira felt nervous and twitchy as she approached Garld's door. She could feel herself losing grip on her edir and it flared out in waves. The walls of the Pillar resonated in response. Nyth pulsed in confusion.

Not now, Nyth.

She felt an image conveyed back to her; an Honorsword in golden armour, and Nyth's double helix blade, hilt deep in the gilded breastplate.

You do understand me, don't you? But that wasn't what she wanted. She didn't want to fight any Honorswords. She didn't want to kill *anyone*—even if they were murderous zealots.

Femira was about to barge into the office but restrained herself, rapping her knuckles against the wood instead.

"Enter," she heard from inside and swung the door open. Garld sat alone at his desk poring over documents. Femira wanted to confront him immediately about what Daurond had said but she knew what Garld was like. He would respond poorly to her lashing out. She needed to bring it up calmly.

"You're early. I wasn't expecting you until..." Garld trailed off and looked up at her with narrowed eyes. "You're losing control of your edir. How long has this been happening?" there was genuine concern on his face.

"Daurond said that we're going to Keiran?" Femira burst out, unable to restrain herself any longer. "Is this true?"

"Ah," Garld replied, visibly relaxing, "he shouldn't have told you that. I wanted to brief you after the War Council today."

"So it *is* true?" there was a panicked edge to her voice, "Garld... I can't."

"Compose yourself, soldier. You don't even know what the mission is yet," Garld raised his hands in a calming gesture.

She felt Nyth hum inside of her. *Not the time, Nyth.* The image of hands holding a skull entered her mind. *What? Stop that, go away, Nyth.* She focused her edir to try to shut out Nyth's buzzing.

And then she noticed it.

A tiny tendril of Garld's edir, so subtle she never would have noticed if she'd not been looking. It was stretched out to her, as indiscernible as a single spider's thread. Garld always had immaculate control of his edir.

This is no mistake.

Nyth thrummed and Femira listened, greeted by a chorus of strange images. A river feeding a canal. A human-shaped creature but with the features of a bird, dancing under starlight. *I don't understand these, Nyth.* Sunlight, distorted through the light of a diamond. *A diamond... mindstone!*

Femira met Garld's eyes. She could feel the fury rising in her. She clenched her jaw, her heart was like a bird thrashing inside a bone cage. *The fucker.*

In her mind, she knew it. She'd known it for a while. Garld had been manipulating Femira's emotions using a mindstone. He'd likely been doing it since the moment they first met. Her bloodshedder training had shown her how to recognise the effect from a foebreaker. The abrupt and forceful shift in emotion along with mental techniques to overcome it. But Garld's touch was so sophisticated and subtle in contrast to what she'd seen with foebreakers.

Nythilium interferes with mindstone. That was what Landryn had told her. Nyth was preventing it from working. *And Garld doesn't seem to realise.* She made a show of appearing placated although internally she was seething. *How dare he?!*

Garld had been speaking the whole time that Femira had been dealing with this revelation. She picked up what he was saying. "The mission to Keiran is a delicate matter," Garld said, "but ultimately, it is a distraction from what is happening today. We must focus on the War Council. Put Keiran out of your mind and we will discuss it later." *You want to send me back there. Where the dead lie rotting under a blazing sun and none will bother to bury them.*

"Of course, sir," Femira shrugged in a show of nonchalance, "I trust you." *You fucking liar.*

She didn't know how to process this. A big part of her wanted to lash out at Garld, to berate him for lying to her for so long, for manipulating her. But that would give away that she knew what he was doing. Garld never responded well in the past to her outbursts, she needed to remain composed. She needed to make him believe that she was under his control while she figured all of this out.

"Good," Garld indicated for her to take a seat, "So. Tell me, what was discussed between Mattice and Prince Lukane?" Femira diligently recounted the conversation to him. While in the back of her mind trying to work through all the times Garld might have manipulated her like this. The small nudges in her emotion to push her towards what he wanted. Femira found now that she regretted not telling Landryn about how Garld had asked her to spy on him. How he'd told her to hide Daegan's death from him. Everything that she was hiding from Landryn was all at Garld's command.

Garld seemed pleased with what she reported. He'd suspected that Mattice would eventually make a play for more military control with Lukane.

"You're certain they both aligned towards war with Rubane?" Garld asked.

"Unmistakably, sir."

"Good, good."

"Is that what you want?"

"My concern is always the defence of our country and our people. And of those under my command."

Femira wondered how many times Garld used his little mind tricks to dodge her questions without her even realising it. She decided to test out asking him direct questions and seeing how he reacted.

"Sir, what is umbra?" Femira asked, thinking back to the conversation regarding soulforging she'd had earlier with Vestyr. Soulforging was still a topic she knew very little about, despite it being such a prevalent thing in her life. It was something Femira felt Garld had deftly distracted her from.

"I see you've been reading the Art of Soulforging" Garld remarked. She hadn't. It was still in her room in the barracks. Left there untouched since the night she'd stolen it from Landryn's office. With her busy schedule the past week, she'd barely had time to sleep, let alone read.

"No, actually... it's just something Vestyr mentioned in our sparring session."

"I wouldn't pay any heed to his remarks," Garld dismissed, "we must focus on the task at hand..." again, Femira felt the subtle touch of his edir on her mind and Nyth responded, interrupting the effect on her. *The sneaky bastard!*

"You are dismissed until after the War Council."

"You want me there?" Femira tested and Garld shook his head in response.

"The War Council consists of the King and his Royal Council, along with our army's senior leaders. This is where we meet to determine the course of action for the various military factions. It differs from the Military Court held in Judgement Hall that you've attended in the past. The Military Court is what Landryn presides over to impose the will of the War Council."

It's not that different to gang leaders. Lichtin's crew had been part of a wider gang of criminal activity. Lichtin himself would go to meet with other crew leaders where they'd decide which rich person they'd target next. *Except instead of some rich noble, the target is an entire country.*

"So Landryn can only act upon the direction of the War Council," Femira considered. *In other words, they treat him like a puppet.*

"Precisely. It is often the will of the King that directs this, but Abhran is not deaf to suggestion. Landryn himself as Commander does hold much sway within the War Council; he has proven himself at Altarea as a strong leader."

As far as Femira knew, Garld was unaware of her growing relationship with Landryn. Whenever Landryn did speak of Garld, he did so fondly, like a child telling stories of his favourite uncle. There was a very clear paternal dynamic between them but Femira doubted that Landryn would tell Garld about how he'd been spending every night with her the past week. Now, she wondered if Garld was manipulating Landryn too.

"Do you think Landryn can convince them that the draega threat is greater?" Femira asked, realising now that she had no idea what Garld wanted in all of this. Garld told her time and time again that he served Landryn but yet he'd had her spy on him. Had her withhold information from him. His actions did not align well with his words.

"Landryn's grief may still impact what he will decide at the War Council," Garld answered and Femira felt her stomach knot with the amount of people that would die because of that decision.

"Is there anything that *I* can do to stop this?"

"Landryn did argue to have your testimony heard by the War Council on the draega. I believe the King's Council decided it wasn't prudent." Femira felt a swell of pride rise in her with the knowledge that Landryn had wanted her there. It also suggested that Landryn intended to push *against* the war in Rubane and to focus their efforts on the draega. "So no," Garld continued, "I believe we have done as much as we can."

"What will you do?" Femira probed, "regarding Mattice and Lukane?"

"Truthfully," Garld replied, "nothing." She raised her eyebrows at his candour. "Mattice already controls the bulk of the army's rank-and-file. His division has command of ten thousand spearmen, four thousand crossbowmen along with three hundred battle-trained runewielders. In addition to this, many of his spearmen are being retrained as riflemen. This is more than half of our entire military."

Garld leaned forward. "A war with Rubane will be extensive," he intoned, "Altarea was a single island state; one battle and the war was won. Rubane by contrast will involve exhaustive campaigns ranging for months, maybe even years.

I do not want our bloodshedders deployed to Rubane unless absolutely necessary. Therefore, I am inclined to allow Mattice to deploy his own soldiers for this effort rather than sacrificing ours." Garld's continued commitment to the bloodshedders was heartening, but that feeling conflicted with Femira's prevailing anger with him.

"That's *if* it comes to war." Femira noted.

"War with Rubane is an inevitability," Garld sighed, "King Abhran's retribution will wash over Rubane as immutable as the great tides of the Altasjura."

"Is there nothing we can do to prevent it?" Femira implored.

"I believe prevention is out of our grasp. All that we can do is minimise the damage."

CHAPTER 48
Revelations of the Soul

Both moons were full bright orbs in the sky. Ecko was a brilliant iridescent blue, Luna a warm lustrous red. It was Lua Nova, the turning of a new year. As with Unionsday in the summer, it was a time when both moons were full, bathing the city of Epilas in bright moonslight.

A sailor had once tried to explain to a young Femira how complex the phases of the moons were and how they affected the great tides of the Altasjura seas. What she'd grasped was that the moons would both be full on different days depending on where you were in the world. So even though it was Lua Nova here in Epilas now, the northern reaches of Rubane would have already celebrated the turning of a new year a few days ago. And the people of Keiran wouldn't celebrate it for maybe another few weeks.

That truth had awakened young Femira to the realisation that Lua Nova and Unionsday didn't actually mean anything important. They were just days that people celebrated for no other reason than both moons were full. The temples tried to preach that they were gifts ordained by the gods, that there was meaning behind the cycles. But the truth was that this was simply the way the natural world was. The only reason this day was special was because people decided that it was.

Knowing this didn't mean that Femira couldn't appreciate the beauty of both moons in their splendour. She stood dressed in her black uniform—the winter variant with a black overcoat. She looked up at the moons from the largest balcony in the Pillar, the twisting fountain behind her.

The city of Epilas sprawled out before her. The twinkling lights of gaslamps were still lit despite the moonslight providing ample illumination. Fireworks burst in fantastical plumes of colours and Femira could see the tiny dots of thousands of people revelling in the streets.

Despite the festivities, Lua Nova was a perilous time. The full moons working together made the Uniontide which drew back the sea for miles, revealing swathes of exposed shoreline. She could pick out tiny motes of light out in the bay where delvers risked the treacherous sea floor searching for pearls. When the tide came roaring back, Wavecallers would be manning the city coastwalls to guide away the strongest of the swells from the city. Flooding across the kingdom was the norm and many rural people travelled inland or to the cities for the festivals, and to avoid the floods.

Femira thought about how different her life was now compared to her past Lua Nova's spent on the rooftops, taking advantage of the festivities to break into stores and homes. She turned to look at the amassed highborn on the balcony and those who milled into the galleries and halls in the Pillar. She hadn't expected anything less for a night as important as Lua Nova.

Like many of the other guests present, Femira waited in anticipation for the arrival of the King and his family. It was no secret in the Pillar that the War Council had met earlier that afternoon. It was expected that the King would make a declaration at the feast. *Festival be damned if it interferes with Abhran's lust for war.* Abhran likely thought the festival was the perfect timing to announce the invasion of a neighbouring nation with all his gathered subjects.

Femira made her way to the main gallery, deftly avoiding the various nobles that attempted to engage her in conversation. Garld had also wanted to discuss the mission to Keiran with her before the feast, and likely to discuss with her the outcome of the War Council. She found that she had little interest in speaking with him. A part of her still seethed at what he'd been doing. She wanted to find Landryn. She was hoping to pull him away from the festivities for a time so that she could talk to him about it.

Femira spotted Landryn across the crowd of nobles. They were all less important than him. Everyone in the world was less important than him. He was dressed in a military style suit, black with silver trim. She couldn't help but smirk when they met each other's eyes. Then she felt a spike in her heart as she noticed Rhianne with him.

The raven-haired woman leaned into Landryn, snaking an arm around his torso, while talking to another noblewoman in their group. The woman looked frustratingly beautiful, dressed in a fine gold and blue dress, her hair falling in immaculate, waving curls.

The look Landryn gave Femira filled her with longing. Femira knew that he wanted to be next to her. She could feel it. There was the slightest sadness in Landryn's expression and it wrenched at Femira's heart.

Rhianne, by contrast, looked exuberant. The woman laughed at something someone in their group said and looked up at her husband. Landryn pulled his eyes from Femira and gave Rhianne a false, sympathetic smile.

In that moment, Femira had never felt more like a thief. She was a crook, and she'd stolen his heart... and she'd meant to. Even after she'd known that Landryn was married, she'd pursued him. Throughout all her years as a thief, Femira had never thought of herself as doing something wrong.

Maybe... am I... am I a bad person?

The question had never drifted into her mind before. She was always able to justify what she was doing. First, she'd stolen to eat, to clothe and shelter herself. After that, she'd stolen from the rich who had too much anyway. She'd stolen Annali's name and hadn't given six shits for what had happened to the woman... and now, what was she doing? She'd stolen Landryn's heart... and she'd stolen lives... Selyn and Drad... the stormguards on that ship.

A knife sliding into an eye socket.

Why am I feeling this way? It wasn't supposed to be like this.

"You don't look as though you're enjoying the festivities," Femira heard Vestyr's voice pulling her from her train of thought. The Aeth youth wore a fine doublet of green and silver. His white curls were pinched back, exposing his elongated ears.

"Parties like this aren't really my thing," she replied, quietly.

"They do not celebrate Lua Nova where you are from?" His Aeth ears picking up her words despite them being barely a whisper in the din of celebration.

"They do... I just usually don't."

"I see," Vestyr looked out across the crowds of colourful people, "it is very different to my home also. In Evier, Lua Nova is a much... quieter celebration."

"I didn't realise you were feeling homesick, Vestyr," a feminine voice said. Femira turned to see Princess Allyn stepping towards them through the guests. The nobles parted, making way for her, bowing and flattering as she moved past.

"Lua Nova is important to my people, Princess," Vestyr bowed, taking the girl's hand and kissing it. Femira had learned enough to know when others bowed, she should too. "We sing the songs of Aldar to the moons," Vestyr continued. "A tradition I have long enjoyed. This is my first Lua Nova away from the forests of my home. My father is likely leading the song of the winds right now."

"You don't speak of your family often," Allyn replied.

"No," he smiled sadly, "I suppose I don't. My father is 'First Whisperer of the Winds.' A grandiose title but carries much weight with my people. My decision to come here... it didn't sit well with him."

"Well... *I* am glad that you are here," Allyn said warmly.

Allyn turned to Femira and inclined her head respectfully.

"You look radiant, Princess Allyn," Femira said, and genuinely meant it. The girl was dressed in a splendid dress of black slashed with white. It made her look simultaneously beautiful and strong.

Femira would typically be judgmental of such an ostentatious dress but she liked Allyn. In no small part that was because of Landryn, and how highly he spoke of his sister. She was apparently a runewielder with phenomenal natural talent.

"Lady Annali," Allyn greeted her with a warm smile though her eyes danced warily between the two, "I've not had the chance to express my gratitude to you for your recent accomplishments. You saved Landryn's life, as I understand it. You have my deepest thanks, he is very dear to me... he and Daegan both." Femira noted that Allyn did not mention her eldest brother Lukane.

"Landryn means a great deal to me as well," Femira replied.

"As a friend, I'm sure."

"Of course," Femira returned the Princess' knowing smile. Femira and Landryn's growing relationship could only stay a secret for so long.

"My father will be making his announcement soon," Allyn turned to Vestyr. "They've told me nothing but everyone here knows where this is going."

"From what I gather," Vestyr said, "this war is inevitable. Mattice, I hear, has already recalled the majority of his forces from the Reinish border."

"Mattice's forces will be the anvil," Allyn said suggestively.

"You've been reading Ayden," Vestyr rose his eyebrows at the Princess.

"It is important for the eldest daughter to be familiar with military tactics," Allyn shot back playfully, "and a broad stroke of interests is valuable... Lady Annali, what do you make of it?"

Allyn turned to her. It was a question that many of the highborn had been posing to her over the past few days. Garld had instructed her to be ambiguous when asked, that she would follow as the King decides. She didn't think that Allyn would be satisfied with that nothing response however, and a part of her wanted the Princess to like her.

"Truthfully," Femira replied carefully, "I do not wish to see us at war with Rubane."

"Really?" Allyn asked with surprise, "you do not seek vengeance for my brother's death?"

"It's not that," Femira replied, "forgive me, Princess, but I did not know your brother. I would like to see justice done for him—for yours and Landryn's sakes... and for Daegan's... but I do not think that an invasion of Rubane is that justice."

"Are you not a bloodshedder?" Allyn asked, her interest piqued. "I would have thought the war was in your interest."

"The bloodshedders are not about war. We're about preventing it... protecting people. Not killing them."

Allyn and Vestyr shared a confused look. The Princess opened her mouth to speak but then was distracted by trumpets sounding at the other end of the gallery. All heads in the room turned to the dais, upon which a plush throne-like chair sat raised above the guests.

The conversations in the hall died away as a man dressed in an ornate gold and black threaded suit arrived, flanked by a full dozen Royal guards. Even at a distance, Femira could see King Abhran's resemblance to Landryn. She could make out the definitive shape of his jaw and his strong bearing. The King had a fierce gaze that he held over the amassed nobles. Any who were sitting, rose to standing as he made his way to his chair.

"My Lords," King Abhran spoke, "you have my gratitude for joining us tonight. Many of you have travelled far for this year's Lua Nova festivities. Even during such dark and grieving times, we must always celebrate the traditions of our country. I am grateful to all whom have expressed their condolences for the death of my son. Daegan's murder is an insult against *all* of Reldon, and our reprisal for this must reflect the power and might of all Reldon." The nobles and military officers in attendance responded with aggressive affirmations, each trying to sound more emphatically patriotic than their peers.

Femira was watching Landryn as his father spoke. She noticed the crease in his forehead, the cracks of his grief showing through the mask on his face. Her heart ached with the desire to comfort him. *He's the only one really suffering here.* She schooled the anger from her face. *None of these people cared about Daegan Tredain. None of them loved him as Landryn had.* They didn't have the right to use his death as a means to further their own goals.

"We will bring back Arch-duke Edmund's head on a spike, your Grace," Femira heard Mattice declare from close to the dais.

"His city will burn," Highlady Ingel's voice could be heard above the clamour, "Rubane's lands and resources will be claimed as tribute to the crown."

"Your avarice for vengeance is admirable," King Abhran raised his hands to the crowd's growing chorus, "I have met with the War Council and we have determined that the Dukes of Rubane are to blame for this injustice. War with Rubane is an inevitability. As immutable as the great tides of the Altasjura, our retribution will wash over Rubane."

There was raucous approval from those in the gallery. Femira met Landryn's eyes, she could see the concern in them. *This is not the fight we should be focused on.*

"We sit upon the dawn of a new year," Abhran continued. "Three hundred turnings of the stars since my ancestor founded this great nation. However it is not simply a new year that lies before us, but a new age for all of Reldon. I confirm here and now that we have re-discovered the ancient art of soulforging. The power which gave the Sorcerer King's of old their omnipotent and supreme rule of these lands is now ours to command." There were audible gasps of surprise in the crowd followed by a tumultuous murmuring. *So the secret's out then.* She wondered how Garld felt about that. Femira glanced over at Landryn who was now making his way towards the dais.

"We sit upon the precipice of greatness, my Lords," Abhran continued. "Join us in celebration of our new era. You all know my son, Prince Landryn Tredain, Commander of our armies. Landryn is one of the first among us to become soulforged. The feats of his bloodshedders have become renowned across our nation." Femira felt her stomach clench in a knot.

"The soulforged will be the spearhead that we drive into the heart of Rubane," Abhran declared. "It is time for the world to see our power. The soulforged will instil fear into the hearts of our enemies, they will be the sword by which this world will bow.

However, the crown is not without mercy. My enmity is for the Dukes of Rubane and I do not wish for needless bloodshed. I will be content with annihilating the Dukes and their rule, but the people of Rubane need not suffer for the actions of their maladroit leadership." *How very magnanimous of you.* Femira thought bitterly.

Femira felt nausea rising in her at the thought of the amount of people that would die because of this decision. She fixed her gaze on Landryn.

Say something! Stop this! Femira pleaded in her mind.

Landryn stood up onto the raised platform and stood next to his father's throne.

"It is with a heavy heart that I issue this charge," Landryn began formally. "The Dukes of Rubane have plotted and murdered my brother, Prince Daegan Tredain, in an attempt to sow sedition within our borders. Under the authority of my father, King Abhran the First; I declare war upon the nation of Rubane. From this day forth, all Rubanian peoples are considered enemies of the crown. The Arch-duke Edmund must be de-throned and the lands of his Dukes surrendered to Reldon."

Femira's heart sank as Landryn spoke. How could they be so reckless? They were talking about tens of thousands of people that were going to die. Her hands were shaking and her chest fluttered. She glanced around at the zealous intent of the highborn as many cheered their support. A few had the decency to look anxious or scared. Allyn beside her looked horrified, Vestyr wore a matching expression.

"We must go Vestyr," Allyn said, pulling the Aeth's arm, "there is much to do."

"This," Femira breathed, "this is all wrong."

"*This* is what the bloodshedders do," Allyn turned to her and spat with vehemence, "your thirst for blood has thrown us into war with one of our longest-standing allies. *This* is not justice for Daegan," Allyn choked, her eyes glistened. "This is greed and my father's reckless ambition."

Femira was taken aback by Allyn's sudden outburst. The girl was already moving, Vestyr trailing after her. Allyn and Vestyr clearly knew more about what was going on then she did. Femira needed to understand what was happening so she decided to follow after them back out onto the balcony. All of the nobles had gathered inside to listen to the King's speech so the balcony was now empty.

"Allyn," Femira called out as she caught up to the pair, "you're wrong! This isn't what the bloodshedders were created for."

Femira shook her head as she spoke. She refused to believe that Landryn had willingly gone along with this. It was surely the will of the King and the War Council pushing him.

But then... why would Landryn agree? Would he not have stepped down rather than have issued that order? *It doesn't make any sense.* Or did it? Landryn was still grieving for his brother. He wanted justice. *He wants vengeance.*

"This is *exactly* what you were created for," Allyn looked pained as she spoke, "to kill."

"No!" Femira retorted, "that's not right, we're supposed to protect people! I don't know why Landryn is going along with this"

"Because he's not the man I believed he was," Allyn snapped, "I was wrong about him. How could I have been so blind…" Everything seemed like it was spiralling out of control. She needed to speak with Landryn. She needed to understand what was going on.

"This will mean more soulforgings," Vestyr said to Allyn, his voice heavy with concern. "We cannot allow that to continue."

"What is your problem with soulforging?" Femira whirled on Vestyr.

"It's barbaric," Allyn hissed, "offering people as lambs for sacrificial slaughter." Femira recoiled at the anger in Allyn's tone. Vestyr was nodding emphatically in agreement.

"You fucking hypocrite!" Femira spat at him, "*you're* soulforged!"

"I tried to explain this to you earlier," Vestyr said with reproach, "you and I are *not* the same. The power of my umbra is enhanced through a process called soulbonding. It is an ancient and non-destructive form of soulforging that my people have practised for centuries. What Garld and Landryn have been doing is sacrilege, it is a mockery of the gift of life."

"You don't know…" Allyn's face dropped. The anguish on her face was enough to make Femira frown. "They didn't tell you!" Allyn shook her head in disbelief.

"Tell me what?" Femira growled.

"The process that Garld uses," Vestyr explained, "it is known to my people as soul*rendering*. It is where the soulforger rips the souls of his victims apart. I told you earlier of the umbra, this is the part of the soul that gives us life. It is our quintessential life essence, it powers our runewielding and gives strength to the edir, it is the inherent nature of our very being."

"What does this have to do with me?"

"An umbra can grow itself over time. As one hones and strengthens their edir, the umbra grows with it. But the accelerated rate that soulforged like you demonstrate is impossible with a natural umbra. Your umbra has been infused."

"Of course it has," Femira countered, "it's been infused with the earthstone—aradium!"

"Not just that… it's been infused with the umbra of others. Your soul has absorbed the life essence of innocent people. Garld ripped apart their souls… tearing the umbra from their soul and suffusing theirs into yours."

Femira's dread grew as she listened to Vestyr. All the lies Garld had been feeding her and the ways in which he had manipulated her made her see truth in Vestyr's words.

"… And what does this 'soulrendering' do to these people?" Femira asked, her tone heavy with worry.

"What do you *think* it does?" Allyn admonished, "*death* is the only way to break the soul apart."

"It is worse than that," Vestyr added sadly, "the umbra is the part of the soul that returns to the great sea of souls. It is the fragment of eternity in our soul that can live once again. This is why it is often referred to as the Life Essence. Not even

Ashamei—the Hollow of Death—can lay claim upon it, it is bound to our world and can be given life once more in rebirth. Garld has utterly destroyed their umbra and augmented yours with theirs. He has stripped them of their natural right of rebirth, all so that *you* could be a more powerful soldier. So that you can reap more death and destruction upon this world."

"How many?" Femira breathed, "how many people were killed for my soulforging?"

"I don't know," Vestyr replied, "I've been trying to figure out Garld's exact method so that we can expose what he's doing. Judging by the jump in your abilities and that of other bloodshedders I have been observing, the umbra of three people, perhaps more... I can't be sure."

Femira's mind raced. She thought back to her own soulforging. Her brain had blocked out much of the memory because of the physical pain. But the dungeon-like room beneath the barracks where it had taken place was distinct in her memory... along with the five unconscious soldiers.

"Five people," she whispered.

Garld had killed five people so that she could become stronger.

Five innocent people had died because of *her*. Because she had craved more power. She felt sick. The image of blood running in the gutters came unbidden into her memory. Of an Honorsword in golden armour shoving a sword into elderly man's chest. Femira knew the man. His name had been Faiza and he'd taught Femira how to read and count.

Five people with lives and families had been killed for no other reason than she had asked for it. She had *demanded* it of Garld. Demanded their sacrifice.

She felt Nyth murmuring inside of her in worry. It was confused. Confused why she was hurting. It sent Femira the mental image of the coiling armour wrapped around her. It was sent as a question. Like an offering. *No, Nyth. I don't need armour.* She could feel her shoulders shaking, her breaths coming in short. She felt a coldness growing in her stomach and realised she was about to be sick.

Then Nyth sent her another image. It was an Honorsword only the face was wrong. The man was not Keiran, the face shifted and blurred and settled on Garld's image. Kept blond hair and clean shaven, standing with a bloodied sword. *You're right, Nyth.*

And then another image. This one taken directly from Femira's own subconscious of Garld in the dungeon, grasping a shining stone in one hand. His other hand placed on her forehead. And in the corner of her vision, the bodies of five people withering, their skin shrivelling and flaking away like ash.

Nyth sent her more images of scenes she didn't recognise; a man in fine robes covered in glowing runes, a shining soulstone held overhead before a field of bodies. Another of a male human-like creature with jet-black skin and bright blue eyes, soulstone in hand, a human woman at his feet, her body decaying in moments. These were images of Nyth's memories? These were the Sorcerer Kings of Old, wielding soulstone and shaping people into monsters.

"You're right, Nyth," Femira muttered. Vestyr and Allyn watched her with confused expressions. Femira met their eyes, trembling.

"Garld... h-he has to be stopped," Femira said with quiet intensity.

"That is what we're trying to do," Vestyr expressed.

"It's not so easy," Allyn added. "My father and Lukane see the soulforged as a means to fulfil their goals. They will throw the continent into decades of destruction if it means they will come out on top. And they'll sacrifice as many as they need to do it. I had thought that maybe Landryn could convince them otherwise... but I was wrong."

"Because he trusts Garld too much," Femira realised, "but that's because Garld has been manipulating him. For *years*, Garld's been grooming him for this."

Suddenly everything began locking into place in her mind. All the spying that Garld had her doing, all the secrecy and hiding. It was all to hide the truth of what soulforging was. But it was more than that... Ferath Vitares. The piece of this that still didn't make any sense. He was soulforged. He was one of them and he turned against them. He'd killed Daegan Tredain and... he was a bloodshedder! It was suddenly so painfully obvious. Garld had done this. *Garld* had ordered Daegan's death. But then what were Misandrei, Jaz and the others doing up in Rubane if not looking for Ferath...

"I have to go," Femira said with determination, making for the stairs.

"Where are you going?" Vestyr asked.

"To find proof." Femira wasn't so naive to think that Landryn would believe her outright. She'd lied to him so much already and Garld was his mentor. Garld had decades of carefully laid manipulation. But if she could uncover evidence that Garld had ordered Daegan's death then she had a chance to stop this.

This war could still be prevented.

CHAPTER 49
Rhyme & Reason

The soulforging room beneath the barracks was no challenge to break into. Femira as a full bloodshedder had almost unrestricted access in the barracks. The dungeon beneath however was off limits to anyone without Garld's prior approval. This didn't particularly matter to Femira who could easily step through walls and evade guard detection when needed.

Femira had been surprised to discover a complete absence of guards on the lower levels. The long hallway had no illumination so Femira focused her edir into her hands, the amber light of her runewielding ability emitted from them to guide her. She moved quickly, scurrying along the hallway towards the soulforging room. She reached the familiar unadorned steel door and, unsurprisingly, found it locked.

She recalled Garld telling her that most of the rooms in the lower levels were shielded with steel. She pushed out with edir senses to the surrounding walls and indeed found that it was lined with steel beneath the stone. That was still no barrier to Femira. She placed her hand on the steel door and felt the vibration under her hand. The door puffed into a cloud of silvery dust. She stepped through the cloud and reformed the door behind her.

She found the control for the gaslamp in the room and twisted the pin on the control causing the wick in the gaslamp to spark alight. The other gaslamps in the room also fluttered into light, illuminating the room as she remembered it. As before, there were six beds arrayed along the back wall, and along the walls were tables with stacks of notebooks and various surgical tools. All six beds were empty.

Femira set to work rifling through the notebooks although she wasn't entirely sure what she was looking for. A part of her still struggled to believe what Vestyr and Allyn had told her. She knew it was a vain hope. The truth was irrefutable, soulforging worked by killing other people and absorbing their life essence—their 'umbra' as Vestyr described it.

The notebooks were filled with complex diagrams and equations that Femira couldn't understand. In many cases the notes looked to be written in a completely different language. In some, she could recognise some sentences written in hurriedly scrawled handwriting. Femira was consumed as she frantically skimmed over notes, moving through the notebooks one at a time.

She found one journal with her name in it. Not her real name of course.

Subject: Vreth
Affinity: Aradium

Formula seventeen has been stable in almost all cases. Earlier iterations of the ritual seemed to incur accelerated rates of degradation. Formula seventeen is confirmed to be the most reliable.

There were some sections she couldn't understand until the very last paragraph.

Subject has demonstrated phenomenal growth over past weeks. Other subjects have since proven unstable under formula. Suspected soulforged lineage affecting the stability. Likely that this case will be unreliable to replicate at scale as formula seventeen has proven a failure in non-soulforged descendants. Potentially still a candidate for higher nobility with confirmed lineage.

Femira wasn't sure what 'formula seventeen' was but she could infer that it was likely some method that Garld had employed in her soulforging. She felt her anger rising at the knowledge that she had been a test subject. They *all* had been.

She pored over more of the notes. There were dozens marked as 'failed.' Then she landed on one and felt her hands tremble holding it.

Subject: Aden Lestras
Affinity: Aquamarine

Formula fifteen had proven to be drastically unpredictable for safe replication. For this test subject, attempting a new formula derived from a combination of Elyina's journals and texts recovered from Altarea.

A series of complex diagrams followed this entry and Femira noted that one was in a pattern strikingly familiar to Nyth's double helix blade.

Nyth resonated eagerness inside of her as she pictured the blade. *No, Nyth. I don't need a sword right now.*

She steadied her breaths and continued reading. She already knew what she would discover but it still hit her like a punch to the gut when her eyes landed on the subject status: *Failed.*

Aden had chosen aquamarine in the end… Femira recalled how he'd been torn by what to do. He'd known there wouldn't be much military use for wavecalling but had been drawn to the practice all the same. Her vision blurred with tears. But she didn't stop reading. She furiously wiped at her eyes and frantically pored over more of the notebooks.

Femira recognised some of the names but most were unfamiliar to her. All of these "failed" test subjects were dead. She knew it. There was no other explanation. Where else could all these soldiers have gone?

There was one leather bound archive that contained page after page of detailed information of people she'd never heard of. There were names, along with lineages, physical characteristics, and varying degrees of runewielding ability. At the end of each profile was a note: *Contributed to subject,* followed by a name of a bloodshedder.

Femira's mouth went dry when she realised what the archive was. It was the record of sacrifices. Her heart pounded and her fingers fumbled as she flicked through the pages until she landed on a series all with the same final note. *Contributed to subject: Vreth.*

She felt bile rise in her throat. There were five of them, just as she remembered. Three women and two men, all of them soldiers in another division. Each of them with lives and families, aspirations and desires. Each of them dead. Worse than dead… they'd been *consumed* into her. Their very souls amalgamated into hers. Her whole body locked up. Her hands gripped the archive tightly, convulsing with tremors.

She was going to be sick.

Femira dropped the archive, pages spilling out. She turned away, and vomited onto the floor. The acrid bile stung at her throat. Her eyes watered. She was horrified... *disgusted*. She felt as though she could feel the souls of these people inside of her.

Watching her. Hating her. Blaming her.

Her mind flashed back to that day in Keiran. An Honorsword in golden armour killing people in the street. They were killed for hiding her. Hiding her existence. They'd died because of her.

Nyth buzzed. An image entered her mind depicting the double helix blade slicing at the Honorsword's neck. Only that's not what happened. That Honorsword had slaughtered the entire village.

The word *karasi* was spat at her. The woman who had been her mother wept for everyone who had protected her. Had wept for all the death and destruction that Femira had caused... only that Femira hadn't done anything. She had done nothing other than existing. That was not her fault.

She couldn't be blamed for that.

Just as Femira couldn't be blamed for this.

She'd never asked for these people to die. She hadn't been the one to tear these people's souls apart and force them into her. It had been Garld. It had been Garld all from the beginning, orchestrating all of it. He'd been guiding her to this since the very moment they'd met. He'd lured her in with promises of power and he'd garnered her trust by delivering it. But it wasn't truly earned, he'd stolen that trust from her. He'd stolen all of these people's lives—their *souls* and mutilated them. Femira's jaw clenched, her hands balling into fists.

Her anger flared. Femira wanted him to suffer. He needed to be stopped.

But it wasn't so simple as killing Garld. Femira needed to *expose* him. She needed the truth of his actions to be laid bare so that she could prevent everything he'd started from escalating further. She gathered as many of the notes as she could and bundled them into the archive containing the list of sacrifices.

Femira realised that this alone wouldn't be enough. This only highlighted what Garld had done in soulforging rituals. She needed more to prevent the war with Rubane. She needed evidence that Garld had ordered Daegan Tredain's death. Garld's office seemed the most logical choice for something incriminating.

Femira made her way back up to the main barracks. She kept the fury burning in her stomach. It quelled the disgust she felt at having other people's souls woven into her own. She needed to focus on the anger.

Garld's office had no sentry outside it. That didn't bode well for anything incriminating being inside. She might have to try his office in the palace afterwards —or even his home. She didn't bother with the door, stepping right through the stone wall next to it.

Femira immediately set to digging through his records. There were briefing reports from various bloodshedder missions over the past weeks in his desk. Garld had marked stars next to performances and even made notes on their progressed runewielding stability. The report detailing the battle with the kragal was amongst them. *Exceeding all expectations,* the notes read; *Formula seventeen again proving considerable enhancements for stonebreakers.*

There was nothing about Ferath Vitares that she could find. Nor the mission that Misandrei and the others had been sent on. Garld had told her that he'd received word from Ferath, and that he'd left instruction for Misandrei's team to meet him in a place called Urundock. But she couldn't find anything that noted any of these details.

She did find one note—written by Garld—that was in a pile to be sent out by carrier pigeon to Rubane—Rubastre specifically:

Promises from beforehand agreement will be held. The Guild will be unspoiled during assaults. Titles and lands will be rewarded for ongoing assistance in coming weeks.
Garld.

There was no indication who the note was for. Garld had also not included any other identifiers for himself as a General in the Reldoni military. Femira was about to start sifting through the books on the shelves for hidden documents when the door swung open.

Light poured in from the corridor outside and Femira met Garld's eye. She restrained her surprise at seeing him in his office at such a late hour—on Lua Nova of all nights.

Garld's face showed outright shock. He had a revolver in hand.

"I must admit," Garld began, "when my sentries informed me that someone had broken into my office. I never suspected it would be you." *Sentries?* What sentries? Other than the patrolling guards in the barracks, Femira had spotted no one. It seemed Garld had tighter security than she'd anticipated. There was no explanation that she could think of for why she was rifling through his office. Her anger also couldn't be as easily contained as her surprise.

"You lied to me," Femira hissed.

"Have I?" he pondered, a serious edge in his tone, "enlighten me."

"You want me to tell you so that you don't reveal more than I've already discovered," Femira replied, bitterly.

"You know," Garld started, and Nyth resonated inside her, letting her know that he was attempting to manipulate her emotions. "I often overlook how clever you can be."

Femira indicated internally to Nyth to allow the emotional manipulation. She wanted to see what Garld was trying to do. She felt the subtle change. Her anger dissipated. Pride swelling at his comment. She felt like a child, eager to please a parent.

Okay, Nyth, you can block him again. This was the game Garld wanted to play. He still wanted to keep her on his side. She could leverage that.

"I know how soulforging works," she let slip intentionally, "how it *really* works. All those people dead," she pointed at the leather archive she'd left on his desk. "You hid this from me." She needed to get him to admit to ordering Daegan's murder. That's what she needed proof of.

"Believe me," Garld said earnestly, "it pains me each time." Her anger flared at his words.

"*Pains* you? You've sacrificed *hundreds* of people! How can you justify all of the innocent people that have died for this!"

"So that we can build a better future!" Garld argued, "can't you see that? You defeated a draega of legend. Your actions have saved thousands of helpless people from the creature, this was only possible because of soulforging. We are doing what we must!"

"You're *insane*," Femira fired at him, "we were supposed to protect people!"

"This is *how* we protect people! We build our ranks and we become unstoppable."

"And Rubane?" she led him.

"The Rubanians have resources we can use to build an army the likes of which this world has never seen. The power of the Sorcerer Kings is returning and we must be at the forefront of it. We must be the shield that protects our people from it." *Fucking hypocrite.*

Femira still didn't believe that he would admit it to her just yet. She needed him to believe that she agreed with him. But she wasn't done yet. She had anger to vent, and he would be suspicious if she didn't at least put up some resistance.

"And Keiran?" Femira pressed, opting for a different tactic, "what do you want me to do there? What is it that you've been training me for all these months?" That last question was a genuine slip of her frustration. She tried her best to school the anger from her voice but she could feel the sting in her tone.

"You are an exceptional runewielder, Vreth," Garld said. Femira felt Nyth buzzing, praise coupled with an emotional push seemed to be a favoured tactic of his. "I want you to do the impossible." He held her gaze with a serious expression. *Now he's appealing to my ego.* It galled her how easily she'd fallen for all of this before.

"I want you to assassinate the Emperor of Keiran. As Annali Jahar, you can step closer to the Court of the Sun than any of my other agents. With your skills and abilities, you can do what no assassin has achieved in history, and kill the Keiran Emperor himself."

Femira felt her jaw go slack, the bold audacity of his plan left her speechless. The Court of the Sun was the most heavily guarded government in the world. The Emperor had an entire army protecting his palace, and was never left unattended by his personal guard of Honorswords.

"The Warlords of Keiran will descend into civil war," Garld continued, "already they nip at each other's heels, and none would suspect Reldon having a part to play in this. The Warlords would be at each other's throats for decades over his death. The fall of Keiran would be inevitable. A unified Keiran is the only nation that could stand to rival us, but shattered it is inconsequential."

"Tens of thousands of people will die," Femira breathed in disbelief.

"And what happened to the girl who wanted to prove herself no matter the costs? What happened to the girl who was bold enough to steal her way into the Altarean Palace—while it was under attack—for her prize?" Garld posed. There was an almost playful manner to his question. He was testing her. Testing how she actually felt about it all.

On the periphery of her senses, Nyth continued to alert her to Garld's attempts to manipulate her. She would really need to figure out a method of getting Nyth to tell her what emotions were being forced upon her, one that didn't involve her actually feeling them. It was too risky with Garld to be caught up in his manipulation to allow them through.

"I never wanted anyone to get hurt…" Femira admitted truthfully, "I never wanted anyone to die." Garld had always been a master at detecting when she wasn't being entirely truthful with him. She would need genuine honesty here to convince him.

"Would knowing have changed anything?" Garld asked pointedly, "knowing how soulforging worked? Would you really have refused this power?"

"I…" Femira trailed off. This was something she admittedly hadn't considered. She remembered that time during her training, only a few months ago. Her hunger for more. Would she have been satisfied knowing that others had this advantage over her?

Another part of her mind recoiled at the thought. Horrified that she would even entertain it. But would she truly have cared what stood between her and power? She tried to remember when that had changed in her. When had she started feeling this way?

A memory came unbidden into her mind of a knife sliding into an eye socket. The grinding of the blade against bone, and her stomach twisted. It had changed when she'd first taken a life with her own hands and the primal revulsion of the action. Her soulforging hadn't been that long before then. Maybe before that she might have thought differently.

An idea struck her.

"Could..." she started softy, looking at Garld with as much helplessness as she could muster. *The innocent lost child act.*

"Could it have changed me?" Femira asked, pushing a pleading tone into her voice. "My soul was reforged with theirs..." she looked towards the archive of names. "I was reshaped by them... could it be possible that the souls I absorbed... could they be impacting how I feel... how I think? I feel like my emotions are not my own..." That last point to drive home the idea that Femira didn't suspect Garld of using mindstone.

His face softened. Garld portrayed nothing but the visage of a concerned father. It sickened her.

"My poor child..." Garld said, oozing pity, "I understand your turmoil, I truly do. It is possible... our understanding of soulforging is still in its infancy." *I'm fucking aware of that you lying sack of shit. You've been experimenting on us.*

"Trust me when I tell you that we will fix this," Garld continued. "Now that we're aware of this, we can take steps to rectify it. Allow me some time to research... however you must be resolute in your trust for me."

Femira remembered the feelings of trust she had been flooded with when Garld had performed her soulforging. That sense of connection she had with him, a sense of protection and caring she'd never felt from anyone before in her life. All that was left in her now was the hurt of betrayal. It was all lies.

"I trust you," Femira let her voice crack. She even let tears well up in her eyes. They were the tears of a shattered heart. "I need you to trust *me*," she pleaded, "please. Stop hiding things from me. I can take it."

In her mind, Femira instructed Nyth to let the guard down and she felt the push of emotion on her from Garld's edir. It was... *confidence?* He was trying to embolden her, to strengthen her arrogance. She let the emotion pour into her and plastered on a wicked self-assured grin.

"I can kill the Emperor," Femira asserted proudly, as if being given the honour was the most elevating thing she'd ever heard. "I will be the greatest fucking assassin you've ever seen," she smirked.

Garld's own face broke into a wide grin. She had him, she realised with excitement—but then again, was that confidence part of what he was feeding her? She quickly dismissed the thought. She couldn't doubt herself now. Although she did instruct Nyth to shield her emotions again, just in case.

Femira decided to press on to what she needed. "What is Misandrei's team really doing in Rubane?"

"They're going to succeed where Ferath Vitares failed," Garld admitted, finally seeming to accept that Femira was fully committed to his cause. "They're going to kill Daegan Tredain."

"So you did order his murder?" She didn't say it accusingly, trying to seem like she was merely putting pieces together.

"War with Rubane is in our favour," Garld replied defensively. "The Rubanians have yet to discover soulforging but it's only a matter of time. They have their extensive Ironworks, and their advancements in weaponry are excelling far beyond our own. Rubane is a powerhouse that we cannot allow to grow unchecked. Right now, we have a superior military but we must look toward the future... we simply needed a just cause for an invasion."

"What about Landryn?" Femira asked, "he surely couldn't have approved that?"

"Of course not," Garld admitted, "his attachment to his cripple brother is too great... but Landryn trusts me utterly. I am more of a father to him than Abhran ever was."

It pained Femira how much Garld's betrayal would destroy Landryn. But it had to be done. She couldn't allow Garld to throw the world into chaos. But it also highlighted a truth that Femira wasn't ready to face. Landryn was unlikely to believe her over Garld.

She needed definitive evidence that Garld had orchestrated this. She needed to prove that Ferath Vitares had been working on Garld's orders. She needed... she needed Daegan Tredain!

In her revelations Femira had missed that crucial statement. Ferath Vitares had failed. *Daegan Tredain is alive!* At least for the time being.

"Daegan Tredain is in Urundock?" Femira asked, "that's where Misandrei and the others are heading, right?"

"Indeed," Garld said, "they will soon have Ferath's mess rectified. However, we are digressing from your own mission."

"Of course, sir," she replied, "let's go over the details."

Garld proceeded to fill Femira in with the details of the mission to Keiran; the ship that he had chartered to ferry her to Keiran, along with the names of agents and contacts that would assist her in reaching the Court of the Sun in the heartland of the Keiran Empire. None of the details mattered to Femira. She already had what she needed for her true mission.

All that was required now was to play along with Garld. Let him believe that she was on board with his insane plan. Femira knew what she needed to do.

A part of her wanted to seek out Landryn and warn him of Garld's subterfuge. She wanted to tell him that his brother was still alive. But her path was clear; it would be easier to disappear. Se couldn't bear to give Landryn that hope if she was wrong... or if she couldn't make it in time.

She was going to find Daegan Tredain and she was going to bring him home.

CHAPTER 50

Fight Further

"It's been two days," Tanlor shook his head, "I don't think shit-digger is going to pull through."

"He's trying," Daegan argued.

"Last night he brought us a pouch of rocks," Tanlor gave him a levelled stare.

"How is he to know that's not useful, he's probably never seen runestones up close."

"He should be trying to get the revolver, that's got everything we need in it."

"You know he can't," Daegan contested. "That big one over there—Razef, shit-digger calls him—he took the revolver and hasn't let it out of his sight since that other one blew his brains out."

"Well maybe he needs to take more risks," Tanlor grumbled, "no wonder he's the runt."

"Let's just give him a chance."

"He's had *lots* of chances. Let's try to convince that one," Tanlor nodded to a bigger rak youth. Daegan had noticed that one before, shoving the others around.

"A bully like that," Tanlor continued, "reminds me of my cousin Boern. I'd bet he would leap at the chance for some power."

"One more night," Daegan offered, "if shit-digger doesn't pull through we'll try rak-Boern, deal?"

"Deal."

A new wrench had been thrown into their plan when more rak had arrived at Twin Garde late the previous night. They didn't look to be the same group that had left with Rowan and the others but it was hard to tell most of the rakmen apart from each other. This group however was a larger force, bolstering the rak in the keep to thirty at Daegan's count.

Razef seemed to be the new leader. He carried with him the garnet crystal dagger that the former chief had carried. Daegan felt anxious every time he spotted it, sheathed at the rak's hip. It no longer glowed with the internal light of a runestone as it had that night in the tower. So far, Daegan had not seen Razef use the dagger's strange murderous effect on anyone.

Along with the new group of rak was a pair of creatures that had made Daegan's jaw drop.

"What are those?" Tanlor breathed.

"I-I don't know," Daegan stammered and felt a chill running down his spine. When they'd first been marched through the gate, Daegan mistaken the creatures as bizarre carts, his mind refusing to comprehend what he was looking at.

Their round flat bodies were covered in a blue carapace and sharp spines jutted out along the chitin. The creatures scuttled forward on six thick insect-like legs and they had two enormous pincer claws—like a crab—that were strapped shut with leather belts. The belts strained against the creatures' movements.

There were no other indicators of restraints and the creatures appeared to be compliant, taking direction from a handler carrying a long barbed pike with a hook at the end. Occasionally, the rak would tap the side of the creature's carapace with the flat of his pike to direct it.

The arrival of the new rak and the creatures had not deterred Daegan and Tanlor from their intent to escape, instead fuelling their commitment to it. Neither wanted to risk waiting for whatever the rak had planned for them.

Daegan was glad he'd convinced Tanlor to wait one more night because sure enough shit-digger shuffled over to their cage after most of the other rak had fallen asleep.

"*I have it,*" shit-digger said with grim determination. He had a cloth-wrapped bundle in his hands.

"Excellent." Daegan beamed and flashed a satisfied grin at Tanlor. "*Quickly, give it to me. The first thing I will show you is how to hold it without killing yourself.*"

Shit-digger passed the bundle through the bars, casting a worried glance back at the sentries on the walls.

"For fuck's sake," Daegan growled, pulling the cloth off the object. "*This!*" he spat at shit-digger, "*is a fucking crossbow… it doesn't even have a bolt!*" Daegan cursed in frustration and caught Tanlor smirking at him.

"*Is the same thing, no?*" Shit-digger retorted in offence. Daegan let out a suffering sigh.

"*No,*" he said with as much patience as he could muster, "*it is not the same. We need the runestones! The glowing stones, remember? This is how we teach you.*" Understanding dawned on shit-diggers face.

"*You need to get the revolver now, tonight! Razef is asleep, you can take it from him.*"

"*Razef will kill this one,*" shit-digger moaned, "*I cannot.*"

"*Well then we will teach another. That one,*" Daegan pointed to rak-Boern, sleeping next to the fire. Shit-digger's jaw worked in anger.

"*No,*" shit-digger spat, "*no. You will teach me. I will get it.*"

"*Get it now.*" Daegan hissed after him as the rak youth scurried away from their cage.

"You really think he'll manage it?" Tanlor asked.

"There's a high chance Razef will kill him," Daegan conceded.

"Yep," Tanlor agreed, "we should've gone with rak-Boern."

***

The cold winds stung Ardy's face, his cloak billowed as he pulled the rope of the main sail. He leaned back, hanging off the edge of the iceraft. He felt the rig shifting direction, the course altering with his weight. He couldn't resist the grin that pulled at his lips when he did this. The exulting joy he felt when working the rig at full speed across the ice was a rush he hadn't felt working any other vessel.

The grin was quickly replaced with a scowl as he heard a voice call out from behind him.

"How close are we?" the infuriating Reldoni woman asked over the howling winds. Ardy pretended he couldn't hear her and allowed himself to enjoy the wind billowing in his hair and rushing in his ears a while longer.

"Master Ardy!" The woman called out again, this time with forcefulness.

"Not far now," Ardy called back.

"How can he even tell, there's no markers out here." Ardy heard one of the younger Reldoni say—Jaz, they called him. Likely the boy didn't think Ardy could hear him. But Aeth ears could pick up a lot of sound.

Soon. Ardy reminded himself. *Soon, you'll be rid of this nasty business.* His chest tightened as he thought about what lay only an hour further into the flat of the ice sheet.

Many considered the ice sheet to be utterly barren. But barren did not mean not empty. Ardy glanced up at the sky. Lua Nova had just passed, but both Ecko and Luna were almost full, illuminating the outlines of the sparse cloud cover with silvery lines tinged red and blue. Every now and then, one of the moons would peek its face out, peering down at the world.

Ardy had learned the cycles of the moons in his youth but only in his years at sea did he really come to appreciate how powerful they could be. Their phases played havoc with the currents and tides of the oceans. Ardy wasn't sure how many other people would be aware of how they affected the ice of Nortara. Perhaps that was simply from the amount of time Ardy spent on the ice. He could feel the moons' pull on it now, the incredible mass shifted and groaned at the whims of the moons.

It was the predictability of the moon's phases that gave Ardy the confidence to know exactly where they were. He looked up and saw Luna's face; a warm bright spot in the otherwise dark coldness of night. He raised his thumb to the moon. Angled it slightly until the constellation of the sword started right at the tip of his nail. He frowned, he had made a slight miscalculation.

"Two hours," Ardy called back to the group.

"See I told you he's just guessing," Jaz said.

"You just focus on restraining that edir of yours," the one called Endrin chided, "and try not to melt the ice around us again."

"Yes, sir," Jaz replied, suitably chastised.

"The Shrydan brothers should not be underestimated," one of them said and Ardy felt his grip slacken on the rope. He slipped back and caught himself quickly. He didn't dare look over his shoulder. The man had barely spoken since he'd stepped onto Ardy's raft the day before and Ardy had spent much of the time actively avoiding looking at him. He peeked back at the man now.

Ferath wore an unremarkable black cloak, the cowl pulled up over his head but his eyes glowed with unnatural amber light. Ardy cared little for runewielding and hadn't bothered to learn any of the basics of the practice. But he knew enough that glowing eyes was a marker for an unstable runewielder. A person who was drawing more power than their bodies could naturally handle. Ardy recalled seeing the same eyes in his youth at Evier in some of his peers that had undergone the soulbond to enhance their runewielding. Those with glowing eyes were usually sequestered, sealed away so that they couldn't hurt themselves or others with their powers.

The glowing eyes alone would've been enough to frighten Ardy. But this man had also chased Ardy, Tanlor and Dessie through the streets of Urundock barely a week past, hurling spears of stone at them.

Dessie. The man's face came into his mind. *Prince fucking Daegan Tredain.* That was who the Reldoni Captain—Misandrei—had said he was. Not only had Ardy broken his only rule of never dealing with Reldoni but it was with a moons-damned fucking Prince of Reldon!

"The Shrydans are just ordinary men, are they not?" Misandrei responded to

Ferath's comment.

"They are not soulforged if that is what you mean," Ferath granted. "But they have managed to interfere with my assaults… twice now."

"This is a result of your affinity instability," Misandrei replied, "Garld will rectify this upon your return to Epilas."

"You're also not fighting like a soulforged yet," Endrin added, "you were among the first of us to undergo the change. We've incorporated our enhanced abilities into a new combat style that better suits it. The newest bloodshedders have benefited more from this as we've been training them for enhanced abilities. You've not been, you'll need to unlearn all of your bad habits."

"Do not speak to me as if I'm an amateur, Endrin!" Ferath snapped.

"You are," Endrin rebuffed, "tell me, did you rely upon your sword skills in your encounters with the Shrydans?" Ferath did not reply.

"If you'd had the time to train with us before this mission, you'd never have let yourself get engaged in melee combat like that. You should have dusted their weapons. There are dozens of different strategies you could have opted for, but you're still thinking like a regular soldier."

"You can't dust steel that quickly," Ferath shot.

"Yes," Endrin replied "we can… and so can you."

"Daegan's revolver is also a risk," Ferath continued, "the rate of fire is considerably faster than that of a regular pistol. Keep an eye on him if you're engaging all three together."

"None of that matters, you know," Ardy interrupted, pulling the attention of the others.

"They're all likely dead already. Those rak were storming the towers by 'time I got out."

"The rak are not a concern," Misandrei said, foolishly, "we take out any we come across but the priority is ensuring Daegan Tredain is dead."

A gracious man might have felt guilt at ferrying these assassins to Dessie, but Ardy couldn't have given a swimming shit. It was Dessie—Daegan's—fault that Ardy was wrapped up in this bloody mess in the first place. Ardy was beyond done with the man. This would be his last dealing with him. It was now his only rule.

**

Tanlor watched in appreciation as Daegan and shit-digger exchanged words in Old Esterin. He'd never seen anyone speak anything other than the language of blades with a rak before. And here was Daegan convincing this one to inadvertently help them. *I suppose he's pretty good at that.*

Daegan unwrapped the new bundle as shit-digger nervously licked his lips. Tanlor smiled as the soft glow of the runestones came into view along the cylinder of the revolver. Daegan quickly passed it to Tanlor—as they'd planned—and kept talking to shit-digger. *Naive little bastard.*

Tanlor worked quickly, placing a hand over the aradium gemstone. Focusing his edir, he felt the tingling vibration from the rest of the metal in response. He set his mind to dissolving the metal around the two runestones, filling the aradium with the material. It would take him a few minutes to dissolve that much metal. He could feel it slowly wearing away under his hand.

Daegan kept shit-digger distracted, speaking quickly in that harsh language and using emphatic hand gestures. Tanlor had no idea what Daegan was saying to keep the youth's attention but whatever it was, he seemed rapt in Daegan's words.

Daegan mimed an explosion, and then raised a warning finger, then spoke again quickly. He then started patting his hands as if putting out a fire and shaking his head vigorously. He seemed every inch a firm instructor and shit-digger was nodding along, completely absorbed in Daegan's bullshit lecture.

Tanlor felt the aradium and topaz loosen and continued wearing it down, holding his gaze on shit-digger and Daegan's conversation. Occasionally, he would glance up to the sentries on the wall to see if anyone had spotted the suspicious interaction. The cages weren't well illuminated which was a benefit tonight.

He felt the runestones slip under his grasp, finally separating from the device. He cleared his throat, giving Daegan the signal that he was finished. Seamlessly, Daegan reached out a hand and took the revolver back.

Daegan didn't break stride in his conversation with shit-digger and demonstrated holding the weapon. He gripped the handle and held his arm out straight, looking down the barrel. Without the runestones it was now useless, whatever mechanisms of gunpowder made regular pistols work were not present in this device. It worked solely off the runestones.

Daegan pointed the wheel-lock gun out towards the campfire where many of the rak were sprawled out. He continued to lecture then pulled the trigger. It clicked and Daegan blew out a breath through pursed lips, mimicking a blast. Shit-digger was nodding along, eagerly licking his lips. Daegan held up a warning hand and spoke firmly again. He then gently offered the revolver back, handle first.

Shit-digger took the weapon almost reverently. He nodded to Daegan then hurriedly wrapped the thing back up in the cloth and slinked away from the cage bars.

"What did you tell him?" Tanlor asked once shit-digger was out of earshot.

"That we've disabled the firing action so that he can practise with it. I told him that we trapped a spirit inside, and that it needs a few days to get used to him as its master. He just needs to keep it on him and keep it hidden. I said that the revolver needs to 'attune' to his presence before it will work for him, otherwise it will try to kill him if he doesn't wait."

"And he bought that?" Tanlor asked incredulously.

"It helps that Razef had been carrying it on him at all times,"
Daegan shrugged, "they seem like the kind of people that believe in spirits."

"They're not people," Tanlor replied.

"No, they're not," Daegan agreed and eyed the corner of the keep where two monstrous crabs were being kept.

"When should we make our move?" Daegan asked.

"I'm going to work on dissolving the lock now," Tanlor said, "those clouds are getting thicker, I say we wait an hour or so, hope that it gets a bit darker and then we'll move on to phase two."

Daegan glanced down to the cage where the other three soldiers were sleeping.

"Let's hope they'll be quick to move," Daegan said, nodding towards the soldiers.

"Leave that to me," Tanlor replied, "and you focus on getting to that weapons rack."

***

The torches of Twin Garde appeared, twinkling in the distance like a single dancing candle. The wind rushed past as Ardy's rig glided along the ice. Ardy felt the knot in his stomach grow tighter. There was no way of knowing if those were rak torches or not. He thought back to the dust falling from the rafters as grenadiers explosions rang outside.

"Ain't no hope in hell I'm gonna bring you right to the docks," Ardy called back, "that's as good as driving this rig right off the side of the icesheet."

"You can land us a half mile from the keep," Misandrei shouted back over the wind, then quieter to her companions. "From what I gathered at Urundock, this outpost has a timber wall and battlements. The main two defensive structures within the walls are towers of stone. Neither should impede us much."

Ardy doubted either tower survived the rak assault. He remembered watching in terror as the tops of those towers were lit up like bonfires. *This is a fool's errand.* Daegan was doubtlessly dead.

Not for the first time on the trip, Ardy considered leaving the Reldoni as soon as they disembarked. It wasn't as though they could follow him back to Urundock. And he would have plenty of time to make his way to Edas, find work on a sea charter and leave all of this mess behind him... but then he wouldn't get paid. Fifty marks was no small chunk of silver. Ardy could live on that for months.

"Jaz, you can light up those walls?" Misandrei asked the sweaty youth. Ardy had been surprised by him, most southerners couldn't hack the cold. They wrapped themselves up in layers of furs and wools, and moaned about the winds. Ardy had not seen the young Reldoni man wear anything heavier than a linen tunic

"I can," Jaz replied, confidently. "All this heat has to go somewhere." If it were not for the pulses of coral light that emitted from the youth's skin, Ardy would've suspected he was feverish and refused him entry on the raft. But this was something else. This was some kind of runewielding nonsense that Ardy wanted no part of. *Don't fuck with runewielding.*

"Good," Misandrei said, "I want any defenders on that wall choking in smoke before we get anywhere close. When those walls are more ash than wood, you're to join Endrin. I want you both to stay to the rear on ranged support.

Endrin, I want you to blast them with stonespears until we reach the towers. Then I want you to make us a door. Loreli and I will be the vanguard. With our aeristone affinities, we're a lot faster than the rest of you."

"Where do you want me?" Ferath asked.

"You've aradium affinity, so you're with Endrin on ranged attacks. You're to defer to his authority."

"He's lower rank than me," Ferath balked.

"But *he* has control of his abilities," Misandrei retorted. "*You* do not. You're also still injured, and to be frank, Ferath, I do not trust your judgement. So you will defer to Endrin for this assault, am I clear?" There was a tense pause from the group as palpable as the winds buffeting them.

"You have been operating solo for some time, Ferath," Misandrei continued, "I need to know if you can still work as part of a team. Otherwise you will be too much of a risk on this mission."

"Daegan and the Shrydans are mine," Ferath hissed, "you cannot take that from me."

"I understand that you are bitter bu—"

"*Bitter?*" he spat, "I am not bitter. Daegan has shot me fucking *twice*! The Shrydans have been a thorn in my side this entire mission. I am not bitter, I am resolved. This is *my* mission."

"That you failed," Misandrei cut him off sternly, "twice, as you so eloquently pointed out for us. We are here because you failed to kill a cripple. Now *we* have to clean up *your* mess. So you will obey your orders, and defer to Endrin's judgement, am I clear?"

Ferath's jaw was tense. If Ardy's edir senses had been sharp enough, he would've detected Ferath's flaring out from him in petulant bursts. However Ardy's edir was a rusty tool, long since discarded to the back of the toolshed.

"I understand," Ferath conceded, but glowered at Endrin as he did.

"Good," Misandrei responded, "if our Aeth friend is correct, then we will have a war party of rakmen to deal with beyond those walls. There are only four of us, but we are bloodshedders."

Oh bloodshedders. Such a big scary name. Ardy scoffed, earning him an angry glare from Misandrei. Ardy quickly averted his gaze as if he hadn't been listening and coughed as though he had something in his throat.

Soldiers and their dramatic titles.

They were worse than the Elders at Evier. Ardy's own brother had been granted the title of 'First Whisperer of the Winds' which Ardy had teased him for relentlessly. "Why don't you go gossip about it to the breeze," had been the last thing Ardy had ever said to his brother.

Ninety years ago... he didn't think about Varestyn often. His brother had looked so pitifully hurt when he'd caught Ardy, rucksack on his back, skulking away from their home. Varestyn would likely weep if he knew what Ardy was doing, leading a bunch of self-proclaimed 'bloodshedders' to do their bloody work. Probably babble something about the sanctity of life and the soul or some shit.

***

Tanlor made his way towards the imprisoned soldiers in a crouched run and wasn't surprised at the pain in his legs. Not only had he spent the past six days in a cage with no room to move around but the skin on his legs was still raw, and the material of his breeches chafed against his burns with every movement.

"Wake up," Tanlor hissed into the cage with the Rubanian soldiers, "and stay quiet." He immediately set to work on dissolving the metal lock of the cage.

Yaref, the grey-haired healer, was the first on his feet, his eyes wide in surprise. The other two followed him quickly, each looking to Tanlor with hopeful faces.

"How did you get free?" Yaref whispered.

"We're not free yet," Tanlor replied in an equally hushed tone, "give me a few minutes to dissolve this lock."

"You've got aradium?" one of the others asked, he had a badly scabbing wound under his eye.

"Either of you a stonebreaker?" Tanlor asked.

"I am," the wounded man replied, "name's Tar. Puck's a grenadier," he nodded to the other soldier. "And Yaref's a healer."

"I'm sure Mr. Shrydan remembers me," Yaref said.

"Here," Tanlor reached his hand into the bars to Tar, "take this. You can probably work on this lock a lot faster than me." He dropped the dimly glowing aradium into Tar's hand.

"You're really like him, aren't you?" Tar asked, getting to work on the lock, "yer da, I mean, I'm named after him, Taran, yer da. You're a hero like him aren't you, you're going to get us out of this."

"If you stop blathering and break that lock, he will, yes?" Yaref slapped the younger man on the back of the head.

"I've only got the one topaz, which I'll hold onto for now," Tanlor said to Puck, pointedly ignoring Tar's comments about his father. "If we come across another, it's yours. Are you lads able to fight if we need to?"

"Aye," Yaref replied, and the other two were nodding, "but we've got no weapons."

"Daegan is sorting that."

***

Daegan grinned as he pulled open a sack of thick cloth, revealing a stock of small grenadier-pouches. Each of them was prefilled with a measure of gunpowder. Grenadier-pouches were often dyed with a red band to denote the explosive material inside and even Daegan could recognise these. There were easily a dozen pouches in the sack.

Daegan hoisted the sack over his shoulder. He already had two swords and a pair of hatchets tucked under his arm. The grenadier-pouches coupled with the topaz they already had would be a considerable benefit.

He had been expecting a better haul from the weapons rack, but the rak preferred to keep their weapons on them. The weapons he'd collected were merely spares looted from the bodies of soldiers. The swords and hatchets were also smaller than typical rak weapons which better resembled greatswords and battleaxes in size.

The weapon rack was situated only a few feet up from where the cages were and was, conveniently, just as poorly lit. Daegan glanced up at the sentries on the wooden walls again. There were only eight of them and none of them seemed to be monitoring the inside of the keep.

Daegan would need to pass under the light of one the torches to make it back to the cages. He didn't want the metal of the blades catching the light and pulling the attention of the sentries but he had little choice.

As quickly as he could, and without making the weapons rattle, Daegan shuffled along the wall. When he passed into the light of a torch his heart leapt with adrenaline. He maintained his pace, moving towards the end cage where he could see the dark shape of Tanlor huddled at the door.

"I got these," Daegan said in a low voice when he reached them. He carefully laid the swords and hatchets quietly on the frost covered ground.

"No greatswords?" Tanlor asked with thinly veiled disappointment.

"Afraid not," Daegan replied.

"This'll do so," he picked up one of the swords, "it'll kill a rak bastard all the same."

Tanlor quickly introduced Puck and Tar as a grenadier and stonebreaker respectively. Tar was still working on dissolving the cage lock.

"Can I have that other sword? I'm not too bad with one," Puck asked and Daegan handed it to him.

"I've also got about a dozen pouches for you," Daegan grinned.

"Really?" Tanlor's eyes widened in surprise, he then turned back to Puck, "here, you'll be more effective with this than me so." Tanlor proffered the topaz through the bars which Puck accepted.

Puck breathed a sigh of relief as he grasped the runestone. Daegan guessed the topaz-wielder was not accustomed to feeling the natural cold.

"Just these left for us then," Daegan offered one of the hatchets to Yaref who took it eagerly.

"I'd like to sink it into one of those fucker's skulls," the healer divulged.

"Ok," Daegan snorted, "I can get on board with the bloodthirsty attitude, I like the enthusiasm." Daegan grinned at them, "you've gone over the plan, Tanlor?"

"I have," Tanlor replied just as Tar finished with the lock, the door to the cage creaking noisily as it shifted.

"Well then, let's get to it," Daegan said.

***

Baroc's ears twitched as he heard the shuffling of feet approaching the radius of his chain. Usually only his handlers came within his reach but the rak he smelled approaching stank of the same watery broth that he was fed. He could also detect adrenaline in their scent. He took a sharp sniff without opening his eyes. *Restless... but eager.*

Eager for blood.

He felt the fur on his back bristle in response to the presence. Two of the rak approached him with hesitant steps. Baroc's eyes snapped open and he gave the pair a low warning growl. He had expected the rak youths but to his surprise it was the small pale ones that had been imprisoned in the cages opposite him. Their skin looked eerily bright in the torchlight, like the face of the Red Moon.

Up close, he could smell the differences in them from the other rak. The one with yellow fur had a deep inherent scent of sulphur. *Like the old chief had.* Baroc had learned to recognise the scent as that of the rak shamans—those that could conjure fire from nothing. They were the most dangerous.

The other—the one with dark fur—did not have the scent of a shaman about him. Both were very small for rakmen. There were three others further back keeping watch.

The pair closest to him began murmuring to each other in a tongue that Baroc could not understand. They seemed to be arguing about something. Baroc decided he didn't like the way the shaman kept glancing at him, sword gripped in his hand.

Baroc rose from his sleeping position, holding the gaze of the shaman. His growl was instinctual—despite what his handlers thought. As soon as he felt threatened it rumbled up from the depth of his throat.

The yellow one sensed the hostility and the point of the blade was raised. Baroc didn't like that. His lips peeled back showing his fangs. The dark one pulled the shaman back by the shoulder and hissed something in that strange language of theirs.

Baroc got the distinct impression that the shaman wanted to kill him. Although he wasn't sure why. Sure, Baroc had killed the other pale rak that had run away but he had no animosity towards them. He only did it because his handlers would have beaten him if he didn't. These ones had been caged too, surely they understood this.

Then the dark-haired one stepped forward, within clawing distance. Baroc could smell his steely determination. His eyes moved suspiciously to the hatchet gripped in the rak's hand.

"*If I come closer do you promise not to kill me?*" the rak asked in Old Esterin.

***

Daegan's heart pounded as he moved closer to the dogman. Dogman was in fact a very poor name for the creature now that Daegan could get a good look at it. Broad-shouldered and standing a foot taller than Daegan, the bipedal creature more closely resembled a mountain lion. His face was rounded, more similar to a cat, its nose bridge flatter than a dog's. Its ears pointed out from tufts of fur. In the moonslight, the creature's exposed fur was a silvery grey, streaked with black, like a tiger.

"*If I come closer do you promise not to kill me?*" Daegan asked hesitantly in Old Esterin. He could feel Tanlor's disapproval as a palpable aura behind him. The dogman turned its head slightly at Daegan's question and Daegan realised that it was foolish to assume this creature could speak the language—if it could speak at all.

Then it gave Daegan a definitive nod.

"*What is your name?*" Daegan tried.

"*Baroc,*" the creature's voice was like a rumbling mountain. Its mouth was restrained in a muzzle but it could still get the words out.

"*If I free you, Baroc,*" Daegan offered, "*do you promise not to kill us?*"

"*Free…*" Baroc mused on the word, "*Why would rak scum help Baroc?*"

"*We're not rak. We're men… humans. We don't want to hurt you.*"

"*Smell like rak… look like rak. Rak lies.*"

"*We're smaller,*" Daegan tried, "*and look—our skin, it's different.*" He gestured to his face.

"*You see me,*" Baroc replied cryptically, "*you see another like me with different colour fur. Is not same?*" Daegan had to admit that the dogman had a point there. The fact that Daegan had thought of him as something akin to a dog or a lion was an example of that.

"*We're not the same,*" Daegan implored, he took a step closer to Baroc, dropping the hatchet and raising open palms.

"*We just want to get away from here, away from these rak,*" Daegan pleaded, "*I think you do too.*"

Baroc was quiet for a moment. He watched Daegan with large round eyes, the light of the torches dancing in them.

"*Shaman wants to kill Baroc,*" Baroc growled, and gestured towards Tanlor with a point of his nose. *He's not wrong there.*

"*My friend thinks you will kill us,*" Daegan said honestly, "*I'm hoping that you won't.*"

"*Shaman could kill Baroc now. While Baroc is chained.*"

"*Yes,*" Daegan nodded.

"*But you won't let him. You are chief.*"

"*Yes,*" Daegan said.

"*If Baroc is free. What will chief want? Baroc has no wish to be slave again. Not to you. Not to anyone.*"

"*I promise you that you won't. If I set you free, will you help us fight these rak and escape with us? After that, you're a free… uh,*" Daegan had no idea how to finish that sentence as he didn't want to offend Baroc by calling him a dogman. "*You will be free.*" Daegan concluded.

A horn echoed loudly. Three harsh blasts interrupting the conversation.

***

Even being soulforged, Jaz could not create heat out of nothing, everything must be drawn from another heat source. However, his body could now draw upon and target that heat far faster, and on a much greater scale, than ever before.

To burn the walls of Twin Garde, he needed a source blaze strong enough to pull on, and he needed it going quickly before any of the rak came to investigate.

For this, he would need something more effective than regular fuel. Which he had. Slung over Jaz's shoulder were ten wineskins, all of them full of dragon-oil. It was too risky to attempt getting the dragon-oil close to the walls so instead he poured it around a copse of trees in sight of the wall. Once ignited, that would be the source he could pull on.

He moved quietly and slowly, hoping to avoid the detection from the sentries on the walls. Misandrei and Loreli were close by, taking down any scouts that were patrolling the woods.

Once he started burning the walls and it spread far enough then his target would become sustainable for him to draw upon, and further accelerate the spreading. With that much fire, he could syphon off heat and centralise it to focus points and have parts of the wall reduced to cinders in minutes.

The key problem was that it would take a few minutes for the heat of dragon-oil fire to burn enough for him to use effectively. That meant a few minutes of a giant fire burning only a few yards from the keep walls. Needless to say, that would quickly draw the attention of the defenders.

Endrin would need to start taking down sentries on the walls and the defenders would be quick to re-man them. They could expect arrows to rain down on them so Jaz would need to work *very* quickly for this plan to succeed.

Sweat dripped from Jaz's chin as he poured the last wineskin. The heat inside of him was now desperate for release. He restrained, holding in his edir as tightly as a scared child clutching a parent's hand. He whistled one of the bloodshedder's bird calls, indicating he was ready.

He heard a whistle in response. It was the go-ahead from Misandrei. They were all in position.

The heat poured out of Jaz and flames erupted on the trees.

***

A horn echoed loudly.

Three harsh blasts. Daegan's eyes widened. His head bolted towards the sentries on the battlements, expecting bows to be drawn in their direction. But they weren't, all the rak on the walls were facing *away.*

A rak sentry was fired off the wall, a spear rammed into his chest. Another sentry was struck, sending the rak hurtling off the wall. Someone was attacking Twin Garde.

"Duke's men?" Daegan asked Tanlor with a hopeful enthusiasm.

"No idea," Tanlor shrugged, then he raised his sword, his attention pulled towards the campfires where the rakmen were jumping to their feet.

"Fuck," Tanlor cursed, "they won't be long spotting us. Time to make a decision," he nodded to Baroc.

Daegan turned back to face the beastman. His facial expression was unreadable, his teeth were bared, but that could be a smile for all Daegan knew. *Fuck it.* He stepped close to Baroc, right within mauling range. He held up his hands in a calming gesture. Baroc held his gaze with a warning intensity.

Daegan placed his hands on the iron muzzle. It was a simple enough contraption, locked into place and connected to the collar. Daegan was hoping there was a simple clasp, something he could unpin easily. Looking down at Baroc's hands, Daegan could see they were thick paws with large claws. The beastman could grip a weapon, but delicate handwork would be beyond him.

Daegan hoped the rak had decided to use a... *that's it!* His fingers found the locking pins. He twisted the pins and pulled them free. The collar and muzzle simultaneously clicked open and tumbled to the ground.

For a brief moment, Daegan and Baroc simply stood watching eachother, Daegan's heart pounding in his ears. The sounds of horns and the rushing movements of the rak were abound in the periphery of Daegan's senses. Baroc's eyes were locked on him. *Oh fuck.* The realisation that he'd just made a huge mistake rising up from the pit of his stomach.

"*What are you doing?!*" Daegan heard the rasping cry of a rak behind him. Daegan turned his head and saw a rak holding a pike, signalling that he was one of Baroc's handlers.

Everything happened in the blink of an eye. Daegan felt the rush of wind and saw a blur of black as Baroc charged past him. In three bounds, Baroc was on the handler. The pike was cast aside, Baroc's huge form tackling the rak to the ground. The rak screamed as teeth sunk into flesh and claws ripped at muscle.

"Daegan!" Tanlor's voice pulled his attention from the spectacle. Daegan looked to Tanlor and saw the group of four men gathered together with weapons raised. The battlements were aflame and smoke filled the air, obscuring the view of the keepyard. *How did they burn so quickly?* Flames were lapping up the timber like they'd been doused in dragon-oil.

Daegan grabbed his dropped hatchet and rushed to Tanlor's side.

"There must be an army of grenadiers out there," Puck said with awe, "we're saved!"

"I don't think we should take the chance that whoever is on the other side of that wall is our saviour," Tanlor replied.

Daegan looked back to Baroc and saw that the beastman had already moved on from his handler, and was now mauling another rak defender.

The camp was in chaotic disarray with rakmen rushing to the battlements. But the fires deterred them, penning them back towards the towers.

"What do we do?" Yaref turned to Tanlor and Daegan. Tanlor glanced at Daegan with uncertainty. *You guys are the soldiers here.*

"We should use the confusion to slip away," Daegan proposed. "We try make for the docks and steal an icecraft."

"Any of you lads know how to work one?" Tanlor asked the others, jumping to Daegan's beat.

"Aye, I used to do runs when I first got stationed here," Puck offered.

"*Hey!*" All heads turned to the rak advancing on them. It was a fully grown warrior, flanked by two youths; rak-Boern and another that Daegan didn't recognise.

The men reacted quickly, Tanlor dashing forward, sword raised, the others raising their weapons. The rak warrior opened with a wide swing which Tanlor ducked under, attempting to step in close where his blade could do more damage.

Puck jumped forward, his sword raised and pressed hard against the other rak youth. Puck had the grenadier pouches but Daegan figured the man didn't want to draw the attention of the entire camp by using them just yet.

Despite being one of the youths, rak-Boern was still as tall as Daegan and wielded a thick heavy blade. He advanced towards Daegan with an eager expression. Yaref was already trying to flank the warrior that Tanlor was fighting and Tar was attempting to form a stone projectile. *Oh shit.* Daegan realised that *he* would have to deal with the oncoming rak.

He backstepped as rak-Boern took a swing at him and the tip of the blade brushed Daegan's shirt. His adrenaline peaking, Daegan tightened his grip on the hilt of his hatchet.

Rak-Boern was off balance from his swing and Daegan's boyhood training kicked in. He stepped forward bringing the hatchet down on the rak's forearm. The blade didn't break through the rawhide armour but it was enough to push the youth further off balance.

Daegan then followed up with a punch. His closed fist connected with rak-Boern's face. He felt the nose break under his knuckle and carried his weight forward, pushing the rak back.

Daegan then brought his hatchet down for a killing blow but rak-Boern recovered, bringing up his thick sword in defence. The hook of the hatchet caught on the blade and Daegan pushed down on the hilt, straining with all of his strength.

Daegan's face twisted into a snarl, baring his teeth at the rak. His opponent matched Daegan's expression, his fierce blue eyes screaming anger and death at Daegan. The rak might've been stronger than him but Daegan was pushing down with all of his weight, he was slowly gaining ground and the rak knew it.

Rak-Boern twisted, pulling his blade free but the action exposed his side. Daegan slipped forward, but he planted a foot and swung his hatchet hard, sinking it into rak-Boern's flank. The blade managed to cut through the rawhide and found flesh underneath.

Rak-Boern cried out, dropping his sword, and staggering forward, the hatchet still lodged in him. Daegan wasted no time, picking up the heavy blade in both hands. He kicked at rak-Boern's rear, toppling him forward and drove the blade down into his back. The rak made a gurgling gasp as he fell forward on his face.

Daegan glanced around in time to see Tanlor thrust upwards with his sword, driving it up through the rak warrior's chin. Blue blood that looked black in the torchlight poured out as the warrior slumped back. The other rak youth was already on the ground, Puck pulling his blade free.

The walls of the keep were completely ablaze and shadowed shapes moved through the din of thickening smoke. Daegan reached down and wrenched his hatchet free from the dead rak. He then pulled out the heavy rak blade. Stepping towards Tanlor, he offered the hilt to him.

"This will work as a greatsword?" he asked and Tanlor nodded, giving Daegan a shoulder pat of approval.

"Nice work," Tanlor said, nodding to rak-Boern's body and taking the large sword from Daegan.

"We're not done yet," Daegan replied and turned to the others. "To the docks!"

***

Loreli burst open the smouldering gate with a powerful blast of wind. Burning chunks of timber and white hot iron rained down on the rak defenders in the keepyard.

The smoke was thick but Loreli sent forward a gust that dispelled it in front of her. The purple light of her amethyst aeristone burned inside her chest and she felt weightless holding all of that energy inside of her. Weightless and omnipotent command of the very air around her.

With a light touch of wind at her back, Loreli shot forward. In easy bounds, she cleared the smouldering debris, and landed into the yard of the keep. Her mind worked fast, flagging the discernible human shapes through the haze.

Misandrei landed beside her and the pair rushed forward in unison. The smoke dispelled revealing a cluster of eight lithe figures, clad in black hide armour. Theirs was roughshod unlike Loreli's own perfected dragonhide.

Loreli closed the distance to the closest one. It swung a greatsword at her which she evaded easily, then she sidestepped a pike thrust from another rak. In a fluid motion, Loreli whipped her curved blade up, slicing efficiently along the neck of the one wielding the greatsword.

As the rak fell, Loreli pushed out the energy inside of her, sending a resonating force blast of wind, pushing the group that had been circling her back.

The pikeman was first to his feet and came in with another jab but she was too fast, leaping out of the way. The rak locked eyes with her and for a moment Loreli was taken aback by how strikingly blue they were in the jet-black face.

The rak came forward with another jab in a pathetic attempt at keeping her at bay. She wind-slapped the blade away, sucking air from the side. As the pike flicked to the side she gave it another shove of wind, pushing the rak off-balance.

Loreli pushed forward and her sword flashed out, slicing cleanly across the pikeman's face. She didn't bother finishing him. She knew that wound was deep enough that he'd bleed out in seconds. She turned to see that Misandrei had already made short work of four other rakmen, leaving only two remaining.

Loreli moved to engage the final pair when a noise that chilled her to her bones sounded from within the smoke. It sounded alien, like the chittering screech of a giant insect. A dark shape loomed in the haze and, on instinct, Loreli sent a blast of wind towards it.

The smoke dispelled away revealing a creature taller than a horse and as wide as a wagon. The light of the burning walls illuminated the carapace and casted dancing shadows along the spines. The creature scuttled forward on black spider's legs with enormous snapping claws.

What the fuck is that?!

Loreli's wind blast had done nothing to deter the monster as it charged towards her. The thing moved at a terrifying pace, but Loreli was more terrifying. She pushed at her flank with wind, sending her into a roll.

She rounded the thing and attempted to slice at the creature's legs but her blade glanced ineffectively off the carapace. The monster swung a claw around at her and she easily ducked beneath it. Loreli then pulled air into her and blasted up above her head with as much force as she could muster. As the claw passed over ahead it was knocked upwards, exposing the underside of the creature.

It was an educated guess that the underside would be its weak point but Loreli was reluctant to step under the monster in case she was wrong and it came down on her hard. Instead, she whipped out her blade at the joints that connected the legs to the shelled body. As she'd hoped, the edge of her blade sliced satisfyingly into the rough flesh, but the thing had *very* thick hide, whatever it was.

The creature let out one of its blood curdling screams and Loreli leapt back, giving herself an extra push of air to be out of the monster's range. She looked over at Misandrei who was fighting another one, neither of them had been expecting *these* things. *We need Endrin so he can smash these things apart with stonespears.*

***

Jaz continued to fuel the flames. The forests behind him blazed, the dragon-oil having given more than enough to start a growing wildfire. Even if Jaz wanted to stop it, he doubted that he could pull enough heat to kill it.

Jaz was no longer in control, he was simply the conduit by which the flames of the wildfire tunnelled through to the battlements. He could feel the fires scourge his body... and he grinned maniacally. The sharp pain of the burns inside his body felt *euphoric*. This was what his body had been craving for weeks. Pure unrestricted release.

Jaz's eyes flicked to a shape emerging from the smoky corridor where the gate had been. It looked like a portal into a hell world of ash. More human-like shapes followed. They were too large to be Misandrei or Loreli.

Jaz felt the will of the wildfire coursing through him. It demanded more. Thirsted for more. Jaz felt his lips peel back in a demonic grin, and outstretched his hands towards the defenders. The heat melted out through his edir. It felt as though the wave of heat was solid and tangible, like anything caught between him and the rakmen would be incinerated in seconds.

The hide armour of the foremost rak erupted in flames, followed by high-pitched screams. Jaz did not relent, he pushed more heat forward. He could see veins of growing red light under the skin of his forearm. His skin began to char and flake but Jaz didn't care. The fire *needed* to be out of him.

The armour of the other defenders caught alight, and their weapons turned white-hot, melting in their hands. The body had a staunchly immutable resistance to direct heat manipulation and Jaz could feel the untrained edirs of the rakmen working to resist his fire. He didn't need to target the body to burn a person, however. Hide armour and steel were nothing to the fires of his soul.

A deep shadowed part of his mind screamed restraint at him. His childhood mentor had instilled in Jaz the dangers of pulling too much heat. But that was the concern of weaker men. *Mortal men.* Jaz had stepped beyond that. His soul had been reforged with the fires of his topaz. He was one with the elemental fury of the world. He had transcended beyond the limitations of man. Jaz was inexorable—a creature one with flame and fury.

Jaz took a step forward, raising his other hand. He drew in more from the wildfire behind him. The flames shrank back to only the green and purple flame of the enduring dragon-oil.

He channelled the fires forward and the walls erupted in flames. *Burn it all.* His eyes glowed with an orange-red intensity. He could feel nothing beyond the searing pain of the fires. But he couldn't restrain himself. His soul desired more.

Portions of the wall collapsed in falling cinders and ash, the flames eating at everything. Great plumes of smoke billowed up in the air. Jaz looked down and could see embers in his charred skin. He was confused by this. How could he burn? The fires could not consume him. He *was* the flame.

More rakmen emerged from the smoke, fleeing the suffocation. They amassed around the gate and Jaz felt the rage build in him. *How dare they deny my fire.* They were nothing but fuel for the flames. He directed his hands towards the group.

As before, many of them burst quickly into flame. But then there was a sudden and direct draw on Jaz's edir. It pulled at him as efficiently and maliciously as Jaz drew fire.

He felt like a drowning man breaking above the water and sucking breath. His fire was syphoned away faster than Jaz could direct it. As the pure and true rages of the flames diminished from him, Jaz felt an offensive and petulant anger rise in him. It felt all too incredibly *human.*

This was not the rage of a god, this was the sullen and perverse fury of a man. Jaz felt more of his fire syphoning away from him and he desperately attempted to retract it.

At the heart of the group of rakmen was a single dark figure, holding something above its head, radiating a brilliant scintillating light of red and white. Jaz could feel the light drawing in everything. It was like an infinite void that drew all the power of his fire into nothingness. An all-consuming hunger, stronger than that of his flames.

Jaz fell to his knees. The searing pain diffused, leaving him only with the after effects. The pain of his cracked and broken flesh now screamed at him. He could feel the watery sting of his tears on his burnt cheeks.

He was still just a man.

Then he felt the void pull more. It sucked at his edir beyond just that of his fire. Whatever that light was, it wanted *more* of him. It wanted every piece he had. Every shred of his soul.

Jaz stumbled back. The snow around him had long since melted, then evaporated, and the ground beneath him had been withered and blackened by his fire. His hands scrambled on that charred earth now, backing away from the approaching light.

He could not see the wielder of the light anymore. It was a shadowing form in the face of the brilliance of whatever was emitting the light. It reminded Jaz of the light of the soulstone. An incandescent white with cascading rainbow colours although red was most prominent.

Jaz felt a pain similar to what he'd felt when being soulforged. Only it was different. This was not the pain of change. He was being pulled, drawn out like evaporating water to steam.

Jaz looked down at his hands. They were grey and shrivelled, sucked of any life that once coursed through them. His flesh flaked away like ash. Every part of him screamed in agony. And he could see nothing but the brilliant light until everything went dark.

***

What the fuck is Jaz doing?! Loreli glanced at the walls turning to ash. The flames were so bright and hot that she felt they would jump right out and take her. She easily kept the flames and smoke at bay from her with a bubble of air, but they needed Jaz in the fight.

Loreli couldn't spare more than a passing thought for Jaz. She had her own problems to deal with. The shelled insect creature was proving to be a far more difficult opponent than she'd anticipated. Luckily, Endrin had finally arrived into the fray, emerging from the smoke and striking the monster with stonespears.

She kept the thing occupied and distracted from Endrin's assault but she wasn't used to being the bait. Loreli was usually the spearhead of the attack. Endrin was the guardian and shield. This role reversal for them was not something they'd had much experience with.

Endrin was also diverting his efforts between both of the monsters that Loreli and Misandrei were fighting. Every now and then, Loreli would catch sight of a rak attempting to flank her. They were easy to take down, they couldn't keep up with her superior speed and they fell quickly to her blade.

The creature's claw came at her again and Loreli airpushed herself out of the way. The monster launched itself after her and she found herself performing a series of evasive manoeuvres to simply flee the damn thing. *This was supposed to be an easy job. Kill one fucking hindered Prince, isolated and alone in the wilderness.*

The fight was chaos. These things were monsters from hell. All Loreli could think of was draega monsters, stories that the temples told from ages long past. This was *not* what she signed up for when she became a bloodshedder. She'd never thought she would fight literal monsters!

She dodged another claw swing, leapt back again, and a stonespear smashed into the creature's shell. Endrin had been taking his sweet time on that one. Endrin then followed up with another, and she could see the shell finally beginning to crack.

Loreli saw a shape move to her side and she struck out, catching the blade of a rak. This one was quick and parried her next attack. The two became embroiled in a rapid succession of attacks but Loreli was still faster and the precision of her attacks would eventually win out.

But she could see the lumbering form of the insect creature shuffling back to its feet. *Shit! Come on, Endrin!* She saw another rak carrying a pike approaching from her left. *Oh no.* She would need to deal with the pikeman quickly. The rak swordsman was too skilled to dispatch fast enough.

Loreli's edir was still focused on both the air bubble and blasting the insect monster off-balance to do much else. The swordsman rak advanced on her, not allowing her to disengage from him. *Shit.* The pike to her left also pressed in.

Loreli took a bold move, redirecting her edir to windblast the swordsman away from her. She turned to face the pikeman but another dark shape leapt out from the smoke tackling the rak to the ground. Claws slashed and she heard what sounded like snapping jaws and tearing flesh.

Loreli didn't know what the fuck that thing was but it seemed like it was on her side for now. She didn't have time to watch further as the insect monster was launching itself at her again. Loreli airpushed herself out of the way again.

Why can't these shell monsters attack some of the rak?! She thought bitterly.

***

Smoke filled Daegan's lungs and he coughed as he ran through the haze. Orange light and heat permeated through the smoke. The group needed to get away from the fires or they'd all suffocate.

Daegan could just about discern the shapes of Tanlor beside him and the other men following behind. He covered his mouth and nose with his sleeve but it did little to protect him.

"Quickly!" Tanlor roared. The plan had fallen to shit in the moments following the horn. They'd fought another set of rakmen while the fires were growing on the battlements. But now the smoke was too intense for anything but fleeing.

Daegan took another step and it was as though he'd stepped through a wall into a clearing. He stood at the edge of a clear dome, the smoke held at bay by some invisible barrier. The others followed through, each of them with matching expressions of surprise.

Thick tendrils of orange and grey curled around the barrier of the dome but were unable to permeate through. Within was utter chaos; the two crab-like creatures were scuttling about while a pair of human fighters leapt out of the way of strikes.

Bodies of rakmen littered the ground and the two warriors moved like shadows with inhuman speed, zipping about and jumping at impossible heights. *Who are these people?*

There was another human, running about the dome, conjuring up stonespears and flinging them at the crabs. Daegan watched as the man formed a set of three stonespears but before he could fire them, a pair of rak warriors moved to intercept him. The man shifted the trajectory of the two spears to take them down, the third flying off into the smoke.

A rak standing on the other side of the dome blew a rallying call into a horn. More and more of the rak warriors emerged from the smoke. Many of them were coughing and spluttering. Daegan began to lose count of how many. *A dozen, maybe more?*

"We should help them," Tar said, he'd picked up the sword that Tanlor had left. Daegan and Tanlor shared a look. They both suspected who these newcomers were.

"I think that's Misandrei," Daegan pointed to the woman with short red hair skirting around the crab monster, teasing out weak points in the carapace. "The others I don't recognise."

"That man's not Ferath," Tanlor said, indicating the bald man, "but his runewielding is a match for his."

"This is something to do with those injuries you had?" Yaref asked them pointedly. Both Daegan and Tanlor nodded.

"Not sure if they're worse than the rak, truth be told," Daegan said and Yaref sucked a breath through his teeth.

"Enemy of my enemy?" Yaref offered.

"Is still my enemy," Daegan finished.

The bright orange glow dimmed noticeably as the flames suddenly dampened, like a wind blowing out half the candles in a room. Smoke still filled the air outside the dome but it came in lighter whisps than before. The shapes of the towers were now visible again, and Daegan could see that large portions of the wall had completely collapsed in heaps of ash.

"The docks are that way?" Daegan pointed to an area of the wall that had completely disintegrated.

"Aye," Tar acknowledged, "I think I can see them." The younger man was squinting through the smoke.

Daegan glanced back at the battle unfolding in the dome. Misandrei had disengaged from the crab monster to fight three rak warriors. She moved through them savagely, cutting them down with ease.

"These are Landryn's soldiers," Daegan said. His brother had given them some silly name that he couldn't recall.

"This is the quality of Reldoni soldiers?" Tanlor sounded worried.

"I think they're considered the elites," Daegan clarified.

The other Reldoni warrior was a blond woman. She moved like a shadow, ducking between blows of the crab monster and turning to dispatch any rak that approached her.

Daegan spotted Baroc in the fray, taking down a rak and mauling them. The beastman's attacks were a terrifying sight but his aggression seemed solely targeted towards the rakmen.

"We've lingered too long," Tanlor asserted, "we make for the docks."

"I agree," Daegan turned to the others, "you lads can stay if you want but Tanlor and I are getting out of here." The three men shared looks between them and none looked eager to join the battle happening within the dome.

"We'll follow you, lad," Yaref said.

***

Ferath stumbled through the smoke. He'd lost sight of Endrin ahead of him and got turned around. Jaz had finally restrained his fires and the smoke was beginning to dissipate. Ferath could hear the sounds of battle, and the blaring of the rak warhorns, the shouts and cries of them as they fell to the bloodshedders' attacks.

Ferath had to admit that he was impressed—and outmatched—by their collective skill. Misandrei, Loreli and Endrin had launched themselves into the battle and Ferath had been left straggling behind.

Endrin had been forming four—sometimes five—simultaneous stonespears, and striking the rak defenders on the walls. Ferath's own stoneshaping granted him two, but even then he fumbled control when his edir would slip from his grasp.

He saw shadows moving about through the smoke and moved towards them. He stepped into an empty air bubble. He could feel Misandrei and Loreli's edirs jointly maintaining the bubble, keeping the stifling smoke at bay. The battle was in full swing and Ferath could see from the scattered corpses of rakmen that the bloodshedders were slowly gaining the advantage.

Ferath could see that there were little over ten remaining rak in the keepyard. Unless there were more hidden within the keep or towers, but Ferath doubted that. Then he spotted a group of five smaller figures running in the opposite direction of the battle.

They ran towards a section of the destroyed wall. Through the clearing smoke, Ferath saw the reflection of moonlight illuminating the ice of the Nortara Sheet. He could just about make out the thin dark outline of the dock.

The frustrating memory of Daegan and Tanlor fleeing to the docks in Urundock entered his mind, and Ferath knew with certainty that Daegan was in that fleeing group.

Ferath snarled and darted towards them. He was not about to let Daegan cowardly weasel his way out of his grip again.

As Ferath ran, he caught sight of Endrin's bald head. The man was turning to bark an order at Ferath. *As if I would ever take orders from a commoner him.* Before the man had even made eye contact, Ferath conjured a stonespear and loosed it towards Endrin. Not anticipating an attack from his own allies, the hit landed and Endrin was thrown the ground. Ferath wasn't sure if it was a killing blow or not—and he didn't care. Daegan was his only objective.

***

Daegan glanced over his shoulder at the high-pitched sound of a hissing screech. He saw one of the crabs buckling under a barrage of stonespears. *They've taken one down.* Daegan felt a rush of fear that they might not escape in time.

Despite the monstrous nature of the crabs and the rakmen, Landryn's elites instilled in him a far greater fear.

The group approached the heap of cinder and ash that had once been the wall. "Puck, can you clear us a path?" Daegan pointed towards the heap. Flames still danced up from the smouldering mound. They didn't want to run straight through an open fire.

"Uhm, yeah," Puck stammered, "I can." The man raised his hands to the fire and the flames slowly began to recede.

"This topaz is really small," Puck explained, "the draw is slow, but I should be able to make a path through. Just give me a few minutes."

Daegan and the others waited impatiently, looking back at the battle with apprehension. A lone figure approached from the fighting, running towards them. Daegan could see an amber glow emitting from the man's skin. In the smoky haze, the light appeared like a nimbus aura around him.

Daegan didn't need to discern the details of the man's face to know that it was Ferath. His curved sword was drawn, catching the light of the fires.

"No more running, Daegan," Ferath's voice cut through the sounds of battle, "this is the end of the road. This ends now." There was unfettered rage in Ferath's words, as though Daegan's persistent reluctance to die was some grave insult to him.

"What do you expect of me, Ferath?" Daegan spat the words, hoping to delay the man long enough for Puck to make them a path through the flames. "You expect me to simply accept death?"

"It is an inevitability," Ferath replied. Ferath no longer had the cold impassiveness he once held. He was frayed... unhinged.

"Stand down, Vitares!" Daegan recognised Misandrei's voice call out. She appeared a moment later in a gust of wind that billowed forward. The gale washed away the remnants of smoke and fanned the embers that Puck was trying to snuff out.

Tanlor took a step in front of Daegan, his rak sword raised. In that moment Daegan felt an overwhelming sense of love for the man. Tar and Yaref also raised their weapons despite neither man understanding the severity of the situation.

"His death is *mine*!" Ferath whirled on Misandrei, an arm outstretched. In the blink of an eye a shell of stone formed around the woman.

"*You* cannot escape me again, Daegan!" Ferath shouted, "the fury of the earth flows within me." The light grew in him, his eyes shining amber. With the smoke cleared, Daegan could see the features of Ferath's face; parts of skin had taken on the appearance of stone. It cracked and crumbled as his face twisted into a snarl.

"You are nothing!" Ferath took a step forward.

The earth at their feet began to rumble. "Weak... pitiful creature," Ferath continued, "I am ascended. My power is inexorable. With your death comes the dawn of a new age."

"You're not a god, Ferath!" Daegan shouted, "you're just a man that's lost his *fucking mind*."

Daegan wished he had his revolver. That egotistical rant would be cut short by a few bullets to the face.

Ferath took another step towards them, his hand raised. Debris exploded out from him and coalesced. It began forming the length of a spear in the air. Tanlor rushed forward. The man closed the distance between them in two bounds and brought the large rak blade down on the forming stonespear.

Daegan darted after, keeping his gaze on Ferath, clutching his hatchet. The weight of the weapon in his hand gave him reassurance. Another stonespear formed and Tanlor smashed it.

The ground cracked and shifted, trembling underfoot. Daegan jumped over a fissure that broke open in the ground, closing the distance between him and Ferath.

Daegan was done running. He was done being afraid.

Daegan was not nothing. He was not weak. He was not pitiful.

He swung his hatchet at Ferath. The man's sword whipped up, deflecting the swing and catching the hook of the axe blade. Daegan hung tight to the handle and twisted, freeing it before Ferath could disarm him.

Tanlor appeared at his side. The thick dark metal of his sword blurring past. Ferath was suddenly pressed with the pair. Tanlor and Daegan worked in tandem in a series of blows so that Ferath could do nothing but focus on parrying the attacks.

The ground continued to shake, Feraths eyes glowing with brighter golden light. His movements slowed and more of the man's skin took on the appearance of stone.

Tanlor's blade struck Ferath's arm. The blade cut into the dragonhide armour and caught the flesh underneath. Only it wasn't flesh. The blade crunched against stone. Hardened chips of Ferath's flesh crumbled under the blade and fell away.

"I am the power of the earth," Ferath intoned, "I am the quiet resolute fury of stone and steel." The light of aradium runestone emitted in the cracks of Ferath's skin as he spoke. Ferath's free hand grabbed at the blade of Tanlor's sword. In the breadth of a second, the blade exploded into dust.

Daegan lost his footing as the earth shifted at his feet. A large crevice opening between him and Tanlor. Tanlor had to jump back before the crack in the earth swallowed him.

Daegan swung forward with his hatchet but as the blade approached Ferath's head, the metal dissolved away to dust.

Daegan followed through with the swing anyway and the wooden shaft of the hatchet connected with Ferath's skull. The shaft broke and Daegan's hand reverberated as if he'd struck a boulder. Cracks of light appeared at the side of Ferath's head where he'd been hit.

Ferath's movements were slow and laborious as he turned to face Daegan, baring his teeth.

"Accept your fate," Ferath growled. Daegan tried to take a step back but he felt rock rise up behind him, penning him in. The rising mounds reminded him of the pillars of stone his father had once used. His chest locked and his throat tightened. Phantom pain flared in his shoulders.

Ferath's arm moved slowly, raising his blade.

And then his eyes widened.

The light faded from his eyes. The lines of light in the crumbling cracks of his skin snuffed like a candle under a glass. The tremors in the ground below abruptly stopped and the fissure that had been growing in the ground stopped deepening.

Ferath staggered back, his sword still raised overhead.

Behind Ferath, Daegan could see a brilliant white light. It tinged with the golden light that had been emitting from Ferath.

Daegan wasn't sure exactly what was happening but he could see that *something* was draining Ferath's abilities. Sucking it away from him. If he had a moment to think about it, Daegan likely would have remembered the bloodstone dagger that the rak chiefs had somehow used to negate runewielders.

Confused horror painted across Ferath's face and the stone-like appearance faded away, replaced by raw and broken skin.

"W-what are you doing?" Ferath stammered. "How are you doing this?"

The look of helplessness that covered Ferath's face struck Daegan. It was not so different to how he'd felt the night Ferath had attacked him back in the Arch-duke's palace.

He'd asked Ferath that same question. *What are you doing…* Daegan gritted his teeth. His fist closed around the broken hatchet handle. It had broken in a sharp spike.

"It's nothing personal," Daegan said coldly and grabbed the back of Ferath's head. With his other hand, Daegan rammed the broken shaft into Ferath's neck.

Ferath's blood flowed hot and sticky over Daegan's hand and down his arm. He pushed deeper, shoving the wooden handle further into the man's throat.

"You're not a fucking god," Daegan hissed at him, letting go. Ferath's body crumpled at his feet.

He reached down and picked up Ferath's sleek curved blade. Daegan recognised the hawk embellishment on it. It was a gift that Landryn often gave to his most loyal soldiers. Daegan had known it for a while but the truth stung him hard.

Landryn orchestrated this. His own brother had ordered his death. The sword was not the deciding evidence, but it was just another amongst Daegan's mounting suspicions.

"Undak!" Daegan heard the deep angry voice of a rak. He looked up and saw one of the rak warriors approach. Daegan recognised him as Razef—the new chief.

Well, I killed their last chief. Razef carried the bloodstone dagger as their last chief had. It now shone with an iridescent white light.

"*I killed your last chief, Razef. You would risk attacking me?*" Daegan said coldly. He couldn't escape. The cleft in the ground loomed to his left and the stonewall that Ferath had raised penned him. The only direction was forward. Towards Razef.

"*You deny the Khandamos his sacrifice,*" Razef approached, he nodded to Ferath's body as he spoke. "*The umbra of this one is strong. The Khandamos will not be pleased that you have stolen this from him.*"

"I don't give a fuck about your Khandamos." Daegan realised that the word 'fuck' probably didn't translate well in Old Esterin but he didn't care.

Daegan gripped Ferath's sword in his hand. He'd killed one rak chief already this week. What was one more?

***

Tanlor watched in amazement as Daegan drove the hilt of the hatchet into Ferath's neck. They were separated by a chasm in the ground. *Too far to jump.* He could see Razef approaching Daegan, the glowing dagger in his hand and realised that he needed to pull Razef's attention.

Tanlor glanced back at Puck, who was still focused on dulling the embers for a path through the fire, and dashed towards him. He'd made a mistake giving that one the topaz.

"Puck! Give me the topaz," Tanlor ordered.

"I almost have—"

"—it doesn't matter," Tanlor grabbed the front of his tunic, "give it to me." Puck, in his surprise, offered out his hand and Tanlor grabbed the tiny chip of topaz. It glowed brightly and felt hot in his hand. Tanlor then pulled one of grenadier pouches from Puck's belt. Tanlor didn't waste any time, releasing Puck and darting back to the chasm.

Daegan and Razef were speaking to each other in that strange language. Tanlor flung the grenadier pouch across the chasm. He focused his edir on the pouch as it arced in the sky, sending out his edir and drawing on the heat of the topaz. There was so much fire around that there was no shortage to fuel it. He continued to feed in heat until…

Boom!

The pouch exploded and Razef was thrown backwards from the blast. Daegan ducked against the stone wall, he had still been far enough away from the rak that the blast didn't reach him.

Razef climbed to his feet quickly, recovering with surprising speed.

"*Undak Savara'an!*" Tanlor heard Razef roar and the light of the dagger in his hand began to shine brighter.

Tanlor felt the heat syphon from his edir. It was drawn from him like blood from a wound and felt like someone was sucking his breath right out of his lungs.

Tanlor staggered to his knees, pain spreading out from his chest to his limbs. The burns on his skin blazed in agony. He looked up, across the chasm, and could see Razef standing with the dagger overheard. He could feel his life being drawn into it.

And then a silver sword burst from Razef's chest.

An arced length of metal that caught the light of the fires. The chief slumped, the bloodstone dagger tumbling from his hand.

Razef fell forward, revealing Daegan. The rak's blood appeared black across the man's face. Daegan bared his teeth at the fallen rak, then reached down and picked up the bloodstone dagger.

END OF

PATH OF THE STONEBREAKER

BOOK 1

Epilogue

The Will of the King

Landryn Tredain scowled as he climbed the stairs to his father's throneroom. Lukane was already there—alone and dressed in his white and gold military suit. His older brother had taken to the style since the announcement of the invasion.

Lukane stood admiring the throne on the dais. It was an ostentatious thing in Landryn's opinion. Dozens of delicate gilded wings had been crafted on the edges of the throne by Landryn's great-grandfather. He'd then renamed it as the Sky Throne. It would've been an apt name without the wing decorations as the walls of the throneroom were entirely glass, allowing for a full panoramic view from the highest point in the Pillar.

"Little brother," Lukane beamed as Landryn mounted the steps, "a fine day is it not?" he gestured out to the blue winter sky, there were scatterings of white and grey clouds. Frost covered the edges of the glass.

"Indeed," Landryn replied, "however I should be overseeing the deployments to Rubane."

"Allow Mattice to manage that," Lukane chided, "when the King summons you, you do not grumble. Respect for the crown is paramount."

"Father's not even here," Landryn retorted.

"When *I* am King," Lukane began and Landryn felt his eyes roll, "I will expect you to show deference. Your attitude has become tiresome of late. Do not think yourself better than me simply because you are soulforged." Landryn opened his mouth to throw an insult but then heard another set of footsteps following up the stairs.

"My sons," Abhran's voice came, "why must you bicker like children." Their father was similarly dressed to Lukane. The black nythilium crown atop his head.

"Father," Lukane bowed, which Landryn matched.

"Join me, my sons. Today is a momentous day." The King walked confidently to the edge of the room, inches from the glass. Landryn felt his jaw tighten at his father's friendly demeanour.

The great height of the Pillar was usually enough to make people weak at the legs, but Abhran showed no discomfort, looking down at the city, hundreds of feet below.

Landryn and Lukane joined their father next to the window. There was a balcony a few levels below the window so a direct drop wouldn't likely be fatal. However, the expanse of air to the city and bay beyond was usually enough to have people recoiling from the edge. Landryn could sense the billowing winds, beyond the glass, rushing past the tower. His edir resonated with them, and the winds responded in kind.

"Sixty warships," Abhran began, "carrying over twenty thousand soldiers; the courageous men and women of Reldon." The King's gaze was locked upon the warships floating in the bay. Many were already sailing around Heraldport in the distance.

"We are on the cusp of a new age," Abhran continued, "our legacy shall be written over the coming months. Rubane will fall beneath our might, the free cities of Athlin brought to heel. The proud defences of Ard-Rien reduced to rubble. The glory of our ancestors will be restored, with us at the very peak of it all."

Landryn had heard variations of this speech many times over the years. His father's avarice for this war had been brewing for as long as he could remember. He didn't have time today to listen to the old man drone on and on about restoring the greatness of their ancestors. He had work to do and at this rate it would be long after midnight before he found his bed. Not that he had any desire to return to it.

It had been three weeks since Lua Nova. Three weeks of war preparations. Three weeks since Femira had disappeared. She had vanished from his life as abruptly as she'd stepped into it. A bright spark in a dark room. He felt his face lock into a frown at the thought of her. She'd left without a goodbye—not even a note.

When Landryn had gone to Garld to ask where she was, his mentor had insisted she was fine. That she was on assignment in Keiran. Of course Landryn had known that Garld had agents in Keiran. He also knew that Femira—under the guise of Annali Jahar—was in a unique position to be a valuable spy. But he couldn't believe that she had left without telling him.

He'd been furious with Garld for not clearing the mission with him first. Shamefully, Landryn had reverted to a teenage boy, throwing a tantrum but Garld could always calm him when the rage took over.

"I know you two were close," Garld had said, putting a hand on Landryn's shoulder. "But you have a duty to this country, Landryn. As does she. We must all play our parts." He knew Garld was right. He was always right. He was the only one whom Landryn could trust utterly.

"The time has come, Landryn," Abhran said, pulling him back into the moment. "It is time for your brother and I to join you in the ranks of the soulforged. The power of the soulforged is unrivalled, and the process, as I understand it, is now perfected. You yourself have shown no signs of degradation."

Landryn felt his shoulders tighten. He'd known this day would eventually come. That didn't mean it didn't anger him.

"Indeed, father. Garld suspects it is our lineage. Those with suspected soulforging in their ancestry seem to have more stable results."

"Elyina," Abhran spat spitefully, "the great shadow and deceiver of our nation. The hypocrite! Had she not smothered all the knowledge of soulforging, Reldon would have become the greatest nation in the world." Landryn chose not to point out that if it had not been for Elyina's journals, they would not have pieced together the formulas for soulforging in the first place.

"Our glory will overshadow even Elyina's legacy," Lukane said, pandering to their father's ego. Landryn had little interest in standing around listening to this.

"It might be prudent to wait a little longer," Landryn suggested.

"Nonsense," Lukane dismissed, "father has announced that soulforging has been rediscovered. Already the highborn are begging us for the privilege to join the ranks.

It would be an opprobrious position for the King himself to not be among the most powerful in our country."

"The Tredains must always exemplify the strength of Reldon," Abhran said, "we must never show weakness in our family. To cower in fear of this power would be a weakness."

"We still have yet to determine how to infuse more than one runestone," Landryn advised, "you would need to choose an affinity and be locked into this."

"An inconsequential price," Abhran contended, "in the face of the power of the soulforged. Annali Jahar was a novice a year ago, and now she stands amongst our most prominent elites."

"We *must* become soulforged," Lukane put in, "we have suffered the stain of Daegan's affliction on our name long enough." Landryn felt his entire body tense at the mention of their younger brother. His stomach turned to ice water.

"Yes, yes," Abhran agreed, moving away from the window and towards the throne. "At least in death, Daegan's life can finally have value to us," he said bitterly.

Landryn felt a flare of rage at the comment. Lukane turned to follow after their father but Landryn kept his gaze fixed upon the warships. He couldn't trust his restraint if he looked at them.

"Who would've thought," Lukane pondered, "that when we sent Daegan to Rubane, it would accelerate to war within a few short months. Quite convenient that… it was you yourself, Landryn, that recommended Ferath Vitares as Daegan's bodyguard, were it not?"

Ferath Vitares. The name sparked inside of Landryn. He could feel the tempest building inside. His fury. The chaotic winds of his edir swirled inside of him, and at the very center of it was Ferath Vitares.

"He was your man," Lukane continued, "loyal to a fault, you claimed." Lukane was taunting him. His brother had always been a cruel bastard. He was trying to trigger Landryn's guilt. An attempt to stir Landryn's temper as he had done so often in the past.

"Yes," Landryn forced the word from his lips.

"It was a good spin you achieved there," Lukane continued, "convincing the noble houses of your grief… that Ferath had been turned traitor by the Dukes of Rubane."

"Lukane," Abhran said with warning, "do not badger your brother so. Daegan's death is indeed felt by all of us." Those words stabbed into Landryn's back like a knife. *How fucking dare he.* How dare his father claim that he was grieved by Daegan's death. That he gave a single fuck about him.

He was so infuriated by Abhran's statement that it had taken Landryn a moment to process what Lukane had said. He whirled from the window.

"What do you mean what *I* achieved?" Landryn said, an accusatory edge in his voice.

"Come now, brother, there is no need to hide," Lukane smirked, "I know that Ferath would never have betrayed you. It was quite genius… you even challenged me on the decision to send Daegan to Rubane. But it was all a tactful play to divert any suspicion, and it played out spectacularly."

"It's alright, Landryn," Abhran spoke, his face every inch that of a doting father, "you do not have to hide from us. We commend what you've done. You've given us justification to finally take Rubane. The Houses would never have aligned on this before. To be truthful, I didn't think you had this in you. But you have proven me wrong, and for that I am glad. You have earned your place as my left hand, alongside your brother. My sons… together, we shall usher in a new era for Reldon. Our glory will be remembered across the aeons. We shall be the sword that this world shall bow to."

Landryn felt a pounding in his chest. It felt like a storm was raging inside of him, battering at his ribcage. *They think... they think that I did this?* That he had ordered Ferath to do what he did? That *he* was the one who had ordered Daegan's death?!

Daegan's face forced its way into Landryn's mind as it so often did these days. The memories of his brother were always dancing on the periphery of his mind.

His teeth ground against each other in anger.

"You should include us in these schemes in the future," Abhran continued, "I appreciate what you've done for us. But we are a family, Landryn. You need to trust us."

"Trust you..." Landryn's voice was ice.

The moment was poised on the edge of a knife. Landryn could feel the rage burying itself into the depths of his soul. His fury woven into it as intricately as the amethyst runestone that enhanced him.

"Because we are family," he felt the words leave him but he couldn't hear it over the building tempest in his ears.

The memory of Daegan trapped in a prison of stone spikes flashed in Landryn's mind and he locked eyes with his father. He was a youth again, returning to the training room hours later to find his brother rasping for breaths, barely clinging to life.

Landryn had dismissed the stones with ease and taken his brother in his arms. Landryn had felt *shame* then. Shame that he was helping Daegan. Shame that he was nurturing his brother's weakness. He'd been disgusted with himself and when Daegan's hand had grasped his shirt. When he looked at the pleading in his brother's eyes and turned his back on him, he'd believed he was doing the right thing. Landryn believed their father. Believed that Daegan was weak.

"Daegan was your son," Landryn growled.

Resume your attack! His father's voice roared in his memory. And Landryn had swung. Again and again as Daegan pleaded for him to stop.

"And you always fucking hated him."

"Do not speak to your King like that," Lukane snapped.

"And *you*," Landryn's death stare landed on his older brother, "you were worse. Taunting him, berating him, making him feel like he was nothing."

"Enough of this Landryn!" Abhran commanded. "Do not push your guilt upon us. It was your hand that has done this. And we are proud of you for it, accept it, and let us be done with the matter."

Landryn had held the blade tip over Daegan's face, covered in blood and tears. His eyes begged for Landryn to stop. And their father's face had been mask of unrestrained hatred.

Landryn's visage cracked, his mouth twisting into a malevolent snarl. The aeristone inside of him sucked at the howling winds outside. The windows shuddered as the gales began to whirl around the top of the Pillar.

"Do not be so melodramatic," Abhran said in disgust, "you let your anger control you. It is a disappointing failing in you and is unbecoming for a Prince of the realm."

"Unbecoming..." Landryn seethed, "*my* rage is unbecoming."

Landryn's mind was blanketed in a red fog. His thoughts weren't forming correctly. If he'd been thinking clearly, Landryn would have called his father a hypocrite. He'd have cursed him as an abusive and cowardly man whose failings as a father and a King had twisted him into the miserable hateful wretch that he was. Instead, Landryn clenched his jaw, his gaze locked on his father.

The winds outside, whipped into a frenzy, slammed against the windows. Darkening clouds were spiralling around the top of the Pillar.

"You left him to die," Landryn hissed.

"Easy brother," Lukane had the awareness to realise that Landryn's anger was building beyond which he could contain. He glanced nervously between Landryn and the growing storm outside. Landryn's hand reached for the hilt of his sheathed sword.

"You would dare threaten me?" Abhran asked, incredulous. Landryn tried to breathe through the growing fury. He could barely hear his father's words. The windows reverberated, the storm winds desperately trying to force their way inside.

"Stop this, Landryn!" Lukane shouted, he had his ceremonial blade drawn. Landryn turned slowly to face him. He felt all other emotion melt away, leaving only a cold, detached enmity.

Lukane was weak. He couldn't stand against Landryn. Not when he had omnipotent command of the storm.

Lukane was a highly competent runewielder and like Landryn he had trained from a young age. He would have aeristone on him, amongst others. But he wasn't soulforged and he couldn't move like Landryn could. The storm was both outside and within Landryn's chest. Its power fuelled his body.

In a single bound, Landryn was within range of Lukane. His sword flashed out of the scabbard. Lukane reacted quickly, bringing his own blade up to block. For the barest second, Landryn and Lukane locked eyes. Landryn's were alight in the roiling purple and blue of aeristone. Lukane's had an edge of panic and fear.

"Cease this absurdity!" Abhran's voice cut over the tension. Landryn pushed forward and his edir sucked at the tempest outside.

A blast of the winds shattered the windows and shards of glass rushed in at them. Landryn knocked Lukane back. His brother staggered but kept hold of his sword. Landryn's blade flashed again and flicked Lukane's from his grasp. Then, with an effortless jab, Landryn drove his steel into Lukane's chest, red spreading out on his immaculately white suit.

"What have you *done*?!" Abhran roared over the winds. Landryn could feel his father's attempts to still the storm, the man's pathetic edir desperately trying to repel the winds.

Landryn turned to face his father as lightning flashed outside and thunder boomed. There was no fear in Abhran's eyes, only confused outrage. The winds whipped at the King's white and gold cloak.

The ground at Landryn's feet shuddered. He recognised it immediately and leapt to the side. Stonespears materialised in front of Abhran and shot forward. Landryn easily evaded them and closed the distance between them.

A set of six glassblades formed around Abhran, hovering in front of him. *Pathetic.* Landryn gave them a strong push of wind and they were cast out of Abhran's control. The wind pushed the King backwards. He fell back, stumbling onto his golden throne.

Landryn took a step forward, the wind rushing in his ears. The tendrils of his edir guided the wind around him, and bore down against his father. Abhran tried to push against it, but he was too weak.

The King was pressed against the back of the throne and Landryn pushed more, focusing on the throne. The metal scraped against the stone floor. It edged closer and closer to the edge of the dais it sat upon. Abhran's edir feebly tried to divert the flow but Landryn's storm was relentless.

The wind pushing against Abhran was too strong for him to speak but there was a desperate pleading in his eyes. It fuelled Landryn's anger how much his father looked like Daegan in that moment. That matching look of terror and fear.

Landryn screamed, his palm shot forward and all the strength of a hurricane compacted and condensed into a single blow.

Lightning cracked, striking at the Pillar.

Deafening thunder peeled.

And both the throne and King were thrown over the edge. Blood pounded in Landryn's ears. His breaths were ragged. In the distance, he could see the metal throne falling, a smaller darker shape hurled through the air. Landryn's outstretched hand wavered. The storm inside wasn't satiated. It craved for more.

The wind carried his father until he was a mere dot, falling into obscurity.

Landryn had killed his father. He'd killed the King. The gravity of that thought stilled him, the tempest dying down around him. Behind him, Landryn could hear the gurgling chokes of Lukane grasping to a few more moments of life.

Landryn turned to him. His brother's white suit was entirely red with blood. Landryn knelt down next to him.

"B-blu-blu–st-stu," Lukane spat blood as he spoke, his hand reaching for something at his chest. Landryn could see it already; a silver pin with a red bloodstone inlaid.

"You want this?" Landryn tore the pin off him. He held it up, out of Lukane's reach. His brother's wound was fatal, it was unlikely that bloodstone would do anything to save him now. But a dying man will grasp for any hope.

"Who told you I ordered Daegan's death?" Landryn demanded.

"Lan," Lukane gasped, his hands weakly reaching up for the pin. "Gah," the man coughed up more blood, "Gah-Gahl," he spluttered. He was too far gone, there would be no answers from him. Not unless Landryn healed him. There could still be time to save him.

Landryn *could* have called for the healers. *Could* have made some attempt to save his brother's life.

It didn't matter anymore.

The dead with the dead.

Lukane's eyes bulged. Veins popping in his forehead. Landryn's lip curled, and he flung the bloodstone pin off into the sky. Landryn rose, turning his back on his dying brother and looked to the empty space where Abhran's throne had been.

To Landryn's surprise, his father's crown had been caught by a broken window frame. It hung there, as casually as a hat on a rack. The smooth finish of the black metal reflected the amethyst glow of Landryn's eyes. That same light traced along the veins of his forearms.

The storm wanted more.

Landryn reached out and grasped the crown.

Acknowledgements

Thank you to all of my amazing readers for following Daegan and Femira's journeys. I sincerely hope that you enjoyed it. I would love to know your thoughts on the book and I am always happy to connect on social media.

If you've not reviewed the story yet, it would really make my day if you did.

There have been so many people that have contributed to the writing of this book over the course of the many years I've been writing it, to name them all would make this book longer than the maximum allowed page limit. But I will highlight some notable people who helped bring this story to life.

My incredible partner and mother of my children; Brana, who has zero interest in fantasy yet encourages the monologuing of all my meandering ideas. While also being my editor, meticulous proof-reader and sounding board, she is my biggest source of encouragement and confidence.

Sam Whitling, without whom this book would likely never have been written; my writing partner, editor, co-worldbuilder and friend.

My amazing parents who have always encouraged their nerdy fantasy-loving child to pursue his love of writing.

I would like to give special thanks to some of my friends for their help and encouragement through the years of trying to write this story; Tomás McNamara and Luke McDermott for introducing me to my first fantasy worlds. Claire Kane and Niall Kennedy for providing much appreciated words of encouragement and edits. Fellow authors and members of my writer's circle; S.R Fauth, Matthew Seymour and my cousin; Sean O'Connor. All of their books are excellent and can be found on Amazon and other online sellers.

To all of my loyal fans and readers on Royal Road; I cannot express to all of you how helpful your words of encouragement have been throughout the journey. I don't think I would have finished book 1 in anywhere near this time without you all.

If you would like to hear updates on the progress of Stonebreaker Book 2 and others in this series you can sign up for my newsletter at https://rdrenworth.com

I am also on Instagram, Discord, Reddit and Royal Road, and I would love to connect with any fans of the series.